BOOK TWO

PLAZA MAYOR

By

John S. Halbert

"Plaza Mayor," by John S. Halbert. ISBN 978-1-62137-333-9 (Softcover)

Library of Congress Control Number: 2013912427

Published 2013 by Virtualbookworm.com Publishing Inc., P.O. Box 9949, College Station, TX 77842, US. ©2013, John S. Halbert. All rights reserved. No part of this publication may be reproduced, stored in a retrieval system, or transmitted in any form or by any means, electronic, mechanical, recording or otherwise, without the prior written permission of John S. Halbert.

Manufactured in the United States of America.

To Salem

PROLOGUE

A WEDDING IN MOSCOW

Moscow, Saturday, August 13, 2011:

The guests stood by the curb, watching, as the receding red tail-lights of the enormous ZIL limousine turned onto the wide boulevard and blended into the late-evening Moscow traffic. Jim Randolph put his arm across Terenty Suslov's shoulder as they made their way back toward the pavilion. "It's official, now! Our two families are connected across the distance."

The Russian patted the American's back, smiling. "This is a happy time for all of us."

Nearby, Nixie Garten Leeds took Kip Leeds's hand and looked with admiration at her husband's profile. "I, too, am happy these young people found each other." She spoke to the hosts in Russian, then in English with an accent that was German, her native language.

Jim's wife, Texas native Sloane Ferry Randolph, reached for the hand of Tamara Suslova in the Russian custom she had observed the past few days since they arrived for the wedding of Nick and Larisa. "That time Larisa came to Texas to visit us, I believe it was love at first sight between those two." Sloane glanced at the smiling mother of the bride and once more marveled at how attractive and young-looking the woman was. She and Tamara were about the same age, she guessed, but there was not the slightest trace of gray in Tamara's magnificent long auburn hair. She still looked almost the same as that day back in Madrid nineteen years earlier, when they had first seen each other as they crouched together under the outdoor restaurant table for protection from the deadly gunfire.

After that, the two families had kept in touch, at first through Holiday greeting cards. Then when Terenty had retired from the

Russian military, he and Tamara had visited Jim and Sloane in Texas. Shortly afterward, Terenty had joined Jim Randolph, Kip Leeds, and the other men in the international crime-fighting operation. Two summers ago, when Larisa came to visit them in West Dallas, the girl, about to start her first year at Moscow State University, and their son, Nick, also headed for his first college semester, became fast friends. In time, their relationship led to Moscow, and their wedding-registration today at the *'Department of Registration of Civil Statuses'*, a classic Soviet-era-like wedding hall; then the vows before the Orthodox priest and all the guests.

Glancing about, Sloane saw several mixed couples around the tables—young Russians and Americans—who seemed to be hitting it off. The language differences did not seem to matter, she observed, as most of the *'Muscovites'* she had met so far spoke English just fine. Probably their schooling, Sloane guessed. And in the few days they had been in Moscow, Sloane had been impressed by how beautiful many of the Russian girls were. In particular, she had noticed one of Larisa's attendants, a brunette teenager with flashing, dark-blue eyes, who had caught the attentions of the younger male guests, with whom she seemed very popular. Several of the young men had sought her out during the dances, including Kip's and Nixie's outgoing son, Bart Leeds, who looked to be about her age and who now held her attention in an animated conversation. Wouldn't it be interesting, Sloane thought, if someday there was *another* wedding between an American and a Russian! For Sloane's first exposure to Moscow society had introduced her to a culture that she was enjoying very much.

She looked around the table at the other women and smiled. "I am glad we will be here a few days more—there are a lot of things I want to see. This city fascinates me." Nixie Leeds nodded in agreement.

Tamara leaned across the table. "We will go to the Kremlin tomorrow . . . then on Monday to *'Arbat Square'* and the *'White House'*, where we saw Yeltsin climb up onto the tank, that time," she said in accented English.

Sloane's and Nixie's eyebrows went up. "You were *there*?"

"We were in the middle of it—Terenty and I, and my cousin and her boyfriend."

Just then, Tamara's mother and a middle-aged woman took seats at the table. "This is my 'Aunt Helen'," Tamara said, in her measured English, then translated for the newcomers. The women extended their hands.

Sloane had seen the middle-aged woman at the ceremony and had thought she looked solemn or perhaps even sad; certainly not as joyful as would have been expected on this occasion.

"Aunt Helen is the mother of my cousin, who is not here, now." Tamara saw Sloane's uncertain look. "'Galina' died in a plane crash . . . she was the wife of our friend, 'Gennady', who was shot in Madrid, that time, as I am sure you remember."

Of course, Sloane could never forget that terrible day at 'Plaza Mayor'. Except for the aunt, the bridegroom, and the priest, all the adult guests she knew at the wedding had been there.

"We named our son after him," Tamara added. Sloane remembered the handsome, light-haired adolescent who had been in the wedding group, whose name was "Gennady".

Tamara turned to the older women and said something in Russian, then in English. "My aunt's husband, who was once Terenty's commanding general, died not long ago."

No wonder the woman looks sad, Sloane thought.

Nixie turned to Tamara. "Kip tells me you and your husband met when he saved Larisa from being run-over by a streetcar."

Tamara translated for the two Russian women, who nodded, then told Nixie and Sloane about the time when she was a young single mother, Terenty had run into the street to pull back her little daughter from in front of a speeding tram. "Larisa was only two years old."

The other two gasped, their eyes wide."My God!" Nixie burst out, "how heroic!"

Tamara looked across the way where her husband was in conversation with the men at the other table. "Terenty has *always* been my hero." Her words prompted nods from the others, as she translated for the other two women.

She turned to Sloane. "How did you and your husband meet?"

The dark-haired American woman told about being kidnapped by the "Cartel's" agents and stuffed unconscious into a wooden coffin-like crate; how she was discovered in a trailer-truck at the Mexico border of Texas by Customs officers; and that she and Jim Randolph had met when he had taken over the case as a government investigator. After the tragic event at "Plaza Mayor" in Madrid, they had continued to see each other and were married the next year. "Then we had our daughter, who is over there." Sloane motioned at a slender teen-aged girl with long, dark-brown hair who was talking and laughing with her new Russian friends. "She was very happy when Larisa wanted her to be an attendant."

Vera Kuznetsova, Tamara's elderly mother, said something that her daughter translated into English. "She says the girl has beautiful hair."

"She got it from my mother, who was from Australia. She and my father met there." She paused. "My mother died of cancer when I was eleven."

"My father passed ten years ago," Tamara said. "My mother has lived with us ever since."

"My father lives by himself—he's pretty independent!" Sloane put in.

"It is *difficult* to do that, in Moscow—but things are getting better." Tamara turned to Nixie. "How did you and Kip meet?"

The blonde woman told the others how she and Kip had first seen each other at the Frankfurt airport while waiting for a flight to Lagos, Nigeria; that they had talked to each other on the airplane; she had been a flight attendant and a translator. Nixie went on about how Kip had later called her to "translate" for him in Madrid at the time of the event at "Plaza Mayor"; that afterward they had traveled to Germany and had met her family; how she had moved to Dallas, Texas, USA, and that she and Kip had been married seventeen years. Nixie glanced across the pavilion at her husband, who was talking with the other men.

* * *

At a nearby circular table, two upper-middle-aged individuals had motioned for the other men to sit with them. "You remember the general," Terenty said to Kip Leeds and Jim Randolph.

"General Golubko!" There followed a round of bonding hugs and male kisses in the Russian custom that the American guests were still getting used to.

The former Russian general nodded. "It has been a while since we were all together."

To Kip, the man's excellent English, with no discernable accent, sounded perfect. He wondered how he did it—most of the "Muscovites" he had met so far spoke English with a noticeable brogue.

Kip put out his hand to the next man. "Livshits! It is good go see you, again."

The angular Russian nodded, at the same time pushing his plastic-rimmed eyeglasses back up on his nose.

The five men took seats, leaned across the table with their heads close together, and began what the other guests would have taken to be a convivial conversation with much nodding. A waiter came around with a fresh Vodka bottle and filled their glasses.

From one end of the pavilion came a sudden burst of music from accordions and a red-colored, triangle-shaped, guitar-like instrument. A fit-looking young man in shiny military boots, a red bandana around his neck, bounded out in front of the musicians, crossed his arms across his chest and dropped to his haunches in a furious bouncing-kicking dance, then leaped into the air, his outstretched fingertips touching the toes of his boots—again and again to the music and to the shouts and applause of the guests.

The men stopped their conversation; the music was too loud for talking. Livshits spoke over the sounds. "Let us meet at my office Monday morning!" The husbands broke away to re-join the women. Livshits motioned to General Golubko. The two men turned in the direction of the bar.

* * *

Tverskaya District; Moscow, Monday August 15, 2011:

Terenty Suslov maneuvered the Mercedes along broad, bustling *'Tverskaya Ulitsa'*. In the front passenger seat, Jim Randolph gazed out, fascinated by the massive, Stalin-era buildings they were passing. He glanced at Terenty, then turned about to Kip Leeds, who was sitting in the back seat. "It looks about like I would have expected," he said, "except for all the shoppers."

Terenty motioned at the pedestrians stepping along the sidewalks and in crosswalks. "This is one of the main shopping districts in Moscow," he said. "Tamara is taking the others to the markets, today." The Russian turned the vehicle onto another street, swinging the wheel to avoid a delivery truck that pulled out in front of them. "We are not far from the Kremlin."

"The Kremlin, yesterday, was terrific!" Jim Randolph spoke up. "Nixie and our son, Bart, were fascinated by all the jewels and the buildings. It was not what we had expected."

Terenty laughed. "Did you expect a 'concentration camp', or something? I believe if you Americans would spend more time, here, the world would better off!" The others chuckled. Terenty went on, "Tonight, we will go to *'Arbat Square'* for dinner and then walk out to the *'White House'*." He pointed at a massive, yellow-hued, columned building to their left, glowing golden in the morning sunshine. An equestrian statue stood on top of it."That is the *'Bolshoi Theater'* . . . they are closed, now, because the dancers are on tour."

"We will go there, next time," Jim said. He knew that Sloane and the others already wanted to come back to Moscow for more visits.

A few blocks farther on, Terenty turned the car into a narrow cobblestone driveway and pulled up behind an older-looking, yellow-stuccoed house surrounded by tall flowering plants."This is Livshits's place—the others will meet us here. *'Tarliani'* flew-in from Zurich, yesterday."

Terenty stepped out of the car. "General Golubko will be here, too."

"How about *'Watering'?*" The American was one of the founders of their crime-fighting organization.

"He could not be with us . . . he is working on a drug case at the border of Colombia and Venezuela."

Livshits answered Terenty's knock. The men stepped into a parlor furnished with an overstuffed sofa and chairs with slipcovers; the papered, flower-print walls were lined with books; white lace curtains covered the windows.

Two other men came into the room. The four greeted Tarliani, the Swiss investigator, and the former Russian Special Forces general, Rodion Golubko, another partner.

While they shook hands all around, Jim Randolph glanced about. One wall was covered with framed commendations—some from the *'KGB'*; others from the *'Federal Security Bureau'* that Jim knew was the current name of the Russian investigative apparatus. Livshits had retired from that organization to help them start the private anti-terrorist venture, then Terenty Suslov had come on board. When Rodion Golubko had left the Russian armed forces with the rank of "Major General", Terenty had jumped at the chance to take-in his former "Spetsnaz" leader, who now headed the paramilitary arm of their group. Randolph also knew that Kip Leeds had invested much of the twenty-million dollars he had obtained from that "black-money" Nigerian deal to underwrite the operation that had scored many successes against worldwide crimials—including some of the "black-money" men, themselves. The returns from the private operation had made all the men in this room wealthy.

Jim spotted on a buffet table a brass, pot-like object with a slender cylindrical chimney atop it, under which glowed tiny coals. The soft bubbling sound of boiling water came from it

"Tea?" Livshits noted the American's look of interest as he pulled some porcelain cups from a shelf. "It is what we call a *'samovar'* . . . for boiling tea." To Jim, the perky little boiler seemed to epitomize the congenial culture the Americans had found in Russia.

Tarliani motioned for the men to gather around a large table. "We will now review the history and progress of our organization," he said. Stepping up, Kip saw that documents and photographs were laid out on the tabletop.

Tarliani held a picture of a heavyset black man. "Busa!" Kip burst out. "The guy who disappeared that time with the receipts for the fifty-thousand dollars I deposited in that Lagos bank that started it all."

"'Busa' was the 'front-man' for the 'Cartel'. He duped people into working without their knowledge for the criminals' purposes."

Kip laughed. "But I turned the tables on them—*I kept their money!*"

Jim Randolph looked at him. "You never told us how you did that."

"The Nigerian judges ruled that since the money had been signed-over to me by a government representative—a very corrupt government, for sure—the money was mine." Kip gave a smirk. "I paid the judges a million dollars for them to rule in my favor!"

"Did you say the money was *blackened*?"

"As part of the agreement, I got the formulas for 'cleaning' the money and I was able to convert the bills back to original. Then I deposited them in a numbered account, arranged by Tarliani, here." He glanced at the Swiss agent. "Tarliani, Livshits and Watering came to me with the plan to put together an organization. That's how we started." He looked around at the men. "I'm sure you will agree it's been a very good investment for all of us." The others nodded.

Tarliani lifted a picture. "This woman was a real success story." The men passed around the photograph of an attractive-looking female. "She and two other agents fed 'INTERNOL'—the international police organization I was with at the time—vital Intelligence about the 'Cartel' that operated out of the *'Tanuta Refinery'* in Nigeria."

Livshits pulled a rolled document from a shelf. "By the way, do you want to see what the 'Tanuta Refinery' now looks like?" He spread out the paper that looked like a large aerial photograph of a forest. The Russian tapped the print. "The refinery's wreckage is underneath this jungle cover—they never rebuilt it."

Kip stared at the featureless foilage "I had heard of it, but never saw it." On the outsized picture he recognized a tiny object at the edge of the jungle as the remains of a truck that gave the leafy green canopy its awesome scale.

Livshits shrugged. "After a few years, the jungle re-claimed it."

"And to think—at one time, it was the center of the world's terrorist network!"

Tarliani picked up a picture of a light-haired man. "This fellow was American and helped this other electronics expert." He pointed at the picture of a young-looking, cream-colored female. "They installed the system. We believe they set up a control link from the 'Tanuta Refinery' to 'Tora Bora' in the mountains of Afghanistan and northwest Pakistan. It used computer chips in their wrists—very clever of them. They actually hijacked a channel one of the American military satellites and used it to relay back-and-forth their coded messages!"

Jim Randolph spoke up. "Where did you get all these pictures of people?"

Tarliani tapped the pile of photographs. "Most of them came from our agents, using tiny cameras. Livshits's operatives were responsible for the others."

He pulled from the collection another photograph of the light-skinned black woman. "This female was the brains behind the Cartel's electronic operations—her name was 'Lisa Anaya'. She designed the 'chip implant' system for Retchko. She and the American put it together." The Swiss Inspector paused. "But 'INTERNOL' later believed that she and the American man were duped—or forced—by Retchko to do it."

Rodion Golubko spoke up. "We used the same type system of wrist-chips in Russia."

"They gave our 'K-G-B' agents a tremendous advantage over the 'C-I-A'," Livshits put in. "Using satellites, we could track our people to anywhere on the planet, right down to the very room they were in!"

Kip was looking at a paper. "What about the 'invisible technology'? I was told the United States never used it."

Tarliani shrugged. "Your government killed it—very foolish of them. But the man we called, *'Agent U'*, the Middle-Easterner—*his people made it work.*"

"They used it for a long time on the Texas-Mexico border," Randolph said, "in the people- smuggling operation."

Kip was incredulous. "They made people *invisible* to take them across the border?"

"They did it for many years!"

Kip stared at a photograph of another blond man and a young woman. "Who are these two?"

General Golubko squinted at the picture of the man and an athletic-looking female. "That woman looks familiar, to me." His eyes went wide. "Of course! I trained her at the 'Spetsnaz Academy'! One of two females we ever had! She was a tough little fighter. She actually bested some of our men in hand-to-hand combat exercises! But how did she get to Nigeria?"

Tarliani turned over the photograph. "Her name was *'Marisol Montoya'* and she was a Havana policewoman . . . she flew to Nigeria on the Cartel's cargo airplane. Retchko gave her security duties.

"The American's name was *'Landay'* . . . *'Lawrence J. Landay'*. Went under the name, *'Larry Landay'*." Tarliani read more off the back of the picture. "He was a fugitive from American Justice. Landay helped 'Lisa Anaya' build the 'chip-implant' system for Retchko. We believe the Cuban woman and this Landay are now somewhere in South America."

Tarliani shuffled the prints and came up with a photograph of a large airplane. "This was the Cartel's 'Seven-Forty-Seven'. They used it to carry contraband military weapons and hardware all over the world. Even nuclear materials!"

"They really were big-time!" Kip Leeds burst out.

Randolph stared at the picture of the enormous aircraft. "How did they *obtain* this plane? A 'Seven-Forty-Seven' is a big thing to have."

Tarliani tapped the photograph. "When Iraq invaded Kuwait back in 'ninety, all the *'Iraqi Airlines'* airplanes flew to Iran. The 'Cartel' bought one and stripped it out to carry cargo. It was spotted all over the world—people remember it because it did not have any markings or numbers on it. It flew for several years." The Swiss Inspector shrugged. "It disappeared in the mid-'nineties—we believe the American air force shot it down between Cuba and lorida." He glanced at Rodion Golubko. "We know some former Soviet bomber pilots were flying it."

Kip saw a blue vein come up on the Russian general's temple. He had issues with that, evidently.

Kip picked out a photograph of a trim, very dark African in a three-piece business suit. "I remember this guy! *'Doctor Krasheev',* they called him . . . he was a big man with the *'Nation Bank of Nigeria'.* I signed the papers for the twenty-million dollars in his office."

Tarliani glanced at Kip and gave a smirk. "What happened to Krasheev was ironic—when the 'Seven-Forty-Seven' flew out of Nigeria, it carried the bad guys first to Madrid, where everything happened at 'Plaza Mayor' . . . then, it went to Libya, and on to Iran. But Krasheev missed the plane when it left Lagos! 'INTERNOL' arrested him on a warrant issued by the United States. The evidence against him for racketeering and having illegal overseas bank accounts was so solid, even his friends in the Nigerian government would not help him! We believe he is somewhere in prison, now."

Kip picked up a portrait of a very dark man. "This guy followed me on the airplane that time I came back from Nigeria. He kidnapped and mis-treated Sloane. We rescued her at the border."

Jim Randolph frowned. "His name was 'Ezego'. I hated him for what he did to her."

Tarliani gave a sneer. "He is—ah . . . 'no longer with us', as they say."

Rodion Golubko spoke up. "That was the first time we all worked together on a mission."

Kip pulled up a photograph of another very dark African. "This was *'Adwadube'*—the Nigerian lawyer."

Jim Randolph looked over his shoulder and frowned. "God! Look at those eyes!"

"His eyes were horrible-looking . . . scary—creepy." Kip went over how the man had demanded a huge sum of money from him to "clean" the "black money".

"We were never able to pin anything on him," Tarliani said.

Kip sifted through the loose stack of documents and pictures on the table. "Ah, yes! This is *'Ajiboy'*. He was the security man at the Lagos airport after the end of the Cartel." Kip looked at General Golubko. "I saw him a few days ago . . . he gives you his regards."

Rodion Golubko nodded. "Ajiboy was one of the few in Nigeria who was honest. After Retchko got away, we worked with him to clean up the terrible situation at that airport."

"It's now one of the best, anywere," Kip said. "But it sure wasn't the *first* time I was there! I thought I would be killed." He recounted to them his narrow escapes at the airport. "When I was leaving, Retchko's soldiers were pulling some Americans off the airliner at gunpoint!"

"Many people were killed at that airport while Retchko was there."

Kip lifted the photograph of a small-looking, bald-headed black man in a three-piece suit. "This man was the manager of the bank in Lagos. We now know he was the real 'Chief'' of the Cartel. He still owes me the fifty-thousand dollars he took from me."

Tarliani gave a sneer. "Good luck on that—he is now one of the Finance Ministers of Iran!"

"Our most important operation, of course, was when we found and disarmed that nuclear device that the terrorists had planted in Houston."

"A very close call!" Jim Randolph said. There was a nodding of agreement among the men.

Tarliani passed around several photographs. "This was the bomb." The pictures showed a regular-looking shipping container in a small warehouse. In the background, loomed a "Port of Houston" crane; the device had been located on the "Ship Channel", at the "Turning Basin", near downtown. A close-up showed cables leading from a control box into the big wooden crate.

"In another two minutes, the whole of downtown Houston would have gone up in a nuclear fireball. We calculated that all of the skyscraper towers would have gone down in the blast— two-hundred-thousand would have been killed at once." Tarliani tapped a chart. "Ten-square miles of central Houston would have been too radioactive to enter for weeks or months."

Jim Randolph spoke up. "The detonator was rigged to go off on a code signal from a telephone—probably from somewhere overseas. Somebody would have called the number, entered some figures on a keypad and the bomb would have gone off."

"We kept it out of the newspapers and off the TV. There would have been panic."

"That was our most important success," Randolph added.

Tarlini looked around at the others. "We now know that the culprits were 'Agent U' and Retchko, and their criminal organization."

Livshits pulled a picture from the stack. *"Agent U'!"* the men said in unison, as they stared at the familiar form of the man who for years was known world-wide as the most dangerous of all the terrorists.

"He was in the mountains of eastern Afghanistan for years until the Israelis killed him in a commando raid."

"Retchko is still in Pakistan, we believe," Tarliani said.

The Swiss Inspector pointed to a grainy picture of a bald-headed white man. "You all remember 'Retchko', of course."

Kip stared at the telephoto of the man taken at Plaza Mayor, at the time of the event. Who could forget the man who remained one of the most wanted fugitives in the world? His eyes widened—in the same picture he spotted Nixie in the background. It was when she had gone to Madrid to "translate" for him and they had gotten caught up in the events of that awful day.

"That is the only photograph we have of Retchko, other than—*this* one." Livshits held up another print. "This picture was taken by the security camerat the Moscow train station the same night he got away." The Russian agent tapped the picture. "It shows a different-looking "Semen Putridchenko" of the

"Academy" in Moscow. At that time, he was bushy-haired with a dark mustache."

General Golubko, who was staring at the picture over Kip's shoulder, spoke up. "Only minutes before, I had stopped him from shooting Yeltsin and Gorbachev at the 'White House'!"

Tarliani glanced at the silver-haired, retired Russian Special Forces officer. "You still have a personal *'vendetta'* against him, do you not?"

The blue vein stood out on the general's temple. He nodded. "'Putridchenko'—that is his real name—had been a security officer in the G-R-U Division of the Soviet General Staff at the Defense Ministry. We found out he had been giving the Chechen rebels advance information about our movements. Many of our brave Russian soldiers died in Grozny because of what that traitor did. I have wanted to catch him ever since."

Terenty spoke. "He captured my best friend while we were in Chechnya and made him work for the 'Cartel'." He picked up a picture of a handsome, blond-haired young man in a military uniform and stared at it with grim lips, shaking his head. "It is difficult to believe he has been gone now almost twenty years..."

Tarliani looked around the table at the other men. "Gentlemen—and 'comrades' . . . we shall now pledge to keep after Retchko and the other criminals . . . for the peoples of the world—and for ourselves." The partners in the crime-fighting organization nodded; they were all now well-to-do from the proceeds of their efforts over the past several years. Their private war against international criminals and terrorists would go on.

The Swiss criminologist spoke again. "For a long time, Retchko and the others have been our enemies . . . we must continue our efforts to kill or capture them."

~~~~

PART ONE

THE CARTEL

-1-

Nigerian Airspace; Tuesday Morning, December 17, 1991:

The climbing 747 nosed up through the cloud layer into a dazzling realm of blue. General Leonid Efimovich Retchko jabbed the seat-recliner button, settled back, and looked out the window. The pudgy, hairless Ukrainian gazed down at the carpet of cottony cloud-tops receding beneath the airplane to the roar of the great turbines that were thrusting the gargantuan cargo-passenger jetliner ever higher into the sunshiny West African sky.

Then the former Soviet general, the Cartel's "Chief of Security", snapped open his briefcase. Leafing through papers, he scanned down pages of notes concerning the recent events that had brought him to this seat on this airplane, for he was now headed toward important destinations and people he would seek to bend to the Cartel's—*and to his own*—advantage. His plans would be world-changing.

Before leaving Lagos, Nigeria, he had been tipped-off that the *'Interrepublican Security Service'*, the successor to the *'KGB'*, was searching world-wide for him. He trusted that his new name and his new appearance would be good enough.

* * *

Interrepublican Security Service Headquarters, Moscow; at the Same Time:

Livshits stood at the upper-floor window and stared down at snowy Lubyanka Square, where *'Iron Felix's'* statue had stood during the Soviet years until the hooligans had pulled it down last August. Recently given back its original Czarist name, the grim-looking, snow-covered plaza seemed to symbolize the uncertainty that had settled over this vast land during the past several weeks

3

as in inexorable stages the Communist Party had lost its grip. Then Yeltsin had dissolved it completely a few days ago. To Livshits, the leaden December sky that draped over Moscow at this season matched the mood of the whole country. Now he was hearing that some of the bigger parts of the old Soviet Union, including Russia and Ukraine, along with Belarus, Kazakhstan and some of the other former Republics, were about to re-constitute themselves into a non-binding, so-called "Commonwealth of Independent States", with Moscow at the head. The new arrangement would have been anathema to Lenin, a true believer in an all-powerful *Central Authority*.

And right now, there was not even a worthy security apparatus: the old "KGB" was no more and its successor was having to endure the tepid title, "Interrepublican Security Service", although he knew it would soon become the "Federal Security Service". Not the universally-feared impact of "KGB", of course, but better than its current name. But the Intelligence and security agency was floundering for leadership; no one expected the man in temporary charge to stay much longer. Livshits gazed out the window at the fluttering snowflakes and shook his head. None of this bode well for Russia.

He lit a cigarette and thought on. What the Bureau needed was a better name and an assertive someone at the top with the skills and the political connections to get the organization back to where it should be. When he had been posted in Dresden, East Germany a few years ago, he had known such an individual: *'Putin',* had been his name—*'Vladimir Putin'.* Livshits drew on his cigarette and remembered. Putin had been a capable, ambitious, and intelligent young agent who had impressed his superiors; a family man with an attractive wife and good-looking offspring. Slight of build, the resourceful, aggressive KGB agent, who kicked a ferocious foot in martial arts contests—a fact to which Livshits's own chin would attest—had the personal attributes and political aptitude that could, given the right circumstances and connections, carry him far in the uncertain Russia that was soon to come. He would keep watching Vladimir Putin.

Livshits had considered making a run for the Bureau's head job himself, then decided better of it, for now. There would likely be several more shake-ups at the higher levels after the Kruychkov fiasco: the bespectacled former KGB chief was now in prison, charged with leading the abortive coup last August. Everyone was looking over his shoulder, these days—who would want *that* job, right now? Livshits would wait until things had settled down before looking for any bigger desks at which to sit. Besides, he had a score to settle with that traitor "Semen Putridchenko".

His attention went back to the intriguing reports from Nigeria about a mysterious "Soviet general" about whom the Bureau in Lagos kept hearing, who seemed to be involved in some sort of activity—perhaps military; perhaps some other type of operation—in that African country. Since he knew there were no actual "Soviet generals" in Nigeria, he would instruct his agents down there to look into it.

* * *

Aboard the 747 over West Africa:

Retchko's humorless eyes scanned down his notes. "Larry Landay", the American, new on the scene at the refinery, and "Lisa Anaya", both electronics engineers, were making progress with the satellite setup. When the system was operating, he would be able to control his agents around the world with chips implanted in their wrists. But to make it work, they would have to find a satellite channel for the tracking system. Based on the arrangement he had used back in Moscow before he had fled from the aborted August *'coup'*, they would tap into a military communications satellite and "hijack" some of its circuits to run the system. In Russia, the security services had employed Soviet satellites; this time, he would have to do it without the host knowing what was going on. Landay seemed to have knowledge about military communications that the Cartel could use without him realizing his contributions. And Lisa was unaware of the true nature of the system—she was telling the American that they were setting up an industrial data link with the U.S. equipment he had brought from California, using shipping documents from Nigeria that they did not know were actually faked. How ironic, then, that the United States authorities now wanted to arrest Landay on a variety of charges of which he was not even aware he was being sought!

But something about the fair-haired American unsettled him. The hairless European sat back in the airliner seat and narrowed his eyes. On several occasions he had detected Landay and Lisa interacting in certain ways that were far too casual for a strictly professional relationship. He had not thought much about it at the time, but at the beginning Lisa had been quite anxious to have the American work with her. By now he was fairly certain that they had known each other before—*as lovers, perhaps?* He was not going to allow *anyone* to get ahead of him with the youthful woman until he had exacted his just dues from her; he was serious about that. Ever since that time when he had saved her life by mouth-to-mouth resuscitation after a lightning strike, he had promised himself he would seduce the slender, cream-skinned young Nigerian woman. If it came down to it, he would use Landay's expertise to the fullest, then kill him. He had done such things before; he could do it again. Then he would make his move on the girl.

Some movement up front caught Retchko's attention; through the open cockpit door he could see his Ukrainian compatriots working the airliner's controls; the former Soviet bomber pilots were talking back and forth over the airplane noises in their native tongue. How good it was to be speaking again with the pilots in rich, robust "Russian", instead of having to use that gross "English" with those people back in Nigeria! And how surprised he had been to learn that these pilots had left the *'USSR'* the same way he had—by stealing away from the military that for years had trained and nurtured them.

But drastic changes were now taking place back in the vast country they had always known as the "Soviet Union"—that nation was now coming apart. The supposed magic creations that Gorbachev had called "Peristroika" and "Glasnost" had been unmasked as unworkable frauds. Now it looked as if both

"Comrade Mikhail" and the longstanding Marxist-Leninist ideology were going down together. Yeltsin, that pompous fool, was talking about something he called the "Commonwealth of Independent States", through which he would try to hold together everything. In this, of course, he would not succeed. *Nothing* succeeded in Russia, except the military, the space program, and the KGB—and now even that once-respected State Security apparatus had fallen into itself. In its place they were putting up something to be called the "Federal Security Service" that could not possibly do as well as the old Intelligence and State Security operation had done. Even worse, except for the "Strategic Rocket Forces", that were still intact, the once-invincible Soviet military was now fracturing into an impotent aggregation of squabbling, unpaid malcontents. Unless the downhill slide was reversed—and fast—before long, the country might not even be able to defend itself against the Imperialists except as to launch a pre-emptive nuclear strike against the Americans, which was unthinkable.

But his secret contacts back there were also telling him that the elite Special Forces, the "Spetsnaz", were as robust as ever. Retchko thought about his former friend, "Rodion Golubko", now a Spetsnaz operations leader. Wonder what he was doing, right now? Still training the misfits he kept having to defend to his superiors for breaking the rules? He remembered in particular a very promising pair—"Suslov" and "Lychin" had been their names; he would never forget them—who kept getting into trouble. Were they the soldiers of Russia's future—stubborn individualists who would now succeed through *'initiative'*—the opposite of the old Soviet System, with its "Political Officers" and rigid Marxist military theories and formulas that controlled everything? All those ideologies were now being shoved aside. The changes underway back there were going to be fundamental and sweeping.

* * *

"Damn!" The female "National Security Agency" analyst frowned into the viewfinder—the parking apron at the Lagos airport was vacant; the subject 747 was gone. Less than twelve

7

hours ago, the INTERNOL agent there had passed information that the international police organization had relayed on a secure circuit to the Americans that the aircraft, surrounded by fuel trucks, was loading many crates and containers and looked to be readying for a long flight.

The woman pulled up images from a satellite pass taken eleven hours earlier. There they were—the large fuel trucks, the forklifts and the crates and pallets around the mysterious jetliner, suggesting it would soon be leaving on a lengthy trip. She zoomed down the viewfinder: there was something on the side of one of the big boxes, but from far above in orbit, even with magnified side-scan, she could not make it out. For a long moment she thought it might be the nuclear symbol, then dismissed that possibility—there was no atomic capability in Nigeria.

* * *

Benina International Airport, Benghazi, Libya; Mid-Afternoon That Same Day:

The probing tires of the 747's landing gear grabbed the pavement with a rubbery cry and a cloud of blue smoke; the behemoth Boeing was returning to earth. While the airplane taxied toward the line of hangars, Retchko fingered once more through his notes. The airport here at Benghazi, Libya would be the first stop on his journey—at this coastal North African terminal the cargo jet would off-load the automatic weapons and ammunition onto trucks that would take it the twenty kilometers to the Port of Benghazi. The general read the manifest with admiration for those who had put together the plan: Under a heavy guard the goods would travel by a disguised boat through the Bosporus and the Black Sea to a friendly northeastern Turkish port; across Iran by special arrangement with that country's Revolutionary government to the Caspian Sea; around by boat to another port; then overland to Grozny, Chechnya. These thirteen-thousand *'Kalashnikov AK-74'* automatic rifles had already had an adventurous career: manufactured in the Soviet Union;

8

shipped to Cuba; used by the *'Castroites'* in their Angolan intervention; recently brought from Angola to Nigeria by this same airplane; and now on their way to Chechnya to battle the Russians who had made them in the first place.

As the pilots cut the engines, Retchko snatched up his briefcase and made for the spiral staircase. At the rear of the main deck, a motorized, scissors-type, heavy-duty-looking elevator was already raised to cargo-deck-level; ground-crewmen had swung aside the big doors and other workers were taking away the straps that held crates to the floor. One of the workmen started the forklift that had made the trip inside the airplane. Three tractor-trailer trucks roared up and came to a stop; a ground-crewman motioned for Retchko to step onto the elevator platform to be lowered to the pavement.

"General Retchko?" The Ukrainian turned about to see a slender, turbaned Libyan. "I am 'Ahmed'," the young-looking fellow spoke in accented Russian, "I am your translator."

Inside a hangar, another man, also crowned with a turban, gestured toward an open door. The general stepped into a conference room where a number of men, all but one in casual civilian clothes, were sitting around a long table. At one end sat a dark-haired man in a conspicuous beige military uniform and an embroidered *'fez'* atop his head.

"Be seated, general." The turbaned man then spoke some words in his native tongue to the other men that set them nodding in what Retchko took to be some sort of approval. "These are our scientific advisors." He turned to the uniformed individual. "I now introduce you to the head of our nuclear program."

The Libyan arose and spoke in the direction of the visitor; his bushy eyebrows arranging and re-arranging themselves as he talked. Even though the North African's words were incomprehensible to the Ukrainian, Retchko thought he looked and sounded businesslike; a good sign.

"He says he sends greetings to you from *'Our Esteemed Leader'* who is familiar with the objectives and capabilities of your organization. He is seeking to develop a nuclear program for his country. He believes you can help us."

The Libyan spoke again, then stopped for the interpreter.

9

"So far," Ahmed translated, "we have obtained technology through a certain scientist in Pakistan who is acting outside the government of that country. Also, much of Libya's nuclear equipment and technical help has come from North Korea."

Retchko knew the airplane was carrying hundreds of crated North Korean-made gas-centrifuge devices to Iran. He nodded at the Libyan then at the linguist. "Ask him what he wants from us."

The official and the turbaned technician talked for some moments, then the translator turned back to the visitor. "He says he needs plutonium pellets . . . he wants to obtain an amount for breeder reactor research."

Retchko had the authority to make such arrangements; the *"Chief"* had made it clear to him before he had left Lagos on this trip that the objective of the journey was to establish connections between the Cartel and other organizations, including governments. "I can offer you pellets in lead containers," he told Ahmed the interpreter, who relayed the information to the researcher.

The man listened, then spoke back something. "Libya will be pleased to pay you in jet fuel."

Retchko tapped his fingertips together in the mannerism he had picked up from the Capitalist bankers. "The contract must give the value of the fuel in American dollars with me as the broker."

While he waited, the gesturing North Africans talked among themselves in their language. Sitting expressionless across from them, the bald European felt pleased with himself; the fuel would go to the Cartel; he would take two-percent of the total dollar value of it as a broker's fee, as he had learned by observing the refinery's purchasing and sales departments. He would have them transmit his funds electronically under blind cover to his new, secret bank account in the Cayman Islands. The dollar amount of this transaction alone would be more than he could have made in comparable Soviet rubles in two decades as a military officer back in Moscow. If this was Capitalism, he was all for it.

The interpreter spoke for the men. "When can we expect delivery?"

Retchko gave a half-smile he trusted would mask his cynicism. "As a matter of fact, we can deliver the pellets very soon." His fingertips tapped together faster. "Let us prepare the papers."

The interpreter said something to one of the turbaned men; the fellow left the room. Right away, the Libyan came back with a sheaf of printouts in his hands. Retchko was surprised at the man's quick return—these people were proving to be rather more sophisticated than he had at first thought.

The man handed the sheets to the scientist in the uniform, who scanned each section and scratched something on several pages, then passed the forms to Retchko. The first document concerned the nuclear pellets, described as "Crated Fruit".

Another sheet of paper crossed the table. "These cover the refined fuels," the interpreter said, pointing to a space for the Ukrainian's signature. "We will make Amsterdam the contract delivery point."

Retchko knew that the Cartel had an office in Amsterdam under the cover name of *'Hannecker- Johannanvelt, Ltd.'* From what he had learned about petroleum shipments, he also knew that the actual jet fuel would never leave Holland; they would receive the amount from stocks along the way of the Cartel's aircraft on their journeys—the big jet engines' thirst for fuel had to be satisfied wherever they went. Double-blind electronic funds-transfers from the Libyans to local suppliers would take care of the payments.

Retchko produced a lopsided smile; he had a secret he knew would enhance his credibility that he would now spring on them. "The pellets you requested are aboard the airplane, *now*."

All the Libyan eyebrows went up. The uniformed man said some rapid words to the turbaned linguist. "He wishes to examine the container."

"We can do that now . . . after brokerage is done, you can load it onto your truck right away." "Brokerage" would be his two-percent commission to his account at the Cayman bank.

Ahmed, catching the researcher's gesture, nodded toward the open door. "Let us see the pellets."

11

"You can see the *container*, now. The actual pellets are highly radioactive, of course."

There was a scraping of chairs as the men arose and filed out of the building into the chilly afternoon sunshine. A blustery wind out of the north had come up; for the first time since leaving Moscow, the bald Retchko missed having the Russian fur cap he had left behind.

He and Ahmed joined up with the uniformed man and the others and made their way across the apron toward the 747, where the trucks were already loaded with the crates of rifles and ammunition. The scientist said something to the interpreter, who turned to Retchko. "No papers to sign?"

"There will be no written record of the armaments," the Ukrainian said. The answer seemed to satisfy the Libyans. Retchko watched the trucks carrying the crates disappear out of sight; soon the weapons would be in action in Chechnya against the Russians.

And his money was already electronically posted to his account in Grand Cayman.

Retchko called up to a workman at the open rear door of the airplane's cargo deck. After an exchange of words using the interpreter as a go-between, the fellow disappeared into the forward part of the cabin. In a few minutes the forklift appeared with a wooden box about six feet square perched on its front forks; the universal "Nuclear" symbol was stencilled on the crate's side.

As the forklift and its load descended on the scissors elevator, Retchko stepped forward to examine the wooden case when it reached the ground. But just as his hand touched the big box, a gust of wind blew off a tarpaulin tied across its top that billowed around the front of the forklift's steel frame. His view suddenly blocked, the driver tramped hard on the brake pedal, causing the big box to rock forward onto its bottom front edge, gouging the pavement! Wide-eyed, Retchko and the Libyan technicians backed away in a hurry and gaped at the crate, now perched at angle, its bottom edge lodged on the end of the forks.

A cargo handler ran up, grabbed the wayward canvas and tugged it aside. After holding onto the big box for a moment to try to keep it from tipping over all the way, the fellow hopped back as the shouting, swearing operator put the vehicle in gear and scooped up the rocking box back onto the machine's forks. Turning about, the roaring forklift carried the weighty plywood crate to an awaiting nearby truck and deposited it onto its trailer.

The 747's captain stepped up just then. "The aircraft is fueled," he said in Russian, pointing at the big rear door, still open from delivering the weapons and the pellets."

Retchko turned to the turbaned Libyan. "I see you speak several languages."

"I know Arabic, Farsi, Russian and English," the fellow said with a quick on-and-off smile. "I attended the *'Soviet Academy'* in Tripoli during the time they were helping our country with oil exploration and building our military. I do translation—I could go with you." He looked hopeful.

The Ukrainian squinted in thought at the younger man "We *will* need a translator where we are going . . . could you come along with us on this trip?" Retchko mentioned an amount of money in American dollars. "We will be gone for some days. We will then return you to Libya."

The young man brightened.

"I will speak to your superior." The Ukrainian stepped over to the uniformed nuclear scientist, who was giving instructions to the driver of the truck carrying the plutonium pellets.

In a minute, Retchko returned. "It is arranged . . . you are coming with us!" The fellow's face lit up. "Get your things and be back here in half an hour. We will be leaving as soon as it is dark."

Ahmed turned toward the office, nodding. No one saw him grinning to himself.

One of the Libyans was motioning at Retchko. He followed the man and the others toward a low building next to the hangar. Inside, the aroma of food reminded him he had not eaten since before they had left Lagos some hours ago. The advisors from the conference room were already there, loading their plates.

By the time he had downed his share of the local fare, evening had come to Benghazi. The chief pilot gestured toward the door. "We must be leaving," he said in Russian.

Outside, the Libyan atomic researcher offered his hand to Retchko and said some words to him in his language.

Ahmed, who had just come back with his travel bag, stepped forward to translate. "He says he is pleased with the pellet arrangement and wants to work with your organization in the future." The head nuclear scientist, still gripping Retchko's hand and staring straight into the bald Ukrainian's eyes, said something else to the general with a glance at the young man. "He says *'The Leader of the Country'* will be much pleased."

Twenty minutes later, the enormous airplane lifted from the runway into the North African night and set a southeasterly course over the sandy Sahara in the direction of Khartoum, Sudan.

-2-

KRT Airport, Khartoum, Sudan, 3:34 AM, Local Time, Wednesday, December 18, 1991:

A jarring thump against the side of the airplane jolted Retchko awake. Looking out the window, he was surprised to see that the 747 was parked at an airport. It was dark outside; he had slept through most of the latest leg of the trip and the entire landing. Some of the pages of his notes he had been reading before he dozed off had slid from his lap to the floor. Down below, shouting grounds-crewmen were bustling about a set of portable steps that were rolled up against the side of the fuselage; over a dim light on a hangar was the single word in faded letters: KHARTOUM. His watch showed it was about half-past three in the morning, local time.

The slumbering Ahmed, sprawled across a row of seats at the rear of the upper cabin, would now have to wake up and start earning his keep. Retchko observed that the fellow still had on his turban. Are those things *that* important to these people? They must be, he decided.

Outside, a slow parade of headlights was advancing across the dark, dewy pavement in the direction of the airplane; these would be the passengers who would be coming aboard—Saudi Arabians, as he already knew, whom the cargo airliner would take to Pakistan. From there, Retchko would go with them overland to the mountains of "Tora Bora", on the Afghanistan border. In that remote area, the Cartel would build an underground headquarters for these men.

The men coming aboard were led by a young man who was setting up an operation to attack Western interests—the United States in particular. Retchko already knew that the fellow, who was traveling under the code name of *'Agent U'*, had a considerable personal fortune; had a thorough fundamentalist religious education; had been in Sudan for some time; and was now going to the inaccessible region of Tora Bora to train his followers for religious warfare. The man was ambitious, rich, was driven by ideology, and had long-range goals—just the type individual with whom Retchko and the Cartel could do business.

As the bald man sat taking it all in, a dull headache he had noticed earlier seemed to be getting worse. He figured he must have slept in an awkward position the flight down from Benghazi. Retchko arose from his seat and walked up the aisle; if he got up and moved around, perhaps the throbbing pain would go away.

* * *

This was no ordinary headache. When the crate of radioactive pellets had slipped off the forklift at the Benghazi airport, a heavy side plate on the big lead container inside the wooden crate had snapped several bolts, opening a seam. In the half-second before he stepped back, an invisible shaft of radiation had focused directly on Retchko's forehead, delivering a concentrated beam to the frontal lobe of his brain concerned with reasoning and personality. At once, millions of his brain cells had begun to die or mutate.

The man who had grabbed the container to steady it had received a lethal dose—even now, back at Bengazhi, he was becoming very ill with undiagnosed radiation sickness and would die a terrible, mysterious death in three days.

When the forklift had re-scooped the crate, the plate had slid back into place and the radiation leak had stopped.

* * *

There came a bustling down on the main deck; a half-dozen bearded, turbaned men in flowing, shawl-like outfits were trudging up the steps. Retchko guessed the next-to-last man in the contingent was the group's leader. As the Ukrainian stepped aside and the men shuffled in single file toward the back of the cabin without speaking, he thought they looked fatigued, as if they had been on the move for some time. Ahmed, who was now awake, stood up and said some words in Arabic, motioning for

16

the newcomers to sit down. The swarthy, young-looking "Leader" took a seat on the back row and looked around with liquid brown eyes as he fastened his seat belt. Meanwhile, bumping noises from the bottom of the airplane suggested that the men were bringing a lot of personal gear with them.

Then came the muffled sounds of airplane doors closing; the vehicles and the portable steps that had delivered the men and their baggage were pulling away. With the usual whines and vibrations the engines started coming up. In another minute, the 747 made a turn and lunged onto a taxiway, its landing lights showing the way. As the huge airplane rocked along the taxiway in the gloom, it seemed to Retchko as if the pilots were in a hurry to get the aircraft away from Khartoum. The careening cargo jetliner leaned onto the lighted runway and at once the engines went to takeoff power. In another forty-seconds, it arose into the Sudanese night.

There was another sharp pain in Retchko's forehead. Strange, he winced; he had never had many headaches. The roaring of the aircraft's engines and the air against its aluminum skin grated against his eardrums. He fumbled for the recliner button and settled back. He was sweating.

* * *

Aboard United States Navy "Ticonderoga" Class "Aegis" Cruiser in the Persian Gulf:

At the lower left edge of the circular screen, a bright green dot was blinking. The specialist squinted at the air and surface scan radar set of the *'Aegis Combat System'* and spoke into a headset microphone. At other consoles in the "Electronic Warfare Suite", tracking radars converged on the aircraft as it entered the monitored airspace.

"No identification signals."

The watch officer spoke some words to the executive officer on the bridge, then felt the deck tilt as the cruiser leaned into a left turn and came about on a northerly course parallel to the Iranian coast that was about fifteen miles to starboard. At the warship's bow and stern, gun turrets swung to port; amidships, muzzle covers dropped from the multiple barrels of the portside *'Phalanx'* anti-aircraft gun-battery as it trained and elevated in the direction of the unidentified aircraft.

Coded signals from the cruiser beamed over to the nearby aircraft carrier; two minutes later a pair of F-14 *'Tomcats'*, their twin orange-blue exhausts following behind them in the pre-dawn darkness, shot off the flight deck on an intercept course. Climbing out, in a few minutes the fighters drew alongside the unlighted mystery aircraft. The flight leader and his wingman took positions behind and below the airplane and took out hand-held lights they shined over the fuselage and the bottom of the wings of the four-engine airplane.

"'Boeing Seven-Forty-Seven '. . . no markings," the flight leader radioed.

The voice from the carrier came back. "No markings?"

"Negative. Aircraft has no markings."

"Roger that. Maintain contact to the Iran coast."

In a few minutes, when the mysterious airplane passed into Iranian airspace, the Navy jets turned away. The 747 continued on its way toward the northeast.

* * *

The captain glanced over his shoulder at Retchko, who was standing behind him, then turned to the co-pilot and the flight engineer and let out a long breath. "They are leaving, now." The four men watched the flashing strobe lights of the American fighters swing away into the gloom.

"When we were flying the *'Tupolev One-Sixty'* supersonic bomber over the northern oceans," the pilot said, "we had this happen many times . . . the Americans tried to intimidate us." By the lights of the instruments in the darkened cockpit, Retchko caught the man's smirk. "What those bastards did not know was that we had them in the sights of our concealed side-aimed laser defenses all the time they were beside us—very close beside us— *they would never have known what hit them.*" The co-pilot was nodding, as was the flight engineer. "There were times I was—"

the pilot held his finger over a button on the center console—
"this close to starting a 'World War'."

Retchko was proud of these airmen; even though he and the
pilots had served in far-separated branches of the Soviet military,
all along they had been on the same side in the so-called "Cold
War" against the Imperialists.

The determined, resourceful insurgents the Cartel now
supported—even though grounded in an ideology based on a
religion incomprehensible to Retchko—possessed great resources
and stood to very much benefit the *"Organization"*, which was
the cover name of the Cartel that would supply their weaponry,
training, and technical expertise. Standing in the darkness of the
airliner's cockpit, the bald man grinned to himself; even though
he was athiest, those religious zealots were going to put more
money into his pockets than he could have ever imagined.

Ahead of and to the right of them, the purple line of dawn,
topped by a thin, curving layer of orange, spread across the
Iranian horizon, breaking his reverie. Retchko stared at the
colorful spectacle. "How long to Teheran?"

The co-pilot punched some figures into the flight computer.
"An hour and twenty minutes."

The captain called out to the flight engineer. "Turn on the
transponder." At his rear console the third pilot moved a switch.
"We are in Iranian airspace—they are expecting us."

"You are just now turning it on?"

"This is a secret mission outside the normal communication
and navigation channels. That was why the Americans were
looking us over with lights . . . it is their standard procedure.
When we crossed over the Iranian frontier they turned away
without doing anything."

The Ukrainian returned to the cabin and dropped into his
window seat. All the Arabs except the fellow who seemed to be
their leader were in slumber. A reading light was on over the
rearmost seat, where he and Ahmed were talking.

Too keyed-up to sleep, the general leafed through some more
pages, then stopped at his notes about the Cuban girl. At the start,
he had been unsure about her—she was a *female*, after all—but
the fact that the young woman had graduated from the "Soviet

Special Forces Academy" was proof she was up to the task; not only were its physical, mental and political standards very high, once she got out of there she would have had all the necessary skills to carry out any assignment. He remembered how she had overpowered one of best (and biggest) local soldiers in a mock hand-to-hand combat exhibition the other day back at the refinery. The fellow had thought she was going to kill him. What the soldier did not know was that her next move *would* have killed him. Based on that, and her knowledge of investigative work from having been a Havana policewoman, he had left her in charge of security while he was gone.

And the intelligent, athletic young Latina had come to him as much as a gift. She had stolen-away on the same 747 he was now aboard when it had flown from Havana to Nigeria. Something about a personal matter, she had said. He once heard the American, Landay, describe her as "wiry"—trim waist; defined arms and shoulders; firm chest; tight hips and muscular legs—female attributes he had always favored. The girl had all kinds of possibilities; indeed she did.

The Ukrainian's thoughts turned to Betty Nkrume. She was now at Tanuta City; he had seen her several times about the plant with her husband, who now held the title of "Refinery Manager" in name only—and knew it. The African was looking more de-spiritied by the day, which was fine with Retchko; his plan to push the man aside and get his wife for himself was taking hold. Retchko thought about those several occasions recently when he and Betty had been in close company and the cream-colored young woman had given him knowing, discreet looks—but nothing that would give away what was already between them. He was certain that what had happened that time at the *'Temple of the Terrarianists'*—operated by that ridiculous "Adept", as the bearded, robed old mystic had called himself—had been merely a foretaste of what would come later in generous amounts. He could already imagine her supple body next to his.

How could he have ever imagined all this when he got on that train back in Moscow, when he had fled Russia in disguise to escape retribution for having been on the side of the anti-Gorbachev plotters? A few minutes later, the Libyan translator slid into the aisle seat next to Retchko. "General, the man back there"—Ahmed gave his head a toss toward the turbaned fellow in the rear seat—"wants you to meet with the scientist in charge of the Pakistan nuclear program."

The Cartel's Chief of Security's eyebrows went up. He remembered that the Libyan in the military uniform back at Benghazi had mentioned something about a "Pakistani researcher" who was working on his own nuclear projects, as well as with the government. *Was this a new opportunity?*

Retchko nodded. "When we get to Islamabad, ask him to take us to the man."

The young interpreter noticed the older man wince "Is there something wrong?"

The pale Ukrainian put his hand to his bald forehead. "I have a headache."

Ahmed stepped to the rear of the cabin and said something to the Arab, then came back with a small bottle in his hand. "He says to have these." Retchko took the little plastic container and read the the label printed in Arabic and English, *'Al-Shifa Aspirin'*. The pills had a Khartoum, Sudan, manufacturing address. Retchko frowned. "They make *aspirin* in Sudan?" The general swallowed a fisful of the tablets. In a few minutes the devilish headache seemed to better; it was all probably just tension. But he was now very tired.

* * *

Mehrabad International Airport, Teheran, Iran; Wednesday, December 18, 1991; 7:17 AM:

The 747's four jet engines whined to a stop; Retchko squinted out the window at a sign on a low building in black English letters: **TEHERAN**. Above it, a swirly green script spelled out what he assumed was the same word in the local language.

In what to Retchko seemed to have become a standard ritual, a vague thump ran through the airplane as ground-crewmen shoved portable steps against the upper front fuselage. As he

21

watched, a motorized, scissors-type elevator moaned up into position at the rear cargo door. Some trailer trucks had moved up to load the crates of hundreds of North Korean gas centrifuges the cargo plane had brought from Pyongyang through Lagos, Nigeria.

The Arabs were awake; the man known as "Agent U" was talking with Ahmed the interpreter, their heads close together, nodding.

The translator came forward and once more dropped into the seat next to Retchko. "He says he has important people he wants you to meet here in Teheran."

* * *

Mountain View, California; That Same Day:

Joe Anglin stood in shock and consternation as the men with **FEDERAL AGENT** in bold yellow letters on the backs of their black leather jackets pulled yellow tape around the little building housing Larry Landay's business. The men had showed up a few minutes earlier with an arrest warrant that read, *'The United States of America vs. Lawrence J. Landay', Also Known As Larry Landay'* and had ordered him out of the place before he barely had time to turn off the coffee maker. He had had to convince the officers he was not, in fact, "Lawrence J. Landay", but was, instead, his friend. Armed federal officers took up positions around the place. With a groan of dismay, Joe realized the decoder he would need to contact Larry in Nigeria was still in there. Now, he had no way to warn his friend at the Tanuta Refinery that he was a wanted man and that the equipment he took with him to Nigeria was embargoed!

A pair of serious-looking agents were walking toward him; one held a paper in his hand.

"Joseph Anglin? I have a warrant for your arrest—you have the right to remain silent . . ."

While the agent recited Joe's "Miranda" rights, the other whipped the stunned prisoner's arms behind him, slapped handcuffs on his wrists and gave him a quick pat-down!

"No weapons."

Someone pressed down Joe's head and shoved him from behind into the back seat of an un-marked government car.

* * *

Federal Court House, San Francisco, California; at the Same Time:

"These indictments are the beginning of a major push against international arms merchants who are involved in illegal technology transfer and those supplying weapons to terrorists." On the sidewalk outside the San Francisco Federal Building, the Prosecutor held up some manila envelopes to the reporters. The rumble of a passing sanitation truck momentarily drowned out the snapping and whizzing of news cameras.

A female television reporter spoke up. "Are there local people or companies involved?"

"I cannot give you specifics, but there is a *'firm'* in the 'South Bay' area that is now under indictment, along with some of its officials. We have arrest warrants working for those individuals."

"Which company is it? Which people?" The reporters were clamoring for attention.

"I cannot tell you at this time. But we believe its chief operating officer may have fled the country."

* * *

Tanuta Refinery, Tanuta City, Nigeria; Later that Day:

Larry Landay hung his hard hat on the washroom hook and turned for the showers, peeling off his shirt as he splashed along in the damp, muggy space toward the stall. "Man, it was hot out there, today!" he muttered, reaching for the shower handle. Tanuta City was close to the Equator.

As the water cascaded over him, his thoughts went on. For the past several days, he and Lisa Anaya had been installing the equipment racks in the transmitter building for Retchko's system. Even though he told her he was curious what it was all about, it seemed she was being close-mouthed—evading the questions, even. Today, he had asked his former girlfriend from college about tuning a dish antenna and she had snapped back at him. What was so secret about the new communications link with the refinery's Lagos headquarters?

Maybe it was time for a nighttime visit to the beach with her for some after-hours canoodling. Then he remembered the crocodiles that infested the area. That might not be such a good idea, after all. Trying to be discreet in this coastal African town was turning out not to be easy—so far, there had been no opportunity for them to "get together" like they had in the past.

He pulled on clean clothes and loafers and opened the door to the corridor, where he almost walked straight into Marisol Montoya, the former Havana policewoman who had flown with him to Nigeria and was the acting "Head of Security" while Retchko was away. The young Cuban woman glanced around; they were alone in the hallway.

"Señor Larry . . ." She lowered her voice. "I must speak to you . . . meet me at the pump-house after dark."

"The pump-house? What for?"

"Señor, it is '*muy importante*' for us . . . that is, for *all* of—" Footsteps sounded from around the corner. The girl backed away, blinking. "Okay?"

"Okay."

Larry turned about just as Lester Nkrume, the refinery manager and his wife, Betty, came up. Nodding, the two kept going in the direction of the exit to the parking lot. As the American stepped down the hallway toward the dining-room, he thought it remarkable how much the woman and her sister, Lisa Anaya, resembled each other. In fact, all of this seemed unreal; he actually *was* all the way down here in Nigeria working on this project alongside the same Lisa Anaya from his past. Who would have ever thought it? Larry remembered Joe Anglin at the office back in Mountain View, who was keeping his marketing business going while he had brought the electronic goods from California to here. Wouldn't he get a kick out of all this! Then it occurred to him he hadn't heard from his friend in a while.

PENINSULA DAILY NEWS

**LOCAL COMPANY IMPLICATED
IN INTERNATIONAL ARMS SCHEME**

**INDICTMENTS LEVIED AGAINST MTN. VIEW
FIRM; TECHNOLOGY TRANSFER AT HEART
OF CHARGES;**

COMPANY OFFICIAL MISSING

**(San Francisco)—Federal Prosecutors announced a
sweeping crackdown against alleged illegal transfers
of classified technology from the Silicon Valley to
foreign governments and terrorist groups.**

A Mountain View firm was included in the dragnet.

**Sealed indictments opened today named Landay
Marketing, LLC, and its chief officer, Lawrence J.
Landay, as defendants. Another person allegedly
affiliated with the company, identified as Joseph W.
Anglin, 34, of Santa Clara, was arrested.**

**The office of the firm in Mountain View was sealed-
off by U.S. Marshals.**

**A spokesperson said the charges include conspiracy
to defraud the U.S. Government; Violation of Technology
Transfer Statutes; Illegal Possession or Sale of
Classified Goods to Prohibited Countries and/or
Terrorist Organizations; Collusion, Conspiracy, and
Racketeering.**

The spokesperson also said that Prosecutors believed Lawrence Landay had fled the country. The company's bank accounts were frozen.

Conviction the charges carry a penalty of up to twenty years in Federal prison and a fine of $10 Million.

-3-

Larry Landay elbowed his way through the tall grass toward the boundary of the refinery complex. Behind him, the western purple sky announced that evening had arrived; ahead, in the gathering gloom, stood the vague, gray shape of the pump-house. What was so important, he wondered as he thrashed along, that he had to meet Marisol out here like *this*? His hasty retreat from the dining hall may have made Lisa suspicious. Over dinner, she had apologized for being testy with him that day. "We must finish the project before General Retchko returns," she had told him. Larry thought she looked stressed. "He is most insistent about completing it in a few days, and I am having trouble securing a satellite circuit." She caressed his forearm, oblivious to the glances of others. He'd gotten the impression she wanted to spend the evening with him, and his turn-down had produced a disappointed look on her face. The nocturnal rendezvous with the young, female, temporary "Head of Security" had spoiled what might have been the renewal of his college-days relationship with the cream-colored electronics engineer. This meeting with Marisol had better be good, he thought.

The front iron gate of the fence surrounding the concrete structure loomed up in the shadows. There came a rustling, then a slender female form, backlit by the distant lights, appeared around the corner of the building

"Larry?"

"Right here."

The *'Latina'* stepped forward and with a little jingling of keys, unlocked the gate. "I sent the guards on another assignment," she said, pulling aside a grated metal door for him, then re-locking it. She touched his elbow. "Come with me." She led him around to the side of the isolated outbuilding opposite from the refinery. The girl stopped in a thin beam of light and turned to face him. Larry stared at her. Marisol's tight, tanned skin caught the rays from the other refinery across the way.

"Why are we *here*? Could we not—"

"'Americano', listen!" Her stacatto voice cut him off. In the half-light her eyes glinted into his.

"Señor Larry—something bad is going on at this refinery." She gave a shudder. "This is a dangerous place."

His forehead creased into a frown. "Why is it dangerous?"

"I found a listening system that hears everything going on in the plant. *Everything.*"

"So what? Wouldn't it be normal to have such a thing for security?"

"Larry, General Retchko records everything people say! I listened to some of the tapes. He has much private information on people. In Cuba, I was used to this sort of thing—I was a policewoman in Havana, remember—but this is even beyond what I saw there!"

"*He is recording what we are saying, right now?*"

She shook her head. "I disconnected the microphones out here in the pump-house. That is why we are here. Also, there are none in the new building with your equipment." In the dim light the young woman stared straight into his face. She swallowed. "Señor Larry, I must ask you some questions."

"Okay, shoot." A confused look came over her face. "I mean ... 'keep talking'."

Marisol took a deep breath; the mounds of her chest rose and fell. "Señor Larry, how well do you know Lisa Anaya?" The American frowned; the young woman went on, speaking fast. "I know that she and you have some kind of ... 'arrangement'—"

Larry felt his face reddening; in the shadowy half-light the girl did not seem to notice.

Marisol looked up into his face. "Tell me about this 'project' you and Lisa are working on."

Her questions about Lisa were bothering him; he was having a hard time getting his thoughts collected. "Well, it's a—a communication link from here to the refinery's main office in Lagos."

She reached out and touched his forearm. "Oh, Señor Larry! You do not know—?" The young woman looked exasperated. "When General Retchko went on his trip and I became the security person for a while, I was curious, so I started looking around. I cracked his computer password code and found his safe combination in a file. Inside it, I found some notes he had made. They were in Russian, but I can read and speak Russian, no?"

Larry heard his pulse swishing in his ears.

The girl swallowed and went on in a hurry as if to rush something out before she thought better of it. "What you and Lisa are building is a secret tracking system that will use computer chip implants in people! He will be following many *'hombres'* with it from space." Marisol was shaking her head. "Oh, Señor Larry, you are so—what is the word?—*'naive'!*" She reached for his hand. "I found paperwork in the safe that proves this refinery is part of a 'Cartel' that is supplying weapons to what you 'Americanos' call 'terrorists'! Your satellite system will control people all over the world from here! Many countries are involved." She squeezed his hand in both of hers. "Do you not see? That is why they repaired your big airplane in Havana so fast. The Cuban government is in on it, too!"

He recalled how the 747 had been damaged on takeoff from Mexico City and Soviet airframe men in Cuba had repaired it at the Havana airport in only two days. Still, her claim that his equipment would be controlling terrorists sounded pretty far-fetched. "How are you so sure about all this?"

"Remember all those automatic rifles the airplane brought from Angola?" Larry nodded. On the flight from Havana they had stopped there. "I found records that show he is taking them to Chechnya."

"Chechnya!" Larry's eyebrows went up. "Against the Russians and all that?"

" *'Exacto'.* He also is taking nuclear materials to Iran! And he has connections with North Korea and Iraq and Libya and Cuba! And other places."

"How? Isn't he supposed to be a *Russian* general, or something?"

"He *was.* But something happened, and now he is here. There is something bad about him, Señor Larry. Something very bad."

"How does that affect me?"

"You brought the equipment here from America, no?"

"Well, yes, but—"

"Does America know what you are doing?"

Then Larry remembered that *all the paperwork to bring the electronics to Tanuta City had been handled "from Nigeria"*—there had been no American export documents, even though the goods were sensitive. A cold feeling came over him. Maybe that was why somebody had shot-up the airplane when they were taking off from Mexico City! And he had personally brought the shipment to Nigeria, which made him culpable. If Lisa had known all along that the satellite system was to be used for criminal activities, then she was part of a conspiracy! Had she duped him? If Marisol's allegations were true, he now faced a whole list of problems; not just with Lisa but also with his home country. What about his friend, Joe Anglin? If something was not right about all this—would he be dragged into it, too?

Larry was perplexed. "I've known Lisa for a long time. I cannot believe she would do anything wrong."

Marisol shrugged. "I hope I *am* wrong, but the evidence—"

"Evidence can be wrong." Larry was groping for excuses and knew it. He was concerned there was nothing wrong with her evidence.

Her eyes were focused in the distance." We must be going, now. The guards are coming back."

Larry turned about and squinted. A couple of hundred meters away a pair of wavering flashlights probed along the outer fence in their direction.

Marisol grabbed his forearm. "Señor Larry, you must not tell anyone what I said. I am trying to protect you." She glanced off; the flickering beams were coming closer. "Come!" she whispered in a breathy voice. "I do not want anyone to find us here."

The two made their way back out through the gate. After Marisol re-locked it, she led Larry into the tall grass, where, hunkered down, they loped through the dew-covered reeds.

As they stepped along, Larry spotted a low, elongated mound ahead of them in the grass. When they were about to pass it by, to his horror he realized the object was animal! Just then, whatever it was raised up and opened a huge snout, exposing the white inside of a mouth! Marisol screamed and grabbed Larry.

The mouth belonged to a twelve-foot-long crocodile!

The reptile, thrashing its tail in the grass with a loud swishing sound, stood on its thick, dumpy legs and, hissing, lunged at the terrified girl. Shrieking, she managed to side-step the thrust, but the animal snapped out again and raked her shin with its front teeth! Larry pushed her back as the crocodile made ready for its next leap. With a purposeful swishing of its rippling tail the crocodile loped toward them, its cottony mouth wide-open. But as the pair backed away from the enraged crocodile, they both tripped on something in the grass and went stumbling backward, onto the ground! Marisol, screaming in terror, tried to scoot back, but there was no escaping the beast!

Just then, Larry saw in the murky half-light that the object they had fallen over was a *pipe*. He grabbed the rusty, six-foot-long section of iron, just as the horrid creature came at him. When the thrashing, hissing reptile made its next lunge, Larry rammed the two-inch-diameter shaft down the crocodile's throat with all his might! There came a gagging, gurgling sound and dark liquid spurted out the end of the pipe and from the toothy mouth! Larry jerked back the section and swung it as hard as he could onto the clawing creature' eyes and head, again, and again as it rolled and writhed in the grass!

With one last twisting convulsion, it lay unmoving. The bloody crocodile was dead.

The hysterical girl leaped up and grabbed Larry around his neck. With a glance back at the hideous creature's ghastly form in the grass, the sweating American and the shaking Cuban girl stumbled across the shadowy field toward the looming lights of the refinery.

Still holding onto each other, the two lurched up the front steps of the employee dormitory into the common living room. The residents gasped at the whimpering young woman's gashed and bleeding foreleg. Larry lowered her onto a sofa. "Get a towel and some peroxide!" he said to the first person who rushed up.

At once, more people were standing around; all were talking at once.

"What happened?"

"Her leg is hurt!"

The sandy-haired American glanced up. "A crocodile attacked her!"

The onlookers gasped.

Frank Ogawan, the office manager, spun the dial of the lobby telephone and spoke some hurried words into the handset. "The medical officer is coming!"

Aroused from her book by the hubbub coming from downstairs, Lisa Anaya, still miffed by Larry's earlier turndown, set aside the reading and stepped down the stairs to the living room. At the far end some residents were gathered around a sofa. On it was a female in red shorts; a male was leaning over her, caressing her shoulders, her neck; her face. The tanned arms of the young woman were draped around the fellow's neck.

Oh, Larry! You killed it! You killed it!" the shaking girl in the shorts was gasping.

Lisa elbowed past Frank Ogawan, who stood aside. She gaped, wide-eyed."Larry!"

The American located the source of the voice. "Lisa!"

The cream-colored electronics engineer was frowning; her eyes darted back and forth between him and the girl on the sofa. Blushing, Larry pulled Marisol's arms away from his neck. He took a quick look at the temporary Head of Security, , then back at Lisa.

Larry missed the jealous glare that passed between the two young women.

* * *

Aboard the 747, at the Same Time:

The huge departing aircraft banked, displaying Teheran's vast sea of evening lights below the end of the wing. Retchko sat back in his seat in the darkened cabin, taking in the view, thinking it had been one hell of a good day. Even as he had gone down the steps from the airplane that morning, the Defense Minister of Iran had been standing; waiting for him. From there, they had gone in a caravan through Teheran to a big building in the center of the city, where they had feted him with a feast they called "Persian". Then, the men had stepped into the nearby hall with its high ceilings, marble floors and other trappings evoking their ancient heritage for their meetings that had lasted all day.

When it was over, he had stared up in satisfaction at the ornate, gilded columns and crystal chandeliers as a turbaned, bearded older man wearing eyeglasses with oversized rims droned on in a nasal monotone to the assembly of likewise bearded, turbaned eyeglasses-wearing men sitting stiffly around a long table. Even as the dutiful Ahmed had whispered the translation into his ear, the Cartel's Chief of Security's own thoughts were elsewhere. It was remarkable how much those Iranian leaders and the "Organization" had in common, particularly in their loathing of America. They and "U", the rich young Saudi they had brought from Khartoum, were driven by the same fervor, it appeared, even though they seemed to be from different branches of their religion, none of which made any sense to Retchko, although he believed he could use the differences to his advantage. During the talks, the young Saudi revolutionary had struck an arrangement with the Iranians to obtain small nuclear devices along with chemical weapons, with the Organization to obtain and transport the goods—for a hefty fee, of course, which included a commission for himself he had built-into the total price.

After Retchko had negotiated the future delivery of Soviet miniaturized warhead designs and other technology, to which he had access from his sources in Ukraine, workers had unloaded the North Korean gas centrifuges from the airplane. The impressed Iranians had promised him additional business.

In the late afternoon, following another sumptious meal, the Iranian officials had bid him and "U" and the others a cordial farewell. Retchko smirked; here, he could do well for himself.

Now the outskirts of the capital city were passing below, and except for the flashing strobe light at the end each wing, the outside soon became completely dark. The captain had told him that this next leg of the trip, to Islamabad, Pakistan, would be a nighttime flight of some three hours.

The bald Ukrainian closed his eyes; starting tomorrow, he would need every gram of energy he could muster for one of the most important days of his life.

* * *

Light knocks sounded on the dormitory door. Lisa Anaya dabbed her eyes and arose from the sofa. "Who is it?" A male voice other than Larry's came back. She pulled on the doorknob. "Oh . . . Frank, it is—you." The young woman blinked at Frank Ogawan, the office manager. The angular, dark-skinned fellow stood facing her, a sheaf of papers in his hand. She crumpled the tear-soaked tissue and dropped it aside.

"I have the report you wanted about the refinery . . ." he said, swallowing. Looking at her standing in the shadows of her darkened room, he thought she looked upset about something; not her usual self. The gangly African handed the documents to her. "I say, are you all right?" he blurted out.

Lisa stepped forward and, grasping his forearm, tugged the shy young man across the threshold. She nudged the door shut. In the darkness she heard his breathing. "I need a friend, tonight."

"Miss Anaya, I—"

Her fingertips against his lips cut off his words. The papers scattered across the floor. She was fumbling with the buttons of his shirt.

* * *

Larry Landay lay on the narrow mattress in his muggy dormitory room, thinking. The sweaty T-shirt and boxer shorts prickled against his skin; the air conditioner seemed to be losing its never-ending battle against Tanuta's heat and humidity. In the damp darkness he stared at its shape protruding from the wall. Was it acting up, again? Or was it working fine and it was *he* who was overheated from the awkward situation in which he now found himself?

After Lisa had spun about and bolted back up the stairs, Marisol had made her way, limping, toward her own quarters,

34

waving off all offers of help from the others. Everyone else had gone back to whatever they had been doing. Lisa did not answer his knocks on her door. He decided not to pursue Marisol—two women were more than he could handle right now. Instead, he had come back here to try and sort out things.

Marisol had said things back at the pump-house about weapons sales and satellites that could control people. On the flight from Angola, he had seen thousands of automatic rifles on the airplane and he had supplied the satellite dishes and other hardware to this so-called "Organization", whatever it really was. But for what true purpose? He had already concluded that some things about this place—and Retchko's involvement, in particular—did not add up. To connect Lisa with the bald, lumpy Ukrainian and his suspicious activities would be a terrible disappointment. The American squirmed about on the dank sheets, trying to convince himself that Marisol's assertions were only her personal opinions. But she had sounded pretty certain of her facts. And those facts—or opinions, or whatever they were— seemed to suggest that she could be right.

For a long time he gazed up at the textured patterns in the ceiling, barely visible in the thin shafts of light coming around the edges of the curtains. At length, he decided not to say anything about any of this to Lisa—if she would speak to him at all. In the meantime, he would keep his eyes and ears open for clues that would either confirm or refute Marisol's allegations.

* * *

Marisol Montoya lay on the bed in a fetal position, her mauled leg throbbing beneath the bandage. The girl caressed her aching shoulder where the injection had gone. "You will be all right," the medical officer had said, "it will just take some time."

But she was *not* all right. And time was *not* on her side. All along the youthful Cuban policewoman had masked her feelings about the sandy-haired American with stony professionalism and steely bravado. But the scene in the living room had uncovered the truth. And Lisa Anaya now also knew it, even if the unsuspecting Larry Landay did not.

35

* * *

Frank Ogawan leaned against the closed door in his darkened dormitory room; his heart pounding; his flushed face stinging. When Miss Anaya had started unbuttoning his shirt and he realized where she was leading him, he had frozen. Her warm breath and the sweet aroma of perfume came over him as she undid another button. "Ah, Miss Anaya . . . I am not—"

Another fastener came open. Panicked, he took a step backward.

She stayed with him, easing the loosening shirt off his shoulders, rubbing his chest. "I want you to be with me tonight."

His shaking hand had fumbled for the door behind him. With one motion he pulled it open and backed out into the corridor.

The cream-colored young woman's eyes went wide. "You coward!" she glared, nostrils flaring. Then she had slammed the door shut in his face with such force as to rock a nearby picture off the wall.

Now, alone in his quarters, waves of humiliation and regret rolled over him. Her mocking words still rang in his ears. The girl he had thought and dreamed about countless times had been in his grasp and he had run away! He could have caressed her and told her how much he loved her like he had always imagined it would be. But she would have found out he didn't know what to do next and would have laughed at him. With a groan he dropped onto the sofa in the dark dormitory room and put his face in his hands. It was then he realized his shirt was still open.

* * *

"United States Consulate General", Lagos, Nigeria; the Next Morning:

Barclay thanked the employee and scanned the new report; it was the daily advisory of Americans wanted by international authorities. Today's missive concerned a one *'Lawrence J. Landay';* also known as "Larry Landay", no other known aliases; last known address, Mountain View, California; wanted on

Federal charges of Conspiracy to Defraud the U.S. Government; Violation of Technology Transfer Statutes; Illegal Possession Of, or Sale Of, Classified Goods to Prohibited Countries and/or Designated Terrorist Organizations; Collusion; Consipiracy and Racketeering. Believed to have fled the United States, possibly to Nigeria. INTERNOL notified. A picture of the suspect was attached to the information sheet.

Barclay handed back the report to the clerk. "Post this on the bulletin board."

* * *

INTERNOL Headquarters, Geneva Switzerland, the Same Morning:

Tarliani puffed on his curved pipe as he looked over the morning's new case-reports. One in particular from the "Agency" in Washington, about an individual named "Landay" who was wanted for illegal technology transfer and now believed to be in Nigeria, caught his attention. The agent sucked on his pipe; something clicked in his mind. As the smoke roiled over his head, he stared down at the sidewalk on the *'Rue de la Croix-d' Or'* and tried to remember. Tarliani fumbled in his desk drawer and pulled out the Lagos agent reports about a mysterious "Soviet general" who was setting up what amounted to a police state there at the International Airport. Here it was: "Leonid Efimovich Retchko" was the man's name. Tarliani thought some more. His agents in Lagos were telling him that unaccountable happenings at the airport involved high-technology electronics, much of it American. Could "Retchko" be connected to the hardware that had somehow been taken from the United States? Was he in league with this "Landay" individual? A long shot, perhaps, but worth looking into.

Tarliani picked up another report. It was from a very secret connection in Moscow. Two years earlier, at an embassy function, he had made acquaintance with a man who let it be known that he was well-connected to Soviet Intelligence. "We are really on the same side, are we not?" he had said with a florid-faced smirk, over Vodka. "We do catch common criminals, sometimes." Now that the Soviet Union was imploding and great upheavals were taking place there, just the other day he had received a message from the man, who called himself "Livshits", regarding a missing Soviet general named "Putridchenko," whom he deemed to be of great danger to people and governments on both ideological sides. Did INTERNOL have any information that might be of assistance to him? Then followed a description of the man, whose last known whereabouts were in Madrid. Livshits had said he would keep his correspondence with Tarliani secret. Intriguing; but there did not seem to be any connection between his case and Livshits's. He would, however, keep open the avenues of communication with the Russian. One never knew when such connections might prove valuable.

* * *

The big Boeing came to a stop at a cargo terminal. Retchko looked at his notes: the "Islamabad International Airport", also known as the "Chaklala Air Base", shared space with Pakistan's Air Force. Well and good; he would prefer to be removed from prying civilian eyes. And as they would later be going in a caravan into the mountains, security would better from this starting point. They would later meet the airplane in Kabul, across the frontier in Afghanistan. For he had important business to conduct there with the *'Taliban'*, who were seeking to take over the government of that country. Even though those native paramilitaries had, up to now, been supplied by the Americans while they had fought the Soviets, he had secret information that they would soon turn against their current benefactors. And the Cartel stood ready to supply their needs—with due compensation, of course. That they had defeated the Russians was, to Retchko, reason enough to side with them. Working with the Taliban, there could soon be great financial and political benefits for the "Organization". And for Leonid Efimovich Retchko.

Much would depend on "U", and his associates. Based on what the Ukrainian had already learned, the young Saudi wanted to establish an alliance with the Taliban to use Afghanistan as a base for future operations against the West. Success for the man's organization would also be very much to the Cartel's advantage.

Down on the apron, a quartet of limousines awaited the men. The Saudis, plus Retchko and Ahmed the translator, got into the cars. The vehicles pulled out of the airport and headed toward the center of Islamabad.

Before long, the caravan drove up to a white, block-long structure with a lone flag flying on top that Retchko took to be Pakistan's parliament building.

The men filed past the decorative front entrance, through a big open lobby into a paneled room where several men in military uniforms were sitting around a long mahogany table. One of the men said some words and motioned at empty seats. Ahmed repeated the man's instruction in Russian. Retchko settled into a chair and looked around at the Pakistanis, who were scrutinizing him and the turbaned visitors.

The first man spoke something to Ahmed, who turned to Retchko. "He says these men are from the 'Pakistan Defense Group' . . . they wish for you to tell them what your organization can offer to them."

The bald Ukrainian nodded at his hosts as he stood before a map on an easel and began to describe, with Ahmed translating, the scope and operation of the Cartel, leaving out details that did not concern the Pakistanis. After an hour, he sat back down, feeling satisfied he had made a strong presentation.

The man who had spoken earlier said something, then paused for Ahmed's translation. "He says the government of Pakistan is familiar with the operations of your 'Nigerian Supply Organization', as he puts it, but is not, at this time, prepared to use any services from you. This instruction comes from the highest levels of the Pakistan government." Retchko frowned as the local man went on speaking, then paused for the translation. "They are authorized to end these proceedings at this time—"

Retchko reddened; he had expected a more favorable reception. The men in the uniforms nodded at each other, then stepped from the room in single-file. Except for the first Pakistani, who had done all the talking for his side, none of them had reacted much during the whole meeting.except for shaking their heads from time-to-time and raising their eyebrows.

"U", who had sat listening, spoke something to Ahmed that he relayed to Retchko. "He wants you to go with him . . . he has arranged another meeting."

Outside, the limousines were gone; a half-dozen all-terrain-type vehicles painted in camouflage colors had taken their places. At the rear was a panel truck that Retchko supposed was carrying their luggage and supplies. The men settled into the seats. The Saudi hauled himself up into the leading vehicle's front passenger's position, motioning for the Ukrainian and Ahmed to take the rear seats. As the machines rumbled out into the mid-day traffic, he turned and spoke something to the interpreter. "We will be leaving the city and going to the Pakistan nuclear facility," the Libyan said, as the turbaned fellow's shimmering brown eyes darted back and forth from the translator to the Cartel's Chief of Security.

Before long, the procession was at the outskirts of the capital, headed in the direction of some mountains in the distance. As they rode along, Retchko gazed at the snow-covered peaks. It had become a gray day; here and there a snowflake fluttered down; it seemed the temperature had dropped since they had arrived in Islamabad. The man felt his bald head and once more wished for the fur hat.

The young man up front wearing the turban happened to glance back and caught the hairless man touching his head. He gestured for the driver to stop. The vehicle pulled to the side of the road; the others followed and stopped. The man got out and stepped to the panel truck. In a minute, he came back and handed Retchko a turban-like cap made of wool. The Saudi spoke to Ahmed, nodding. "He says to take this with his compliments. It will keep your head warm."

Retchko pulled the headpiece over his shiny pate. Although he was glad to have it, he felt awkward wearing a symbol of the man's religion, in which he had no interest.

For an hour, the vehicles drove away from the city across a landscape of patchy snow. "U" stared straight ahead; Retchko got the impression the young man knew where they were going. He remembered that the fellow had said something earlier about a nuclear facility.

After some time, a sprawl of low buildings materialized ahead of them against a backdrop of the looming white mountains. As the procession drew closer, the riders could see clusters of buildings, all surrounded by a high barbed fence that went off for some distance to the left and right. Slowing, the vehicles pulled up to a gatehouse where several guards in dark overcoats and fur caps, all holding automatic rifles, motioned for them to stop. Then commenced an animated verbal exchange between one of the sentries and "U". At length, the gatekeeper stepped back and waved them through into the big enclosed space.

The machines lurched in single file up a muddy, rutted road past many structures. As they jostled along, the Ukrainian gazed out at narrow, pot-holed byways that led off in every direction toward what looked to be laboratories and barracks. Here and there, featureless men and women wearing dark overcoats and fur caps plodded along slushy sidewalks. To Retchko, the bleak, isolated place seemed to give few hints of its actual role in Pakistan's atomic ambitions.

A swarthy, middle-aged individual in a long coat and cap stepped from the curb and raised his hand, pointing at the lead car with a motion toward the roadway's mushy edge.

As the passengers got out, several other men stepped up. The turbaned "U " shook their hands, bowing with them with what, to Retchko, seemed to be a certain familiarity. Then the Saudi pointed to the European with some words to Ahmed, who nudged him forward.

"He wants you to meet these men," the translator said.

The Pakistani in the fur cap said something else to Ahmed, who turned to Retchko.

"This man is the chief atomic scientist in Pakistan," he said. The pale Retchko and the darker-skinned researcher shook hands. "He says he is interested in working with you," the interpreter went on. "These other men are specialists."

The group stepped along to the nearest building. Inside, they filed into a big room where technicians in white smock coats and

41

hair-nets, some of whom wore medical-style white breathing masks, were working over what to Retchko seemed to be complicated instruments and devices. The general looked around at a roomful of upright stands bolted to the floor, upon each of which was a whirring device connected to a control panel. He recognized them as gas centrifuges of the type they had taken to Teheran.

The scientist was talking. "He says these are gas centrifuges'," Ahmed put in, "there are thousands of them here in these laboratories."

"These must be pretty important," the Ukrainian said. Ahmed relayed the comment to the scientist. The man nodded and made a statement in his language.

"They separate low-level uranium into 'highly enriched uranium' that is weapons-grade. He says it is a slow process, but very effective." There was a pause as the Pakistani went on speaking. "It takes twenty kilograms of weapons-grade uranium to make one nuclear weapon." That answered Retchko's next question. The man was speaking again to Ahmed, who turned to the general. "He wishes to obtain many more of these machines, but are having problems with 'ring magnets', as he calls them. The man's laboratory desires to purchase these on the world market . . . but he does not wish to draw attention from the international 'non-proliferation' treaties and regulations."

"We can secure these," Retchko said, "tell him we have reliable sources of supply."

The man looked pleased when Ahmed relayed the Ukrainian's words."He says his organization has three-thousand in operation and has about ten-thousand more. But the ring magnets are stopping them. He will pay a bonus price for more of them."

"Is not their government involved?"

"He says the laboratory here operates *outside* the regular government."

Retchko was astonished—*this man was running an independent nuclear operation!* Since the government officials in Islamabad had reacted earlier with indifference to his proposals, much of what they produced here had to be going somewhere else. *But where?*

"Who are your customers?"

The chief scientist spoke some words with deliberation, which Ahmed passed along. "Of course, the Pakistan military gets most of it." The young fellow paused as the older man went on, "he says they also send enriched uranium *and 'other technology'* to certain other countries. He says it brings considerable revenue to the laboratory."

Retchko realized that here was a great opportunity for the Cartel. "Besides producing 'weapons- grade-uranium', what else does this place do?"

The researcher regarded the foreigner for several seconds, then spoke. "We are working on another important project . . . you can help us."

The chief scientist gestured toward the door. Outside, the man strode up the mushy walkway, then turned up a side street, with the others following. After slogging along the snow-piled byway for several blocks, the man led the troupe to a hulking, warehouse-like structure. Inside, the Pakistani researcher took brisk steps down a corridor, followed by the others. For an intellectual, he seemed to be in good form, the general thought, puffing.

The scientist stopped and opened a heavy-looking, stainless-steel door. Retchko stepped into a roomy space and his eyes went wide. Cradled in a sturdily-built, all-terrain-style, self-propelled weapons-carrier with multiple axles and very large tires was a ballistic missile of a size that left no doubt it had a range of hundreds or thousands of kilometers. The general frowned; something about the rocket looked familiar. Then he realized it was almost identical to a missile he had seen one time when he was on a secret military mission to China with some Soviet scientists! Were Pakistan and China working together? Or, better put—was *China and this laboratory working together?* If so, this operation was having a great and probably secret influence on global politics. If the place needed specialized instruments, Retchko thought, his former connections to certain North Korean laboratories could be very helpful. If he could resurrect those contacts, there could be great rewards for the Cartel. And, of course, for himself.

"... are working to reduce the size of payloads—" Ahmed relayed the man's words to the general. "He says they also seek to improve their rockets' accuracy."

The important man paused, for Ahmed's tranlation.

"They need some components for guidance systems," the young Libyan said. Retchko caught the speaker's eye and nodded.

A pleased expression crossed the fellow's face. The bald Ukrainian thought about his secret Cayman bank account.

"He wants to know if you can get nuclear triggers," Ahmed whispered.

With the melt-down of the Soviet government now taking place, Retchko guessed that some of the scientists he had known in the past, whose jobs could now be uncertain, might be willing to share Russian State secrets with him—for a price. He would seek to re-establish those connections. The guidance systems might be more complicated, since the Soviet Union's main strategic rocket production center was located in Ukraine.

Retchko stared into the man's eyes in his proven strategy of taking over a conversation. "The 'Organization' can supply the triggers and the guidance systems," he said, with a fixed, mechanical smile.

The man in the smock coat blinked, as if coming out of a momentary trance, then nodded. "Very well . . ." He blinked some more. "We will retire for the night while my people prepare specifications. I assume you will be ready to talk on the morrow?"

An assistant gestured for the visitors to follow him. In a few minutes, Retchko found himself in a dormitory-like room.

The Cartel's Security Chief pulled out a notebook and began writing. In a few hours, he would begin negotiations with these people that could alter the world's strategic balance for decades to come.

* * *

Federal Court House, San Francisco, California; the Next Day:

"You came out of this a helluva lot better than you could have!" The court-appointed attorney watched with narrowed eyes as the clerk behind the glass stamped the court-order that freed Joe Anglin on bond. "The magistrate could have held you until your trial, you know."

Larry's friend could still hear the prosecutor arguing to the judge that he was a threat to national security. Thank God this attorney, for the time being, had been able to convince the court otherwise.

The man put out his hand. "I'm 'Michael Parsley'. . . the court appointed me to represent you." Joe shook the man's hand with a fervent hope the lumpy-looking fellow could get him out of this mess.

The pale-faced lawyer stuffed the papers into a battered briefcase and buttoned his rumpled suit-coat. "We're going to my office for a long talk." He led the way outside and hailed a taxi. The two bundled into the back seat.

"It's a good thing you were able to find my dad for the bond money."

"He was about to leave with his girlfriend on a two-week cruise," the attorney rasped. "We caught him just in time at the dock down in San Pedro. He wasn't happy to part with the twenty grand, you know. He wants to know what the hell you've been up to. And so do I."

In the Pacific Heights District the cab pulled to the curb. The lawyer paid the driver and motioned toward a building entrance. On the eleventh floor, next to a heavy-looking, varnished wooden door was a plaque proclaiming the office to be that of *'Michael B. Parsley, Esq.''*

"Here we are," the chubby, forty-something man said, opening the door. The lawyer motioned for his new client to take a seat. Parsley scrambled around on his piled-up desk until he found a crushed pack of cigarettes. "Smoke?" Joe shook his head. "My doctor says these things are gonna kill me, someday." He lit-up and narrowed his eyes at a looping blue circle wafting over his head. "Perfect," he smirked. "Just perfect. Looks like a halo."

His eyebrows stitched together in a frown. "They're sayin' you're a frickin' risk to flee the country, you know—just like your partner did."

"But he didn't *flee* the country!"

"Then—where is he?"

"He was headed for . . . that is, he—I haven't heard from him in a while. We weren't really partners. He hired me to help him."

"You'd better come clean with me, or I can't save you in court. Now, where is this Lawrence J. Landay? He's the key to getting you off."

"We call him 'Larry'. I think he was going to Nigeria. Some place called, 'Tanuta City'."

"You think?"

"We used a kind of—code machine . . . on the phone. One-here-one-there. I'm not sure exactly where the other people were, though."

The lawyer ran his fingers through his thinning hair. "We can trace the numbers."

"The machine is locked-up in our office. I can't get to it."

"I can claim we need some things from the place for your defense. They have to let us in. The telephone company will have the records." Parsley scratched notes on a legal pad. "Now, where did you say this Landay is? Stop talking in circles. Start from the beginning."

Joe took a deep breath, swallowing. "All right, here's what I know . . ."

* * *

Pakistan Nuclear Research Center; That Evening, at the Same Time:

Retchko sat at the desk in the dormitory room and scribbled some notes about the negotiations with the nuclear scientists. Working out the details had been so involved that he and "U" and the others would have to spend another night here at this research center.

But the extra time would be productive for the Organization; the Chief would be pleased. He had agreed to supply the laboratory with guidance systems and other rocket hardware, plus gas centrifuges for their atomic projects. He had been surprised how far along they were with their work; it looked as if Pakistan was serious about being a full-fledged member of the "Nuclear Club"—and if the Cartel had anything to do with it, other countries would soon follow their example.

Now, he must track down the Ukrainian rocket experts he had known in the past and convince them to part with secret Soviet guidance hardware and deliver it to Pakistan. Also, he had promised the researchers thousands of gas centrifuges, plus rocket components from North Korea.

The payoff would be enormous. And part of the electronically-transferred funds the Pakistanis thought they were paying to the Organization would go instead into his secret Cayman account.

-4-

Michael B. Parsley, Esq. lit another cigarette and squinted down at the pedestrians bustling along below on the San Francisco sidewalk; it was getting along toward lunchtime. He turned back to Joe Anglin, who sat fidgeting in the leather chair on the opposite side of the desk.

"So the satellite tracking system—not approved by the government for export, as it turns out—went to 'Tanuta City' in Nigeria?"

The defendant nodded.

"You say a *'girl'* ordered it and this 'Larry Landay' went with it on ships and airplanes to install it down there? Did Landay know this girl?"

"He said he knew her from grad' school . . . they were both in electronic engineering."

"What was her name?"

"I think he called her 'Lisa'."

"Why would this 'Lisa' order embargoed electronics from Nigeria?"

"I don't know. She just did it."

"What were they going to be used for?"

Joe shook his head. "I'm not sure."

"What about those 'code machines' you say he used to send and receive messages?"

"They had built them as a school project . . . Larry showed me how to use it. She had the other one in Nigeria. He told me it was a secure communications link."

"Why all the secrecy?"

"I got the idea there was something . . . 'different'—about all of it."

"Different? In what way?"

"Well, the way some of the things were handled made me a little—uneasy. I told him one time that it looked like a flaky deal to me."

Parsley's eyes bored into Joe's. "Go on."

48

"Well, for one thing, there were no government documents—everything was handled from Nigeria."

The attorney's eyebrows went up. "What? You mean, he didn't have export licenses . . . clearances—things like that?"

"Like I said, it looked strange to me, but he seemed to know what he was doing. I believe that Lisa had him convinced everything was all right."

"Does he know that he, and his business and you, are charged with all these alleged 'crimes'?"

"Probably not."

Parsley shook his head. "Man, oh, man," he muttered to himself. This case was getting more complicated by the minute; it could involve whole countries, even. He would have to petition the court for a bigger budget.

* * *

Security Service Headquarters, Lubyanka Square, Moscow; the Next Day:

A functionary stepped into Livshits's office. "Comrade Inspector, a message has come from Zurich. It is addressed to you."

The Intelligence officer took the paper from the fellow's hand, nodding. He waited until the man had turned about and closed the door, then looked at the missive:

MAY HAVE GENERAL INFORMATION ABOUT SUBJECT.

PARTICULARS TO FOLLOW.

-T-

He knew the cryptic message was from from Tarliani. The words, "general" and "subject" would mean he had information for him about General Semen Putridchenko.

A loud *THUMP!* jolted Retchko awake. He had dozed off. The general lifted the wool cap and looked around. The procession had stopped at ancient-looking stone structure that resembled a castle with a masonry archway over the road supported by battlements on each side. The driver was speaking to a sentry. The Ukrainian narrowed his eyes at a sign in the local language; on it were the numerals, "30". "It is thirty kilometers to the summit of *'Khyber Pass',*" Ahmed said.

Another thud sounded: military guards were inspecting the vehicles. The rear door opened and a turbaned, bearded individual in a robe-like outfit took the back seat next to Ahmed. Retchko gaped at the automatic weapon the man laid across his lap.

The fellow said something to "Agent U", then to Ahmed. "He will be going with us to our destination," Ahmed said, "he is a guard."

"We need guards in the Khyber Pass?"

The translator and the newcomer had a short conversation. "He says there are still insurgents beyond the summit—in Afghanistan." There came the sounds of several car doors slamming behind them. The fellow said something else to Ahmed. "He says that guards are in the other vehicles, also. They are *'Pashtuns'*—native peoples who are friendly with the Taliban."

The general remembered the Taliban had connections with the Russian-hating *'Mujahideen',* whom the Americans had armed during the Soviet invasion of Afghanistan that had lasted until recently. Retchko knew that the "Mujahideen", who were mostly Pashtuns, were soon going to turn against the Americans and to try to overthrow the Afghan government. To do this they would need weapons and technical advice—from the Cartel. That explained why the fellow was with them.

The head of the military guard detail waved the procession through the gate.

As the vehicles splashed past gesturing sentries, under the stone archway and onto the paved highway leading in the direction of the summit thirty kilometers ahead, it occurred to Retchko that the exchanges between the military men, the Pashtun guards and the Saudis had been, at the very least, cordial, *almost as if they all already knew each other.*

The trail soon began to climb; the driver dropped the machine into a lower gear. As they whined upward along the winding road, the procession passed one mule caravan after another trudging on gravelly ruts running alongside the uncertain pavement; Retchko observed that each file was accompanied by several armed guards. The Pashtun fellow in their vehicle cocked his automatic weapon and commenced scanning their surroundings; his eyes darting to and fro.

After a while, they passed a religious temple and a military-like fort that looked to Retchko to be a way-station to rest the pack animals. Then the pavement and the rocky caravan lane came to a deep cleft in the mountain where the bluffs rose a hundred meters or more on each side; in some places only fifteen meters or so apart. As the roar of the engines echoed off the crowding cliffs, the guard fingered his weapon and cast about, frowning.

A little farther along, the roadway made a slight turn and opened out, revealing another huddle of buildings up ahead. The vehicles passed a sign in the local alphabet in front of the weathered-looking, colonial-style structures. Ahmed gazed about. "We are at the summit of 'Khyber Pass'," he said.

Then the roadway took a downward slant that soon led to sloping, desert-like terrain. In a while, they came to a checkpoint manned by robed guards whom Retchko recognized as Pashtuns like he had seen back at the other end of the pass. "U" got out and had a quick, gesturing conversation with the swarthy, turbaned men, then got back inside the vehicle.

Ahmed pointed at a vertical white line on the side of the guardhouse as they drove past a raised barrier. "This is the Afghanistan border," he said.

Sometime later, as the lowering sun shined into their faces, the procession came to an isolated crossroads. The Saudi in the front passenger's seat gestured for the driver to turn right onto a newer-looking road. Ahead in the distance, a range of snow-covered mountains had a pinkish cast from the setting sun. Gauging by the direction of the dropping orange disc, now to the left and a little behind them, Retchko decided they were headed northeastward.

At length, the driver made a sharp right turn onto a rutted road that led toward some low hills. After bouncing along the corduroy lane for about a kilometer, the vehicles passed over a rickety plank bridge spanning a small stream and came up a short, flat rise to the foot of a rounded, rock-faced hill. As soon as they were stopped, the base of the mountain started moving outward! Staring at the astonishing sight, Retchko saw it was a camouflaged entrance, wide enough for several cars to pass through at the same time. As the mammoth door swung aside with loud moaning and creaking noises, the general saw that inside the hill was a lighted cavern about as big as a medium-sized airplane hangar.

"U" nodded toward the opening; the driver put the vehicle in gear and drove into it. The other machines followed.

When they were stopped, the turbaned man alighted and stepped toward the other vehicles, saying something to Ahmed over his shoulder.

"He says we are transferring to helicopters."

Sure enough, when the general stepped from the utility vehicle, he saw, parked in a far corner, a pair of rotary-winged military-type aircraft that bore no markings. Some men were working around them. Retchko recognized the helicopters as Soviet-built *'M-I Twenty-Fours';* with their ferocious firepower, the best assault helicopters in the world. What NATO had called the "Hind", the Russian soldiers had given the vicious-looking warplane the more colorful nickname, "Krocodil". Hundreds were still in service by Russian forces and client states. This pair, probably captured during the invasion of Afghanistan, looked to be in perfect shape.

As the men piled out of the utility vehicles, "U" shouted something at the helicopter crewmen. One man, wearing a leather aviator's cap with goggles pushed up on his forehead, came across the stony floor, hewn from solid rock, to the turbaned Saudi. While the others watched, there followed a loud conversation under the bright lights in what Retchko took to be Arabic, or a language that sounded like it, punctuated by gestures.

The pilot returned to the aircraft and shouted something to the ground crewmen. One of them stepped up to a tractor and attached a towbar to its front. In a few minutes, both aircraft were at the entrance, surrounded by men. A fuel tanker, diesel exhaust billowing from it, rumbled up. While the truck pumped jet fuel into the helicopters' tanks, workmen loaded the travelers' bags into rear compartments. When the tanker had finished topping-off the aircraft, the tractor tugged the ungainly-looking war machines out to the flat space in front of the hill.

Retchko frowned at elongated structures welded to the rear of the twin jet engine pods of the helicopters. The pilot saw his stare and said something to Ahmed. "He says they deflect and spread the exhaust so satellites cannot spot them from space. They are safe from detection."

All at once, the lights inside the rocky hangar went out, plunging the place into darkness. In the gloom the camouflaged hangar door started closing. By the dim cabin lights, Retchko, Ahmed, and the guard from the car, along with a half-dozen others, crowded into jury-rigged jumpseats welded inside the narrow fuselage. The other men climbed into the other aircraft as the engines whined and the rotors began turning. A few minutes later, the two helicopters performed a short roaring takeoff run across the flat space and lifted away into the night.

As they pounded along, from the sudden twists and turns the aircraft was taking, Retchko sensed they were flying very close to the ground. The general knew that some of these helicopters had the terrain-following radar like Soviet bombers used and felt a flush of admiration for the designers of these machines. Then he remembered he was no longer associated with the Soviet military—in fact, he was now wanted by them for desertion and other charges. Retchko felt under the turban at his bald head; so far, the disguise and the name change had fended off the pursuers he knew were after him.

* * *

Security Service Headquarters, Lubyanka Square, Moscow; the Next Morning:

Livshits stared at the photograph that had arrived by facsimile machine; even though it was not signed and lacked an originating telephone number, he knew it was from Tarliani in Zurich. The picture was of a crowd of people at an airport. The face of one of the many individuals in the scene, a bald white man in civilian clothes, was circled. There was no further description. The Russian compared the faxed picture with the grainy security camera photograph from the Moscow train station taken the night Putridchenko had disappeared. Yes, the two men looked very much alike. Then he noticed in the background of the airport picture a large poster of a black man in a military uniform. The strongman leader of some country in Africa—perhaps Uganda or Nigeria?

* * *

Tanuta Refinery; at the Same Time:

Marisol Montoya frowned at the Russian handwriting. This morning while she was showering, random thoughts had led to the subject of the safe in Retchko's office. Ever since a few days ago when she had cracked its password and the safe combination, the temporary security head had intended to look more closely at its contents. Today the young former Havana policewoman had come to the security office before the others arrived; had locked the door, and opened the safe. For a while, she would have the place to herself. Being busy would also take her mind off Larry Landay and that other woman, Lisa Anaya.

In the strongbox, the first sheet of paper was a list of people she did not recognize: *'Lychin'; Putridchenko', ' Suslov'; General Krolov';* some others also with Eastern European names.

At the bottom of the page, in Retchko's handwriting, alongside someone named *'Golubko';* was the single word: "Regret". Marisol shook her head; none of this made any sense to her.

The next page was a list of names she recognized as those of people at the refinery. In the margin were other notations. The new detective read on down the page, then frowned. Next to Lisa Anaya's name were the words, "Owes me". *Owes me what?* Marisol wondered.

Beside "Lester Nkrume's" name, the man whom she knew was the husband of the woman, "Betty", was the notation, "Eliminate". This was a word, she thought, far too intense to apply to an everyday co-worker. Beneath the plant manager's name was Larry's, with the same scribbled commentary: "Landay—Eliminate". Marisol's hand flew to her mouth to stifle a gasp. For there was only one possible explanation: Retchko must have marked Lester Nkrume and the blond American she admired for death! But *why?* What had they done to bring about such a threat?

Her heart pounding, she scanned down at other names on the paper. There were no notes in the margin next to the name, "Busa", the overweight man she had seen around the refinery.

The same for someone he had listed as the "Chief", but had not identified by name.

One name she did not recognize: "Ezego". But from Retchko's evaluation, the general must consider him either a potential ally or rival, for the comment on this individual read, "Useful but block his ambitions".

She located her own name toward the bottom of the page. "Marisol—possibilities." Possibilities for *what?* she wondered. A chill ran down her back as she stared at the ambiguous word the enigmatic Ukrainian had written about her.

Another name caught her attention: "Colonel Ajiboy". Next to the name of the Army officer in charge of security at the Lagos airport was the word: "Replace". Since Marisol had overheard Retchko complain several times about security at the airport, it seemed as if the only question was whether he would just relieve him or have him killed.

There was a cryptic comment beside "Betty Nkrume's" name: *"Satin!"* Marisol frowned; how did the general connect the attractive young woman, who was also Lisa Anaya's sister, she had learned, with a word that had such erotic connotations?

"Satin" in relation to a man and a woman suggested a bedroom and sex. *Was something going on between Retchko and Lester Nkrume's wife?*

Scanning down, the last comment on the sheet of paper concerned Frank Ogawan. She looked across the page to Retchko's evaluation and again caught her breath. "A fool," was the notation, "No value—decide later what to do with him". Marisol frowned; in the time she had been here, she had found the shy young office manager to be intelligent and capable at his job. So why did Retchko have a negative opinion of him? It almost looked as if his life was in danger.

Then it hit her: *At this refinery, everyone's life was in danger!* For the handwritten notes pointed to a cold, calculating man who would use and discard people at his convenience.

The next page looked like some sort of accounting report, with columns of figures that seemed to be sums of money—very large sums of money, in fact; all in American dollars, placed next to corresponding dates. The most recent entry would have been just before Retchko had left on his trip. The only identification was a number consisting of many digits at the top of the page.

Just then, Marisol heard a whining vehicle crunching across the gravel parking lot outside. In a hurry, she stuck the papers back inside the safe, making sure they were arranged the same way she had found them, then closed the door and reset the combination dial. Grabbing a handkerchief from her handbag, she wiped the safe's door, the handle, and the dial clear of her fingerprints. Then, she stood up and opened the office door, just as Lester Nkrume stepped across the front door threshold. She nodded at the man as he walked by, then again closed the door. Marisol dropped into the desk chair and stared at the ceiling. She had looked into Retchko's mind and did not like what she saw. But what could she do—if anything—with this information that had such frightening implications? No one around here was safe from this man. And one of the most endangered seemed to be Lisa Anaya.

* * *

Marisol did not notice that when she withdrew her right hand from the safe, the emerald ring on her second finger, when it raked across the frame of the strongbox's opening, slipped off her finger and dropped into the safe.

* * *

"Power is on!" Lisa called out to Larry, who was scanning the needles swinging around in their dials and the little lights holding steady as each instrument came on. Electronic sounds came from an overhead speaker.

"We have acquired the signal! You hit the jackpot with the satellite!" Larry stepped around to where the girl was smiling."We did it!" he beamed, "it works!" On impulse, he gave her a hug. The cream-colored young woman stiffened and stepped back. She looked about; no one else seemed to be near the little concrete building at the edge of the refinery's parking lot. "Larry, we need to talk." She looked down, then straight into his eyes. "I want to know what is going on with you and that— Cuban girl. I mean, how did you and this 'Marisol'—whatever her name is—manage to come to Tanuta City together and she was bitten by a *crocodile?"*

Larry turned red. He did not want to divulge anything about what he and the temporary "Head of Security" had talked about at the pump-house. He remembered Retchko's microphones, then recalled Marisol had told him that there were none in this new building—yet. For now, he could speak freely, here.

"We talked about some—'security matters'. On our way back, we ran into a crocodile. It attacked us and I killed it with a pipe. It was all business . . . that's the truth."

"Larry—she has a 'thing' for you. I'm a woman, and I know it when I see it."

An awkward grin crossed his mouth. "Don't be silly—I believe you're jealous!"

"Well, look, things have not been exactly like they were, before. And now, along comes this—"

"I'm not involved with her, and you and I have been busy, and this place is . . . crowded."

She brushed his forearm. "Very well, 'luv'. I shall see if you can solve this 'crowding' problem, as you put it." Larry was conscious of her British accent. "I am hoping—"

Grating footsteps sounded outside. "Someone's coming!" he said.

A moment later Lester Nkrume stepped through the open doorway. For a split-second, the "Plant Manager" took in the two engineers, who were standing close, facing each other. "Lisa, we need to go over some paperwork."

As Nkrume and the man's sister-in-law stepped away, Larry saw him glance back over his shoulder; a knowing look on his face. Their gravelly footfalls faded away.

Larry turned turned back to the equipment rack and tried to make some adjustments to one of the receivers, but he could not concentrate on the electronics. He kept remembering that Marisol had told him Lisa might be involved in illegal schemes with Retchko. A feeling of dread came over him—*what if she was right?* It just didn't seem possible that the cream-colored electronics engineer from his past could be into any criminal activity, but, according to the temporary Head of Security, the evidence she had found looked incriminating. Maybe Retchko was using her without her knowledge! From what Marisol had told him, the ruthless foreigner was capable of doing that.

As he tried to work, other thoughts crowded into his mind: Lisa's notion about Marisol having a "thing" about him was preposterous, of course; he and the Cuban girl were strictly business. But he remembered the Latina's smooth, tight skin, her trim figure, and the light touch of her fingers on his forearm in the dim light at the pump-house and all at once he was not so sure about that. And whatever differences he and the street-savvy former Havana policewoman had, they seemed to get along together well. Then he realized that neither he nor Marisol would be alive right now were it not for each other: the young "Cubana" had twice saved his life when pirates had attacked the freighter carrying the electronic goods, and he had rescued her from the murderous crocodile.

As Larry stood there in the sun-drenched outbuilding in the equatorial heat, he was having a hard time concentrating on the satellite receiver. His clothes were soaked with sweat.

* * *

Inside the office building, when Lisa and her sister's husband had stepped down the corridor, out of habit she had glanced in the direction of Frank Ogawan's cubicle. Hearing their footsteps, the office manager looked up from his desk. Even as he and Lisa saw each other for less than a second, both his and her eyes widened. While she went on, Lisa felt a tingling flush and gasped to herself without knowing why. Meanwhile, Frank Ogawan turned away, then slumped in his seat. In a daze the young man stared glumly at the papers on his desk. He felt as if a sledgehammer had slammed into his chest.

* * *

In the transmitter building, Larry forced himself to try to think about business as he fine-tuned the signal from the American military communications satellite. Turning on the encoder, he wished Lisa were here to see this—all her efforts had led to this success and her brother-in-law had come along just now to take her away from her moment of triumph. For the downlink signal was strong and steady. He turned on the carrier wave and transmitted a coded burst. In its stationary orbit over the equator, the American satellite responded with a signal that was the exact answer he had expected. He keyed the transmitter and sent the code twice more; both times the orbiter returned the proper response. By now he had forgotten the heat and humidity of the sunbaked place.

Just then, Larry heard footsteps outside.`"Lisa, you're missing the show!" he called out, turning around.

But in the doorway stood—Marisol Montoya.

"Oh . . . I thought—"

The Latina pushed back her hair from her eyes. "Well, sorry to disappoint you." She glanced around and saw that she and Larry were alone in the isolated radio shack.

He motioned at the racks, where little colored lights flickered across the front panels of several pieces of equipment; wavering electronic sounds came from the overhead speaker. "It's just that—well, something very interesting and exciting has happened. We're getting signals from the American satellite!"

"Señor Larry, we must talk."

"Like last time? More secrets? More bad news?"

"Oh, Señor Larry, you do not understand!" She cast another look about as if to confirm they were alone. "Meet me again at the pump-house, tonight."

The American caught his breath; he had planned to get together with Lisa at that time. He could not afford to again stand her up.

"We're by ourselves, right now—can't we discuss it here?"

The girl wrung her hands and gave another glance to the outside, as if to make sure no one could hear them. "'Americano', you are in bad danger, here!"

"Really, now? You keep telling me that."

"You are such a fool! I went through General Retchko's safe, again, and found some writing he made about you—about everyone here, in fact. He has you on a list to 'eliminate,' as he wrote it."

"'Eliminate'?" Larry looked puzzled. "What would he mean by that? I hardly ever see him."

"I do not know. But he is bad man, señor. He says bad things about everybody here." She stopped and looked into his eyes. "Your friend, Lisa, is in bad danger, too."

"Lisa is in danger? How?"

"He writes beside her name, 'Owes me'. I do not know what it means." Marisol glanced out the open door. "What I am telling you is a secret between us."

"But if Lisa is 'in danger', as you say, then I must warn her."

"Señor Larry, *por favor,* do not say anything to her, right now . . . I shall try to find out more before the general returns from his trip. Nothing will happen until then, I think."

"Maybe I can help you."

"I will let you know."

She turned and stepped out through the open door and walked toward the office building. Just as she reached the door, Lisa Anaya came out. Both looked at the other without speaking. For a fraction of a second, their eyes met.

Irritated that it seemed Marisol had been with Larry at the transmitter building while she was gone, Lisa made her way with purposeful steps in its direction—she had some pointed questions to ask him. But when she got there, she made an alarming discovery. "Larry . . . the transmitter is on!"

The American came around the console. "Oh, my gosh!" he said, flipping the key to the "off" position. "I did some tests while you were gone, All the satellite links are working!"

"But we are not supposed to keep transmitting—the Americans might locate us!"

"Sorry about that. I was interrupted."

"By the Cuban, I see."

"She just came by with some—information." Larry wanted to change the subject. "Let's get together in my quarters, tonight. We can be alone." He grinned. "There will be less of a 'crowd', there."

She reached across the console and brushed his forearm. "That sounds fine, 'luv'. After dinner?"

* * *

Signal Intelligence Office, National Security Agency, Washington, D.C.:

The operator stared at his monitor screen—there had been an apparent anomaly aboard the relay satellite in syncronous orbit over Manaus, Brazil. Something had activated one of the standby sideband modules for several minutes in the past half-hour.

A standard scan on the circuit showed nothing had been on it. Perhaps sunspots or a glitch in the electronics had caused a spurious signal surge. He would pass along the information to his superiors.

* * *

Khwaja Rawash International Airport, Kabul, Afghanistan; Evening of the Same Day:

The two darkened helicopters dropped into lantern-lit circles at the outskirts of the Kabul airport. Retchko watched as gesturing, turbaned men ran to open the doors, even as the rotors were still turning. "He wants us to follow him!" Ahmed shouted, unbuckling his seat belt. The passengers alighted and, hunched down, loped behind the scurrying men toward an outbuilding fifty meters distant.

As they came closer, the general saw in the uneaven light that the place was surrounded by robed, bearded men, all holding assault rifles. One of the guards motioned the muzzle of his weapon toward a lighted doorway. Just inside, another man gestured for the newcomers to hurry along down a short hallway, where they turned into a stark-looking, dimly-lit space that had been set up with battered chairs arranged around a long table. Several black-bearded men wearing turbans stood about. Retchko looked around the room that was lighted by weak lamps casting dim shadows along cracked stucco walls. The setting gave an impression of intrigue.

The man at the head of the table stepped forward to "U" and kissed him on both cheeks, then turned to Retchko, who returned the wet kisses of the man.

The fellow spoke some words, after which Ahmed turned to the Ukrainian. "He says we are safe at this location—the government is weak and will not bother us." The turbaned man was still talking. "He is a leader of the 'Mujahideen'—Pashtuns, the fighters who threw the Russians out of this country. He has many heroic stories to tell."

Retchko nodded; he had no sympathy with the now-evicted Soviet invaders of Afghanistan.

The man gestured for the visitors to take seats around the long table, pushed his big-framed eyeglasses up on his nose, then spoke. Ahmed listened, then translated the man's words. "He says that, until now, they had been working with the *'American Special Forces'* and *'Central Intelligence'* agents. But the Americans were not sympathetic with the aims of the Mujahideen, except as to help them rid the country of the Soviets. The infidel Americans are now gone." Ahmed interpreted as the man went on. "He says they shall now operate against the puppet government the Soviets left here . . . they will need assistance with arms and training. They have heard of your organization and seek to work with you."

The insurgent leader glanced around at his comrades, and at "U", who was nodding. The Afghan and the Saudi began talking to each other with rapid words, gesturing with upraised palms as they spoke; their conversation punctuated with frequent grins and nods.

Ahmed translated into Retchko's ear. "They are going to join forces to oppose the Afghan government. They will enlist many young men and set up a training camp in the mountains." Ahmed gestured at "U". "He has much resources to finance it."

The general already knew about that; their talks over the past day at Tora Bora had keyed around the young Saudi's fortune that would pay for the instruction of recruits and their weapons. The Organization would supply those armaments, along with training the irregular troops in their use. Retchko could hardly contain himself at the prospect of the Cartel being involved in an enterprise that would soon operate on such a vast scale. Already, this journey had achieved great success.

He thought about his growing Cayman account. Its secrecy was secure, of that he was certain; the information about the balances and other private information in the safe back in his office were under layers of code numbers and lock combinations that would be impossible for anyone to break.

* * *

Frank Ogawan stepped into the executive dining-room and frowned; all the tables were taken. Then he saw a hand waving at him across the crowded space. "Señor Frank . . . have dinner with me!" came an accented female's voice over the room noise.

"Ah, Miss Montoya, I am very late. There is no other place to sit."

The Latina motioned at an empty space across the table from her. "You have no choice," she said with a wry grin, "this is the only empty seat in the room."

Taking his place, he saw out of the corner of his eye, Lisa Anaya and the light-haired American sitting at a table for two in a far corner and looking to be engaged in a convivial conversation.

Marisol gave him a forced smile. "So, how are you doing?"

Frank sighed. "Many things to do, these days; many things." He stole another glance at Lisa and Larry, who were clinking their glasses together. "We are closing the books on the year."

The waiter took their orders, then left. There was an awkward silence, then Marisol picked up the conversation. "I understand you called the doctor when the crocodile bit me."

"Oh, Miss Montoya, you looked so . . . *hurt.*"

Marisol felt a tug of empathy for this young man; his uncomplicated innocence was refreshing. "Señor Landay and I were inspecting some 'things' and the crocodile attacked us. He killed it and saved our lives."

The office manager gave a quick glance at the two in the corner, then back to his new table companion. "You think a lot of him, do you not?"

Marisol felt a flush on her face. "The ''Americano'? He is— *'nice'*, as they say." Her eyes flickered to the other table. Lisa and Larry were refilling their wine glasses. "We first met when he came through Cuba on his way to here. I came along with— the airplane. I *had* to leave Cuba, and he was on the airplane." She realized she was repeating herself. "There was nothing there for me, anymore. All my family was gone away and I had the chance to get on that airplane. It is a long story."

The food arrived, just then. The two attacked their shark steaks on their plates with knife and fork. Frank looked at her. "I have the time . . . *tell* me the story."

"Okay, I was a policewoman in Havana. I was trained in Russia—that is how I got this job. General Retchko needed someone with police experience and he knew I had trained, there."

"You went to Russia?"

"*Si*—yes. I trained with 'Soviet Special Forces'." The young Cuban woman sliced off a piece of steak. She held up the fork and cocked her eyebrow with a grin. "Do not provoke me—I am dangerous, señor!"

Frank Ogawan laughed. "I must say, I am impressed, ma'am."

Marisol glanced across the room. The other diner took a subconscious cue and did the same. When their eyes came back to each other, they realized what they had done. The young woman's face felt a rush of heat.

The African sighed and looked down at his plate, embarrassed. He took a stab at the fish steak. Marisol was looking at her right hand. "That is strange . . . my little emerald ring is gone." She felt the empty space on her finger where it had been. "I must have lost it."

Just then, there came motions from across the way; Lisa and Larry were getting up from their seats. As they passed by, for a second, all four glanced in each others' direction.

At length, the *'Cubana'* set aside her napkin. "Frank, we must talk some more." She pushed back her seat. "Let us go outside."

Marisol led the office manager toward the direction of the little satellite transmitter building. In the shadows, she touched his forearm. "We can talk, here." She looked up at the sky, as if trying to formulate what to say to this earnest, otherworldly young man. The moon was going behind a scudding cloud; it looked like rain was not far off.

She spoke in a low voice. "Frank, what do you know about General Retchko?"

The office manager swallowed. "Well, ma'am, things have been . . . 'difficult' since he came here." His dark face glinted in the refinery lights. Marisol kept silent; she wanted to hear him speak without prompting. "I mean"—Frank was choosing his words carefully—"he has changed the place very much. He took over Mister Nkrume's office and put him in a regular cubicle. Everyone noticed that. He walks around giving big orders."

"What else?"

The young man cast about, wide-eyed, as if fearful someone was overhearing what he was saying. He leaned toward her and spoke in a whisper. "There have been rumors—" He stopped short. "Everybody is afraid of him."

"Do not worry, this is between us, okay?"

Somewhere off in the nearby jungle, an animal cried out.

"Frank, I have found out some things . . . I cannot say much, but I want you to watch out for yourself . . . and for Lisa Anaya— it is important."

The whites of the African's eyes caught the refinery's lights. "I do not understand."

"Things are dangerous, here. I wish I could tell you more. Be careful."

Just then, a truck turned into the driveway; its headlights sweeping across the parking lot. The two dropped back into the shadows of the little outbuilding as the machine whined past them toward the lighted refinery towers; its driver and passenger looking straight ahead, not noticing them.

The slender office manager shook his head. "I must get back to my room. I have to give Mister Nkrume some reports tomorrow morning."

"Remember what I said . . . and watch out for Lisa—she needs your protection."As he turned to leave, she touched his forearm. "Do not tell her what you are doing."

A hopeful expression passed the African's dark face. "Thank you, ma'am."

The two stepped out of the shadows and made their separate ways back to the dormitory.

After Frank had left her, Marisol headed up the stairs; she had decided to say some more words of warning to Larry. On the third level she stopped in front of his door. It was then she remembered he was with Lisa Anaya.

The Cuban girl hung her head and trudged to her quarters.

Retchko wrote in his notebook with masculine strokes of triumph. What a day this had been! The general was not given to useless, time-consuming celebration, but today he and these men had joined together in an alliance that would affect the course of history; in the future, this day would go down as one of the most important dates of all time.

Their day had started hundreds of meters beneath one of the mountains of Tora Bora, where the men from the helicopters had spent the night in one of the former CIA-built underground bunkers. The empty, multi-story cavern, hollowed-out by the Americans during the time they were working with the "Mujahideen" and later abandoned by them, was one of several in the isolated area that the Cartel would soon transform into impregnable, self-contained, undetectable fortresses from where the new paramilitary organization would direct its operations. When they were finished, those caverns, Retchko wrote with a rare literary flourish, would make old Hitler's bunker back in Berlin look like a chicken house by comparison.

For now, his main concern was to organize their physical upgrading and to outfit the electronic suites. For that, he would enlist Lisa Anaya, and perhaps, the American. *At all costs those two must never know the location of those facilities or their actual purpose.* The two would design the hardware and program the software to run the system from Tanuta, based on the specifications he would give them. His own operatives would bring the equipment to the Tora Bora command-and-control center and install it. Soon everything would be tied to the new satellite setup in Nigeria that Lisa and the stooge—"Landay'" or whatever his name was—were just now finishing; by now, they should have it up-and-running down there. Retchko frowned; they had *better* have it up-and-running down there.

The leaders of the new common-cause were very pleased when he had described to them the chip-implant system; the scheme would be perfect for controlling the agents and the operational cells that would soon be springing up around the world.

They would develop supply lines to Tora Bora such as they had done with shipping weapons to Chechnya. He knew that the Chechens, in due time, could train these mountain men to become capable paramilitaries and demolition experts. The Chechens had described to him how they specialized in bombs that would cause massive lower-limb casualties to civilians in crowded places as instruments of institutionalized terror. Moreover, in a few days, he would meet with the warlord he had worked with in the past in the former break-away Soviet Republic and iron-out details of weaponry and training for the new recruits, who would soon be coming. The Saudi, "U", had already agreed to pay for the start-up, which would benefit the Cartel right away. Continuing funds would eventually come from sympathetic ethnic nationals in many countries and from the sale and processing of opium poppies, which was a staple crop of Afghanistan's peasant farmers. The Cartel would take advantage of the fact that Afghanistan was the leading supplier of heroin on the world's drug markets. And the refinery's profits, handled through multiple-layers of Swiss and Cayman bank accounts, would add its considerable financial contributions.

Then Retchko added a post-script to his notes: As long as the electronic engineers, Lisa Anaya and the American, Landay, kept contributing to the aims of the Organization—provided they never learned the true nature of what they were doing—he would consider allowing them to live.

* * *

Signal Intelligence Office, National Security Agency, Washington, D.C.:

"There it is—right there." The analyst pointed at the zig-zagging line on the circular screen of the oscilloscope. "Run it, again." Once more the electronic signal analyzer displayed the jagged, jumping yellow shape. "Stop!" the analyst held up his hand. The recorded signal stood frozen on the screen. "That's what I saw—what is it?"

The chief engineer moved a knob; the display enlarged. The man squinted. "I believe there was a sub-carrier signal on the module," he said, "it responded to a command."

"We did not send it any 'command'."

"Well, somebody did." The technical director turned to an assistant. "Put a continuous monitor on that module. If it happens again, let me know right away."

* * *

On a Fishing Trawler in the Caspian Sea off Baku; Two Days Later:

Leonid Efimovich Retchko held on to the rail inside the pilot house of the pitching, rolling fishing trawler and peered out through the spray-drenched window as the bow of the little ship took the gray water in the heaving Caspian Sea. The captain lurched up next to the general on the deck and grabbed the bulkhead handle. "Sir!" he shouted above the roaring swell, "we will be arriving in Baku, soon. You should prepare to go ashore!"

The Ukrainian gazed out at the frothy whitecaps all around and the low scudding clouds clipping across the undulating wavetops, and considered how he had come to be aboard this wave-swept vessel. Two days earlier, while staying over at the Kabul airport, he had made contact with a man he had known before, who was a leader of the rebellion in Chechnya. When he had told him in couched terms what he had in mind for training and equipping paramilitaries in Afghanistan, the man, who had an important post with rebel forces who were trying to wrest the region from being part of the Soviet Union, had suggested that they meet on a fishing trawler off Baku. Offshore, safe from prying eyes and ears, the two men could speak freely. Today, the revolutionary leader had joined him on this sturgeon trawler that usually worked to supply caviar to the elites. Today, however, the vessel had had a much different function: as a platform upon which they had made plans for actions that would, in time, bring down those same privileged societies.

It had been a congenial meeting; the Chechen had come aboard from another trawler drawn alongside in the heaving Caspian seaway, expecting to be greeted by the burly General Semen Putridchenko he had known from his past. Instead, a bald man—a completely bald man—had pulled up along the plunging railing, his chubby hand outstretched.

"Putridchenko?" the visitor had said, with raised eyebrows, looking Retchko up and down. The host had given the newcomer a nod and a half-smile and showed the visitor below to a small wardroom that served as a meeting place. In the warm space, over a narrow table supplied with mineral water and caviar, the Ukrainian had explained his new identity and his new career, leaving out details the other man had no need to know.

Retchko had known the rebel leader ever since he had been an officer in the "GRU" Section of the Soviet General Staff at the Academy, and with whom he had secretly worked at the same time to undercut the Russian efforts in Chechnya. The general explained that there was now an opportunity at hand to bring down reactionary governments worldwide, along with their social structures, including those of the United States and countries in Western Europe. They, along with some prosperous nations in East Asia and South America, would be easy prey when confronted with the determined alliance that was now coming into existence. He told the Chechen leader that an undertaking dedicated to re-aligning the world order, to be controlled from the Afghanistan mountains, was being put together; could the new operation count on them for support? Already, people were using the word, "terrorists', to describe their kind of people, which fit the image they were seeking to develop. In return for helping to train new recruits, Retchko offered the Chechen rebels a reliable supply of modern weapons for their fight against the Russians. The Balkan groups, aligned with the "Organization", as Retchko called the Cartel operating out of Nigeria, could eventually control most of the world through terror and intimidation. Working together, he said, they could cause great disruption and fear among the decadent democracies that would be made to pay ever-increasing prices for petroleum, one of the prime objectives. The task in the short-run would be to gain control of the

70

governments that oversaw Middle Eastern oil supplies. Full-scale assaults—economic, at first; military, later—on the Western societies would begin in due time.

The man had grasped the concept; he would take the plan back to his compatriots in Chechnya.

Departing onto the pitching deck of the other trawler, the warlord had pumped the hand of his old comrade, Putridchenko—*"Retchko"*, the Ukrainian had reminded him—and said he would be hearing from him again very soon.

Now, as the general's boat drew near to the Baku dockside, he felt satisfied that the journey was a complete success; far beyond what he had originally envisioned. In a little while, he would be on the private jet, supplied by the Iranian government, on his way back to Teheran, where "U", Ahmed, the others, and the 747 were awaiting him. In a couple of more days, he would be back at Tanuta City, ready to press ahead with his plans.

* * *

Private Chambers of Judge Jerrold Greeley, United States District Court, Washington, D.C.:

The Federal Judge leaned back in his high-backed leather chair and put his hands behind his head. "You say you believe somebody is hijacking one of your *satellites?"*

"We're getting signals from an intelligence satellite we use that are unusual. Somebody is tapping a module on it . . . somebody very clever. It could be a national security issue."

"How does that affect this court?"

"Well, I remembered last year when you gave a couple of kids who were computer hackers suspended sentences. It made all the news."

"Oh, yes . . . they got into a computer and caused all the office lights of the Federal Building to spell out some girl's name in the windows. When we finally found them, our technical staff found some pretty exotic stuff on their computer."

"Intelligence satellite intercepts, as I remember."

"I doubted if they realized what they had—but they had the potential to cause problems. I thought if they could channel their efforts in the right direction, they could do more good than harm. The prosecutor and their attorneys cut a plea bargain and I sentenced them to community service. They re-programmed all the traffic lights in the city and it's saving the voters millions of dollars in fuel this year. The mayor is taking credit for it in his re-election campaign. They still have some hours to go, by the way. But why are you interested in them?"

"Our technical people want to use experienced hackers—to get their perspective, how they operate, that sort of thing."

The judge lifted the telephone receiver and pushed a button. "Bring the 'Suggs' and 'Habbler' files to me, please."

* * *

Tanuta Refinery; Two Days Later:

Leonid Efimovich Retchko sat his desk behind the locked office door, finalizing his report to the Chief. When he had talked to him by telephone this morning; the leader was buoyant about what he had achieved on the trip. Tomorrow, he would travel to Lagos to relate the details to the head man in person. For now, he would polish the report and get caught up from the policewoman Montoya what had been happening in his absence. He already knew the electronics engineering pair had the satellite system operating, which was a great step forward in his plans. Next would come the chip implants. They needed to get it perfected right away; the new allies in Tora Bora were anxious to use the satellite-control technology.

More good news: a coded cable this morning from his old-time rebel associate in Chechnya had promised support and cooperation with the Cartel, "U" and with the Afghanistan group.

Obtaining the North Korean centrifuges and rocket components for Iran would take a little longer due to the distances involved, but he was sure he could work it out. During the next few days, while he was in Lagos, he would go to their embassy and get things started.

For now, "U" would operate out of Sudan; the 747 had dropped him and his men off at the Khartoum airport in the middle of the night. Later, as the reconfiguration of the mountain caverns continued apace, the intense young Saudi would return to Tora Bora; they had reckoned it would take some months to outfit the fortresses. In the meantime, the man would finalize his plans for the recruiting and training of thousands of volunteers for whom he would soon begin casting his worldwide net. At the same time, Lisa Anaya and Larry Landay would design and arrange to manufacture the implant chips and the gear along with the software to make it all work.

Picking up Ahmed had been a stroke of luck; looking back, he realized the mission would have been stymied without his language translations. Taking him back to Libya was the least he could do for the fellow. He had arranged to take him along on future trips.

Retchko shut the notebook and focused his eyes on the safe; he would put the report in there for safekeeping.

* * *

When he opened the armored door, the little emerald-jeweled ring that had fallen off Marisol's finger dropped further down onto the bottom shelf's loose papers, out of sight.

* * *

The bald Ukrainian pulled out the top papers and scanned them; everything was he had left them, of course. Soon, the Cayman bank would send him an updated statement. As he thought about its growing balances, a cynical smirk came to his face: *Moscow was never like this.*

The general closed the door to the safe and went outside. In the short interval it took him to step across the sun-broiled parking lot to the new satellite building, sweat broke out on his bald head. Remarkable, he thought, that two days ago he was surrounded by ice and snow.

A scraping outside the door of the radio shack caught the attention of Larry Landay, who was inside adjusting a control. A moment later, a rotund, baldheaded man lunged through the open door.

"General Retchko! Welcome back—" The sandy-haired American offered his hand to the Ukrainian, who proffered his own pudgy grip. Lisa Anaya, overhearing voices, came around the equipment rack and gave a start the Chief of Security noticed. She put out her own hand.

"I am told you are finished with the satellite radios," the stocky European said in his Slavic accent, looking around the room that was crammed with electronic gear. "To me, it is most mysterious."

"Well, general, it's what you ordered," Larry put in. The enigmatic man seemed to be in an expansive mood.

Retchko turned to the girl. "You have the specifications for the wrist implants, already?" When she nodded, he went on, "I want the finished product ready in thirty days."

The foreigner took one more look-around, as if satisfied with what he saw. "Very well, carry on." He turned and stepped out the door. His crunching footsteps faded away.

"Well, I guess—" Larry stopped; Lisa had a concerned look on her face. "Something wrong?"

"Not so much *'wrong'* . . . it is just that he wants me to do something in a few days that would usually take months." She was shaking her head. "Larry, you must help me find a circuit board manufacturer, right away."

She turned back to the transmitter and sent a coded signal that was acknowledged by the satellite.

* * *

Signal Intelligence Office, National Security Agency; Washington, D.C., at that Moment:

Jamey Suggs stared at the squiggly line dancing across the little round screen. "What do you think, Buzzy?"

His friend blinked at the yellow waveform. Is this in real-time?"

"It's coming from the satellite, right now," the technician said.

"I would say the module is relaying a command." He snapped his fingers. "A *'sideband'!* The waveform is a 'sideband' transmission!"

The jagged lines kept up their frenetic zig-zagging on the screen.

A knowing look came on Buzzy Habbler's face. "Look at the way that square-wave forms at the top of the positive peak. I believe this signal is *'ultra-modulated'.*"

"Of course! A sideband would mask an ultra-modulated signal!"

The technician looked perplexed. "You mean, where they over-drive the positive peaks and take it off the negative peaks? Some old *'A-M'* radio stations used to do it to get a louder sound on the air. But I never heard of such a thing from a satellite."

Jamey straightened up. "It's hard to lock onto a sideband that has ultra-modulation imbedded in it, except by using custom equipment at both ends. Somebody very clever is behind this."

Buzzy Habbler was nodding. "It's even harder to detect if it's encoded—and I'll bet it is."

* * *

"Okay, everything checks out." Lisa moved a lever that took the transmitter off the air. "We won't need any more code tests until we have the chip implants ready." Standing next to her, Larry flipped a row of switches; one-by-one the instruments in the equipment racks went dark.

* * *

Even as the technical man and the two boys stood watching the waveform, all at once the squiggling yellow line flattened; the oscilloscope went blank All the needles on the dials were at "zero". Jamey Suggs stared in surprise at the featureless screen. "What happened?"

"The transmission's stopped." The technician adjusted a knob with no results.

"Well, gee . . . things were just getting interesting. Any idea when it'll be back on?"

"Who knows?" The three gaped at the screen. The electronic specialist shrugged. "We'll keep a monitor on it and let you know if something happens."

-5-

Tanuta Refinery, Christmas Day, 1991:

Leonid Efimovich Retchko gaped in amazement at the headlines splashed across front page of the morning paper. "Well, I will be damned!" he said out loud to himself. "Sons of bitches! They finally did it!" The bald Ukrainian flattened the pages on his desk:

Tanuta Times, Wednesday, December 25, 1991

SOVIET UNION COLLAPSES

YELTSIN TAKES OVER FROM GORBACHEV

HAMMER AND SICKLE COMES DOWN FROM KREMLIN

REPLACED BY OLD FLAG

CITIZENS DANCING IN RED SQUARE

HUGE COUNTRY FACES UNCERTAIN FUTURE

After Retchko had read and re-read the stories about the events in the Far North that he knew would re-shape the world, he set aside the newspaper, put his hands behind his bald head and leaned back in the chair with a lopsided grin. "Now, things are *really* going my way!" he said, loud enough to be heard through the closed office door. But he knew there was no worry about anyone else overhearing his grunts of satisfaction; the whole place was vacated for their holiday. He looked out the window at the shut-down refinery that epitomized his perceived weakness of these people and their "Christmas Spirit;" as they put it. For days, now, he had had to endure the record player in the lobby and its imbecilic screeching about "Happy Holidays", and "Deck the Halls," until he was ready to smash it. On top of that, the employees had hung the silliest kinds of decorations around their offices to the point he could hardly stand it. The whole thing reminded him of the New Year's celebrations back in Russia. Here, they even had a fat, red-and-white costumed fellow they called "Santa Claus, who looked a lot like the juvenile Russian "Grandfather Frost"; both gave out presents and looked and acted childish.

Today, the revelry was gone; all the offices were empty; only a few maintenance workers were out in the plant; all the equipment was idle. It was a day of lost business, as far as he was concerned.

But there were compensations. In the absence of prying eyes, there was much he could accomplish today for himself. Retchko picked up the coded message that had come in from Pyongyang overnight on the secret circuit: the North Koreans would be pleased to supply the items he had requested. Of course, they would. They would make hundreds of millions of American dollars off the deals.

Other things—personal things—were also in the works. He would send Lester Nkrume to Lagos on a supposed business errand, and he would never again have to put up with the aggravating plant manager. After that, he would have a clear shot at the man's young wife.

* * *

Tanuta Refinery, Thursday, December 26, 1991:

"I must have the system ready to start in two weeks," Retchko was saying, "you must do the designs in a few days and have them ready to give to the makers of the 'circuit board', as you call it."

Lisa Anaya sat across from the big mogahany desk as he rasped on about the implant project."We will have the computer-assisted designs finished in a couple of days," she put in when the pale Ukranian paused, "Larry says he has found a circuit board manufacturer in Lagos. He is going there next week."

Retchko tapped the desktop with his fingertips. "I am sending the security girl along with him. I want her to do some work for me at the Lagos airport." The "Chief of Security" arose, signifying the meeting was over.

Stepping out into the hallway, she was not happy that the man was putting Larry and Marisol together on the same trip, but she knew she had no choice in the matter. And she wondered about the twitching she had observed around the man's mouth as he spoke. She had not noticed it before.

Just then, Larry stepped out of the room of office cubicles and came in her direction When he saw her, he grinned; he too still felt the warm glow from what had happened in his apartment last night. He pointed his finger at his watch. "It's lunchtime . . . let's eat."

"And I have some things to tell you." Looking around and seeing that no one else was in the corridor, the slender young woman slipped her arm into his.

* * *

When the girl had closed the door, the bulky European had leaned back and grinned; with both the American and the Cuban woman gone, he would also now have Lisa Anaya to himself.

The pain hit in his head just then. Retchko reached into a desk drawer and pulled out the aspirin bottle. These damnable headaches were getting worse and more frequent, it seemed.

* * *

Late Afternoon; the Same Day:

Marisol Montoya squinted into the setting sun as she walked across the parking lot toward the office building. She had been looking into a reported break in the security fence, and was now headed toward the main building for dinner. Then she heard a male voice coming from off to the side."Miss Montoya!"

She turned and saw Frank Ogawan stepping in a hurry toward her, his hand up-raised. "Miss Montoya," he gasped as he trotted up out of breath, "I am glad I found you . . . General Retchko wants to see you right now in his office. He says it is important!"

"Now? At dinnertime?" As they stepped inside the entranceway, the aroma of food came to them. Trying to forget she had not eaten in many hours, the young woman turned in the opposite direction from the dining hall toward the Security Office. The fellow called back to her over his shoulder. "I will save a place for you!"

* * *

A half-hour later, when Marisol walked into the dining-room, she saw an arm waving at her from the far corner. "Over here—!" Frank Ogawan called out across the crowded space.

As soon as she took a seat across from him, he thought she looked stressed; perhaps tired. She hadn't been that way when he talked with her just a little while before. "I say, are you all right?"

"Well, yes . . . no—I just found out I will be going to Lagos next week for some days."

"What is so bad about that?"

She looked at him for a long second, then leaned forward. "We will talk later," she mouthed, with a grave gesture toward the ceiling. Marisol had remembered the listening devices.

* * *

The two stopped in the dark shadows behind the new little microwave building on the outskirts of the office complex. "Why are we here, again?" Frank asked.

"I have found out that this whole place is bugged with microphones. I also know this new building is not, yet." In the gloom Marisol saw the outlines of Frank Ogawan's frown. "I do not have a good feeling about leaving, right now," she said in a hoarse whisper. The young woman pursed her lips. "I guess it was the *'way'* that Retchko spoke to me in his office just now." She looked around as if to make sure no one was overhearing her; they were alone. The former Havana policewoman went on. "There is something about him I do not trust. He gives me—as the 'Americanos' say—'the creeps'." Marisol looked straight in the young office manager's face. "Frank, do you remember the other night when we talked out here? When I told you I thought people were in danger?"

"Well, yes . . . but you did not say how."

She gripped his forearm. "Frank, I found some of Retchko's papers. I think he is sending me away on purpose so I will not be here for some reason . . . I believe he will be moving against some people while I am gone. Lisa may be in *'especial'* danger—perhaps you, too."

The African looked shocked. "Miss Montoya, what do you mean by that?"

The Latina spread her hands. "I am not sure, but I sensed it again when Retcko and I talked just now. There is no real reason for me to go to Lagos—something is not right about this. And Lester Nkrume is going with us. I wonder why."

"What can I do?"

"I asked you before to watch out for Lisa and you will have to do that. Stay with her as much as you can. I am sure she would not mind."

He remembered the humiliation of the other night. Most likely, she *would* mind. But he could not tell Miss Montoya about that.

At that moment there came a loud blow-off from one of the refinery's vent stacks that cast a garish, flickering orange light over where they were standing! At once Marisol pulled back Frank---but now they were in the lights from the main building. The young woman's eyes went wide. Across the way, General

Retchko was standing on the porch smoking a cigar! The man was turning away. *Had he seen them?*

The Chief of Security went back inside, irritated as always by the ear-splitting racket from the tower. When the torch-like flame had erupted with startling suddeness, searing the calm night with its blinding glare and fiendish uproar, the wincing man had turned at once and had returned to his office. As he finished his smoke at his desk, he thought about how, as he had stood on the porch, torching the rolled Cuban tobacco while staring idly at the new building across the broad parking lot, he had remembered it did not yet have the microphones. The general scratched some notes on a pad to have his "special" technician—the man who was sworn to secrecy in the electronic evesdropping project—to install them.

And to tell the truth, he was getting bored with this backwater place; perhaps he would go to Lagos, too. Then the image of Betty Nkrume that time they had had their first—and so far, only—carnal get-together rushed back. She would be here while her husband went with the other two back to the capital city. Both sisters would be available to him. What a convenient arrangement! Of course, Lisa would not likely be a willing participant, but did it matter? She owed him a debt for saving her life in the lightning storm and he was going to collect it. As for her sister, Betty's body language had been telling him all along that she was not only willing but anxious to renew their previous liaison. Boredom could have its compensations.

* * *

Murtala Mohammed Airport Lagos, Lagos, Nigeria, Monday, December 30, 1991:

The Aero Commander's twin propellers subsided to a whisper, then stopped turning. Marisol reached back over the seat and nudged Larry, who had dozed off during the flight from Tanuta City. "Wake up!" she grinned, "we are here at Lagos, now."

82

The American sat up and gazed about the big airport. Even as he yawned and rubbed his eyes, a grounds-crewman trotted underneath the high wing and tugged open the side doors. Muggy morning air, mixed with the smell of jet fuel and engine exhaust, came into their faces. He and the young woman, along with Lester Nkrume, who had kept to himself during the flight, pulled their luggage bags from a rear compartment and made their way across the apron to the hangar building.

While Nkrume turned up the corridor in another direction, a military man man motioned for Larry and Marisol to follow him down a short hallway. They turned into a meeting room, where a trim man in an Army uniform, wearing military-style sunglasses, stood up. Larry recognized Colonel Ajiboy from when they had embarked on the freighter. "Good to see you, again!"

The officer shook Marisol's hand then Larry's. The colonel waved away the attendant and closed the door.

"Señor Landay"—Marisol motioned to Larry—"will be in Lagos on a business matter." She nodded at the Nigerian military man. "General Retchko wants me to inspect the security arrangements here at the airport."

Larry thought he detected a look of alarm pass over the African's face.

"Ah, yes . . . the general said something about that." Ajiboy swallowed, then called out to the enlisted man who had directed them to the room. "Get tea for these visitors."

Marisol looked out the big panoramic window. "I see many guards around here."

"Yes, General Retchko has done much to strenthen security here at the airport." Larry noticed the military officer kept licking his lips.

Just then, the corporal came back with a tray. "Let us now have tea," Ajiboy said, motioning at the table. After helping themselves, the three stood around, sipping from delicate porcelain cups that struck Larry as being out-of-character in this masculine environment. "Tea-time' is from the British colonial days. We do it in the morning and afternoon," Ajiboy offered. Well, that answered *that* question, Larry thought.

The American set down his cup. "I'll need a taxi to take me downtown."

Colonel Ajiboy called to the soldier. "Show him to the cabs."

Larry picked up his luggage, then he and the other fellow headed for the door. "I'll be at the hotel later this afternoon," Larry said to Marisol, over his shoulder. The three visitors had arranged to stay overnight at a place called the *'Roomland Hotel'*.

Marisol looked out the window, then at Ajiboy. "I wish to see the airport, now."

The colonel stepped to the doorway and spoke some words to an enlisted man standing in the corridor, then motioned to the young woman. "Come with me."

Outside, Ajiboy and the Cubana dropped into the rear seat of an olive-drab Army sedan. The officer gave the driver some orders; the vehicle moved off. Rounding the corner of a hangar she spotted the familiar 747 parked on the flight line in the morning sunshine. Marisol felt a tingle as she remembered hiding in a box on that very airplane to escape Cuba and becoming acquainted with Larry during the long flight through Angola, where they had picked-up the AK-74's, to Nigeria.

The vehicle gained speed and bounded across some taxiways. At length, they pulled up at a fence near the end of the main runway and got out. As the two made their way across a grassy space to the outer barrier, Ajiboy pointed at an electrical cable that came out of the ground. "The fence is electrified," he said, "and there are ground sensors all around. General Retchko ordered it to be done."

"We have just completed electrifying the fences at the refinery," Marisol said.

"The sensors took the place of many soldiers," the colonel went on. "Watch out!" the man shouted all at once, grabbing her arm. The officer pointed at a low mound in the grass. "Land-mine!"

The young woman stepped back, her eyes wide. One of these could blow off a leg.

Ajiboy swept his arm around at the fences. "There are several rows of them. They are very effective in keeping intruders from getting into the airport." Marisol was sure she observed a fleeting wince cross the African's dark face. "Some people were killed by them at the start, but it was General Retchko's plan for that to happen. Now that people have learned of the consequences, there are fewer attempts at intrusion." Marisol got the impression the colonel was not altogether happy about the anti-personnel mines.

The two got back into the car and rode around the perimeter of the airport. At length, as they came up to the backside of the main security area, the colonel stared at a small, concrete-block outbuilding. A thin column of gray smoke was rising from a stovepipe stack on its roof. The young woman detected a sweet-like odor as they passed by. She noticed the officer was frowning. "That is strange," she heard him mutter, as the car drove past, "I thought they were not going to—" Then he caught himself and glanced at her, almost, she thought, as if to see if she had overheard him.

Inside the crowded terminal, Marisol observed squads of soldiers marching shoulder-to-shoulder in the big open terminal and up-and-down the concourses; a rifle was balanced on each of the mens' left shoulder. There came a shouted order; at once some men in battle gear marching by broke into slamming goose-steps! Marisol jumped; people in the surging throng reacted with gasps and looks of shocked awe. Ajiboy squinted at the high-kicking troops as they thundered past. "General Retchko set up a high military profile at the airport," he said, when the noisy soldiers had tramped away from them.

For the second time Marisol noticed that the colonel had injected the general's name into a context that included drastic—even deadly—security measures at the airport; that he kept repeating how the former Soviet had devised the various new methods. Like so many others, did the colonel also fear the bald Ukrainian? She thought about the contents of the safe. What was it Retchko had marked beside Ajiboy's name? "Replace".

Marisol felt the skin on the back of her neck prickling as she realized Retchko's diabolical tentacles could extend out and envelop with dread even this officer who was perhaps in reality more diffident than he outwardly tried to appear. That Retchko held such power unsettled her.

"Come with me," Ajiboy said, turning down a corridor off the main concourse. At a metal door he stopped and punched a keypad next to it. There came a loud "click", then the door swung open by itself. Her eyes adjusted to a narrow, musty hallway that went away for a short distance. At a dead-end, the colonel clapped his hands twice. At once, part of the end wall creaked inward, revealing a stark, white-painted room.

Marisol eased through the door and looked around. A single metal chair sat in the middle of the gloomy space. She noticed it was bolted to the floor; what looked like leather belts with buckles dangled onto the dull-red linoleum floor. A bare light-bulb hung on a cord from an overhead socket; a porcelain lavatory hunched in a corner. The place had a clammy feel; the young woman shuddered. Other than the moving wall, the only other entrance seemed to be another metal-type door next to a white metal cabinet.

All at once, the metal door burst open and two muscular Africans bounded into the room. Without words, they pushed past Ajiboy, who looked surprised, and grabbed Marisol by both her arms! The girl screamed; her purse went flying; one of the powerful pair pulled her into a headlock while the other man flung her, flailing, onto the chair, at the same time reaching for the leather restraining straps!

"Stop! Stop!" the colonel shouted, tugging at them.

The violent intruders stepped back, almost robot-like, and turned their heads as one toward the speaker. Marisol burst into tears.

The Army man glared at the assailants, then spoke something in a rapid dialect the shaking Cubana barely heard; her cuffed ears were ringing. The two dark men frowned, shrugged, then spun on their heels and stepped back through the opening. The door slammed shut.

Ajiboy, looking mortified, snatched up a hand towel, wetted it in the sink and handed it to the shaking Marisol. Looking around, he retrieved her purse from where it had scooted into a corner. "I am sorry, madame, they mistook you for someone else."

The young woman wiped her face, trying to compose herself. She felt her neck; something cold had been on the man's hand that had gripped her. With horror she realized the giants had been wearing brass knuckles!

Marisol dabbed her eyes. "Why did they do that?"

"It is all on General Retchko's orders." He swallowed. "They 'take action' when his officers bring in someone." He glanced about as if making sure he could speak freely with this woman. "I do not personally sanction it," he said in a low voice, "but it is beyond my control."

"God, I was so scared!"

"Madame, please—it was a mistake." The uncomfortable officer patted her shoulder.

She stood up and looked around at the tight space with a shudder. "In Havana, the 'P-N-R; have the same thing . . . for 'counter-revolutionaries'."

"The 'P-N-R'?"

"*Nacional Revolución ary Police*'—the secret police of Cuba. I was a Havana police officer." She grimaced at the horrid torture chair. For the first time, she saw little crimson blotches on the floor. *Bloodstains?*

Ajiboy seemed to not have noticed her observation. "You are from Cuba?"

"It is a long story."

* * *

Larry Landay paid the taxi driver and turned with briefcase and luggage bag toward a low building with a sign on its front that proclaimed the place to be the headquarters of "Ikoye Printed Circuits, Ltd." At the front desk the receptionist looked up at him.

"I'm Larry Landay, and I have an appointment with your Chief Engineer." The girl lifted a telephone handset and repeated the American's name.

* * *

In a laboratory behind the reception area, another American cocked his head. "Larry Landay?" Where had he heard that

87

name, before? Then he remembered: an American by that name was wanted by the authorities back in the United States and was believed to be in Nigeria! The envoy had seen the announcement on the bulletin board at the United States Consulate General's. What a stroke of luck if he happened to be in this very place! The man peeped around the corner for a split-second and saw a sandy-haired fellow, perhaps in his mid-'thirties, standing in the outer room, who looked like he might be the guy in the picture he had seen.

* * *

Then the receptionist called the subject's name and the suspect stepped away.

The electronics expert with whom the consular employee had been working on a technical matter came back just then and as the two went on with their discussion, the American kept his ear attuned to the receptionist area in case the fellow left the building. The man strung-along the talk until at length he heard the visitor's voice in the lobby, then the unmistakable sounds of the front door opening with a burst of traffic noise from the outside, then closing.

The man from the United States Consulate General took his leave. At the curb, he spotted a receding taxicab rounding a corner a couple of blocks away.

"Taxi!" He stepped off the curb and called out to a cab driving by just then. In a moment he was telling the driver to follow the other vehicle that was just coming into sight on the thoroughfare up ahead. The car settled back to follow the other cab. After some kilometers, including driving across a very long bridge, the lead taxi drove down an exit and ran along a service road. The second car followed along. Not long after leaving the main road, the first vehicle slowed at a turn-around and after a short distance pulled in at a mid-rise building. The American envoy's cab swung about, passed a big police station and came up to what he now saw was a hotel. "Turn here!" he told the driver. The car stopped in front of the "Roomland Hotel."

The man stepped out and paid the driver. The suspect had gone inside. The official went into the lobby and made a quick survey: the sandy-haired individual was standing at the front desk; his back was to him. The fellow had not noticed his pursuer. The second man slipped back into an alcove off a stairwell and stood, listening. At length, he heard the desk clerk say, "Room six-ten." That would be his room—"six-ten". He watched as the fellow stuffed some folded papers into a pocket and sat down on a sofa facing away from him, next to his luggage bag.

Just as the consular man was trying to decide his next move, the target individual stood up and called out to a smallish, tanned young woman who was coming in the front entrance. While the two went to the main desk together and talked with the clerk, the consul agent stepped boldly into the lobby and took a seat with his back to the counter. "Room six-twelve . . . the top floor," he overheard the hotel man call out the girl's room number, as he feigned reading a magazine. Glancing up, the agent got a good look at the pair's backsides as they headed up the main staircase. The two were acting friendly with each other, he observed. At the first landing, they turned out of sight.

The envoy looked at his watch; it was half past five in the afternoon. He went to the front desk. "A room for the night, please," he said to the clerk, scribbling on a pad the fellow had pushed across the counter at him. "Do you have something on the top floor—I don't like street noises."

"Ah, yes, we do, as a matter of fact." The fellow ran his credit card and handed him a key. "Room 'six-fourteen'. It is the only vacancy on the top floor. We are pretty busy, tonight."

The new guest stepped across the paneled lobby's carpeted floor to the bottom of the steps. As he turned to go up, he caught sight of a room full of television monitors in a room off the staircase; a uniformed guard sat at a console watching several jerky screens as they switched from scene to scene. The place seems to have a pretty good security system, the man thought. Then it occurred to him that perhaps they were *spying* on the hotel's guests.

The man puffed to the top of the staircase, wishing he had taken the elevator. Then he recalled he had not seen an elevator in the lobby and there was none on the sixth-floor—it looked as if the place had *no* elevators. Trying to catch his breath, he took careful steps down the over-lighted hallway and stopped at room "six-twelve", which he had overheard the desk clerk speak out where the woman would be. He stuck the key into the lock of the next-door room, number six-fourteen, and stepped inside. He would wait until the suspects had retired for the night before making his move.

* * *

Retchko dropped the telephone receiver into its cradle on his desk and gave himself a grim smile of satisfacton. The cryptic call from his new ally Norbert Ezego had just confirmed that the Plant Manager had disappeared. The fierce-looking man had told him it had happened without Ajiboy's knowledge.

The tough Nigerian, Ezego, had passed his first test and would figure greatly in future plans.

* * *

Marisol looked out the window of her top-floor hotel room. Down below, in the early tropical evening in a palm grove an outdoor bazaar was going full-blast. The young Cuban woman stood watching the scene below, with its dozens of little lighted lanterns hanging on palm fronds swaying in the breeze as she listened to the muffled, rhythmic thumps of African drums and steely native music.

There came a knock on the door. She walked over and peered through a peep-hole at the compressed view of Larry's face in the tiny viewer.

"I was looking for Nkrume," the American said, stepping into the room a little out of breath. "The front desk guy says he's not yet checked-in. I would have thought he would be here by now."

His eyes fell on a menu next to a telephone on the writing desk. "I don't know about you, but I'm hungry. Let's call room service."

A few minutes later, there was a rap on the door. "Room service!" an adolescent-sounding male voice cracked from the corridor. Larry paid the boy and took the tray to a low table in the middle of the room that was surrounded by a grouping of stuffed furniture.

Marisol made a show of turning the deadbolt on the door. "Something about this place I do not trust." She wrapped her arms around herself and dropped onto a compact sofa across from the coffee table and leaned forward to see what Larry had ordered. *"'Pollo'?"*

Larry grinned. "*Native* African chicken."

"You say Nkrume is not here?" Marisol said between bites. "He is always on time for everything."

She was right, Larry knew. From observing Lester Nkrume the American was aware that, although the man's title of "Plant Manager" had become meaningless ever since Retchko had taken over his duties and even his private office, as others had told him, Lisa's brother-in-law had carried himself with dignity in the face of all that and with an obvious lack of support from his flighty young wife. For he had seen observable differences in the personalities and in the depths of character between Betty Nkrume and her sister, Lisa Anaya.

"I'll go down to the front desk again to see if he's checked in," he told Marisol when they had finished. "Lock the door and I'll give you a special knock when I get back."

Downstairs, the desk clerk fingered through his registration cards. "No, sir, Lester Nkrume has not yet arrived, but his room is still reserved for the night."

Back in the room, Larry relayed the information to Marisol, who was frowning. "It's strange," he said to her, "it almost looks like something might have happened to him."

"And he is such a nice man."

"He didn't say where he was going?"

"I remember he did not say much on the flight up from Tanuta City, this morning," Marisol said, "when we landed he went off in a hurry, as if he had something important to do." She shrugged. "He is probably still busy."

"This late at night? I wonder." He looked at his watch. "Well, I'll leave, now . . . we have to go to the American Consulate General early in the morning."

Larry caught her sudden shudder. "I am nervous about this place," she said, wrapping her arms around herself as before.

The American chuckled. "You—the confident woman—are afraid to be alone?"

"Something about this hotel frightens me." She shook her head, trying to suppress the shaking.

"Well, I'll be next door in case ghosts come to get you."

"Señor Larry, that is not funny!"

He gave her a smirk and closed the door. From inside, the lock gave a loud click behind him.

* * *

In the room next to hers, the consular envoy heard the doors opening and closing. Good; the suspect was retiring for the night. He would wait a little while, then make his move. When he captured the fugitive, he would get recognition. Perhaps even a promotion.

* * *

The bulky man huffed in a hurry through the darkened main gate of the refinery and turned onto the gravelly shoulder of the black asphalt main road, barely visible in the pale moonlight. Ahead, in some deep shadows, beneath a leafy canopy of overhanging tree branches, was a parked car. With stealthy steps he came up to it, opened the passenger-side door and slid onto the front seat. "It is done," the stocky individual told the driver in a low voice."

The person behind the wheel took the night visitor in her arms; in the humid darkness the two gave themselves over to a tight embrace.

The female disengaged herself and reached for the ignition switch. "Let us go now to my house."

* * *

Marisol Montoya sat up in the bed, her eyes wide; in the shadowy darkness of her hotel room the young woman's hand flew to her mouth—the door was rattling. Someone in the hallway was trying to jimmy the lock to her room!

At that moment, the house detective stepped from the staircase onto the sixth-floor and reached for his billy club. Down the corridor, a middle-aged Caucasion man in a sport coat looked to be sliding a credit card into a door frame; he was trying to break into the room. "Halt!" the detective shouted, "Stay right there—do not move!" The uniformed man bounded forward and grabbed the suspicious individual by the shoulder of his coat.

The white man whirled around and acted startled. "Oh!" he gasped in seeming surprise, making a show of glancing at the number on the door. "I have the wrong room!"

"I saw you! You are trying to break and enter! I watched you on the security monitor!" The African detective whipped around the suspect's arms and snapped handcuffs on his wrists. "Come with me!" the scowling man said, brandishing his billy club.

"You can't arrest me! I have 'diplomatic immunity'!"

"Sure, you do!" The security officer's voice was sarcastic. He jerked the protesting prisoner toward the staircase-landing.

Marisol, her heart pounding, stood next to the door and cocked her ear: no sounds were now coming from out there. Peering through the peephole, its fish-eye viewfinder seemed to declare an empty, brightly-lit hallway. The young woman pulled open the door a little and looked up and down; the corridor was vacant. Unmindful that she was clad only in a long T-shirt, she tiptoed over to the next room and knocked on the American's door. "Larry! Larry! Open up!" the young woman called out in a hoarse whisper.

The door cracked aside; a surprised Larry Landay gaped at her. Before he could react, in a second, Marisol edged through the opening and stood next to him, shaking. He closed the door and twisted the deadbolt. "What—?"

"Someone was trying to break into my room!" The Latina flung her arms around his neck in a tight hold. "Oh, Señor Larry! I heard noises at the door . . . someone was trying to open the lock!" The girl pulled her arms tighter on him. "I do not want be alone, tonight! *Por favor!*"

"Well, I guess you can stay here . . . ”

In the dim light filtering through the window-shade the two looked into each other's eyes for a long moment; the girl blinked, her mouth opened a little. He was aware of her T-shirted chest against his, her taut shoulders; her tense upper back.

Larry eased her clinging arms off his shoulders and motioned at an empty bed in a corner. "You can sleep there—I'll be over here."

Marisol pulled the chair from the writing desk to the door. Larry frowned. "What are you doing?"

The Cubana put her finger to her lips for quiet. "We must know if intruders come," she whispered, bracing the back of the chair under the door knob. The former Havana policewoman tested the arrangement; it seemed secure. "Now, no one can get in here."

The girl glanced down at herself, then gave a gasp. "Señor Larry, all my clothes and everything are still in my room! I am almost naked!"

Larry already knew that; when she had grabbed him, he could tell she was wearing only the T-shirt. "We'll get your things in the morning . . . let's try to get some sleep." He was trying to steer away from the subject that he knew was on both of their minds.

She stepped to the second bed and pulled down the covers; in the dim backlight of the window he could not fail to catch the outline of her figure. Larry felt his blood pressure going up. He took a deep breath; this was going to be a night of extreme self-control. The American dropped onto his mattress and tried not to be tense.

He heard the girl sliding about on the sheets close by; her every movement, amplified in the quiet, shadowy room, was if a symphony orchestra was playing. For the presence of the pretty young Latina, lying in the same hotel room near to him, whom he knew was wearing almost nothing, was torturing him, even though she didn't know it. Larry wondered what it would be like to make love to her. He tried to drive away that notion by remembering how it had always been with Lisa.

But as he lay there in the darkness, he knew he was not in love with the beautiful, brainy electronics engineer. He liked her a lot and enjoyed being with her. Ever since he and the cream-colored graduate-student had first been together in the moonlit surf one night in Hawaii when they had been there on a school trip—now so long ago and so far away, it seemed—he had thought of her always in physical and intellectual terms, he now understood, not with any particular emotional attachment. Larry squirmed on the bed, thinking. Try as he might, he just could not envision a future with Lisa that included little offspring crawling on the floor and intrusive in-laws always coming around. But how could he tell her without creating a scene? They were almost finished with the satellite project—perhaps he could just leave, and that would be that. But he knew it could never be so simple; women never let such things go by without repercussions. Besides, if he left Tanuta City, he would also be leaving Marisol Montoya.

His thoughts drifted over to Lisa's sister, Betty Nkrume. A number of questions had formed lately in his mind about the plant manager's wife; some things about the young woman just didn't quite add up. He had noticed several times how she treated her husband with an obvious disdain that was painful to watch. Larry had overheard others talk about it, so it was not just his observation, alone. He was starting to have sympathy for the melancholy, older man. Tomorrow, when they returned to Tanuta City, he would make it a point to try to be more friendly to him.

On the next bed, the sheets rustled; Marisol was still awake, he guessed. From the time he had first seen her as a policewoman at the Havana airport, it seemed she was always connected to intense events; the latest was the encounter with the crocodile. He was going to have to be honest with himself about this tough, straightforward little woman with the trim figure and the leggy good looks—he was attracted to her and had been all along. For Lisa's sake, up to now he had managed to fend her off, for the main reason that she came from such a different background from his—she had even trained in Russia with Soviet Special Forces! All he knew about her personal life was what she had told him: that her relatives, except for one uncle and a few who had escaped to Florida by boat, had been ground-up in the political machinery of the Castro régime, which was the reason she had stowed away on the 747 to get out of Cuba. Other than that, she was a mystery.

Once more, he heard Marisol softly moving about; he visualized her squirming bare, toned legs caressing the sheets and the long, clinging T-shirt, which was all she had on. Maybe they could talk. But he knew if he were to say something—anything— to her right now, the dam holding them back would burst. As enticing as that prospect might be, he was not yet ready for that.

* * *

In the darkness, Marisol Montoya listened to Larry's breathing. There came a rustling and some mattress squeaks; he was still awake. Intense urges, nurtured in Cuba, the land of physical release, welled-up in her taut, tense body; she would be sleeping in the same room with Larry Landay! As she listened to his sounds, she wondered what it would be like to make love with him. But that was impossible, she knew; he was already taken by Lisa Anaya—besides, he had shown no interest toward her in that way—or in any other way. A tear, then another, then rivulets of drops ran down her cheek, dampening the pillow.

After a while, Larry's slow, rhythmic breathing told her he was asleep.

Sometime later, fatigue overcame her and she, too, dropped off into slumber.

* * *

Tuesday, December 31, 1991:

Larry and Marisol gaped at the desk clerk, frowning. "You say he did not come in last night?"

"No, sir; madame. Mister Nkrume did not arrive." The fellow behind the counter shook his head.

The American pulled her out of earshot of the man. "I don't like this! Something must have happened to him!" He knew that Lagos was a very dangerous city; one of the most risky places in the world. The travelogues even said so.

"Oh, Señor Larry, what can we do?"

"Maybe he went straight back to the airport, last night."

The girl blinked. "Let us hurry to the Consulate General's, then go back there to find him."

Larry needed to update his visa to return to the United States—a reminder he would soon be leaving Nigeria to return home. He glanced at Marisol's bare, tanned shoulders; this morning she was wearing a Cuban-style sundress that exposed a lot of skin. The prospect of leaving the lithe young Latina at Tanuta City was unappealing now, after the hard decisions he had taken last night about Lisa. But he also had his business to run back in Mountain View. Everything was becoming so confused.

Parked outside was a beat-up looking taxicab. "To 'The American Consulate General'," Larry told the sleepy driver.

Minutes later, the smoking sedan pulled up at a gate where a uniformed United States Marine raised a white-gloved hand. The fit-looking young man leaned over and frowned into the little car. "Business?"

"I want to update my return visa," Larry called out to the guard, holding up his passport.

The corporal looked the driver up and down and shook his head. "*You* will have to park over there and wait for them." He pointed to a space nearby, then motioned for the American and Marisol to alight from the vehicle. "The office is through that door," the soldier said, nodding at a nearby building.

Inside, a native receptionist took their names and made a telephone call. Then the girl pointed toward a hallway leading off the lobby. "Third door to the left," she said.

In a minute, the American and his young woman companion were sitting in front of a desk, facing a middle-aged white man who was leaning back in his big leather chair, his fingertips touching. "I will be returning to the 'States in a few days, and I need to update my passport, "Larry said, handing the blue book across the desk.

The official turned to the identification pages and hesitated. *Did he do a double-take?*

"'Lawrence James Landay . . . born in California'?"

Larry nodded.

The man scrambled around on his desk and pulled up a sheet of paper. He held it up where the others could not see it and looked it over, squinting. "They call you 'Larry'?"

"Yes." The Californian felt himself stiffening. *How did he know that?*

The envoy frowned at the document, then at the passport and back at the visitor, as if comparing some things to be sure without question; a silence hung heavy in the room. Marisol noticed the paper was shaking in the man's hand; he looked nervous. She glanced at Larry; her instincts told her something was not right.

The man clenched his teeth and reached for a telephone. "'Code-Seven' in the passport office," he said into the receiver in a strained voice, glancing again at the younger man. Marisol saw that he was breathing in shallow gasps. He leaned forward, frowning, and clasped his fingers on the desktop. *As if waiting?* He stared past the two sitting before him at the direction of the door. Larry felt himself breaking into a cold sweat. *What's going on?*

There came a shuffling sound behind the visitors. Larry turned about and tensed in alarm.

Two husky-looking Marines, both popping billy clubs into the palms of their hands, stood in the doorway, their boots planted wide!

The official behind the desk pointed at Larry. "Take this man into custody—there is a warrant for his arrest!"

Marisol bolted from her seat and lunged at the two soldiers. Before they could react, with a shout the "Spetsnaz"-trained young woman launched herself feet-first at the guards and caught both of them square-on in their faces! All three came down in a heap; the two men's heads rammed hard against the opposite wall of the corridor! Frothy fountains of red bubbled at their noses and mouths.

The girl, breathing hard, stared for a split-second at their inert forms, then jumped up. "Come on!" she called out, reaching back and grabbing Larry by his wrist. The diplomat at the desk, his face ashen, was punching some numbers on the telephone.

Outside, the young woman and the blond man raced across the open space toward the gate. As they came up to it, the Marine they had encountered earlier stepped from the guardhouse, making a motion for them to stop. Marisol flung herself at the unprepared American and slammed the heel of her hand hard across his face, laying his nose over with a *"SNAP!"* The guard screamed and dropped to his knees grabbing at his face, a flood of crimson coursing through his fingers. The girl leaped high, clasped her hands together and came down on the back of his neck with all her might!

The soldier fell onto his face, not moving.

The second Marine, hearing the commotion, appeared in the doorway, fumbling with the holster of his sidearm. With a shriek, the young woman leaped, twisting, at him feet-first and rammed him stiff-legged in his face with the heel of her shoe! His white helmet flew off; with a groan he went down, his head striking the edge of the desk with a loud noise and was still.

Marisol shot up, grabbed Larry's hand once more and tugged her stupefied companion past the first guard, who was groaning on the ground, to the iron gate.

The gate would not open!

She ran back to the guardhouse door and shoved a knob on the wall labeled, "Gate Control". The sentry stirred by the desk; blood was gushing from his nose all over the place. She dashed out to Larry, who was edging through the gate that was starting to open.

The girl pointed at the taxicab, still waiting in the parking place. "Over there!" The two jumped into the back seat, catching the dozing driver by surprise. Marisol shook his shoulder, rousing him. "To the airport! Hurry!"

The sweating fellow started the engine and threw the vehicle in gear. The smoky little taxi hopped off the curb and turned onto the main road, with the young man behind the wheel furiously working the pedals and the shift lever.

Larry's eyes were wide. "You killed them!" He gaped at her—it had all happened so fast.

"I *could* have . . ." she gasped over the noises of the rattling car's whining gears and worn-out, clacking engine, "but I only broke their noses. It stopped them!"

Looking back, the two saw a knot of men run into the street, pointing in their direction. Then, just as their chugging car lurched through an intersection, a *'Humvee',* its big wheels spinning, shot out of the gate and churned after them. Inside the taxi, the two passengers stared in horror as muzzles of automatic weapons poked out the chase car's windows in their direction!

"Go faster!" Marisol shouted to the driver.

But the fellow could not coax any more speed out of the wheezing taxicab.

Larry was frantic. "We're not going to make it! They're going to catch us!"

-6-

The lugging little car had managed to crawl only about a half-block farther along when the howling Humvee swept through the intersection behind it and began chewing away at the distance between it and its quarry. Flashing bursts of orange ringed the vehicle. Automatic weapons fire! Chunks of gouged pavement rattled against the struggling cab's backside; Larry stared horrified at sudden cracks tracing across the rear window!

At that moment, the slab-sided bulk of a moving van backed out of a driveway straight into the path of the onrushing U.S. Government vehicle. As Larry and Marisol stared wide-eyed, the military machine jumped the curb, clipped the rear corner of the truck—ripping-off its own front bumper that went tumbling down the sidewalk into a plate-glass storefront window! The zig-zagging, out-of-control-vehicle careened into a power pole, knocking it away, its trailing wires sparking, and with a screeching of metal, the Humvee skidded to a stop on its side! Gray smoke started billowing from under its skewed hood.

Larry, aghast, gaped at the now-receding wreck, where men were crawling up and out through the splintered holes where windows had been.

The taxicab's engine started coughing and sputtering. Larry and Marisol spun about and stared in consternation at the driver, who was trying the whinnying starter to no use, as the hapless sedan rolled to a stop in the middle of an intersection. We are out of petrol!" the sweating fellow called out over his shoulder.

"Come on!" Marisol shouted, jumping out with her travel bag. Larry grabbed his and bailed out the other door. Just then, a big sedan pulled up at a nearby traffic light. The girl bounded up, yanked open the door and hauled out the surprised driver. "Sorry, but we need your car!" she gasped to the well-dressed, middle-aged Nigerian, "you will get it back!" She made quick motions for Larry to get in. The Cubana flung her carry-all onto the rear seat and slid behind the wheel. At the same time the American with his luggage dropped onto the passenger front seat.

"Hey!" the indignant man shouted, banging on the window as Marisol put the car in gear. The expensive automobile, its tires spinning with unaccustomed vigor, roared away, trailing a cloud of blue rubber-smoke.

The American looked back at the man in the middle of the street. The fellow was jumping up and down, waving his arms wildly. Larry hung on to the armrest as the heavy sedan scruffed around a corner and picked up speed down a side street. A few blocks farther on, Marisol spun the wheel and ran the car up a ramp onto the main highway, past a sign pointing to the airport, thirty kilometers ahead.

The young woman glanced into the rear-view mirror. "We left them back there!" she shouted, pounding the steering wheel.

Larry turned about and slapped the girl a high-five.

Marisol gave the big car more gas; she watched as the speedometer edged up toward one-hundred kilometers an hour, then lifted her foot as the sedan merged into a line of slower traffic. Larry kept his eyes on the crowded lanes behind them; no one seemed to be following their commandeered getaway car. "You threw them off!" he shouted.

In a few minutes, the hulking airport terminal building loomed ahead. Marisol, frowning, looked back and forth. "Which way do we go?"

Larry pointed at an "Air Freight" sign with an arrow directing. The young woman twisted the wheel; the car shot past the airport buildings and pulled around to the rear.

"There it is!" Larry pointed at a sign over a glass door that announced the security office.

The vehicle screeched to a stop and the two hopped out. One more time Larry looked back. "The coast is clear!" he huffed, as he dashed toward the door.

Marisol motioned at Larry. "Hurry!"

The two ran, gasping, into the office, where Colonel Ajiboy, startled, dropped his feet from the front desk and stared openmouthed at the newcomers."What—?"

"Where are the pilots?" the girl shouted, looking about, "we must leave at once!" She tossed the car keys onto the counter.

"There is a black car out there—get rid of it! Put it in the parking lot! Anywhere but here!"

"We took it!" Larry put in, "they're after us!"

"Where is Nkrume—the other man who was with us?"

"The tall man? He is not here."

"Que?" Marisol, surprised, looked at Ajiboy then at Larry.

The American stared at the Nigerian. "You're sure he didn't come back?"

"I have not seen him since yesterday morning."

Marisol slammed her palm on the counter. "Then we will have to go without him! Find those pilots!"

* * *

Tverskaya District, Moscow, Early Evening The Same Day, December 31, 1991:

Terenty Suslov grasped the bag of wrapped gifts in one hand; balanced the bundle of long-stem flowers in the crook of his other arm; at the same time fumbling for the door handle to the apartment building's first-floor entrance.

His fellow Russian Special Forces officer and friend Gennady Lychin, who was doing his own balancing act of gifts and flowers, grunted as he stuck his knee out at the elusive door to help Terenty hold it open. In a moment, they were both inside, beyond the icy blasts of winter that had come down on Moscow on this last evening of the year nineteen-ninety-one.

Terenty launched up the lighted stairwell with Gennady on his heels. "I cannot wait any longer to see Tamara!" At the fourth level, the two stopped at the head of the stairs in front of the door to the flat where the Kuznetsovs lived. The young soldier adjusted his coat collar, re-situated the gifts and flowers in his arms and took a long, deep breath. "Here goes!" he said, knocking on the door.

In a moment, there came a clicking of quick footsteps from inside, then the metallic grating of the dead-bolt turning. The door opened and a slender young woman stepped forward. Her long auburn hair swished onto Terenty's shoulder as she threw her arms around the uniformed officer. Terenty felt the soft skin of her neck and her firm shoulders beneath her party dress; there was the aroma of perfume. His heart was racing; the girl was even more beautiful than he had remembered.

From behind Tamara, a young woman in her mid-'twenties with short black hair rushed up. "Gennady!"

Terenty's friend edged past the embracing pair and grabbed her in his muscular arms.

"Uncle Terenty!" came a child's voice from just outside the room. A light-haired little girl ran out through the archway in the apartment, threaded herself between the adults and grabbed Terenty's trouser leg, hopping up and down on her tiptoes.

The young man leaned down and picked her up, kissing the beaming youngster's cheek, not caring that his packages were sliding to the floor. "Ah, my little Larisa, I have missed you very much!" he said, tweaking her tiny nose and pulling on the pink ribbon in her blonde hair with a glance at her mother, whose glowing expression made the months of separation now seem to be fading away.

Vera Kuznetsova stepped into the little front parlor and grasped Gennady's arm, then Terenty's, for two-sided kisses. "It is so good to have you two here, again . . . we have all missed you so much!" Tamara's mother glanced at her grown daughter, who was staring into Terenty's face.

Tamara's father came into the room. "Welcome, comrades!" he said. The older man kissed the visitors' cheeks on both sides, in the Russian fashion.

"Let me help you with your coats," the older woman said, as the officers pulled off their long overcoats and billed gray hats with military insignia on their front crests. "Oh, you look so handsome!" she said, eying the young men in their dress uniforms.

"Yes, I know," Tamara put in, looking Terenty up and down with a slight flush. Galina held Gennady's hand with a dreamy look on her face. Little Larisa had not stopped grinning.

Terenty looked around at the small room, with its seasonal decorations. A lighted, meter-tall figurine stood on a pedestal in the corner with wrapped packages piled at its ceramic base. "Ah,

'Grandfather Frost' is here!" he said, scooping his own gifts off the floor and putting them with the others. Gennady did the same with his.

"Look over there," Terenty said, nudging the little girl toward a present on top of the others. The child tore off the wrapper.

"Clothes for your doll!" Tamara laughed along with the child, who ran out of the room and came back a minute later with the doll Terenty had given the girl right after he and the young mother had met when he rescued the little one from being run over by a streetcar. Their relationship had grown since then.

The young men had presents for the older people, who gave them gifts in return. After a while, the little girl yawned, and put her arms around Terenty's neck; sucking her thumb. The four young people glanced around at each other and at the gifts remaining under the "Grandfather Frost" figure.

"I will put Larisa to bed," the older woman spoke up, taking the nodding little girl from him.

Both of Tamara's parents left the room.

Tamara motioned for everyone to sit on the floor next to the statue's pedestal. "We have some things for *you*," she said, reaching for a package and handing it to Terenty. Tamara's cousin pulled a wrapped gift from beneath the icon. At the same time, Gennady lifted a ribboned box and placed it on Galina's lap.

"I want you to open yours, first," he said.

The girl lifted off a box cover, revealing a pair of fur-lined leather boots. "I had to ask around to find your size," Gennady grinned, as she pulled off her high-heeled party shoes. "They fit!" she said, wriggling her toes inside the new footwear. "What is this?" She had spotted a smaller wrapped package inside the bigger box, "another one?"

"Ah, wait until she opens hers," Terenty spoke up, motioning at the ribboned package on Tamara's lap.

The auburn-haired girl tore into the box. "Oh, Terenty, it is beautiful!" she said, holding up a red knitted sweater. "There is more?" She had also noticed a smaller box inside her larger one.

"Now, you can open them," Gennady said. Both girls' eyes went wide.

"Tickets to the 'Bolshoi' for tomorrow's matinee`of '*The Nutcracker*'!" Terenty said, as the auburn-haired girl stared at the little cards, open-mouthed, "all of us are going."

"Larisa will love it!"

"We had to try very hard to get them; the performance is very popular, as you know."

Terenty nodded. "Our Colonel Golubko knew someone at theater. He got them for us."

"By the way, how *is* he?" Galina spoke up, "the last time we saw him, he was very angry with us, remember?"

This was a reminder of the time when the two girls had innocently stepped into '*The Academy*', and were nearly shot as intruders. "We have been training with him," Terenty said.

"He is very tough on us." Gennady was staring at the floor, a serious look on his face. A pause came over the room.

"Ah, yes," Terenty said, "but he said we did well and this was our reward."

"Your training must have been difficult . . ." Galina reached for Gennady's hands; for the first time the young woman noticed how rough and calloused they had become.

"Our training was.*'intense'*," Gennady said, picking up her reaction; groping for some words to satisfy her curiosity without going into detail.

* * *

A fellow officer of their unit had sunk out of sight to his death in a swamp some weeks before while under the orders of a Special Forces instructor; the 'Spetsnaz' régimen was brutal in the extreme. On another training occasion, only a timely action by Colonel Golubko had saved Gennady's own life.

* * *

"Open your presents," Tamara said, "it is your turn, now." Terenty pulled a scarf from his package. "It is just what I needed," he said with a grin, "they do not supply us with these. And we are very cold, sometimes."

Gennady lifted the same type wind-breaker from his box and held it up. He turned and kissed Galina's cheek.

"We knitted them, ourselves," the dark-haired cousin put in, pulling Gennady's new scarf around his neck, touching a fingertip to the end of his nose with a flourish, "your last letter said how cold you were out there. It gave us the idea for the scarves."

"Oh!" Galina said, with a glance at her cousin, "we have something else for you." She motioned for the other girl to go with her through the archway. In a minute they came back with tiny velvet boxes. Both put the boxes into their companions' hands. Gennady and Terenty lifted the little lids.

"Crosses . . . ?"

Galina draped the miniature Orthodox icon around Gennady's neck. Seeing the uncomfortable look on his face, the girl spoke up in a hurry. "Now, with the Communists out, it is all right to wear this—it is a reminder that God is with you, always."

Tamara took the one out of the box in Terenty's hand and lowered it around his neck. "Wear this wherever you go. I will pray for your safety."

She stood up and poured a round of Kvas. "Let us celebrate the season!" The four young people lifted the drinks in a holiday toast.

Galina reached for Gennady's hand. "Come with me to my flat." She pulled him closer to her. "I decorated it for you . . . you must see it."

Tamara glanced at Terenty, who had a wry expression his face. "Go with her," he said, "you may learn something!"

The two took their leave; Terenty and Tamara were alone at last. She turned a switch; the room darkened except for a tiny light-bulb on the "Grandfather Frost" figure in the corner. "Now, we can talk . . . I want to hear about what you have been doing." She drew him down onto the sofa.

Terenty put his arm around her shoulder and the young people held a lingering kiss; her long, luxurious auburn hair, backlit by the figurine, flowed over their faces. "I have waited a long time for this . . . " He whispered into her ear, caressed her neck, her shoulders, her face.

Tamara touched his face."I feared you would never return. Larisa asked about you every day.

"We were very . . . *busy*." He pulled away and looked at the young woman's face; little strands of her hair caught the light. "You cannot imagine all that we have been through."

Tamara leaned over and kissed the back of his neck."It was bad?"

"It was *intense*. There were times I did not know if I would survive."

"Terenty!"

He leaned back and stared at the shadowy ceiling. "I cannot tell you much, but I will say this: we are training for a special mission . . . an important mission for the country."

"The country?" Tamara shook her head. "Gorbachev is gone. My mother says, 'be gone with him!' She disliked him very much—our country even has a new name and a new flag. What is going to happen?"

"I am sure we will be all right."

"Tell me more about what you have been doing."

"We went to the far north to the 'Karelian Peninsula'. It was very cold there." Terenty took a deep breath; something seemed to be on his mind. "They took us outside for survival training and long marches that sometimes lasted for days." He reached for her hand.

Tamara caught her breath; something was bothering him.

He paused for a moment, then went on. "One day, we went on a full-gear march near some geysers, where the ground was not frozen as hard as we were used to, one of our men—one of our best men . . . a good fellow named 'Misha Kerebets'—stepped onto soft ground and sank all at once out of sight. He completely disappeared—vanished!" Terenty leaned forward and put his face in his hands. "I can stll hear his—his 'gurgling . . .'"

"Oh, darling!" Tamara leaned over and caressed his back; kissed his neck.

He looked around at her. In the dim light she saw his eyes were reddened. He spoke in a croaking voice. "But that is not all!

Gennady was right behind him. He tripped into the mud and started sinking in it, too! Colonel Golubko ran up and grabbed his fingers just as he was going under! He pulled him out. He saved Gennady's life!"

Tamara put her hands to her face. "Oh, God! What are they *doing* to you?" She pulled him to herself in a tight embrace.

He went on in a low, deliberate voice. "We are a special military group . . . our training goes far beyond that of regular forces." He shook his head. "I am saying too much—there is much more I could tell you, but I cannot . . . regulations; rules—"

"I know."

Terenty came against her with a long, wet kiss; he tasted her salty tears. He could feel the mounds of the young mother's chest against his tunic. "It is warm in here," he said, pulling off the uniform coat and tossing it aside; rolling up his sleeves.

The girl gave a little laugh, pointing at him, her fingertips on her lips. "I think it is *you* who is warm, in here!" They came against each other in a new embrace. The girl flipped off her strappy party shoes and pointed her newly-painted toes at the floor. Terenty saw this and thought the motion reminded him of a ballet dancer. They would be going to the Bolshoi, tomorrow. She tucked her feet underneath herself and kissed his neck "I have missed you so much," she whispered, pulling him close.

"It has been so long—" Terenty fumbled with the back of her party dress; the tiny top clasp came loose; the zipper started down; his groping fingertips unhooked the back of her lingerie top.

Tamara felt herself loosen beneath the dress. "Not now . . . not here—" The girl gave a glance at the archway; beyond it the parents and the little one were sleeping. Her arms went around his neck. "They will hear us," she whispered. The zipper was past her waist; the back of the dress fell open, then dropped off her shoulders. He caressed her bare back, kissed her shoulders; her neck.

Just then, a light came on in the inner hallway. "Someone is in the bathroom!" the girl gasped, pulling back up the thin dress and reaching around to re-hook and re-zip in a hurry. Then, there was a click and the bathroom light went out. A rustling came from down the short corridor, then a door closed. "It is time for you to sleep"—the young woman gestured at the sofa—"out here, where you belong!" She turned through the archway. "I will be back." In a minute she returned with a bundle of bedclothes. "Make yourself comfortable, comrade, and I shall see you in the morning."

Tamara gave him a quick kiss and with the smile and the little wave she always gave him, the girl stepped beyond the archway into the darkness. Terenty heard the door to her room click shut.

He looked down at the lumpy pile of things she had brought. The young officer arranged the sheets and the blanket on the sofa, pulling everything tight at the corners, like they had taught him all the way back in the "Pioneers" of his Soviet youth. He turned out the light, and lay down. As Terenty squirmed about in the darkness, trying to get comfortable on the couch cushions, he detected the tiny aroma of Tamara's perfume still in the air. Terenty stretched out and thought about her warm, supple body; her breath on his neck, on his face; her soft, fluttery kisses; her smile that transformed a room. How he had missed her! And it seemed to be a miracle that he was here, now, after all that had taken place during these past grueling months of training. For he had not told her everything; not at all. She must never know how they had taught him to pursue and kill with a vicious cast that he would not have imagined of himself before now. Terenty pounded the pillow with his fist to fluff it, almost like a move the Spetsnaz instructors would have taught him to do to an opponent. He took a deep breath and lay back, thinking more about Tamara. He would have to be careful with her; a little while ago, in this very room, they had been very "close to the line"—a phrase he had heard the Americans use back in Washington where his parents had once been diplomats. For everyone's sake, he must restrain himself; the beautiful, wonderful girl had been through a lot of grief, he knew. The grim vision of her former husband— "Pavel Drubkin" had been his name, he remembered after a moment—lying dead in a pool of blood at the "Academy" with General Putridchenko glaring at his torn, bleeding form, flashed across his mind. It had been the morning after he and Tamara had first met. The fellow had followed Gennady and him back to the secret school, "The Academy", and had been shot dead by a guard.

Then Terenty recalled Colonel Golubko saying something recently about General Putridchenko having disappeared—an unaccountable development, as his commanding officer had put it.

As he lay there in the darkness, staring at the ceiling in the diffused light that forced its way through the window curtains, from all across Moscow, bells began pealing in the New Year. As the hollow, melancholy sounds went on—the first time they had rung-out since Communism fell exactly one week ago—he pondered the changes that had come about in the past few days, and what they portended for the future. Flashes of light, followed by the distant booms of fireworks started coming from the direction of the Kremlin. Closer by, he could hear shouting in the streets.

As the revelry went on, so did his thoughts. Terenty found himself wondering what it would be like to be married to Tamara—that is, if she *would* marry him. Even though he had thought about it many times while he had been away—mostly at night in the barracks, while he tried to rest and recover from the harsh régimen of training—the full import had only come to him this evening, even as she had opened the door to him. *For he loved Tamara Kuznetsova and little Larisa*—both of them; there was no denying it. But how could they ever adapt to the demands of his career? Colonel Golubko had admonished his charges again and again about the distractions females could cause to career military officers—particularly Spetsnaz officers.

Something slid across his chest onto his shoulder. Terenty felt for the little cross on the chain around his neck and fingered it. Another vision came to him; a remembrance from his childhood: his mother holding his hand as she walked him as a little boy to the shabby church in their town near the Urals.

After some time, the vague light from the street filtering through the curtained window became a blur and he fell asleep.

* * *

111

A short distance from Terenty, Tamara Kuznetsova lay awake; in the darkness of the little bedroom, the soft breathing sounds of her daughter in slumber next to her rose and fell.

She listened to the bells and the fireworks announcing the New Year. What would they bring? *Hope*, please, God? The past two years had been difficult, what with trying to balance the paltry clerical job with the needs of Larisa. There were times at the beginning, when the baby had demanded constant attention without Pavel being there to help her. For the thousandth time she wondered why she had been so foolish as to marry him in the first place. Lack of experience, of course—she had not realized at the time she could have told him *"nyet"*, and that would have been the end of it. Talking with other girls who had fended off insecure, immature young men like Pavel had been a revelation to her, except by then it was too late. From the beginning, he had struck her, in particular when he wanted to take her, which he did with force much of the time. He had had to "beat-her-up-to-get-it-up", as one of her friends had put it, confiding that her husband did it to her, as well. Before long, it had reached the point that anything she had felt for him at the start was squeezed-out until there was nothing left. Not long after their daughter was born, she had taken the necessary steps and filed for divorce. But then Pavel had started following her around; pestering her at unexpected times and places.

Now, her former husband was dead, a victim of the military—or so they said. All they had told her was that he was killed while riding in a taxi that collided with an Army vehicle. But was that not the *same* story they had told Galina when her former fiancé, Sergei, was killed? There were still many questions remaining to be answered about the two dead young men; questions that, to her, cast a pall over the military and everything connected with it. It had even had a subtle effect on her relationship with Terenty, although not as much as it had earlier, and she was trying very hard, for his sake—and for her's, and for Larisa's, as well—to give him and the government the benefit of the doubt. But as impressive as his uniform was, it still was a reminder that the military's mission was death and destruction and that Terenty and his friend, Gennady, were part of it.

Larisa whimpered and moved about underneath the blanket, then went on sleeping. Tamara ran her fingers through the little girl's fine, blonde hair with a sigh. True; she had married Pavel and together they had produced this wonderful daughter. And for valid reasons, she had also divorced him. Though it had saved her sanity and perhaps even her life, the experience had left her and the child with an emptiness that had lasted until Terenty came into their lives last summer when he had saved Larisa from being run-over by the streetcar.

The young woman lay back on the pillow and brushed her long hair out of her face. Through the window came the flashes of the distant fireworks that painted the room in fleeting oranges and reds, along with the faint sounds of the New Year's celebrations taking place across the vast city. Tamara stared at the stark rectangular shape of the bedroom door, etched by the intermittent bursts of light, and knew that, on the other side of it, down the short hall and through the archway, Terenty lay alone on the sofa in the parlor.

His presence here in the same apartment right now was both exhilarating and troubling to her: "exhilarating", because he was here at long-last, and she had missed him terribly during the months of separation—she could almost feel his presence next to her, right now—"troubling", because he had given no real indication that he wanted his future to include her and the little one. Terenty, after all, was a military man whose duties would keep him away for extended periods of time—a dreadful prospect for her and Larisa. And it was clear that the régimen was causing him much emotional distress; in particular what had happened to the other soldier and to Gennady in the swamp. Terenty had said they were preparing for a secret and dangerous mission. All at once, Tamara felt insecure for herself and for her daughter.

And what was she to think about how Terenty had come on to her a little while ago? His hand on her back had evoked tortured memories of her former husband's oafish groping; recollections of Pavel's fists; the boy's sneering, hateful words. At the same time, she wanted to believe that Terenty's masculine, yet gentle touch had meant he had a special love and concern for her—and for her daughter, as well, since they were inseparable. While Tamara lay there and thought more about what had happened tonight with Terenty—as brief and basic as their little interlude had been—she realized it was the first time she had ever experienced anything like that without Pavel's terrorizing tactics. Even though she had been surprised when Terenty started undoing her dress, she had felt safe in his hands; with a tingle, Tamara could still feel his caress on the bare skin of her back. As the New Year's faraway fireworks flashed and rumbled through the lacy window curtains, she felt an unexpected flush come over her with the reality she would have probably gone much further with him had the others not been close by.

Tamara remembered that Galina and Gennady had gone up to her cousin's apartment "to see the decorations", as they had put it; a flimsy excuse to get away, she thought with a drowsy grin, even as she fell into sleep next to her little daughter.

* * *

"You almost drowned in a swamp?" Galina held Gennady in a tight embrace; her hot tears dropped onto his shoulder. "Oh, God, what are they *doing* to you?"

"It is a part of our training. It is difficult—" His words stopped; her lips smothered his. She rolled him back onto the sofa; the fluffy cushions gave way as she lay herself onto him. The girl fumbled at the brass buttons of his tunic; one-by-one they came undone.

"I cannot bear that you would be in danger!" She kissed him; in the dim light he saw her moist eyes were red.

The young officer found the buttons of her thin party dress and slipped them out. His hand felt down her backside; the little hooks came loose; she felt her breasts come free. He ran his hands down her back, across her shoulders, on the nape of her neck. His palms and fingertips caressed her back. "I want to make love to you," he whispered.

Her reddened face moved back and forth on his shoulder, damp with her tears. "We cannot, Gennady. I made a vow; I promised God." Her arms tightened around him; her shoulders shook a little. "Sorry, comrade—not without a ring on my finger." The dark-haired schoolteacher raised up and looked at him; her blue eyes shimmering. "Gennady, listen to me! I want babies . . . I want children . . . I want a family . . . do you understand—?" Her tears dropped in a steady flow onto his shirt, leaving little dark, expanding spots where they fell. She wiped her eyes with the back of her hand.

The young military officer looked up into her shimmering dark-blue eyes, framed by wet mascara. "Galina . . . Galina. You cannot imagine how many times I thought about you on those long marches and while I was searching in the woods for food."

"Searching for *food?*" She blinked past her tears with a puzzled look; a choking laugh.

"They sent each of us alone into a forest for many days to find food and water from natural sources—from nature." A grin passed over his face "I found that some worms taste very good, raw!"

Galina was incredulous. *"You ate raw worms?"*

". . . and raw rats; and raw field mice; and raw lemmings; and raw mushrooms—I had to be careful about the mushrooms, though, some were poisonous—I ate boiled leaves; boiled tree bark; and raw—well, many other raw things. It was part of our training; it kept us alive."

She was gasping. "Why did you *do* all that?"

"We were training to—that is, we . . . will be going out of the country soon on a mission. We must be able to live off the land a thousand kilometers behind enem—behind lines." He shook his head; he was about to say too much! "All I can say is that what we do soon will be important for the country."

"The country?" There was sarcasm in her voice. "The 'country' is falling apart, have you not heard?"

"It is not as bad as all that. And our missions will go on, no matter who is in charge."

"'Missions'? You have more than *one* mission?"

"We will always have missions to perform for Russia. Galina, have you ever heard of 'Spetsnaz'? We are the best

Special Forces in the world. Everyone in the West fears us—even the Americans!"

"Oh, Gennady, this is too much!" The slender young woman dropped down and pressed herself gainst him; her pale, angular arms tightened around his shoulders. He felt her chest against his; her slim fingers at his back. She blinked through wet lashes; rubbed her eyes with her hand. He caressed her face, her neck.

The dark-haired cousin raised up and saw that Gennady was looking away, like he was thinking; as if he had decided something. The young man tapped the end of her reddened nose with his fingertip. "When I return from the—from the 'mission'—let us talk more about . . . what we talked about . . . just now—"

* * *

Noontime, Wednesday, January 1, 1992:

Galina glanced at her reflection in the full-length mirror, then to another dress on a hanger she was holding up in front of herself, then with a fast swap back to the first one. "The long one?"

Tamara looked her cousin over from her seat on a wooden chest at the foot of the bed. "I think the shorter dress looks better . . . it shows off your legs." A quick grin flashed across the auburn- haired girl's face. "It will perhaps also give him something to look forward to, some day."

Galina caught Tamara's grin. "I made him sleep on the sofa, last night. I told him, 'Nothing without a ring on my finger, comrade!' He is at least thinking! What about you and Terenty?"

Tamara looked down and shook her head. "We have not talked about . . . *that*. Just about what they have been doing and what they are going to do. And most of it seems to be a secret."

"Gennady told me they are going on a big mission, soon— somewhere out of the country. He did not say to where." Galina glanced at her watch as she pulled on stockings. "You had better get going; the 'Bolshoi' starts at two o'clock."

116

* * *

"You told her about the *swamp?*" Gennady rinsed the blade shaver and stowed it in his travel bag. He saw Terenty in the mirror behind him, nodding, "I told Galina, too. She was very upset." He pulled down a towel.

Terenty spread shaving cream on his face. "Tamara took it pretty hard, too." In the mirror he observed that his friend had a frown on his face. "You think we told them too much? Colonel Golubko said not to reveal anything to outsiders."

"How much *is* too much? The girls deserve to know *something* about what we do."

"Yes, but telling them about Kerebets would scare them."

"It scared Galina. She was all over me."

"Speaking of *that*—did you do any good, last night?"

Gennady knew what he meant "She is a—she will do everything but *that'* . . ."

Terenty rinsed the razor and dragged the blade across his chin. "You mean she is still *'Virgo Intactus'* after spending the whole night with you? Comrade, I shall report you to the 'Commissar' at once!"

"Oh, come on. I will not force myself on her. Besides, Galina is most conventional—she says she wants children."

"She wants a *husband*, first." Terenty glanced in the mirror at Gennady, who was buttoning his shirt. He rinsed his face and reached for a towel. "If you ask me, it sounds like she is setting you up for it."

"Tamara has that look, too, you know."

"Oh, I do not know. I am a military man. Military men do not get married . . . look at Colonel Golubko." He took a quick glance at Gennady. "I mean, would she want a soldier who was always going off to war?" He stuffed an arm into his shirt. "Ah, but she is beautiful, she is . . . and the little girl is fond of me, I know that . . . and I am fond of her, too. When we return—*if* we return—"for a moment Terenty thought about what he had just said—"I do not want Tamara and Larisa to get away from me."

Gennady was thinking. He remembered Galina's tears on his shoulder; her declarations for him; her slender arms clinging to him; her perfume; the feel of the soft skin of her back. He knew he could not live without the poignant, sentimental schoolteacher. She tugged on him wherever he went and with whatever he was doing.

"Did you tell her the mission will be to America?"

"Of course not. I am having a hard time believing it, myself."

"Perhaps we are both fools, talking like this. These women are . . . are—"

". . . are going to be late to the 'Bolshoi', if we do not hurry!"

Terenty opened the door and almost tripped over Larisa, who was standing in the narrow hallway in her new dress, holding her doll; sucking her thumb. The little girl lifted her hands for Terenty to scoop her up in his arms. "Mommy says we are going to the . . . to the—?"

". . . to 'The Nutcracker', sweetheart. You will like it."

* * *

Tanuta Refinery, at the Same Time:

Leonid Efimovich Retchko stared out the window at the refinery towers, idle today in the early-morning holiday sunshine. At least "New Year's" was a day to which he could relate—it was, after all, one of the biggest celebrations in Russia—unlike last week's mindless carrying-on about "Christmas", as these people had called it.

The bald man leaned his elbows on the desk and held his head in his hands; last night's staff party in the dining-room still buzzed in his brain; even though for a short while, the festive food and drink had numbed the recurring headaches. But the pains in his forehead were back this morning, worse than ever. The party would have been better, of course, if Betty Nkrume had been there, but she had gone to Lagos to go through the motions of looking for her missing husband, leaving him without her carnal company. For their discreet new relationship was the only diversion he had at this godforsaken place; remarkable, he

118

thought, since they had had such different past lives. And she seemed quite ready to keep it going.

He shook his head. Another matter loomed before him: before long, he would be going to Pyongyang to polish the arrangements for the North Koreans to supply military goods to the Organization; their coded messages were in his safe. On impulse, Retchko rose and wobbled unsteadily over to the strongbox—God, he felt dizzy, today!—and turned the combination. When he pulled out the papers, a green jeweled ring dropped out onto the floor with a little "clink". A *woman's* piece of jewelry! *What was it doing in there?* Whose was it? Frowning, he put it back into the safe. He would figure it out, later.

* * *

Moscow, Late Afternoon, the Same Day:

Terenty looked into Larisa's happy face. "Which part of 'The Nutcracker' did you like the most? Was it the princess? The prince? The dancing? All of it?" The little girl held her doll, wearing its own tiny fur-trimmed coat, close to herself and nodded. As they stood waiting at the Metro trolley stop, he turned and scanned for the bus across the broad, snow-covered cobblestone space in front of the Bolshoi Theater

Tamara rubbed her daughter's coat with a gloved hand and adjusted the little one's ear-muffs under the fur hat, then put her arm around Terenty. "You liked it all, did you not, honey?" she said, tweaking the child's reddened nose. The young mother gave a slight shiver as a cold movement of air came along just then; sparkles of ice crystals shook loose from the overhead trolleybus electric cable and hung in the street-lights like a prism for a few seconds, then swirled away. She pulled her muffler tighter around her neck, then reached up and did the same for Terenty's New Year's scarf.

Larisa's little voice spoke up. "Can we go again to the—the . . .?"

"The 'Nutcracker'? Perhaps sometime soon."

119

"I see the bus coming!" Gennady's voice broke through the crisp, late-afternoon air. "It is a block away . . . I still have time to freeze before it gets here!"

Galina, standing arm-in-arm with him, swatted his shoulder with a hand. "You are bad!" Then she, herself, gave a shiver. The cousin clasped her gloved hand to Gennady's as the sparking trolleybus screeched to a stop in front of them. The little group and some others waited in the overcast, late-afternoon Moscow air for a line of arriving passengers to drop off the bottom step into the slushy curbside snow, then they climbed up into the warm, spartan interior of the electric bus. With a moaning lurch, the coach headed down the boulevard. As they took their seats, Larisa turned about in Terenty's lap and pointed back at the receding buff-colored Bolshoi Theater building, its yellow columns and the horse statue on top of the front portico glistening in the streetlights."I liked it!" she said, grinning, holding her doll close to herself.

At the red-painted Arbatskaya Metro Station the group got off. Gennady pointed at the yellow, triangular-shaped "Praga Restaurant" across Arbat Square. "It is still early, let us get refreshments."

Terenty looked around as they took their seats in the saffron-hued dining-room trimmed in gold leaf, surmounted by glittering crystal chandeliers. "Remember the first time we were in here? It was the same night the tanks came to Red Square."

Galina shook her head. "I thought we were going to be arrested. Or killed." The young woman looked out the front window at the fresh snow on Arbat Square, where a few pedestrians strolled along, taking advantage of the remaining hours of the holiday. "Things have changed, since then. The Communists and Gorbachev and all the rest of them are now gone and in their place we now have—Yeltsin!"

Tamara frowned."My mother says she is not sure things have changed all that much. She did not like 'Comrade Mikhail Sergeyevich' . . . and she thinks 'Comrade Boris' is—well, she has some questions about him, too."

"But the country goes on, Gennady said. *And so do our duties.*"

There was a pause; Gennady's remark had reminded them that he and Terenty would be leaving tonight to rejoin their unit. Before long, they would be going on a dangerous mission that the girls only knew would be somewhere outside of Russia.

Larisa, not understanding their conversation, pointed at a picture of an ice-cream dish on the menu. "Cream—"

"Vanilla ice-cream for all of us," Terenty told the waitress who had stepped up just then,"and a pitcher of kvas."

"While they ate, Gennady glanced at his watch, then at Terenty. "Remember, we have to be back at the barracks by midnight."

Galina gave out a long sigh. "How long, this time? How many months before you return? *Will you return?"* Her voice had a desperate-sounding edge to it. Gennady thought she was being sarcastic. Tamara had stopped eating and was looking down. All at once her eyes were blinking.

Gennady reached for Galina's hand. "They have not told us, but if we are 'successf—if everything goes as planned," he changed his words—"I believe we will be back here in a few days. I will bring you a souvenir."

Terenty called for the bill. "We really have to be going, comrades. Tomorrow is going to be a big day for us."

At the Arbatskaya Station, the "Metro Line Four" to Tverskaya rumbled up. A half-hour later, they were getting off a short distance from the apartment building. No one had said much on the ride home. Larisa was dozing in her mother's arms.

"I will see Galina to her place," Gennady said, as they went up the stairs.

Terenty kissed Galina's cheeks in the traditional farewell. He noticed they were damp. "I shall see you again, soon," he said, squeezing her hand.

In the bedroom, Terenty looked down at the sleeping little one, her doll still tucked under her arm. "This is just like last time," he said, feeling an all-too-familiar sadness as he caressed the child's blonde hair. "I already miss her very much."

Tamara led Terenty to the darkened living room and pulled him down onto the sofa. "Terenty—" She leaned onto his shoulder. "I cannot take these separations." Her shoulders gave a sudden heave. "And it is so hard on Larisa. She will be so sad when she knows you are gone."

"I do not know what to say—it is my duty." A pause came between them; Tamara put her arms around his neck; he felt her tears. "Look, I am sure we can work this out . . . when I return from the mission to Am—from the *'mission'*—we will talk."

* * *

Upstairs, Galina held Gennady in a tight embrace. She had not turned on the lights; only dim, fitful rays from the outside filtered their way into the room. "I cannot stand this!" Her tears dropped onto his shoulder. The girl shook her head, suppressing a sob. "Why did I have to fall in love with a military man? I do not even *like* the military."

Gennady felt as if an electric bolt had shot through him. "You . . . love me?"

"I have always loved you—from the time we first met. I pray for you all the time." She nodded on his shoulder as if something had come to her mind. "I am sure God was listening to me . . . to my prayers for your safety when you fell into that swamp."

Over her shoulder, Gennady saw the outlines of her home altar with its icons and the candles on it. She felt for the cross on its chain around his neck and held it up; in the shadowy darkness it managed a tiny sparkle. "Promise me you will always carry the cross. It will remind you that 'The Savior' is with you, wherever you go . . . all you must do is ask 'Him' for 'His' protection. 'Ask and you shall receive'. I want you to remember that."

Such talk made Gennady uncomfortable, but he knew he would need all the assistance—from whatever source—he could get on the upcoming mission; the little cross would at least be a connection to her, since she had given it to him.

"I promise," he said. There was another pause. "I am going to miss you. I love you, too."

She wrapped her arms around him; caressing his neck, his face, his shoulders "Oh, Gennady, I—"

He pulled her to him for a long, deep kiss.

There was a knock. When Gennady opened the door, Terenty was standing there, grasping the two officers' kits. "Sorry, comrades . . . we must be leaving, now."

Tamara was with him. She located her cousin standing in the shadows behind Gennady, adjusting her dress. "We can go with them to the tram stop," she said.

In a few minutes, the two girls stood in the slushy snow and watched the rear of the streetcar as it groaned away down the cold boulevard into the night. Galina gave a whimpering sigh. "There they go," she said, reaching for her cousin's hand; leaning against her, "and to where, I do not know."

* * *

INTERNOL Headquarters, Geneva, Switzerland; the Next Morning:

OUR CONTACTS INFORM US THAT THE SUBJECT IS A FORMER GENERAL OF THE GRU DIVISION OF THE SOVIET GENERAL STAFF. HE IS NOW SEEKING TO ESTABLISH AN INTERNATIONAL ORGANIZATION TO SUPPLY ILLEGAL CHECHNYA REBELS AND OTHERS WITH MILITARY HARDWARE.

WE BELIEVE HE IS SOMEWHERE IN NIGERIA.

ANALYSIS INDICATES STRONG PROBABILITY THE SUBJECT PHOTOGRAPH YOU PROVIDED IS SAME INDIVIDUAL WE ARE SEEKING.

SUGGEST WE REMAIN IN COLLABORATION ON THIS MATTER TO COORDINATE OUR EFFORTS.

REGARDS, LIVSHITS,
INTERREPUBLICAN SECURITY SERVICE, RU

To Tarliani, the message from Moscow pretty much confirmed that his and the Russian Livshits's investigations were aimed the same man.

INTERNOL's own informants had also heard that the individual who had been seen at the International Airport at Lagos, the bald-headed man who was believed to be the mastermind behind the recent stepping-up of security at the airport to the level of a police state, had been a former Soviet general. But his name and other details about the man were not yet known.

* * *

Tanuta Refinery, Later That Same Day:

". . . *a warrant for your arrest?*" Lisa Anaya stopped what she was doing and stared at Larry while they worked in the hot tropical sunshine pulling electrical cables at the new satellite transmitter building. He was telling her about what had happened at the American Consulate General in Lagos.

"If Marisol had not gone after those guards like she did, I would probably be in jail, right now! As it was, we barely got away at the airport. I saw police cars pulling up as we were taking off in the plane!"

"But *why* are they looking for you? What did you do?"

"I don't know—and I can't get through to Joe Anglin. I was going to call his house, but thought they might trace the call, if I'm in trouble, or something."

"Does he not know where you are? He could call you."

"We had everything set up on the code machine. He doesn't know any phone numbers, here."

"Marisol has been a big help to you, has she not?" Larry detected an edge to Lisa's voice.

"She says she trained in Russia with their 'Special Forces'. She really went after those big guys, back there, I'll say! Whatever kind of training she had, it got us out of there."

He had not told her all the details of their escape; how she overpowered several United States Marine guards; coming within a hair's-breadth of killing one or two of them.

"But what am I going to do, now? I'm trapped, here."

She rubbed his forearm, in the gesture she liked to use. "Well, luv . . . I guess you are stuck with us, as they say."

It was beginning to look as if she was right. Then a fleeting remembrance of Marisol squirming under the sheets in the next bed at the hotel in Lagos ran across his mind. Things were becoming very complicated; very complicated, indeed. He sighed to himself. "Any news about Lester Nkrume? How is your sister taking his—disappearance?"

Lisa shrugged. "It is as if he had stepped off the face of the earth. She says no one has seen him since he got off the airplane with you and Marisol, the other day. She came back this morning, by the way. She says the police will notify her if anything turns up."

Larry tightened a cable connection. "I received a fax from the circuit board company in Lagos, this morning. They will have our etchings ready in a few more days. I told them we will send someone up there to get them." He straightened up. "I won't be able to go myself, of course. If the *'Feds'* are looking for me, I'd better stay here."

Lisa looked at Larry. "Maybe I could go," she said. "I would only be gone a day and I could take one of Ajiboy's men with me."

"That's a good idea."

She shook her head. "Larry, this whole setup looks strange, to me: chip implants in the workers; satellite tracking of people; and did you notice how *many* of the wrist chips he ordered? *Hundreds* of them! Larry, we do not have that many people, here! Where are the rest of them going? And look at the number of channels we are putting in—far more than we will ever use! On top of that, he wants us to build *more* satellite receivers to go somewhere! What is going on?"

Larry recalled Marisol telling him about a so-called "Cartel" she said she had uncovered that would supposedly be controlled from here. At the time, he thought she was exaggerating. But as he looked around at the scope of the installation he and Lisa were putting together, for the first time he had real questions about what they were doing. He was about to say something, then he remembered Marisol's admonition not to tell Lisa anything; at least not now, while the young detective continued her investigations.

Larry's stomach gave a hunger pang. He glanced at his watch. "It's time for lunch."

As the two passed Retchko's open office door, his accented voice came at them. "*Amerikanski!* Come in here!" Lisa waited in the corridor while Larry turned and stepped into the plain office. Once inside the stark little space, he saw that Betty Nkrume was standing beside the desk. The bald Ukrainian was holding a folded newspaper in his beefy hands. "My, my," the man said, handing the section across to Larry, "for being in such an obscure place—" he gestured at the window and the refinery outside—"you certainly are becoming famous!"

As Larry read an article from a British newspaper, his eyes went wide in shock and dismay:

SEARCH WIDENS FOR FUGITIVE ELECTRONICS EXECUTIVE

(San Francisco, USA*)***—The search for Lawrence J. Landay, wanted for transfer of sensitive and classified electronics hardware, has gone international. INTERNOL, the police organization based in Geneva, Switzerland, has launched its own investigation, a source at the crime-fighting group told news outlets yesterday. There was an unconfirmed report that the suspect had been spotted in Lagos, Nigeria.**

Larry looked up from the newspaper at the hefty, middle-aged white man sitting behind the desk and the slender, cream-colored young woman standing next to it. The room seemed to be moving around. *"What in the world . . . ?"*

"Betty—ah, 'Madame' Nkrume—saw the article yesterday while she was in Lagos."

126

"I thought you would be interested in seeing it, yourself," Lisa's sister said, in her broad British brogue, looking straight at him, her eyes narrowed, "so, I brought it with me."

"What is happening?" Lisa Anaya stepped through the door opening just then, giving a perfunctory nod when she saw her sister, then turned to Larry. "I thought we were going to lunch."

Retchko grunted. "'Comrade Amerikanski' is reading his life's story!"

His face drained, Larry dropped into an empty chair. "'The suspect's company'," he read aloud, "'Landay Marketing', of Mountain View, California, was seized in a raid by Federal agents. Landay's alleged accomplice—*'accomplice'?*"—Larry gasped, then read on, "... identified as 'Joseph Anglin', thirty-four, of nearby Santa Clara, was arraigned in Federal Court on charges of 'Conspiracy'; 'Conpiracy to Defraud the United States Government'; 'Violation of Technology Transfer Statutes'; 'Conspiracy to Sell Classified Goods to Prohibitied Countries', and 'Racketeering'. The same criminal charges were previously leveled at Lawrence Landay, who authorities believe has fled the country'."

Larry dropped the newspaper into his lap and looked about at the others in a daze. "Fled the country?" There was a pounding in his ears; all at once his mouth felt as if it was stuffed with cotton. "Good Lord! I had no idea about this!"

He got up and shuffled out, with an absent glance at Lisa. "I've lost my appetite for lunch."

* * *

"They were going to *arrest* Mister Landay in Lagos?" Frank Ogawan set down his fork and gaped at Marisol Montoya. "But *why*?"

"I do not know. But we barely got out of that consulate. We had to race ahead of them to the airport. It is a long story."

Just then, Lisa Anaya came in alone and took a seat across the room from them. Frank's eyes went wide for a second, then he returned to his food. Marisol finished her meal in silence.

At length, he dropped his napkin onto the table and stood up. "We are putting in a new computer program, this afternoon, so I will be going, now."

Stepping outside, Marisol headed toward the outer boundary near the pump-house, where she was supposed to inspect a new double-row fence like the one she had seen at the Lagos airport. When she had talked to Retchko about it, he had wanted to put one around the refinery right away.

"Saboteurs . . ." he had groused in his clumsy English, "we must guard in the most strenuous way against intruders."

At the pumping station, she turned to the left and made her way along the high, twin-row, chain-link barrier, topped by coiled razor-wire. Marisol took a blade of field-grass and touched it. There came a tiny spark and a faint snap: the fence was now electrified. The general had not wasted any time.

As she walked along through the grass, cut low where they would soon be laying land mines, she spotted a figure some distance ahead, standing alone by the fence in some shadows of the nearby refinery towers. When she came closer, she recognized the light-colored hair and slim form of Larry Landay. He seemed to be staring out at the other refinery across the fields, not noticing her approach.

"Señor Larry!" she shouted out, as she came closer. The American turned and saw her, fifty meters away, stepping through the grass along the fence toward him. "What are you doing out here?" she went on, breaking into a run.

When the young woman came up, he reached out and touched her hand. "Thinking, I guess."

Marisol wished he would have kissed her cheek in the Cuban fashion, but he had not. He was not Cuban, she reminded herself. "Thinking about what?"

He told her about the newspaper article.

Marisol put her hands to her cheeks. "Oh, Señor Larry!" She reached for his forearm.

He shrugged. "And all I did was fill Lisa's orders for all that equipment and bring it here and now they say I've committed all those crimes! I can't believe it!" His eyes narrowed. "You think that Lisa—?" He shook his head. "No . . . Lisa would not do that to me."

"Retchko is behind all this, I am sure of it!" Marisol's flashing hazel eyes looked into his. "He does not care what happens to you or anyone else as long as he gets what he wants!"

Larry started to say something, but Marisol spoke again. "The other day at the Lagos airport when I was with Colonel Ajiboy, smoke with a strange smell was coming out of a little building. I remember he acted surprised. And in the room I told you about where they beat-up people, there were some dried blood drops on the floor! After we landed, we did not see Lester Nkrume after he left us! They—"

". . . beat him up, killed him and cremated him!" Larry gasped; his eyes wide. "Great Scott! That would explain how he disappeared in such a short time! And if you don't think Ajiboy knew about it, then, who did?"

"*Retchko.* Somebody else killed Nkrume on his orders. I am telling you, we are all in danger, comrade."

"And I can't even leave this place—I'm a wanted man, remember?" He frowned. "How does Nkrume's wife—Lisa's sister, Betty—fit into all this? She spent the whole week in Lagos looking for him."

"I cannot not say," Marisol said. *But I am not comfortable playing word games with him; for now, I will continue my investigating. At the same time, I will have to be on guard, lest Retchko should suspect me. I know that for all of us, our lives are in a delicate balance.*

Larry, not aware of what she was thinking, went on. "Marisol, I haven't thanked you for 'saving' me the other day, back in Lagos. That was quite a performance, I must say."

"Well, señor . . . 'Spetsnaz' at your service."

He had heard Marisol talk about "Spetsnaz" once before, but knew little about whatever it was. "What is this 'Spetsnaz'?"

Her eyes narrowed. "Remember I told you I trained in the Soviet Union? Well, I was with the very best Special Forces on the planet, señor. Let me tell you—your *'Delta Forces'* and *'Navy Seals'* and *'Army Rangers'* and *'Marine Force Recon'* and the others—all are helpless against 'Spetsnaz!'"

"Oh, come on—"

"*Ask them, yourself.* Ask your military people about what they think about 'Spetsnaz'! If they would admit it, they would tell you that the very mention of the word makes them uneasy. Their reputation follows them all over the world." She was as much as glaring at Larry. "Remember those beautiful-looking United States Marines we saw back there in Lagos? Well, Señor Larry, those men are alive right now *only* because I let them live. I could have killed them in a fraction of a second, *each!* They would not have known what hit them. You see, the Russians are not bound by your stupid laws that tell your Special Forces not to do a lot of things."

Larry stared at her, dumfounded.

"You want more? How about this: your government made laws to keep your forces from assassinating foreign government leaders, okay? Spetsnaz's *'mission' is* 'assassination', along with demolition, and reconnaissance! If the Warsaw Treaty forces had been ordered to invade Europe, the first forces in would have been the Spetsnaz! They would have gone in behind your lines without your people knowing they were there and would have taken out *whole governments*, señor—killed them all in one stroke . . . probably while your important people were asleep! Your missiles would have been dead, your pilots would have been killed while asleep in their barracks; your generals dead in their homes! Warsaw Treaty Forces would have taken over all of Western Europe before NATO could have ever reacted. I trained with those people, señor. They are the best."

The American was shaking his head; all this was news to him.

Remember when Soviet forces invaded Afghanistan? The night before they went in, Spetsnaz troops killed most of the government while they slept! The next morning, Soviet troops landed and took over the country."

"But they didn't stay there."

"That was the fault of the politicians. Soviet Special Forces performed very well."

"How did you get involved with—with . . .?"

". . . 'Spetsnaz'? I was a Havana policewoman, remember? My police superiors selected me and some others to go to Russia, to the Special Forces Academy. There was another woman, by the way, who went. That is where we learned all those things. The training was *extreme*—and brutal." Marisol looked Larry in his face, "But those U.S. Marines were nothing. As I said, I could have killed those guards, no problem. That is how we got away, the other day."

"Man, you're something else!"

"Señor Larry, I am a *woman*. Have you not noticed?"

"It's what we Americans call a 'figure of speech'. Of course, you're a woman."

Larry looked her up and down with a little grin to himself; her expatriate Havana police outfit did indeed reveal certain essential elements of her design in startling detail. To him, her question ("have you not noticed?") was preposterous—with the girl's every breath, the points of her very feminine chest rose and fell in vivid clarity; the outlines of her trim figure were not lost in the white blouse and the short, tight, blue denim skirt that traced her hips and showed off the fine shape of her tanned legs; she even wore a red scarf tied around her neck to one side. Today, he thought, Marisol looked the part of a true Cuban revolutionary, and a right pretty one, at that. Larry had to remind himself she had already saved his life three times.

"What I mean is, you are a loyal *'friend'* who is looking out for me—protecting me, I guess you could say—in a lot of ways. Like with what happened back in Lagos."

"And while you are being so 'complimentary', let me remind you about the mean and evil General Retchko."

"You really think he's all that bad?"

"Señor Larry, I have found out some terrible things about him." She looked about; they were standing beside a secluded part of the outer fence at the edge of the refinery that shielded them from the office side of the complex. Marisol decided to tell Larry more things. "I am sure it is safe to talk; his listening microphones do not come out here."

"You mean it's *that* secret?"

She took a deep breath. "I am sure Retchko and Betty Nkrume are involved with each other."

"What!" His eyes went wide. "You think they conspired to do away with her husband? If that's true—" For the first time, Lisa's sister looked suspicious to him.

"Oh, Señor Larry, but that would be terrible! Poor Señor Nkrume! And what about Lisa?"

"I'm sure Lisa had nothing to do with it."

There was a pause. "You will not tell her?"

The American shook his head. "No, I won't say anything. Not now, anyway."

He looked out across the way at the distant silvery stacks and towers of the other refinery, glimmering in the sunshine; his head full of thoughts. For Marisol's question came to the heart of the dilemma with which he had recently been wrestling. *Of course I like Lisa, but my feelings for her fall short of the emotional intensity I believe is the essential ingredient for a permanent relationship. Yet, it seems that Lisa takes it for granted she and I are "together", which makes it uncomfortable for me at times and limits my options, which, of course, is probably what she has in mind. But on the other hand, a couple of times lately I think I have detected an interest from Marisol toward me. Going back to the night we spent together in the Lagos hotel bedroom—in separate beds—I have become more aware of her, too. But how could we ever bridge the differences between us?*

Marisol was oblivious to his thoughts. "Oh, Señor Larry, I feel so sorry for both of you." She reached for his hand.

Her touch felt as if it was charged with an electric current. He looked down at her tanned hand in his; it was perfectly manicured. "First of all, will you stop calling me 'Señor Larry'? You can cut out the formal stuff. This is not Cuba!"

"All right . . . 'Larry'." Marisol looked up in his face and gave a sudden laugh; it was the first time he had ever heard her laugh that did not involve escaping from the bad guys. This laugh had a happier sound he had not noticed before.

"Marisol, let me tell you some things." Her mouth opened a little; her hazel eyes blinked several times. "Lisa and I have known each other for a long time; we were in the same engineering school in California. One day, long after we had graduated and gone apart, she called me with the proposal for the satellite dishes and the chips—all this electronic stuff. Anyway, I came down here with it and we are setting it up. We are really just old friends."

"Come on . . . I know for sure you two are—" She was about to say "lovers", but held back.

He knew he would have to measure his words so as not to make it sound as if he was belittling Lisa, whom he liked and respected a lot. He swallowed and began, "Well, whatever our relationship has been, we're not getting married, or anything like that."

She looked into his eyes. "I remember the night we were in the hotel."

A quick grin flickered across his face. "So do I."

"I heard you on the other bed."

"I heard you on your bed, too." He paused a moment. "I thought about you a lot, that night. Every time you moved, I thought about you."

"You did? Then, why did you not say something to me?"

"Because I knew if I did, no telling what would have happened. I was not ready for—that."

The girl looked up at his face. "I am Cuban, remember?"

"That's what I mean—look how different we are. We hardly know each other."

"Larry, I graduated from the university—in Cuba. My field was psychology. You want me to 'psycho-analyze' you?"

Larry's sudden laugh was of surprise. "Marisol, you amaze me. You save my life three times, and now you are inside my head! What's next?"

"That is up to you, Lar—"

Just then, one of the nearby towers erupted in a shrieking blow-off that went on for some seconds. When it was over, Larry spoke. "We must be going back . . . the others will be suspicious."

"They will think we are in love, or something." A grin crossed her tanned face. "Cubans are always in love."

133

7-

Frank Ogawan heard footsteps. Crawling out from behind a panel where he had been hooking up a cable, he looked up at Lisa Anaya. "Ah, Miss Anaya, what—?" The young man, flustered by her sudden appearance, stood up and dusted-off his pants. "I mean, *'what'* can I *'do'* for you?"

"I want you to tell me about the new computer program."

Was she putting him on? Ever since that night he ran away from her advances, he had felt like she thought he was a fool—or worse. She had called him a coward, even. Her door slamming at his back was if she had taken away his manhood. Now she was here asking him questions about his *computer operation?* Maybe she was serious. Maybe it was another ploy to put him down. He rubbed his sweaty palms on his trousers.

"Well, ah, sure . . . where do we start?" He felt himself breaking out in a cold sweat. "Ah, it is a digital operating system that comes from the 'States—the 'United States', that is." His mouth felt dry. "It will do a lot of things."

"Tell me about them."

For the next half-hour the office manager described to her the features of the computer system. Here and there Lisa would ask a question that the young African answered.

When he had finished, she shook his hand—a gesture he found a bit unusual, given they were colleagues in the same office—and left. As she walked across the open space toward the main building, he watched her receding backside through the window. But just for a moment—he did not want her to turn about all at once and see him staring at her.

* * *

At her office cubicle, Lisa Anaya stared at her disorderly desk; perhaps she should straighten it up; cleaning the clutter would use up some of the nervous energy she felt right now. As she moved papers and other things around and out of sight, she kept thinking about her conversation with Frank. While she was there, some things had caught her attention. From observing his diplomas on the wall of his private office as they spoke, she had discovered something she had not previously known about him: he had a Master's Degree in Business Management from the famous Economics school in London, which meant their educations were on the same level, although in different disciplines. *Complimentary* disciplines, given the right circumstances, she decided. And they were both about the same age.

Lisa felt sudden guilt; slamming the door at his back and her words to him that time—sarcastic words—had been unkind and unnecessary; cruel, even, as she now realized. Ever since then, she had had the impression he was avoiding her. Understandable; she would overlook it. Frank was a decent, honorable young man, but his obvious lack of experience with women was holding him back. *Holding him back from her.* There had been plenty she could have taught him that night if she had not been so abrupt with him. Of course, she would have had to massage his male ego, which sometimes got in the way of a man with a woman (and the woman with the same man, as she remembered from some past relationships), but the results might have been worth it. What kind of student could he have been? Perhaps there could be other times to find out.

Lisa turned toward the filing cabinet and looked straight at the little home-made, wooden-box code machine sitting on top of it; the device with which she had placed the orders to Larry.

Larry. The reason she had tried to seduce the office manager in the first place had been because she was burned by her old friend and lover's too-familiar association with that Cuban girl. They had come in together that night after an altercation with a crocodile—so they said—and were touching and feeling each other in a way that had made her jealous. So when Frank had knocked on her door a little later, on impulse she had seen him as a substitute for the roving American. Only he had failed the test, and she had thrown him out—two rejections in one night had been too much for her. But it had been unfair to Frank that he had

had to bear the brunt of her frustrations, she now understood; somehow she would try to make it up to him.

And she felt terrible that Larry was now in a lot of trouble with the authorities back in America on her account. But it was Retchko's fault! All she had done was to go along with his plans; how in the world could she have known that the arrangement would run afoul of American laws? The possibility of such a thing happening had never occurred to her. God, what a mess! And what could she do to help straighten out things?

Lisa slumped in her office chair and stared at the desktop. Her eyes, swimming with the emotions of the moment, fell on a little manual Frank had given her about the new computer program. She picked it up and idly flipped through some of the pages. None of it made any real sense to her right now; she would have to go over it in detail, later. Then, inside the front cover, she came across where he had written in his own hand, "Frank Ogawan". She stared at the concise cursive, realizing he had signed it himself. All at once, through the letters of his name on the page, without knowing why, Lisa felt an uncommon sense of attraction to the young man. How could *that* be? He was so different from other men she had known; so earnest, so innocent; such a change from her worldly lifestyle that went back to her youth. Could such a combination of someone like her and someone like him ever work? Stranger things had happened, she knew.

And she was ready for a more settled existence. But all her recent thoughts about the possibility of life in the long-term with Larry Landay had come up inconclusive; for some reason, the idea just didn't click. Here they were: working alongside each other on the project every day and the routine had become just that: *routine*. She had come to understand with a great disappointment that their relationship was based pretty much on intellectual and physical attraction alone, and left off something else. That missing ingredient was emotion—that thing called 'love'. She wanted a loving husband, children, a standard, everyday family life. *That* was the kind of routine she could live with.

But not here. Not in this swampy, isolated place, cut-off from the rest of the world. And, as she had lately realized, not likely with Larry Landay, either. She liked and admired him very much, but he was not for the long-haul. Not for her, anyway.

Footsteps sounded in the corridor. She turned about and caught a glimpse of Larry and the young Cuban woman coming into the building together.

* * *

José Marti` International Airport, Havana, Cuba, Two Days Later:

Terenty Suslov stared out the window of the *'Ilyushin IL-62'* as it taxied toward the Havana terminal. As the *'Aeroflot'* jetliner turned onto the apron, he looked out in wonder at the palm trees of Cuba and the flowers growing alongside the taxiway; he had never before seen such tropical plants. But neither had he ever been this far south. A grounds-keeper on a tractor drove by on a side taxiway; he noticed the fellow was in short sleeves—it must be warm, here, he guessed. Compared to the ice and snow of Moscow they had left thirteen hours ago, this was indeed different. He wished Tamara and Larisa could be with him to see this, but there was business ahead. Serious business.

A few rows behind him, Gennady Lychin also watched the palms pass by. Since he had already seen tropical vegetation during a posting at Sochi, on the Black Sea, he already knew what to expect. For the thousandth time, he thought about Galina. Would she ever like to see this! He was already missing her very much. But he knew there was grim work to do and many thousands of kilometers to travel before he would again see her pretty face and feel her warm body.

The long, pencil-shaped airliner lurched and there was a thump from up forward. Then the four turbofan jet engines at the rear of the big airplane whined down to a stop. They had arrived in Havana.

At once, the nearly two-hundred passengers—mostly Russian diplomats, Intelligence along with military officers

137

traveling incognito, such as the Spetsnaz group—stood up, jamming the aisle, and started pulling down their things from the overhead.

Just past the arrival gate, the Special Forces men, wearing civilian clothes, who had been seated separately on the airplane so as not to compromise their secret status, saw a man standing off to one side, gazing about in a nonchalant manner. But on his lapel was a button with a large number *"6"* on it. This was a code to the men to go to baggage claim gate number six. Stepping along in the surging crowd of arriving passengers, the young Russians came to where the other passengers's bags and parcels were going around on the carousel. By prior arrangement, the men's luggage would go straight to their muster station on the other side of the airport, but they were to go through the regular motions in order to throw-off any inquisitive types, such as American agents. Terenty looked around and spotted another man dressed in the same type of suit as the first, standing to the side. On his lapel was a button with the number *"3",* on it, which meant the number of the bus they were to take. Out of the corner of his eye, Terenty spotted the others, including Gennady and Colonel Golubko, making the same connection and heading through the throng toward an automatic door with a sign over it announcing the direction to ground transportation.

Outside, looking down a line of smoking buses and taxis, Terenty located a bus with the number "3" on it, climbed aboard and took a seat. Several others who looked to be Russians were already seated; Terenty guessed they were security police. The rest of the group elbowed down the aisle and also sat down. Colonel Golubko, the last man to arrive, motioned for the driver to close the door and get moving. The fellow behind the wheel, whom Terenty observed was wearing a holstered pistol, put the vehicle in gear with a loud grinding noise. The bus groaned out into traffic.

In a few minutes, the machine lurched up to a very large, white-painted hangar building. Through the big front doors of the enormous structure, he saw some Russian-built airplanes in various stages of repair. Even from a distance, he could see that the mechanics were Russians. He had heard of this place, with its

Soviet, and now, Russian presence; it was about what he had expected.

Terenty joined the others in a line of men making their way in silence toward a door in the side of the hangar. None had spoken since they had gotten off the airplane; no one was to overhear their language and accents. A young-looking Cuban military officer directed the men down a hallway and into a classroom-like space. On a wall was a big portrait of Fidel Castro. The fellow motioned for the men to be seated at some school-type desks.

Colonel Golubko stepped into the room and nodded at the Cuban, who stepped outside and closed the door. "Well, comrades, here we are in Havana." He paused for a moment and went on, "This is our first stop on the mission to bring the agent out of the United States." He looked about at the Special Forces men with another nod. "Now, you may speak freely." A more relaxed air settled over the room. Gennady, sitting across the aisle from 'Terenty, turned about and gave his friend a thumbs-up.

The fit, older officer looked at the group. "Comrades, our training has been exacting and has focused on this mission . . . we are now ready to undertake the task before us." When he pulled down a map, Terenty was impressed that it was of northern New Mexico; preparations for their arrival had included having the specific map in this Cuban classroom. He glanced at Gennady; his friend was staring intently at the big chart.

"This is the plan we will follow," Colonel Golubko said. The officer drew down a second map alongside the first; a map of Texas and New Mexico. "We will fly from here to Monterrey, Mexico. From there, we will travel by vehicle to Nuevo Laredo. Getting across the border should be a simple matter—the Americans are very lax with security at this checkpoint." He gave a smirk. "In fact, the Americans are very lax with their security at *every* checkpoint! We will take advantage of that." He took a pointer and traced their itinerary. "From Laredo, we will travel to our Spetsnaz facility outside of the town of 'Cuba, New Mexico'."

"*'Cuba,'* you say?" One of the young men spoke up. "We are going to 'Cuba'? In America?" Some snickering went around the room.

The colonel nodded. "That is correct." His pointer aimed at the small-looking locality on the map. "This place is on a road that will allow us secure movements, should it become necessary."

He moved the pointer to an isolated-looking area. "Our agents found some hidden caves in what they call a 'National Forest'. They set up the training and supply facility. It is very secure. There, we will issue our gear and weapons." He moved the pointer. "This is where the Americans have their big atomic laboratory—right there, at 'Los Alamos'. They developed the atomic bomb, there, during the 'Great Patriotic War'; or 'World-War-Two', as they call it." The colonel paused and gave a significant wink. "Ah, but comrades, our K-G-B agents were there! Everything the Americans did they relayed to Russia—to Stalin. But the Americans did not know about it until it was too late for them. Our own atomic bomb came soon after." He smirked. "We have *always* had agents at Los Alamos!"

This information brought about a general shuffling in the room. Terenty was impressed.

"Our K-G-B agent—or 'Security Service', they now call it—our agent has been working there on their 'invisible technology' project we showed you once before."

Terenty thought about General Putridchenko and his demonstration with a vanishing car back at the Academy one time. Once more he wondered about the general's disappearance.

Colonel Golubko was going on. "Our academicians have not been able to perfect the light-cancelling technology to go with the sound-eliminating and radar-deflecting part that we already have. But the Americans have achieved the breakthrough . . . our agent has gathered the information in a secret form and we will lift him from the laboratory and return him to Russia."

One of the men raised his hand. "Colonel, how does the agent know we are coming after him?"

"He has the same communications equipment—supplied by the agents at the pre-positioning facility—that we have. He uses the burst transmitter. Our satellites pick up his information and relay it to Moscow. But the time has come for us to extract him. We have information his cover is about to be blown. That is why we are performing this mission at this time, and why you have been selected to do it, with your specialties."

Terenty remembered the colonel had told them when they joined the GRU that his own specialty in electronics and Gennady's in tactics and planning had figured in their selection for this mission. Others in the group had specialties that would also be important in the upcoming operation. Rodion Golubko would be the leader. The planning looked to be very thorough.

The colonel adjusted his eyeglasses and scanned his small audience. "Something else . . . from now until the conclusion of the operation, we will speak only English. Even though some of you speak Spanish, we will stay away from people in Mexico and use translators, as if we were tourists. We shall *never* talk in Russian; to do so would draw suspicion—security is of primary importance. We will have our final briefing at our destination."

The young men stared at the officer in silence.

"One more thing. The laboratory is very heavily guarded by the best defenders the Americans have—our skills will be put to a strenuous test. We must work together as we were trained in order for the agent to survive . . . and for *us* to survive."

* * *

Tanuta Refinery; Afternoon, the Next Day:

Larry looked at the little clear-plastic package in his hands; turning it over and around. "These implant chips sure came out small, didn't they?" He held it under a magnifying glass, squinting at the near-invisible circuits in a flat wafer-like chip not as big as a small coin.

"Small enough to put under our skins." Lisa Anaya held up one to the light. "This was a real job of miniaturization, I will tell you. Direct satellite links do not get any smaller than this."

"When will they put the implants into the peoples' wrists?"

"Retchko says the doctors will be here next week. By then, we must have the transmitters on-line and he wants the design of the hardware that will go to the other places ready by this weekend."

"Let's do high-speed bursts tonight to test the satellite system."

* * *

Washington, D.C.; Late Afternoon, the Same Day:

Jamey Suggs's telephone was ringing. "Yes? . . . Okay, I'll call Buzzy Habbler."

"Buzzy? Guess what! The're getting more signals from the satellite! Yeah, they want us to go there right away! They say they may have a fix on where it's coming from!

* * *

Tanuta Refinery, at that Moment:

Larry moved the switches that turned off the uplink transmitter and the receivers. "Everything is working like it's supposed to," he said, jotting an entry into the technical log."Who will get the implants?"

"Most of the people, here; that's what he tells me." Larry looked at Lisa, with a frown. "To tell you the truth . . . I'm not sure I *want* somebody knowing everywhere I am and what I'm doing! It sounds creepy, to me."

"I heard it is mostly for the plant workers." She gazed at the cases of the wrist implants on rows of shelves, each unit packaged in a stainless-steel container labeled, *'Sterile-Programmable'*. She shook her head. "Where are they all going? There are hundreds of them."

"That's somebody else's worry." Larry looked at the clock on the wall. "It's dinner-time, you want to join me?"

Lisa gave him a side-glance. "Ah, I am having dinner tonight wih Frank Ogawan."

* * *

The "Noches Hotel"; Havana, Cuba, the Next Morning:

Colonel Golubko surveyed the young men standing at the curb in front of the hotel holding their travel bags. Already Terenty felt sweat under his civilian clothes; he would never get used to this warm winter weather here in Havana. The leading oficer spoke up. "Listen for your name . . . "Malinovsky . . . Lychin . . . Suslov . . . Blagron . . . Grishinov . . . Zabresky . . . Chernenko . . . Navarin—" Each of the young men spoke up in turn; the last three had been added since the original training selection; their specialties in weapons and tactics would be important for this mission and brought the number of men in the group to nine; the standard size of a Spetsnaz squad. Terenty glanced at Chernenko, who had taken the place of Kerebets, the trainee who was lost in the accident. Although the rugged, red-haired replacement fit-in well with the group, every one of the original regulars missed the popular, capable young soldier who had perished in the Karelian swamp some months before.

"Here it comes!" Petr Blagron, another red-headed soldier, pointed at a long, black automobile that had just nosed around the corner up the way and was now gliding down the narrow side street in their direction. In a moment the limousine, with a red flag on each of its front fenders, squealed to a stop at the curb. A military driver got out and opened the trunk and all the doors. While the fellow stuffed their gear into the rear compartment, the men scrambled into seats. Terenty took one of the jump seats, just behind the division-window glass.

"We are going to the airport!" Colonel Golubko told the driver, who saluted and slid behind the steering wheel. The big vehicle pulled away down a wide boulevard lined with palm trees.

As they rode along, Terenty gazed about inside the enormous, impressive vehicle. He knew that the red flags up front meant it was the private limousine of a high-ranking Russian

143

general, probably one of the few ranking former Soviet military men left in Cuba after the recent changes back in the mother country had put such a strain on relations between Russian and Cuba.

Then his eyes fell on a bronze plaque under the center of the division glass. Terenty gave it a quick glance, then did a double-take. On it, in Russian, was the name, "Pavel Drubkin", whom the plate identified as the person who had installed the luxurious interior of the car, a "ZIL". Pavel Drubkin! That was the name of Tamara's former husband, the fellow who was shot and killed at the Academy that time by General Pudridchenko's guards! Then he remembered Tamara had once told him that he had worked at the ZIL factory in Moscow—what a coincidence that he had helped construct this very vehicle!

Terenty motioned to Gennady, then pointed at the little plaque. Leaning forward and reading it, Gennady's eyes went wide in recognition.

Large buildings came into view up ahead. The big conveyance lumbered across an intersection and made its way past security guards in military gear and through a gate. Crossing an open space, the ZIL drew up to a one-story building situated off by itself.

"Here we are, comrades," Colonel Golubko said, swapping his ever-present cigar from one side of his mouth to the other, "we will have breakfast and return to the main terminal." As the colonel got out, Terenty saw him give a sneer and flick his cigar in the direction of the long black car. Was it because their leader believed it was used by some high-ranking officer who was enjoying an easy life at this tropical posting far removed from the realities of Russia? The colonel had already registered his contempt for upper-level officers not pulling their weight—the lower ranks performed the real work, he had said, one of the reasons the men under him respected the demanding, yet fair-minded man.

* * *

"Pancake House"; Capitol Beltway, Silver Spring, Maryland:

"Well, it was a good try, I guess." Buzzy Habbler shook his head as he dug into a plate of bacon and eggs after a fruitless post-midnight session at the National Security Agency's Signal Intelligence Office.

Jamey Suggs poked at his omelet. "Jeez, by the time we got there, the signals were gone . . . and how could they have so mistook the direction? Even *we* could have told them nobody would be transmitting those kinds of signals from the 'Gulf of Alaska'!"

"It didn't take them long to find out that no ships or airplanes or submariness or anybody else were up there. And it was too bad the signal lasted only a few seconds. It was all over by the time we got there. Good thing they recorded it."

Jamey stopped and stared at the far wall. "You know what? Maybe we went about it wrong." The youth jabbed at his hash-browns. "When I get home, I want to get a world globe and look at something." His friend was frowning. "Look at it this way: what if the satellite had it right, but we got the directions wrong?"

"What do you mean?"

"If the signal came from the *opposite* direction from the Gulf of Alaska to where the satellite received it over Brazil—" He did some quick mental arithmetic—"that would mean it came from somewhere in Africa!"

* * *

Terenty Suslov heard and felt the "thumps" as the landing gear came up; their next stop would be Monterrey, Mexico. From there, according to the colonel's briefing, they would take a van to northern New Mexico in the United States to extract the agent. Why did they call it *'New Mexico'*? Then he recalled that several states in America had the word "New" in front of them. He loosened his seat belt; the Cuban breakfast he had eaten a little while ago had settled heavily on his stomach; the blintzes back in Russia were better, he decided.

And in their Havana hotel room they had encountered the biggest, scariest-looking insects he had ever seen.

A flight attendant came down the aisle taking drink orders; something about her caught Terenty's attention. Then he realized her hair was the same brownish-red color as Tamara's. Terenty took a deep breath and looked out the window at the gray-white clouds shooting past the climbing airliner. Much would happen before he would see her again—*if* he would see her again. For the task ahead was going to be difficult—and dangerous.

* * *

Sunan Airport, Pyongyang, North Korea; 6:55 AM Local Time:

The engines whined down; the 747 had arrived at Pyongyang. Retchko gazed out the window of the upper cabin at the trucks parked in front of the terminal; the North Koreans were already preparing to load the military goods and other hardware onto the airplane. A motorized stairstep truck, trailing blue exhaust smoke, drew up to the lower-left front door of the jet. The bald Ukrainian grabbed his briefcase and swung down the spiral staircase to the main cargo deck, puffing to the exit door just as it swung open. Standing by the bottom step, a Korean in a greenish military uniform looked up at him without expression. A black Mercedes limousine had pulled up nearby.

As the general, still unsteady after the long flight, bumped down the stairsteps, a middle-aged man hauled himself out of the car's back seat, straightened his starched tunic and ran his hand through bristly, graying hair. The fellow spotted the pale European on the stairs and gave a toothy grin. A serious-looking young woman wearing horn-rimmed glasses stepped up next to him.

The Korean put out his hand and spoke some words that she translated in a monotone into passable Russian."Welcome to the *'Democratic People's Republic of Korea',"* the girl relayed for him.

146

The Korean gestured at the open rear door of the limousine. "We will now go to the place of the meeting," the girl echoed the man's words, waiting for the guest to take his place in the plush rear seat, then dropping into a jump-seat behind the division glass. As the big car moved past the terminal building, the general stared at the line of flat-bed trucks loaded with machines and crates—the first installment he had brokered for the North Koreans to sell to the Iranians, the Chechen rebels, and to the bearded revolutionary; the young, rich Saudi, code-named "U".

The automobile moved onto a thoroughfare devoid of other vehicles except for an occasional military truck and a bus here and there, but jammed with what looked to be hundreds, if not thousands, of people on bicycles; all pedaling at a brisk pace toward some buildings in the distance—the city center, Retchko guessed. Most of the riders, he observed, held onto briefcases as they rode. Everywhere he looked, outsized posters with the portrait of the country's leader stared down from the sides of buildings and billboards, along with red-trimmed banners with slogans in the native language. Murals depicting heroic workers were on practically every building. As they drove along, the road became a wide, divided boulevard with scrubby trees on the esplanade and flanked on both sides by drab-looking concrete structures that looked to the Ukrainian like many he had seen in "Eastern Bloc" capitals.

As they drove on, Retchko noted that neither the Korean man nor the female translator had said anything since they had left the airport.

In a few minutes, the car pulled onto a circular drive in front of one of the nondescript buildings. When he got out, Retchko was struck by the almost absolute silence of his surroundings— the only sounds were those of a policewoman's whistle in a nearby intersection and a truck rumbling along a block away, with an occasional voice of a pedestrian. Even by his own standards, he thought he had never seen such a dreary-looking city—and a *capital* city, at that.

The man in the starched suit gestured toward a glassed front door and finally said something. "We shall go in there . . . they are waiting for us." The girl repeated his words in Russian.

Retchko assumed "they" were the committee with whom he had been communicating through a secret circuit about the arrangements for the goods.

At the door a military guard passed them through, then another woman, almost a carbon copy of the first one, Retchko thought, led them to a bank of elevators. Several stories up, the door opened into a paneled room dominated by a heavy-looking conference table where sat about a dozen men and one woman, all dressed in the ubiquitous Korean-style jackets. A man in a black Westernized civilian suit motioned to an empty seat. While the general was taking his place at the table, the man said some words at the bald Ukrainian in his incomprehensible language.

"Greetings from the 'Democratic Peoples Republic of Korea'. We trust your stay here will be enjoyable." As the man spoke in a sing-song dialect, the girl repeated in Russian what he said in a whiny, level voice. Retchko wished for several cups of strong coffee.

The general glanced around. On the opposite wall hung an oversized picture of the country's leader, who seemed to be staring straight at him with a baleful expression. Bunched in the middle of the table were bottles of mineral water along with vases of cut flowers that Retchko thought looked out of place in these plain surroundings.

The important-looking woman said something, then pushed some papers at the Organization's Chief of Security; the pages were printed in Russian. "These are the agreements," the translator said, as the woman kept speaking, "The 'Democratic People's Republic of Korea' will supply these items—"

She then read aloud the shipping manifest of the goods that matched, she said, what was sitting on the trucks at the airport, waiting to be loaded onto the 747.

". . . three-thousand separation centrifuges . . . one-hundred grenade launchers; twenty-thousand rocket-propelled grenades . . . ten '*Scud-D*' ballistic rocket bodies with guidance hardware . . . ten guidance systems . . . ten warhead re-entry vehicles . . . one ballistic missile erector-launcher—less transporter truck that will follow later—twenty-thousand anti-personnel land-mines . . . five-hundred packaged and shaped plastic explosive charges . . . forty burst-transmission radio units—"

The list went on for several pages that she read aloud as Retchko followed along, checking the items against his own inventory sheets.

"Payment has already been received in Zurich," the woman said, dropping her papers to the table. Retchko knew that "U" had transferred the funds, totaling tens of millions of U.S. dollars, into a numbered Swiss account controlled by a company operated by the Koreans as a cover. It reminded him of a similar arrangement they had once used when he was negotiating here for the Soviets.

In short order, Retchko and the North Koreans signed all the papers. The man in the suit stood up. "Come, let us have a meal," he announced, motioning toward a side door as the severe-looking girl translated. Even as she was still speaking, the door opened and a Korean man dressed in a butler's outfit gestured for them to step into a room where a long table with silver place settings awaited. From a side room, waiters came in bearing steaming tureens of Asian-looking foods.

A little later, while they were eating, the man in the civilian suit turned to Retchko. "Two years ago, there was a Soviet delegation that negotiated with us. I remember there was a man on the Soviet side who spoke just as you do . . . for a moment, you reminded me of him."

Retchko felt himself turning red. When he had negotiated a military pact for the Soviet Union with these same North Koreans, he had indeed been in this room. The expatriate Ukrainian offered a measured smile. "With so many Soviets, many of us were looking alike, I suppose—"

The disguise was working; they did not recognize him.

The woman spoke up. "Workers at the airport are loading your airplane, now."

The Cartel's Chief of Security stood and proposed a toast. "To every success," he said, as the girl translated. Everyone in the room stood and raised a glass of mineral water.

With handshakes and much bowing from the toothy North Koreans, the general, along with the man who had met him at the airport, and the ever-present girl translator took their leave.

Forty-five minutes later, the limousine drew up to the 747. Retchko, looking about, saw that the trucks were bare. "The airplane is loaded," the chief pilot said, stepping up as the general got out, "we will be leaving right away." He handed the manifests to Retchko.

Shaking the hand of the Korean man and the bespectacled girl translator, who managed a slight smile, the first expression from her round, impassive face she had exhibited since his arrival, Retchko and the pilot went up the stairsteps into the cabin. As he turned toward the spiral staircase, he looked back through the vast cargo fuselage that was now jammed to the overhead with crates and the massive bulk of the missile erector that filled the space amidships, all strapped-down to the deck He knew that, according to the manifest the pilot had given him, the bottom-deck cargo holds were also loaded with goods. From the serious expressions he had noted on the faces of the pilots, he guessed this would be a maximum-weight takeoff.

After a long takeoff roll, the airplane lifted from Pyongyang's runway and set a course toward the South China Sea. According to the pilot's plan, out of sight of land, they would turn toward the west to Islamabad, Pakistan, where "U" was waiting at the airport to take his goods into the Tora Bora mountains. Next, the Boeing would head for Teheran, to unload the three-thousand centrifuges, plus the missile erector and its ballistic rockets that would soon be going to the Chechen rebels. Then the airplane would make the long haul to Havana to pick up another load of infantry weapons. Retchko was pleased that the jet fuel arrangements with the Libyans were functioning perfectly; at every stop, right on schedule, trucks had driven up to replenish the 747's tanks.

* * *

International Bridge; Laredo, Texas:

The uniformed U.S. Border Patrol guard stepped up to the van waiting in line at the border crossing and looked the vehicle over.

"Destination?"

Colonel Golubko, sitting in the front seat opposite the driver, a Russian agent, leaned over. "Señor, we are headed to San Antonio . . . we will be in the *'fútbol'* tournament, there," he said in the Spanish accent he had learned in language school.

The officer, frowning, stuck his head in the window and looked at the occupants, all dressed in casual civilian clothes. "Where is your equipment? Your luggage?"

"It was all shipped in advance, señor. We always do it that way—'fútbol' rules. The colonel nodded at the officer with an indulgent grin.

"You don't look Mexican." The pale Russians sitting in the rear rows stared ahead, not moving.

"We are from *'Distrito Federal'*, señor. Our ancestors were the *'Conquistadores'*."

The border guard shook his head and waved the van past the checkpoint.

* * *

At the Law Office of Michael B. Parsley, Esq.; San Francisco, California:

"No, I won't do it." Joe Anglin was shaking his head.

"But it gets you a lighter sentence for pleading guilty to a reduced charge and turning 'State's Evidence'." The lumpy-looking attorney handed the legal papers across his piled desk at the younger man. "This 'plea-bargain' is your only chance to avoid a trial—and perhaps a conviction."

The accused man scanned the sheets. "But I *didn't* do all these things . . . I mean, all I did was pack up the stuff and get it ready to ship! Surely that's not 'conspiracy'and 'racketeering' and all—all . . . *that*." He looked at the papers and shook his head. "Come on! This is not real."

"You'd rather go to trial? You could get twenty years. This Federal Prosecutor is up for re-nomination by the President, you see. A conviction—*your* conviction—would look good for him at the White House." The lawyer walked around his desk.

Joe threw up his hands. "Look, if Larry was here, we could straighten all this out."

Michael B. Parsley, Esq. narrowed his eyes and got his face down close to Joe Anglin's. "Are you coming clean with me? Are you *sure* you don't know where this guy Landay is? It's important."

Larry's friend shook his head. "We packed the stuff to go to Acapulco on a ship. He went along with it. That's all I know." He fingered the pages and looked again at the plea offer. "Let me think about it."

* * *

Chakala Air Base, Islamabad, Pakistan; the Next Morning:

As soon as the big jet came to a full stop, Retchko looked out the window and spotted the trucks already driving up, their whining engines audible through the airplane's windows. A robed, turbaned individual, whom the general recognized right away as "U", dropped from the running board of the first machine and began issuing orders to about a dozen other similar-looking fellows who hustled toward the aircraft. At once, came the "thumps" of the doors opening down below. By the time the bald Ukrainian had reached the rear of the main cargo deck, the first crates of rocket-propelled grenades and other weapons were dropping to the ground on a yellow scissors elevator. The lower cargo doors were also swung-out.

"Hallo!" the fellow called out, and went on speaking at the hairless general who was framed in the main-deck cargo doorway.

Seeing Retchko frowning, a grounds-crewman cupped his hands and shouted up in Russian. "He says he will have the cargo unloaded in a short time!" The Ukrainian stepped onto the elevator platform and rode it to the ground.

On the pavement, the wealthy revolutionary came up and gave the general a bear-hug, nodding and speaking in his language. "He says he is glad to see you, again, and trusts you had a safe journey." the translator went on.

The Cartel's Chief of Security opened his briefcase. "These are the manifests," he said, handing the young man a folder. The interpreter relayed Retchko's words. The bearded, turbaned leader looked at the documents, then said something with a slight grin.

"He is glad they are in Arabic," the translator said. Retchko glanced at the fellow's copy that he noticed for the first time were printed-out in the squiggly-looking cursive of the other man's language. He was grateful the North Koreans had thought to do that—then it occurred to him that perhaps they had done that sort of thing before. The fellow flipped through several pages, then signed the top page, handing it back to Retchko and keeping the other sheets.

Just as the tanker drivers were disconnecting the fueling hoses from the bottoms of the wings, the elevator deposited the last crate of the shipment onto the ground, where it was scooped up by a forklift and raised onto a truck.

"U" came up and said something. "He wants the communications equipment as soon as possible," the translator said.

"Tell him it is being prepared now, and will soon be here."

The answer seemed to satisfy the young man, who put out his hand to Retchko and said something.

"He looks forward to seeing you again, soon," the translator relayed to Retchko. With that, "U" turned and hoisted himself into the cab of the leading truck. Other vehicles, including several vans and military-looking machines, swung into position in front of and at the rear of the procession that began moving away.

In a few more minutes, the big 747, now considerably lighter, alighted from the runway and set a course toward Teheran.

* * *

Tanuta Refinery ,that Same Day:

Larry Landay stood in the doorway, watching; the conference room had been turned into a surgical ward. At the rear wall, where a single table was set up, the company doctor was examining the left arm of a refinery employee. As Larry watched, the physician injected anesthetic into the man's forearm, just below the elbow. The worker grimaced and looked away as the medical man took a scalpel and made an incision in the man's upturned wrist. An assistant blotted blood, then the doctor took forceps and eased one of the wafer-like computer chips underneath the patient's skin. Within a couple of minutes, the physician had stitched the cut and applied a bandage. The fellow, holding his wrist, arose and walked unsteadily out the door.

The doctor looked at a chip, then at a list. "Number twenty-three?"

Another man the American recognized from the plant stepped forward and took the seat. Before long, he too walked out the door, holding a bandged left wrist.

Larry knew that on Retchko's orders every refinery worker was having a tiny transmitting and receiving unit placed under his skin. He and Lisa had programmed each chip with personal information about each worker and assigned it a number. The little wafer would identify the person.

There was a touch on his shoulder. "How many, so far?" Larry turned about to see Marisol standing next to him.

"About two dozen. At this rate, they'll be finished in a few hours." He looked around "Where's Retchko? Shouldn't he be here to see what's going on?"

"He is on a trip." Marisol made a slight motion to him to step away. Out of earshot of the others, she said in a low voice, "Meet me out by the fence in twenty minutes . . . we must talk."

The American sauntered back to the doorway and watched another implant go into a worker's wrist, then made his way outside. In a few minutes, he spotted Marisol at the outer fence

154

beyond the last refinery towers, near where they were the other day. "What's up?"

She looked up at him, her hands in her jeans pockets. "Larry, I have a question." The Cubana was frowning. "Did you say there are many more of the implant chips than there are people, here?"

"There are hundreds more."

"Just as I suspected." The compact female detective kept her gaze into his eyes. "Remember when I said I had gotten into Retchko's safe? At the time I did not think much about it, but I saw some notes about these implants. There was something about 'agents' and 'control' and a diagram that included a satellite and some aerials and something like a place very far away." Her eyes bored into his."Now I am sure of it—this is part of a spy network, or something like it! He is controlling many people from here. Larry, these implants are part of it!"

"How would these workers be spies?"

"I believe this is a test."

"You mean these men are like 'guinea pigs'—to see how the system works?" Larry looked away for a moment, then back at her. "You are right . . . there are only a few dozen company employees here at the refinery and back in Lagos, but there are hundreds of the implants! We designed and built two complete systems to program chips and register people entering and leaving a place. One of the units is at the refinery, here. We crated the other one." Larry stared up at the refinery towers. "That means it's going somewhere else—but to where? And where are the other chips going?"

Marisol was thinking. "Perhaps I can get back into the safe and find out."

"Be careful!" He gave a visible shudder. "It would be a disaster if Retchko knew you'd opened it." He looked down at her tanned face, framed by the thatched halo of bronze-colored hair that caught the noontime sun. All at once Larry felt a rush of admiration and concern for this young woman who was putting herself on the line to oppose the general. He glanced at his watch. "It's lunchtime."

As they came across the open space between the refinery and the offices, there came the distant sound of the rear screen door of the main building clattering shut; two people were headed away from them in the direction of the smaller computer building. They were Lisa Anaya and Frank Ogawan. The two were talking in animated fashion; their laughter came across the way. Larry took a quick look at Marisol; she gave him a side glance. The two watched as the receding pair, who seemed to have not noticed them, made their way across the parking lot.

* * *

Mehrabad International Airport, Teheran, Iran; Late That Afternoon:

Retchko, puffing, pulled himself up the stairsteps into the 747's forward cargo cabin; on the concrete below, an armed caravan, four trucks in the middle of it, was pulling away in the direction of the lowering sun. Soon, two of the trucks would arrive at the nuclear research laboratory some kilometers outside the city with their cargoes of three-thousand gas centrifuges. The other truck, with some of the guards going along with it, was headed north to a port on the Caspian Sea to be loaded onto a coastal steamer. From there, the "Scud" erector-launcher, along with the crated cargo of rocket-propelled grenade launchers and the grenades would travel to Chechnya to be picked up by the rebel warlord Retchko had met on the tossing ship.

In the upper cabin, as the general strapped his seat belt, he reflected that the Iranians had been very pleased with his prompt delivery of the instruments from North Korea and had promised him even more business for their expanding nuclear program. They had told him that if the "Outside" should catch on to their plans, they would insist the centrifuges were part of the research necessary to build nuclear electrical power generating plants—a plausible cover, they had said, to use while developing atomic weapons in secret for possible use in the fight against their enemies, the Zionists, and their lackeys, as they described them—Britain and America. For a war of civilizations was starting, one of their generals had told Retchko, and incredibly, the expected enemies did not yet know it. In time, they *would* know it. Along with the Cartel and other organizations, including the fast-growing new group headed by the wealthy and ambitious young man, code-named, "U", the targets were already being selected. And among the first, he said, would be a pair of iconic landmarks in New York City.

* * *

Tanuta Refinery, That Evening:

Someone was knocking on Larry Landay's dormitory door. He pulled it open and gaped in mild surprise. "Lisa!" The American pulled the door aside. Lisa Anaya stepped into the apartment.

"Larry . . . ah, Larry—" She wrung her hands. "Oh, Larry, something has happened!"

"You're pregnant!"

Lisa glared at him. "Is *that* all you can think about?"

He had to control an impulse to laugh. "All right, what is it? What's going on?"

"Ah . . . Frank Ogawan and I have been seeing each other." She stopped, as if waiting for him to react or to say something.

"Okay, go on." He thought he knew where this was going.

"That is, we have been talking, and we are going to be seeing each other, from now on."

"Well, I guess that's good for you."

"You can now . . . I mean, that is, you and the Cuban girl—"

Larry started to speak, but she came out with what she had to say in a hurry. (Almost as if she had rehearsed it, he thought.) "I mean, I have known ever since she came here that she liked you. I told you that once before, remember? And that night you said she got attacked by a crocodile.she was all over you on that sofa."

"She was hurt—"

"And I have seen you talking with her a lot, lately."

"Sounds like you're jealous!"

"Oh, come on! I guess I thought if you came here to Tanuta City—"

". . . but things changed." He finished her sentence.

Lisa took his hand. "Well, look, you are a great guy, but I am going in another direction, now."

The cream-colored girl leaned forward. "This is for old-times' sake." She lightly kissed his lips. Then Lisa dropped his hand turned about. "I will find my way out," she said.

In the split-second that Lisa stepped through the opened door and as she pulled it shut, he saw the beginning of her hand moving toward her eyes. Then she was gone.

Larry sat down on the sofa; his head felt like it was spinning. "Well, I say . . ."

Then the American realized he had used one of Lisa's British expressions. The image of Marisol Montoya formed in his mind. All of a sudden, things were completely different.

* * *

Cuba, New Mexico, that Night:

The headlights of the van shined on the welcoming sign proclaiming, "Cuba, New Mexico" to visitors and townspeople alike. The Russian Special Forces driver, looking the part of a local rancher, reached across the console and nudged the dozing Colonel Golubko. "Here we are, in Cuba, sir."

The senior officer pushed up his glasses and looked around as the vehicle slushed slowly through a dimly-lighted village; it looked like there had been a recent dusting of snow. "This is the place?"

"The camp is ten kilometers from here."

In the short time it took the passenger van to pass through the town, some of the others had also aroused and were gazing about at their surroundings, with its dimly-lighted streets and a gas station; open late. To Terenty, this hamlet looked like legions of nameless ones he had seen in his own country, except for all the private cars parked about—in Russia, all vehicles out at this time of the night would be either police cars (bribes accepted), or military trucks.

Not far outside of town the van took a right turn onto a narrow road that led into some woods. "This is part of the '*Santa*

Fe National Forest','" the driver said, as the way became more narrow and rutted.

Before long, the driver swung to the right and stopped. In the headlights, he got out and pushed aside a fence-gate, then climbed back inside. The van lurched through the opening. When he had tugged the swinging barrier back around and secured it, he swung up into the driver's seat and turned off the headlights leaving on the amber parking lights. As Terenty and the other passengers watched, fascinated, twin rows of reflector-type lights, attached to tree trunks, shined-up, one after the other, guiding their way up a narrow forested lane between ghostly trees and snow-laden saplings that slapped against the side of the vehicle.

After jouncing along several hundred meters in the dark woods, the driver steered the van up to the side of an overhanging cliff, lighted by some shaded, emergency-type red light-bulbs, and pushed a button on the dashboard. While the passengers gaped, a section of the escarpment swung aside, revealing a lighted space inside the hill. As soon as the van bounced forward into the rocky-rimmed cavern, the driver punched the button once more and the rock wall behind them rumbled slowly back into its original position.

Colonel Golubko opened his door. "This is the place," he told the others, "we shall now go to our quarters. In the morning, we will have our final briefings and draw our equipment."

* * *

Tanuta Refinery; the Next Morning:

Marisol Montoya locked the door to the Security Office. After peeping around the edge of the window curtains at the parking lot, it's dew-covered surface glistening orange in the sunrise, and cocking her ear for people sounds, of which there were none, the young woman knelt in front of the safe. Spinning the dial several times, there came the little "clicks." Then she moved the shiny handle, and with a groaning of hinges, the heavy steel door swung open.

As her eyes adjusted to the dim interior, she spotted a tiny, shining point of light at one side on the bottom shelf. When she picked up the pebbly source of it, her eyes went wide in shock and dismay. *It was her missing emerald ring!* "My ring!" she gasped. A wave of horror rolled over her as she realized General Retchko had doubtless been in the safe since she had last opened it and had found it! He must know the only way it could have gotten into the safe was if someone had been in there! Marisol's mind was swirling; her hands shook; her breath was coming in little gasps. "You must stay calm," she said to herself. There was no choice but to trust that Retchko had never noticed she used to wear it.

Steeling herself and pulling on gloves, Marisol lifted the bundle of papers from the safe and leafed through them. "Aha!" she said to herself; here it was: the pages about the satellite implant system. Commiting the important points to memory in a particular pattern she could remember later, the young woman put the stacks back into the safe in careful order as they were before and placed the little gemstone ring in the spot where it had been.

She had just closed the heavy door and was wiping the handles with her cotton gloves, when the first footsteps of the day scraped on the front porch. In a hurry, Marisol clicked off the office door lock, tossed the gloves into a drawer, scooted behind the desk and sat down.

Hardly was she situated than the door opened and Larry Landay stepped in.

"I am glad you are here," he said, glancing over his shoulder at the empty corridor and around the stark, un-decorated office. "I was hoping you'd be here—before the others arrived."

"I came in early, today. When the general is away, I have many things to do." Marisol frowned. "Are you all right?" *He looks nervous; not like the usual Larry.*

Larry closed the door behind him. "Well . . . something has happened."

She gaped at him. "'Something'?"

"Marisol, I need to talk to you about—we need to talk." Larry took a seat across from her; his forearms on the edge of the

160

big desk. He clasped his hands, rubbed his palms together, interlaced his fingers; cracked his knuckles.

Marisol blinked at him. First the emerald in the safe; now Larry was acting strangely—and the day had hardly started. "Talk about what?"

"It's something that's going to affect us—you and I, that is. Lisa came to see me, last night."

Marisol had a sinking feeling. *What had they done?*

"Lisa told me she and Frank Ogawan are getting together."

"'Getting together'? What do you mean?"

"I mean, they 'like' each other. They are serious about each other."

Marisol sucked-in her breath; her eyes went wide. "*Que?* But I thought—"

"Remember, I said Lisa and I were just friends? Well, it looks like she's found someone who is more to her than just a 'friend'—Frank Ogawan."

Marisol thought she detected a tone of regret in his voice; she understood that he and Lisa had been lovers. "*Frank Ogawan?* But I thought she did not—"

"... I guess things change."

"How does that affect us?" She was afraid of what he would say.

"Well, I don't know how to put it, but do you remember when we talked about staying in the hotel room together? About how I heard you on the bed but didn't say anything to you that night because of Lisa? Well, now there's no more Lisa."

Marisol swallowed and started to say something, but Larry went on in a hurry. "Well, the fact is that I think about you a lot."

"I saved your life three times, comrade. I guess that is good for something."

Larry gave an ironic laugh. "It's more than that; a lot more than that." He stopped, as if trying to find some more words. "The first time I saw you, I didn't like you at all . . . I think I told you that."

Marisol nodded, swallowing again.

In Cuba, I thought you were an arrogant bitch."

She managed a shrug. "I *was* an 'arrogant bitch'. I had to be to survive."

"You told me that, one time." Larry rubbed the back of his neck, trying to think of what to say next. "Well, I want you to know that I guess we have come a long way since then." He wrung his hands. "I'm saying I want to know you better . . . to do things with you—if it's all right with you."

There was a roaring in her ears; Marisol forgot she was supposed to breathe. Was this conversation really happening? "Larry, I—"

At that moment the door flew open. A security man stood there, panting. "Come quick! There is a dead man by the fence!"

* * *

Near Cuba, New Mexico, Several Hours Later; Early-Morning Local Time:

Terenty Suslov squirmed about, trying like the others to get comfortable in the student-type desk that was far too small for his husky frame. As he sat there, he looked about the little room that was hollowed-out of solid rock; it was hard for him to believe they were hundreds of meters below a mountain peak, hidden under the massive bulk of what the Americans called the "Rocky Mountains".

Gennady Lychin was having his own hard time getting used to the miniature desk that seemed to be more suited to pre-adolescents than fully-grown men, he thought. As those in the room became quiet for the colonel's arrival, he heard the soft whirring of blowers nearby that were responsible for bringing down to this subterranean space the crisp, pine-scented mountain air from the outside that had been such a comfort last night while he slept. Whatever were the deficiencies of the Americans—and there were many, he knew—their country had good air.

Colonel Golubko strode in just then and stood in front of the eight Spetsnaz men who came to attention. "I trust you all slept well!" He grinned as his troops once more took their seats. "Comrades, today is the big day—or should I say, *'tonight will be the big night'*—" The fit, older officer paused. "We are at the time and the place for which we have all been training."

162

The colonel reviewed the plan, diagrammed the upcoming operation on a chalkboard; answered questions; made assignments.

The van driver stepped through the doorway into the room. "Ah, yes, our comrade driver, 'Mister Alex Adams . . .'" The officer nodded at the man who had driven the passengers all the way from Monterrey to this underground outpost in northern New Mexico.

The middle-aged agent stepped before the soldiers assembled in the stone-surrounded space, into the garish light of bare overhead bulbs. He looked around and nodded, then began speaking in Russian.

"My given name is 'Alexei Konstantinovich Adamov' . . . I was assigned by the 'G-R-U' to develop this place near the American *'academician center'* at Los Alamos. I came here about five years ago and found this cave while searching through the forest."

The man switched to English and went on, "I told the people here I was looking for farm land. I used identification documents provided by the G-R-U and became a cattle rancher."

To Terenty, the Russian, who spoke with a flawless American accent, looked and sounded like a citizen of the United States; a local rancher. His cover was perfect.

"All the while I was raising cattle, I used helper-men on the ranch that the people around here thought were Mexicans—but they were actually our disguised agents. We built this training location here in the cave. It is so well hidden that the people of the town do not even know it is here."

One of the soldiers raised his hand, looking around. "Why is all this down here? For what purpose do you use it?"

"We use this as a staging-location for our agents and for secret operations against the Americans all over their country. When there is an explosion in a military factory, for example, or a big power blackout, our people are probably involved. All the time since the 'Great Patriotic War' of the nineteen-forties—that the Americans call 'World War Two'—*we have had agents at Los Alamos, getting information.* Only once, in the nineteen-forties, did they catch on to one of our men, who got the secrets of the original atomic bomb for Russia. He was a true hero of the Soviet Union. But there have been many others, including the man there now . . . the comrade we will bring out."

A soldier spoke up. "Why can he not just leave? Is he not a scientist? A civilian?"

"The Americans consider him very important to their cause. The man is in a section that is very guarded—some parts of the laboratory are *not* well guarded, by the way—it will be necessary to get past the guards to get to him." The Russian agent-rancher gestured at Blagron and Zabresky "You two soldiers will 'eliminate' the sentries." He looked around at the other young men. "The operation is set for exactly one hour past midnight."

"That is it, comrades," Colonel Golubko said, "now we will draw our equipment and rest until after dark. Then we will get started."

* * *

Tanuta Refinery, Early That Evening:

"Where did you *get* this?" Marisol Montoya gaped at the tall bottle as Larry Landay stood in the compact kitchen of her apartment, twisting the corker. "I have not seen rum since Havana!"

"'Seek and you shall find', as they say. I asked the guy at the commissary and he hauled it out. Got it at a good price, too." The American poured a pair of shot-glasses to the rims and handed one to the girl. "To success." The two clinked their little tumblers together and downed the amber liquid in quick swallows. He poured another glass.

She tasted the second round, then pulled him by his forearm onto the sofa beside her. "Are you trying to get me drunk? Next, you'll be trying to seduce me!"

"Not so fast! We're supposed to be talking about business, remember?"

The Cubana set her glass on the lampstand, kicked off her sandals, leaned forward, fluffed her fingers into her yellowish-red hair, and looked at him. "All right, but first let us talk about today. Seems it started with something about your . . . 'friend'— and her 'new' friend."

"Ah, well, Lisa is history as far as it was between us." The American upturned his glass, then refilled both. He upended the shot-glass, squinted at Marisol, who was blinking at him, and shook his head. "This stuff's getting to me, already. It's been a while since I've had anything like this." He rolled the glass back and forth in the palms of his hands. "What about that dead man they found, this morning?"

"The guards said the 'hombre' was trying to climb over the fence. As soon as he touched it, he was electrocuted. Dead on the spot. Probably he did not know it had electricity on it."

"Why was he trying to break-in? What's so interesting about a *refinery?*"

"I found something on him."

Marisol stepped toward the kitchen. As she strode away barefoot, Larry stared at her trim, tanned figure; the lithe little woman's tight shorts and halter top, backlit by the kitchen lights, were fueling his imagination. Was it because of the rum that she looked more appealing than ever—or now that Lisa was out of the picture, he no longer had to hold in check his thoughts?

In a minute she came back and handed a sheet of paper to him. "I kept this."

Larry pored over the paper that had creases in it, like it had been folded. One side was a hand-drawn diagram; on it were some lines, identified as "pipes". Other lines were shown as "wires". On the edge were wavy lines, evidently a water symbol—the ocean, he figured—with the word, "Inlet", and a rendition of a fence and a building. An arrow pointed to the building with another word, "Computer?" in the margin. The question mark was underlined.

He shrugged. "What does it all mean?"

"I do not know, but is it not interesting that the big hombre, Busa, was here almost as soon as we found the body?"

When the portly man had come puffing up that morning in his garish, flowing, flowery outfit, the American had recognized right away the very dark African he had seen several times. Larry recalled something the man had mentioned that morning. "He said he came from another refinery—was it the one next door?"

Marisol nodded. "Remember how he acted like there was something he did not want us to see?"

"You're right! Busa went through the dead fellow's pockets in a hurry, like he was trying to find something."

Marisol held up the paper. "*This* was what he was looking for, I am sure. But I already had it."

"Good girl!" Larry cocked his eye and again scanned the drawing. "Maybe the fellow was checking on something before he got zapped by the fence—like he wanted to confirm something or another. Why else would he be over here trying to climb the fence to get in?"

He traced the lines with his finger. "Perhaps this is a diagram of some sort of computer and the pipeline of *our* refinery. But why would that be?" He pointed at the wavy lines. "There's the other refinery's terminal where their tankers off-load their crude." He traced the line labeled "pipe" with others marked "wires" that led toward their own refinery, through the "fence" into the building labeled "computer" with the underlined question mark.

As Larry stared at the paper, all at once everything on the page seemed to leap out at him as a perfect three-dimensional picture. His jaw dropped. He gasped. "Of course! This refinery's stealing the other's oil—that's what this diagram is all about!" With his finger he again traced the lines. "Now I see it! Computers here are controlling a diversion of some sort! The guy from the other refinery came over here to try to confirm what he had figured out was going on and got killed by the electric fence!" Larry's eyes went wide; again he sucked-in his breath. "*Lisa!* Oh, my God . . . *she's the only one here who could have created such a setup!*" His head was swimming at what it implied. "Is she into some sort of—?" The answer was unthinkable; all of a sudden the piece of paper in his hand felt hot. "And how about the others? Frank Ogawan? Betty Nkrume?" He voiced the questions aloud. "*Retchko!* He's behind all this, I'm sure of it." Larry gave a perplexed shrug. "Are they *all* involved?"

For the first time, the American had reason to suspect there was a lot more going on here than he had ever recognized, and that some people he had trusted all along were perhaps in the middle of it!

"How about poor Lester Nkrume . . . he seemed honest—you think he found out what was going on and they got rid of him?"

Larry's face was still stinging. "The implants! The satellite links!" He shook his head. "Lisa and I designed and built it all and now some of it's going somewhere else—but to where?"

Marisol told him about what she had found in the safe that morning and what it seemed to suggest about the scope of the implant and tracking system.

Larry groaned. "And to think I'm involved in it, too!" He leaned forward, his head in his hands. "And they're looking for me all over the world . . . what a fix I'm in!"

Marisol poured the last of the rum into their two glasses. "Señor Larry, we must not worry ourselves with these things, right now." She lifted her glass to his. "Let us celebrate the moment."

Larry sighed. "Yeah . . . celebrate." He narrowed his eyes and held up the glass for some seconds, as if the rum could solve his problems, then upended it.

Marisol sipped some of her's, then set it on the lampstand. "I am sure everything will be all right." The Cubana touched his shoulder and looked into his face; Larry saw her hazel eyes catch the yellow lamplight. "Think 'Cuban', Señor Larry . . . with us Cubans, things are always all right."

He shrugged. "I wish I could believe that."

Marisol leaned him forward and began to massage between his shoulder blades. "In Cuba if we have *'problema'*, first, we try to feel good." She moved her hands down his back, then up to his neck, alternating her palms and fingertips in a circular motion. "Señor Larry, things are always better when we feel good."

He felt himself relaxing. "You're supposed to call me 'Larry' . . . remember?"

She stood and grasped his forearm. "Come with me— 'Larry'. We can do better in the other room." The Latina led the American into her tiny bedroom. "Stretch out on your stomach," she said, as he dropped onto the sheet. She tugged on his shirt. "Shoes and socks off . . . shirt off." It occurred to him that the bed was already pulled down. Did she plan this? Right now, he didn't care.

Marisol kneeled next to him and began pressing his back; he could feel her rhythmic hand-and-fingertip motions working between his shoulders toward his waist. As she moved back and forth, her bare knees came in contact with his shirtless torso; then away; then they rubbed him again, and again.

Larry was at the point of no return. He drew her down to him and they shared their first kiss, ever.

The girl reached around and pulled on the backstrings of her halter top. "I want you to stay the night with me . . ."

~~~~

PART TWO

ENCOUNTER

-8-

On Highway 126, Five Miles West of Los Alamos, New Mexico:

"Everyone synchronize your watch—the time is now twenty-three-fifty hours." Colonel Rodion Golubko spoke to the others from his front seat as the white van slushed its way through the night along the narrow, two-lane highway, its headlights casting ghostly shadows on trees and fences in the white, wintery world of high-altitude northern New Mexico.

Terenty Suslov set the controls on his special chronometer; its soft background light cast a glow as he pushed the buttons; the others were doing the same. He fingered the *'AK-74'* across his lap, knowing from countless checks and re-checks that it was in perfect condition. The other men were making their own last-minute inspections of their equipment. Considering the magnitude of the task ahead, Terenty thought the gear they had been issued was surprisingly spartan: in addition to the automatic weapon and spare magazines, each Spetsnaz soldier carried a folded shovel, sharpened around the edges to almost that of a razor blade, along with the sheathed bayonet knife that doubled as an anti-personnel weapon, intended for quick, silent assassinations. The men were all dressed in white, to blend-in with the snowy landscape, with white scarves and white face-paint. Chernenko, who carried the burst transmitter-receiver around his waist in addition to his other gear, was already picking-up signals from the embedded agent and would remain in communication with the driver, Alexei Adamov—"Alex Adams"—who would meet them at the pre-arranged pick-up spot after the extraction of the incognito Russian researcher.

"Turn here," the colonel said, pointing at the arrow where "Highway 4" bore off to the left. "This road takes us to the backside of the laboratory." The driver twisted the wheel and the van leaned onto the state highway.

Colonel Golubko turned about. "Chernenko—status?"

"He is sending burst-coordinates every ten seconds," the radio operator said.

"From now on, if we need to speak, we will speak only in Russian." The ranking officer turned back and scanned the roadway.

The vehicle sloshed past a closed gas station and rolled on at a steady pace through the rural night. Terenty looked out the window; overhead, in the black sky, dotted with the white pinpoints of countless stars; the ethereal glow of the "Milky Way", that he had seen only a few times in his life, cast its vague, ivory swath across the sky.

The driver turned off the headlights and pulled down a night-vision visor over his eyes. The others donned goggles, as well. There were no other vehicles along the way; so far the van had had the road to itself. As the van picked its way slowly along, Colonel Golubko, using an infared flashlight whose beam his goggles picked up, gazed at a single barbed wire strung atop some weathered wooden posts.

"Is this all the Americans have to keep people out of this place?" The question came from Malinovsky in the back of the van.

Adamov, the driver, spoke up. "I drove down this road the other day and thought the same thing. There is a guard-post around the next bend."

The colonel looked back at two of the soldiers. "Blagron and Zabresky . . . get ready—your job is to eliminate the guards." Terenty heard the young men fingering the safeties of their Kalashnikovs.

Rodion Golubko shined his infared flashlight at a sign and uttered an expression of ironic mirth. "'No Trespassing!'" it says. Well, comrades, we shall not 'trespass'—we will only 'enter without permission'!"

Ahead, darkened buildings loomed over some scrub trees. "'Technical Area Thirty-Three'," he said, comparing the structures to a map he was scanning in his lap with his flashlight. He shined the infared beam onto the upper side of the metal building. The numbers, "33-234" came up in the light.

The officer frowned at his chart, then back at the hulking edifice. "That is the building, all right."

"The agent is at the side of it," Chernenko spoke up, pressing the radio earphone to his ear, "by a metal out-building away from the main one."

* * *

An American Intelligence satellite, passing in orbit overhead just then, picked up the burst transmissions and relayed them to Cheyenne Mountain at Colorado Springs. Deep underground, on the monitor of a duty officer, a flashing dot of light zeroed-in on a map of the laboratory, pin-pointing the source of the signal. At the same time, a tone signal sounded in his earphones. The Intelligence officer punched a button on his console and spoke into his headset microphone.

* * *

"Blagron . . . Zabresky—deploy!" The van stopped and the two Spetsnaz troops hopped out. In a fraction, they disappeared into some brush alongside the road. Zabresky pulled out a meter-long wire with clips on each end and clamped them onto the fence. Using a special cutter, he snipped the barbed wire and laid it onto the ground. The clamped wire would bridge any electrical circuit that might be on the fence as part of a warning system.

The pair stepped across the opening and made their way forward in the sagebrush, past some scrubby trees. Topping a low rise, the two picked-out a small building about fifty meters ahead. A light shined through a single window on the side—it was the sentry shack. In the greenish view of the night-vision goggles, the soldiers saw movement; a guard outside was walking around. A spot of light glowed in front of his face for a moment, then moved away; the man was smoking a cigarette.

Blagron motioned to Zabresky, who made his way, crouching, around the backside of the tiny guardhouse and came up on the other side. At the same time, Blagron, hunched-down, moved forward, his bayonet in his hand. Without making a sound, he stepped up behind the smoking sentry and whipped the blade across the front of the fellow's neck, nearly decapitating him, then stabbed him three quick times in the chest, just below the ribcage. He dragged the man to the rear of the little building.

The other guard, hearing some sounds, came outside and looked about. "Charlie?" he called out.

For a split-second, he was aware of the crunch of snow behind him. Before he could turn, a razor-sharp blade slashed his neck to his spine, then three knife jabs ripped into his chest.

Zabresky dragged the lifeless American to the rear, next to the body of the other man. The two Russians then pulled the dead guards twenty meters behind the shack into a clump of trees. There, using their special shovels, they covered the corpses with snow, shoveling-under any flecks of blood and smoothed the path along where they had dragged their quarry. For the time being, no one would be able to tell the bodies were there; the snow was as pristine as before:

Blagron motioned to the other Russian. The two turned about and, re-tracing their steps, loped down the side of the low hill. Behind them, inside the guardhouse, the telephone was ringing.

While this was happening, the van had turned around and was now parked alongside the road a hundred meters back in the direction from which it had come. Where the fence ended, next to the "No Trespassing" sign, the others, including Colonel Golubko, dropped from the vehicle and made their way through the snow, past a cluster of low trees, toward a looming, boxy shape up ahead. From their briefings, the men knew it was an outbuilding of "Technical Area Thirty-Three", where they were to meet the agent.

The colonel motioned to the soldiers to deploy around the buildings. Gennady led four other troops to the left; Terenty moved with the colonel along with others around to the other side of the structure. As they crouched along in the starlight, Gennady noticed there were no lights in the buildings and so far, they had not seen any guards. He knew such lax security in Russia would be unthinkable; there, an important installation such as this would be surrounded by layers of armed sentries and anti-personnel devices. What was the matter with these Americans? Had they never heard of intruders or saboteurs?

There was movement next to one of the outbuildings. In his green-hued goggles, Terenty saw the outline of a man stepping toward them. Colonel Golubko held up his hand said a word to the newcomer; both nodded. The officer gestured for the others to surround the fellow, who was holding a satchel. Terenty saw a bulge in the man's overcoat that he knew was the burst transmitter.

The group made their way in silence back toward the farthest outbuilding, where Gennady and the others, who had gone the other way around the small building, were waiting for them.

Gesturing, the seven troops, plus the researcher, stepped toward the road, beyond the fence, where the van was supposed to be waiting for them.

Just as they reached the downed barbed fence, all at once, there came the flickering glow of headlights and the rising whine of vehicles from the direction of where they had dropped-off Blagron and Zabresky!

"Get back!" Colonel Golubko called out in a hoarse whisper. Gennady grabbed the shoulder of the scientist, who seemed unsure of what to do, and shoved him to his knees. As the men back-tracked on their hands and knees, the approaching lights topped the rise and materialized into a line of military vehicles! The headlights sprayed their revealing beams squarely onto the van, which was parked fifty meters down the road from where the Russians were crouching in the snow-laden underbrush.

Terenty recognized the trio of machines as American "Humvees" of the latest type that had been so prominent in the recent "Gulf War".

The combat cars slushed to a stop behind the van. Bright lights on the front of the vehicles came on, turning the scene as bright as day. In his goggles, Terenty could make-out the snowy fields on each side of the road for some distance. An armed man dropped from the right front and rushed up to the driver's door. "Get out! Get out!" the Russians heard the man shout. The soldier yanked open the door and waved inside the weapon to-and-fro, looking to the van's rear interior. "Empty!" he yelled, as Americans jerked open the other doors.

The fellow motioned for some of his men to take up perimeter defense; casting about with his own goggles, he led the others in the direction away from the hidden foreigners.

Just then another soldier, who was standing in the open seat of the topless second vehicle and was wearing night goggles, let out a yell. "I see movement! Over there!"

Wide-eyed, Terenty and the others followed the man's motioning arm and saw that he was pointing in the direction behind and above the crouching Russians.

"Get them!" The officer in the opposite field scrambled in the snow back toward the road. More Americans jumped from the Humvees and dashed across the road into the ghostly, snow-covered field.

Alarmed, Terenty realized they must have seen Blagron and Zabresky returning from taking care of the sentries! The ten Americans, all dressed in combat fatigues, ran with their automatic weapons at the ready across the pavement a few dozen meters from the hiding Russians.

Colonel Golubko made some quick, decisive motions that the troops understood. "Deploy shovels!" Leaving the stupefied scientist in a low ditch, the Russians, their razor-sharp utility spades in their hands, deployed in a semi-circle in the darkness behind the Americans, who had not noticed their presence.

The first pair of American soldiers were a few meters from them when Blagron and Zabresky, in a slight depression, realized troops were approaching. Acting on the instincts of their training, the two whipped their shovels from their belts, flipped them down into position, and as their adversaries came over the little rise, the two Spetsnaz troops lunged up at them with quick slicing motions of their razor-honed shovels, catching the two Americans straight across their throats! The pair went down, jerking; foaming dark liquid spraying the snow.

Blagron motioned for Zabresky to follow him to the right, toward the road. In his infared glasses, he spotted the outline of the other oncoming Americans, back-lit by the lights of the Humvees.. Then they saw their own Spetsnaz troops following them, advancing row-by-row across the undulating field. It did not seem they had been discovered. From countless exercises of this sort, Blagron and Zabresky dropped down into another low place and began making their way back toward the van, still parked in the garish glare of the Humvees' lights.

In a minute, the Americans advancing across the field came upon the corpses of the two soldiers. "Oh, shit!" came a Yankee voice across the snowy landscape. The Americans stood about the dead men in the snow, their backs to the road; oaths filling the air.

The squad of Spetsnaz soldiers in line abreast lunged over a low rise just behind the unsuspecting Americans, and without making a sound, swung their shovels into the backs of their necks between their shoulder blades. One American, dodging his assailant, fingered his rifle in the split-second before a Russian, whom Terenty recognized as Gennady Lychin, lunged his shovel into the throat of the fellow, who went down, gurgling, beside the others.

All the American soldiers lay dead in the crimson-soaked snow.

Colonel Golubko shoved his goggles up onto his forehead and gazed at the bloody bodies. "They were stupid," he breathed hard, shaking his head, "they forgot to cover their rear perimeter."

Blagron and Zabresky came up, holding their shovels that were stained red. "The sentries are taken care of," Blagron told the colonel, taking in the scene, "and we killed two more."

"Come on!" the officer said in a hoarse whisper, motioning, "get that agent and let us get out of here! Blagron! Zabresky! Go secure the van!"

The two turned and made their way straight toward the vehicle that was down and across the road. When they were some distance from the vehicle, still shining in the spotlights and headlights of the Humvee, Zabresky grabbed the other soldier's arm with a "get down" motion. He held up his finger and pointed, the signal that he had spotted movement near the van. *Their driver, Adams?* Then an American soldier, looking to and fro, stepped out from behind the boxy rear.

Blagron looked about and found a good-sized rock. He threw it over the van, where it landed in the snowy field beyond it with a soft *'plop'.'*

"Jerry, is that you?" came a voice. The two Russians watched the fellow step off the road's shoulder into a darker place some distance beyond, below the level of the pavement. "Hey, Jerry? Are you taking a leak?"

Blagron gave a "come on" motion, and in the darkness behind the last vehicle, the two trotted across the road and crouched behind the rear-most Humvee.

It was then that a second American came up the slope from the front direction and climbed into the right front seat of the van, shining a flashlight around the interior.

Zabresky hunched-down and tiptoed down the line of military vehicles. At the same time Blagron took the opposite side and came back around the front of the boxy vehicle and hunkered down below the view from the front seat.

Zabresky poked the van's rear door with his shovel handle, creating a loud *"BOOM!"*.

"What . . . ?" came a surprised voice. The springs lifted as the fellow alighted and scrunched in the snow toward the rear of the van. At the same time, Zabresky tiptoed down the left side of the van toward the front. When the American came to the rear corner, Blagron came up from behind and grabbed the fellow around his neck, slicing open his throat with a quick slash of his bayonet, then plunging the blade into the man's back. The soldier went limp in Blagron's arms and dropped to the snow. The Spetsnaz trooper dragged the fellow around behind the first Humvee, out of sight.

"Tommy?" came a voice from down the way. The other American was coming back! Zabresky cocked his ear to determine where the fellow was headed, which happened to be toward the same right front seat as the other man had occupied.

As the unsuspecting soldier stepped up to the van and reached for the handle, the Russian lunged around the front corner and plunged his knife straight into the fellow's throat, catching him by surprise.

Clutching his neck, gurgling, the man dropped to his knees, then fell flat onto the snowy gravel without making a further sound, thrashed a moment, and was still.

While this was happening, Colonel Golubko and the other Russians had been trotting across the field toward the road. They came upon the researcher, still hunkered-down in the depression. The officer tapped his shoulder, motioning for a soldier to carry his satchel. "Let us leave, now!" The men trotted toward the vehicles, a short distance down the road.

When they got there, "Alex Adams" was coming up from the low ravine. "I had to kill one down the way!" he said, gripping the handle of his shovel that was stained red around the blade-edges.

Rodion Golubko made terse, incisive gestures at the van. "Get in! We must leave here at once!"

As the others climbed into the passenger vehicle, including the scientist, who looked to Terenty to be very nervous, the colonel ran back to the three Humvees and smashed all their headlights, taillights, and spotlights with furious jabs of his shovel handle. The whole scene was plunged into darkness.

The van pulled away, leaving the three Humvees alone beside the road. With its lights off, the vehicle, its driver wearing his night-vision goggles, re-traced its way westward on "Highway 44".

Just after they had passed the spot where "Highway 126" joined up, from ahead came the glow of headlights. The oncoming machine slowed and swung around behind the darkened van.

Flashing blue and red lights burst out atop the sedan. The vehicle was a State Trooper's cruiser!

Groaning, Adams pulled the van to the side of the road.

As there came the clump of the driver's door of the police car closing, Colonel Golubko glanced back and spoke in a low voice. "Grishinov, take care of him."

The Russian moved the handle of the right-side rear door; it slid open only enough to let him get out. The van's interior light did not come on as it had been disabled before they had left the cavern. He tiptoed around the dark-side-front of the van just as the trooper looked in the driver's window.

At the same instant the officer saw Adams sitting in the darkened driver's seat, staring straight ahead, and was about to speak to him, Grishinov lunged at the fellow, pulled his elbow around the man's neck and jerked *hard.*

There was a *"Pop!"* that everyone inside the van heard as the American's spine snapped; the officer went limp. The Spetsnaz soldier dragged the lifeless patrolman around the front of the vehicle, rolled his body into a ditch, and climbed back into his seat.

Colonel Golubko grabbed his shovel, ran back and smashed the running lights and the flashing lights on the trooper's car. As before, darkness took over.

The whole episode had lasted less than two minutes.

Once more, the darkened van made its way down the road. After another mile, the driver turned on the headlights and increased speed.

Fifteen minutes later, the getaway vehicle came to a stop inside the hill with the camouflaged rock-doors closing behind it.

Adams took the satchel from the newcomer, who looked both relieved and bewildered. "Come with me," the agent told the scientist, "we will begin the de-briefings in the morning."

* * *

At the Underground Spetsnaz Training Center near Cuba, New Mexico, USA; the Next Morning:

"Comrades! Come quick!" Alex Adams shouted down the dormitory hallway. "See this!"

Terenty stuck his head out the door to his quarters and looked up the corridor. "What is it?"

"The television!"

All the men, including the researcher, who padded down to the viewing room in robe and slippers, crowded into the space.

On the screen, a florid-faced, middle-aged newscaster sat at a desk next to a young blonde woman whose facial expression alternated between a fixed smile and a fixed frown. On a screen behind the two was a picture of the three Humvees the Spetsnaz troops had encountered the night before, surrounded by squads of police officers and military men. In the background dozens of red and blue lights were flashing.

". . . about this startling development at the Los Alamos National Laboratory," the newsman was saying, "right now, we go to Dick Trushy at the scene . . . Dick—?"

A mature-looking man in an overcoat appeared on the screen. "Tom and Jan, what we know at this point is that, sometime last night, eleven United States Marines, all assigned to guard the Los Alamos Laboratory, were killed in what one military officer told me was the most brutal assault he had ever seen outside of combat." The screen showed a panning shot of the three Humvees alongside the snow-covered shoulder of the road, as the reporter went on. "It began, we understand, when the soldiers responded to what was described as an 'event' taking place on 'Highway Forty-Four', close to a section that is believed to be involved in some of the most secret research here at the laboratories, where two security guards and another Marine are missing."

The reporter came back on the screen. "I have been told that officials are concerned that one of their top researchers, whom they will not identify, is unaccounted for. A search is now underway for him."

"I cannot comment on the type of research," a professorly-looking man in a white smock coat said into the camera.

"They will never finish their project," the spy said to his rescuers seated in the viewing room, "I have the files with me . . . and I ruined all the records that are still there." He grinned and there was some scattered laughter in the room. "Their 'invisible technology' research is now stopped—they just do not yet know it!"

"You must tell us all about it, later." Adams directed their attention back to the television.

The reporter was squinting at the camera. "In addition to the eleven Marines, an unidentified State Trooper was found dead in a ditch about four miles west of here. We understand all the victims had deep cut wounds, except for the patrolman who had injuries authorities would not specify. A State Police officer told me a short while ago they have found matching tire tracks on the shoulder of the road in front of the Humvees, and at the scene a few miles away in front of the police cruiser. All the tire tracks seem to match, I am told."

Alex Adams sat up straight. "I must change the tires on the van."

The reporter consulted his notes that were flapping in a slight breeze. "If the tire tracks from both scenes are the same, it would suggest that the same people were involved in both crimes. A military spokesman told me it would take many strong men to take out all the Marines at once, like this—"

The man paused and seemed to be listening to an earpiece. "I'm told all the exterior lights were smashed-out on the military Humvees and on the highway patrol car, adding to the mystery, here."

Just then, a hand appeared from off-camera with a paper that it passed to the reporter. He looked at it, then at the camera. "They are now saying *two more* bodies, perhaps those of the missing sentries at the guardhouse near here, have just been discovered."

He again scanned the missive. "It says here, from an unofficial source, that these latest bodies were buried in the snow behind the guard shack and were found by police dogs." The man paused for a second, as if doing some mental arithmetic. "This would mean a total of thirteen fit, well-trained security men have been killed and one is missing in a mysterious, ambush-like mass killing at a location close to one of America's most sensitive and secret research laboratories. The investigation is just starting. Now, back to you, Tom and Jan—"

Agent Adams flicked his remote and the screen went blank.

"The de-briefings begin in an hour." Colonel Golubko looked at Terenty. "It will be your function to coordinate the information and the oral reports." To Gennady he said, "You will catalog the armaments and make a report." In turn, the leader gave each of the other troopers an assignment.

After a Russian breakfast, Terenty stepped down the rock-hewn hallway and opened the door to a small meeting-room. In the center was a table; a small crystal light fixture hung from the stony overhead, the only concession to luxury Terenty had seen in the entire place.

The middle-aged researcher shook his hand. My real name is 'Boris Arvidovich Glinka'. . . at the laboratory I used the name, 'Doctor Barry Glenn'."

He speaks perfect English, Terenty thought. "'Terenty Suslov' . . . my specialty is electronic warfare."

Ah, 'Comrade Suslov', we understand each other already, eh?" he said, switching to Russian.

From briefings, Terenty already knew that the man had infiltrated the "Los Alamos National Laboratory" several years earlier, using false identity papers supplied by the GRU and had top-secret American clearances; that he was a ranking researcher on a project in which the Americans were seeking to cancel waveforms; that the laboratory had made a recent break-through in the technology, and that he believed he was about to be exposed as a foreign agent, making necessary his extraction, along with important research materials.

"The Americans are working on 'radiant-spectrum wave-cancelling' using the principle of *'de-coherence and the collapsing of waveforms',* " the researcher said.

Terenty leafed through some of the papers on the tabletop. "Most impressive . . . I see the technology involves a revolutionary application of *'quantum mechanics'.* " From his study of physics, he was familiar with the principles, although not as applied to this type of technology.

Over the next two hours, the man outlined how the concept worked, using papers he had brought and computer disks he had taken. As they went along, Terenty began to realize the awesome military potential of the process.

"You say you destroyed their research on this?"

"In a way—yes." The Russian pushed his shock of graying hair out of his eyes and leaned back with a grin. "I infected their computers with an un-detectable 'stealth-virus' that will cause their conclusions to be slightly off at all times. The Americans will never be able to duplicate what is on these disks, here—and they will not know why."

The door opened and Colonel Golubko stepped in. "Comrades, are you making progress, here?"

"Yes, sir," Terenty said, standing and saluting the officer, who was still wearing his paramilitary outfit. "This information will be of great value to Russia."

"That is good." The colonel re-opened the door and looked back at them, nodding. "You can take a break, now, and resume later, if you wish."

The younger man glanced at his watch. "It is already past noon!" he said, surprised, "time to eat!"

At the same time as the two stepped into the rock-walled, brightly-lit hallway, there came a voice from the television set down the way. The men turned in the direction of the sound.

". . . makes the death toll in the attacks now fourteen." The same reporter they had seen that morning was delivering a new report. "A short while ago, investigators located another dead soldier in a ravine some distance from where the other bodies were found . . . the condition of this Marine was reported to me to be roughly the same as the others."

"He was the one I killed," Alex Adams said, as others gathered in the viewing room.

The newscaster was speaking. "We now go to Washington, for a news conference just starting at the Pentagon—"

The scene shifted to a silver-haired man in a military uniform emblazoned with ribbons, standing before a blue curtain, blinking in the glare of floodlights. Gripping a podium, the man looked around at an audience of news reporters sitting shoulder-to-shoulder in an auditorium-like room.

"Ladies and gentlemen, I have a short statement to make, and I will have time for a couple of questions, afterward." He gazed about at the news people and went on. "This morning, at approximately zero-one-hundred-hours, local time, the Marine Security Post at the Los Alamos National Laboratory at Los Alamos, New Mexico, received information of an 'event' taking place at or on the grounds of the laboratory, which extends over several dozen square miles . . . the post dispatched eleven United

States Marines in three Humvee vehicles to the scene. When, after some time, they did not respond to our routine queries, we sent another squad to investigate. When they arrived a short time later, they found the original Humvees abandoned. Investigating further, they discovered ten of the Marines from the first group. All were deceased. Another Marine was just located in the last few minutes—also deceased. Two sentries who were missing have been discovered . . . deceased. A Colorado State Trooper was also found four miles west of the original site . . . he was deceased. A wide-ranging investigation is now underway."

The man looked around the room. "Questions?" He pointed at a man who was standing in the glare of the lights; a boom microphone appeared at his face from the side.

"You said there was an 'event' . . . what type of 'event' was it? And what was the source of the 'information' you said they received?'"

"Usually these are minor breaches or animal activity that sets off automatic alarms. But we always take these 'events' seriously. The source of this particular information is not being revealed, however."

"Are you saying that this 'event' may have been *different*?"

"I cannot comment on that."

A young woman stood; the boom microphone materialized in her face. "How were they killed?"

"All I can say at this time is that they all suffered fatal wounds consistent with being physically attacked."

"Who do you think might be responsible for this?" The question came from an older, heavyset, jowly-faced woman in the front row. "Do you think it might have been a response from those opposed to the recent Gulf War? Could the Administration have prevented it?"

The uniformed man rolled his eyes, as if there was someting out-of-line with the question. "We do not know at this time who the perpetrators were. And, no, ma'am, there is no evidence of any anti-war faction having anything to do with it." The man nodded at the group. "Thank you very much—"

To a chorus of questions that he ignored, the high-ranking officer turned and left the stage.

The scene transitioned to a studio desk, where a newscaster was sitting, along with an older man and a middle-aged woman, all facing the cameras.

"There you have it," the newsman said, "the statement from a Pentagon officer about the events today in New Mexico." Below him on the screen, superimposed letters identified the man as a network correspondent.

The fellow turned to an older man in a tan suit, who looked slightly uncomfortable. "Here, now, we have our military consultant . . . retired U.S. Army Colonel 'Morris Tredd'."

The man nodded at the camera as the newsman went on, "Colonel Tredd, maybe I'm jumping to conclusions, but is there not something sinister about this? I mean, thirteen Marines and a state trooper all dead in this manner?"

"Well, not only is it sinister, but considering where it took place, it has serious implications."

"Implications for *what*?"

The fellow squirmed in his seat. "Let me make one thing clear: Los Alamos is one of the two most important nuclear research centers in the whole United States—the other is the 'Lawrence Livermore Laboratory' in California—and as such, there are many secret projects going on at those places. I can't talk much about them, but they are there, believe me. For one thing, that's where they design some of our nuclear warheads. So it's a really important place. Now, to have what looks like a successful armed assault on this place is serious, to say the least. Some questions come to mind right away: 'What happened during the time the Marines left the post and when their bodies were found? We know a scientist at the laboratory can't be located. What else? That's what the chain all the way to the White House is concerned with, right now."

"It is *that* serious?"

"Look, whoever attacked and killed these men—who were very-well trained in self-defense, by the way—used tactics and techniques not usually seen against our personnel . . . certainly not within the borders of this country. I understand they were attacked in the most extreme manner." The man shrugged. "If I

186

didn't know better, I would say they were killed—defeated—by highly-trained foreign paramilitaries."

The newscaster looked astonished. "'*Foreign paramilitaries*'? From where?"

"In Vietnam, toward the end of the war, there, we faced some terrifically-effective enemy soldiers who we later found out were trained as 'Spetsnaz' troops . . . they were trained by the Soviets."

The camera cut again to the newsman, who looked perplexed.

The expert went on. "'Spetsnaz' is the Russian equivalent of our 'Army Rangers', or the 'Delta Force', or the 'Navy Seals', among other organizations we have. They go back to Stalin, who first organized them, which should tell you something. The difference from us is that they have a reputation for audacious, vicious tactics and methods far beyond what our Special Forces are held back from using. Political assassinations, killing off whole governments in the middle of the night—stuff like that. *Ours can't do that.* I'm told our military and our Special Forces have a *very* strong respect for Spetsnaz." He spread his hands. "And frankly, this looks to me like a Spetsnaz job." The man shook his head. "And if it is—this is a security breach and a military defeat of the first order!"

The news anchor was frowning. "A defeat? That's a strong word."

The retired colonel's voice was shrill. "I mean, we have a unit of our best soldiers—U.S. Marines, for God's sake—lying dead in a killing field right next to one of our most important installations!" The man's eyes bulged. "Hell—that's a defeat!"

The middle-aged woman on the panel looked indignant. "You're telling me that these so-called, 'whatever-they-are-Russians'—did this to our men right here in our own country?"

The man looked straight at the camera and touched his fingertips together; his eyebrows knitted. "*Somebody* thought it important enough to use those kinds of people against ours at the most secret weapons development center in the United States!"

* * *

"Mind if I join you?" In the rock-walled dining-room, Terenty set his tray on the table opposite Gennady. "We have not talked for a while."

"We have been very busy."

"The operation seems to have gone well."

"So far—but we still have to get back home."

"The colonel told me that is what he will talk about."

Gennady noticed Terenty was picking at his food. "Where is the appetite? After last night, I thought you would be hungry like I am."

"I killed a man . . . I have never done that, before.

Terenty jabbed at the potatoes on his plate."I thought the training would keep me from thinking about it. But I can still see that American . . . the surprised look on his face."

Gennady shrugged. "It was either them or us." He would try to change the subject. "How did it go with the academician, this morning?"

"Very well, I should say. The technology the Americans were using is very clever. It will be most helpful to us."

Gennady picked up a little glass salt-shaker and rubbed it in his hands. Then he twisted off the shiny top and dumped the spoonful of salt into a saucer.

"What are you doing?"

"I told Galina I would bring her a souvenir. Since 'salt-with-bread' is 'good luck' in Russia, this will hold the salt." He gave a grin. "I wish I were holding *her*, right now!"

"You are serious about her, are you not?"

"I have some things to tell her when we return."

Terenty gave a grin of his own. "Same with Tamara."

Gennady was about to say something else when Colonel Golubko's voice came from the doorway. "We will have our meeting in five minutes."

* * *

"Comrades, here is the man we brought back with us, last night—'Academician Glinka'." The colonel motioned for the man to step to the front.

188

The wispy scientist stood before the men and pushed back his touseled hair. "Ah, comrades, as I told your Major Suslov, I have been working on the 'invisible technology' with the Americans." He grinned. "Of course, they did not know I was also working with the G-R-U!"

For a half-hour the man talked about his duties and the work that was going on at the laboratories. When he described how he had infected the Americans' computers with a virus that could not be traced that would prevent them from achieving anything meaningful, the others in the room laughed.

"So you see, comrades, what you did to bring me out will have great benefit to Russia."

Colonel Golubko stepped once more to the speaker's stand. "I will tell you what will next happen." He pushed up his eyeglasses and looked at some notes. "We will leave tonight for the border the Americans have with Mexico—we will be disguised as Mexican workers. Major Suslov, who speaks Spanish, will ride in the seat next to the driver . . . should we be stopped by the authorities, he will convince them we are workers. We will drive to El Paso and cross the border, then we will go to Monterrey and fly by commercial plane to Havana. In Havana, our agents will meet Comrade Glinka and de-brief him." The leader looked up and gave a grin, "and we will have a short holiday in Havana."

Handclaps and grins greeted the announcement. .

"Now, we will rest. We will put on our disguises and leave after midnight, when there is no interference from the citizens."

* * *

Aboard the 747, on Landing Approach to José Marti` Airport; Havana, Cuba:

Sunshine streamed into the upper cabin of the huge cargo jetliner—by the changing pressure in his ears, Retchko knew they were letting down. The Ukrainian looked at his watch; it was just after seven o'clock in the morning—it seemed as if they had been flying forever since the last refueling stop in Benghazi, Libya.

Cuba, he knew from having been there before as "Semen Putridchenko", was a far cry from some of the bleak-looking places where he had lately been. Pyongyang, in particular, was the most depressing place he had ever seen and seemed to get more grim every time he went there.

The general leafed through his notes, then set them aside. Even though he would be busy organizing the latest shipments from the Cubans, he would try to give himself a little time off. The sunny beaches and the just-as-sunny Havana women were the best, he knew from past experiences, and he also needed a mental break. Being there would put his cover to the test, of course, but if the Koreans had not recognized him, he felt confident his hairless disguise and name change would hold up.

* * *

At the International Bridge, El Paso, Texas; Late in the Same Morning:

The van slowed, then pulled up at the rear of a long line of vehicles waiting to cross the border into Juarez. Colonel Golubko leaned forward from one of the middle rows and called up to Terenty. "Remember—we are farm workers returning to Guadalajara."

At a crawl, the white vehicle started-and-stopped in the teeming traffic as it made its halting way to the front of the procession. Just as the temperature gauge on the dashboard was climbing past the red "Overheat" line, a U.S. Customs officer stepped back to Adams's open window.

The uniformed man looked the van-load of men over. He frowned at the driver. "Where did you come from in the United States?"

Adams spoke up, although Terenty had been told to do the talking. "We . . . from El Paso," he said in deliberate English, with a try at a Mexican accent. The officer stared at the disguised Russian, then at the others. Terenty hoped the brown face-paint and dark conact lenses were masking his and the others's pasty Slavic skin and blue eyes.

190

"What is your destination?"

Terenty leaned over. "'Que`?" He shrugged, as if he did not understand the question.

The man scowled. "Where are you going?"

Terenty gave exaggerated head nods. "Ah, señor officer, we—going to . . . Guadalajara!"

The officer narrowed his eyes, then stepped back and walked around the vehicle; he got down on his hands and knees and looked underneath it.

At length, the border agent came back and gestured at a parking space off to the side. "Drive your vehicle over there!"

Terenty glanced at the driver, who was doubling his fist. After a long second, Adams put the van in gear and maneuvered it to where the official was pointing.

"Everyone out of the van!" the man said, as two other border guards came over. Terenty saw one un-snapping his gun holster; the other stepped to the rear and began taking down the license number.

Glancing around at each other with impassive faces, the disguised foreigners dropped from the van—this was the last thing they had wanted. Colonel Golubko, looking nothing like his usual self in his made-up brown face and hands, was frowning. Terenty walked around to the border officer. *"Problema, por favor`?"*

The fellow pointed at a sticker. "Your registration is out of date."

Adams, who had overheard what the man had said, stepped up. "Ah, señor," the Russian said in an exaggerated Mexican accent that, to Terenty, did not sound convincing, "there is *no* 'problema! I have 'sticker' right in here." He scrambled around in the dashboard compartment and came up with a peel-type paper. "Here it is."

The officer took it and walked to the left front, to the vehicle's identification numbers behind the lower windshield glass. In a minute he came back and gave it to the driver. "Put it on, right away."

Just then, the officer with the writing pad ran up. He was holding a walkie-talkie-type radio. "This van is *not* from El

Paso!" The man pointed at the driver. "It is registered in Cuba, New Mexico! Hold these men!"

Adams had forgotten El Paso was in *Texas—the van had a New Mexico license plate!*

There came the sound of a siren, then the rising whine of a vehicle's engine. Everyone turned about. A police wagon, lights flashing, was racing straight toward them! At once, the three officers pulled pistols and aimed them using both hands at the van's occupants. "Hands up!" the guard shouted, "you are all under arrest! The charge is fourteen counts of murder—this is the van that was at the Los Alamos attacks!"

-9-

His hands held high, Colonel Golubko cast about, sizing-up the situation. With a nod that the other disguised Spetsnaz troops observed, he started making minute motions. As Terenty, Gennady and the others gave quick glances at him so as not to arouse suspicion from the glowering guards, the senior Russian officer made hand, head, and body signals that were the instructions—undetectable by the Americans—for quick action as they had practiced many times in training. And there was no time to waste; the shrieking police wagon was now only a few hundred meters away.

The colonel made a quick motion to look over the shoulder of the man holding the gun on him and gave a loud shout. "Hey!"

The guard turned for a split-second to look back. That was all the Spetsnaz leader needed—in a flash he lunged forward and knocked the weapon out of the fellow's hand! Before the wobbling pistol had even clattered to the asphalt, the older but powerfully-built Russian brought his clasped hands down onto the back of the reeling border-guard's neck, dropping him senseless to the ground!

At the same instant, as the second man also let down his guard to glance back, Gennady gave the distracted officer's wrist a mighty kick, sending his weapon spinning to the pavement. Then he performed a leaping, twisting kick at the fellow's face with the heel of his shoe. The man's head snapped to the side, blood frothing from his broken nose as he went down, his yell joining the shrieking siren of the onrushing police wagon.

Before the third guard could react, Malinovsky lunged at him, knocking away the gun, catching the heel of his hand at his chin with a mighty jab, jerking his head back, and smashing down on the back of the fellow's neck. The American dropped to the pavement face-first and was very still.

While all this was happening, Adams had yanked open the driver's door, clawed up onto the seat and started the engine.

By now, the howling police wagon was nearly upon them. The scrambling Russians dived into the van, some on top of each other in their haste, as it started its run toward the bridge, fifty meters distant. Gaining speed, the vehicle's flat-front flung aside the wooden barrier. The van rocketed onto the open span, past a line of screeching pedestrians, who fell back against the outside railing as the rocking, thrusting machine lunged by!

At full throttle the van shot across the center of the bridge into Mexican territory, slowing at the opposite guard-house while Adams tossed a fistful of American hundred-dollar bills out the window and kept going. As the fleeing van disappeared down the street into teeming traffic, Gennady looked back and saw the local guards on their knees, scooping up the currency. Back on the other side, the police wagon was stopped beside the inert security men.

El Paso Record-Gazette:

ONE OFFICER DEAD, TWO CRITICAL AFTER ATTACK AT BRIDGE

Investigators are seeking the men who attacked Three Border Patrol Officers at the International Bridge yesterday, killing one and leaving two in critical condition at a local hospital.

Officers who arrived at the scene moments after the Incident occurred said they saw a white van break through the barrier and cross the bridge at high speed.

Pedestrian eyewitnesses who were on the bridge said the van was occupied by several men who appeared to be Mexican nationals.

José Marti`International Airport, Havana, Cuba; Two Days Later:

"I am glad to get all that face-paint off me!" Terenty said, as he toweled off in the military maintenance bathroom at the Havana airport, "and the shoe black in my hair was the worst!"

"Same with me," Gennady said, tying his shoelaces," and I would not make a very good Mexican, either . . . I do not speak Spanish!" He looked at his watch. "The colonel said for us to meet him at oh-nine-hundred in the classroom, and it is past that, already."

". . . the rest of us will be on—" Colonel Golubko glanced from his notes as Terenty and Gennady took their seats in the same stuffy classroom where they had gathered on their first arrival in Cuba, some days ago. As before, Comrade Fidel's portrait stared down at them from a side wall.

The older officer, dressed in combat fatigues and cleaned of his brown-skin-black-hair disguise, pointed at his wrist-watch. "You two are late, as usual, but I will overlook that fact this time, since our mission was a success." The Spetsnaz leader glanced at his notes. "As I was telling the others before you got here, Comrade Glinka is now being de-briefed by G-R-U Intelligence officers who flew from Moscow to interrogate him."

The man looked around at the seated soldiers. "Comrades, the Los Alamos operation was a success worthy of the glorious operations of the past. It has already been determined that the materials we obtained from the American laboratories will now complete our own 'invisible and silent technology', and is therefore of great importance to Russia." He paused, then said, "For that reason, our superiors have granted you some rest and recuperation time."

Colonel Golubko nodded at a door attendant, who stepped into the corridor and returned a moment later with a slight, middle-aged man in a white pullover shirt. 'This is 'Comrade Trini', who will be your guide around Havana."

The angular fellow with bristly, graying hair that stood straight up, motioned at the assembled group.

"Come outside with me," he said in English, with a choppy Cuban accent. The eight young men, minus Colonel Golubko, who stayed behind, followed the man, whom Terenty had already decided was somewhat eccentric, to the parking lot. There, a small bus, enveloped in black diesel exhaust, was waiting, its engine idling. A bored-looking young man sitting in the driver's seat watched as they clambered aboard. "You will have to excuse the bus," Trini said in his broken English, "she is old and shook-up."

The driver clashed the shift lever into gear and with a shuddering turn the machine lunged around toward an exit, rocking along on cracked pavement pitted with pot-holes and punctuated by lines of grass that poked through here and there. Gennady saw that most of the cars and trucks in the parking spaces looked very old-fashioned—then he remembered the Americans had had an embargo against this island for many years and that no new Yankee cars had come to Cuba in decades.

They passed a huge parked aircraft Gennady recognized as a Boeing 747, that was loading cargo. As the sunlight caught the fuselage, he saw the faint words *'Iraqi Airlines'* on its upperworks, as if they had been rubbed out, and the curious airplane had no numbers on it. The outer wheel rims on the right side were an odd yellow-green color. From where did it come, he wondered, and what is it doing here?

As the groaning, swaying bus bounded onto a broad roadway, Trini the Cuban, waving a cigar, spoke up. "We will see Havana, today," he said, above the moaning engine and the rush of humid air swirling through the open windows, "and I hope you enjoy our island."

* * *

"There is a Russian group here, right now . . . some 'Special Forces' men, I believe." The chief maintenance man was speaking to Retchko at the counter in the cargo section. "They are from Moscow, I remember their leader had said."

The bald Ukrainian narrowed his eyes. "What is their leader's name?"

The fellow leafed through a stack of papers. "His name is . . . 'Golubko—Colonel Rodion Golubko'." He looked up. "Do you know him?"

"Ah . . . no—" But Retchko felt as if he had been struck by lightning. *Golubko!* His once and former friend and now

196

adversary was right here in Havana! The hairless man ran his hand over his shiny pate, already becoming sunburned in the Cuban tropics. Now, his disguise would *really* be put to the test, for he had no doubt that they would meet-up sooner or later.

Retchko started back in the direction of the airplane. Just then, from around the corner came the very Rodion Golubko he was just discussing with the Russian mechanic!

Trying to appear calm, the general stepped past the man, who nodded and kept going.

He could not believe it! He had been within a couple of meters of the former Soviet officer he had once known as a friend—and the man had not recognized him!

The portly man took deliberate steps toward the airplane. They must complete the loading and depart as soon as possible—Golubko must not know he was in Havana! Above him, he spotted the chief pilot standing just inside the rear cargo door of the 747. "When will we be ready to depart?"

The round-faced aviator looked at the loading chart in his hands. "We can leave as soon as they bring two more crates." He squinted in the direction of the hangar. "They are coming, now." Retchko turned about and saw a sputtering tractor pulling two rubber-wheeled trailers, both bearing a large wooden crate, in their direction.

"Very well," the general called up, as the clatter of the rickety tug's engine grew louder. "The customer for these goods wants them as soon as we can deliver it."

Just then the tractor gave a loud noise and the engine stopped! The general spun around; the machine was giving off oily black smoke—already the Cuban driver was dropping down to look at it. Several workers and some of the Russian technicians were making their way across the apron to see it for themselves.

One of the men was Rodion Golubko!

The bald Ukrainian stood rooted to the spot; there was nowhere for him to go! Steeling himself, he walked toward the disabled tug, trusting that his disguise would once more cover his true identity.

"What is the problem?" he asked the driver in a different-sounding voice from usual, seizing the conversation before the others came up.

The fellow shook his head. *"Que?"*

Retchko realized the man did not speak English. As the others drew about, he edged around behind a heavyset Cuban worker; it would best if he kept away from Golubko as much as possible. Several of the Russians did appear to speak the local language, however; they began a halting conversation with the tractor driver. He overheard one of the Russians say "old", which probably meant the machine was worn out. Retchko groaned to himself—of all times! The tug was a mere fifty meters short of the airplane.

The Ukrainian glanced at Golubko, *who was staring at him!* Then the man Retchko had known before in another guise was stepping in his direction!

A problem with your loading?" Golubko's question was casual.

"Ah . . . yes." Retchko again tried to change his voice so his former fellow officer would not recognize it. *So far, the man did not recognize who he was!* "We are leaving for—our destination—as soon as we can get these crates—loaded," he said in halting Russian.

Rodion Golubko was about to say something, when a rumble came from the direction of the hangar. Everyone turned toward the source; another tug was headed toward them. The newer machine pulled up and the drivers hitched the two trailers behind it.

"Well, I must be going," Retchko nodded at the other man, and turned away.

To the Ukrainian's relief, as he stepped onto the scissors elevator, he saw that the others, Golubko included, had turned about and were now making their way back toward the hangar.

* * *

Photographic Analysis Section, National Security Agency; Washington, D.C.:

"Well, I'll be—!" The lady analyst called to her superior. "Come look at this!"

The middle-aged man squinted into the eyepiece, and grinned. "That's it, all right . . . our old friend." He stood up. "Zoom down and see if we can tell what the cargo is."

The technician punched a button several times; each jab gave a closer view and more resolution. "The trucks are covered with tarps . . . can't make-out what's underneath them." After a few more taps on the button, a bright spot appeared beside a scissors elevator next to the airplane. "Looks like somebody's bald head down there is getting a sunburn."

The Chief Photo Analyst looked at his subordinates. "I want a non-stop surveillance on this aircraft. I don't want it to get away, again."

* * *

Colonel Golubko stood at the maintenance counter with the chief aircraft mechanic, a Russian. The Spetsnaz officer stared through the picture window at the flashing red lights on the top and the bottom of the 747 and listened, frowning, to the whine of its starting jet engines coming through the glass. "Who was that man on the cargo airplane?"

"I do not know who he was. The pilot signed all the papers."

"What is its destination?"

"Angola. It makes a run from Havana to there." The round-faced Soviet shrugged. "The Cubans are pulling out of there, you know. It was a disaster for them."

"What is the cargo?"

"General cargo to Angola, according to the manifests. They take the Cubans' weapons out of there."

"Do they bring the weapons back here?"

"Now that you mention it, I cannot say if they actually do."

Rodion Golubko stared at the behemoth aircraft as it waddled out the taxiway on its veritible forest of struts and wheels and made a slow, stately turn. "To where does it go?"

The Russian airframe man shrugged. He tapped the countertop with his ball-point pen as he also watched the receding big Boeing. "That is the same airplane we repaired some time ago," he remarked, matter-of-factly.

The colonel was interested. "What kind of repairs?"

"We had to make repairs to the landing gear and the airframe . . . it had been shot-up taking off from Mexico City—something about its cargo on that trip from there had caused problems, as I understand it."

This was intriguing information. "What kind of cargo was it?"

"Electronics . . . I believe it was mostly military communications and radar equipment."

"Military radar equipment? From Mexico City?"

"I know that the cargo originated in America." The fellow thought some more. "There was an American on board, I now remember. He was taking the electronics to somewhere in Africa."

The Russian Special Forces officer gazed at the airplane, now far out in the distance and turning for its takeoff run. Something about the big jet unsettled him. No, it was not the airplane, he thought; nor was it the electronic cargo from that earlier flight. It was the stocky, bald-headed man with whom he had just briefly spoken. It was almost as if he had seen him before, somewhere.

A voice sounded behind him. "Colonel, they want you in the de-briefing room." One of the GRU Intelligence officers from Moscow had come up. "We have some more questions about the agent rescue."

* * *

"This is a *big* difference from the last hotel when we were here!" Gennady gaped around at the palatial suite. "Even our luggage was already here!" He picked up a postcard from the desk." *'Hotel Nacional de Cuba'*, it is." He glanced at his watch; it was past two o'clock in the morning.

Terenty dropped onto one of the big beds, put his hands behind his head and gazed up at a crystal light overhead. "I believe I am liking Cuba very much."

After today, who would *not* like this place . . . oh, man!"

Terenty glanced at his watch. "We were out ever since *yesterday* morning."

The colonel said we could sleep late."

"I do not feel like sleeping. I still remember all the dancing girls at the 'Tropicana'."

Gennady laughed. "We must not tell Galina and Tamara about what we saw!"

"And we saw just about *everything!*"

Gennady nodded and let go with a laugh. "Nice looking . . . but not for me—I will take Galina over any of them!"

"That fellow, Trini, he was a character, no?"

"What is the plan for tomorrow?"

"We go to the beach."

"Trini said the colonel wants us back at the airport tomorrow night. I suppose we will be leaving for Moscow."

"And I am ready to get back to Moscow." Terenty was thinking about Tamara; he had some important things to say to her when he returned.

* * *

Havana Beach; Noontime, the Next Day:

"Now, *this* is the life!"

Gennady, propped on his elbows, looked out in relaxed satisfaction at the roaring white surf, chased by heaving dark-gray offshore rollers as it crashed down onto the sandy beach up and down the way. Screeching seagulls spun and looped about overhead. Some of the Russians, stretched-out on oversized towels, were soaking up the warm tropical sunshine; a couple of others over at one of the thatched-roofed gazebos among the palm trees were practicing their Spanish on tanned, barely-clad 'señoritas'. From the looks of things to Gennady, the girls seemed to be taking to the pale, muscular young men.

"This makes all that effort back there in America worth it," the officer went on.

Terenty picked up the camera he had borrowed from the airport and took a round of pictures. "Wait until Tamara sees this!" he said, snapping a shot of the surf. He waved at Trini, who was sitting on a barstool at one of the surfside huts nearby, smoking a cigar.

Up on the road, a half-dozen young men who had alighted from a 'fifties-vintage Chevrolet station wagon were making their way toward the beach, each carrying a pastel-painted surfboard under his arm. Then one of the Cubans spotted the girls who were talking to two young men. Turning toward the gazebo, he motioned for the others to follow him.

As Gennady watched, frowning, the talk among the young people looked to be taking an untoward turn, judging from gestures and the voices he could hear above the surf. Gennady called to the others to pay attention to what was happening on the beach down the way.

Then one of the locals punched at one of the foreigners as the girls, shrieking, dropped back.

Grishinov, the Russian, pointed at the Cuban in what seemed to be a warning to the fellow.

Navarin, the other officer, doubled his fists.

As the others looked on from a distance, the tanned, muscular interloper lunged forward and took another swing at the Spetsnaz soldier. Grishinov, ducked underneath the punch, pointing at the fellow and his friends and seemed to be cautioning them stay away. By now, Gennady and Terenty, along with the others, were making their way in a hurry across the sand. But before they could get there, the fellow who seemed to be the leader of his crowd motioned to his fellow Cubans who rushed at the two Russians, holding their surfboards up as clubs and shields.

The first to reach the scene, Malinovsky, grabbed the back end of one of the flat boards, wrenched it out of its owner's hand and threw it to the sand. The surprised fellow whirled about just as a fist slammed into the side of his face! As the girls screamed, the surfer dropped to the ground, senseless.

At the same time, Grishinov, with a loud grunt, delivered a flying kick with his bare foot squarely into the face of the youth who had been doing the talking. The Cuban's head snapped to one side and he fell to the sand without another word. Navarin's fist shot forward and caught another surfer flush on the jaw with a roundhouse right that propelled the flailing fellow backward, his knees buckling.

The other Spetsnaz officers made quick work of the remainder, a couple of whom had dropped their surfboards and were trying to flee across the slip-sliding sand.

The girls backed away, wide eyed; all the Cuban male bravado had been replaced by groaning young men rolling on the sand. Two were out cold.

Grishinov stepped toward the young women, who kept backing away.

"Señoritas, we have—" he said in broken Spanish, motioning to the prone antagonists, whose surfboards lay in disarray around them.

But one of the girls was glaring at him. "He is my *brother* . . ." she hissed, kneeling down at the first of the Cubans, who was moaning. She looked up at the foreigners with a look of contempt. "He was trying to defend my honor . . . he did not know you." The young woman kissed her relative's forehead. "You Russians are pigs! Go away!"

Trini loped up just then and said something in rapid Spanish to the girls, then turned to the visitors."I told them you did not understand their motives," he said, switching to English, "and that I saw how the Cubans had started it."

Just then, a policeman dropped down through the sand toward the scene of the recent fight. Trini stepped forward and said someting to the man, who was pointing his billy club up at the main road.

Terenty turned about and was shocked to see that a police wagon, its emergency lights flashing, had pulled up into the parking area! Several uniformed officers holding night-sticks piled out of more police cars and started running and sliding down the sands toward them.

The first officer motioned his club at the swim-suited Russians and said something. "He says to get your clothes," Trini told them, "they are taking you in for questioning!"

"What!"

Trini said something to the officer, who replied in rapid Spanish.

"You are not under arrest—yet. But the Cubans may want to press charges!"

Terenty glanced in the direction of the old Chevrolet, toward which the bikinied young women and their unsteady male friends were walking. One of the girls turned about and glared at the foreigners.

Groaning, the young men retrieved their things from where they had been, all the while surrounded by serious-looking officers fingering their clubs. They bundled the Russians into the wagon.

"Colonel Golubko is not going to like this," one of the young officers said, glumly, as the jammed vehicle started moving. Already it was sweltering inside the box-like space.

After some minutes of bumping and rocking along, during which time the vehicle ran over several deep pot-holes, knocking the men about inside the van, the pavement smoothed out and the police wagon ran up a short incline and shuddered to a stop.

There came a rattling of chains and a scowling, uniformed officer pulled open the rear doors, gesturing for the prisoners to get out. "Hands up!" he shouted at Gennady, bashing him on the side of the head with his club. Resisting the impulse to kill the man on the spot, which he knew he could easily do but did not dare to try, the Spetsnaz officer obeyed the fellow's order and followed him, along with the others, down an odorous, peeling hallway to a small room with bars on the outside windows.

"In there!" the policeman said in Spanish, motioning at the door. When all the Russians were inside, the officer slammed shut the heavy metal door, followed by a series of loud clicks. They were locked-in!

The small room was packed with seething young men. Malinovsky clenched his fists. "Someone will be in trouble for this!" The others ruefully agreed with him.

Terenty turned to Grishinov, whose troubles with the young Cubans had started everything. "What happened?"

The powerfully-built Russian shrugged. "Navarin and I"—he nodded at the other officer—"were having a 'friendly' conversation

204

with the three girls and those fellows showed up. Next thing he was threatening and pushing me. I tried to warn him to back-off, but he started a fight. You saw what happened next."

Navarin was shaking his head. "And we had gotten along well with the girls, up to then."

"I hope Colonel Golubko understands—" This was from Chernenko, who had not said much. The others groaned; everyone knew he was telling the truth about what their no-nonsense superior might do when he found out about this.

An hour went by; most of the detainees paced back and forth as there were no seats. A couple of the young men propped themselves against the dingy wall; one of them dozed off, sweating, in the muggy, airless space. Everyone else was becoming more and more concerned as to what might happen to them.

There came a rattling and a clatter, and the door swung aside on creaking hinges. "Trini!" one of the young men shouted, and he was taken up by the others. The slender Cuban stood outside the door with Colonel Golubko and one of the policemen. The policeman was impassive. The Spetsnaz leader was frowning. Trini was grinning.

"Señor Russians . . . all is 'hokay'!" the middle-aged man said. The police officer gestured with his billy-club for the prisoners to step outside. As they filed-out into the corridor, the heat of the hallway felt like a cool breeze compared to the oven-like room where they had just been. "I told the officers what happened and they are going to let you go," Trini said.

Observing the Cuban guard's subsided demeanor and Rodion Golubko's clenched teeth, Terenty guessed the colonel had also had something to do with their release. The officer's eyes narrowed. "I *told* you women were trouble—will you believe me, *now?"*

Outside, the old bus was waiting, surrounded by its everlasting cloud of black diesel exhaust. "We will return to the airport," Colonel Golubko said, as they clambered aboard, "the Intelligence officers want all of us to be on the Aeroflot flight to Moscow, tonight. They wish to return Glinka to Russia right away—his information is urgent, they say."

The bus rattled around the edge of Havana Bay, past the midtown section of Havana that Terenty recognized from yesterday's all-day tour with Trini, and on out the broad thoroughfare along the seawall that he remembered as the "Malecón". As they rode along, Terenty gazed out at tanned, bikini-clad young women on the stone walkway, some in explicit embraces with male companions.

"Those girls were not fair," he said aloud, voicing what he knew was on the others' minds. *"Their* fellows started everything."

"I am just ready to go home . . ." a tired-sounding voice said from somewhere inside the bus to a general agreement from the others.

* * *

Photographic Analysis Section, National Security Agency; Washington, D.C.:

"Dammit! It's gone, again!" The middle-aged female analyst stared into the eyepiece. "The Seven-Forty-Seven at Havana . . . it's not there—"

The Section Chief came over. "How long since the last satellite pass?"

The woman pulled up some information a screen. "The over-flight was one hour, twelve minutes ago."

"Plot co-ordinates and do a time-distance search in every direction."

* * *

As the Aeroflot "IL-62" banked into a steep, climbing left turn, Terenty stared out the window at the blaze of evening lights that defined as well as illuminated Havana. While the Cuban capital scrolled past underneath the end of the dipped wing, he dropped back the seat and started thinking about what had happened since they had left Moscow just a few days ago.

For the most part, he had been pleased with his own and the group's performance in the recent operation; the only discordant note had been having to kill those Americans. From the days when he had lived in Washington with his diplomat parents, he had always personally liked them. But his first allegiance was, of course, to Russia. His Spetsnaz training had prepared him to do without flinching whatever was necessary—up to and including meting-out the "ultimate punishment" to those who got in his way.

"Vodka—straight . . ." he said to the smiling female attendant, whose admiring eyes were unabashedly surveying his well-built physique.

Settling back, as the liquid refreshment took hold, Terenty went on with his reflections about the mission. From what he had already learned by talking with the agent, Glinka, the information the man had taken from the Americans was so important as to sharply alter the strategic balance of power in favor of Russia. Putting together what their country's academicians had already learned about the invisible and sound-cancelling technology with Glinka's new information would give Russian diplomats unassailable geo-political advantages—backed by irresistable military power—against the West. What was it General Putridchenko, the high-ranking officer back at the Academy *(Where had he gone?)* had said when they were in training? *That the Imperialists would soon be helpless before a technology that rendered Soviet—now Russian—warheads invisible to American radars.* Now, all the elements would be completed, thanks to their efforts at Los Alamos.

For that, they must give most of the credit to Colonel Golubko. The man and his experience stood far above them, Terenty knew, and certainly above their opponents. It intrigued him that their leader had never told them much about himself, except that he had once trained with the cosmonauts—thereby enhancing his own mystique. Typical of his "focused" style, even as the others had gone on Trini's sight-seeing excursion around Havana, the colonel had stayed at the airport, working on operational reports to Moscow. And his account to headquarters would tell of a near-perfect mission: the successful extraction of

Glinka from America's most prestigious and secret research laboratory without a single injury or mishap to their group. Terenty knew it was all the result of the colonel's personal drive and his attention to planning and detail.

He thought it remarkable how far the young officers had come since that day, months back, when they had first sat in the anteroom at the Academy, waiting for Rodion Golubko to interview them.

At about the same time, he had first seen the beautiful Tamara and her winsome little girl walking past a sidewalk kiosk as he sat spellbound; and later, he had rescued the child from the onrushing streetcar. So much had happened, since then.

Terenty felt in his pocket for the little velvet box he had bought at the Havana airport. He hoped Tamara would want what was inside it.

* * *

A few rows behind Terenty, Gennady stared out the window as the last of Havana's lights faded below the long, slender airliner and darkness took over. The young Russian military officer sat back and ordered a drink. He pulled a tiny velvet box from his pocket, lifted the little cover and admired the shiny gold piece within. When he had suggested to Terenty that they buy the special jewelry for both of the girls at the airport's duty-free store, without hesitation, his friend had pulled out convertible currency and paid for one, guessing about Tamara's finger size. He had done the same for Galina. He knew that his and Galina's lives would be forever changed were she to accept the gift he was bringing to her from Cuba. Gennady grinned to himself; likely the colonel would grouse if he knew about it, but the young officer was excited about again seeing Tamara's slender, dark-haired cousin. He fingered the smooth, velvety box that was no bigger than the end of his thumb. Its shiny contents, Gennady knew, would create a sensation.

And it was a quiet, peaceful ending to the deadly job the men had taken on when they left Moscow just days before.

From the start, they had been told the mission would be difficult and would likely involve injuring or "eliminating" their opponents. Not a problem; their training always focused on accomplishing objectives using unusual and overwhelming force without political or ethical constraints. For *'Mother Russia'* demanded and expected the utmost from her heroic soldiers. And it was beyond dispute that Spetsnaz troops, ever since the "Great Patriotic War", were the best-trained and most lethal Special Forces in the world. And their little squad had just pulled off one of the most successful and important operations in the history of the Force. Gennady tallied the score: At Los Alamos they had killed fourteen of their opponents, plus one more at the border crossing, without so much as a scratch to themselves. The Americans—their pius moralizing and smug claims of their "superior" technology notwithstanding, had been puny push-overs when confronted with the Spetsnaz onslaught—and deep inside their own country, no less.

The result had been an Intelligence coup that would alter the balance of power in the world.

* * *

At the Office of "The Chief"; Lagos, Nigeria, the Next Morning:

"You say you have contacts in the Philippines who want us to supply armaments to their forces?" The slight, baldheaded man leaned back in his leather executive chair and tapped his fingertips together as he regarded Leonid Efimovich Retchko and Norbert Ezego, who were sitting across from him.

"Yes, sir, the revolutionary we call, 'U', who is now in Sudan, says his operatives in the Philippines are organizing and wish us to supply training and arms to them." Retchko glanced at the very dark African sitting beside him. "'Ezego', here, who is my deputy, will go on the cargo 'Seven-Forty-Seven' to Sudan to pick up a relative of 'U' and take him to the Philippines. On the way, they will stop at Pyongyang and load weapons the North Koreans will supply . . . then to Manila and by boat to Mindanao

Island, in the south. We may also start supplying a new group affiliated with 'U' in Bali—in Indonesia."

"Everything is arranged?"

"Payment through the usual channels. The Philippine insurgents are willing to pay the premium to get the weapons right away." *The Cayman bank balance will swell.*

"Very good." The Chief narrowed his eyes at Ezego. "You are leaving, soon?"

"I will be on the way, early tomorrow."

The little man stood up; the meeting was over. Ezego took his leave.

"Just a minute," the Chief said to Retchko as the two watched the other man's broad back recede through the accounting office, with its roomful of clacking posting machines, and on out beyond the glass lobby door up front. "I have some questions." He closed the door.

The short man in the brown three-piece suit turned his eyes on the Chief of Security "You trust Ezego with that much responsibility and authority?"

The question caught Retchko off-guard. "Yes, sir. because he is 'realistic', as I am. Ezego has worked logistics with me on other arms deals. He will be perfect for the job."

The Chief' took a deep breath. "All right, but report back to me about what he is doing." The small man bored his eyes on the bald European. "What are *you* doing in the meantime?"

"The airplane will return to Lagos and pick up a load of arms and satellite equipment to take to Teheran, then the shipment will go on to Chechnya. The Iranians are now cooperating with us on transporting our goods across their country," he said, nodding. "I will go to Chechnya where we will be setting up the chip-implant system for the warlord's soldiers."

"How about the refinery?

"For now, the office manager, Frank Ogawan, is in charge until we resolve the 'Nkrume affair'." *I detest the weakling Ogawan. In my scheme, there is no place for anyone without a strong will. But because I need him, for now, I will let him live.*

* * *

Tanuta Refinery; Late Morning, the Same Day:

Frank Ogawan stared at the computer screen, frowning. The new operations program showed that with the quantity of oil they were off-loading from the coastal tankers it was not possible to supply the amount of finished product they were shipping out. Even the gasoline they produced required more crude than they were taking in, and the plant also produced raw asphalt for the State Road Department that used mostly leftover crude components for which the readout could also not account. He ran a scan on the hard disk; the discrepancy was still there. The temporary refinery manager pulled up the old program. It showed that the former one also displayed the difference. Strange. Since it was Lisa Anaya's program, he would ask her about it.

Just then, Lisa stepped into his office. "Ready for lunch?"

He would bring up the subject of the oil with her some other time. The two stepped out into the noonday sun and headed across the parking lot toward the main building.

While they stood in the doorway to the dining-room for a few seconds, waiting for their eyes to adjust from bright sunshine to the subdued indirect light of the interior, Frank caught sight of someone waving. Larry and Marisol were calling to them from a table across the room.

As the newcomers took their seats, nodding and smiling, Marisol gave a discreet glance at the cream-colored female electronics engineer sitting across from her; how remarkable, she thought, that the two couples had as much as swapped partners. It occurred to her that this was the first time the four had actually been together since it had all happened. The Cuban girl had already noticed that the office manager seemed to be walking with a new spring in his step these days. Marisol guessed that, because of Lisa, he now had much more amorous experience than before. She had seen such transformations happen.

After they had ordered, Frank spoke up. "Lisa says the implant system is now in place."

"We ran our first full-scale test this morning," Larry said, buttering his bread, "and everything checked out . . . even the encoder worked perfectly."

"Retchko wants us to ship a satellite dish system to Lagos," Lisa put in. "He says it will be going overseas."

Marisol's eyebrows were upraised. "Overseas?"

"Retchko is handling it."

The Cubana rolled her eyes. "Let us not talk about Retchko—or I will lose my appetite."

* * *

Signal Intelligence Office, National Security Agency, Washington, D.C.:

"I *told* you it was coming from Africa!" Jamey Suggs pointed at the plots on the monitor screen that seemed to back-up his earlier contention. "All you had to do was reverse the phase, and—Presto! There it was—straight-up from West Africa to our satellite, then down to us!"

The Chief Engineer, tuning the receiver, nodded his head. "The last transmission was very short—less than two seconds, just enough to trigger our automatic scanners—so we couldn't get an exact fix on where it originated. But we now have something to work with."

Buzzy Habbler frowned at the oscilloscope as the technician ran and re-ran the recorded signal on the screen. "What are they saying?"

"It seems to be encoded—and not like anything we've seen before . . . like it's relaying a signal from somewhere else through our own satellite!" The electronics analyst looked around at the others, then back at the screen. "Let me tell you something: I've seen a lot of things come through here, but whoever is behind *this* setup is *very* clever."

* * *

Tverskaya District, Moscow; That Evening:

Tamara Kuznetsova gaped at the gold band in the tiny velvet box; her hands were shaking. "It is a. *'wedding'* ring, is it not?" She blinked at the shiny circle.

Yes, it is," Terenty said, watching her stunned face, gauging her reaction. "I brought it all the way from Havana, to you."

"You were in *Havana*? In *Cuba*?"

"Si señorita! I will tell you about it, some time!"

The young woman gave a laugh. "I forgot you speak Spanish."

"The Cubans, I found out, are big on romance. The women at the airport store there helped me pick it out. "

"But it is a . . . *gift*?"

Tamara, *it is a wedding ring.* I want to put it on your finger in front of the *'Marriage Registrar'* . . . I mean, I want you to, ah—marry me."

The girl gasped. "Oh, Terenty, I never thought—"

"You never thought I would *ask* you? Tamara, I have always wanted you . . . from the time I first saw you and Larisa at the kiosk that day, I wanted to know you. I just did not know how to make it happen—the streetcar did it for me!"

"But you are gone all the time, and you are busy, and you do not have time to—"

". . . be quiet and kiss me. . .that is, if you will marry me."

The girl's long auburn hair tumbled over both their faces as she pulled herself to him. Terenty could feel her trembling. Her lips probed for his; her joyful tears dropped onto his cheek.

"When the mission was finished and we were in Havana, I had much time to think—time to think about us. And when we were at the airport, getting ready to leave, Gennady and I saw a jewelry store. Both of us had the same idea at the same time."

"Gennady bought a ring for Galina?"

"He hopes she will take it."

"Oh, she *will!* I am sure of it!" Tamara wiped her eyes with her hand, nodding. "We must tell my parents and Larisa. They will not believe this." She took his hand pulled him from the sofa toward the archway.

In another part of the block-long building of flats, Galina held Gennady in a long, tear-streaked kiss. "Oh, Gennady! I was so afraid I would never again see you . . ."

"It was when we got back to Cuba, that Terenty and I decided to buy one for each of you."

"Terenty got one for Tamara?"

"He was afraid she would not want it."

Galina wiped her eyes with her hand."Believe me, *she will take the ring!* Tamara worried and prayed for him every day. I did the same for you. She told me how much she loved Terenty and was afraid she would not see him again—that something might happen to him."

Galina lifted the gold band out of the little box. "May I put it on?" The young woman slipped it onto her ring finger. "It fits! But how did you know the size?"

"The woman at the airport store had fingers about the same as yours."

She put her arms around his neck and whispered in his ear: "Let us go to the 'Marriage Registrar', tomorrow and to see the priest. We must have a wedding in the church."

Gennady swallowed. "After all we went through, that would be all right with me."

"Well, *that* is a change of heart!" Galina rubbed her fingertips across his shoulders and kissed his neck. Then she saw he looked serious. "Are you all right?"

"Galina, you were closer than you thought when you worried we might not get back."

The girl was frowning. "What do you mean?"

How much could he tell her?

Gennady took a deep breath. "We went to America on a very important mission—a secret mission I cannot tell you much about.

The dark-haired girl said nothing.

His shoulders gave a shudder. "Galina, I had to kill someone . . . I had to kill an American—we killed some American soldiers."

Galina's hand went to her mouth to stifle a gasp. Her eyes were wide. "Gennady! *What—?*"

"I felt terrible about it, but at the same time, I was . . . *pleased.* Pleased with myself. I had performed my duty to Russia. *All* of us performed our duties to Russia."

The girl's face looked stricken. "You were 'pleased' to kill someone?"

"In the sense it was my duty, *yes*—but you must understand that it was either us or them. It was terrible . . . exhilarating."

He was close to telling her too much.

"I mean, the mission was so important to our country . . . you cannot understand how important it was. Am I making sense?"

Galina's eyes were wide. Her breath was coming in short gasps. "I do not know what to say."

"Say you understand. Say you love me, anyway." He leaned forward, his face in his hands.

"Of course I love you." She grasped herself against his back, her slim fingers digging at his shoulders. "But why did you have to 'kill Americans'?"

He turned to look into the girl's face; the lamplight over her shoulder outlined her short, black hair, framing her pale face; she blinked her wide blue eyes. "Galina, we are the first line of the Russian military . . . we go in ahead of all other forces when our leaders give the order. We are the most respected in the world of what they call 'Special Forces' . . . our job is 'assassination', 'demolition', and 'reconnaissance'—if you know what they are." Her mouth was open; speechless; her eyes blinking. The young officer took a deep breath and went on. "All I can say is that in America we surprised and destroyed our opponents to accomplish our mission." He straightened up and looked at her. "Our commander, Colonel Golubko, was a tremendous leader . . . we would not have gotten out of there, otherwise." Gennady hesitated for a moment. "But all the time he tells us that women are 'problems' for career military officers." Galina was frowning; he went on in a hurry. "I do not believe him, of course, nor do the other fellows. You should have seen some of them go after those Cuban girls on the beach at Havana!"

"You went to the beach with Cuban girls?"

"Ah . . . one day we went to the beach and they were there."
He touched the tip of her upturned nose. "Terenty and I just lay in
the sun while the others chased the women." *I will not tell her
about the fight on the beach and being taken away by the police
wagon.*

Galina looked into his face and saw pride in whatever it was
he and his comrades had done. It was then the young woman
understood she no longer held the military in contempt. But she
was sure he had not told her everything that had happened while
they were in America.

"Oh! I almost forgot!" Galina gave him a quick kiss and
swung off the sofa. "I will be right back!" In a minute she
returned with a packet of papers. "I got this from the 'Ministry of
Education'."

Gennady read the letter. "You are invited to *Iran?*"

"They may want me to go with a group of teachers . . .
culture and friendship, they call it."

"You are going?"

"I have not yet been officially accepted, but I hope I can go. I
have never been out of Russia."

"I will miss you."

"I would not be gone for long. Only a few weeks this
summer."

He pulled her to him for a long, liquid kiss; at the same time
his hand felt up her back to the little hooks. Galina stiffened. "No
. . . not until we are married—remember?"

With a grin he pointed to the gold band. "*There* is the ring . . . it
is on your finger, already!"

She pulled it off with an exaggerated tug and rustled about
on the sofa for the little velvet box. "Tomorrow, we will go to the
'Marriage Registrar'. It takes a month to get everything in order."

"A month, you say? How did you know that?"

"I have always hoped—" Galina pulled her angular arms
around his neck and pressed her mouth to his. She stifled a
sudden yawn with a sleepy smile. "Tomorrow is a big day. For
now, *you* sleep here on the sofa. I am going to bed—*my* bed . . .
alone!"

216

* * *

Ninoy Aquino International Airport; Manila, the Philippines:

The 747 braked to a stop before the freight terminal and the pilot cut the engines. Norbert Ezego stretched and reached for his briefcase. God, was he stiff and tired—hardly any rest since leaving Lagos two days ago, and now, here he was—out here in the western Pacific in the Philippines.

From several rows of seats behind him came stirrings as the turbaned young man and the half-dozen others with him gathered their things. Fortunately, one of them spoke passable English, so he was able to speak sensibly with the man he would be ferrying to the port of Cogayan, on the northwest coast of the island of Mindanao, in the south of the country of many islands. Further inland, they would deliver the supplies to a recruiting and training camp in the countryside of "U's" new operation, just getting organized down there.

And from what he had already learned, the potential for the Organization in the rural southern Philippine islands was immense. Not only that, but there was talk of setting up a camp still farther south, in Indonesia, a mostly-agricultural country with plenty of places to conceal secret activities. All this, of course, would mean more financial gain for the Cartel, with political advantages, as well, since many of the local governments down there were sympathetic to revolutionary movements.

The very black man looked out the window. Down on the pavement, the procession of trailer trucks was pulling up alongside the airplane right on schedule; already grounds-crewmen were positioning a scissors elevator alongside the rear cargo door; from down on the main deck, came the staccato sputter of the forklift swinging into action. Ezego nodded at the men in the rear of the cabin; all moved toward the stairwell, then back through the main cargo deck, stacked high with small crates suitable for pack animals.

According to the plan, there would be a short drive by truck to the Manila docks, then a journey of some days on a freighter through the islands to Cogayan. After a train trip, a pack animal caravan would haul the goods through the jungle to the new training grounds in the middle of Mindanao Island, in the far south of the vast island chain.

In the blistering morning sun the African stepped across the pavement, through waves of heat, toward the freight office where he would send a cablegram to Retchko. His boss would be pleased to know that he and "U's" relative and the other men had arrived in the Philippines with the armaments and supplies they had picked up in Pyongyang and that they would soon be on their way south.

They would unload the 747 quickly; it would return to Lagos to get Retchko, along with the weapons from Cuba and the satellite dish equipment. In Sudan, the cargo jet would pick up "U" and his associates, then fly to Teheran, and on to Islamabad. In the Pakistani capital, they would join-up with the translator Ahmed, who was flying-in by special permission from the Libyan government to meet them. From there, the men and the goods would go overland to Tora Bora, where "U's" construction batallion had about completed refurbishing the big under-mountain caves that would be headquarters for the upcoming operations, and where they would set up the satellite controls, deep underground.

* * *

Tverskaya District, Moscow; the Next Day:

"You can have the registrations and the church weddings on the same day?" Vera Kuznetsova leaned over her daughter's shoulder as Tamara, Terenty, Galina and Gennady all sat around the kitchen table, reading and talking about the requirements for Moscow weddings. "It is more complicated than last time—" The woman reddened and put her hand to her mouth in embarrassment. It would be Tamara's second wedding ceremony.

218

Terenty looked up at the girl's mother and laughed. "I am honored she has selected me to spend the rest of her life with her."

"Actually, Terenty selected *me!*"

Little Larisa climbed up onto Terenty's lap. "I believe we all selected each other," he said, rubbing his hand through her downy-blonde hair. The child reached her arm around his neck and put her thumb into her mouth.

As Galina watched the little scene between Terenty and Larisa, maternal instincts welled up in her taut bosom—the upcoming marriage could offer her children of her own.

Vera Kuznetsova leafed through the stapled, mimeographed pages. "I see the 'Department of Registrations' requires a month of waiting."

Galina held Gennady's hand. "For us, our waiting period started today."

Tamara spoke up. "The priest said he has a time for the church wedding that same afternoon. He says that does not happen very often . . . usually people have to wait several days before a church wedding can take place, and the official registration has to happen first. For us, it will all be on the same day."

Terenty looked at Gennady. "Now, we have to tell the colonel."

"Your commanding officer?" Tamara's father frowned. "Are you concerned about what he will say?"

"He sees women as distractions from our duties." Terenty nodded at his friend's remark.

"Oh!" Galina straightened, as if to change the subject. "One of the neighbors down our hallway is moving, soon." Her eyes were bright. "I will talk to the Rent Committee and see if you and Tamara can live there."

"I am sure there is already a waiting list," Vera Kuznetsova said. Terenty got the impression the woman would prefer that he and his bride should stay with the parents.

Terenty took a deep breath, glanced around at Gennady and stood up. "I guess we had better go see the colonel.

* * *

219

"Getting married? Both of you?" Rodion Golubko's eyebrows were up; behind his glasses the silver-haired man's eyes bulged more than ever. "Do you two not *ever* do things like you are supposed to?" His pale hands gripped the edge of his desk; the purple vein on his temple stood out. "Who *are* these . . . these— *women?"*

"Comrade colonel, sir, they have never interfered with our duties," Terenty went on before the older man could react further. "Let us tell you about them."

The young officers in turn told the older man about the two young women. "Believe us, sir, we can perform our duties while we are married."

"It is difficult, though," the colonel said, seeming to measure his words, "I know—because I was married at one time."

The younger men were surprised. *"You were married?"*

"My wife died young . . . in childbirth. The baby died, also. After that, I put everything into my duties to the country."

"I had no idea." Gennady shook his head, as did Terenty. This added a whole new dimension to the man.

"Very well, I can see you two are serious about this. We . . . that is—the others in the group and myself—are invited?"

"Comrade colonel, we would be honored."

"Perhaps I can do something for you." A grin flickered across his face. "You need limousines? A honeymoon spot?"

"We had thought of that, but with things like they are right now in Russia, we were not—"

Rodion Golubko held up his hand. "I have 'connections' to the senior officer's automobile pool," the colonel interjected, "I can secure all the big black cars you want—with drivers, even!" The mouths of the two grooms-to-be dropped as the man went on, "I also have access to a *'dacha'* in the country for your honeymoons. I will arrange leave for both of you to get . . . ah, *'acquainted'*—with your new wives."

"Colonel, I . . . we—do not know what to say."

"Consider it a reward for a job well done in America. You two deserve it." He leaned back in his chair and clasped his hands behind his head; his eyebrows raised. "You should know that the information Glinka brought back was more vital even than they first realized. It puts us years ahead of the Americans with the invisible technology." The man nodded. "You two were an important part of that."

"Thank you, sir."

"One more thing: I have put in for promotions to 'Major' for both of you. It was supposed to be a secret, but I will tell you, now. More rubles, better housing. The others are getting promotions, also."

Terenty told the man about the possible arrangements at the apartment building.

"All right, then you can use the allowance for the rent."

The man stood. "Well comrades, I am glad you two came here to tell me this in person . . . let me be the first to give my congratulations." He put out his hand to both, shaking them. Saluting, the younger officers turned and took their leave .

* * *

Vera Kuznetsova's hands were at her face. Tamara and Galina gaped at the young men. Vasily Kuznetsov stared at the grooms-to-be, then at his friend, "Comrade Renko", from down the corridor, who was visiting. "You say your *commanding officer* will have a honeymoon 'dacha' for you in the country? Limousines? Housing allowances?"

"Promotions, even!" Terenty tapped the table with his fingertips.

"And he wants to come to the weddings . . . along with the rest of our unit."

Tamara's mother glanced at a list in her lap. "Oh, dear, we must prepare more food!"

"Oh!" Galina spoke up as if she had just remembered something, with a look at Tamara and Terenty. "While you were gone, I spoke with the head of the Rent Committee, and he will put you at the head of the list for the vacant apartment."

Tamara's mother was fidgeting. "We must get started on the dresses and the shoes—"

Gennady glanced at Terenty with a grin. "I am almost glad we will be training until then."

-10-

Central Mindanao; the Philippines:

Norbert Ezego wiped the sweat from his forehead; the heat and humidity in this swampy, insect-ridden jungle was, if anything, worse than it had been back in Nigeria—which was saying a lot. Since their arrival yesterday after four days on the slow steamer, then the train ride, followed by two days of trying to balance on the back of a swaying mule while branches and saplings slapped in his face as he rode along in the caravan of fifty pack animals to this godforsaken place, the very dark man had been trying to adjust to the soggy climate; so far, without much success.

But the weapons and the other supplies had gotten here in good order; already the men had stowed-away everything in the camouflaged bunkers hacked-out of the jungle canopy. And "U's" relative and his men were busy signing-up new recruits, some of whom were already waiting for them when they got here; from the looks of things, there would be plenty of manpower to get the training program started. A dozen or so Afghans—Talibans, plus interpreters, all experienced in irregular warfare—were already here when Ezego and the others had arrived. Now that they were supplied, the real business of training the recruits could get underway.

The African stepped out onto the porch of the sapling-built shelter and looked around. This place, far removed from any habitation, was the perfect cover for what they would be doing; they could even fire medium-sized weapons here without anyone else knowing about it. Dense greenery overhead would prevent any observation from the air and at least the men would not have to endure direct sunlight down here in the perpetual shade of the jungle floor. Amazingly, in one section among the trees were several storefront-style buildings the early arrivals had constructed. When he had asked, "U"'s relative had told him, through a translator, that they would be used for training the men in urban warfare.

"Hot, is it not?" One of the bi-lingual trainers, his handkerchief busy at work, came up the low steps onto the unsteady floor of the hut, elevated about a meter above the ground, "to keep out the dragons," as one of the natives had put it. Ezego guessed the "dragons" were snakes. Or worse yet, the giant lizards about which he had heard. He hoped he would not meet up with any of them.

As they stood, the African's eyes narrowed. Across the way, a *white* man—then another; two of them, together, along with a native-looking man, well dressed—were walking in the direction of the biggest hut, the headquarters of the operation. Ezego pointed. "Who are they?"

"Americans. They have been here several days."

"What are they doing, here?"

"They are learning how to build and explode bombs. Big bombs in cities, like in trucks."

"*Truck bombs in American cities?*"

"They want to learn how to destroy government buildings in America. They are from a place in the middle of that country, I believe. We are training and financing them."

"Who is the other man?"

"He is the head of the local committee."

Ezego was impresed. If these people were training *American* saboteurs, they were indeed thinking big.

"There are others, here, some Middle-Easterners who are training to blow up buildings in other American cities—like 'New York'. *They say they have big plans for New York.*"

The Nigerian took a deep breath. The scope of this setup was far bigger than he had imagined. What would the "Chief" think about this! The man looked around—there was plenty the Organization could do to help these men, who were obviously driven by their ideology *and well-financed*. And of course, this would mean even more payoffs for the Cartel. A surge of anticipation came over the African. For certain, the boss would be pleased with his report.

* * *

Tora Bora Mountains; at the Northeastern Afghanistan-Pakistan Border:

Retchko stood at the upper cave-opening of the mountaintop lair with "U" and followed the man's pointing finger as he and the bearded revolutionary gazed at the razor-edged, pink-hued snow-tops glimmering in the late afternoon sunshine far away in the distance. The fellow said something in his language.

"He says those are the Himalayas," Ahmed the translator relayed to the bald Ukrainian, as the robed man went on talking, "it is disputed territory between Pakistan and India, called *'Kashmir'* . . . he will soon start a campaign there to destroy the Indian influence."

The Organization's Chief of Security nodded; the upcoming actions would mean new business for the growing Cartel—and for his secret Cayman accounts.

"U" spoke rapidly, at the same time gesturing for the men to go back inside. Ahmed repeated the man's words. "Satellites can spot people from space, but not from inside the mountain."

As they made their way down a hollowed-out tunnel, lighted by electric bulbs strung along the stony corridors, they passed room-after-room where technicians, recruited from affiliated cells in Europe that were already in operation—mostly from northern Germany, Retchko had learned—were busy installing the electronic equipment they had brought from Nigeria. Stopping for a moment to watch, Retchko recognized satellite transmitters and receivers the American had brought from the United States, along with a row of equipment racks of chip-implant sending and receving devices that were going in. Other workmen were uncrating the dish-domes that would be camouflaged to look like boulders when they were set in place outside.

"We want to implant the chips in the men as soon as possible," Retchko said to Ahmed, who relayed his words to the robed man.

The fellow said something in reply. "He says the doctor who will do the procedures will arrive tomorrow from Islamabad."

Farther down several flights of stone steps, the men came to a dormitory-like space. The bearded man said something to Ahmed. "This is for the workmen. Our quarters are on a lower level."

As they kept descending into the mountain hideaway, down narrow stone stairs, from time-to-time, as the men passed an open hole in the wall, a current of air came over them as they went by. "Those are ventilation tunnels," Ahmed said, in response to another comment by "U", "fresh air is essential to the men's health." Retchko shook his head in amazement; these men seemed to have thought of everything.

On one level the men passed by a larger-than-average hollowed-out room fitted with tables and chairs. On the opposite stone wall was a display of religious icons, none of which made any sense to the athiest Ukrainian. "The cafeteria," Ahmed said, responding to what "U" had told him.

In a closed-door room stood a pair of dynamos connected to thick electrical cables; the ends of their shafts turned in their massive housings. From out of one end of each generator a rotating shaft ran into a narrow horizontal tunnel.

The translator relayed "U's" words. "The electricity is from hydroelectric turbines, using heated snow outside as a water-power source. Diesels take-over when snow-levels are low."

A couple of levels farther down, a young, turbaned, brown-skinned man pushed open a copper-colored door. Beyond it, were other doors along a stone corridor that was well-lighted by bulbs strung from the overhead. "These are the quarters," Ahmed said.

Retchko stepped into a compact room, dominated by a wooden bedstead; a Persian rug covered most of the rocky floor. His luggage was already there. The cave's transformation since he was here the first time, he thought, was incredible.

* * *

Central Mindanao; the Philippines:

"You say there are *three* Americans, here?" Norbert Ezego's eyebrows were up. Across the lunch table, the native wife of the well-dressed *'Filipino'* he had seen earlier, the man whom he had learned was the second-in-command of a paramilitary group working with "U's" organization, had just delivered some interesting information.

The woman leaned across the table and spoke again in a low voice. "They tell me that one of the men—the fellow with the big eyeglasses—is learning how to explode trucks at American government buildings in the middle of the United States. The other man seems to be someone he knows. The third man is another American who lives here in the islands. He brags that he has connections to some Middle-Eastern people with lots of money to spend on weapons and things like that."

Ezego thought fast: should he approach these Americans—or were they amateurs better left alone? He decided to play it safe; before long, one way or the other, they would tip their hands. He was fast learning that this place was swarming with all kinds of people, all bent on becoming irregulars or paramilitaries for one cause or another. He knew that some would succeed; some would not. At any rate, the prospects for the Organization were looking better all the time.

There was a tap on his shoulder. Turning about, "U's" relative and the translator were looking down at him. "When you are finished, come to my office." The man spun about in military fashion and strode away with the other man tagging along at his heels.

"I will talk with you, later." Ezego dropped his napkin and arose, nodding at the woman who had been a gold mine of information—probably without her realizing it, the Nigerian thought.

Outside, stepping along through the shadowy world that was the training camp, the stocky man thanked his stars for not having to spend any time in the direct sunlight.

At the biggest elevated hut, Ezego climbed a low-ladder, pushed aside a muslin curtain and stooped through the opening into a reedy conference room built of saplings and other woven foilage. Around a cane table sat "U's" relative and the three white men, along with the translator.

The Middle-Easterner voiced some words. "We will refer to everyone here with a shortened name," the interpreter said, motioning to a slight man—not yet middle-aged, Ezego judged—who wore oversized, dark-rimmed glasses. "This is 'T—'"

The fellow stood, almost losing his balance for a moment when his bamboo chair got caught in the matted floor. Ezego shook his hand, noting the American's grasp was limp. From the way the foreigner blinked his eyes all the time and kept rubbing his hands together, then on his pants, the African got the impression the American was suffering from nerves.

"This is 'E—'." The man motioned to Ezego, "and "M—'." The interpreter gestured to the second of the three white men, a younger, taller fellow compared to the first. "And, finally, we have 'J—', who lives here in the islands." The third man, a little older than the other two, rose unsteadily on his feet, his hand outstretched. But he missed Ezego's proffered hand on the first try, finally making solid contact on his second attempt. The African dismissed this individual at once; the fellow was inebriated *(on drugs?)* and obviously too unstable to trust.

Over the next hour, as the men talked, to Ezego the question as to whether or not to make an offer to the Americans resolved itself—none made any impression on him; on the contrary, if they were to somehow succeed with their plan to blow up a United States Government building in the middle of America, it would be as a result of sheer luck and not much else, he decided. Even then, Ezego thought it unlikely they could cover their tracks well enough to keep the authorities from catching up with them. The Organization needed people with more intellectual promise and operational savvy than these unlikely bumblers could offer. If their so-called "financial backers" wanted to bankroll them; fine. But he would not promise any of the Cartel's money or support to these men.

* * *

Tora Bora; Two Days Later:

"Did everyone get their implant?" Retchko, standing in the dining-room of the rocky redoubt, watched as the last of "U's" men shuffled from the subterranean cutaway, holding a bandaged wrist.

The doctor said something in his own language as he stowed his gear in a black leather bag. The man nodded at the translator, who repeated the words in Russian. "He says he has implanted all the men who were on the list—including the big man, himself."

At first the general had been surprised "U" had wanted to have the procedure on his own arm, until the man had told him that should there ever be a need for his men to find him were he to be kidnapped or lost, the satellite could pinpoint his location to a few meters anywhere on earth. When the Head of Security had pointed out his enemies could also use the same system to find *him*, the bearded leader had dismissed the possibility with the logic that before long his organization would be so strong as to make such a thing impossible. At least the Middle-Easterner had plenty of self-confidence, Retchko thought. Such a positive attitude could carry him a long way.

The Pakistani physician narrowed his eyes at the Ukrainian. "Do *you* have an implant?

"Yes," Retchko lied.

Before the doctor had a chance to pursue the subject further, the bald European turned away toward rocky steps, followed by Ahmed the interpreter.

In the electronics center, right away he saw that the technicians had made headway with the installation of the gear; already, little lights were blinking in the equipment racks.

A workman caught sight of the newcomers and stood up, saluting. "Ah, Comrade General, we are ready to test the relay through the satellite to Nigeria," he said. Retchko remembered the fellow was East German, still in the mental orbit of the Communists, he guessed, although the Party was now "officially" gone in that unfortunate, re-united country. *But not really re-united, he knew. Not yet, anyway.*

Another man moved some switches; in the racks more instruments started coming to life. Several monitor screens lit up.

The fellow called out; two more men came into the space and took seats before consoles. With a nod, one of the technicians moved another switch and pressed a series of buttons on his console. Indicator lights began flashing on the face of one of the cabinet components; then more lights on other instruments in the room took up the beat. As Retchko looked on, wide reels on a tape machine began turning.

One of the men called out something; another fellow reached for a knob and made an adjustment.

"They are transmitting," Ahmed said.

All the men were staring at their consoles and monitor screens. After about a minute, the tape machine stopped; reels on a second tape recorder began moving. Then the flickering lights went out and a needle in a big dial stopped moving. There came a noticeable relaxing of tension; men began nodding, looking around at each other; a couple of them were smiling.

The man who seemed to be in charge said some words to Ahmed. "The test is a success. A reply came back from Nigeria through the satellite link," the young Libyan relayed to the general.

* * *

Tanuta Refinery Satellite Receiving Station:

"They are transmitting!" Lisa Anaya called out to Larry Landay, who stood before an equipment rack, chronometer in hand. "Strong signal!"

"Exactly on time!" The American focused on the sweep-hand of the time-piece.

The young woman pressed a button and a tape machine came on. "One minute . . . stop!"

Larry moved a switch; most of the lights on the rack went out. "Transmission ended!"

The young woman turned to the blond associate. "Well, it looks like we are in business."

"Yes, but I wish I knew what the 'business' really is and where the other station is located."

"Retchko said not to ask questions."

* * *

229

Buzzy Habbler fumbled for the nightstand light switch; the telephone beside the teenager's bed was ringing. In the blaze of sudden light, he lifted the receiver. "Hello . . . ?" An excited adolescent voice crackled from the other end. As the earpiece squawked on, the young man sat up; his eyes wide; a grin on his face. "They have a strong signal through the satellite, you say—from *southern Asia,* this time? You're sure it's the same people?"

* * *

Central Mindanao; the Philippines; the Next Day:

"You want to learn bombing techniques?" The eager-looking, just-arrived young Filipino sitting across the table from Norbert Ezego nodded to the question through the interpreter.

Shouts came from the outside; the black man glanced out the open side window of the bamboo hut at some sweating recruits in their first day of basic training on the parade ground.

The Cartel's emissary looked at the expectant newcomer and spoke to the translator. "Tell him we will have some Chechen explosive experts here in a few days." The third man passed the African's remarks to the young native Filipino. Ezego motioned toward the parade ground. "But he must first learn the basics."

The fellow, still nodding, arose and stepped through the cloth curtain to the porch, then down to the outside to join the other young revolutionaries.

Out on the broad matted forest floor not far away, one of the Afghan trainers was shouting at some recruits, who were trying to follow his directions after a translator had repeated the orders in their several languages. Ezego watched, wincing, at the speeded-up-then-hesitating cycles of motions the trainees were going through in the steamy jungle. At this rate, it would take a long time to whip these raw recruits into a cohesive force, he thought, but at least everybody was trying. He pulled out his well-used handkerchief and wiped the sweat from his face.

The curtain parted again. "Ah, it is the 'cousin'," Ezego nodded, using the nickname he had given to "U's relative, as the trim, swarthy fellow took the seat just vacated by the recruit.

230

"I have a message from my cousin," the young man said, waving a sweat-dampened piece of paper in the humid air, "it came from Davao through wireless and runner."

"Davao is two-hundred kilometers away . . . it must be important."

"He wants us to go to Indonesia." The revolutionary stood and turned to an old-looking, large-scale map thumb-tacked to the bamboo wall. "We will be going . . . 'here'—" He pointed to an island labeled, *'Celebes'*. "They now call it *'Sulawesi'*, he said. "We will travel by freighter to Makassar . . . the training camp is ninety kilometers to the northeast." The man indicated a spot on one of the legs of the big, oddly-shaped island east of Borneo that reminded Ezego of a mis-shapen scorpion. "It will take us about a week to get there," he went on, through the translator, "two days by mule, four days at sea . . . then another day to travel to the camp." The bearded young man gestured at the cloth-covered doorway. "We will leave late this afternoon."

* * *

Tverskaya District, Moscow; Six Days Later:

"They say we can be married *this* Saturday!" Terenty waved a paper. "These are the orders."

"Oh, dear—" Vera Kuznetsova fanned her face with a notebook, gaped at her daughter, then at the young men. Larisa leaned back in Terenty's lap, her thumb in her mouth. The older woman was shaking her head. "We have not yet finished your dresses."

"We can borrow the neighbor's sewing machine." Tamara looked into Terenty's eyes. "But why—*how* did they speed it up? It takes a month to go through the registration process."

Gennady leaned over and patted her shoulder. "Connections, my lovely comrade . . . connections."

Terenty flipped the official-looking paper through his fingers. "Our colonel told the commanding general of the school and it happened in a hurry."

"Colonel General Krolov called us into his office this morning and told us he could supply all the food and drink, and that he and some other officers could attend the weddings."

"He said we can use a government pavilion for the party."

"And the limousines—many limousines."

Galina ran her fingers across Gennady's shoulder. "But why are they doing all this for us?"

"I guess they want to think that the country is back to normal." *But he knew the real reason.*

* * *

Sulawesi Island, Indonesia; the Next Day:

The translator leaned forward; the older man in the white robe and cap was gesturing; his rasping voice hung heavy in the equatorial southwest Pacific humidity. "He says he is pleased you are here and is looking to work with you in his plans." The bearded individual said a few words more, then came the translation. "He has funding through Middle-Eastern sources and wishes to establish a training camp here for young men dedicated to his cause."

Ezego was frowning. "Ask him to explain to me what is his 'cause'."

The young fellow who was acting as the go-between for the African and the religious leader spoke to the older man, who said some more words in his own language, nodding at the Organization's emissary.

"They will disrupt the social order in Indonesia by selective bombings of tourist and government places. Already there is much sympathy among the people to do this . . . eventually, he will send men who are trained here and in the Philippines all over the world to function as suicide bombers."

"They will blow-up themselves?"

After some words the young fellow turned to the African. "They consider it a high honor to do so."

Ezego had never before been with people who seemed to think it was better to be dead than alive. If that were true, the

232

process would require a steady supply of new recruits, which would, of course, mean more training, more supplies—and, in the end—more profits for the Cartel. Maybe there was something to be said for religious suicide.

Ezego looked around; the setup in this place was quite similar to the one they had left back in central Mindanao except that there was no jungle canopy overhead; here he would have to get used to the everlasting sun shining down on the open drill-fields and the huts during the long hours of daylight. Even where they now sat, underneath an open, thatched-roof bamboo pavilion, the dark-skinned visitor was already sweating; he pulled out his handkerchief and put it to work.

The older man was again speaking. Turning to the African, the translator repeated the man's words in English. "He says They will require supplies in the form of automatic weapons, plastic explosives, and bomb-making materials, plus training for the recruits, as in Mindanao. He says he is hearing good things about what is happening in the Philippines, and he wants to do the same thing in Indonesia."

Across the way, a local trainer was leading a ragtag-looking squad of men in calesthentics; their grunts matched the cadence of their movements. But as Ezego could see, they were a long way from becoming any sort of effective force. The Organization's man smiled to himself: they would need *everything* over a long period of time. At a price, of course.

* * *

Tverskaya District, Moscow; the Following Saturday:

"Do you wish to marry?" The well-dressed, slightly-heavyset woman stood behind a dark-oak table. There was a shuffling of shoes on the marble floor as others of the party moved closer. The young people glanced at each other, then looked back at her. The woman beheld first one and then the other beaming, yet nervous, couple standing before her. Over the years she had observed these same expressions on thousands of faces.

"*Da—*" The four said the word together.

233

The woman nodded at the group; she had not observed such a scene since Brezhnev. For there were about a dozen military officers in the party, and from their insignia, she knew that some of the older-looking men were of high rank. The grooms wore dress uniforms, also. They had all arrived in a procession of black government limousines the likes of which she had not seen since the glory days of the Soviet Union. It had all started when an officer of the Defense Ministry had come by the other day and insisted the twin ceremonies take place *this* Saturday, for some reason or another. She had had to re-schedule a half-dozen other weddings to accomodate the official's demands.

The matronly-looking registrar nodded at a young woman off to the side at another table. A scratchy symphony sounded from the speaker of a record player; Gennady recognized the piece as the *'March of Mendelssohn'*.

As the echoing strains of the orchestra soared around the high-ceilinged room, Terenty glanced about at the big, brightly-lit space with its overhead crystal chandeliers and golden light sconces along the gilded marble walls. Substantial-looking, varnished double-doors led away to other wedding halls. Out of the corner of his eye he spotted Galina's mother, whom he had just met this morning when she arrived by train in the city. The trim widow looked remarkably young for her age, he thought. A nervous thrill ran through him; he could feel Tamara's arm entwined in his as they stood before the official. At some point in the music her fingers squeezed his forearm. Terenty looked down for a moment at the red carpet upon which they were standing; it was hard for him to believe he was actually here in this place he had heard of many times to register his own marriage. Next to him stood Galina; Gennady was at her right. The dark-haired cousin's rapturous face was bathed in a beam of light shining down from above.

The woman nodded at the couples. "You may now exchange rings." At the same time Terenty slid the little gold band from Cuba on Tamara's third finger of her right hand, Gennady was doing the same with Galina's. Then the brides placed rings on the young men's fingers.

"You may now kiss each other." With self-conscious grins, the four matched lips with their respective new spouses.

As she stood there behind them, Vera Kuznetsova wiped a tear from her eye, then reached for her husband's hand. The other military officers glanced around at each other with the smirks reserved by young men everywhere for such an occasion. General Krolov stood attention, a pleased look on his weathered face; Colonel Golubko likewise stood straight, betraying no emotion.

The woman opened a large book and pointed at a page. "You may now register your marriages with the authorities."

In turn, the four signed the book-bound forms.

The general stepped forward and with a big hand put his signature, "Antonin Krolov" on the line for witnesses; Rodion Golubko did the same.

"Best wishes on your marriages," the woman said, closing the book.

She gestured to the young female assistant who scurried out one of the big varnished wooden doors to inform the next wedding party they would be ready for them in a few minutes.

One of the officers stepped forward with flowers he handed to Tamara and a bouquet to Galina.

The general nodded at his adjutant, standing in the back of the room, who came up with a bottle of champagne as another aide handed out glasses. General Krolov hoisted his glass, bowing to the young women as a flashbulb went off. "A toast to the brides!"

As they were leaving, Gennady had a fleeting glance of the general talking to Galina's mother; the senior military officer, his gold-braided hat under his arm, was shaking her hand; the woman was smiling.

Moscow Review, Monday, May 4:

**Residents of the Tverskaya District were treated
Saturday to the spectacle of a ceremony that was
almost like the pageant-filled days of Leonid Brezhnev.**

235

In the afternoon, a caravan consisting of a dozen or more very black limousines drove up to the Orthodox church on the Garden Ring Road and unloaded their cargoes of important-looking military officers, all in the finest tradition.

Almost lost in the uniformed pagentry were the two brides, who led the others into the little church. After a while, the bells started ringing, and the brides and grooms, along with the military types, got back into their cars with the priest waving his holy water dispenser at them.

Neighbours said they had not seen anything like it in years.

At the Academy; One Week Later:

"Well, I trust you two had—*(ahem)*—'successful' honey-moons." Colonel Golubko gave a wry grin as Terenty and Gennady stepped into his office, past the other young officers who were already there. One or two gave knowing smirks as the newly-minted grooms sat down.

"Most successful, sir."

The colonel called for all the young men in the crowded room to listen-up. "'Comrade Majors'—I am pleased to say that, with your new promotions—it is now time for us to get back to work."

"'Da', Comrade Colonel!" All the younger voices spoke as one.

The senior officer pulled down a map. "Recognize this?" He aimed a pointer at the large, colorful chart. "It is, of course, the place where the *'Great War'* started in nineteen-fourteen. These are *'The Balkans'*. Comrades, we will be going . . . *'there'*—" The officer tapped the pointer at a particular spot. "'*Sarajevo'*, to be exact. Our mission will be to seize the airport."

To Terenty, it sounded like an easy assignment until the colonel went on. "The airport is occupied by unfriendly reactionary forces . . . we know the Americans also want the airport . . . we must take and hold it before they do."

One of the men spoke up. "Sir, *why* is it important?"

"The question is not for us to ask. It was a political decision at the highest levels." Colonel Golubko looked around at the men. "We will join with other units and will practice parachute warfare for the mission." He gestured at the door. "Draw your gear . . . we will be training at the airport, today. The mission is set for four mornings from now."

* * *

United States Navy Aircraft Carrier in the Adriatic Sea; The Same Day:

"All right, listen up!" The United States *'Navy Seals'* commander stood at the front of the pilot's ready room where the mixed Special Forces group was assembled, popping a pointer in his palm. Around the enclosed steel space sat a couple of dozen men in comfortable leather chairs usually reserved for pilots; more men in combat fatigues stood around the bulkheads. The fit-looking man pulled down a map and tapped the pointer at a place on it. "Gentlemen, this is the objective: the airport at Sarajevo . . . we will make a parachute drop at dawn and take it." He nodded at another officer who came forward.

"Thank you, Commander Wicker . . . this is the operational plan." The Navy Lieutenant pulled down a second map. "Our force will consist of a 'Task Unit' of forty 'Navy Seals' and a platoon of *'Army Rangers'*, backed by forty-four *'Marine Recon'* troops—"

The officer held up from speaking as the ship leaned over in a steep, shuddering tilt. The deck heaved, sending a notebook from an officer's knee-desk onto the deck; the speaker at the front lunged by rote to maintain his stance; the hulking flattop, plunging into a long swell at flank speed, was turnng into the wind to launch planes. The deck straightened; with a distant roar and a thump from the flight deck directly above them, the supercarrier catapulted an *'F-14'* of its "Combat Air Patrol" off the flight deck, followed by another.

"As I was saying, gentlemen, our objective is the airport at Sarajevo." The officer tapped the map depicting the runway of the airport. "Right now, the airfield is occupied by local irregulars, so there should be little opposition—we will effect a quick takeover of the objective. *'Zero Hour'* will be at zero-six-thirty, local time, four mornings from now."

* * *

Dyagilevo Air Base, Ryazan, Russia; 2:35 AM; Four Days Later:

The *'IL-76MD Heavy Lift Airborne Troop Transporter'* lifted from the *'Dyagilevo'* runway, outside of Moscow, and turned onto a south-southwesterly heading.

Gennady Lychin squirmed around in the plain bucket seat; wearing full battle gear, like the forty-seven other Spetsnaz troops on board, he would have to make himself as comfortable as possible for the three-hour direct flight to Sarajevo. The landing at the objective airfield was set for zero-four-hundred hours, local time. A half-hour earlier, they had watched as two other military lifters, painted in commercial colors, had taken off for Sarajevo carrying long-term supplies for the occupation. The airplanes would land after the Special Forces had secured the airfield.

Although Gennady knew he and the others were ready for the mission, he was already homesick for his wife. As the airplane droned on, his mind once more brimmed with the recollections of the wedding and the honeymoon week at the country estate that was so spacious he and Galina never saw Terenty and Tamara, who were also there.

After the church ceremony, he and his bride had ridden around Moscow in the limousine for three hours, until the early evening, visiting historic places in the city, in the Russian tradition. At the same time, Terenty and Tamara were doing the same. What had made their twin ceremonies different from most couples's was that they had had the big government cars and the general's drivers to take them around. Also, at the suggestion of Colonel Golubko, who already knew they would go into immediate training exercises for this mission as soon as they returned from their honeymoons, they had shortened the reception from a standard two-day-long affair to the single all-night program. Even at that, the wedding had caught the attention of the Moscow news media. He patted a newspaper clipping about it in his pocket; he was taking it along on this mission as a connection to his wife.

His thoughts went on. After the ride around the city, they had arrived at the pavilion near the Academy provided by General Krolov. The other officers and the neighbors who had been invited were already there, ready to go after them with all the nonsensical poetry and practical jokes and the dancing that were typical of Russian wedding receptions. The whole thing had gone on until almost the next sunrise, with prodigious quantities of Vodka consumed to the point that some of the guests had turned staggeringly drunk; another Russian tradition. Even Galina's mother had downed her share of adult libations. Interesting too, was how the Academy's commanding general had taken to the young-looking widow, so it seemed.

At long last, still very much awake, he and Galina had arrived by limousine at the senior officers' "dacha" in the wooded countryside some distance outside of Moscow. From the first glance, he had realized the advantages of being an upper-level officer in the Russian military; its manicured grounds and the spacious setting were worlds apart from anything that regular Russian soldiers would likely ever see. Inside, they had been met by white-gloved servants and led to the suite that would serve as the bridal chamber. When he had carried Galina into the room of luxury, they had found their things already in place; the bed was even turned down. As General Krolov had told him at the reception, "Work hard and make the right political moves, comrade, and you can have access to that kind of place all the time."

"I am so happy," Galina had said, kicking her feet in the air, her strappy shoes dropping to the floor as he closed the door and moved the lock with his fingertips while he balanced her in his arms. Even as he had lain her on the satin sheets she had put her arms around his neck, pulling him down. "I have waited all my life," she had whispered in his ear, "for this moment."

Gennady fidgeted in the uncomfortable military aircraft seat, his blood pressure rising, as he remembered that first time with her. From the moment they were alone in the room—in the daylight, no less; the yellow morning sun had beamed in through the lace curtains the whole time as if some wonderous, benevolent muse was watching over them, orchestrating their every move.

He had expected Galina to be timid, perhaps even with tears; in the past she had always stopped him at a certain point, but she resisted not at all and he beheld his bride's entire slender body from her head to her toes for the first time and she looked even more perfect than he had ever imagined she would be and he told her he loved her and she was a willing, learning participant in what happened next . . .

But now, she was back at work teaching the primary grade and getting ready for the big trip to Iran, set for two months from now—for when they had returned, the envelope from the Education Ministry was waiting for her. Until then, he would stay busy with the unit; they would see each other on the weekends, when possible.

When they came back, they found that something else had happened while they were gone. Vera Kuznetsova told them that the day after the reception, the widower Colonel General Krolov had taken Galina's mother, Helen Gavrona, to the railroad station in his personal chauffeured limousine for her to catch the train back to Tula. "As an *'Inspector-General'* of the Army, I will be in Tula in two weeks with General Lebed's troops'," he had said, "would you like to go to theater with me?"

Gennady wondered what it would be like to have his commanding general as his father-in-law.

The young soldier squinted at his watch; in the darkened cabin its radium dial showed about one hour to go until they were over the drop-zone at Sarajevo.

* * *

Across from him, Terenty Suslov was lost in his own thoughts as the big four-engined transport roared on through the night. He knew he must keep focused on the current business; fortunately, this mission should be a quick, easy affair—nothing like the recent mayhem back in America. They would drop onto the Sarajevo airport before dawn, sieze it from the local insurgents, hold it until their regular occupying forces arrived, get back onto the airplane and fly home. At least that was what they had told them at the briefings. He ran and re-ran the operational plan through his mind.

But his new wife and step-daughter were always there. From the start, it had all seemed like a dream; at some point he must surely awaken and find himself back in reality. But it was true: he and Tamara were married!

Terenty squirmed about on the metal bucket-seat trying to get comfortable and returned for the hundredth time in his mind to how it had been.

The pink sky of dawn was glowing over the treetops as the limousine had pulled up at the dacha in the wooded countryside east of Moscow. And the place was enormous; palatial.

"Oh, Terenty, this is beautiful!" the girl had gushed as the ZIL came to a stop in front of the classically-styled Russian mansion. Silver columns of water shot twenty meters into the air above a sculptured fountain out front; formal gardens went off as far as they could see in the vague light of dawn.

A wispy-looking, middle-aged man in formal attire and white gloves stepped from the curb and opened the right rear door. "Welcome to this place!" he said, "I shall take you to your quarters." As Tamara took the man's hand and alighted from the long vehicle, the driver pulled open the left-side rear door. As Terenty stood up, on the other side, the first man looked across the big car and gave the new groom a nodding wink that the bride did not see.

Terenty stepped around and took his new wife's hand; at the same time he gave her a quick kiss to her neck. The newlyweds put their arms around each other's waist and mounted the steps onto a columned portico.

"Right this way," the servant said, opening the French-style doors and nodding at the limousine driver behind them who was carrying their luggage. The troupe stepped into a well-lit, tall-ceilinged foyer surmounted by a massive, lighted overhead crystal chandelier to a red-carpeted staircase with dark-wood balustrades that led up to a second floor landing. Upstairs, they made their way along a red-carpeted corridor with crystal light sconces along the walls to a mahogany door with brass fixtures. "In here," the fellow motioned, moving the handle and pushing the door open for them. The driver stood uncertainly in the corridor for a moment with their luggage. Terenty dug around in his pocket and dropped coins into the two mens' hands.

The driver set the luggage bags on the floor next to an open door of a big closet.

Terenty shook his head. "We can do it ourselves—we will have plenty of time, in here . . ."

The older man and the driver smirked at each other: they knew what the groom had meant. The two turned about and left. The door closed. Terenty reached down and flipped the lock.

"I will be right back," Tamara said, giving him a quick kiss, lifting one of the smaller bags. With a grin and a glance over her shoulder at him, she stepped into the bathroom "It is really nice in here," he heard her say through the closed door.

"This whole place is nice." Terenty pulled off his shoes and socks onto the deep, dark-red carpet. The bed was already turned down—a nice touch, he thought; someone had already anticipated what would soon happen here. Terenty fluffed the pillow, put his hands behind his head, lay back, and looked around at the sumptious suite. Period furniture graced the space; the bed was shiny brass. Above, on the tall, textured ceiling, hung a glittering crystal chandelier; around the rose-colored walls, soft lights glowed from alabaster sconces; classical busts stared out from little lighted alcoves. A fully-stocked bar stood at one end of the room. For a place operated by and for the military, they seemed to have thought of everything, he grinned to himself; it would not take much imagination to picture jowly generals romping with mistresses in this very room.

There was a "click" and the bathroom door cracked open. Tamara peeped out, then stepped into the bedroom, her bare feet stroking the carpet. Terenty's eyes went wide—over the beautiful girl's shoulders draped a diaphanous negligee; as she came toward him, her hands brushed across her chest in a time-honored female ritual; through the window curtains, the morning sunrise caught Tamara's backlit figure's every detail.

She looked him up and down with a wry grin. "You are still dressed?

The two took care of that in a hurry.

The youthful bride lay next to him and gave him an enduring kiss; her splendorous auburn hair flowed down onto his face. As long as he lived, he would never forget those magnificent moments with the exquisite female, now his wife. "Oh, Terenty, be gentle . . ." Tamara had whispered. He had kissed her, caressed her tenderly, held her with great feeling as the beloved young woman came to him for their first time together in the ultimate embrace . . .

Terenty took a deep breath as he thought about the glorious nights and days they had spent at the *'Grand Dacha'*.

* * *

But now it was back to the roaring reality of jet engines; the rush of air against the big military transport; the four-dozen fully-outfitted Spetsnaz troops slouching in their bucket seats, trying to get some rest before the action. Up toward the front of the darkened cabin, Colonel Golubko was leaning back, his eyes fixated in thought—the sensible, competent man would be the leader of the operation to capture the Sarajevo airport.

Terenty dozed. Some time later, when the airplane made a sudden lurch, he snapped awake. Yawning, he looked at his watch: the drop would take place in a little less than hour.

-11-

Aboard United States Navy Aircraft Carrier in the Adriatic Sea; at the Same Time:

As the ship with the iconic name in American history plowed across the central Adriatic, in the glare of floodlights on the supercarrier's vast flight deck the rotors of the four *'Sea Stallion'* helicopters were turning at full power to the screams of their jet engines; the streaking blades howling in the steady wind across the open deck from the flattop's thirty-one-knot forward motion.

High on the "island" structure, inside "Primary Flight"— known to the crew as "Pri-Fly"—the "Air Boss" watched the numbers on the digital clock count to "zero-three-thirty". A buzzer barked; the commander gave the order that resounded from the ship's squawk boxes: "Launch Helicopters!"

Below, the red light on the outer face of the glassed-in control position changed to green; at the same time, high on the upper mast, a white light started blinking a pre-arranged signal to the pair of frigates following along outside the enormous ship's churning wake that turned the black water phosphorescent in the pale rays of the lowering three-quarter moon. The shrieking five-bladed rotors changed to angry *"SNAPPING!"* sounds as the blades twisted to takeoff pitch. First one, then the other three choppers in turn lifted from the deck, hovered a moment, then eased off the portside over the water.

In a minute, the quartet of rotary-winged machines, their navigation lights turned off, using focused-beam lights on their rear fuselages to maintain line-ahead formation, were on a course east-north-eastward. At sunrise—at zero-six-thirty hours—they would drop United States Special Forces paratroopers onto the Sarajevo airport, where they would sieze the airfield from an insignificant number of insurgents who were reported to be there. It should be an easy mission, according to the latest briefings to the men of the mixed force—any opposition would be light to non-existent.

In the lead helicopter, Navy Commander Wicker and his second-in-command synchronized their watches: the flight time to the drop zone at the Sarajevo airport would be three hours.

* * *

Colonel Golubko sent back the word: go to the facilities— better to take care of things now than to be found wanting later. It was standard procedure before a Spetsnaz mission like this. One-by-one the young men groped forward to the lavatory behind the cockpit to relieve themselves.

The airplane had been descending for some time, then it made a sudden turn to the left and straightened. Terenty took a deep breath and caught Gennady's eye in the shadowy gloom of the cabin and gave a thumbs-up gesture that his friend returned. Other fellows of the familiar group looked around at each other, exchanging expectant glances. He made one last check of his equipment: all the straps were tight, everything was it was supposed to be.

The engines slowed some more. Colonel Golubko stood up and spoke in a loud voice. "To the doors!" The men arose and trooped past tied-down vehicles toward the front of the airplane; at the same time the pilot adjusted the aircraft's trim. In a few minutes, all of the soldiers were assembled in position, one behind the other, in two lines at the front end of the deck.

The speed and altitude continued to drop; Gennady opened his mouth to relieve his ears.

Then the two front side-doors opened into the slipstream and the air rushed past with a shriek and a roar of the nearby jet engines that was almost earsplitting. On the front bulkhead of the main deck a red light glowed at them. On the ground, a little smudge of white, then another, came into view. They were starting to move over the Sarajevo airport. "Ready!" the tethered jumpmaster called out.

Then the light turned green. The crewman pulled back a hinged red-and-white barrier and slapped Colonel Golubko on the shoulder. The leader took two quick steps toward the open left-side door and dropped out of sight followed at one-second intervals by the others in the left-side and right-side lines. In less than a minute, all four-dozen paratroops were swinging through the darkness at the lights below them; the landing target was a grassy open space just to the rear of the main terminal building.

Then the ground was rushing up; one-by-one the Russians plopped onto the soft earth. Terenty un-hooked the shroud lines, and, gripping his short-stock AK-74, loped as fast as he could toward a cluster of comrades who had already joined up. In a few minutes all the others were there.

Even as Terenty ran up, Colonel Golubko was issuing silent orders; a squad dashed for the door at the base of the control tower—they must sieze it before anyone could sound an alarm.

Other troops, led by Gennady, dashed into a dimly-lit hangar building that looked to be deserted. From the direction of another hangar came the snap of automatic weapons fire; then all was quiet.

One of the men was pointing upward. "Control tower!" From inside the glassed-in position above them a flashlight signal was blinking that it was now in their hands.

"Tell them to find the switches and turn on the runway lights!" the colonel shouted to one of the men who carried a radio backpack. "Call down the aircraft!"

A couple of minutes later, white lights alongside the runway came up; in the distant blackness, the landing lights of a big aircraft stabbed the sky as the first Russian supply transport swung onto its final approach.

Even as the first of the three "IL-76MD Heavy Lifters" shrieked up to the concrete apron at the rear of the terminal building and cut its engines, out on the runway the second aircraft was dropping to earth. Minutes later, the third screeched down. By the time it had turned off onto the taxiway, the first two transports were already discharging their armed vehicles and other gear off the rear ramps.

In short order, all three airplanes stood empty in the shadowy pre-dawn light; under the colonel's direction, the men and their machines were already deploying around the vast airfield. "Very good work, comrades," the colonel told Terenty and some others standing nearby. The officer looked at the pink sky off to the east; overhead, the sky was turning from black to gray; it was going to be a clear, cool day. He glanced at his watch. "Zero-six-fifteen," he said with a pleased nod, "we accomplished our mission ahead of schedule." The colonel motioned at Terenty. "You and Lychin and the radio operator, come with me . . . we will set up our headquarters in the terminal building. The occupation force will be here by nightfall." He turned and headed toward the glassy structure, backlit by the brightening sky, followed by the three others. Terenty grinned at Gennady and the radioman —all three knew what the others were thinking: *They would be out of this place and headed toward home by tomorrow.* This had been one of their easiest missions, ever.

* * *

Six kilometers to the southwest, the four "Sea Stallions" circled and landed in a sunrise hay meadow. One of the officers ran from one helicopter to another, shouting instructions at the pilots; then he hauled himself back into the first chopper. His and two others lifted off; each aircraft with thirty-four paratroopers aboard. One stayed on the ground, its rotors turning.

Scrambling for altitude, the two flying helicopters headed over a rise toward the airfield. At the chopper that stayed behind; its thirty-four "Marine Force Recon" soldiers were already hopping off—they would infiltrate across country on foot to act as a backup for the first-landers.

In the lead helicopter, the pilot pointed down at the terminal area. "Three aircraft!" he shouted at the force commander, sitting behind him. "There's the drop-zone behind the terminal!"

The three "helos" stood off in a wide circle over the end of the runway, gaining altitude. Two machines moved-in alongside the lead helicopter, then all three turned and made for the airspace directly behind the larger main building that stood-out down below; its expanses of glass reflecting the orange sunrise. Next to it, the trio of four-engine aircraft, now seen as large airliner or transport-types, glinted in the dawn's light.

Rotors roaring, the American helicopters began a pounding pass over the airfield at an altitude of five-hundred meters.

* * *

Hearing the thumping noises that were becoming louder by the second, Rodion Golubko hustled out the rear door of the terminal and joined the others who were looking up and pointing. The four-dozen Russians stared stupefied as dots started dropping out of the ungainly machines roaring over their heads—then appeared the unmistakable puffs of parachutes pulling away from the tiny images, now visible as *men* directly above, swinging under canopies straight toward them.

"Unidentified paratroopers!"

"Defensive positions! Take cover!" Colonel Golubko thrust his fist at the direction of the radio operator. "Broadcast we are under aerial attack!"

Chernenko, the communications officer, turned and ran for the control tower, taking the steps two-at-a-time up the tight inside stairwell—he would use the tower's topside antenna to get more range. In a minute, he had located the cable to the overhead aerial and pulled down its connector, which was the standard type, as he had hoped it would be. In a hurry the young officer connected it to his back-pack transmitter and keyed a message in plain language to theater headquarters. As soon as he was finished, there came back a snappy reply: "Received."

But now from down below came clattering, booming sounds of a gun-battle breaking out.

The first paratrooper had plowed down onto the open grass. Blagron, crouched behind a parked truck, loosed a burst from his AK-74. Red froth sprayed off the man, who never moved.

But other soldiers were dropping onto the concrete closer to the parked Russian airplanes—these men, dodging a furious fusillade of fire, ran for the bulky landing gear of the three big Ilyushin transports and took cover. Terenty peered around the front of a tractor-tug and saw one of the aggressors shouting at his men; others, gripping automatic weapons, were running up. Terenty took aim and fired his Kalashnikov at one of the men who fell onto his face, not moving; then at another aggressor, and at another with the same results. But two dozen were now sheltered behind the parked airplanes' lumpy mounds of wheels.

248

All around the backside of the main building, Spetsnaz troops aimed automatic weapons fire at the pinned-down intruders. Meanwhile, other paratroops were landing farther away.

Inside the nearest hangar, Gennady bounded onto the back of one of the newly-landed weapons carriers and grabbed a 14.5-millimeter cannon, stand-mounted at its rear, as another trooper jumped behind the wheel. Even as the machine careened out of the big open hangar, Gennady let loose with a cannon-burst at a cluster of exposed troops out in the field who were scrambling for non-existent cover. The heavy caliber rounds, intended to bring down aircraft, tore through the men, flinging crimson and pieces of their backpacks into the air. By now, more vehicles had taken up the charge; out at the perimeter of the airfield the enemy—whoever they were—were taking defensive positions and returning fire. Breaking glass sounded from the terminal building.

Gennady's vehicle turned about and blasted away at the men beneath the aircraft; then as aggressor bullets zinged past him, made for a hangar. Inside, the men grabbed their automatic weapons and laid down a continuous fire at the men crouched underneath the airplanes.

* * *

Even as Commander Wicker was still two hundred meters above the ground, he knew things were going terribly wrong—from below, came the stutter of automatic weapons fire. Then he saw them: unknown troops moving about; then a stupendous roar of many weapons assaulted his eardrums. Casting about at the target zone uprushing toward his boots, the American force commander was appalled to observe that all his men who had already landed were sprawled unmoving on the ground in grotesque positions of death.

Who were these enemy shooting at them?

Whoever they were, they were ripping-up the "Navy Seals" who were landing around the parked airplanes—his troops were the dead he had seen from the air. Even as bullets whanged around him, chewing-up chunks of concrete, the American force leader managed to unhook his shroud lines. Gripping his *'M-16'*, he ran for the nearest airliner, a few dozen meters from where he had landed; its big wheels and tires were the only cover in sight. All about, other men, attempting to run the gauntlet of deafening gunfire, were spinning to the concrete, not moving.

Somehow, the Navy commander made it to the relative safety of the airplane's landing gear, even though he knew the respite would be only temporary. For a trio of small armored vehicles were wheeling behind them, raking the men with heavy-caliber fire. More Americans were dropping from fatal gunshot wounds.

* * *

"Quick-time . . . *MARCH!*"

The major leading the two squads of "Marine Force Recon" troops through the woods called his men into a fast trot—sounds of gunfire were coming from the direction of the airport, just over the rise ahead of them. In a couple of minutes, they topped the low hill and charged up to a tall fence at the southwest corner of the airfield that ran off diagonally in both directions. From around the terminal building, where it was obvious a major fire-fight was taking place, loud booming noises rent the morning air; already a blue-gray cloud of gunsmoke was drifting skyward over the central part of the airport, catching the orange rays of the rising sun. Sounds of heavy gunfire seemed to be coming from around three very large airliner-looking aircraft parked on the apron behind the terminal.

"Move it!" The officer motioned to the right—he had spotted a gate about a hundred meters from them. "Let's go!" Keeping to the cover of the woods that came up to the fence, the men thrashed their way along to the gate. The leader pointed at a padlock. "Break it!" A corporal with cutters stepped-up and snipped the latch; it fell aside. In single-file the men side-stepped their way through the narrow opening.

"Get down!" The major had spotted a detachment of soldiers in unknown uniforms ahead, facing away from them. Squirming along in tall grass, they elbowed closer. Whoever they were, they were directing a heavy volume of automatic-weapons fire at some Americans who were pinned-down behind an outbuilding. Across the runway toward the main structures, another ring of the enemy was firing at a squad of American troops who looked to be taking casualties. All across the airfield, concentric circles of the marauding weapons carriers roamed back and forth, directing large-caliber fire at clusters of pinned-down United States "Special Ops" troops.

As the Marines watched, a pair of the mobile machines criss-crossed behind a squad of "Army Rangers" who were hunkered-down behind a shed not far away, raking them with heavy bursts of automatic fire, dropping several.

Just then, from the direction of the terminal building there came an earsplitting *"BOOM!"* that rolled across the landscape, deep and terrible, that drowned out the gunfire. One of the large airplanes had exploded in an orange fireball that was climbing above the height of the terminal's rooftops! Another, then a third ground-shaking blast rocked the landscape as two more big transports blew up, hurling whirling, flaming chunks of the aircraft through the air in all directions!

* * *

Crouching underneath the three airplanes, Commander Wicker and his other Navy Seals had been in a desperate spot: if they stayed there, they would all soon be killed. As the Force Commander, he would have to get the men away from these aircraft to the better cover of the building, forty meters away. But the enemy—*whoever they were, they were damn good*—controlled with heavy fire the space between where they were and the rear doors of the terminal. The officer motioned to one of his men. "Ordnance!" As bullets zipped around him, the corporal, head down, loped behind the fat wheels and tires to the senior officer, who shouted and gestured: "Blow-up the planes!"

The young man hunched-over and made his way back toward the rear of the clustered main landing gear. Using hand signals, he caught the attention of fellow "Seals" behind the two other parked transports. Nodding, the second soldier understood the order: they would explode the airplanes and use the resulting confusion to escape to the building. Commander Wicker knew his "Seals"—experts in close combat—could overpower the defenders no matter who they were, and in any case, they must get out of here—this space behind the airplane's fat tires was a death-trap.

The corporal reached into his backpack and pulled out a reddish-brown, doughy-looking block about the size of a brick that he molded in his hands and stuck onto the bottom of the airplane. Into it he pushed a cap with a thin wire attached to it. Crawling along, unrolling the wire—not easy; as bullets were flying all about him the whole time—he used his hand to affix another, then another—four in all—along the bottom of the hulking fuselage over his head. Then he crawled back between the wheels and stuck the wires into receptacles on a little box. "Ready!" he shouted to the commander.

Underneath the nearby pair of freighter aircraft, two other demolition experts had been doing the same. The troops, who had been watching, looked to the commander. Wicker gave a quick motion: "Go!" The corporal pushed his thumb into a depressed switch on the detonator; they now had ten seconds to get away.

The Americans's sudden dash from underneath the airplanes seemed to catch their opponents off guard—only scattered shots sounded, striking none of the leaping, bounding "Navy Seals".

Just as they dived headlong behind a row of trucks, first one, then the other two enormous transport aircraft exploded in ear-shattering blasts that sent whole sections of their fuselages erupting into the air and all around! With one roaring crash all the windows of the terminal building blew-in from the concussion! As the Americans hunkered-down, their heads covered with their hands, trying to make themselves as small as possible, white-hot chunks of metal slammed against sides of the trucks. In the next second, radiant fireballs climbed off the ground, taking much what was left of the three airplanes with them

* * *

All at once, Gennady saw an astounding sight: the enemy were running in his direction! Before he could react, two-dozen or more soldiers scrambled behind nearby trucks and dropped to the pavement, holding their heads. Startled, he recognized an exercise the Spetsnaz troops practiced in their own training. On impulse he looked out at the nearest airplane just as there came a triple-flash, seconds apart, and all three big Ilyushins erupted into fireballs with concussions that rocked Gennady backwards—out of the way of a big piece of metal, trailing smoke, that went tumbling onto the spot where he had been crouched! Behind him there came a big smashing noise as the whole glassed side of the terminal blew inward. Heavy black smoke and orange flames boiled from the blasted shells of the three bombed airplanes.

Even as the plane pieces were still swirling to the ground, one of the enemy was shouting at his other men who jumped up and ran for a blown-in double-door at the rear of the building. But they were headed straight at the Russians, who were hidden behind vehicles and pallets stacked high with just-unloaded cargo.

The Spetsnaz troops were ready for them. When the shooting had first started, Colonel Golubko had shouted for them to pull out their shovel-weapons. As the enemy stampeded past the truck, Gennady lunged at the nearest man, catching him in his throat with the deadly spade, nearly taking off his head. Before the next enemy could react, Gennady swung the razor-sharp edge of the shovel at the man's neck. The fellow's head lifted from his shoulders and lobbed through the air—his torso, gushing red, staggered forward one step then fell; it's hands opening and closing spasmodically; his automatic weapon clattering to the concrete. A third man, realizing what was happening, tried to stop and turn about, but went limp as the spade drove cleanly through the back of his neck. All around him, other Russians were dealing the same treatment to their surprised opponents, who seemed to have no defense against this sudden eruption of shovel-swinging soldiers.

By now, the Americans had no doubt that their opponents were as skilled as they were—perhaps even more so—and that their tactics were far more vicious than anything they had ever encountered. A few raised their M-'16s but were cut down at once by Kalashnikovs, their weapons skittering to the ground. One-by-one those still standing dropped their automatic weapons and uplifted their hands.

The prisoner who looked to be the detachment's leader uncertainly raised his own hands. Malinovsky stepped up and prodded the man *hard* in his stomach with the stock of his AK-74.

Rodion Golubko, a fierce look on his face, stormed forward and glared at the gasping, doubled-over man. "Stand up!" he shouted in perfect English, jerking high the man's elbows. "Who are you and why are you here?"

I am Commander Wicker . . . United States Navy . . . who are you—?"

"Do not address me in this manner!" The purple vein stood out on the Spetsnaz leader's temple. "You do not belong here!" Colonel Golubko motioned to Blagron and Grishinov, who were standing by, aiming their automatic weapons at the Americans. "We should kill you all!"

Pounding noises coming from somewhere in the distance were becoming louder.

Chernenko ran out the door of the control tower, waving his arms. "Helicopters are coming!"

* * *

—(WIRE SERVICE)—1:14 AM EDT—(BULLETIN) REPORTS OF A GUN BATTLE BETWEEN AMERICAN AND RUSSIAN FORCES AT THE SARAJEVO AIRPORT IN BOSNIA.

* * *

Out by the far fence, the twenty-four soldiers of the "Marine Force Recon" detachment had squirmed through the high grass, their rustling noises drowned-out many times over by the non-stop crashing and booming noises of the pitched battles going on all across the airport. Little-by-little the men had closed-in on the detachment of enemy soldiers facing away from them who had the American "Ranger" unit pinned-down with heavy automatic-weapons fire.

One of the adversaries turned about and spotted the Marines thirty meters behind him and shouted a warning to his compatriots. As they were swinging their weapons around, the Marines opened fire, dropping two on the spot. Looking surprised, the others, seven of them, let their AK-74's drop to the ground and raised their hands, casting nervous glances at the men lying unmoving in the grass.

The American major nodded for some of his men to cover the captives and for others to confiscate their weapons. The Army Rangers who had been under their fire until a few moments ago ran up; their automatic rifles aimed at the captured men.

One of the foreigners spoke some words in a language the Marine major recognized as Russian.

While all this was going on, thumping sounds began coming from beyond the northeastern boundary of the airport. The major searched in the direction of the pounding noises, becoming louder by the second in the concussions of the gunfire going off all across the expanse of the smoke-layered airfield. In the hazy distance, a big helicopter was approaching. The Marine officer motioned to a pair of his riflemen, who took aim at the aircraft that was in now in sight, headed in their direction. The chopper was swinging about a few hundred meters before them as if it was about to land. The American commander hesitated—he did not recognize the type. Then he saw the red star on the side of it. *The helicopter was Russian!*

Just as he was about to order his marksmen to open fire on the big aircraft that was now setting down in a swirling cyclone of dust, *another helicopter*—an enormous machine they had not noticed in all the uproar going on about them—swept straight over their heads at very low altitude, pounded over the Russian 'copter whose rotor blades were still turning, and dropped down some distance away in a violent landing maneuver, even as bullets from somewhere kicked up clumps of grass all around it.

Not sure what was happening, the Marines and their Russian prisoners stared at the two aircraft, from which men were now jumping. "Binoculars!" the major shouted. Focusing the eyepiece, the Marine saw that the newly-arrived chopper had United States markings on it—a *Ch-57 'Seahorse'*, one of the biggest of the American helicopters.

The major was shaking his head; frowning. *What's going on, here?* The Russian and the American helicopters were parked near to each other in the midst of what was obviously a major firefight, for the gunfire had not slackened; indeed, since the two aircraft had set-down, the noises of shooting seemed to have increased all across the beleaguered airfield. But the helicopters were not exchanging fire and even as the major watched, men in military uniforms from the two aircraft were running across the field in each other's direction, waving their arms.

The American swept his binoculars. around the landscape; the heavy black smoke of the burning airplanes that he could now see were big transports continued to boil into the sky. The rear of the terminal building looked like it had been bombed. Panning the glasses, he saw that some pitched battles were still going on all along the airport's expanse of runways and taxiways and off into the open fields. In places, it almost seemed as if some of the American forces were shooting at their own men; a prospect that made the major wince. Striated layers of smoke hung over the entire airfield.

The officer swung back and focused once more on the men from the two helicopters, who were standing in a grassy space between the two aircraft. As he watched, they appeared to be shouting and gesturing among themselves and pointing off in different directions. Then the cluster of men—all of them high-ranking officers from both sides, he saw—broke apart.

The American major checked the captives; his men had everything under control. The officer told the radio operator to report to theater headquarters that they had taken Russian prisoners—what were their instructions?

When he looked back toward the helicopters, the men were running in twos and threes across the field, waving their hands and shouting—through the crashing, booming fray, he could faintly hear their thin-sounding voices.

There was a momentary pause in the shooting, then the racket came back. It looked like whatever the helicopter men were trying to do—stop the shooting, as it appeared—was not succeeding.

Outside the concussion-crashed rear door of the terminal, the head American officer was squirming in protest. "This is a violation of the—"

"Shut up!" Colonel Golubko was in no mood for diplomatic niceties. "You come here and shoot at my men! You have no orders to do so!" He nodded at Blagron and Malinovsky, who still aimed their Kalashnikovs at the captives."Take these prisoners inside! I will decide later what to do with them!"

* * *

—(WIRE SERVICE)—1:48 AM EDT (URGENT) WASHINGTON-MOSCOW HOTLINE ACTIVATED CONCERNING MILITARY INCIDENT AT SARAJEVO AIRPORT BETWEEN AMERICAN AND RUSSIAN FORCES THAT REPORTEDLY HAS BEEN GOING ON FOR AN HOUR.

* * *

—(WIRE SERVICE)—1:54 AM EDT (FLASH) RELIABLE PENTAGON SOURCES REPORT THAT UNITED STATES STRATEGIC NUCLEAR FORCES HAVE GONE TO FULL ALERT.

* * *

—(WIRE SERVICE)—1:57 AM EDT (URGENT) PRESIDENT REPORTEDLY NOW BEING TAKEN TO SECURE LOCATION.

* * *

The radio operator ran into the debris-filled waiting room, side-stepping broken glass strewn all around from the explosions and saluted the colonel. "The gunfire has stopped!"

Just then there came the sound of voices—angry-sounding voices, speaking in clipped English and Russian—that burst through the ruined double-doors to the outside. Terenty stared at the newcomers: there were the familiar uniforms of a Russian "Colonel General", plus several lesser-grade generals and two colonels. With them came a half-dozen men in uniforms he had not seen since he had lived in Washington as a teenager—senior American officers. The American prisoners stood in a tight circle, surrounded by Russian troops aiming AK-74's at them. Their leader had been shoved into a chair. The Russian generals took purposeful steps in the direction of the colonel and the others.

While the other officers held up, the highest-ranking Russian general stepped to the group. "Who is in charge, here?"

The colonel came to attention and gave the open-style Russian salute. "Rodion Golubko, Comrade General . . . *'Vityaz Spetsnaz'*—"

Terenty happened to be looking at the American commander when Colonel Golubko spoke. At the words, "Vityaz Spetsnaz", the man had visibly blanched. Terenty remembered that "Spetsnaz:" carried a world-wide reputation for uncommon, effective methods. And "Vityaz" was an elite force *within* the Elite Force, specializing in deep-penetration and counter-terrorism missions. He stood straight as the grim-looking Russian general stared hard at the captive Americans, then spoke in Russian.

"These are your prisoners, colonel?"

"*Da*, Comrade General."

"Very good work, colonel!" He glared at the seated American officer and switched to accented-English. "And who are you?"

"Wicker . . . Commander . . . United States Navy . . . serial num—"

"*Shut up!* I am not interested in your goddam serial number! What the hell are you doing here?"

"We were ordered to take the airport . . ."

"*Whose* orders? You have no such authority!"

"NATO's orders."

"To hell with 'NATO'! *'Our'* orders came from the *'highest'* authority! You have no right to be here!"

One of the American generals spoke up. "Ah, general we—"

"You be quiet! I am in charge here!" The red-faced Russian's fists doubled. He nodded at two Spetsnaz soldiers. Navarin and Blagron lowered their Kalashnikovs on the Americans.

"This is most irregular . . . "

"'Irregular'—Bah!" The Russian spat on the floor. "You attack our soldiers without reason! You *'Americanskis'* are the 'irregulars', general!"

"Perhaps we can work this out . . . peacefully—"

"Ah, yes"—the colonel general's voice dripped with sarcasm—"you Americans dropped-in, 'peacefully', of course, and started shooting at our troops and exploding our airplanes!"

The AK-74s waved back and forth at the U.S. generals, whose eyes were wide.

The senior Russian officer pointed to some overturned furniture in a far corner. "Bring that table and those chairs out here! We shall have 'peace', all right . . . *on my terms!"*

* * *

—(WIRE SERVICE)—4:02 AM EDT (URGENT) THERE ARE UNCONFIRMED REPORTS THAT THE CONFRONTATION AT SARAJEVO HAS ENDED.

* * *

—(WIRE SERVICE)—4:04 AM EDT (FLASH) PENTAGON NOW CONFIRMS THAT THE MILITARY STANDOFF BETWEEN AMERICAN AND RUSSIAN FORCES AT THE SARAJEVO AIRPORT IN BOSNIA HAS ENDED.

* * *

The female news anchor looked at the camera. "Good morning . . . and this is 'The Early Morning News Hour', thanks for joining us." The young, attractive woman shuffled her script and went on speaking. "While Americans were sleeping, last night, events were taking place in an obsure corner of southern Europe that might have brought about a war between the United States and Russia by this morning." A dark-haired, middle-aged man, holding a microphone, came on a screen behind her. Now to our Pentagon correspondent . . . Albert Montroy—"

The reporter's image went full-screen. "From what Pentagon sources are saying, an American 'peace-keeping' force landed at the airport at Sarajevo . . . in Bosnia . . . to take over the airfield—not knowing that a Russian force was already there. The result was a gun-battle that went on for some hours and—from what we are told—nearly got completely out of hand." He looked down, listening to his earpiece. "A Pentagon briefing is just now starting . . ."

The scene dissolved to a darkened room where a contingent of correspondents sat in chairs; the tops of their heads visible from the straight camera shot from the rear of the room. At a podium, a close-cropped, silver-haired military officer in a dark uniform, service ribbons across his chest, had stepped into floodlights in front of a bright blue curtain with a *'Pentagon'* emblem on it and was starting to speak.

" . . . 'States Special Forces landed by parachute and were immediately taken under heavy fire by forces whose identity were unknown at the time. According to *'Central Command',* the situation got out of control when neither side knew that the other had orders to take the airfield and both sides thought the other force was an enemy."

A map came down behind the man. The officer pointed at the spot where the encounter took place. "The airport at Sarejevo had been under control of insurgents and American troops were ordered to fly-in and clear them out. We do not know all the details, as yet, but we do know there were American casualties. How many, we do not know at this time. The President was notified in the early hours of this day and went to the underground shelter, which is standard procedure. The 'Washington-Moscow Hotline' was activated and leaders of both countries were in contact with each other." The man looked around at the room."Questions?"

At once, a middle-aged man, noted for his direct manner, stood and spoke before any other reporter could say anything. "General, there were reports that U. S. nuclear forces were on special alert. Is this true?"

"As a precaution we activated some of our forces to the highest level." There was a murmur as the officer went on, "Let me clarify that this is standard procedure in such situations."

A man came up and handed him a piece of paper, that he looked at, frowning.

"How many Americans were killed?"

"We have just been notified by our people at the scene that there are more than twenty."

There was audible murmuring in the room.

"How many Russians were killed?

I do not know the answer to that question."

"How dangerous was this situation?"

"We believed it had the potential for . . . 'other eventualities'—"

"You mean war? *War with Russia?* I thought they were now our friends."

"I cannot speak for the diplomats, who, incidently, were very busy during this 'situation'. But our new relationship with the former Soviet Union is now such that we believe we can de-fuse these kinds of situations without resorting to something that neither side would want."

The man's lips continued moving, but another voice came on, then the picture switched back to the chisled-featured, blond-haired man on the news-set. "This was the Pentagon's 'Briefing Officer' with the latest about what happened in Bosnia overnight—"

The fellow moved a paper on his desk, then looked at the camera; on the screen behind him appeared a middle-aged, close-cropped, thin-lipped man in a tan suit. "Now we go to Austin, Texas, where our military consultant, retired Army Colonel Morris Tredd, in our affiliate's studio, has been following these events all night."

The man nodded, as his image became full-screen. Behind him was the Austin skyline.

"Colonel Tredd, we know that some Americans and some Russians got into some sort of battle over there at the Sarajevo airport . . . can you tell us what you know about it?"

"Well, an American mixed Special Force—men who do things out of the ordinary behind enemy lines—in this case, as I understand it, 'Army Rangers', 'Navy Seals' and a lesser-known group called, 'Marine Force Recon'—parachute-dropped onto the main airport at Sarajevo, in Bosnia, to take it. No one in particular was supposed to be there, I am told . . . but when they landed, they found that another force was already in position. It turned out, they were an elite Russian force known to our military as 'Vityaz Spetsnaz ', a particularly effective branch of their Special Forces. Now, this 'Spetsnaz' group opened fire on the Americans and killed some of them, my sources tell me."

"Why were the Russians there?"

"Most likely, there was some kind of mix-up . . . at least that's what everybody's saying, right now. Anyway, our men landed there and came under heavy fire. Naturally, they shot back. From what I know, it was a very intense and confused affair that went on for some time."

"There was a report that the President went to his special underground shelter. Does that mean the situation was more serious than they are letting on?"

"From what I'm told, the 'Washington-Moscow Hotline was activated. Except for tests, they don't do that unless it's something important. By the way, our nuclear forces went on alert."

"So it was a dangerous situation?"

"It could have easily led to much bigger things in a hurry. That's why the 'Hotline' was used. I'm told our President was communicating directly with Yeltsin."

"How about casualties? We are told by the Pentagon that twenty or so Americans were killed in this *'battle '*—or whatever you want to call it."

"My sources say *twenty-three* American Special Forces were killed. We know of two Russians that the Americans killed. There may have been more. If it is true, then this does not bode well for our 'Special Forces', I must say." The military consultant paused, then went on. "One thing about who we were facing: this Russian force that they call 'Spetsnaz' has a reputation among our American military---those who will say so, privately—as being frightful; indimidating, because they are vicious and are not bound by laws or other restraints that would hold them back . . . we know that the 'Spetsnaz'—which was set-up by Stalin, during World War Two, by the way—employ tactics that our Special Forces are forbidden by law to use."

"You are saying these Russians are *better* than our Special Forces? And our *laws* have something to do with it?"

"Well, in the sense their missions, as I have studied them, are quite different from what we would do . . . for example, the Russians deal in things like assassination of government leaders and other important people, which our forces *at this time* are forbidden by Congress to do. In Afghanistan, when the Soviets went there, the night before their troops landed, Spetsnaz men infiltrated and went into the home of the Afghan President and killed him and his family, along with almost all of the military officers. They were all gathered together and shot. So when the Soviets landed their main force the next morning, they took the capital, Kabul, without much opposition. We understand that no matter how helpful or important it might be to us in a wartime situation, our forces can't do anything like that. One more thing: had the 'Warsaw Pact' ever invaded Western Europe, as everyone assumed might happen to start *'World War Three'*, Spetsnaz could have gone in and assassinated every government leader in Western Europe before the war started—probably at night, in their beds, right past their bodyguards. Also, they could have killed most of the NATO military officers, cutting-off the command and control of the organization. They're that good."

"I, for one, have never heard of this 'Vityaz Spetsnaz", as you call it.

"Well, our military knows about them, all right—and have for a long time. I'll tell you what: mention the word, 'Spetsnaz' to some of our officers at the Pentagon and watch their reaction. That'll tell you."

"You say they assassinate *whole governments?* Come on, nobody can do that."

"Well, they are very good at getting behind the lines of an enemy and causing a lot of trouble. Remember not long ago, when there was some kind of 'event' at Los Alamos, New Mexico where some of our soldiers were killed—killed *viciously* by an unknown force? Now, we suspect that Spetsnaz operatives were probably behind it. It matched their way of doing things like we know they have done in the past.

"The Russians were in this country?"

"I don't think with our extremely porous borders they would have had much trouble getting in. Maybe they were already here to begin with—who knows? All I can say is that if our borders stay open like they now are, someday we're gonna have something really, *really* big happen here in, say, one of our cities, that can be traced back to somebody coming across—somebody we should have stopped. And *would* have stopped, if we were like they are in most parts of the world. Try swimming across the river *into* China—they will meet you with a hail of bullets. For that matter, if you swim *into* Mexico from the United States, the same thing might happen to you. But *not* the other way around." The man's face was tight; his teeth were clenched.

"Isn't that a little far-fetched?" The voice-over newsman sounded skeptical. "Shooting people swimming across the Rio Grande *from* Mexico?"

"And let's don't forget, either, that huge border up-north with Canada. It's a lot tougher world out there than most Americans— including some of our leaders—seem to realize; that's all I'll say. *We may have to learn some hard lessons, someday."*

"But back to the Sarajevo thing last night . . . how did it end?"

"I'm told there was a lot of harranguing at the airport terminal between our generals and their generals—it probably got pretty hot in there. Anyway, they got it stopped."

"I have to break away now, because we are getting word the Russian Embassy in Washington is going to have an announcement. Colonel Tredd . . . Colonel 'Morris' Tredd, our military consultant from Austin, Texas, thank you for joining us."

The man in the tan suit nodded, then the picture rolled and changed to a dark-haired man holding a microphone, blinking his eyes and adjusting his earpiece as the studio newscaster voiced-over: "Now to our Diplomatic Correspondent in Washington, Irving R. Flessner..."

The reporter brushed a shock of windblown hair out of his face, glanced at a substantial-looking building behind him and spoke. "At the Russian Embassy, we are waiting for the Ambassador to appear. I am told he has a statement about last night's incident at Sarajevo."

As he spoke, the screen took a close-up of a door that was opening, then closed back a little, then swung open. In a moment, a graying, middle-aged man of considerable eyebrows and girth was coming out. A man in a decorated military uniform, looking grim, followed him and moved to the side. Two younger uniformed men exited the door with rigid movements and came to stand by the others, stamping the stocks of rifles they were holding on the concrete with a single *"WHAM!"* the microphones caught, then holding the weapons out attention.

"The man in the suit is the 'Ambassador', and the uniformed man is the 'Military Attaché," the reporter was saying in subdued tones, as the diplomat arranged some notes on a slender podium. He pushed up a pair of thick, plastic-rimmed eyeglasses, then began speaking in English with a discernible accent.

"This morning, the government of the 'Russian Federation' lodged a protest in the strongest terms with the American government over an incident at Sarajevo, in Bosnia."

The paper fluttered and there were some wind noises in the microphone.

"The position of the government of the Russian Federation is that our troops were authorized to be at the airport at Sarajevo from a resolution of the United Nations—*that America signed*—that gave the Russian Federation full authority to take and hold the airport on behalf of the *'Coalition Forces'*."

The man turned the page and went on talking in a heavy monotone voice. "The government of the Russian Federation holds that 'NATO' was also aware of the lawful and legitimate duties of the Russian Federation to take and hold the airport in accordance with the resolution of the United Nations, and any orders to the contrary given to or by America were illegal."

A gust of wind came up just then, prompting the military man to step forward to hold down the notes. As the man in the suit started to go on reading, again, the television microphone picked up chanting by some protesters somewhere off-camera. The Ambassador looked over the rims of his glasses for a second, then went on, even as another wind gust momentarily drowned him out.

"The landing of American troops at the Sarajevo airport and their firing on the troops of the Russian Federation and the wanton destruction of aircraft owned and operated by the Russian Federation was illegal, and the Russian Federation demands an apology and compensation from America for their illegal and unjust activities against the personnel of the Russian Federation who were carrying out their lawful and just duties in accordance with the resolution of the United Nations."

The man in the suit turned to the Military Attaché, who stepped to the microphone.

"The Armed Forces of the Russian Federation performed their duties in a thorough and efficient manner. Let it be known in the strongest terms that any attack upon the military forces of the Russian Federation will always be met with the strongest response. The aggressors must always understand this—"

Then the officer turned, ranks of medals on his chest catching the sun, and accompanied the Ambassador back through the open doorway into the building, followed by the sentries, and some others who had been standing on the porch.

The television correspondent came back on camera, caught in the act of pushing his blowing hair from his face. A box at the bottom of the screen identified him as *'Irving R. Flessner, Chief Diplomatic Correspondent'* of the network. "That was the very strong statement from the Russian Ambassador about the military confrontation between the Americans and the Russian forces that took place in Bosnia, overnight. Recapping . . . from his point of view, the Russians blamed the United States and NATO for what they said was an 'illegal attack by American forces' on what he called 'the lawful Russian troops' who were there on what he said was a 'United Nations resolution' that the Americans signed." The middle-aged correspondent glanced at his notes. "We are looking, now, to find that resolution and see what it really said."

WASHINGTON NEWS EDITORIAL PAGE:

SARAJEVO INCIDENT

"World War One" started at Sarajevo, and "World War Three" almost started there the other day, as well. From what we now know, both the Americans and the Russians were preparing to take direct action against each other's country if the airport battle had gone on much longer; a horrifying prospect, to say the least. It was indeed fortunate that the situation was de-fused in time.

But the confrontation brought some sobering conclusions For American military chiefs. It now appears that the Russian force thoroughly whipped the Americans in the battle for the airport: according to sources who were at the scene, the tally was twenty-three U.S. dead and no more than *two* Russians were killed, in heavy fighting. If this is true, then something is amiss with either the training or the tactics of U.S. 'Special Forces'— supposedly the elite troops of the American military.

Not only was the U.S. military performance found wanting, but liaison between the American diplomats and their own military failed terribly. For it now turns out that the Russians had every right to be at the Sarajevo airport and were occupying the airfield from a mandate of the United Nations. Somehow, the American forces did not know this, which led to the confrontation. Embarrassing—and very dangerous.

On a positive note, the "Washington-Moscow Hotline" seems to have performed well.

-12-

In the Mountains of Central Bali, Indonesia:

Norbert Ezego slumped at the crude table on its elevated, lashed-cane porch beneath a canopy of woven leaves, fanning himself in the sweltering heat of the mountainous jungle hideaway. If anything, hot, sticky Bali was even worse than the last island where he had been—as soon as he had arrived, he had arranged for a bath, but its benefits were now gone; here, non-stop sweating seemed to be a part of everyday life. An attendant came up and handed him a glass of fruit juice. At least he would not die of thirst.

Out in an open area, young men were jumping to calesthentics; others jerked wooden poles around in the rudiments of weapons training. Right now, they looked just like the fellows back on Sulawesi Island had been to start—ragged, but with potential. One had to begin somewhere.

And they were enthusiastic; some of the trainers who had come with him from Mindanao were already at work, politically indoctrinating overflowing classes of young recruits who were flocking here from all around the islands of Indonesia.

It was obvious they were going to need everything. Even now, the African was scratching-out a long list of equipment and supplies to order from the stocks in Lagos and from North Korea; all to be paid for, of course, by the financiers. As he sat writing on sheets of paper, a smile came to him—the totals added up to an enormous sum. And with some judicious inflating of the prices here and there, he could exact a nice return for the Organization—and keep the excess for himself. He had learned of Retchko's Cayman accounts from some papers he had seen on the Chief of Security's desk. Quick work at a copy machine before the general had returned to his office had nailed-down the information. His own Cayman account, of which the bald Ukrainian had no knowledge, was now set-up and ready for future deposits, the first of which should soon happen.

The Nigerian turned to a map thumb-tacked onto a reedy wall behind him. According to the chart, this new training camp was going up in the center of the island, far from any village that might harbor prying or dangerous eyes. Before they had even arrived, the basic layout had been in place. Ezego turned back and watched native men hacking through heavy underbrush with machetes, cutting away even more open space. From what he had learned, the response for volunteers in Indonesia, teeming with a restless population, was already most satisfying.

Behind him, the porch squeaked; the man who was in charge of the local operation was hauling himself up the lashed-together ladder of the temporary headquarters. The Nigerian turned about and saw that the turbaned, middle-aged fellow had a long, rolled paper in his hand.

"Ah, Ezego, I trust you find everything satisfactory."

The African pushed the written proposal across the knotted table. "This is a list of what you must have to get started."

Across the way, the young recruits were shouting and grunting in their exercise exertions. Ezego motioned at them. "As you see, those men need everything."

The Indonesian put on eyeglasses and scanned the pages. "How soon can we get these things here?"

"Probably several weeks. Everything will have to come by boat from North Korea."

The man unrolled a map of Indonesia; Ezego had not known it was made up of so many islands—the archipelago spanned all the way from southern Malaysia to northwest of Australia.

The local leader pointed at the map. It showed that Bali was located to the east of Java, the main Indonesian island. "We chose Bali because it has this secluded part where we can train without interference, and because the island is big on tourists." Seeing the African's frown, the man went on, "our objective is to discredit the government—to make it unstable—and the best way to do that will be to disrupt the tourist trade. Bali is a big destination for people from all over the world—Australia, Europe; America—we plan to start a campaign of random bombings in tourist places. We will start here in Bali, and go all over Indonesia. Before long, the tourists will stop coming and the government will fall and we can set up one that is more to our 'liking'." The fellow looked hard at Ezego. "For this, we will need men trained in bombing techniques, bomb materials, and the like."

"It will take time to do this."

"We have plenty of time—years, if necessary."

Ezego stared out. On the field, the young men kept up their shouting to the cadence of calesthentics.

* * *

Grozny, Chechnya; the Next Day:

"We have sent some of our explosives experts to The Philippines and Indonesia." The turbaned warlord held up a glass of cider to Retchko in a toast of greeting. "Your man seems to be doing a very good job of organizing the revolutionaries, down there—what did you say his name was?"

"'Ezego '." The hairless Ukrainian downed the liquid in thought. He was pleased, of course, that his assistant was making headway on his Southeast Asian assignment, but he would have to keep a close watch on him, lest the man gain too much power and influence—it was a fine line between being exceptionally capable at what one was doing and becoming *too* strong for his—Retchko's—own good.

"I am still having a hard time getting used to your bald head," the bearded old man went on, an allusion to when the general, as the dark-haired, mustached "Semen Putridchenko" from Moscow had come in the past to Grozny for secret meetings with the breakaway region's leaders.

"It is most necessary." Retchko wanted to deflect the conversation toward something else. "I have a new identity and new duties."

The Chechen revolutionary and some others sitting about a table nodded, looking satisfied with the response. "So you are now part of the Cartel that supplies 'progressive' causes?"

Retchko knew he was trying to draw him out, but what the hell—since he had no more connections with the Russians, he decided to level with these people. Between long draws on the communal smoke-pot, he told the men the whole story of escaping from Moscow in the aftermath of the aborted coup against Gorbachev and making his way in disguise to a whole new career in Nigeria; to working with revolutionaries all over the world.

The wizened man pulled on the gurgling water-smoke-hose. "You have certainly changed, all right."

The general pulled some papers out of his briefcase. "These are the plans I have put together for our collaborations." The men drew up their chairs as the Ukrainian went on. "We will have a two-way partnership . . . our 'Organization' will supply weapons to you at discounted prices . . . you will send to us men to train some others of our clients."

The older man was frowning. "Who are these 'others'?"

Retchko opened a world map and spread it on the table. "We are supplying 'Agent U', in Tora Bora. He is setting up cells everywhere to wage urban warfare against the Imperialists."

He pointed to Iran. "We are supplying centrifuges for their nuclear research operations."

His finger stopped on the Philippines. "In Mindanao, we are selling weapons and helping train insurgents in the south." Retchko looked at the warlord. "You are helping us, there, with instructors."

He moved down to Indonesia. "In these islands, we are opening camps to teach young men how to build and explode bombs and how to subvert the government through underground political and paramilitary cells. They plan to someday take over all of Indonesia—with our help, of course."

His finger pointed at North Korea. "The Pyongyang government is being very helpful in supplying military goods for some of our clients . . . so far, we have been able to count on them for many things we need and their prices are reasonable."

The bald man moved across the map and tapped Cuba. "The Cubans have a surplus of weapons—mostly left-over Russian equipment they are giving us at a very good price. Also, we have helped them get their military hardware out of Angola, now that their adventure there is ending."

"How do you move all these things around the world?"

"We have our own cargo aircraft and we use freighters and boats. Our prices include shipping."

"Very good, general . . . impressive."

Retcko moved a stubby finger up the map and stopped on the United States. *"In America, we have big plans."* Retchko glanced up; the men were staring at the map. "'Agent U's' Tora Bora group is working with us to set up cells in America to attack and bomb buildings, poison water supplies and inject nerve gas in subways, and—perhaps you can help us on this—obtain nuclear devices to smuggle into America to detonate in cities like New York, Washington, and Houston. An atomic explosion in a crowded city means many casualties, which is good for our cause."

The Chechen leader was rubbing his chin. "I know sources in Ukraine where we may be able to get such nuclear devices . . . small, but powerful ones, even—" The fellow looked around at his compatriots, who were nodding.

The hairless man could hardly contain himself. "That would be great!"

The Chechen motioned at one of the others, who arose and came back with a map. "These are *our* areas of control," he said, running a nicotine-stained finger across the paper, "as you can see, we are holding back the Russians. In some areas, we are moving ahead, but the Russians are not giving up."

The other revolutionary spoke up. "We need more weapons."

Retchko looked around; all the men were staring at him. "Make a list and I will get started."

He was thinking about the automatic weapons they had brought from Cuba, some of which were already here in Chechnya, but there were many more stored in the Organization's hangar back at Lagos.

"There is something else we are doing that will be very useful to keep control of your men." He told the insurgent leader about the chip implant system.

" . . . and you say we can know where they are at all times?"

"Exactly."

The grizzled men looked around at each other. "When can we do this?"

"I will get our technicians started on it right away."

* * *

Tanuta Refinery, Three Days Later:

"Well, look at this!" Larry Landay handed Lisa Anaya printout. "It's an order from Retchko for *another* complete satellite system!"

The young woman fingered the paper. "Our first real message—" She read the equipment requisition in detail, which was several pages long. "It will take us some days to put it all together . . . we had better get started on it right away."

* * *

Signal Intelligence Office, National Security Agency, Washington, D.C.:

"More signals came down overnight." The technician handed a paper with unintelligible printing on it to the agent in charge of intercepts.

"So far, our decryption people have not been able to make anything of it. They say it resembles an old Soviet code, but it has a lot of new things thrown in. They are working on it."

"Maybe we should just turn off the module in the satellite. That'd stop whomever's using it."

"But it'd also keep us from trying to trace the sources. The 'Director' says he wants us to stay on it."

* * *

Tverskaya District, Moscow; Three Weeks Later:

"*You* will be gone to Iran and *I* will be gone to Chechnya . . . then, we will both come back at the same time and everything will be normal, again."

Galina felt tense. "But Gennady . . . *Chechnya!* It is such a dangerous place." She remembered he had told her once how

273

terrible it had been that first time he had been there. And the insurgency now seemed to be much worse—every day it seemed more Russian soldiers were dying down there; one of her co-workers at the school had recently lost a cousin in Grozny. She had also heard that Chechen rebels were bombing places in Moscow and around the rest of the country. "I wish you were not going."

"We are on a special mission that should not last long. They are telling us perhaps three weeks. And that is how long you will be gone to Iran. So the timing will be perfect!"

Gennady propped himself on his elbow and looked at Galina's pale, slim figure on the satin sheets."Since we are both leaving Moscow tomorrow . . . everything will work out just right," he said.

"But what about the *next* time you are gone and I am here alone, and every time after that?"

"We will always make up for it when I return—to what city in Iran did they say you are going?"

"The letter said it was some place called *'Bandar Abbas'*. It is on the Persian Gulf, where our group will be teaching." She pointed at the top of the bureau in the little bedroom. "My passport finally came in the mail, today. It is in the clear waterproof bag, where they said it would be safe from the humidity, there."

All around the room, her clothes were in various stages of packing into luggage. By the door, Gennady's gear was already stowed in a duffel bag, ready to go.

"Talking about passports makes me miss you already." He rolled over to Galina and gave her a long, deep kiss; caressed her shoulders; her neck.

The girl gave a gasp. Oh, Gennady, I will miss you so much while I am gone." She pulled herself to him. "Love me one more time."

* * *

". . . and I feel so badly for Galina and Gennady—" Tamara, lying in the warm, early-spring half-light of their flat's bedroom, was whispering to her husband. "They just got married and already

274

they are traveling away from each other. They are so in love . . . Galina is so happy. But now, they will be apart for a while."

"Remember, *I* will be leaving, too, and we are in love, are we not?" Terenty propped himself on his elbow and turned to his bride with a grin she saw in the semi-darkness. Then he pulled his wife to him and embraced her; Tamara's long auburn hair settled over them.both.

She whispered in his ear. "Oh, Terenty, I loved you from the moment you saved Larisa's life in front of that streetcar . . . I had never seen anything so noble and heroic . . . and it was *you!*"

"May I be honest? Gennady and I saw you and Larisa coming up the sidewalk that day and neither of us could take our eyes off you . . . we even looked to see if you had a wedding ring—God, you were beautiful!"

She gave a little laugh. "Now *I* will be honest: I was trying to watch you and act like I was ignoring you at the same time— you know how women are!"

"Aha . . . suspicion confirmed!" Terenty grinned. "That day, Gennady and I had just been assigned as roommates at the school—we were finding we had a lot in common."

"I remember how handsome you looked in your uniform." She pulled herself closer to him.

Then Terenty remembered something. "I heard that some of us in our squad may be assigned to diplomatic duty after our next mission. How would you like to live in another country for a while?"

"I have never been out of Russia."

"It is a big world out there."

Tamara took a deep, satisfied breath; he felt the soft, ample mounds of her chest, her whole body against his. All at once he wanted her one more time . . .

* * *

San Francisco, California; the Next Day:

Michael B. Parsley, Esq. leaned back in his scuffed mahogany desk chair and tapped his fingertips together. "You say you *still* can't locate your friend, Larry Landay? After all this time?"

Joe Anglin stared across the desk at his court-appointed attorney. "All I know is that he is in Nigeria, somewhere." He looked glum. "The only number I have is the one we used with the little code machine—and it doesn't answer. I have the machine and the code book with me, now, by the way. They were with the stuff we were able to get out of the office with the court order."

"Well, Landay is the key to your defense . . . but without his testimony, it's gonna be tough."

"You can't really expect him to show up. They'd arrest him on the spot!"

The pudgy lawyer looked thoughtful. "Maybe we could find him in Nigeria and get his side of the story. We might get some facts that would beneficial to your defense, sanitize it, and use it at the trial."

"Some trial—right now they might as well declare me 'guilty' and send me off to jail!"

"Well, remember . . . you're still innocent until they prove that you're guilty."

"Yeah, sure." There was a lack of conviction in Joe Anglin's voice. "Any date, yet, for the trial?"

"We'll file a continuance to hold up the court date some more. The judges are usually pretty lenient about that sort of thing—as long as we show some progress." Michael B. Parsley, Esq. shrugged. "We have a few months, I would say, before we have to face a jury."

"I'll keep trying the code machine."

* * *

Tanuta Refinery; the Next Day:

While Lisa Anaya finished a report before they went to lunch, Frank Ogawan idly picked up the little wooden box on top of her filing cabinet and looked it over. "I have been intending to ask you: What is *this* thing?"

276

She glanced up. "Oh, it's a code machine I made back in college for a course in cryptology."

"Cryptology?"

"Codes . . . cyphers; that sort of thing." She pushed aside the papers. "We—that is, Larry and I—when we were back in grad' school in America we took a cryptology course. We made two of these and sent coded messages to each other. It was a lot of fun, then, and in fact, we used them to order the electronic equipment that he brought here."

"You are still using it?"

"Not now . . . in fact, it's not even plugged up."

"How does it work?"

Lisa located the telephone line outlet on the wall next to the filing cabinet and pushed the machine's telephone plug into it and reached for the power cord. "I had to use a transformer, since the electrical current is different here in Nigeria than what it is in America," she said, plugging the cord into the wall. All we need, now, is a keyboard and a printer and it will be working—except, of course, it has no other machine to 'talk' to, except for Larry's back in California, and since he is here now, it's just been sitting up there on the cabinet." She pulled out a pamphlet-like booklet. "This is the 'code-book' we used."

"Interesting . . . I would like to check it out." He flipped through the pages of the little book. "I will get a printer for it from the computer room."

"Suit yourself. But as far as I'm concerned, it's now just a decoration—a toy."

* * *

International Airport, Grozny, Chechnya; Two Days Later:

Terenty knew the place would look like a war zone, but he was not prepared for anything like this. When they had stepped from the military airliner the day before, almost everything in sight—from the terminal building, to the airplane hangars, to the control tower—looked like it had been shot-up, blown-up, or burned-up.

Now, in their temporary tent barracks behind the blackened shell of the main building, the men of the Spetsnaz squad were sitting around on folding seats, taking a breather in the warm springtime air.

Gennady shook his head. "It looks far worse, now, than it did when I was here last time."

Malinovsky stared at him. "You were here, before?"

Gennady told the others about his tour the previous year and a fire-fight in which he was the only one in his squad who came out alive. "This is a bad, bad place," he said, gripping a glass of kvas. "These people—these rebels—are murderous terrorists who will stop at nothing." He was watching some workmen shoveling dirt into some shell craters out on a distant taxiway. "And they are all around us." He gave a discreet gesture at the local laborers. "Those men out there could very well be after us tonight with scimitars or automatic rifles or grenades."

Just then, Colonel Golubko came up. The young men stood and saluted. "All right, comrades," the officer said, returning their salutes, "get your gear ready, we will be making a sweep through the city, tonight." As the man stepped away, he looked back over his shoulder. "Get used to it—we will be sweeping through the city *every* night while we are here."

* * *

Somewhere in Grozny; Two Days Later:

Retchko popped a fistful of aspirins; he was now having to do it several times a day. These headaches! The bald Ukrainian held his forehead; since he had never had much in the way of ailments in his life until recently, all this was new to him. Once or twice, as he was trying to get off to sleep, he had even noticed little flashes before his eyes in the darkness. What is going on? Thank the stars the aspirins always did their job—for a few hours. Then, it was back to more of the tablets. Probably the stress and strain of putting together all these new elements for the

Cartel was taking its toll. That was what it was. He just needed to slow down.

But not right now; there was too much to do. Yesterday, he had received a communication through roundabout channels from Ezego: the man was making great headway down there in Indonesia, it appeared. The supplies and weapons had just arrived from North Korea, the Nigerian had messaged, and the imported Chechen trainers seemed to be whipping the recruits into shape in the Philippines and on Bali at a faster pace than expected. From the looks of things, before long, they would be ready to start their bombings and attacks against the unsuspecting governments and against civilian targets, which, as they knew, was the most direct route to unsettle the masses.

Another message, this one from the Chief, said that the satellite implant and control system that would come here to Grozny was now in Lagos, ready to go out on the 747. That was good news; the leaders here in Chechnya would soon be able to monitor and direct their agents anywhere, just like "U" was starting to do with his men. Since he and Ezego were both gone from headquarters right now, the 'Chief' would order Busa, the Organization's agent in the other refinery at Tanuta City, to go back to Lagos on a pretext to coordinate the shipment through Libya; across the Mediterranean; around the Black Sea; over Iran to the Caspian Sea past Baku; then up the coast to Chechnya. A long haul, of course, but in the past it had proved to be a secure, if complicated, route.

* * *

Tanuta Refinery; the Next Morning:

Lisa Anaya stepped into her office cubicle and set her coffee cup onto her desk. Turning to the filing cabinet, she did a double-take: the printer Frank Ogawan had plugged into the little decoder was covered by fan-folded paper with printing on it! At her desk, the young woman broke down the sheets into pages, took out the code book, and started decoding. After some minutes, she snatched up the telephone and dialed some numbers in a hurry.

"Larry! Come quick . . . yes, right now . . . hurry to my office! There's an important message for you on the code machine from your friend Joe Anglin!"

* * *

Strait of Hormuz, Persian Gulf; the Same Day:

The captain of the United States Navy "Aegis" Cruiser stood on the bridge of the steely gray warship; his binoculars focused on the tan landmass off in the distance to starboard. The Executive Officer pointed. "There it is, sir, Iranian territory."

Yes, and I intend to pass close by it."

The Exec lowered his spyglasses and looked at the ship's commanding officer.

"Sir, if I may speak."

"You may speak."

"The orders are for us to stay in International Waters."

The captain pretended not to hear. "I want those Iranians to know I am here."

The Exeutive Officer, frowning, stepped to the portside of the command bridge and again raised his binoculars. Across the hazy, shimmering, mid-morning waters some miles away, another large mound of land rose out of the green sea—the coastline of Oman. A few miles farther up the coast, he knew, was the bustling "Principality of Dubai," one of the "United Arab Emirates". He glanced at the radar screen; as its invisible beams crossed over the land to each side every few seconds, the sweep-line on the screen momentarily outlined the promontories in relief on the green circle, then subsided.

The captain turned to his executive officer. "General Quarters! All Ahead full! Max propeller Pitch! I want those Irainians to get a good look at my ship in the Strait of Hormuz!"

The second-in-command repeated the order to a junior officer, who reached out and moved a switch. Throughout the ship an unmistakable staccato of sound jolted every crewmember from whatever he was doing, followed by the three drawn-out notes of the bosn's whistle.

"General Quarters! Man your Battle Stations! This is not a drill!"

Below, in the engine rooms, as soon as the repeater indicated "Full Ahead", the duty operators moved levers. At once the whine of the gas turbines's gearboxes beneath the grillwork deck—jet engines, very much like those on commercial airliners, mounted to reduction gears and long shafts leading to the stern—took on a lower, almost growling sound as the variable-pitch propeller blades moved to maximum thrust against the water. Topside, flecks of spray flung back against the bridge windscreens as the slim, gray U.S. Navy warship, bristling with the latest electronically-controlled weaponry, its crew standing at the ready, lunged into the warm swell at thirty-one knots.

* * *

One thousand meters behind the cruiser on its port quarter, the Watch Officer of the "Arleigh Burke" class destroyer stared through binoculars as the leading ship's "rooster-tail" wake began to rise into the air behind its stern transom in a silvery arc, to drop back into the churning water behind it.

"Captain! Aegis is increasing speed! He is bearing to starboard! He is headed toward Iranian waters!"

The commander of the smaller ship raised his glasses. "He's up to it again . . . that captain over there—he's going to start a war, someday."

"Do we follow him?"

"No . . . maintain course and speed and inform the Fleet Commander of our intentions."

* * *

Tanuta Refinery; at the Same Time:

"I sent Joe all the information he wanted about the case—I hope it helps." Larry Landay was telling the others around the

281

lunch table about the message that had come in that morning on the code machine. "He said he had been trying to contact me for a long time." He looked at Frank Ogawan. "It sure was a good thing you wanted to turn it on."

Lisa Anaya let out a long sigh. "I feel responsible, because I placed the orders that now have you and Joe in so much trouble."

"Nobody knew it would lead to this."

"You're being too kind."

"I gave him a complete run-down, from the beginning—a lot of things he didn't know. I mean, all he did was what I hired him to do. I'm the real bad guy, here. "

Marisol, who had been listening, spoke up. "What *will* you do? It sounds like you cannot return to the 'States, any more."

"Stay here, I guess. I can't even go to Lagos, now. They're looking for me up there, too."

Frank Ogawan had been listening. "Are they really all *that* bad . . . those charges against you back in San Francisco?"

"Unless I can find a way to prove I didn't know the goods were going out of the country, I'm cooked. Unfortunately, I *did* know the shipment was going to Nigeria—I even came along with it! If they were to ever catch me, I'd probably spend the rest of my life behind bars."

* * *

Strait of Hormuz; Sunrise, Eighteen Days Later:

The captain of the Aegis Cruiser was pointing. "Intercept those damn boats! Board and search them!"

The Second Officer of the Watch stared across the crowded bridge at the captain. "Sir, if I may speak?"

"You may speak."

"Sir, we are outside the shipping channel . . . these are Iranian gunboats in Iranian waters."

"I don't give a damn where they are. Those vessels are a threat to my ship!"

The Second Officer of the Watch turned to the bosun's mate. "Sound 'General Quarters'."

The noncom moved a switch on the rear bulkhead. At once the brassy staccato alarm sounded in all corners of the warship. Then the bosun' flicked-on another switch on the communications console and blew his whistle into the microphone. "General Quarters, General Quarters—all hands man your battle stations! This is not a drill!"

* * *

"What the hell is he doing, now?" On the bridge of the "Arleigh Burke" class destroyer, a thousand meters behind the cruiser, the officer of the watch lowered his binoculars. "Get the captain . . . Aegis is turning into Iranian waters—"

"Signal from Aegis, sir. He is going to investigate some hostile gunboats."

" *'Hostile gunboats'?* Has he lost his mind? Those are Iranian boats in their own waters—Aegis is out of position!" The captain turned to the communications specialist. "Send a signal to the flagship at once! Ask for instructions!"

* * *

The executive officer of the Aegis cruiser turned to the captain. "They're off!"

"Note the time."

"Zero-six-forty-eight hours."

"Exec! Take-over the conn!" The captain and the fire-control officer turned and made their way off the command bridge aft to the "Aegis Electronic Warfare Suite", a dimly-lighted place in the boxy superstructure that housed a billion dollars' worth of the most up-to-date naval warfare command control electronics in the world. In a minute his eyes adjusted to the red-hued space, the tense nerve center of the warship's weapons systems, dominated by banks of computer consoles manned by junior officers and seamen specialists, all staring at monitor screens. The commanding officer took a seat in a raised leather chair, much like his "captain's chair" on the bridge. He put on a headset with an integral microphone. The fire control officer took a seat in a nearby chair.

"To captain! Aggressor gunboats firing on our helicopters!"

"Tell my helos to keep them in sight . . . move the ship closer."

"Arleigh Burke destroyer says we are in Iranian waters."

"Ignore that message. Delete from logs."

"Aircraft carrier asks if you request fighter cover."

"Negative, that."

* * *

Aboard the United States Navy "Arleigh Burke" Class Destroyer; on station with the "Aegis Cruiser", the officer of the watch called across the bridge to the captain, pointing. "Sir, Aegis is launching helos!" The commanding officer raised his binoculars and watched perplexed as a second "chopper" lifted from the helo pad at the stern of the cruiser and swung away in the direction of the Iranian gunboats, lying low on the horizon toward the not-so-distant shoreline. The cruiser's wake was lengthening and rising higher; the bigger warship was increasing speed.

"What's he *doing?*" The younger man voiced what everyone on the command bridge was wondering.

The captain shook his head, his forehead in a deep frown. "That stupid bastard—he's attacking them!" The ship's commander turned to the communications officer, standing at the rear of the bridge. "Message the flagship: 'Aegis is attacking Iranian gunboats in Iranian territorial waters!' Send it right now! Hurry!"

The destroyer's captain once more raised his binoculars, just as a flash and a gray mushroom cloud came from low on the horizon in the direction of the gunboats

"It blew up!" the executive officer gasped, as all binoculars on the bridge focused on the scene over the distant water. "One of the gunboats blew up!"

All at once the view faded, then disappeared. "It's a sandstorm, sir!" the quartermaster at the wheel called out. While

284

all eyes had been turned toward the east, toward the Iranian coast, no one had paid much attention to the brownish-yellow cloud closing on the ship from the direction of the Arabian Peninsula, some miles behind them. In moments, the ship was enveloped in a gritty fog that blocked their view of the action taking place eight miles to the northeast.

The captain stared at the opaque curtain outside the bridge windows in consternation—now he would be unable to maintain visual contact with the Aegis cruiser and the sand posed a real danger to the ship's machinery. "Secure for airborne particulate threat!"

"Message from flagship, sir!" The communications officer called out, "addressed to 'Aegis'." The younger officer stepped across the bridge and handed the paper to the captain.

"They're ordering him out of the Iranian waters and to break off the action!" The captain turned to the officer of the watch. "Navigator! Our position to the coast!"

"We are right at the twelve-mile limit, sir!"

"Message from flagship, sir . . . they are ordering us back through the Strait of Hormuz." He handed the decoded print-out to the captain.

The destroyer's commanding officer read the missive. "Come about to course two-one-zero! All ahead full!"

* * *

Combat Information Center, Aegis Cruiser:

The captain glared at the message ordering him to turn about and leave the area at once.

"Bastards! I wanted to take out *all* those gunboats!" The man cast about the red-hued room as if momentarily dis-oriented and trying to get his bearings. "What are the positions of our helos?" The talker relayed the question to the bridge.

The bridge came back. "They are standing-off and taking the gunboats under intermittent fire."

"Tell them to break it off and return to the ship." The captain tapped the leather armrest. "Fire-control! Lay the main battery

285

onto remaining gunboats and keep it aimed until I tell them to stand down!" The captain fingered the headset and called the talker to tell the watch officer on the command bridge to stay just inside the twelve-mile limit.

* * *

Strait of Hormuz; Forty Minutes Later:

Radar! Give me the position of Aegis Cruiser!" The captain of the "Arleigh Burke" class destroyer cursed the sandstorm that still surounded his ship as it plowed blindly across the water toward the south-southwest, guided only by invisible radar beams and the sure tracking of the "global positioning" satellite system.

"Bearing one-niner-zero-degrees, sir, distance, twelve nautical miles. Aegis is still inside Iranian waters."

"Well, at least he is coming after us, now." The captain was shaking his head. What would come of the incident with the gunboats, he wondered—for the Aegis Cruiser was violating orders by going into Iranian waters, he knew. For sure, its captain would face a court of inquiry.

The specialist at the radar binnacle called out. "Sir, we are now passing Bandar Abbas airport . . . distance, thirty nautical miles to port!"

"Maintain flank speed! Aegis cruiser?"

"Still behind us, sir, distance twelve nautical miles . . . still just inside the Iranian twelve-mile limit."

* * *

International Airport, Bandar Abbas, Iran; at the Same Time:

Galina Gavrona Lychina propped her sandaled feet atop her carry-on luggage and looked across the humid, crowded expanse of the echoing waiting room at the Bandar Abbas airport. Outside, even though the sun had been up for only a short while, the orange, early-morning sky already was proclaiming it would be a hazy, dusty day—someone had said there was a sandstorm coming across the Persian Gulf from the Arabian Peninsula. The young woman picked up a newspaper and fanned her face and the head-covering that was mandatory for women in this country. All around, bored-looking adults were sitting in rows of plastic seats awaiting the flight to Dubai; some held restless children in their laps. There would be many children on the airplane—at least a couple of dozen, she guessed. A few of the more adventurous youngsters were running around out in the middle of the space in some sort of "tag" game. Galina smiled to herself; their juvenile antics were almost like the way she and her friends used to play years ago back in Tula, as well as her current students at the primary school in Moscow. Since Galina had been here in this Iranian city on the Persian Gulf, far from the apartment she now shared with Gennady, one thing she had learned was that little ones everywhere were pretty much alike: it was only after the politicians got hold of them, it seemed, that they went off in other, sometimes baffling directions.

The young teacher thought how grateful she was to the Ministry of Education for selecting her to come here; these two-and-a-half weeks had been one of the most enlightening times of her entire life; she would have some wonderful stories to tell the children back at the primary school in Moscow. The assignment had gone by quickly, it had seemed, and had been most enjoyable—except for the heat; nothing had prepared her for the furnace-like climate, here—she had never quite gotten used to it. In this sweltering city on the Strait of Hormuz, the days and nights had been filled with school events and social gatherings with local Iranians she had met. Thinking about it and gazing around at the crowd in the airport waiting area, she had found the people here to be friendly and curious about Russia. It would be good, she thought, to have more travel opportunities in the future.

But she was now ready to go home. Gennady would soon be coming back from Chechnya and she was anxious to get back to being a wife; even now, with a tingle, she could almost hear his sweet words and feel his strong arms around her. Their schedules away from Moscow had almost exactly co-incided, as it turned out; just as Gennady had said they would.

Galina pulled her boarding pass out of her purse; she would need it in a few minutes. According to the flight plan in the packet, the *'Iranian Airlines'* plane would make a short hop over the Persian Gulf to Dubai, then continue on to Teheran. From there, she would take a Lufthansa flight to Frankfurt, then connect with Aeroflot, arriving in Moscow late in the day. During an international telephone call last night, her mother had told her she and her new special friend, General Krolov, would meet her at Moscow's *'Sheremetyevo Airport'* with his limousine.

As the young woman sat waiting for the boarding call, once more the touch of nausea returned. Thank God for soda crackers, she thought, pulling a packet out of her handbag. When she had mentioned her recurring stomach aches that seemed to happen early in the day to an older Iranian teacher, the woman had laughed. "Better get going on those little knit socks!" Could it be true? Could she actually be *pregnant?* As soon as she got back to Moscow, she would look up an obstetrician. The dark-haired cousin thought about Gennady—would he be pleased to learn if he was to be a father!

A metallic voice burst from a nearby loudspeaker, calling her flight number. Galina groped for her bags and made her way into the throng headed toward the gate.

* * *

Iran Air Force Military Hangar; Bandar Abbas International Airport, at That Moment:

On the concrete apron in front of the maintenance hangar, the technician dropped into the cockpit of the parked F-14 "Tomcat", one of the fighter-aircraft left over from the "Shah's" buying spree of American warplanes back in the 'seventies, just before the Revolution. The young man reached down and turned on the transponder for a regular test of the device that answered electronically to inquiries from friendly ships and airplanes. The Americans called it "Identification—Friend or Foe"; "IFF" for short; the Iranians had kept the terminology. Satisfied that the aircraft's device was operating properly, the fellow hauled himself out of the cockpit, leaving the device still operating.

* * *

The destroyer captain was seething. "How long is this damn sandstorm going to last?"

"Language, captain?"

The ship's commander turned about to face the chaplain and his wry grin. "Oh, sorry, *Padre`,* but things are hectic up here, right now."

"Ah, but you must remember that the Lord will never give you more than you can endure."

"I guess you're right—of course, you're right. It's just that we're having a helluva—sorry . . . a 'heckuva' tough time—with the Aegis cruiser, over there. It looks like he's trying to start a war."

"We must always pray for God's peace, captain." The cleric fingered his collar and stepped away.

* * *

Bandar Abbas International Airport, Aboard Iranian Airlines 'Airbus A-300'; Flight 013:

As the airliner turned onto the runway, already several babies were crying; it was going to be a loud flight to Dubai. Galina stared out from the window seat as much trying to ignore the annoying racket as she was interested in the scenery outside. Little dust-devils hopped and swirled along the barren ground; what little plant life that had managed to gain a foot-hold in the parched desert earth alongside this airport runway in southwest Iran was waving back and forth in the hot breeze.

The engines became louder and the ground started moving past. She looked down at the left engine, its curved nose protruding from underneath the leading edge of the wing a few meters below her window, as the pavement swept by faster and faster.

Then came the leaning-back sensation and the "thumps" that she had come to recognize on the flights from Moscow. The first time she had heard the strange bumping noises coming from the airplane, she had been frightened, but her seat-mate had told her that it meant the wheels were off the ground and the landing gear was coming up—all perfectly normal.

As she kept on gazing out the window, trying to ignore the wails from the children, whose ears were doubtless giving trouble as they climbed, once more she felt the tingle of anticipation that had been building up these past few days—she was going home to Gennady! The young woman slipped off her sandals and flexed her toes: she knew it already, just as women across the ages had known it; an instinct, a knowledge borne of human survival, actually, even though it was all new to her: Galina was sure she was pregnant.

* * *

Strait of Hormuz; at That Moment:

"Thank God!" The captain and everyone on the command bridge of the "Arleigh Burke" class destroyer breathed a sigh of relief—the warship had at last run out from under the sandstorm cloud. The warship's commanding officer stepped out onto the bridge wing, now covered by a thin layer of yellow sand that crunched beneath the soles of his military oxfords. The ship's entire upperworks had taken on the color of sulfur—even as he watched, the stuff was blowing off the decks into the wind in wispy saffron sheets. Blinking, the man looked aft; astern, the churning, receding cloud still held the Aegis Cruiser in its blinding grip.

"Signals from Aegis, sir! They are tracking a hostile aircraft headed in their direction!"

* * *

Aboard Aegis Cruiser:

"Unidentified bogey descending in our direction! Range . . . twenty miles, closing rapidly!"

The captain squirmed in his elevated leather chair and frowned. An air of urgency came over the "Electronic Warfare Suite"; every man scanned his console.

"Acquired transponder signals!"

"Ascertain aircraft type!"

"Transponder consistent with 'F-Fourteen', sir!"

The captain thought fast: Iran's military had F-14's.

"Range eighteen miles! Bogey is descending! Speed four-five-zero-knots!"

The captain spoke into his microphone. "Standby *'Standard'!*"

On the ship's forecastle, the deck parted; a pair of long slender shapes leaped upward onto the twin launcher. Following the digital commands from the Weapons Control Center, the gangly mechanism jerked around to port in the direction of the suspicious aircraft approaching from the southeast.

"Visual contact?"

"No visual, sir . . . ship still in sandstorm."

"Bogey still descending, sir! Range sixteen miles! Speed four-five-zero-knots!"

"Warn him away! Radio him to stay away!"

* * *

In front of the military hangar at the Bandar Abbas airport, the F-14's transponder received the signal from the Aegis cruiser forty miles away over the water and dutifully responded its aircraft type and position.

The US Navy warship interpreted the signal as an F-14 hurtling toward it—the particles in the sandstorm cloud were causing ghost reflections that made it appear on the consoles in the Electronic Warfare Suite to be an aircraft descending toward the ship. At the same time, the Airbus was returning a radar echo on a straight line with the responding F-14 sitting on the ground twenty miles directly behind it. The Airbus's transponder was transmitting on a civilian frequency that the Aegis Cruiser was not equipped to receive.

* * *

On the destroyer, the officers standing on the command bridge had been monitoring the signals from the Aegis cruiser with growing concern. From their vantage point twelve miles ahead of the cruiser, they knew that the other ship's bogey was climbing, not descending; was traveling at a ground-speed of only two-hundred-five-knots, not four-hundred-fifty; and was likely an airliner that had just taken off from Bandar Abbas.

The captain suspected the Aegis was mis-identifying the target. "Send a warning in plain language to the aircraft to turn away!"

"Sir, no response!"

"Keep sending! Tell him he is about to be shot down! Tell him to make an emergency turn!"

* * *

The Aegis radar officer was shifting nervously in his seat. "Sir, the bogey is still descending toward us . . . range, thirteen miles . . . speed, four-five-zero!"

"F-Fourteen still transponding!"

"Tell him to climb away! If he comes to eleven miles, launch missiles!"

"Sir, range eleven miles!"

The captain could wait no longer; his ship was under attack. "Launch missiles!"

On the foredeck, an orange flame, then another erupted. Two "Standard" missiles shot from the launcher, followed by gray contrails. The two rocketed away toward the southeast, into the sand-cloud that still obscured everything. But the streaking pair needed no visual aids; in seconds, guided by an invisible radar beam, their infared heat-seeking acquisition systems locked-on to the target's engine exhausts; as the missiles climbed out, their warheads armed themselves. Everything was automatic, pre-programmed; what would happen now was beyond human control.

"Sir, target is turning!"

* * *

292

All at once the airplane gave a vicious twist. Galina grabbed the armrest as a chorus of surprised shouts broke out in the cabin; a flight attendant fell across a seat arm in the next aisle.

Then came something white—something very hot—an indescribable blast of heat and pressure that no one in the cabin felt for more than a fraction of a second. For in a fleeting, along with two-hundred-seventy-nine others on the exploding, disintegrating Airbus, Galina Gavrona Lychina, the slender, dark-haired cousin, stepped across the threshold into eternity.

-13-

"Target destroyed!"

The word from "Weapons Control" to the "Aegis Electronic Warfare Suite" was greeted with desultory applause in the Command Center.

Then a communications specialist handed a message to the captain, still sitting in his high leather chair in the back of the electronics room. The commanding officer scanned the missive and frowned; it was from the captain of the destroyer patroling outside the sandstorm cloud, warning him not to shoot his missiles—he believed the target was a civilian airliner.

The Aegis captain crushed the paper in his hand. "Maintain course and speed."

* * *

The men on the bridge of the "Arleigh Burke" class destroyer gaped at the orange fireball hanging in the sky some miles away. As they watched, from far above, myriad pieces fluttered down along the edge of the sandstorm cloud toward the sea—spinning, twisting, turning; the early-morning sun glinting on some of the swirling sections making the long drop in a dreadful procession that seemed as if it would never stop; many chunks now chased by lenghtening white contrails as they fell; all far larger and more numerous than could have ever been possible with an F-14.

The executive officer shook his head in a hopeless denial of what he was seeing. "They shot down a civilian plane! It's a big one."

The chaplain made the sign of the cross, his lips moved silently; his hands clasped together.

The captain bounded into the wheelhouse. "Left full rudder! Come about to course three-two-zero! All ahead full!" He turned to the communications officer. "Get on the horn! Tell flagship that Aegis has shot down a civilian airliner in the Strait of Hormuz!"

In a few minutes, just as the destroyer was about to re-enter the sand-cloud, the second officer pointed to starboard. "The Aegis!"

Sure enough, the warship that had just downed the civilian airplane burst out from the yellow sand-cloud. "He's going away from the shoot-down!"

"Damn! That sorry—" The executive officer broke off his contempt as the destroyer plowed into the opaque curtain.

After maintaining course and speed for ten minutes, during which time the men had had to retreat back into the enclosed bridge to escape the swirling airborne sand, a lookout on the starboard bridge wing gave a shout.

"Wreckage!"

Many pairs of eyes stared in the direction the man was pointing. As the ship slowed, the executive officer, followed by the chaplain, and other men, left the command center and made their way aft toward the flat helicopter deck at the stern.

About the time they got there, the sand began to dissipate. As the ship coasted to a stop, wallowing in the light swell, sunshine burst upon the scene, its ironic, cheerful rays illuminating a scene of abject horror.

For the sight that met them bore upon the hardened navy men the magnitude of the disaster. All around were bodies— hundreds of them, it seemed—floating in the rising and falling swell along with waterlogged flotsam of all description, including rafts of scorched, ripped seat cushions; all mute evidence of the great flame that had enveloped everything as the airplane exploded. Even as the men watched, a big section of what looked like the airliner's tail turned over and sank in a welter of foam and bubbles. A strong odor of jet fuel hung over the water. As the destroyer came closer, the men could see that many of the bodies were actually only *parts* of bodies—a leg here, an arm there, a ripped torso; a head—many heads, it seemed; many if not most of the corpses were decapitated. Of those that were not, the heads were twisted in grotesque positions on the shoulders of the victims. Calloused crewmen groaned—many of the bodies were of children. All about, the water had a ghastly red hue—the blood of the hundreds floating on the surface. A sailor leaned over the rail, retching.

The medical officer stared at the twisted figures. "They call it 'internal decapitation'," he said to the chaplain, "it happens in a lot of accidents—a sudden motion that snaps the spinal cord but the head stays attached . . . it was if they were hanged." He shook his head. "Those people probably didn't know what hit them." As he looked about the awful scene, he saw that many of the bodies were burned. "It was quick and merciful, actually."

One of the sailors was groping with a long hook for a clear-plastic object floating against the side of the ship's hull. After a few tries, he managed to snag it and pull it aboard. "It's a passport!" he called out to the officers standing nearby, "in a waterproof case."

"Let's see it," the executive officer said, his hand outstretched. When he unzipped it, he observed that the booklet was printed in Cyrillic script. "It's in Russian."

"I know Russian," the chaplain said, taking it. When he opened it to the main pages, he saw the picture of a smiling young woman with short, dark hair. "'*Galina Gavrona Lychina; Moscow*'", he read aloud. "This person was on the plane." The officers and the sailor stared at the photograph.

"She was quite pretty, wasn't she?"

As the chaplain gazed out over the water at the bobbing bodies and bloody body parts, the man of religion knew that somewhere out there this girl was one of those floating in the mangled wreckage. Whoever she was—she didn't deserve this.

None of these people deserved this.

Just then, a pair of strange-looking craft nosed-up from around the other side of the ship. The executive officer recognized the Iranian flag; they were probably the gunboats the Aegis cruiser had recently been engaging. On the small vessels, uniformed men were gesturing and shouting at the American ship; shaking their fists; automatic rifles nosed out from openings in the little boats' sides. Forward, the destroyer's five-inch main-battery turret trained in their direction, its muzzle at full depression. The chaplain, still standing at the stern, gasped. Were these miniature vessels about to resume their battle against the Aegis cruiser with this destroyer?

The sound of the bigger ship's horn broke across the water. At the stern, the water began to move about. "I guess we are going to leave the recovery to the Iranians," the executive officer said, turning toward the bridge as the destroyer made its way slowly away from the carnage; astern, the gunboats were now edging into the macabre floating morgue of wrenched bodies and tangled debris.

* * *

"Good morning . . . and this is the 'Early Morning News Hour', thanks for joining us." The young female newscaster looked into the camera. "The top story this morning comes from the Persian Gulf', where an American warship has shot down an Iranian airliner—apparently by mistake." Behind the anchorwoman a picture of a large airplane came up. "Early reports from the scene say all aboard the 'Iranian Airlines' flight zero-one-three, that was bound from the coastal Iranian city of 'Bandar Abbas' to 'Dubai', across the 'Gulf', were killed."

A chiseled-featured blond man appeared on the screen. "For the story, we now go to our Pentagon correspondent . . . Albert Montroy—"

The dark-haired reporter stared into the camera for a long second, as if listening to his earpiece, then spoke in clipped tones. "It was a terrible mistake, apparently. That's what Pentagon officials are saying as the details start to come in about the incident in the 'Strait of Hormuz' that happened just after sunrise, local time, when a U.S. Navy warship, one of the modern, capable—and very expensive—'Aegis Cruisers', as they call it, made an awful error. Somehow, it's elaborate radars and weapons thought a civilian airliner was an attacking warplane. From what we are learning, the captain of the ship ordered the shoot-down when the airplane did not respond to radioed requests to turn away—"

The picture cut away to a middle-aged, silver-haired man in a blue military uniform who was stepping to a podium. Behind him, on a blue curtain, were white letters that read, "Pentagon", with a white rendering of the distinctive building.

"Now, the Pentagon Information Officer is here, and we suppose he has more details."

The man looked around at the reporters seated in the darkened room. "This morning in the Strait of Hormuz, in International waters, a United States Navy 'Aegis Cruiser' identified an aircraft approaching it at a high rate of speed from the direction of Bandar Abbas, Iran, to be a hostile combatant. Radars on the American ship determined that the unidentified airplane was descending directly at it . . . despite repeated radioed requests, the aircraft continued to descend at a high speed at the American ship in a maneuver consistent with an attack."

The man gripped the podium and went on. "When the aircraft failed to turn away, the captain ordered surface-to-air missiles to be employed to interdict the target. Accordingly, the target aircraft was destroyed. As it turned out, unfortunately, the aircraft was an Iranian airliner that had taken off from Bandar Abbas, a city in Iran at the Strait of Hormuz—I should point out here that the Bandar Abbas airport handles both civilian and Iranian military aircraft. Although the United States regrets the incident, the fact was that the aircraft failed to respond to queries and orders to turn away. The captain of the American warship followed normal procedures to protect his ship in International waters, as per standing orders." The man paused. "Questions?"

A man in the third row stood up; his face pasty in the garish reflected stage lights. "Did the American ship actually *see* the airliner before it shot off its missiles?"

"No . . . there was a sandstorm going on at the time, I'm told. We have no indication that the cruiser acquired its presumed attacker visually since the 'Aegis' system uses radars to track its targets."

Although several other reporters stood up, clamoring for attention, the same reporter managed a follow-up. "How far away was the airplane that the ship shot down?"

"The information I have is that the Aegis Cruiser fired its missiles when the unidentified aircraft was about a dozen miles from it."

An older, stocky woman, well-known as a gadfly reporter of long standing, gave a sneer that the television cameras picked up. "Sir, I have a two-part question . . . you say there was a 'sandstorm'? Ships, as you know, sail on the seas. This navy ship, I assume was on the *water*, sir, *away* from the land . . . so how did it become *blinded by sand,* as you say?"

The officer ignored the sarcastic tone of the question. "Sandstorms are very powerful and wide-ranging in that part of the world . . . you had another question?"

"If this ship had all this radar, then why did it shoot down an airliner full of innocent people?"

"Ah, ma'am, we are looking now into how the Aegis Cruiser mistook it for an attacking aircraft. *That* is the real question at the moment—"

The woman, shaking her head, sat down. The Pentagon Information Officer pointed at a reporter whose hand was up. "Over there . . . your question?"

"Will there be any disciplinary action taken against the captain of the cruiser? It was his order, presumably, that launched the missiles that shot down the airliner."

"The captain of the cruiser has been temporarily relieved of his command, which is normal in a case such as this . . . he is on his way to Washington, now, to tell his side of the story. There will be a 'Court of Inquiry' convened to investigate the matter." He pointed at another reporter.

"My sources tell me there was a *second* navy ship involved. Can you comment on that?"

"There was a U.S. Navy destroyer in the area, but it did not participate in the action."

"What about reports that the cruiser was in Iranian waters when it shot down the airplane?"

"The captain says his ship was in International waters. We are looking at all the data, now, to confirm this." He nodded at the group. "Thank you, very much."

The screen dissolved to the dark-haired network correspondent. "The news conference at the Pentagon concerning the shoot-down of an Iranian airliner early today in the Persian Gulf . . . the Information Officer telling reporters here that the U.S. ship was in

International waters and the captain will tell his side of the story to a 'Naval Court of Inquiry'. Now, back to you . . ."

The chiseled-featured male news anchor came back on camera. "We now go to the White House, where the President is about to make a statement."

The screen switched to a pastel-colored hallway with white trim that receded for a short distance, surmounted by ceiling chandeliers and flanked by sconces along the walls. A podium bearing the Presidential Seal was set up at the near end. The President of the United States was stepping forward on a red carpet toward the cameras, accompanied by other men; some in dark suits. A high-ranking-appearing military man stood to one side of the President.

The Chief Executive spread a paper on the podium, and, in the bright lights, began speaking. "I have this morning sent letters of condolences to the government of Iran, through the Swiss Embassy in Teheran, and to Russia, on the apparent shoot-down of an Iranian airliner by a United States Navy warship. According to their respective governments, on board the airliner were two-hundred-fifty-six Iranian passengers and crew, and twenty-four Russian Nationals, all of whose deaths the Government of the United States deeply regrets."

The President scanned around the space at the assembled news reporters, a few of whose heads were visible in the camera range. Next to him was the glum-looking Secretary of State.

"The Government of the United States re-iterated in the notes that the U.S. Navy warship, an 'Aegis Cruiser', on patrol in the Persian Gulf, was operating legally in International waters and, according to its captain, was being stalked by an unidentified aircraft that was on a descending course toward it at a high rate of speed, consistent with making an attack. The American warship tried to contact the airplane and warn it away. From some electronic signals it was making, and for some other reasons that are classified, the aircraft appeared to be an Iranian warplane. At a certain point, the cruiser—believing itself to be under attack by a hostile aircraft—launched defensive missiles and destroyed the airplane. We now know it was a civilian airliner. The question, now, is *why* was the airliner descending toward the American warship at a high speed in an apparent attack mode? Only the Iranians canswer that question."

The President picked up the paper, turned about, and made his way back down the brilliantly-lighted hallway, followed by his advisors and the others.

The male newscaster came back on camera. "The President telling reporters that the United States regrets the events in the Persian Gulf and the airliner shoot-down that happened today." He paused a moment, as if listening to his earpiece."Now we go to the Russian Embassy in Washington, where our Diplomatic Correspondent—Irving R. Flessner—is standing by . . ."

A middle-aged man was in the act of brushing a lock of graying hair out of his eyes, when, with a start, he looked up into the camera. "We are waiting here in the Reception Room of the Russian Embassy, where the Russian Ambassador is about to make a statement. As you know, it now appears there were about two-dozen Russians on board the Iranian airliner that the U.S. Navy warship shot down, and, from what I am hearing, the Russians are extremely unhappy with what the American government has said so far."

There was some movement behind the man, who turned about for a moment. A heavyset, graying man was stepping toward a bank of microphones, followed by a man in a military uniform, along with some other serious-looking individuals in business suits. The newsman spoke in a low voice into his own microphone. "The Russian Ambassador will now speak."

The foreigner fingered his eyeglasses, then looked down at some papers in his hand. "This morning, the American Secretary of State informed me that one of the American warships patrolling in the Persian Gulf had shot down a civilian airliner— supposedly by mistake. It was determined that twenty-four citizens of the Russian Federation were aboard the airplane, of which there were no survivors. The American government says the airplane was attacking it in International waters . . . by our *'National Technical Means'*, we have determined that the American warship was, in fact, in Iranian waters, acting illegally."

The man glanced at the glowering military man standing next to him, and went on. "The Government of the Russian Federation therefore protests in the strongest terms the illegal actions of the American warship and rejects the so-called 'explanation' that the aircraft was acting in a hostile manner toward the American warship that was illegally in Iranian territorial waters and demands and an apology and compensation for the Russian lives lost in this illegal action by the American warship."

The man glared at the cameras for a second, then stepped back, his place at the microphones taken by the man in the military uniform.

"This is the Russian Military Attaché," the network correspondent's voice whispered, as the man began speaking in a heavy accent.

". . .was unwarranted and provocative, and therefore the Defense Ministry of the Russian Federation is taking the following actions: By the request of the Iranian Government, elements of the Russian 'Black Sea Fleet' will transit to the Persian Gulf to take up stations to insure the safety of Russian citizens in the region, and to insure that American warships will obey the recognized elements of International Law. The Russian Federation warships will operate inside the Iranian twelve-mile limit, only—unless provoked."

The officer's medals glistened in the glare of the overhead lights, as he looked around, then went on. "From this time forward, should any American warship enter Iranian waters illegally, it will be considered as an aggresive action that will be met by strong and effective Russian military and naval forces. *The Americans must make no mistake about this—*"

The frowning man stepped back, as one of the other men in a suit waved his hands at the reporters, signifying they would take no questions. From across the room came the murmurings of broadcast and cable news reporters speaking into their microphones punctuated by the snapping and zipping sounds of still-cameras.

"Strong words from the Russians . . ." correspondent Flessner said, as over his shoulder could be seen the backs of the receding diplomats. "The big story here is that the Russian Navy will now directly confront the U.S. Navy in the Persian Gulf, and seems ready to take on the United States militarily, there. It must be said, though, that the rejection of the American 'explanation', as the Ambassador put it, was almost a foregone conclusion, given how diplomacy works. It remains to be seen how and if the two countries can work-out all of this."

He paused, then went on, "all this is very unfortunate, of course, since after the fall of the Soviet Union last winter, there had been some thawing in relations between the two countries, as the Russians groped toward some sort of new 'Capitalism-based' society. This is a setback for all that, now. This is Irving R. Flessner, at the Russian Embassy, now back to you . . ."

The scene shifted to an older, thin-lipped man in a gray suit staring stiffly into the camera, nodding as the male news anchor voiced-over, "Now, we go to Austin, Texas, and our Military Consultant, Retired Army Colonel Morris Tredd, who's been following this—Colonel Tredd, we heard the President as much as apologize for shooting down the airline . . . at the same time he claims the American warship was under attack . . . the Russians are threatening military action—how do you see this?"

The man cleared his throat. "Well, this event—the American warship shooting down a civilian airliner with Russians on board—is a serious matter. Now, I'll leave 'International Law' to the lawyers and the diplomats, as the military implications are serious, enough." The man squirmed in his seat, and went on. "There are several contradictory factors, here, as I see them, and frankly, somebody is not telling the truth. It remains to be seen if whether the American 'Aegis Cruiser' was in International waters—as the U. S. Government is claiming—or if it was in Iranian territory, as both the Iranians and the Russians are insisting. By now, both sides know the truth, but the claims of both sides are at odds, and may stay that way until the diplomats have had their say."

"Why would the Iranians want Russian warships in their waters?"

"Well, we have known for some time that there is a connection between the two countries—after all, the Russians have been building nuclear reactors for electricity in Iran for some time, and I'll bet that the Iranians still owe them some money. That said, it gives the Russians a chance to flex some muscles after their drop in status and power since the fall of the Soviet Union."

"What did the Russian military man mean by 'National Technical Means'?"

"'Satellites'—theirs and ours—were probably looking down from on-high and saw the whole thing—even with the sandstorm. That's what I mean by both sides knowing the truth, by now. Either we or the Russians will eventually have to back-down on whether or not the American ship was in Iranian waters."

"Why is that so important?"

"You don't shoot down a non-combatant in International waters—for that matter, you don't shoot down a non-combatant, period, in peacetime! Whatever the outcome, to the whole world, it looks bad for the Americans to be killing these civilians. It's like the Korean Airliner 'Double-Oh-Seven' shoot-down by the Soviets back in 'eighty-three' all over, again! They looked like bloodthirsty monsters, then—and that's how we look, now, I'm afraid." The man pursed his lips. "And if the Aegis Cruiser really *was* in Iranian waters . . . well, I don't want to even *think* about how the world would see *that*."

The man went on in his gravelly voice. "One thing I noticed the military man say was that their warships would 'protect Russian citizens in the area', which is interesting in itself. That could mean the Russians may have more going on in Iran than we realized." The man looked thoughtful for a second. "On the other hand, the state of the Russian Navy is nowhere near like it was under the Soviets, so it remains to be seen how they would do this—unless they plan to use submarines, of which they have the world's biggest and the most capable types . . . *now this would pose a real problem for the Americans*."

"All because our navy shot down one airliner by mistake?"

"Like I said, perhaps the Russians tipped us off—without intending to—that they have more at stake in Iran than they have been letting on . . . an earlier press briefing said the Russians on the airliner were 'school teachers', but that could have been a cover for something else. Our Intelligence people are quite familiar with how they use athletes and others as spies and undercover operatives."

The newscaster's voice spoke from off-camera. "There's been talk about an Iranian nuclear program . . . you think maybe these 'school teachers' could have been nuclear scientists, or something?"

"Anything is possible. One thing we do know, now, is that there were many children on the airplane who were killed." The man in the suit shrugged. "That, alone, makes it really unfortunate for the kids—and for the image of the United States."

The male news anchor's voice came on as the man in the gray suit sat, nodding. "Our military consultant, Retired Army Colonel Morris Tredd, on the shootdown of an Iranian airliner over the Strait of Hormuz overnight by a U.S. Navy warship. Colonel Tredd, thank you for joining us this morning."

* * *

Grozny, Chechnya; Late Afternoon, the Same Day:

"Comrades, one more patrol, then we go home!" Rodion Golubko was in an expansive mood; indeed, everyone in the platoon that included the closely-knit group that had been all the way to America recently and had fought other Americans at the Sarajevo airport, were ready for some rest and recreation. "Now is not the time to let-up!" the colonel went on, "it is at times like these that it is easy to let down our guard."

One more night's patrol! Gennady was thinking about it as he adjusted the sling on his automatic rifle. In the corner of the tent, his duffel bag was already packed; by mid-day tomorrow, he and the others would be on the airplane, headed back toward Moscow. He could already visualize Galina, warm and willing, next to him.

* * *

In Moscow and across Russia, the evening newspapers were publishing the names and pictures of the twenty-four Moscow-area schoolteachers and education specialists who were confirmed killed on the Iranian airliner shot down by the Americans; their faces were also on the main evening television news program. One of those on the list and identified with her picture along with the others on the television newscast was: *'Galina Gavrona Lychina, 24, Moscow; a primary schoolteacher of the Tverskaya District'.*

* * *

The old woman cracked open her apartment door and peered out. What was the wailing of voices all about? In the corridor, at a nearby door, stood several people she recognized in the building, along with an older man in a military uniform, and a child; a little girl. The woman frowned. It was the apartment of that nice young couple, a schoolteacher and her husband, who lived there, now. They had just gotten married, someone said. But why were they crying?

* * *

In the Center of Grozny, Chechnya; Post-Midnight:

The flat-bed truck with soldiers sitting on side-benches at the rear drove past the checkpoint. The man in the Russian military uniform saluted Colonel Golubko, sitting in the right front seat beside Gennady Lychin, who was driving, as the big machine rumbled by. But a block farther on, outlined in the headlights, was a *second* checkpoint; its gate, like those all over the city used after dark by the Russian forces, was down. Rodion Golubko stood up in the open seat and looked up and down the street flanked by dark, multi-storied buildings and frowned; they had just gone by a checkpoint—he could still see its vague outline behind them; the next scheduled stop was supposed to be some blocks farther on. The vehicle pulled up on the muddy, cobblestone street in front of the gate and lurched to a stop. A

306

sudden alarm ran through the officer: *Something is not right about this.*

All at once, out of the shadows stepped a turbaned man leveling an automatic weapon at them. "Ambush!" the colonel shouted. "Out!"

As the men scrambled over the sides, the rebel soldier opened fire. One of the Russians went down at once, his weapon clattering across the slippery pavement; most of the others bounded into an alleyway; crouching. From the direction of the first checkpoint, other men were running, shouting in a native language. Terenty realized that both stops must have been manned by Chechens dressed in Russian uniforms, whose job was to pass them along into the trap! Now they were jammed in a pincer between two squads of enemy irregulars!

As he hugged the dark wall there came more yells and gunfire.

Grishinov huffed down next to him. "They got Lychin!" Captured him! Maybe others, too!"

"What!" Terenty gasped, horrified that his friend at that moment was being dragged off into captivity. Chechens had a reputation for torture and murder. Hot lead from automatic fire whanged against a nearby brick wall, gouging out chunks above them. Just then, the personnel truck exploded with a loud *BOOM!* Chunks of ripped-apart steel and glass slammed against the sides of buildings.

Someone shoved at Terenty's shoulder, as flames and explosions rent the narrow street, lighting nearby buildings with flickering orange. Up and down the street, armed rebels, outlined in the flames, dashed about.

"We must get away from here!" Colonel Golubko gestured to his men over the smash of gunfire. "Back that way! Behind us!"

Turning about, Terenty saw a vague opening at the other end of the alleyway. He was torn between the immediate need to escape and going back to look for his friend.

The colonel motioned his weapon, seen by the others in the light of the burning vehicle, toward their rear. "Go! Move it!" Crouching down, the older man covered the others as they retreated, then followed them into the dark, tunnel-like shadows toward the open lights at the other end.

"That way!" Colonel Golubko gestured his automatic rifle up the byway, one block off the ill-fated street down which they had driven into the trap. Hunkered down, they loped up the sidewalk, then crossed to the other side and made their way down another alley one block still farther over. "Hold up!" the ranking officer called, motioning them into a place behind a trash bin. "Sound off!"

Lychin, Malinovsky and Blagron did not answer, nor did Chernenko, the radio operator.

"They shot Chernenko!" one of the fellows gasped, "he is dead."

"They captured the others."

Terenty knew the Chechens usually tortured information out of captives, then killed them—the fate of most of the Russian dead so far in the Chechnya uprising. He thought about his friend with a sinking feeling. *Galina!* A widow, and so soon after she and Gennady were married? An unbearable thought."We must go back!"

"We will wait until dawn, then begin a search." Colonel Golubko's voice sounded resulute, the result, the others knew, of years of training and experience for just this sort of dire situation.

* * *

An automatic rifle muzzle rammed at Gennady's kidney, sending stabbing pain through his whole body as the three prisoners ran gasping down dark alleyways and across several gloomy streets, surrounded by the captors, whom he saw wore hoods over their heads and were talking back and forth to each other in a language he did not understand. As they ran along, the men prodded the Russians with more hammer- like blows to their backs. Gennady could feel liquid dropping down his backside, sticking to his shirt; his own blood, no doubt.

Some blocks farther on, the men shoved him and the two others, whom he now recognized as Malinovsky and Blagron, down what looked to be a cellar door next to a lighted basement window just above ground level.

One of the men pushed aside the door with his rifle stock and stepped into the space. From within, came voices in animated conversation. Gennady recognized Russian. The hooded man came back and motioned with his automatic weapon. Rough hands on his shoulders shoved him, stumbling, along with the two other captives, down some low steps into a dingy cellar lighted by bare bulbs. At the other end of the musty space, beyond row of crates and stacked wooden boxes, Gennady saw a bald, heavyset, older-looking man sitting at a beat-up wooden table, staring at them as they came closer to him. Standing in the shadows was a young, turbaned fellow, whose dark eyes were darting back and forth between the captives and the man at the table.

The man nodded at the captors, who stood aside, their weapons at the ready, then he looked the prisoners up and down. "You are Russian?" he growled in the Motherland language.

The three nodded.

The man's beady eyes focused hard on the trio, in particular at Gennady; a frown creased his shiny, furrowed forehead. "Do I not know you?"

Gennady and the two other prisoners glanced at each other.

"Were you at the 'Academy' in Moscow, last year?"

He nodded. A chill ran through Gennady. *Who is this man?*

"Well well!" the hairless insurgent said, with a lopsided grin, looking Gennady over, leaning back in the squawking chair, "I thought I recognized you . . . you and your friend were always getting into trouble, right? What was your name, again?"

"'Lychin . . . Major Gennady Lychin'."

"'Lychin'! Ah, yes." He gave a sneer that Gennady seemed to recall from somewhere. "You do not remember me? I used to be known as 'General Putridchenko'!"

The three prisoners gave a collective gasp; the guards gripped their automatic rifles tighter. The bald man glanced at the youth standing next to the table, shaking his head. The young fellow with the turban said something to them in a language incomprehensible to the captives. The armed irregulars lowered their weapons.

"You disappeared!" Blagron blurted out."

"Yes, I did, did I not? Now I am here . . . I have another name . . . another look . . . another identity—for you see, I am in the same position as each of you now are—a deserter from the Russian military!"

"We are not deserters! We were taken by these . . . these—"

The seated man shook his bullet-shaped head; in the glare of the garish overhead bulb, he looked more pallid than ever. "Ah, but you *are* deserters, now! You can never return to Russia . . . at least not as *Russian* soldiers. You see, you have those little 'chips' in your wrists, and your magnetized blood has your identity in it—remember? Satellites can track you from space . . . you know the penalties for deserting Spetsnaz." The man gave a frown. *"And now that you know who I am, I will not let you go back to Russia, either."*

Gennady stole a despairing glance at the hooded guards and at the other two captive soldiers. Galina's face flashed across his mind—would he never see her again? They were supposed to be going home, today.

The hairless one at the table was speaking in the nasally voice he now remembered from the Academy. "Comrades, I am prepared to make you an offer—an offer you can accept or refuse." He spread his beefy hands. "Either you become part of our 'Organization '. . . or these men, here"—Putridchenko motioned to the hooded gunmen, who lowered their weapons at the captive trio—"these fellows will take you out and shoot you." He shrugged. "You really have no choice, comrades." The man gave a smirk. "Besides, we can use you; I will reward you with great amounts of money and other advantages."

Malinovsky spoke up. "I . . . that is, *we* do not understand—"

". . . about the 'Organization'?" The bald man leaned forward in his squeaky chair "I suppose I can tell you some things, now; it makes no difference . . . either you will become part of us or you will be shot. Whichever way, you are not going to be telling anybody outside what this is about."

Gennady's face was burning; this could not be happening. He thought of comrades in the unit— surely, they were looking for them, by now.

Galina.

Putridchenko was going on. "We supply and train revolutionary groups all around the world. We are well-connected to many organizations . . . many governments and people of great wealth and power whose aim is to end the control of reactionary governments on the oppressed peoples of the world."

"'Revolutionary groups'?" Blagron blurted out.

"The world is full of people who will give their all—their lives, even—to further their cause . . . and there are many 'causes'." The bald man saw the uncomprehending looks on the young mens' faces. "Our organization has taken advantage of this, much to our benefit, financially and otherwise. We have great influence in this." He paused and spread his hands, again. "You can be a part of it." Putridchenko shrugged. "Otherwise, we will shoot you, right now, and get it over with." The man sneered." Like I say, none of you will be going back to Russia. Either you cooperate—or you are dead." He nodded his shiny head. "Be assured, comrades: *whichever way you now turn, either I or the 'G-R-U' will kill you.*"

The three glanced among themselves; all were thinking the same thing: they would go along and play for time; perhaps there would be a chance to escape.

"And do not think you will ever escape, comrades," the former Soviet general smirked. "For we will devise to not only *erase you from Russia*, but to have you in our—that is, *my*— complete control, always!"

Putridchenko was staring at the three captives standing before him. "Come, come, comrades," he said, raising the remnants of his eyebrows in the direction of his waxy forehead. "It is most simple, actually—cooperate . . . and you will be part of a rich, growing organization." The man shrugged. "If you do *not* go along—" He spread his hands, as if impatient.

Gennady was overwhelmed by a crushing sense of despair— it now looked as if he might never again see or touch his slender, dark-haired wife. To himself, he cursed Chechnya; he cursed the military for sending him here; and in particular, he cursed this gross man who held his life and the lives of the other two captives in his grubby-looking, nicotine-stained hands.

"So, what is it? What is your answer?"

The young men looked at each other; they knew they had no choice if they wanted to stay alive.

Gennady bit his lip. "All right . . . what do we do?"

"Excellent choice, comrades!" Putridchenko nodded and gave an off-center grin that to Gennady looked cynical. He tapped his fingertips together in a gesture of finality—for the Russian soldiers, there would now be no going back. The general motioned to the three hooded fellows, who pulled off their disguises; the trio saw they were swarthy, Middle-Eastern looking; in the glaring lights they looked to be not much older than teenagers, Gennady thought. The man said something to the young turbaned man who had been standing next to the table all this time, whom Gennady decided was the bald man's translator. Putridchenko gestured at the new recruits. "Take them to temporary quarters. In the morning, we will get organized." The translator repeated the words in the others' language.

The guards motioned their automatic weapons for the three to follow them. Gennady stepped along with his two compatriots, with one gunman in front of them and the other two following, down rows of big, stacked wooden boxes. As they made their way through, the young Russians saw, from the stencilled words on them, that they contained crated 'Kalashnikov AK-74's'— thousands of them, it appeared. It occurred to Gennady that if what they had seen so far was any indication, this "Organization", as General Putridchenko had put it, seemed to have plenty of resources to afford all this. What are all these weapons doing, here? he wondered. Then he remembered the hairless man had said something about "world-wide causes". Squinting in the shadowy light, he saw that their guards were brandishing AK-74's, which seemed to offer some sort of answer to his question.

The gunmen pointed into a little lighted room with bunks and a table. Behind a curtain was a privy. One of them nodded, which the Organization's newest "members" took to mean that these spaces were to be their sleeping quarters.

* * *

"I wonder if they are they far from here?" Terenty whispered aloud the question that was torturing the five remaining men of the Spetsnaz squad who were holed-up in a cellar at the back of a building in a central Grozny alley. His friend and the two others had been captured by Chechen insurgents on their last night in this godforsaken hellhole. Terenty pushed back a sudden wave of despair.

How would he ever explain this to Galina?

From what they had been told before they arrived, so far in this conflict very few Russians had survived being taken away by the rebels. There had been rumors that a few—regular conscripts, for the most part—had gone over to the other side, but he knew such a thing would be impossible for elite Spetsnaz officers. Besides, they had the implanted chips: if the three could get back to a friendly area, the satellite system could locate them. The captives would just have to remain strong until the rescuers could get to them—provided, of course, they were still alive.

On his tiptoes, Terenty peeped out a low basement window at street level; the first rays of sunlight were starting to outline their muddy, moldy surroundings. All around them stood the shadowy, blasted shells of two-and-three story brick buildings; their stark walls pointing up at the rose-tinted sky like jagged fingers. They were in the middle of a war zone.

Colonel Golubko edged up and looked out, squinting. "We will begin our search as soon as it is full daylight," he said, running his hand over his stubbly chin.

Terenty took a deep breath and tried to be hopeful, but underneath it all, he knew the chances of ever seeing his compatriots again were small.

* * *

Someone was nudging Gennady's shoulder, prodding him. With a start, he came awake—where was he? From somewhere daylight was filtering into a strange space; in the half-light, a brown-skinned young man wearing a turban frowned down at him. Then it all came back: the midnight ambush; the capture of himself and the two others; General Putridchenko. His back was aching; he could almost still feel the automatic rifle butts jabbing him. Moving about, a tugging pain came to his backside; his shirt was stuck to his skin where he had earlier been bleeding.

Galina. He had to fight off renewed waves of despair that were trying to roll over him—this was the day he was supposed to return to Moscow, to his new wife—by now, she would have returned from her teaching trip to Iran. The young officer knew he must try to drive all thoughts of her from his mind for now and concentrate on staying alive; somewhere out there, he was certain, Colonel Golubko and the rest of the unit were searching for them. He took a deep breath of the musty air and stretched. In the next bunks, Malinovsky and Blagron were also coming around; their initial looks of confusion turning to dismay when they realized they were also in Chechen captivity.

"The general wants to see you now," the fellow was saying in broken Russian, after making sure they were all awake.

"I trust you comrades slept well . . . " The bald-headed man sat at the battered table beneath the glaring light-bulb, twiddling his thumbs at the three unkempt-looking Russians. Gennady and the other two shuffled from one foot to the other, looking about, trying to get some bearings, to sort-out their situation.

"They"—Putridchenko nodded his domed head at three dark-haired youths standing by— "will take you to the facilities for you to clean yourselves. When you return, we will prepare you for the procedures."

With that, the three insurgents motioned for the captive trio to follow them. Gennady frowned. What had he meant by "procedures"?

A half-hour later, the young men were again standing before the bald man, this time outfitted in local garb. "It will not do for you to look like Russians, anymore," he grinned, revealing gapped teeth. Gennady observed that Putridchenko was wearing the same type of old-style civilian clothes as he, Malinovsky, and Blagron had donned.

The Ukrainian stood up. "We will now do the procedures." The three "Organization" inductees glanced at each other as the heavyset man turned toward the rear of the warehouse-like basement. "Follow me."

After a short walk down a cob-webbed aisle of crates, he led the three into a brightly-lit room with a half-dozen white-sheeted gurneys arranged around the walls. Putridchenko motioned to some scuffed-looking wooden chairs. "Take seats . . . the doctors will be with you in some minutes."

Doctors? The three looked at each other, perplexed. Just then a slender, middle-aged man in a medical smock-coat stepped in, followed by two serious-looking younger men in similar attire.

"You are the new recruits?" the first man asked, in imperfect Russian. Gennady gave the fellow a blank stare as the newcomers motioned to the gurneys. "Each of you will lie on a table and put out your left arm. This should not take too long."

While the new Organization men climbed onto the wheeled examination tables, the doctors pulled tubes, packages, and other medical paraphernalia from cabinets. One of the men rolled a chromed transfusion dolly next to each of the gurneys. Another medical man tugged into the room a machine with dials and switches on it.

"What are you doing?" Blagron spoke up, as a thick needle jabbed into a vein in his arm.

"They did not tell you?" The older doctor looked surprised. "We are neutralizing the magnetism in your bloodstream, then we will replace the Soviet electronic chip in your wrist with a new one." The fellow pulled a rubber cord from the Russian's wrist. "When you leave here, you will be like a new soldier!"

Overhearing this exchange from the next table, another wave of nervous uncertainty rolled over Gennady—these men were serious. As he watched a greenish liquid course from the machine into his arm, once more the gravity of his situation was borne upon him; whatever these doctors were doing to him, it meant a total break from his Russian past and an induction into whatever new life was ahead of him. From the expressions on the faces of Blagron and Malinovsky, they were thinking the same thing.

Gennady shook his head on the low pillow of the gurney, trying to fight down the prospect that he might never again see Galina. Would she ever know what had happened to him? Would she think he was dead? If so, would she someday marry some other man? Would she have children with him? It was an unbearable thought. The young man felt sorry for himself. And for Galina.

"Well, that is it . . ." the doctor said, as he stopped the machine. Then he pulled out the needle and put a small gauze bandage on Gennady's arm. "Hold this for a few minutes." Malinovsky and Blagron were doing the same.

One of the other doctors rolled a tray into the room, replacing the bigger machine they had been using. Gennady glanced over; on the portable table were three plastic wrappers. He recognized the little packages as looking almost the same as those he had seen back at the Academy last year when they had implanted the first chip into his wrist.

The doctor gave his forearm an injection; in a few minutes the procedure was completed.

Putridchenko appeared at the doorway, looking impatient. "It is most important to destroy the old chips so they cannot be traced." He motioned. "Follow me."

The three took seats in battered chairs facing the bald man across the table. "You are actually most fortunate," the "Academy's" former "Chief of Security" was saying in his wheezing, high-pitched voice that sounded to Gennady to be out of keeping for such a large man, "our organization has great uses for men with your skills and training." He gave a pause for effect, then went on. "As I said last night, it can be very rewarding to you in money."

Galina. Money could not replace her.

The hairless Ukrainian was talking on. "There is something else that has changed about me, besides the way I look. I am now known as 'Leonid Efimovich Retchko'—'General Retchko'—do not address me by any other name."

"'Retchko' . . ." The three men repeated the word.

"Now—here is what we are doing . . ."

For the next two hours, during which time attendants brought Chechen breakfasts and drink to the men, Retchko, using maps and charts, told them the whole story of the international Cartel, also known as the "Organization", that was supplying arms and training to revolutionaries all over the world; about the Nigeria connection; the Tora Bora group; the Cuban, Iranian and North Korean supply lines; everything about the operation in places as far away as the South Pacific islands. The objective was to foment revolution leading to a new—and far more structured and rigid—world order controlled by clients of the Cartel.

"The world's peoples will soon know what we are doing!" The man gave a lopsided grin. "The Americans, for sure, will find out . . . and we have *big* plans for America . . . oh, yes—!"

For Gennady, it would mean cutting all his ties to the past—including those to Russia and to his new wife. He was in agony about Galina. But he knew he could not go back to his old military unit—on pain of death, he knew. Retchko had made that point very clear. Malinovsky had a faraway look on his face: the soldier had a girl in Moscow; he would not be seeing her again, either. Gennady was unsure of Blagron's former social life; the husky, redheaded young man had kept such things to himself.

Retchko was talking. "Our most important need right now is for specialized ammunition of the 'depleted-uranium' type for anti-tank weapons."

Gennady thought about the Russian soldiers who had been killed by Chechens using such projectiles and felt guilty. His mind was still reeling with the realization that he would now be a part of the broad-based conglomerate providing this kind of weaponry against his friends—his *former* friends, as they now were. For—like it or not—his life was now under the control of these ideologically-driven men and their minions. He frowned clinically at the wrapped bandage on his wrist. Under that gauze, beneath his skin, he knew that that very moment the chip was magnetizing and programming the hemoglobin of his blood to allow the "Organization", as the man called it, to locate him anywhere in the world. And from what he had observed so far, the Cartel's tracking-chip system looked to be at least as effective as Moscow's had been. Gennady sighed: it looked as if he would have to try to forget his past life and everything and everyone connected with it. In truth, he had no choice but to try to make the best of the situation, if he was going to stay alive. Another thought came to him: Retchko had said he would actually make money doing this—as if money could substitute for what he was giving up.

Galina. He was giving *her* up. A wave of regret came over him. What would she ever think? Perhaps all this was just a bad dream; that he would wake up, roll over, hold his wife, and go on to have a normal life. His eyes moved to the guards standing by the cellar door, holding loaded Kalashnikovs. No, this was not a dream; there would be no more wife and perhaps nothing ever again for him resembling a normal life.

"Lychin!" Gennady came back to the present—Retchko was looking at him. "I have an assignment for you men to break into the *'Sulak Armory'.*" His eyes fixed hard on Gennady. "I know you guarded an armory at one time and you are familiar with that type of place."

The general spread out a map. "It is here," he said, pointing to the small town a few kilometers to the north of Grozny, on the short, curved river that drained into the Caspian Sea. "It is still in Russian hands, so you will have to be clever to get into it."

The three young men scanned the landscape portrayed on the page. "There is the armory," Blagron said, his finger on the spot, "we can take a boat right up to it."

"I would suggest a fishing-type boat," Retchko said, looking over their shoulders. "There are lots of them around and would not attract attention."

Malinovsky was frowning. "Where would we get one?"

"Chechens use them all the time . . . they will have one for you."

Gennady had to fight down a feeling of being a traitor—he was talking about attacking his former compatriots. A tug just then on the wrist bandage covering the chip implant brought him back to reality. The mission would go on.

* * *

The command vehicle drew up to Colonel Golubko, who was trudging alongside the muddy street with the remaining men of the unit. Its driver saluted the officer.

"Comrade Colonel, the 'area commander' says to withdraw to the airport and await orders. It is not secure here—there is much rebel activity, today."

The older man looked at his gaunt men, who stood grimy and unshaven, then at the man behind the wheel. Five armed soldiers were with him. "Come back in an hour with a personnel carrier. We have one more place to look."

* * *

Gennady, Malinovsky, and Blagron, along with a half-dozen turbaned Chechen irregulars, stood on a wobbly wooden dock. Before them, a reeking, twenty-meter fishing sloop rocked in the low swells; its glistening hemp lines that tied it to the wharf groaning in the cleats.

One of the Chechens was speaking to a middle-aged boatman in stained yellow-rubber slickers and a floppy, broad-brimmed rubber hat; evidently the vessel's captain. The fisherman kept nodding and producing a missing-toothed grin every few seconds.

Malinovsky turned to Ahmed, the Libyan translator, who was with them; Retchko had sent him along as a linguistic go-between for the men, who spoke various languages among themseves. "What are they saying?" Blagron and Gennady leaned-in to hear the young fellow's answer.

"They are talking about using the sailboat and what this is all about."

The bewhiskered Chechen motioned for the others to come aboard the little ship. The visitors and the local men who would be going on the mission stepped over the gangplank carrying fishing-tackle boxes that contained dismantled AK-74's, burglar-tools, presurized cloroform dispensers, and gas masks. Gennady and the other two had tried to make it clear to Retchko and the Chechens before they left that they wanted to avoid killing or injuring any Russian guards at the armory.

"Just accomplish the mission," the general had grunted.

In a few minutes, they were cast-off and making their way out into the river channel, headed upstream; the vessel's chugging auxiliary diesel engine sending a black cloud of exhaust drifting away into the late-afternoon breeze. A half-dozen swearing crewmen clambered about the rigging and hoisted a rip-repaired, triangular-shaped mainsail up the mast and out the swinging boom.

Gennady looked down into the smelly hold that usually carried iced-down sturgeon and other Caspian catch; on this trip it would be empty, save some ropes and netting heaped at the bottom that would be used later for tying-down the weaponry and ammunition they planned to "requisition" from the unsuspecting Russian armory.

Before long, the sun dropped behind some low hills around a bend in the river and the boat soon became enveloped in darkness. A nearly-full moon came up over the stern, outlining the trees and sandbars along the banks. At the rails, crewmen with flashlights called-out directions to the pilot at the stern tiller.

As the boat made its way west and northward up the narrow river, in a tiny cabin at the stern, its portholes covered by heavy blackout curtains, the Chechen leader, the boat captain, and the Russians, along with the ever-present Ahmed, pored over a map and some coffee-stained charts.

"The armory is about two kilometers beyond the next bend," the green-toothed head of the insurgents said, puffing on a rolled cigarette. From the smell, Gennady concluded the smoke was not from tobacco, an opinion bolstered by the man's increasingly giddy demeanor.

After a while, the darkened shape of a one-story building came into view, its form barely visible in the pale moonlight back in some woods, some distance from the water. The master cut the diesel and let the sail draw the silent boat up toward a low dock, just down a short paved road from the shadowy structure.

Leaning over, some of the crewmen used grappling hooks to snag the wooden pilings of the wharf and pull the boat alongside it. In a hurry a couple of the boatmen hopped off and snubbed the lines around cleats. The Russians followed the Chechen irregulars off the gunwale onto the little pier. In the rays of the moon, the insurgent leader issued silent orders to the men; Gennady and his compatriots would follow the man's directions, as the fellow was familiar with the armory's layout.

Spreading out, some of the men went around the building in one direction; others loped toward the opposite side. In the moonlight, they could now see that the building was surrounded by a fence—no surprise, since it was an important Russian military installation.

All at once, a figure loomed up alongside the fence—a guard! But the fellow seemed to be not paying attention, or perhaps was only half-awake. Blagron pulled one of the aerosol cloroform cans from his pack and tiptoed up alongside the oblivious sentry. In a couple of seconds, the young Russian lay slumped unconscious on the ground.

Malinovsky drew out some snips and cut through the wire-link fence. Then, giving the others a "come-on" motion, he stepped through the opening. Gennady was surprised that no alarm sounded; then he remembered the place had been in darkness from the time they had arrived. Maybe the electrical power was already off; on the boat the Chechen leader had told them they tried to keep the wires to the place cut all the time, to harrass the "occupiers", as he put it.

As they moved around toward the front of the building on the side away from the water, Gennady held up his hand. "Voices!" he whispered. Just then, the Chechens appeared from the opposite side. Gennady dropped below a window that had a tiny beam of light coming through it, and pointed at the apparent source of the speaking—a room behind a metal door. The man stepped around and tested the handle; the door was locked. He made motions for everyone to put on their gas masks and break out the chloroform aerosols; the Chechens gripped their AK-74's. Then to the Russians' surprise, the man stepped up boldly and rapped on the door!

The voices inside stopped, followed by rustling. Then the door cracked open.

The Chechen shoved against the barrier with his shoulder, flinging it back with a resounding *"WHACK!"* then burst through, followed by the others with all their spray cans aimed into the room. There came clattering thumps and sudden darkness; then silence. A couple of flashlights came on, revealing two soldiers lying on the floor amid the glass of a broken table lantern that the pair had knocked over. The room was filled with a cloud of the chloroform gas; everyone's' eyes were smarting.

The leading Chechen said something to Ahmed. "He says for you to locate the ammunition the general wants us to get from here!" The local man motioned to his men; several turned and made their way back outside. "They are going to get the loading carts from the boat!"

Gennady and the two others headed toward the main storage area in the back of the building. In the darkness, Malinovsky and Blagron ran their probing beams up and down down some aisles and along lines of shelves

"Here they are!" they whispered out, almost in unison. Down a dark row, stacks of crates were stenciled with lot numbers and production runs on boxes of depleted uranium shells for anti-tank guns. With a start, Gennady realized this Russian ammunition was the same type he knew the insurgents were using—doubtless, along the way, they had managed to capture many Russian field-pieces. This ammunition would keep them going.

Once more, Gennady was struck by the unreality of it all: two days ago, he was riding along with the Spetsnaz men, looking forward to getting back to Moscow—now, here he was, on the other side. He suspected that Retchko had told these Chechens not to let him escape, or do anything foolish; the general's stiff warning still rang in his ears. He would just have to be patient and try to play along. He was sure the two others felt the same way. Then he spotted the small bandage on his wrist— the chip implant and his now-polarized blood were probably sending signals even at this moment to an "Organization" satellite somewhere in space. There would be no escape.

Several pairs of hands gripped the first box as the group lifted it, groaning together, onto the dolly. "These crates are *heavy*!" Blagron gasped through his gas mask, wiping his forehead. The other men were reacting in much the same way.

Gennady remembered that the secret to the shells' success lay in the fact that they were extremely weighty for their size, as they were made of depleted uranium—one of the most dense of all the elements—that allowed the projectiles to punch right through most targets with ease. If this mission went off as planned, these shells would soon be on their way to the Chechen insurgents for use against the Russians.

But first, they would have to load all these crates onto the boat. One of the turbaned fellows was calling out, pointing. In the corner was an electric forklift—perfect for speeding-up the job.

Using the almost-silent machine, in an hour the men had the boat's fish-hold filled with crates. For good measure, they had also found some automatic weapons and other ordnance that were also now aboard the fishing boat.

As they were leaving, one of the turbaned men came back and said something to the leader, who passed the words along to Ahmed. "They had to give the guards another dose of gas," he said to the three Russians, "to keep them out until we get away from here!"

The Chechen man was looking around with an expression of satisfaction; the shelves were not nearly as filled with goods as when they had arrived. "Let us be going, now!" he said in his language, motioning the others outside. Ahmed relayed the man's words to the Russians.

In a few minutes, the darkened boat was adrift in the middle of the stream. Then the diesel roared to life with a raucous clamor that rocked the countryside all around, punctuating the quiet operation just finished; then it settled down. The vessel came about and started chugging back downriver in the direction from which they had come; the shiny disc of the moon overhead bathed the dark water and the banksides in a soft white light. To Gennady, it looked as if they were motoring down a shimmering, dimly-lit black highway.

They had hardly made it around the first turn when a sudden spotlight snapped-on not far behind them, outlining the fishing smack in a merciless glare! Then came the throaty roar of a powerful engine. What appeared to be a patrol boat shot out of a nearby cove, its spotlight probing ahead of it! "Russian river patrol!" Ahmed gasped.

The captain leaned over the gunwale and squinted back, then called out something to his crewmen..

Gennady was at once concerned and thrilled. *Perhaps he and the others would be rescued!*

Crewmen scrambled to the stern of the boat; in the moonlight Gennady saw an oil drum balanced on the rear transom. It looked as if they were pouring out something behind them.

After a half-minute or so, an small orange flame went over the back-side—a lighted match, Gennady guessed. Immediately, a wall of fire shot up on the surface of the water and rolled right back into where the pursuing patrol craft was headed! The roaring sounds of the Russian engine stopped; fading shouts came from its direction as the fishing boat, its engine laboring, pulled away down-river.

* * *

Outside, the sun was well up over the horizon; in the hideaway basement, General Retchko stood behind the papers-covered table, nodding; pulling on his chin in a rare gesture of approval. "Well, comrades, you passed the test!" Gennady, Malinovsky, and Blagron glanced at each other; even though they were dead-tired from their all-night adventure, the three retained enough wits to wonder what the bald man had meant. "You see," the stocky Ukrainian went on, "I sent you to the armory to find out if I could trust you for bigger missions . . . now, you are ready for some *real*—"

The man stopped speaking; Gennady had picked up a Russian-language newspaper that was on the edge of the table and was staring at it with an expression of horror. The young man was pale.

"Where did this come from?" The paper was shaking in his hands.

"It came this morning . . . it is about two days old." The man frowned. "Why do you—"

Gennady was reading; his lips were moving as he read. Then he snatched open the paper to an inside page. He gasped; dropped the paper, gave a gagging sound, and turned toward the door. The guards were about to stop him when he fell to the dirty floor.

"Galina is dead! Oh, my God . . ." His shaking arms were wrapped around his head; his knees had drawn up.

Malinovsky knelt at his friend who was unconsolable. "Gennady . . . *what happened?*"

"They killed her . . . oh, my God . . . they *killed* her—"

Killed who? What—?"

"Galina . . . my wife. She was on an airplane—they say she is dead!"

Blagron picked up the paper and scanned down the page, aloud. " *. . . captain . . . American warship claimed . . . under attack . . . hostile aircraft . . . 'Hormuz' . . . Bandar Abbas . . . missiles . . . no survivors . . . twenty-four Russian schoolteachers—*"

He retrieved the second section and kept reading. *". . . list of dead from Russia—"* The young man's eyes dropped down the page, then went wide. *". . . Galina Gavrona Lychina . . . age twenty-four . . . primary school teacher . . . Tverskaya District, Moscow—"*

Blagron looked down at Gennady, who was lying very still on the floor, then at the general. "We were at their wedding, two months ago. She was very nice. And very pretty." An empty expression came over the young man's face.

For once, Retchko had nothing to say. He turned away, fumbling for a cigarette.

-14-

Grozny Airport; at the Same Time

"*. . . Foreign Ministry of the Russian Federation rejected the so-called 'explanation' of the American government that the airliner was acting in a hostile manner—*"

Terenty Suslov crushed the newspaper in his hands; his face contorted in anger such as his comrades had never seen before.

"Sons of bitches! Those bastards killed Gennady's wife!" The crumpled pages slid to the floor. The officer dropped onto a stool in the tent, his head in his hands. "Oh, God! Galina—" The vision of the slender, smiling, dark-haired young woman was before him. From the first, he knew his friend was taken by Tamara's cousin; the altar had always seemed a foregone conclusion. Many things about the girl flashed across his mind— how devoted she was to Gennady; how he talked about her when they were apart. Now she was gone—killed by a stupid American mistake, the newspaper said.

"You mean the girl at the wedding? The dark-haired one? She is *dead*—?"

Terenty nodded.

"We must find Gennady, somehow!"

"Our orders are to move out, today. We are already one day past when we are supposed to return to Moscow."

"Perhaps he is dead, now, also."

Terenty shook his head. "I know Gennady—I am sure he is alive . . . and the others, too."

* * *

"I am very sorry to hear about your wife. But you must remember that it was most unlikely that you would have ever seen her again, in any case." Retchko rustled around in the drawer of the desk-table where he was sitting and brought out a cloth.

There was an interval while the young man wiped his face. Retchko motioned at the chairs.

Gennady sat down and hung his head. "Those Americans . . . those damn Americans . . . doing that to my wife—oh, God . . . Galina's gone! I cannot believe it."

The bald Ukrainian waited while Gennady grieved some more.

"But I always thought she would be *safe*—even if I was not with her."

"Because of the 'Americanskis', that was not the case." Retchko drew on his cigarette.

Gennady, still shaking, was trying to compose himself. Blagron put his arm across his friend's shoulder; Malinovsky patted his back. The young men were taking hard the news of Galina's death—the occasion of the wedding and the smiling, pretty young bride with the short, dark hair was on their minds.

Retchko went on. "Now, if we can get back to business . . . as I said, you passed the tests and you are ready for more and bigger things." He held up for some moments. "I have arranged for you to go on a journey."

Gennady, wiping his eyes, frowned. Blagron and Malinovsky stared at the general.

'You will travel to Teheran by boat and overland, using people we can trust—I have used these people before for the same journey . . . at Teheran, you will meet the Cartel's cargo airplane that is coming back from North Korea. The airplane will take you to Lagos, Nigeria." The man waited while the young men absorbed this news, then he went on, "at Lagos, you will meet the 'Chief' and some others of the Organization . . . then you will travel to Havana, Cuba, and on to Monterrey, Mexico."

"Monterrey, Mexico—we were there, once."

"You were *there?*"

"We passed through Monterrey on a Spetsnaz mission—with Colonel Golubko."

The portly Ukrainian thought about that for a moment. "At Lagos, mission experts will give you detailed instructions . . . your final destination will be 'Nuevo Laredo', which is across the river from the United States'." Retchko spread his hands. "Your overall assignment—"he scanned around the space at the three,

Blagron, Malinovsky, and Gennady, who was blinking at the stocky Ukrainian through reddened eyes—"will be to do great harm to the 'Americanskis'."

Gennady clenched his teeth. "I have nothing left—*except* to 'harm the Americanskis'."

Retchko leaned back and tapped the ends of his fingers together, his elbows on the arms of his chair. The man squinted at the young soldier for some seconds, then came forward and stood up. "Very well, we will leave by tonight."

"We—?"

"I am going with you."

* * *

Gennady was *captured?*" Tamara Kuznetsova Suslova held her husband. His things were on the floor where he had dropped them when she opened the door. "Oh, Terenty, this is too much! Galina—now, Gennady!" He felt her hot tears on his neck. "What did they *do* to deserve this?"

There was a tugging on his trouser-leg.

"Sorry, sweetheart . . ." Terenty reached down and picked up Larisa. "How have you been, little one?" He handed her a child's bouquet of flowers.

"Cousin Galina is not here, anymore."

Terenty glanced at Tamara. "Did you tell her?"

The auburn-haired girl wiped her eyes with her hand. "She just knows that Galina has gone away." Tears dropped down her face. "And I already miss her so much—"

Tamara's parents stepped through the archway, just then, and reached for Terenty. Vera Kuznetsova looked about, frowning. Tamara was crying; Larisa looked upset. "Where is Gennady?"

Terenty took a deep breath. "Let us go inside . . . I have many things to tell you."

* * *

Gennady Lychin and the others stood on the same undulating floating dock from which the three Russians and the Chechens had left on the expedition to the armory. Tied-up before them was a good-sized cabin cruiser, much different from the odorous fishing sloop of the mission to obtain the depleted-uranium shells.

Nearby, General Retchko was speaking to the captain. Both men were nodding; grinning. The bald Ukrainian motioned to the others. "Let us go aboard!"

Gennady, Malinovsky, and Blagron, along with Ahmed, picked up their cloth bags of belongings and stepped over the gangplank onto the deck of the well-kept craft.

A crewman came up, gesturing for the men to follow him. The fellow led the way down a steep companionway to a little space with table nooks around the outer bulkhead. In a corner was a bar and galley combination. Glancing around, Gennady saw that it was stocked with several kinds of beer and liquor—at least there would be food and libations during the day-and-a-half voyage.

From topside, came the thumping of feet. The young men set down their valises and climbed back up the near-vertical steps onto the main deck, where they saw that the dock was receding; the yacht had already cast off. Below deck, came a stutter, then a steady rumble, as the diesels took over. Before long, the buildings and houses of the scruffy little port town were dropping toward the horizon; to the west, the orange, late-afternoon sun was just barely peeping over the rims of purple hills above the hamlet.

Retchko came up to them. "Well, in some hours we will reach the next port." The general grabbed the handrail of a steep stairs leading to the pilot house up on the topdeck. "The captain says to try the beer and Vodka . . . they will not allow such things when we get to Iran." The young Russians took their cue and dropped down to the bar and ordered a round of beer. The abstemious Ahmed opted for goat's milk

* * *

Moscow, Two Days Later:

". . . and now Lychin's wife!" Rodion Golubko swiveled his desk chair and stared out the window for a long minute. "I

329

remember those two on their wedding day. Now, she is dead and Gennady is missing—my God!"

Terenty doubled his fists. "Now the Americans admit their ship was in Iranian waters! The whole thing should never have happened!"

"When our Ambassador showed the satellite pictures at the United Nations, it was all over for them . . . even their so-called 'friends' were shocked. They had no defense—there was their ship—caught on camera well inside the twelve-mile limit! The 'sandstorm' that they thought would conceal what they were doing was wide-open to our infared Intelligence satellite that sees through *everything*." Colonel Golubko pulled off his eyeglasses and tossed them onto his desk.

Terenty shrugged. "The news reports are saying that their captain was having an 'uncertain reaction', or something like that, to an aircraft coming toward him—so he fired his missiles. Myself, I do not think the man was *stable* enough to be the captain of a warship."

The colonel clenched his teeth. "I believe it was a crime. At any rate, I am pleased the Defense Minister had strong words for them—the Americans will not be so trigger-happy next time when our Russian warships are in their faces with big guns and rockets aimed and cocked at them!"

"And our silent electric submarines will also be there. *The Americans do not know that.*"

The door opened at the rear of the big gilded room. Terenty looked around; the colonel started to rise. "Keep seats, comrades!" came the booming voice of Colonel General Antonin Krolov. The Academy's commandant returned the adjutant's and the others' salutes and stepped toward the two men at far end of the high-ceilinged office. The attendant came forward and pulled up a chair for the impressive man with the three red-outlined gold stars on his shoulderboards.

"We were talking about Galina," Colonel Golubko said.

"So terrible . . . Helen is devastated. The doctors are giving her sedatives." General Krolov shook his head. "The apartment is like a ghost-place, with both of them gone . . . at the same time, we still hope Lychin and the other two will turn up." The general turned to Terenty. "You were there when they were captured. How did it happen?"

The younger officer told the whole account about the midnight ambush and the three soldiers' disappearance; Colonel Golubko filled-in some of the details. Terenty let out a long sigh. "We did not find a trace of them. But I believe they are still alive. I am hopeful."

General Krolov frowned. "Have there been any signals from their chip implants?"

The colonel shrugged. "It is strange that there have been no contacts . . . it is almost like they did not have them, anymore. Even if all three were dead, their chips would still report."

There was a contemplative silence; the general nodded at the colonel, and toward Terenty. "Did you tell him?"

Terenty was puzzled. "Tell me what, sir?"

"I have put your name onto the Foreign Ministry list for promotion to 'Military Attaché in Madrid." He paused while Terenty was surprised. "We know you were there twice before—the second time as 'Assistant Military Attaché—so this is a promotion." The general spread his hands. "I am sure you will want to talk with your wife about this, since you have a child, now."

"I told Tamara how I was with my parents in Madrid while they were there in the diplomatic corps. I am sure she would want to go there."

There were voices at the rear of the room. A staff officer came up with a paper in his hand. Saluting, the uniformed man handed a note to the general.

Antonin Krolov read the message, frowning, then pushed the paper across Rodion Golubko's desk. The officer put on his glasses and scanned the missive. His face became red; the purple vein on his temple flared.

"You will not believe this," the colonel said to Terenty, holding up the paper, his expression grim. "The news reports are now saying that the whole crew of the American warship that shot down the airliner are getting *'commendation medals'* . . . for doing a good job."

* * *

Gennady Lychin was gazing up at the 747. Blagron and Malinovsky were gazing up at the 747. Retchko was gazing at three pale, round-faced men standing underneath the 747, beside the right-side tires, who were gazing up into the wheel well.

"This is the Organization's airplane," Ahmed was saying as the awestruck Russians climbed out of the military-style vehicle and gaped at the enormous aircraft looming over them. Across the way on a hangar building was a sign in two languages: the writing on top was in "Farsi", Gennady guessed; English letters below it said, "Teheran"—both proclaiming the Iranian capital.

As Gennady walked around the hulking airliner, looking up at it, the sun caught faint lettering on the forward upper-deck fuselage. Curious, the young man stepped back and forth several times to read what the erased, yet still-visible words, were up there. *"Iraqi Airlines,"* he muttered to himself. Movements beneath the right wing just then caught his eye; Retchko and other men were standing beside the outer landing-gear wheels that were painted an odd yellow-green prime color exactly like the 747 in Havana had been. And there had been a bald-headed man with it. Of course! *Now* he remembered: this very airplane had been parked outside the hangar at the Havana airport when the Spetsnaz group went through there with the spy from Los Alamos! The faded lettering, the distinctive paint on the landing gear wheels, the pale pilots and the bald man whom he now knew as "Retchko", were the same as he had seen in Havana! Gennady shook his head; how could he have ever guessed that before long, he would be boarding this same airplane for the "other" side?

"Over here!" The hairless Ukrainian was calling to him. As he walked underneath the airplane, Blagron and Malinovsky were stepping around the right-side landing gear trucks with the painted wheels and the big radial balloon tires. When Gennady came up, he saw that Ahmed was also there.

Retchko nodded at the three slightly-built men. "These pilots were once with the 'Soviet Strategic Bomber Forces '. . . they fly now for the Organization."

One of the pale-faced former Soviets who identified himself as the captain introduced the second officer and the flight engineer. All shook hands with the Cartel's three newest recruits. "General Retchko and Ahmed have flown with us many times," the pilot said in Russian.

Gennady told them about seeing the 747 in Havana. He gazed up at its hulking fuselage. "This airplane seems to go everywhere."

"We are returning from Pyongyang." The aviator pointed to some loaded semi-trucks that were parked inside a nearby open hangar building.

"Those are hundreds of gas centrifuges for the Iranian nuclear program," Retchko put in. Gennady glanced at Malinovsky and Blagron; what the general had told them earlier in Grozny about the worldwide scope of the Organization looked to be true.

Gennady heard shoes scuffing behind him and turned about; stepping across the concrete toward them was a man with extremely black skin that to Gennady looked as dark as coal. The fellow's eyes darted from one of the three new recruits to another as he stepped under the 747's wing.

The general spoke up. Ah, this is 'Norbert Ezego', my assistant from Nigeria." The Russians shook hands with the African. "Ezego is returning from the Philippines and from Indonesia, where they are setting up new training camps."

Once more, Gennady was struck by the extent of the Organization's operations. The black man seemed to be an important player in the Cartel's far-reaching cast.

"The aircraft is fueled and ready," the pilot said, "we will be leaving, now."

The men walked through the vast open cargo deck of the enormous airplane that, except for some crates in the middle portion and a lashed-down forklift, was empty. Gennady was taken aback by the size of the gigantic air freighter—it was far bigger than any Russian transport he had ever seen. At the forward end, they even came to a spiral staircase that led up to another level!

On the second deck the men stepped into a regular-looking airliner cabin with a bar and a galley; no hard metal bucket seats in *this* airplane, Gennady was relieved to see. From their expressions, the others' impressions of the plush accomodations were the same as his.

Outside, the four big engines were already coming up to speed. Gennady fastened his seat belt and looked out the window as the taxiway moved past underneath the leading edge of the wing. Then the monstrous aircraft turned onto the runway. With a distant rumble the four turbofans ran up to full power, easing him back into the superb seat with a gentle shove as the stately aircraft accelerated.

Watching the runway race by, Gennady wondered where all this was taking him and the other two former Spetsnaz soldiers. Then came the thumps and the ground fell away. The young man leaned back and took a deep breath; his fingers gripped the armrests. He glanced across the aisle at Blagron and Malinovsky. For better or worse, the three were now on their way to completely different lives.

* * *

Tamara's eyes were wide; the eyes of her parents were wide; Larisa blinked without understanding Terenty's announcement. The little one held onto her new stepfather's neck and looked across his shoulder at the frowning *'babushka'*.

"Oh, dear . . ." Vera Kuznetsova fanned herself. "You are moving to *Spain?"*

"It is a promotion and will be a comfortable job . . . I used to live there when my parents were diplomats." He grinned at Tamara and the child. "You two will be learning Spanish—and English!"

* * *

Lagos, Nigeria; in the Early Hours of the Next Morning:

The blue Toyota pulled up and stopped in front of a lighted, multi-story building; the overhanging *marquee* proclaimed the place to be the "Roomland Hotel". The very dark young driver pulled open the doors and motioned for them to follow him.

"Your room keys are at the front desk," he said, leading the way into the paneled, carpeted lobby.

As the clerk handed the three guests their room passes, Gennady got the impression the front-desk man not only knew they were coming, but how they looked. The young driver turned and headed up a staircase with the others behind him.

At the end of the sixth-floor corridor, the man turned a key in a lock. With a start, Gennady realized the fellow had had the key all along. The door swung open; the African gestured for the three Russians to enter.

Inside was a good-sized room with three beds. In the center of the space sat an arrangement of sofas and a glass-topped, low-set table; a writing desk was situated underneath a window. On an outside wall growled a built-in air conditioner that sounded as if it was having a hard time keeping up with the equatorial heat and humidity that had been such a shock to them when they had deplaned from the 747 an hour earlier.

The fellow motioned to a dark-wooden *armoire* in a corner. "You can put your things in there," he said.

Malinovsky dropped his cloth travel bag onto the well-used carpet and collapsed onto a sofa. "God, what a day!" He put his hands behind his head and kicked his feet onto the center table. "And to think we started this day in Teheran!"

"With the stop in Libya to let off that translator," Blagron put in. "I am tired."

At the door, Gennady was speaking to the Nigerian who had driven them from the airport. "You say someone else is coming?"

"Mister Busa will be here shortly." With that, he started to turn away, then hesitated and looked back. "I am 'Ivan'," the young man said, "and I will be here in the morning to drive you to downtown Lagos."

"Where are we going?"

"To see the 'Chief'." With that, he pulled the door shut.

Before Gennady even had time to turn about, there came a rapping in a peculiar sound pattern. He glanced at the others, then, frowning, pulled back open the door. At once an obese black man in a flower-print, tent-like outfit bustled into the room. As Gennady stood blinking, the grinning fellow stuck out a pudgy hand. While the Russian gave him a return shake, the man, still showing plenty of teeth, looked around at the others. "'Masobe Busa'!" the African said, pumping Blagron's hand, then Malinovsky's. "You will be going with me tomorrow to meet the 'Chief'! General Retchko tells me you have just joined the Organization!"

The young men nodded.

"Good. We will all meet tomorrow at the office and plan out the details for your assignment." Gennady was about to speak, but the black man was ready with more words. "I shall be here at ten o'clock in the morning to get you." The African tugged the door knob and stepped out into the corridor. "Ten o'clock sharp!"

Then he was gone.

Gennady gaped at the backside of the door for a second, then turned about with a wry grin, "I say!'"

Malinovsky was shaking his head, trying to hold back a laugh.

Blagron spoke up."Do you realize we did not say a word the whole time that man was here?"

"And he will probably have even more to say, tomorrow!"

Who was that European-looking man who came with us from Teheran? The fellow who kept to himself the whole time?"

"Retchko said something about him being an 'electronics expert'."

"And who is this 'Chief' we keep hearing about?"

"I guess we will find out, starting at ten o'clock in the morning."

Blagron looked at his watch. "We had better get some rest . . . ten o'clock will come early."

As Gennady unbuttoned his sleeve, his fingers brushed across the little wrist bandage over the incision for the Organization's control-chip implant.

* * *

In the Mountains of Tora Bora; at that Moment:

The technician adjusted the receiver to fine-tune the signal; out of an overhead speaker came a continuous cycle tone. The man switched to another frequency and made an adjustment; a second tone, somewhat higher in pitch, burst from the speaker. The communications man moved the knob some more; from the reproducer came a lower-pitched sound.

The man in the medical smock coat standing next to him was nodding. "Signals from the three new recruits?"

"Yes, doctor . . . strong, clear reports from each of them—"

"I will inform "U" that the members are now at the location in Lagos, just like Retchko had said they would be."

* * *

Signal Intelligence Office, National Security Agency, Washington, D.C.; at the Same Time:

The technician was frowning as he fine-tuned the satellite receiver. "Inform the Director that we are monitoring continuous uplink-downlink tones through the satellite 'spare channel' re-modulators."

"*Tones,* you say? More than one?"

The man who was plotting on a screen spoke up. "There are three distinct signals passing through the satellite." He moved a mouse and punched a keyboard. More information flashed onto the monitor. "The signals are originating somewhere around Lagos, Nigeria—" He watched as some new blips appeared. He zoomed down at the apparent source of the radio waves. "There are three return signals from northeast Afghanistan." He shook his head. "Strange pattern, though . . . like it could be some kind of monitor and control circuit operating between the two locations."

"The Director will want to notify the President."

* * *

Tanuta Refinery; the Next Day:

"You say the new guy will be working the frequencies?" Larry Landay leaned forward and spoke low to Lisa Anaya as he stirred his morning coffee. He glanced around; none of the workers at other cafeteria tables seemed to be paying attention.

The cream-skinned young woman shrugged. "That is what Colonel Ajiboy said in his call last night. He said Retchko is back in Lagos, and a 'new man' will be arriving, today—a 'communications expert' of some sort." She glanced at the empty seats at the table. "Where is Marisol?"

"It's Saturday—she's sleeping late."

"Frank is arranging quarters for the new man." A quick grin passed across the cream-colored young woman's face. "We can talk freely."

Larry picked up her cue. "You and Frank really hit it off, didn't you?"

She looked away for a moment. "And to think that before I didn't like him much—before you and I went our—separate ways." It was a delicate allusion to the fact she and Larry had once been lovers. Her eyes came back to him. "You and Marisol are doing all right?"

"Of course." Larry gave an enigmatic grin. "And she is very 'clever' about 'matters'."

He had never told Lisa about Marisol's "Russian Connection", or the Cubana's suspicions about some of the people at Tanuta—including Lisa. "Retchko has left her alone. She is about the only one here who can say that."

Lisa cocked an eyebrow. "Is it not interesting that Betty left for Lagos at the same time Retchko came back from his trip?" She glanced around and leaned forward. "I believe there is something going on between those two! My own sister!" The young woman looked down.

Larry's eyes were big. "You don't think she had something to do with her husband disappearing, do you?" He stirred his coffee some more. He knew they were treading onto uncertain ground.

Lisa shrugged. "Sometimes I wonder if I really know her."

"Marisol is a trained detective. Maybe she can dig up something."

Just then, Lisa looked over his shoulder and gave a wave to someone behind him. Larry turned about. Frank Ogawan was stepping through the doorway. A white man Larry did not recognize was with him.

* * *

Gennady fluffed his shirt to create a breeze on his body; the muggy wind swirling through the open car windows was doing nothing to stop the rivulets of sweat he could feel running down his chest, dampening his clothes. And judging from the florid faces of Blagron and Malinovsky, it looked as if they were having their own time contending with the heat and humidity. In the front passenger seat, Busa was working a handkerchief on his shiny, very black face.

The Russian squirmed about uncomfortably in the crowded back seat of the blue Toyota as the little sedan thumped along on the most endless, drawn-out causeway bridge he had ever seen; its every bumpy meter suffused with the stifling smell of septic fish. As they rode, he gazed out at loincloth-clad fishermen standing in sailboats that seemed to hang in midair over the shimmering, sun-saturated waters as far as he could see in the morning haze.

The fresh-faced young Ivan glanced into the rear-view mirror at the three passengers and saw the Russians gazing out at the water. "This is the longest bridge in Africa," he said.

Gennady squinted; in the distance, the vague outlines of Lagos's tall downtown buildings were at long last starting to materialize in the striated layers of smog.

In a few more minutes the Toyota bounded onto land, past a sign that said "Ikoye Lagos", into a battered-looking district that reminded Gennady of Chechnya. From the looks on Blagron's and Malinovsky's faces he was sure they were thinking the same thing, for as they came closer, he could see that many of the tall structures were burned-out shells; some even seemed to be leaning. The sedan dropped down an exit ramp from the elevated thruway and moved along on a surface street, dodging man-sized potholes in the cracked and pitted pavement. Everywhere the passengers looked, bombed and blasted vehicles of all description were parked along the main roads and side streets. Some, with their rusty doors still hanging open, looked as if they had been abandoned in a hurry a long time ago. To Gennady, this was not what he would have expected of a country's biggest and most important city.

Blagron tugged on the front passenger's seat-back. "What happened, here?"

Busa, wiping his face with his handkerchief, turned to him, wincing. "Civil war—"

After several more turns, the Toyota pulled up into a traffic jam. Without the breeze, in no time the Russians were sweating even more in the stifling heat. All around, men were leaning out of car windows; grimacing, gesturing, and shouting at each other over the deafening din of every vehicle's horn going full blast.

Busa looked back at the perspiring passengers. "Petrol rationing," he called, "there is a fuel yard just ahead."

Somewhere Gennady had heard that Nigeria was one of the world's leading petroleum countries. "Rationing? *Here?*"

The native man tapped a pants pocket with his index finger. "Corruption . . . it is all corruption."

After some time, the vehicle crept out of the congestion and turned in at a trim-looking, two-story light-tan stucco building. Dark-green canvas awnings hung out over the front windows and the main entrance; an elegant sign announced the place as the "Imperial Industrial Bank." As Busa pulled open the heavy mahogany front door, Gennady saw identical brass plaques flanking it on each side with a crown insignia on them. Then he remembered that Nigeria was once an British Imperialist colony, such as textbooks and educators had denounced throughout his schooling back in the days of the Soviet Union.

The black man led the three Russians into a tall paneled room lighted by wall sconces and.a crystal overhead chandelier As Gennady took a seat in an overstuffed chair, he glanced over the main doorway and gave a start—hanging on the wall was a life-size painting of a scowling Nigerian in a bemedaled military uniform. The figure's fixed gaze seemed aimed straight at him.

Busa saw his reaction. "He is the leader of the country."

Trying to ignore the aggravating stare, Gennady settled back in the seat. At least the place was air-conditioned, he thought—in the cooler air he could almost feel the accumulated heat radiating from his body.

Just then, a svelte, very attractive, cream-colored young woman in a short, tight outfit came in and took a seat across from Gennady. Out of the corner of his eye, he knew that the female was looking the other two Russians and him over.

Busa was at a receptionist's desk, talking to a girl. Presently he came back. "Doctor Nomoah will be with us in a few minutes."

Hardly had he said that, than a glass door swung open and a business-like female bank employee holding a clipboard came out. She surveyed the visitors. "Mister Busa?" At the dark man's nod, the employee gestured for the men to follow her.

As he stood up, once more Gennady was aware of the light-skinned girl's fixated gaze on the others and him.

The African and the Russians filed through a long, narrow paneled room full of clattering machines and computer screens; all operated by workers at keyboards.

At a mahogany door the female knocked in a sequence, then opened it. "They are here," she said to someone inside. The girl motioned for the visitors to enter. Behind an enormous, dark-wooden desk, a compact, bald-headed man in a brown three-piece suit stood up. Gennady noted that the black man's skin color exactly matched the varnished, ebony-hued desk. Through a big picture-window behind him, a gardener outside was tending manicured tropical plants and flowers.

"Ah, Busa! It is good to see you again!" The banker looked the three young white men up and down. "And these are the new recruits?" The African nodded.

"'I. M. Nomoah'," the little man said, shaking the newcomers' hands in turn, getting their names. "I have heard many good things about you, already—" As the Russians glanced at each other, the diminutive financier went on, ". . . and I am sure General Retchko has told you many things about our 'Organzation'." The three nodded; the black man leaned back in his chair and tapped his fingertips. "The Cartel is fortunate to have three young men as yourselves with us, now." He paused to let the three new recruits absorb this. "You will be assigned to

'Nuevo Laredo, Mexico', just over the border from America. You will be transporting armaments and personnel into that country." A pause; then, "Our objective is to weaken the United States and Western Europe *'and other places'* to where they will be ready for revolutionary takeovers by people we support."

Gennady started to speak, then held back; Nomoah kept talking. "We will accomplish that by destroying important buildings and infrastructure, causing many casualties . . ." He paused, then added, "In particular, we will target schools and other large events, in order to achieve maximum effect. Sports matches will be prime targets, as will be large, crowded arenas and religious gatherings." Gennady's eyes, along with Blagron's and Malinovsky's, were wide as the man kept talking. "All this will take *time*, of course, but 'time' is one thing we have plenty of . . . in fact, I expect it will require as much as *two decades or more* for us to accomplish all this. By then, we will have immense power and influence."

"Are those people now in place?"

The small man nodded. "There are various groups with which we are associated in supplying arms and training, some of which we are still organizing . . . we have training grounds and weapons-storage warehouses in the United States right now. All quite secret, of course."

The young men looked at each other; they were all thinking at the same time about the Spetsnaz cave in the Colorado mountains. But now they were on the other side of Spetsnaz.

Gennady took a chance to speak. "General Retchko has explained a lot of this to us."

"Good. But there is much more. As you go on, you will get a better picture of what our operation is all about."

For a moment the young Russian had a hollow feeling that none of this was real. Then he remembered what the Americans had done to Galina. He would do whatever was necessary to pay them back. It was real, all right.

". . . well-compensated for this," Nomoah was saying, reaching into a desk drawer and lifting out three envelopes with their names on them. "These are your initial vouchers," he said, passing them out, "take these to the 'Nation Bank of Nigeria'.

'Doctor Krasheev', whom you will meet, will set up payroll and expense accounts for each of you."

Nomoah stood, giving notice the meeting was over. "Doctor Krasheev is now waiting for you."

The Russians, led by Busa, made their way back out through the offices to the parked Toyota. The dozing young driver, Ivan, bathed in sweat, bolted awake as the heavyset African pulled on the door handle.

In a minute, the sedan had turned about. As the driver was putting the car in gear, Gennady happened to look back. Emerging from a side door of the bank building was the cream-skinned girl he had seen in the lobby waiting room—the young woman who had been staring at him. With her was a bald, pudgy, white man. She was reaching for his hand. Gennady gasped, his eyes wide. "Retchko!"

* * *

Tanuta Refinery, at That Moment:

The new technician scanned the dials, nodding. "I will now proceed," he said, in an European accent, moving some switches. Lisa Anaya and Larry Landay, standing beside him, watched a monitor screen. While the fellow turned a knob, a display of Nigeria came up, then three blinking dots on the seacoast. As the intent-looking man kept twisting the knob, the city of Lagos filled the screen, then as the view continued to zoom downward, streets began to appear; all the while, the three pin-points of light kept blinking. Then, as a dark, moving, oblong object came into view, the spots tightened inside the rectangle.

"There you are," the technician said, tapping the screen, "your subjects are in a moving vehicle on Ikoye Island in Lagos."

"Who *are* the 'subjects'?"

"Russians—three recruits now working with Retchko. I flew with them from Teheran. They have your tracking chips in their arms." The foreigner gave a professional-grade grin. "Congratulations. The chips work perfectly."

"Thanks—I guess. Where'd you get the street map?"

He held up a compact disk. "At a computer store in Lagos!"

Lisa and Larry were surprised. "How do you do that?"

"It is really quite simple: Once we know their approximate location, we load the software for that area into the computer . . . the system will automatically overlay the location of the subjects onto the display—it will work every time."

"How did you know all this?"

"I worked with 'Soviet Intelligence'. They had a satellite system much like this one."

"So *that's* where Retchko got it! He gave us the basic idea— but we had to figure it out by ourselves."

It was the European's turn to be impressed. "I would say your system is at least as good as the Soviet one—and they had a whole design bureau working on it!"

* * *

Signal Intelligence Office, National Security Agency, Washington, D.C.; at that Moment:

"Come look at this!" The technician at the intercept station called to his assistant. "We are getting multiple-source signals through the satellite." As the monitor tape continued feeding through the recorder, the fellow fine-tuned the rack-mounted receiver for the American signal intelligence satellite.

The second man was frowning at the screen; four separate horizontal wavy lines were now on it. "Get a 'triangulation'. Call up '*Menwith Hill*' and also have '*MAGNUM*' trace the sources."

The expert was already on the secure circuit to the English monitoring station. "They have it!" he called out. A pause, then "Menwith Hill has three signals originating in the Lagos, Nigeria area."

The other man was making an adjustment. "I have one MAGNUM up-link originating from somewhere in the Niger Delta."

"All signals from Nigeria?"

"Looks like it."

"Modulation?"

"Just cycle tones . . . like somebody is testing some circuits."
"Call the Director. *Now* we have something to go on."

* * *

Stepping from the blue Toyota in the equatorial heat, Gennady gaped up at the hulking, four-story, gray-stone edifice that took up a whole city block. "I guess this is the bank," he said to himself. As the others alighted, he looked around. Across the sun-baked street was a multi-floored, factory-looking building surrounded by scaffolding as if it was being renovated; somewhere down the way, multiple jackhammers were at work, their piercing, pounding, pile-driving pulses reverberating against the nearby buildings.

As the men mounted the broad stone steps, Gennady observed brass plaques on either side of massive bronze doors, both bearing the crown insignia, with the inscription: "Nation Bank of Nigeria." More Imperialism from the past, he thought. Inside, they crossed an echoing lobby in which numbers of well-dressed, business-looking people—Africans and some whites—bustled about. When they started up a marble staircase, Gennady was surprised to see a pair of armed sentries in paramilitary dress flanking the foot of the stairwell, their rifles at parade-rest. Out of the corner of his eye he noticed other soldiers standing guard across the big open space.

On the next level, Busa led the Russians down a long, dimly-lit hallway. At the last door, a fierce-faced, muscular-looking African in a white shirt and khaki pants motioned for them to enter a room.

The men filed into an office crowded with stuffed mohair chairs and some tall, dark-mahogany carved objects in the corners that Gennady took to be African art. The dark-red walls seemed to be in velvet, much like what he used to see in elegant Russian houses; overhead, an electric fan swirled casually. Behind an enormous black-varnished wooden desk sat a trim, very-dark middle-aged man in an expensive-looking three-piece pinstripe suit.

345

"'Krasheev'," he said, holding the newcomer's hand in a stiff shake. Gennady could feel the bones of the man's fingers. As Busa introduced the newcomers, Gennady's eyes fell on a brass plate on the man's desk: *'N. B. Krasheev, (Dr.) Director, Intercontinental Remittance Office'*.

"Take seats," the white-shirted African spoke up.

"I will get right to the point," the important-looking man said, his dark eyes scanning from one visitor to another. Busa stepped up and handed Krasheev some packets. The man behind the desk pulled papers from three envelopes and handed them out. "These are your payroll and expense account documents," he went on, as the three foreigners looked at the pages. Gennady observed that they were from a bank in the Cayman Islands. He recalled that the Caymans were in the Carribbean not far from Cuba. Some figures in American dollars at the bottom of the page caught his attention; the expatriate Russian stared at the amounts that were, to him, astronomical.

". . . your opening balances—" Krasheev was saying, bringing Gennady back to the conversation.

The young man glanced at Malinovsky and Blagron; looks of pleased surprise were on their faces, as well. If these sums were any indication, International-Arms-Dealing was lucrative, indeed—and they were on the lowest rung of the "Organization's" ladder.

The banker's eyes kept darting at the three Russians in turn. "You will leave tomorrow on the 'Seven-Forty-Seven' airplane for Havana. There, you will take a commercial flight to Monterrey, Mexico."

He handed Gennady and the two others what looked like half of an index card with jagged edges on one side. "At the Monterrey airport, a man will have the other half of this identification . . . he will take you to Nuevo Laredo. Everything is already arranged for you, there." As Gennady fingered the card, the man kept speaking in a brusque, impersonal monotone. "You will stay there." Krasheev's eyes narrowed. "At Nuevo Laredo, you will receive further instructions."

Gennady glanced at the statements. With this kind of money, he could tolerate many things.

Krasheev stood; Gennady saw that the creases in his expensive suit were aligned perfectly. The "Director of Intercontinental Remittance" put out his hand. "I wish you all success."

With Busa leading, the Russians filed out of the office and made their way downstairs to the outside. At the curb, Ivan, in the blue Toyota, was waiting for them.

"To the airport," the portly native said to the perspiring driver.

Before long, they were back on the thruway headed out of the city center to another thumping, bumping crossing on the causeway over the backwater bay. In a while they came up to an enormous, many-storied white structure. While the sedan skirted the huge building, the young men gazed up at a big sign on its upperworks that caught the afternoon sun: *'MURTALA MOHAMMED AIRPORT LAGOS'*.

At the rear, the Toyota pulled up at a curb near a door over which a small sign signified the office of airport security.

Inside, the men stepped to a counter. Busa called out to what seemed to be an empty room. "Colonel Ajiboy?"

Right away, a uniformed soldier came through a doorway. "Ah, Mister Busa . . . I will get the colonel for you."

In a minute, a tall, well-built military man, whose eyes were obscured by gold-rimmed pilot's green sunglasses, came out. "Busa!" Then he spotted the white men and took on a more serious mien. "You must be the new recruits General Retchko was telling me about."

The Army man sized up the muscular Russians as he shook their hands. "The general says you were 'Spetsnaz'." Before any of the men could reply, Ajiboy motioned toward the inner door. "Let us talk," he said.

* * *

An hour later, they came back out, nodding and grinning among each other. The African officer motioned to a soldier who was lounging about. "Get the car, corporal; we are now going to drive around the airfield."

In a minute, the men—except Busa, who had gone somewhere else in the airport—were in an olive-drab staff car. The vehicle turned toward a nearby taxiway.

As they passed by a small concrete-block outbuilding, Gennady saw Ajiboy look at it and grimace. Gennady was curious. "What is that?" he asked, pointing.

"Ah . . . it is where people who 'die' here are 'taken care of'.'."

An uncomfortable feeling came over Gennady. The other two Russians were frowning.

"People who die here?"

The man stared ahead; expressionless, grim. "The régime here is rigid."

For now, Gennady decided to let the matter drop, as they were approaching a heavy-duty-looking fence at the edge of the airfield.

Ajiboy pointed at the multi-depth barrier that reminded Gennady of the anti-personnel fences behind the recently-torn-down *'Berlin Wall'*. "All these were built on General Retchko's orders. He wants the airport to be secure."

The Russians glanced at each other. Retchko seemed to have his hold everywhere on people.

When the men stepped back into the office, Busa had returned. A soldier was speaking on the telephone. "Ah, here he is now," the young man said, handing the receiver to the colonel.

The officer listened to someone on the line, then spoke some words into the mouthpiece.

Ajiboy hung up and turned to the others. "General Retchko wants you at the 'temple'."

The Russians gave quizzical looks. Busa spoke up. "They will have a dinner and a show for you . . . you will find it 'interesting'."

The Russians and Busa piled back into the staff car. The colonel stayed behind. As they were rumbling down the expressway a few minutes later, Gennady happened to be looking out as they zoomed past the "Roomland Hotel" and kept going at a speed he thought was above the safe limit. Several times, they had to swerve to avoid striking a pedestrian running across the main lanes. But the young Army driver handled the vehicle with alacrity as he dodged Africans dashing across in front of the sedan—some of the grinning fellows were even making daring motions at the cars and trucks as they side-stepped onrushing bumpers and fenders. One time the driver had to whip around a garbage truck stopped in the middle of the highway. Gennady shook his head; not even in Chechnya had he seen such haphazard road manners.

"Where we are going?" he said to himself.

His question was answered in part when the Army car all at once swung off the divided highway and zoomed down an exit ramp. After bumping along on a pitted side road, they made another quick turn and came up to a ceramic-sided, gold-domed structure that reminded Gennady of something he had once read about in *'One-Thousand-and One Arabian Nights'*.

* * *

In the Mountains of Tora Bora; at That Moment:

Inside the control room cut out of solid rock, the pair of European technicians monitoring the signals from the three Lagos wrist-chips watched the cathode screen and the sweep hand of the clock as it came to the top of the hour.

Then came the "blink" as all the electronics reset to the new frequencies, and the little winking dots went on as before.

One of the men started touch a control knob, then pulled away. "No need to adjust," he said, a tone of awe in his voice, "it is locked-on . . . the frequency change went off perfectly."

"The download instructions were correct," the other man put in, "the chips's carrier frequencies will automatically change once a day, from now on."

"It is very clever . . . whoever designed this is a genius."

The men gazed at the screen. The three Lagos blips went on flashing once a second.

* * *

349

Signal Intelligence Office; National Security Agency, Washington, D.C.:

"It's gone!" The signals specialist twisted the tuner knob. "What happened? It was there just a second ago!" He surveyed the meters, but all were flatlined; unmoving. The "carrier" light had gone to red, signifying no signal.

"It's no use," he groaned after several tries. He knew it might take days—if ever—to get back the signal.

He called the monitoring station at Menwith Hill, England. They, too, had lost the transmission.

The man hung up the receiver for a moment, then, steeling himself, lifted it again and punched another number. He would have to tell the Director the bad news.

* * *

"It worked!" Larry Landay grinned. "Break out the champagne!"

In the Tanuta receiving station, Larry, Lisa Anaya and the new technicnan whooped, slapped each other on the back and gave a round of high-fives.

Larry turned to Lisa. "That was a great idea of yours to change the frequencies every day!"

"I figured it would keep hackers from getting into the system."

The new man looked at the girl, grinning. "How does it work?"

"It's a trick they taught us back in cryptology class in college. We just went further with it."

She ran her hand across the equipment rack.

"This is the 'stepping-cypher'. It changes the frequencies automatically with bundled number cyphers that ride on a sub-carrier. At the other end is a de-cyphering machine that strips the code from the cypher. Even if somebody could monitor it, they would be knocked-off after twenty-four hours. To make it run after that, they would have to duplicate the stepping-cyphers without ever seeing one or knowing how it works. It's foolproof."

350

"Oh, man, what a time *that* was!" Malinovsky was grinning, his eyes glazed in afterglow-amazement as he pulled off his shoes and socks .

Blagron dropped onto the sofa and rolled his eyes. "Those girls . . . I mean, they really went after it, did they not? How would you have liked to been one of the boys carrying around a babe like that!"

"And what was it they called that old man in the turban—the 'Adept'?"

"The fat man—'Busa'—told me he is the head of the 'temple', and the girls are his 'priestesses'."

"Something about worshiping the earth. But those leeches— ugh!"

"Some of the food was actually pretty good."

"I liked the girls, better!"

Gennady listened to the banter between the other two with little enthusiasm. As far as he was concerned, the revelry had been at the expense of his late, lamented wife. Even as the beautiful girls had twirled about in the swirling smoke, he had been assailed by waves of remorse and regret. The young man was still tormented by the conviction that if he had been with Galina he could have done something to save her.

Now, he was carrying the *Cartel's* implanted tracking chip in him; his very blood was magnetized on their radio frequency and he was going to some places to do things he would never have imagined a few days ago. Did Terenty and Tamara ever think about him? What about the little girl? Colonel Golubko? What would Galina think if she could know what he was now doing? But he would never again see her, or any of the rest of them— ever.

He must get a grip on himself, or he could lose it all in a hurry.

The Americans. Blame it on the Americans. It was all their fault.

* * *

INTERNOL Headquarters, Geneva Switzerland; the Next Morning:

The Swiss Inspector read the message with interest. The agent in Lagos deserved a bonus.

HAVE NEW INFORMATION THREE SUBJECTS BELIEVED RUSSIAN ARE AT LAGOS. PART OF ORGANIZATION. SOME INDICATIONSTHEY HAVE CUBA DESTINATION. IDENTITIES NOT KNOWN, BUT RECENT RUSSIAN MILITARY SUSPECTED. CURRENT FUNCTIONS UNKNOWN. A FOURTH SUBJECT MENTIONED, LOCATION AND FUNCTION UNKNOWN, BUT NOT BELIEVED LAGOS.

Tarliani groped in his breast pocket, hauled out the curved-stem smoking pipe, loaded the bowl from his tobacco pouch and lit it off. As the sweet-scented blue smoke wafted over his head, the agent read the intriguing message once more. Then he sat back, thinking. Twice before, when INTERNOL had sent operatives into Nigeria, both agents were never again heard from; the last known location for both had been around the Lagos airport that, in the meantime, had developed a reputation as an exceedingly dangerous place. His agents there now were locals who, so far, had remained deep moles. Puffing, the man stared out the second-story window at the sidewalk below and reflected on the recent developments. As he watched the mid-day pedestrian parade along the "Rue de la Crox-d'Or", Tarliani tossed around in his mind the decoded Nigerian dispatch. *Russians in Nigeria?* Most extraordinary. Who else could use this information? The Swiss Intelligence officer would keep his agreement with Livshits in Moscow; the Russian might have insights into the identities of the mysterious four, in which case everyone would benefit. For he had an intuition that there was more to this than appeared on the surface. Then Tarliani had another idea: he would also send the information to Agent Watering at the "Bureau" in Washington. Perhaps the Americans could also make use of it.

* * *

Headquarters, The "Bureau"; Federal Office Building, Washington, D.C.:

Watering drew on his Marlboro and read the message from Tarliani, as the smoke wafted around him. Interesting, he thought, but not really much to go on. Yet it was the kind of tantalizing stuff that appealed to his detective instincts. And he had a strong feeling these "Russians", as Tarliani had described them, were headed in his direction. Nigeria was where the "Organization" seemed to be headquartered, and the fact that they were there, he believed, was significant, although their actual functions, according to the other agent, were unknown. And the information he had so far on the shadowy group that supposedly was was training and equipping "revolutionaries" and "paramilitaries", along with aiding so-called "terrorists", was scanty in any case. This latest information from one of them seemed to suggest that the Cartel was branching out into ever more ambituous ventures. Keeping track of these criminals and contriving countermesures to oppose them was going to tax to the fullest the ingenuity of cooperating counter-terrorist bureaus and friendly governments

He read the message one more time. *Cuba?* Russians were not particularly welcome in Cuba, anymore. No, this was something new and bigger for the Cartel. These three would be moving on to somewhere else, and probably, soon. The fourth subject was a further mystery. *Northern Mexico.* That's where the three Russians would go—he would bet his career on it. Somewhere close by where they would have ready access to the United States yet not likely to be bothered by the local authorities. There were any number of border towns rife with official corruption that would provide perfect cover for such individuals.

It would be even more interesting if it turned out they were connected with that mysterious general whom Tarliani had said disappeared from Russia about a year ago and was now believed to be somewhere in Africa. Were the three new Russians on some

353

kind of mission for him and the Cartel that would someday involve the United States?

Watering nodded to himself. If they were headed toward America, he would be ready for them. And he knew just the agent to put on the case. The man lifted the telephone receiver and punched-in the number of "James Richard Randolph".

* * *

Larry Landay frowned; the new technical man was downloading from a satellite source with which he was not famliar. The American watched the monitor screen as it scrolled in rapid motion what looked to be names and numbers; the words were in a language he did not understand. "What is this?"

"Others on the system."

"Where is this downlink coming from?"

"It is the other system you shipped out. It is reporting to me." To Larry, the fellow seemed to be holding back something.

The man went on about his work. "This is 'Organization' business."

* * *

The Chief leaned back in his executive chair; his fingertips touching. The morning sun beaming thorough the big office window shined on his bald head as the man processed what he had just heard. "You say this 'Agent U', as you call him, wants us to supply a cell in New York City? In America?"

Busa leaned forward in his chair; his fat forearms flabbed across the edge of the gargantuan mahogany desk. "Well, technically, sir, in *'New Jersey'*. But the tunnel goes to lower Manhattan, he says."

"What would be our involvement?"

"He says he wants to manufacture explosives to put into delivery-size trucks and explode at some buildings in New York." The dark man looked earnest. "He says he now has a cell of his people there—they are scoping-out the city for the best targets." Busa paused for effect. "He says they will pay us extra

354

to help them." The portly Nigerian gestured at the other man sitting next to him. "Ezego can go there and get started right away."

The head of the Organization nodded at the two sitting across from him, their faces shining in the light, as he contemplated the plan.

"Very well, you can fly commercial to New York . . . less chance of detection that way."

He stood up; the meeting was over. Busa and Ezego were smiling. The Chief was smiling.

-15-

Tanuta Refinery; the Next Morning:

Larry Landay reached over and jabbed the alarm clock button, quieting the infernal racket. The orange hue of sunrise was glowing through the curtains. He looked over at Marisol; her hazel eyes were blinking; she was awake. She gave a long sigh.

The Cubana kicked down the sheet, raised onto her elbow and looked at his face. "Larry, what are we going to do?" In the dim light he saw that her eyes were brimming. "We cannot stay here forever—but we cannot leave this place, either."

The American stared at the ceiling. "It's been eating on me, too, ever since I found out how they're looking for me all over the world." He gave an ironic laugh. "Can you believe it? 'Larry Landay, The International Fugitive. Wanted by Everyone!'"

Marisol shrugged. "Sometimes, I wonder if I should have stayed in Cuba."

"And miss all this excitement?" Larry grinned at her. "You would not have wanted to miss *me* by staying in Cuba, would you?"

"Of course not." Her eyes looked into his. "But Larry, I want a real future . . . a real life. We must somehow leave this place."

"How could we do it?"

"Retchko is coming tomorrow. I have an idea."

* * *

Monterrey, Mexico Airport; Two days later:

Travel bags in hand, Gennady, Blagron and Malinovsky stepped off the skywalk from the airliner into the muggy arrival terminal. Each held in plain sight their little card with the serrated edge, as Retchko had told them to do.

The three had not gone very far when a dark-haired man, slightly older than they, stepped around some other passengers and looked straight at Gennady. He fingered a card. *"Identificacion?"*

Startled, Gennady put up his. The fellow thrust his card at the edge of the other one; the match was perfect. The cards of Malinovsky and Blagron were also exact fits.

The stranger nodded his head at the direction of a "To Arriving Customs" overhead sign. "Follow me," he said in Spanish that the Russians understood.

They walked at a brisk pace down the concourse. At a currency exchange, he stopped. "Change your Cuban pesos into Mexican ones." The man stepped back.

After they were finished, the four resumed their walk. As they started to pass a restroom, the man motioned at it. "Go in there and place one-hundred pesos inside your passports."

When they came back out, the man was waiting. "Give them to me," he said, taking the little books, gesturing at a departure lounge. "Take seats, and wait . . . I will be back."

Malinovsky sat squirming, looking out at the arriving passengers bustling along on the concourse, taking it all in. The others were doing much the same. "What do you think?" The Russian posed the question in his rudimentary Spanish.

"Retchko said the man will take us to Nuevo Laredo," Blagron put in.

Gennady was frowning. He had noticed a rough-looking male bystander frowning at them from across the way. "Perhaps we should not say much," he said in a low voice, nodding at the direction of the suspicious-looking Mexican male who was now gazing around as if not paying any attention to the three. But Gennady noticed that every few seconds or so the stranger's eyes snapped back in their direction for an instant; then away.

Just then, the first fellow re-appeared, handing the passports back to them, motioning toward the concourse. "We are cleared, now. Let us be on our way."

Outside the man led the three newcomers across a parking lot to a minivan. The vehicle, with their host at the wheel, pulled out of the lot and onto a thoroughfare, passing under an overhead freeway sign pointing its arrow down at a lane marked, "Nuevo Laredo".

After the van had gone a few kilometers, Gennady happened to look out the left-side window and gave a start. *In a truck alongside them, staring back, was the same unsavory-looking individual he had seen in the airport!* The other vehicle, a large delivery-type truck, all at once scraped against the side of the van they were in with a grinding, thumping jolt!

With a yell, the driver ran the passenger van onto the shoulder of the roadway, then jerked it back into the lane, swerving back and forth. *"Banditos!"*

Scowling, the other driver spun his wheel once more; this time the bigger truck jammed against the smaller van, shoving it off the road! Unable to dis-engage, the van bumped to a stop, still locked onto the side of the truck.

At once, the rear cargo door rolled-up and four rough-looking, brown-skinned young men jumped out, each of them holding a knife!

"Defense!" the driver shouted in Russian, a familiar 'Special Forces' order, as he bailed toward the right-front door. At the same time, Gennady, Malinovsky and Blagron yanked open the right-side sliding door and dropped to the ground, just as five grinning, blade-wielding assailants came at them!

When the first fellow lunged at the driver, the well-built man side-stepped his thrust and brought his clasped hands down on the back of the off-balance tough's neck with focused force. There was an audible *'SNAP!'* and the highwayman sprawled still. A second attacker, with an uncertain glance at his inert *'compadre'*, shoved his blade at the driver, who parried his thrust with his fist, then grabbed the outmaneuvered man's flailing forearm. A second later, the thief was also on the ground, not moving, his neck twisted in an impossible position.

At the same time, the other three attackers each came at a passenger—but before any of them could get close enough to engage hand-to-hand, Blagron, Malinovsky, and Gennady, shouting, leaped feet-first and caught the flat-footed desperadoes in their throats with the heels of the heavy, cobbled 'Spetsnaz-issue boots. Down they crumpled, with no further movements.

The van passengers and the driver stared with looks of disgust at the bandits, all lying still on the grass.

"Welcome to Mexico!" Blagron shouted sardonically at them in Russian, over the noise of vehicles racing by on the thoroughfare a few meters away, whose occupants paid them no attention.

The sweating four, breathing hard, hauled themselves back into the van. With some deft maneuvering, the driver managed to dis-engage the left side of the van from the clutches of the delivery truck and steer it back onto the pavement. As they pulled away, Gennady and the others looked back; the driver caught the scene in his rear-view mirror. All five of the attackers lay inert in the grass next to the roaring freeway.

The fellow at the wheel glanced back over his shoulder. "No sympathy for those *hombres!*" For a while the van cruised up the highway without anyone speaking; everyone was thinking about what had happened.

At length, Malinovsky spoke up. "Is Mexico always like this?"

"You have to watch out, all right." The driver looked into the mirror at the young men sitting behind him. "Where we are going—'Nuevo Laredo'—lots of gangs and organized crime."

"Why 'Nuevo Laredo'?"

"That is where General Retchko wants us." The fellow's tone seemed to settle it. The driver took another glance in the mirror; the young men were frowning. "Actually, it is a convenient location to do the things we will be doing against the 'Americanskis'." A pause, then, "Did they tell you what your duties will be?"

"They just said to wait for instructions."

The driver grunted. "Sounds like them, all right." He took another glance in the mirror."Do not worry, we will have many things to do—but first, you will meet some important people."

"What kind of 'important people'?"

"Some politicians . . . some police people; gang leaders; enforcers.You will see." The fellow gave a laugh. "After we meet with the big people, you will be *'hokay'!*"

In the mirror he caught the glances among the young men in the back. "Like I said, no problems with the police or the government—that is one of the reasons we are in Nuevo Laredo."

The conversation faded away; the driver focused his attention on the highway; the passengers settled back and watched the scenery of northern Mexico run past. As they rode along, from time to time Gennady would recognize some place or another from the time the Spetsnaz squad had come this same way when they were headed for the encounter at Los Alamos.

The remembrance of those days brought up in Gennady once more the never-ending ache about what had happened. As hard as he tried to suppress his thoughts, they kept going back to those he had left on the other side—Terenty; Tamara; the older people; the little girl; Colonel Golubko; the once-familiar people, sights, and sounds that were now gone from him for all time.

Galina.

Like it or not—they would be locked-into this "situation" for the rest of their lives. He would take it out on the Americans. They were the cause of all this.

His thoughts were interrupted by the driver speaking. "We will stop for something to eat, now."

The man looked in the rear-view mirror and saw the passengers nodding in agreement.

The van swung off the freeway onto a service road. Presently they drew up to a pastel-painted, stucco-sided establishment with many vehicles parked around it. As they got out, Gennady gaped at a gaudy sign on the upper front with cartoon characters proclaiming the place as a *'Restaurante'*. Lighted *'Cerveza'* signs in neon colors hung from the windows. "World Famous!" another bragged in Spanish. One of the fellows gave a shallow laugh. "If it is so famous, why I have never heard of it?"

"Mexican food—" The driver held open the front door of the establishment for them. " . . . better get used to it!"

Inside, Gennady and the other Russians stared at a menu on the wall behind the order-counter that made no sense to them.

"I will order for you," the driver said in Spanish, pointing toward an empty table in the back of the crowded place.

In a few minutes, he came back with a big tray of food items wrapped in waxed paper. For a moment the little packages reminded Gennady of the kiosk blintzes back in Moscow. *"'Tamales',"* the man said, pulling off the paper from his food item. The three gaped at folded, hard-shell-like concoctions containing meat pieces and lettuce, with melted cheese oozing-out. "They call these *"'Tacos',"* . . . a popular food in Mexico."

A hostess brought a tray of beer in clear bottles, unlike the amber ones Gennady was used to back in Russia. He took a long swallow and looked at the label. *'Corona'*, it read.

"A big brand—you will see a lot of it in Mexico."

As they had not eaten since a Cuban breakfast all the way back in Havana that morning, the young men went after it with gusto.

Malinovsky winced after his first bite, taking several big swallows of beer. "Hot . . ."

The 'Mexican' gave a smirk. *"Everything,* here, is hot!"

Blagron spoke up. "We have not introduced ourselves."

"I guess with all the excitement, we forgot. *'Alexei Sorbetsky',"* he said, shaking theirs in turn. "Here, they call me *'Alex Salinas'.''* The others gave their names and shook his hand. The local-looking Russian squinted at his new compatriots. "You will need new names, here—Mexican-like names," he said. "We will be staying in the same *'casa'*—that is, 'house',"' as they call it." He went on. "General Retchko messaged me we will be working with—"

Sudden movement at a nearby table caught their attention. A swarthy, powerfully-built older man with a huge, gray-black mustache had stood up and was edging his way across the diner toward them between some startled customers of the eatery, some of whom stood and began backing away. The Mexican stopped at the Russians' table and ran his hand through his greasy black hair; his coal-dot eyes darting from one newcomer to another.

He fixed his gaze on Alex. "These are the 'hombres'' you were telling me about?" He scanned the three pale-skinned men sitting at the table.

Gennady, Blagron, and Malinovsky gave quick glances at each other. They had been here only a short time and this part of

Mexico was already looking like it was on edge. It occured to Gennady that the room might be filled with this fellow's friends; all the male customers in the place looked like rough men. He caught the others' eyes and gravely shrugged. They would play along and see what would happen.

Alex looked up at the fellow and gave a big spread-handed grin, gesturing to the three newcomers. "Ah, José! *'Amigo'!* These 'hombres are the *'compadres'* I told you about!" He kept on, in Spanish, "they are here to work with us!"

"'Gringos'?" The man looked over the decidedly un-Mexican-appearing visitors with a skeptical eye. Gennady realized there were probably not many blond, crew-cut native-types in this part of the world, such as himself; nor red-headed ones, such as Blagron. Malinovsky, whose hair was thinning, was still given-away by his light-shaded complexion.

Alex cast about and caught the attention of a waitress. After speaking something to her in rapid Spansh, he gestured for the others to follow him "We will find a quiet place," he said. The Major Mexican seemed to be looking around the room, catching the eyes of some other men at different tables. Gennady noticed that some, pretending to be feigning indifference, were, in fact, taking in what was happening with particular interest. It appeared that the restaurant was probably some sort of regular hangout for these men.

The group stepped into a smallish dining-room, devoid of other customers. As everyone scraped back a chair and took a seat, Alex gestured around the table and at the hostess. *"Cerveza* for each one of us, *'señorita'."*

As the very pretty young brunette waitress wrote down the order, Gennady saw her give furtive looks at the slick-haired Mexican. The writing pad trembled in her hand. The girl looked nervous—*was she frightened of this man?* As the teenager turned about to go place the order, her foot bumped into a chair leg.

Alex was talking with the newcomer. "These fellows, here," he said in Spanish, "are working with the Organization."

At the mention of the word,"Organization", the man began surveying the new Russians; his heavy black eyebrows furrowed.

Alex went on. "They are Russian . . . *as I am.*"

The man seemed to ease off. He nodded and put out a calloused hand. *"Bueno!* I am *'José Aldrada'!"* He gave a heavy-handed shake to each of the three as they told him their first names. "What will be your functions?"

Alex spoke up. "They are waiting for their instructions from Retchko. In the meantime, I will be showing them around Nuevo Laredo."

Aldrada gave a brushy-mustached grin at Alex, then around at the others. "You will see *everyone . . . everything*, then?"

The three gave perplexed looks. Alex saw their confusion. "He means you will get a complete knowledge of the operations, here."

"Operations?"

Before the man could speak, the waitress came back with an outsized tray of beer in bottles. As she handed them out, Gennady watched her. Her hands still shook. Gennady observed that Blagron was staring at her with more than casual interest. He also noticed that the girl had blue eyes, unlike the other Mexicans. And she was light-skinned.

With another glance at the older man, the dark-haired girl turned away. Aldrada leered at her swaying, well-proportioned backside until she stepped around the corner, holding the tray high over her head on her fingertips. She *is* a real beauty, Gennady thought. He glanced at Blagron. The Russian's ruddy face was frozen in admiration.

José Aldrada saw the young man's look. "You like her? Then, I give her to you, someday."

Blagron blinked. "What? I do not understand."

"Ah, you see . . . she is very much afraid that she will be kidnapped into prostitution, like what happens to many girls along the border."

The young man still looked confused.

The Mexican went on. "Señor, we have a prostitution problem—the bad hombres get their girls from"—the man's eyes swept around the crowded dining-room—"places like this." The Mexican gave a little sneer Blagron and the others picked up. "The girl's family is honest but poor . . . she is virgin, you see, but if they come for her, she has no choice. "

"If they come for her?"

"Ah, Señor Russian, I am 'compassioned' man, as you see. But there are men here in Nuevo Laredo—bad men—who would take her away in the middle of the night. But I would never do that to her."

Alex spoke up. "There is a 'gang' here who would kidnap her and rape her and sell her into the 'bordellos'—she is the right age—and she has blue eyes and light skin . . . much liked by the *'bordertown banditos'*. Her work would fetch good prices."

The redheaded Russian looked shocked.

The Mexican pointed at Blagron's "Corona". It was untouched. "Drink your 'cerveza', señor. If you finish, she will come back and bring you another, and you can see her, again—"

Hardly had the man said those words, than the waitress reappeared. "*Mas cervezas,* señors?" she said in a lilting Mexican Spanish. Blagron was looking at the girl, who caught his stare. She glanced at his full bottle, then back at him, her eyes questioning. "You do not like 'cerveza' . . . ?"

"I will finish soon," the young man said in his best try at the local language, taking a quick swallow, his eyes fixated on the delicate-looking, dark-haired girl with the light skin and the dark blue eyes.

Gennady, watching her as she scooped bottles onto a tray, saw that she was indeed beautiful in an uncomplicated sort of way. Such a dainty creature in a brothel would be a sacrilege, he thought.

"I will be back," she said, taking a longer look at Blagron, who was downing his beer in obvious haste. Then she lofted the loaded tray over her head on her fingertips once more and sidestepped her way out past vacant tables and chairs and around the corner.

Gennady looked at the young man, then at José Aldrada. "You will 'give her' to him, you say?"

"It will be a contest with the 'gang '. . . whoever gets to her first—"

". . . gets the girl." Gennady finished the sentence. It was a tough society in this town, he was starting to think. Blagron's eyes were glazed in thought as he swigged his beer.

Aldrada twiddled his calloused thumbs, looking from one of the men to another. "You are all Russians, no?"

Gennady told the man how they had been in "Spetsnaz"; about being kidnapped by the Chechens; joining the Organization—not in a willing manner, but having no choice—and coming here.

"Ah, but the Chief will pay you well." Aldrada tapped his pocket, that the others saw was bulging. "You will have good life, here, you will see."

"The 'Americanskis' killed my wife in an airliner shoot-down," Gennady said. "I will take out my vengeance on them all."

Aldrada was nodding. "That is a good attitude to have in this business. There is plenty to do, here."

"Now that you mention it . . . what *do* you do, here?"

The shiny-haired Mexican gave a gap-toothed grin. "Aside from the usual—ah,'things'—we move 'revolutionary goods' and agents over the border for the Cartel. We have a secret warehouse in Laredo, across the river. We work with Central American revolutionaries, and new groups that are coming along." He looked around to see if anyone was overhearing their conversation, then went on. "Right now, we are starting to recruit in Venezuela and are training paramilitaries in Colombia."

"The Organization has big plans for Venezuela and Colombia," Alex put in.

"Perhaps you will soon meet some of our 'compadres' from Colombia and other places," the Mexican said, pulling on his black, bushy mustache. The fellow lowered his voice almost to a whisper. "In a few days, there will be a meeting at *'Cali'*, in *'Colombia'*, of revolutionaries from Central and South America. They are forming a new 'Hemisphere Revolutionary Council' . . . they say they will work together against governments and against the *'Yanqui Imperialists'*. The revolutionaries are well-financed through cocaine . . . kidnapping . . . extortion—"

"Our Organization has the arms and training to help them," Alex commented. The Russians would appeal to the Mexican leader José Aldrada's instincts of greed and survival.

The man seemed to be pickng up on what Alex was trying to get over to him. The suggestion of a grin appeared beneath his riotous mustache; his well-worn face creased at the corners. "I am sure you would find it advantage to be in Cali."

Alex turned to the new men. "Your timing is perfect . . . I will communicate to the Chief' about this. Perhaps it would be a good assignment for the three of you, since you speak Spanish, to be there and show them how the Cartel can help and work with them—"

At that moment, the waitress came around the corner, holding aloft another tray of the local beer. Aldrada gave her an obvious going-over, then nodded at Blagron. "Ah, señorita`, the young *'hombre'*, here, has eyes for you." The girl took a glance at the redheaded Russian, then looked at the older man, uncertain what he meant..

"He is good young man . . . he will want to marry you."

Blagron's face turned even more red than his usual ruddy cast; at the same time the others around the table all at once were having a hard time keeping straight faces. The girl's eyes were wide. Gennady thought she was going to drop the tray and run.

Blagron came to his own rescue. "Ah, señorita, I am . . . new, here," and I am not familiar with your ways. Mi compadre"—he gestured at Aldrada—is trying to help me."

The light-skinned teenager started taking bottles off the tray and setting them in front of the men. There was a touch of pink on her face as she handed a Corona to Blagron.

The young man was trying to go on. "Señorita, I am *'Pedro Beltran',* from—from—the . . . 'East', and I mean you no harm." His hand was out. *"Por favor, señorita."*

The girl hesitated, then set the tray on the edge of the table. ". . . *'Tatiana Castillo'*—" She shook his hand. She was blushing.

"Pedro Beltran" eased back his seat a little and stood up. "Tatiana Castillo" gave a little gasp; her eyes wide in obvious admiration of his muscular build next to her own slight form.

The young waitress cast about; a look of concern was on her face. "The owner does not allow us to talk to customers."

Aldrada looked straight at her, his mustache twitching "Do not worry, señorita . . . if there are 'problema', *I will take care of the owner."* There was an edge of authority in his voice. "I—that is, *'we'*—are regular customers."

Gennady remembered the others in the diner he had observed earlier; the men he had suspected were with Aldrada. The slender waitress seemed to relax a little.

"'Señor Pedro', here, will be pleased to know you *outside* this place ... *then* he will not be customer, eh?" The girl held her breath. The man went on, "Boss will have no complaint, then, no?"

He looked at the young Russian, whose jaw had dropped. The burly man leaned toward him, his voice in a humorous, growly tone. "Here is where you 'save the señorita, señor!"

"Pedro Beltran" groped for words in his incomplete Spanish. "You have *'telefono'?*"

"He promises to be good." Malinovsky, who had been taking in everything, spoke up in Spanish.

The young waitress wrote some numbers on a paper napkin and handed it to him as if she was unsure of what she was doing. "I will be off, tomorrow night. I will be at that place."

Tatiana Castillo snatched up the tray and stepped in a hurry out of the room, leaving the men staring at her. As she turned the corner, Gennady saw she was blushing.

The Russian took his seat. The others were looking him with wry grins.

"*'Pedro Beltran'?*" Gennady let out a laugh. "Where did you get *that* name?"

"*'Petr'* in Russian ... *'Pedro'* in Spanish." He pointed at a nearby wall. "I saw a poster over there for *'Beltran Belts and Holsters'.*" The young man frowned."What is a *'holster'?*"

Alex pointed at a gun-toting man at a table just outside the room. "See that hombre over there? His gun is in a 'holster'. You will see lots of holsters in Nuevo Laredo, 'Señor Pedro'!"

Aldrada spoke up. "Pretty little thing, that Tatiana, is she not? You will call her, no?"

The redheaded Russian fingered the paper she had given him as if it had certain powers. "Ah, yes, of course." He was embarrassed by the little episode—but the look of anticipation on his face was obvious.

* * *

Tanuta Refinery; the Next Morning:

"You say you want to *leave* this place?" Leonid Retchko leaned back in his office chair; a questioning look on his florid face. The sunlight beaming through the open window reflected off his bald, sun-burnished head. Refinery sounds came from outside. The man cocked his eye and looked down his bulbous nose at the two across the desk from him. "Why do you want to do that?"

"We've done everything we were assigned to do here." Larry Landay motioned toward the outside. "The satellite system is running and—"

". . . the security fences are up and the guards have everything under control," Marisol put in, "we want to have a regular life in the world." She hesitated. "We could work freelance for you.

"I see." The man behind the desk tapped his fingertips together. "I take it you are 'together', as they say—"

Larrry and Marisol glanced at each other and nodded.

"Very well . . . I will release you from here on three conditions . . . the first is that you go to Colombia as 'technical advisors' at a meeting that will take place there, next week."

Larry was frowning. "Colombia?"

"'Cali, Colombia'. It is in South America."

"But how will we get there? Everybody's looking for me. I'm a 'criminal', they say."

"Ah, yes." Retchko ran a hand across his skin-topped dome. "Perhaps you could go in disguise with fake passports . . . dye your hair black . . . grow a mustache; make it black, too. You would look Spanish, enough—you speak Spanish?"

"Enough to get by on."

"The 'second condition' is that you 'consult' with us when we need you . . . you will have to devise some method to communicate back to us."

"We have already worked that out. Lisa has designed a smaller, solid-state version of our encription and decoding machine . . . we can take it with us. It uses a regular telephone line." Larry cocked his eyebrow. "You said there were *three* conditions—"

"Ah, yes . . . the most important one." Retchko leaned back in his chair and looked down his nose at them. The pudgy man tapped his fingertips together. "You will have the chip implants."

Larry had a sinking feeling. Having helped to design it, he knew the purpose of the tiny device was for the Cartel to track to the ends of the earth whoever possessed it.

Marisol was frowning. "Both of us?"

The Chief of Security nodded. "As you are perhaps not aware, *'no one ever leaves the Organization'.*" Retchko's beady eyes bored onto Larry and Marisol. "We fed and housed you all this time . . . you will remain in our service as long as we need you."

Larry glanced at Marisol, who had a resigned look on her face. She seemed prepared to endure whatever it would take to get out of this dead-end place.

The bald Ukrainian stood up. "Come back tomorrow and I will have all the documents you will need." Then he seemed to remember something. "Where will you go after the Cali meetings?"

"Probably *'Medellín, Colombia'.* "There, the United States will not bother us."

* * *

As the Mercedes made the turn onto the approaches to the Holland Tunnel, Norbert Ezego gazed up at the two massive towers of the *'World Trade Center'* that held sway over Lower Manhattan. For long seconds as they drove past, the late afternoon sun caught the contrasting hues of orange and gray on the sides of the hulking glass slabs that soared into the azure sky.

The young driver glanced back and spoke to his passenger in English with a heavy brogue. "That will be our first target. The *'Twin Towers',* they call them . . . *we will bring them down.*"

These people are thinking big, the Nigerian thought, as the sedan hurtled down the ramp into the below-water vehicular tunnel, if they are aiming at such a solid-looking target for their first effort in America.

"The fellows from Chechnya arrived this morning," the youth went on, over the rumble of vehicles in the orange-lit tube, "they are now getting lists of materials together." He swerved around a slow-moving delivery van and glimpsed for a moment in the rear-view mirror at the African passenger. "We already have a place to work in a mini-warehouse."

The tunnel began to rise and up ahead the bright sunlight of New Jersey came into sight.

* * *

Nuevo Laredo, Mexico; the Next Day:

"Alex Salinas" took another swig of his "Corona"; his eyes darting back and forth between Gennady and Malinovsky. "What 'Hispanic' names will you use? They must be convincing."

The young Russian with the thinning hair had been flipping through a book he had found in the apartment, looking for names. "How about 'Andres Martinez' . . . it would be almost like my real name, 'Andrey Malinovsky'—" He handed the book to Gennady.

Gennady ran his eyes up and down several pages of a Spanish 'novella' in his hands. "These names are so different."

Alex spoke up. "How about 'Guido Lopez'. It will be easy to remember from 'Gennady Lychin'." He nodded at both newcomers. "Those names are common enough to get you anywhere without anyone being suspicious."

"'Guido Lopez '. . . I guess that will work."

Alex looked around. "Where is our friend, 'Pedro Beltran'?"

"He is getting ready for his visit to that girl, 'Tatiana'— the waitress."

"I think he likes her."

"I am surprised she actually answered the telephone when he called her!"

"I think maybe she likes him, too.

* * *

Tanuta Refinery, Earlier That Same Day:

"At least it doesn't hurt." Larry Landay stared at the gauze bandage on his left wrist as he dabbled at his lunch.

Across the table, Marisol Montoya rubbed her own forearm that was also wrapped in tape."You say this chip will tell the Organization where we are all the time?"

Larry nodded. He looked around to make sure no one in the dining room was overhearing them. "Retchko says they are now in his agents's wrists all around the world. The new guy has been very busy, setting up the links of all the agents through the satellite—dozens of them."

"Larry, this whole thing frightens me."

"I am sure everything will be all right." But he remembered Retchko's words that "no one ever left the Organization"; that the Cartel would always know where they were. The general had also said, "you will always remain in our service", or something like that. Larry tried to give her a convincing smile. "In a few days we'll be a long way from here and we can start a real life."

Someone tapped Larry on his shoulder. Turning about, he was confronted by a security officer. "General Retchko wants to see you both—right away."

* * *

"You will be on the 'Seven-Forty-Seven' that leaves the day-after-tomorrow for Havana." Leonid Efimovich Retchko handed some papers to Larry, then another packet to Marisol. "When you get to Lagos, your new passports will be at Ajiboy's office. You will have new names and new looks."

"New looks?"

"With black hair, you will not attract the attention of the authorities when you get to Colombia." Retchko nodded his bullet-shaped head at Larry, who had the beginnings of a mustache. "They will be looking for a blond man." He looked at his watch. "Dye your hair now and get the passport pictures taken

371

so our man who is going to Lagos tonight can take them to our printing office, up there."

"What about our names?"

"Your new names will be on the passports." The general nodded at the two. "You will both become 'Colombian' citizens."

The hairless man stood up. "You must memorize the instructions, then shred the papers—and practice your Spanish for Colombia."

Just then, there was a knock.

The office door eased aside and the flabby bulk of Masobe Busa waddled around the frame. The overweight African, sporting his usual ballooning flowery outfit, looked Larry and Marisol up and down. The dark fellow squinted. "Ah, yes . . . I remember you from the day the intruder was killed at the fence."

The portly Ukrainian gestured at the couple and toward the door. "Go now, and have the pictures ready in two hours."

Retchko watched as the door closed, then motioned to sit down. "They are leaving us."

"I did not think anyone could leave the Organization."

"They have the implants—we will be tracking them." The Cartel's Security Chief' rubbed his hands together. "Now that you will become General Manager of the refinery, here, *with other Cartel duties* . . . we must make it look as if we simply hired you away from the other plant."

"To stop any suspicion . . . "

"Of course. Someone will keep the 'crude-oil-diversion' software up-to-date, over there?"

"I bribed one of their maintenance men. He knows what to do."

"Very good. The satellite system is now operating. That girl, Lisa, and a new man are running it."

"You trust them?"

"The man, yes. I have some questions about the girl, though. You will want to watch her." He shook his head. "She is the weak link, here. Even more so than Frank Ogawan."

"Why is that?"

"She is not ruthless, like her sister . . . I believe she could crack."

Busa pondered Retcho's reasoning. "What else?"

"Frank Ogawan, the 'office manager'—" Retchko lit a cigarette and leaned back. "I will want to 'eliminate' him, at some point."

Busa frowned. "Why?"

"The girl, Lisa, and Ogawan are 'together', you might say." He drew on his cigarette. "She is in my debt over a matter—and I do not like competition."

Retchko thought about how he believed Lisa Anaya still owed herself to him for reviving her one time when lightning struck nearby and she was unconscious. He had saved her life. It was a debt she owed to him and no one—certainly not Frank Ogawan, who was becoming more aggravating by the day— would be allowed to interfere. But the young man, a weakling, would have to be done away with. He would bide his time for the proper moment to act. The bald Ukrainian pulled on his cigarette, grinning to himself; it could be sooner rather than later.

Busa squirmed in his chair. "It is that important to get rid of him?"

"Let us say that we will use Ogawan and Lisa Anaya as long as we need them . . . then—"

The unfinished sentence hung in the smoke-clouded air. But its meaning was clear.

* * *

"Pedro Beltran" compared the numbers on the fronts of the plain houses and the address he had written down as he maneuvered the borrowed sedan down the narrow lane, at the same time trying to avoid the man-sized potholes in the crumbling, long-ago pavement. According to what the girl had told him on the telephone, her home was near the end of the short street. At length, he pulled up to a modest pink-stucco house surrounded by a weathered wooden fence. Flowering cactus plants sprouted here and there in the mostly-dirt front yard, like she had described it.

As he was alighting from the car, a young man about his own age came running out through the gate, loped around to the rear of the vehicle and started writing something on a pad, glancing at Pedro several times.

Just then, Tatiana Castillo stepped out the front door onto the porch and Pedro forgot all about the fellow with the pad. For as appealing as she had been in the restaurant was nothing compared to how she now looked. The girl had outfitted herself in a short yellow sundress that displayed a considerable expanse of her pale skin, including, as he could not fail to observe as she came toward him, a great proportion of her chest, in the off-the-shoulder style he had already noticed of girls in Mexico. He felt his face flushing as she stepped up to him, her cheek presented to him for the obligatory kiss Alex had told him was the custom. Hugging her, he was surprised how tiny, almost fragile, she felt.

The teenager brushed back her waist-length black hair and looked up at him with eyes the same color as the late-afternoon sky. "I am glad you found our house," she said in an almost-musical voice, motioning at the modest stucco bungalow.

He was awestruck by how beautiful she was in the daylight. "I—did not know you had—long hair," was all Pedro could think of to say in his halting Spanish.

"We have to keep it pinned-up at the restaurant. I have never cut my hair in my entire life!"

Tatiana took his hand and tugged him through the gate. "You must meet 'mi familia'," she went on, as they mounted some cement-block steps to the porch.

Pulling on the screen door, she ushered her guest into a little parlor crowded with plastic-and-wood furniture and many vases of artificial flowers all around. Several pictures of long-haired men with scraggly beards hung on the walls, along with some objects that Pedro remembered from his grandmother's apartment back in Russia as crucifixes, although of a plainer, different type. In a corner was a cluttered collection of lighted incense candles and more flowers in vases, surmounted by a larger, more detailed crucifix hanging above it.

"Those are 'The Savior' and the 'Saints'," Tatiana said in a reverent tone, "and that is our altar."

At that moment the young fellow with the writing pad pulled open the squeaking front screen door, walked past Pedro and

Tatiana and on through an archway without looking at them or saying a word.

"He is my brother," the girl said, looking down. Pedro thought she was embarrassed. "He does not know who you are, so he took down the license number of your car." She bit her lower lip.

Pedro gave a grin. "I think that is a good idea." He would try to appear gallant. "I have nothing to hide, so what is the problem?"

A look of relief came over Tatiana's face.

Just then, a smallish woman stepped through the archway into the room. Pedro noticed she had the same dark-hair-light-skin coloration as Tatiana.

"Pedro, this is *mi mamá,* 'Belén Castillo'," the girl said, "and this is Pedro , , , Pedro—?" Tatiana blushed, her hand flew to her mouth, her eyes went wide

". . .'Beltran'," he finished with a grin, as the woman offered her hand. To Pedro, *'Señora Castillo'* looked quite young to be the mother of the teenaged Tatiana.

The mother looked him up and down. "You are going out with *him*?" The girl nodded. Belén Castillo frowned. "You are from Nuevo Laredo?"

"I am from . . . the 'East'—"

The woman started to say something, but Tatiana's younger brother came back into the room just then and handed her a paper. Pedro let out a silent sigh of relief—the boy's timely arrival had perhaps saved him from having to answer some delicate questions.

"This is his license plate number," the adolescent said, giving a furtive glance at the husky-looking newcomer.

The mother glanced at the small scrap, then back up at Pedro. "You said you were from—"

"Ah, 'east of here'." The Russian disliked having to play word games with these good people, but he would have to bend things to protect his true identity. Since Moscow was "east" of Nuevo Laredo, technically he was telling the truth. He glanced at Tatiana; she was staring at him, unblinking.

375

The woman's face seemed to relax a little. "Oh, 'Matamoros'!"

Pedro wanted to get going before there were any more awkward inquiries. He gave the girl's elbow a subtle nudge. "We will be going to the movies," he said, pushing open the screen door for her with a wave back at the blinking two in the tiny living room. "We will be back early."

They stepped outside; the mother and son watching through the mesh door as Tatiana and her date got into the car. In a few moments, the sedan had turned about and was gone.

"She will be all right, mamá? We do not know this hombre . . ."

The woman looked down at the paper in her hand that was trembling a little. "I trust to the Lord she will be."

* * *

"That was the first movie I have seen in a long time!" Tatiana Castillo swung into the booth of the Mexican fast-food place, kicked-off her flip-flops, and tucked her feet to the side on the long red-leatherette seat. The girl fluffed her long hair and tossed it back. "I always like *'Cantinflas'* . . . he is so funny."

"He was funny, all right." The redheaded Russian caught the attention of a waitress and ordered two Cokes.

The dark-haired girl's deep blue eyes met his across the table. "I want to sing like the woman who was in the movie."

"You want to be a singer?"

Tatiana gave a sigh. "We cannot afford my voice lessons, anymore." Her eyes looked down. "*Mi papá* is very sick, now. That is why I work . . . most of my pesos from the 'restaurante' help pay for *'medicina'*."

The young man was frowning. "Your father is sick?"

"He is sick from working at the asbestos factory. The doctor is not giving a good report."

Pedro felt uncomfortable. "I am very sorry."

Just then, the colas came. The two jabbed straws at the paper cups and started working on their slushy drinks.

After a few swallows, the girl leaned her elbows on the table and ran her slim fingers into her long black hair, her eyes turned

376

up at him. She shook her head. "It is dangerous for me to work at night. Nuevo Laredo is not safe, Pedro."

"Could you not work in the daytime?"

"I have to take care of 'mi papá' while 'mamá' cleans the rich peoples's houses . . . then I work at night. But I have no choice—" Her fingers were still enmeshed in her hair. He noticed they seemed to be freshly manicured. *For him?*

A girl came by and refilled their glasses. Pedro observed how the waitress's brown skin and eyes, typical of most peoples' he had seen in Nuevo Laredo so far, contrasted with Tatiana's light complexion. "Just curious, but how did you get your blue eyes?"

A flush came onto her face and her chest, very much of which was exposed by the low-cut dress, particularly as she was leaning forward toward him, a fact Pedro could not help but notice. *"'Mi familia'* are from the south of Mexico . . . I was born in 'Cuernavaca' . . . many people there are light-skinned." The girl squinted at Pedro's red hair and grinned. "Some even have red hair." She looked down at her pale hands for a moment, then sat straight up with a deep breath, as if in some sort of defiance. "My people were the Spanish *'Conquistadores*' who married the *'Mayan'* girls, there, long ago."

"Then how did you get to Nuevo Laredo?"

"We came here so papá could get medical treatments across the border in Laredo . . . in Texas. But we cannot get across the border." She wiped an eye with her hand. "The doctors here are not hopeful, for him. It is taking all our *'dinero'* in Nuevo Laredo."

To Pedro, it seemed that her unfortunate family situation had caused her to have to grow up very fast. He looked across the soda-shop table at the very pretty teenager's face, framed by her long, silky-black hair, and realized she was wearing perhaps the only worthwhile dress she had, which, as he could not help but notice, displayed her young assets in the most flattering terms— perhaps more so than she would have consciously planned—in what seemed to be the custom for young women in this overheated border town. Pedro remembered that the older man, José Aldrada, who seemed to know much about such things, had said she was a virgin. A wave of concern for the tiny, vulnerable "señorita" came over him. The young man reached across for her hand and was pleased she did not pull away. "You are not old enough for all this!"

"I am seventeen. And I will be a year older in one week." The girl gave another look of defiance. "I will be full woman, then!"

Some males, all dressed in black, came in and noisily took a table across from them. Out of the corner of his eye, Pedro saw them staring at Tatiana. He recalled what Alex and José Aldrada had told him about kidnappings and prostitution, and that she was about the age that unsavory things could start happening to her. All at once, he sensed they were in an unsafe place.

"Perhaps we had better leave, now," he said, forcing himself to sound calm.

But Tatiana had already noticed the leering "hombres" and was scooting her feet around underneath the table for her flip-flops. She looked at Pedro with a wide-eyed expression of alarm.

The young man tossed some coins onto the table and stood, blocking the mens' view of the girl as she got up. Pedro guided her by her elbow toward the door in a hurry; he wanted to get her away from there, *fast*.

Outside, he bundled the nervous Tatiana into the sedan and dropped behind the steering wheel, reaching for the ignition switch. In a few moments he maneuvered the car onto the main road and gave the engine more gas.

They had gone hardly a block when he saw in the rear-view mirror a pair of headlights sweep out of the parking lot and aim in their direction. "Oh, oh," he muttered to himself.

Tatiana looked back and gasped. "They are following us!" She pointed at a cross-street intersection. "Turn here!"

Pedro twisted the wheel and the sedan leaned into a skidding turn, then straightened as he gave it more speed.

The girl pointed at a small building. "In there!" To the left, outlined in the headlights, was a vacant garage, its overhead door gaping open.

Pedro braked and swung the sedan into the crowded space, jamming to a stop. Jumping out, in frantic haste he tugged down the overhead roll-away door.

Scarcely a second later, the howling sounds of the other vehicle burst around the corner and came tearing close by the closed door of the inconspicuous hideaway, then started to trail off.

In the darkness, Pedro lifted the groaning garage door and peered out. Some blocks away, the red taillights and the muffled engine noises of their pursuers were fading away. The only sounds became the nocturnal buzz of crickets.

He jumped back into the car and screeched it around to head in the other direction; slamming it in gear, stepping on the gas. "How do we get to your house?"

The girl, still breathing hard from the narrow escape, pointed at a street a block away. "Down there! It is only a short way to where I live."

The car pulled up in front of the little bungalow; the two jumped out.

"Inside! Hurry!" Pedro gasped, pulling her up the makeshift steps. The young man guided her into the little living room and doused the lights. He cracked open the door and listened. Everything was quiet. He looked out. No one was there. "Be right back!"

Pedro dashed to the car and started the engine. By the vague lights of some nearby front porches he guided the vehicle around the corner and parked it in some moon shadows behind an outbuilding. Then he ran back back to Tatiana's house.

Even as he hopped onto the porch, the glow of some approaching headlights came pulsating over the roof-tops of houses up on the main road. Pedro gave a quick knock. "Let me in!" The door opened, then closed as he bustled inside. Hardly breathing, the two hunched down and peered around the window curtain, listening for sounds through the open window.

Some seconds later, a darkened van stole slowly down the lane, then stopped at the dead-end just beyond the house. A pause; then came the crunching of tires on the crumbly pavement as it seemed to be turning around. The vehicle pulled up out front and stopped, its engine idling. Tatiana grabbed Pedro's arm. He could feel her trembling.

A heavy male voice came from inside the van. "You *sure* it was *this* street?"

There was an indistinct reply.

After some moments the van, its tires grinding on the gravel, moved off. Through the curtains, the fugitives observed its taillights turn away at the main road. Then it was gone.

The girl collapsed into Pedro's arms, shaking. " I am afraid they will come after me."

Pedro was in a quandry; he was outmanned by the searchers. With a sinking feeling he realized he had neglected to get Alex's telephone number before he left the apartment—a serious oversight.

The young man thought fast. He gripped Tatiana's slender shoulders and whispered to her. "I must go and get help . . . while I am gone, you must hide under the bed . . . in the attic— *somewhere.*"

In the half-light filtering in through the window curtains he saw her pale face nodding.

"I will be back here in a little while with friends." He scooted across the floor below window level, nudged open the door a crack and peered out. In the shadowy blackness of the modest rows of houses nothing seemed to be going on. He squeezed the girl's hand and melted into the darkness.

Pedro had almost reached the hidden car when there came a snapping sound from nearby. All at once, a black cat leaped in front of him, its back arched, its tail swishing, yowling and hissing with glowing red eyes; its white, fang-like teeth flashing in the dim reflected light! Then the creature of the night dashed off into the crackling underbrush, leaving him gasping in surprise; his heart pounding.

Up ahead loomed the sedan, still in its murky hiding place behind a small barn. He opened the door, climbed inside and started the engine. Holding his breath, as if not breathing would somehow quiet the engine sounds, he backed-out the borrowed car and maneuvered it toward the main blacktop road; its headlights still off.

As he drove past, Pedro did not see the dark van that was parked off the side road under some trees, a few houses below the unlighted intersection. When his car was out of sight, three men, all dressed in black, stole out of it and made their way in the shadows toward the short lane. Just before they came to the street crossing, a fourth individual, also in black, reared up out of the blackness making "come-on" motions. The nodding figure pointed at the little pink bungalow near the bottom of the darkened, dead-end street.

-16-

The sedan skidded to a stop in front of the apartments. Dashing toward the row of flats, Pedro saw that the lights in their upstairs place were burning.

Drumming up the stairsteps, the young man burst into the living room where the others, except "Gaido Lopez", were slouched about, watching a *'fútbol'* game on television. Empty "cerveza" bottles littered the floor.

"I need help!" In a hurry, Pedro gasped-out the situation back at Tatiana's home.

Alex was already on the telephone. "Let us go!" he shouted, slamming down the receiver, "José Aldrada will meet us there with some of his men! Bring weapons!"

There was a rush down the steps. Everyone bundled into Alex's van. In scant seconds, the vehicle was rocking down the rutted road. From the back seats came the clacking of ammunition magazines snapping into AK-74's.

Alex called over his shoulder at Pedro. "I know where she lives . . . we have been watching her neighborhood!"

Before the Russian could ask what he meant, the headlights shone on the darkened intersection to the short street. The driver gunned the engine, aiming the van down to the gate of the little bungalow and hung on the brakes, sawing to a stop.

Right away, Pedro had a feeling something bad had happened—the front door was wide open; the living room lights were on. Some men and women were standing on the porch surrounding a woman in a night-gown who was screaming, pulling her hair. As he ran up the cinder-block steps, Pedro recognized Tatiana's mother.

When she saw Pedro, Belén Castillo grabbed him. "They took her! They took away Tatiana!"

Just then, another van scratched to a stop on the pebbly pavement out front. José Aldrada, along with several other men, all carrying automatic weapons, bounded through the gate and ran up to the little gathering on the porch. The neighbors gaped at them and seemed to shrink back.

"Too late! They have her!"

Aldrada gestured to two of the men who were with him. "Stay here and guard this place!" He motioned toward the street. "Come on! I know where they are going!"

The men scrambled back into the vans and the vehicles roared off.

Alex gave the engine more speed to keep pace with the tail-lights ahead of them, as the other van turned a corner and kept going. The speeding machines passed a police car going in the other direction, but the cruiser made no effort to come about and follow them. "Get ready your weapons!" the driver called back over his shoulder.

The van ahead made a sudden left turn. Over the engine noises, came a crashing sound, then the grinding of the other van's gears as it lunged ahead. As the probing headlights swept about, Pedro gaped at a broken iron gate hanging askew, still swinging on a single dangling hinge in the fleeting beams. Farther ahead, up a palm-lined lane, the first van was stopping in front of an enormous yellow stucco house that was blazing in lights.

"'Marco's Hacienda'!" Alex shouted, slamming on the brakes. "Everyone out!"

The men ran up the 'terrazzo' steps to the glass front doors, lighted from the inside by a splendid crystal chandelier hanging in the foyer.

José Aldrada grabbed the door handle—it was locked.

"Break it!"

One of his men crashed the glass with his rifle butt, sending shards flying, then reached inside for the lock-lever. In a moment, all the men were running past the door's jagged remains.

Just as they came into the main hall, a grinning man, dressed in black, came out of a side room. The door clicked shut behind him. When the fellow saw the onrushing intruders, he gave a shout and started to turn about. Before the gang member could take more than a single step, an Aldrada man leaped forward and smashed his rifle stock against his head. The man dropped, sprawling, onto the marble floor and was still.

There came a scream—a female scream—from behind the door.

Tatiana! Pedro was sure of it, probably being—

He left the thought unfinished as with a shout, he lunged his shoulder against the door, breaking it; bounding over and through the collapsing frame into a bedroom suite.

From the side, a shape came at him. He turned about to confront a dark-haired man in a silky black outfit, his fists doubled with brass knuckles. Lunging at him, with both hands, Pedro jammed the rifle stock into his throat as hard as he could. There came a cracking sound, and the man went limp onto the floor.

Another scream burst through a nearby open door. Pedro dashed toward the sound into a very large, palatial bedroom. His eyes went wide—on an outsized four-poster canopy bed Tatiana was on her back, gasping, crying, pushing her arms at an older man who was on top of her, trying to press her down.

"Help me!"

The young man dodged past the surprised fellow's upraised arms and swung the AK-74's gun-stock squarely against his head, propelling him off the mattress onto the opposite floor. The enraged Russian tore around the foot of the big bed, aimed his automatic rifle at the stunned would-be-rapist and pulled the trigger. To the earsplitting crashes of the Kalashnikov, the man's head exploded in a froth of red and gray that splattered onto the walls; across the floor; under the bed. Screaming, the girl scooted back, pulling the sheet around herself.

Shouts and gunfire were breaking out in other parts of the house. Heavy pounding noises came from somewhere.

Pedro dropped the weapon and flung himself onto the mattress next to the terrified teenager.

"Oh, Pedro! Pedro!" She held him in a tight embrace, sobs wracking her tiny body. With a start, he realized that beneath the sheet she was unclothed. Pedro snugged the satin sheet around the shaking señorita and caressed her face. "Are you all right?"

Tatiana nodded, gasping, her tears cascading onto his shoulder.

"Did they—?"

He felt her shake her head.

"I am sorry . . . I should never have left you back there."

"There were many of them. They would have killed you."

He held her in the wrap while she cried some more.

Tatiana wiped her eyes with the sheet. "They were—tearing everything off me . . . I was so humiliated." The girl gave a shudder and cast about the room, blinking. "Where are my clothes?"

Pedro looked around. "I do not see them, anywhere."

He glanced through the open door; on the floor in the other room was the still form of the man with the brass knuckles.

"I promise no one will ever again hurt you." He wiped Tatiana's tears and on impulse gave her a kiss on her forehead. "We are getting out of here."

Pedro tenderly lifted the girl into his arms, thinking how lightweight she was. He stepped with her past the horrid bodies of the dead men, across the splintered door and out into the main atrium.

Just then, José Aldrada and his men hustled down a staircase to the big open space at the front part of the house; thin curls of smoke lifted from the muzzles of their rifles. A quick look at the tear-streaked, sheet-wrapped girl in Pedro's arms told the man something had happened. *"Did they—?"*

Pedro shook his head. "They were about to, but I killed them just before they—"

The Mexican's face erupted into an expression of rage. He looked around with a scowl of disdain at the magnificent foyer, resplendent in its expensive period furniture and artwork. The leader spat on the polished marble floor.

"Marco's blood money paid for all this! He and his henchmen upstairs are now all dead!" He motioned his AK-74 toward the crashed-in front door. "Let us go, *'pronto'*—"

Out front, Aldrada turned about and glared at the hulking stucco mansion, still lighted from end-to-end on all its three floors. He gestured to the other armed men standing with him.

"Burn it!"

The man's *compadres* gaped at him.

"I said, 'Burn it!' Burn it to the ground! Burn that bastard and his gang to hell!"

* * *

" . . . and the firemen, who arrived too late to save the huge mansion, said the fire had started in an upstairs bedroom, probably by a cigarette in bed, and had consumed the place rapidly."

"Guido Lopez" flipped the morning newpaper page and read on aloud to the others. "Police sources say the death of Hector Marco at his well-known 'Marco's Hacienda' will bring about many changes in northern Mexico, mostly to the benefit of 'José Aldrada'. Aldrada, who was reportedly out of town, was not available for comment."

Guido looked up at Alex, who was sitting across the kitchen table from him.." *'Out of town'?* Are they serious?"

Alex took a swallow of his breakfast 'Tequila' and gave a snort. "The newspaper wants to stay on Aldrada's good side. He is busy at work, right now, in his own office." He bit off a gigantic mouthful of his *'burrito'* and gave an ironic, chewing grin. "I am sure Marco's men are 'disappearing', today, as they say. The undertakers will be busy! All the people—the police . . . the 'dealers . . . the politicians—will now turn to José."

He took another gulp of his drink and went on. "Señor Aldrada is *'Primo Importante'* in these parts, now. It is good for us to have him on our side."

"The Organization can now help him very much."

"Ah, yes. And our Pedro's little girlfriend—what is her name?"

"Tatiana—"

". . . Tatiana. She was the cause of Aldrada's good fortune to take over Nuevo Laredo. She will now have much better life."

"Pedro told me Aldrada is arranging for her father to go to 'States for treatments of his sickness."

She was brave one, was she not?"

"Aye, sí . . . and pretty señorita, too."

"By the way, where *is* Pedro?"

"He is with her, today. He will become important, too, you will see."

Alex nodded at the newspaper picture of the flaming "Marco's Hacienda". "It does not say so in the paper, but all the bodies were burned up—everyone knows they were in there."

Guido shook his head. "And to think, I went to the movies and missed all the excitement!"

"Not to worry—you will have plenty to do. Aldrada wants us to help him clear out all the remaining Marco men, starting today." The expatriate Russian smirked. "He likes our style."

* * *

Headquarters, The "Bureau"; Federal Office Building, Washington, D.C.:

". . . *power structure has suddenly switched to a one 'José Aldrada', who had previously held second-place in the long-running gang wars along the Texas-Mexico border in and around Nuevo Laredo.*"

Watering read the morning Situation Report with fascinated interest—this was an unexpected new development. The Marco régime had run things on the border for a generation; Hector Marco, although still a relatively young man, had amassed great power and wealth controlling the immigration rackets along with the flow of drugs and clandestine weapons the "Bureau" knew were coming across the border. Now, this "Aldrada" individual looked to be taking-over it all.

The Agent re-read aloud to himself some parts of the report. "From what we already know, the power-grab by Aldrada has been a particularly violent one; even more vicious than usual for border wars, with some aspects not seen before."

Something clicked in his mind. *"Violent power-grab"*, did it say, *"with some vicious aspects not seen before?"* Watering sat back in his leather executive chair, his hands behind his head, thinking. Could the Russians he had believed were headed to

Mexico—*possibly Spetsnaz-related*, he had since learned—now be there and involved with this new gang lord, "Aldrada"?

* * *

Office of the 'Chief'; at the Same Time:

" . . . and you say this new man—?

" . . . 'Aldrada'—'José Aldrada'—a Mexican man."

Retchko read down the printed-out message from the Organization's contact man in Nuevo Laredo who was going by the name of "Alex Salinas".

"He says this 'Aldrada' is purging his enemies and is ready to do business with us."

"But how did our fellows get involved with them soon?" The small man leaned back in his big chair, tapped his fingertips together; amazement etched on his face. "They just got there!"

The general told him about how Blagron, now known as "Pedro", had right-off become involved with a local girl; about the abduction and the fiery shootout at the mansion; how the powerful man was impressed with the paramilitary tactics of the former "Spetsnaz" men who were now clearing out his opponents in a thorough manner. "I believe those three can become very useful to the Organization . . . we can market their paramilitary skills to train others—for a good fee, of course."

"What else are the Mexicans into?"

"Alex says they do drug smuggling . . . *'Coyote'* activities— a 'Coyote', by the way, is someone who smuggles illegals across the Rio Grande` into America—for a big price." The Chief's eyebrows went up; Retchko went on. "There will be many ways to profit with these people—drugs, in particular."

" Are not our people going to Colombia to meet with the *'Drug Lords'*?"

"The man and woman, Landay and Montoya, are leaving tomorrow on the cargo flight to Havana. They will go on to Cali." Retchko flipped through some pages of Alex's missive from Nuevo Laredo. "Alex says he and two of the new Russians will also be going to Colombia."

"Were there not *three* 'new Russians'?"

"The one with the girlfriend will stay behind and help this guy 'Aldrada' get organized." The general gave a smirk. "It seems our fellow 'Pedro' has already impressed the Mexicans very much."

The chief scanned down his own notes. "How about the guys from Chechnya? Are they still going to New York?"

"Ah, yes. Three of them came in yesterday from Teheran. They are explosives experts. They will go on our airplane to Havana, then to Mexico and cross into America at Nuevo Laredo and go to Newark—near New York City—to work there with Ezego and the others."

"How are the new identities working out?"

"The 'Chechens will use the false Mexican identifications they now have. It is 'Agent U'—the 'Tora Bora' man's—idea. And it is terrific." The bald Ukrainian grinned. "If it works, he says many of his agents can cross the southern U.S. border disguised as Mexicans. And since the Americans cannot tell the difference between Middle-Easterners and Mexicans, they will never catch on, he says." Retchko squinted. "It will also work with the Canadian border."

"How will they do the fake identifications?"

"We expect the printing plant in Nuevo Laredo to become very busy before long, running-off false United States *'Work Permits'* and picture identifications and other authentic-looking materials . . . aged-looking birth certificates . . . so-called 'baptisimal certificates'—whatever they are—for people who want to cross the border." The pale, hairless man gave a lopsided grin. "Alex says the documents are absolutely perfect—the American immigration authorities have not been able to spot them." Retchko paused for special effect. "And the identity cards are almost pure profit. They can do hundreds in a day and generate tremendous income for the Organization."

The Chief tapped his fingertips. "Most extraordinary." For the first time, Retchko detected a touch of a British mannerism in the man's voice.

The bald man ran through his reminder-notes. "Ezego says they will start making a bomb as soon as the materials arrive."

"You mean the ammonium-nitrate fertilizer and the diesel fuel?"

"Everything will have to be bought on the open market without attracting attention. Not only that, but the ingredients must be mixed carefully—it will be highly explosive. *The Chechens, who are working with Ezego and the others up there, have great knowledge of those and other kinds of explosives.*"

"The target is still the 'World Trade Center'?"

Retchko nodded. "They plan to blow-up the buildings next January or February."

* * *

Tanuta Refinery; at the Same Time:

"I don't believe it's really 'you'!"

Lisa Anaya gaped wide-eyed at Larry Landay and Marisol Montoya as the two dropped into dining-room seats across from her. Larry's blond hair, now shiny black, matched his new mustache; Marisol's hair had become blonde. "You said you'd color your hair . . . but I never thought—"

Marisol looked embarrassed. Other diners were looking around at them. "Retchko said to do it."

"Why?"

Larry patted his new locks, as if making sure the coloring was dry. "He said the disguises would keep the police from noticing us."

"I almost didn't notice you, myself!" A pause, then Lisa gave off a sigh that the American thought might be of disappointment or resignation. "You will fly to Lagos, first?"

The American pulled out a paper from his pocket and glanced at his watch. "In about two hours, the itinerary says." He read down the printout. "Our company plane will take us to Lagos, then we catch the 'Seven-Forty-Seven'—our old 'flying friend'." He glanced at Marisol, who reddened a little. "We will fly all night to Havana . . . then by airline to Caracas." He turned over the page and went on, "Then we take a hop to Cali—in

Colombia. That's where we have our next assignment. Then, it's on to Medellin to start a new life."

Marisol looked across the table at Frank and Lisa. "I must tell you something." She leaned forward. "While Retchko was on his latest trip, *I disabled the microphones in this room and we can speak freely.*"

Just then, Frank Ogawan took a seat, giving a start at Larry's and Marisol's new looks. "They are leaving, today," Lisa told him," in a couple of hours."

The dark fellow's eyes went wide. "So you are really getting out of here!" he breathed.

The cream-colored young woman cast around, to see that one in the room was overhearing them. "I wish we could be going with you."

Marisol tried a hopeful grin. "After the meetings in Cali, I hope we never again hear from Retchko." She looked at the little bandage on her wrist where the chip was implanted. "But he will always know where we are, I am afraid." She shrugged. "At least, we are getting out of here, and—oh, yes—we will be getting new names."

The earnest young Frank Ogawan leaned forward. "This is not a good place . . ." His voice was hardly above a whisper. "It never was."

Lisa spoke in a low, dusky voice. "I started getting suspicious when my sister's husband disappeared." A perplexed look came over her face. "And I don't think Betty was ever much concerned about him—I can't understand that." She set down her fork. "I believe Retchko was behind Lester's vanishing, *and perhaps Betty was, too*, because, now, she seems to spend a lot of time with him." The girl shrugged. "She's in Lagos at the company apartment, next to Busa's, where the general is staying." Lisa shook her head. "I'm sure they are together, right now."

"Speaking of Busa," Frank put in, "he is taking-over the refinery. And he is all over the place! You see him everywhere in his big outfits. He spent this morning in my office asking questions—irritating questions—along with that little old fellow,

'Mickey', who follows him around." Frank shot a glance at Lisa. "Mister Nkrume was never like that."

Lisa spoke up. "The new Russian guy . . . what's his name— 'Yegor Boronov'—now has the electronic section pretty well under his control, it looks to me."

Larry frowned. "But he stays to himself, a lot . . . like he has secret things he doesn't want us to see or know about."

"He knows all about the chip implants."

Larry shrugged. "He told me one time he had worked with a setup like it in Russia."

Marisol spoke in a low voice. "Then it all adds up! I am sure this refinery is part of an operation that is doing things—strange things . . . *bad things*—all over the world!"

An uncomfortable look came over Lisa's Anaya's face.

Frank Ogawan looked serious. "Go on."

The Latina drummed her fingertips on the table. "Think about it: Larry and I came to Nigeria on a big airplane loaded with Russian automatic rifles and the American antennas and the electronics . . . and you sent the implant chips to 'who-knows-where?' . . . then this Russian hombre shows up and seems to know all about everything . . . the satellite dishes send and receive signals to places we do not even know where they are! And now, Larry is wanted all over the world by the authorities—"

She stopped at Lisa's look of dismay.

Larry spoke up in a hurry. "It was not *your* fault! You just placed the order to me on Retchko's instructions. He has used all of us for his own evil deeds."

Lisa dabbed at her eyes with a napkin. "I feel bad that I put together the system to take oil from the other refinery . . . at the time, I didn't know that much about it."

Frank put his hand on hers; the young African fellow looked relieved to know the truth. "It now seems as if Busa and the 'Chief'' I keep hearing about—but I do not know who he is— kept from us what they were doing. Then General Retchko came along and had you do the satellites and the chips and the other things, and—even though we did not realize it at the time—we were all involved . . . it was like we have been little pawns on his big chessboard!"

Frank stopped; Lisa's blinking eyes were brimming. He handed her another napkin. "I believe there is a lot more going on here than what we know about . . . things connected to that 'Organization', as you put it, and to Boronov—and to Retchko."

". . . and to the airport at Lagos." Marisol remembered the blood-spattered floor and the room where big men had attacked her before that Army man had pulled them off. She thought for a moment. "I believe that security man at the airport—what was his name?"

"'Ajiboy'—"

". . . Ajiboy. Somehow, he seemed honest." Marisol told them about the assault and how distressed the Army officer had been, afterward. "It is almost like he does not want to go along with some of the stuff Retchko makes him do."

Lisa gave a shudder. "I believe Retchko is an evil man. I want to stay away from him."

Frank looked around; none of the other diners seemed to be paying attention to them. He leaned forward and spoke in a hoarse whisper. "I wish Lisa and I could get out of here, too."

Lisa rummaged in her handbag and came up with a card. "This is my brother's telephone number in London."

Larry pocketed the card.

Lisa looked at both Larry and Marisol. "Call him, if you ever need to get in touch with us . . . maybe we all can get together again, someday . . . somewhere . . . somehow—"

Lisa Anaya pushed back her chair, put her hands to her face and stepped in a hurry past the other tables and out of the room.

* * *

Nuevo Laredo; Later the Same Day:

José Aldrada took four glass tumblers from the office cabinet and turned to the three expatriate Russians. "'Tequila' all right for you?"

"Of course." Alex glanced at "Gaido Lopez" and "Andres Martinez", who were nodding.

"I rather think you like this Mexican brew!" The portly man poured a round and handed out the glasses, then eased himself

393

into an overstuffed leather recliner chair. "It grows on you, pretty fast!" He downed a swallow and leaned back. "A lot better than that damn 'Vodka' you Russians drink, I will tell you. Tried it once. Tastes like hair tonic, to me." He rubbed a free hand through his greasy, graying black hair.

Andres spoke up. "So you now control the border."

"You should have seen the parade of people coming to me, today!" The powerful man gazed around his rustic room, with its stuffed heads of big game on the wall and clutters of Mexican-styled decorations; reveling in his new status. "*Si, Señores!* It is all in our hands, now . . . 'mi compadres' and me!" Aldrada surveyed his three guests and waved the glass back and forth. His face was becoming tinged from the libation. "The other hombre, Pedro—where is he, now?"

"Guido" gestured with his own glass. "He is across the border with the girl and her family—at the hospital in Laredo. They used the new false identifications to get across to Texas for treatments of her father's lung sickness." He looked thoughtful for a moment. "It was the first time we had used the new printed papers and identifications—they worked perfectly, they said—the Americans passed them right through. Now the man will get his medical treatments. The girl and her people are *'muchas gracias'* to you."

"Like I told Pedro that time, 'this is where you save the señorita!'—remember?" The man leaned back and gave a loud guffaw, nearly spilling his drink. "Who would ever thought it would be like this!"

He stood up unsteadily and splashed some more tequila in the direction of his glass. "She brought the whole border right to me!"

The man upended his glass; some liquid dribbled down his chin. "I reward her some more. When they get back in some days, I have moved them to *'hacienda gigante'*, with maids, even. 'Old José', he remember what señorita did for him!" The man took another swallow. "Their new 'casa' was before belong to a 'Marco man'—now fellow no longer need it, because he is on 'permanent vacation'!"

The Mexican wobbled to the pantry, found another tequila bottle and pried it open. He poured another round and settled back down.

"Like I said, señors, they were in here all day long kissing my ring." The powerfully-built middle-aged man gave a smirk. "It is amazing what a burned-down house can do for you—if the house is your enemy's—with him inside it!"

Alex was curious. "You said important people came to see you, today—"

". . . the police chiefs . . . the mayors of towns . . . some high government officials from Mexico City, even. You would not believe how they were swearing allegiance to me!"

Alex glanced at the others, then looked at Aldrada. "What makes the most money for you?"

"Ah, besides drugs—smuggling people across the border is the biggest."

"That much in people-moving? From what I heard, they just swim across the river."

Aldrada gave a big laugh, then chased his mirth with another big swallow of drink. "Señor, it is *mucho* complicated!" The mighty Mexican pulled up a pad and started drawing. "Here is the way it works: Some people who already know a *'Coyote'—he or she . . .* it might be a girl—who pays us 'protection' to operate in our territory . . . they will bribe an American border guard."

"Bribe an American guard?"

"Sí, señor! Say that the 'Coyote' has coffee with an American guard he knows in the early morning. He will mention—casually, of course—that he has a van-load of people coming across at noon."

The Mexican drew something on the pad.

"Now, the American border guards usually work in 'two's'. Maybe one is not so honest—almost all are, by the way; we have to be careful who we approach—so the 'Coyote' slips the 'cooperating' American guard some money, called, *'mordida'*— or a 'bite', as Mexicans say—the Americans call it a 'bribe'. It is all arranged, señor, that during the shift, at noon, 'our' guard will send his 'compadre' to get coffee, or pizza, or run an errand. While the other guard is gone, the van drives through the border crossing without stopping, since the first guard recognizes the 'Coyote', who is driving the van. In a few hours, the van is in San

Antonio, or Houston, or Dallas, and they are off to meet their friends or relatives and go on with their lives in America!"

Aldrada tapped the diagram with a big grin. "It is all simple and easy and everyone makes *'mucho dinero'*, as they say. It happens all the time."

Alex spoke up. "We want to make it even more profitable for us—for you . . ." He pulled a page off the pad and took Aldrada's pen. "Here is what we can do: first of all, we must make it look to the illegals like it is now much harder to get into America."

"Que?" Aldrada was frowning.

"We will tell the 'Coyotes' that the illegals must now have 'certain documents' to go across." He scratched something on the pad. "They will say that the people must have 'identification'. Of course, none of them will have any such thing, so we will, for a fee, provide such 'documents."

Aldrada looked perplexed. "Who will do those things?"

Alex drew some more on the paper. "The 'Organization' has a printing plant, here. Our people can print up very good-looking papers and documents in one day, and charge a high sum for them. These people are desperate enough—they will pay the price."

The Russian connected some boxes on the diagram. "You provide the 'Coyotes' . . . we provide the fake papers and split the profits."

"Ah, Señor Alex! I see what I like! There are many people . . . many 'Coyotes' . . . many 'identificaciós' . . . 'mucho dinero' for us!"

Alex raised a single eyebrow, as if he knew a secret. "There is more we can do for you!" He flipped the page and started another diagram. "Now, in order for you to hold on to your power, you need trained, reliable troops. Not just some armed men—*Army-like soldiers!*"

He glanced at the two other Russians, who knew what he was about to say.

"We are experts in paramilitary training."

The burly Mexican stared transfixed at the page.

"Your rival, *Señor Marco*, never had a real trained force! If he had, we would not be talking together, right now." Another pause, then, "We will provide training . . . armaments—the very best former 'Soviet' bloc anti-personnel weapons. When we complete the job, you will have one of the best-trained paramilitary forces in the world, Señor Aldrada . . . no one will dare go against you, *including the Mexican Army!*"

"Not even the 'Americanos''?"

"The Americans have no stomach for fighting when it gets tough for them. Look what happened to them in Vietnam. When it got too much for them, they cut and ran. In the so-called 'Gulf War', it was over very fast; few killed. With many American casualties, the people would never have let their Army keep going. The Americans are not tough, like other peoples—they will never bother you."

Aldrada looked up. "Our people work hard in America for little wages. Good for America. The poor *'Mexicanos'* send money back to Mexico. Good for Mexico."

"Then the Mexicans will keep going to America and we will all make a big profit!"

The Russian hesitated while the tantalyzing words took hold over the Mexican. Aldrada's eyes, red as they were, narrowed in thought. The tequila, far from dulling his senses, seemed to have sharpened the man's mind to the possibilities Alex had just laid out for him.

"Ah, but there is more!" Alex drew the outline of a bomb on the paper. "Some of our other, ah, *'clients'* seek to infiltrate arms and powerful weapons—*the most powerful even*—into America for future use in urban warfare. *We can work together on this.*"

"Bueno! Bueno! " Aldrada was in no mood for hesitation. "And the drugs—they are a constant money source. How can your, ah, 'people' help us on this? For our mutual profits, of course."

Alex glanced at Andres and Guido, then back at the older man. "We are leaving tomorrow to Cali, Colombia, for the meetings . . . I am sure we will have good information to bring back to you."

"What about Pedro? I want him to stay here. I need him to help me."

The Russian caught the eyes of the other two with him. "Of course."

397

"We now celebrate, señors!" The Mexican reached for the tequila bottle.

* * *

Tanuta Refinery; the Next Day:

"You say you still have connections back in Russia at the 'Academician Center' that is working on the 'invisible technology?'" Retchko leaned forward on his desk at the man across from him, his hands clasped.

Yegor Boronov nodded. "My friends back there send greetings to me through their satellite system to ours here at the refinery. In secure digital code, of course."

"Interesting. You could get blueprints of the devices? The 'invisible' machines? Could you build them, here?"

"I am sure it could be arranged. The academicians there have no loyalty to the new political régime, and our facilities here are adequate to construct the models." The pale, round-faced man pushed a lock of brown hair out of his face. "They may not like the new Russian politics, but they are ready to take advantage of the *'New Capitalism'*, there." A grin crossed the man's face. "They *do* see the advantages of 'money'!"

"We can arrange to pay them well through the Cayman accounts."

"Then I am sure they will work with us."

"How soon can we get the prints?"

"I will message them right away."

* * *

"The Academy", Moscow; Morning, the Next Day:

"Major Suslov, I wish you the best in your new post . . . I am sure you will perform your duties as would benefit the 'Motherland'." Colonel General Antonin Krolov, speaking in the formal Russian style used for occasions of importance, nodded at

Terenty across his massive desk at the Academy. "Send my best wishes to your beautiful wife and daughter, as well."

"Thank you, Comrade General; you have been very fair and supportive to me." Terenty followed the senior officer's speaking style that reflected his deep respect toward the man he had come to know during the intense events of the past year. "I am looking forward to returning to Madrid. I am sure Tamara and Larisa will enjoy the posting."

There came a pause; an unresolved matter was on both mens' minds.

The general shook his head. "Nothing on the three missing soldiers! Not even any returns from their chip implants! Most extraordinary—nothing like this before has ever happened." The man spread his big hands. "Stay aware of things in Madrid, Suslov . . . you might happen onto something."

"I will, Comrade General." Terenty stood to attention and saluted.

Colonel General Krolov returned the salute and extended his hand to the younger officer.

Terenty executed a formal "about-face" and stepped with measured tread across the high gilded room's carpeted floor. The general's adjutant opened the door for him to the anteroom.

A few minutes later, as Terenty made his way across the Academy's, cool, autumn-like grounds, through little drifts of fallen leaves rustling on the sidewalk in a slight breeze, a familiar uniformed figure with a briefcase strode briskly around a building up ahead and came in his direction.

"Ah, Major Suslov!" Colonel Golubko stopped, returning Terenty's salute. "I hear you are leaving, tomorrow."

"Yes, colonel, we catch the early 'Aeroflot' flight to Paris, then on to Madrid."

"Well, major, it has been rewarding working with you . . . even though there have been things that . . ." The officer looked uncomfortable. ". . . many events . . . and . . . our people—"

"Yes, sir, there have been."

"You spoke to the general?"

Terenty nodded. "Yes, sir, I did." It was about what they were both thinking. "He says there is no new information about

Lychin or Blagron or Malinovsky." The younger man shrugged. "It is like they all disappeared from the earth."

Rodion Golubko looked grim. "Well, stay in touch through the regular channels. If you should learn something, let me know. I will do the same for you."

There was a slight pause. "Ah, colonel, sir, I just want to tell you how much it has meant to all of us to have you as our commanding officer these months." He managed a tight smile. "We were more than a little nervous, at first."

"Suslov, those first times you and your friend, Lychin, screwed-up, I wondered if the powers above me had screwed-up, too!"

Colonel Golubko looked away, then back at Terenty. It was plain to the younger officer that the normally-impassive man was wrestling with some personal thoughts. "You and your friend became fine officers for Russia. I am sorry Major Lychin is not now with us."

"I trust he will someday return."

The colonel seemed to brighten a little. "We start a new class next week. Upon my recommendation, the men from the squad—those left—will be working as instructors with me. Based on our experiences, they will have much to teach the new recruits."

"It was an extraordinary year."

The two men looked at each other for a long moment. "Well, Suslov, tell the wife and child 'greetings' from me, and I trust we will see each other again, sometime."

Terenty saluted the colonel, who returned his own salute in a formal manner. As the two stepped away in opposite directions, to the younger man, the older officer's fading footfalls on the leaf-blown sidewalk had an unexpected melancholy sound.

* * *

Signal Intelligence Office, National Security Agency, Washington, D.C.:

"Strong unknown signals processing through MAGNUM!" The assistant at the intercept station called to the other technician. He turned back to the monitor screen and clicked his computer mouse.

400

"Contact 'Menwith Hill'!"

The first man was on the secure circuit to their British counterpart. "Menwith Hill is tri-angulating a transmitting source in southern Russia."

"*Southern Russia? Our* Intelligence satellite is handling a *Russian* signal?"

"Call the Chief Engineer, quick!"

The printer was again.buzzing, The operator pulled off the paper. "'Menwith' is now getting what looks like a return signal from southeastern Nigeria."

"Same setup as before!"

"Some sort of burst-signal, Menwith says . . . not enough time to get a fix on it."

The Chief Engineer stepped into the room and watched the replay of the intercepts on the monitor, frowning. "A 'burst signal', all right—in a digital code just like the Russians use." The man was shaking his head. "If it is, then Russian Military Intelligence has broken into the Pentagon's most secure field-control system." He let out a deep breath. "If the Russians have penetrated MAGNUM, we have a serious security breach of the first order. Get on the line to the Director . . . he will notify the *'National Security Advisor'*.

* * *

Tanuta Refinery, at that Moment:

"You can construct the 'invisible' devices with these prints?" Leonid Efimovich Retchko ran his fingers over the just-arrived blueprints and schematics that were spread out on his desk.

Yegor Boronov nodded. "We can have a working model inside of a week." He tapped one of the papers. "All we need are the parts. What components we do not have here in our workshop, we can get in Lagos."

"Make a list and we will have our people up there get them for us and send them down here on the regular flight." The bald man squinted at the round-faced Russan. "Do not let the girl, Lisa

401

Anaya, know what the devices are, or for what they will be used."

"How *will* you use them?"

Retchko looked-over the drawings that were in Russian, with a cynical, off-center grin. "Comrade Yegor, with these, our enemies will be helpless."

* * *

Private Chamber of Judge Norris Greeley, United States District Court, Washington, D.C.:

The middle-aged man in the judicial robe turned another page of the file documents, his eyes darting back and forth. He lifted a second folder, read some notes clipped to the cover, and opened it. For some moments he scanned the top page, nodding from time-to-time.

He looked up at two youths and a serious-looking individual in a three-piece suit sitting across the desk from him. In the back of the room, the parents of the two boys sat on leather sofas, looking. anxious.

"Well, counselor, these 'letter of commendation' from the Director of the 'National Security Agency', and other important people are very impressive—I happen to know some of these people, and they do not give out such glowing words about just anyone."

The boys glanced at each other, and at the lawyer, who spoke. "Thank you, Your Honor. These boys have been diligent in carrying out your instructions for their suspended sentences."

The judge gave a slight, quick grin, considered by many to be the upper-limit of emotion the usually-dour jurist allowed himself. "I should say they have . . . many people, including the Vice President, himself, have written something positive to me about them."

The robed jurist's eyes darted from one young man to the other. He seemed to be thinking. "Very well, counselor, I will grant your motion to dismiss all charges against these defendants—'George Thomas Habbler', also known as 'Buzzy'

402

Habbler' . . . and 'James William Suggs', also known as 'Jamey' Suggs." The judge looked at certain pages. "Both of you are minors, I see."

The robed man stamped some papers, set aside the files, and pulled up other papers that he looked over, nodding. "Based on these recommendations, the 'Security Agency' is prepared to offer you two young men full scholarships to an engineering school of your choice and full consideration for jobs after graduation."

Buzzy's and Jamey's eyes went wide; gasps came from the sofat the rear of the room; one of the mothers started crying.

The lawyer spoke up in a hurry. "My clients will be happy to accept these offers, Your Honor."

Judge Greeley looked at the two boys. "I trust you will use this opportunity to its best advantage." He paused, then went on, "Is there anything you would like to say?"

Jamey glanced at his lawyer, who was nodding. "Thank you very much sir—Your Honor."

The jurist fingered the files, then leaned back. "Well, boys, based on these reports of your service to the country so far, I— and the American people—should be thanking *you*."

* * *

Alfonso Bonilla Aragón International Airport, Cali, Colombia; Late Afternoon, that Day:

"'Luis Landa'? 'Monica Montero'?" The uniformed man fingered the Colombian passports and glanced up at the man and woman standing at the head of the Customs line. He looked over the most recent visas stamped in the backs of the little books. "You two enjoyed your trip to France?"

"Ah, si . . ." The dark-haired American now known as "Luis Landa" spoke, with a quick look at the trim blonde woman whose eyes darted from him to the uniformed officer. He hoped his Spanish sounded authentic enough. "Paris is pleasant this time of the year."

403

With motions of automatic haste, the man stamped the passports and handed them back over the counter."Welcome back to Cali," he said in his perfect Castillian Spanish.

The two picked up their luggage bags and lugged them toward a nearby waiting area. "Luis" motioned toward an isolated space where there were no other passengers. They made their way over to some seats and sat down.

"They said to wait here with the identification," he said, pulling the serrated-edged card from his pocket with a look-around at the travelers scurrying back and forth on the concourse. A mother stopped in front of the two to attend a complaining child while the husband seemed to be looking them over. "Luis" wondered if it was a setup, like he had heard was common in Colombia. At length, they moved on. But no one else seemed to be taking any particular interest in them. Every few seconds, a nearby loudspeaker said something in the purring Colombian brogue he had come to recognize ever since they had landed a short while ago.

"I hope they hurry!" Monica propped her feet onto her travel bag. "I have heard a lot about Colombia. They say it is a tough place, if you do not know your way around—Cali, in particular."

"It's the reputation." Both knew his comment was an oblique reference to the powerful drug Cartel that was based in Cali.

The blonde young woman pulled out her passport from her purse and looked at it. "I am still having a hard time calling myself 'Monica Montero'."

"And I'm trying to get used to 'Luis Landa'." He looked around to make sure no one was overhearing them.

"But it *is* clever." The new "Monica Montero" glanced at the re-named "Luis Landa" next to her. "It is an old trick, as you say. We used it in Cuba when they wanted to insert an agent or have someone go underground. They would have a new name enough like the old one, so it would be easy to remember, but would still be different enough to get by. And if we said our old name by mistake, people did not notice."

Luis was looking over his new Colombian passport. "Can you *believe* this?" The American leafed through the little book some more. "Whoever printed this passport in Lagos did a great job. It says I was born in Bogotá—" He flipped to the back pages. "... and I just took a trip from Paris, France, to Caracas ... then here to Cali." Luis gave a little smirk. "Well, they got the 'Caracas' and the 'Cali' parts right!"

"You were pretty quick to speak about Paris as if we had really been there." The Cubana stretched out a little and leaned her head onto Luis's shoulder.

He reached for her hand. "Too bad we didn't have a chance to see Havana together on this visit."

She glanced at him. "I had to be careful ... I had 'escaped' from Cuba, remember—'Papá Fidel' does not like people who do that—but at least I got to see my *'Tio Trini'* for a little while."

"I had forgotten Trini was your uncle. It was good he came while we were there."

He remembered *you* after you told him who you were! The disguise fooled even him."

"He seemed to like your blonde hair."

"Did I ever tell you about my cousin, the Miami television star?"

Luis shook his head.

"Her name was 'Sabina'—'Sabina Torres'. Her father was the brother of my Uncle Trini Torres. She was born in Miami, so I never met her, but Uncle Trini and some other relatives and I used to watch her on Miami television with this crazy aerial he had inside the roof of his house ... she did the news. I thought she was very beautiful, with her long, dark hair."

"Now I remember! Trini showed me a picture of her when I went there the first time—after the 'Seven-Forty-Seven' was shot up at Mexico City—when we met. She was your *cousin?*"

A faraway look came onto Monica's face. "Uncle Trini told me that he had learned she was killed in a car wreck, somewhere in the 'States. She had a husband—a detective, or something like that—and a little boy. The boy was killed, too."

"He didn't say anything to me about her being killed."

"I think he found out about it only recently—after we went to Nigeria. Sometimes news takes a long time to get back to Cuba."

Just then, a foursome of bearded men in robes and turbans strode along in front of where they were sitting. Luis squinted at them as they walked past. "How about those three guys on the flight from Lagos who stayed in the back of the cabin and brought their own food?"

Monica was also watching the foreigners go by. "I talked with one of them—he spoke English . . . he said they were from Chechnya—"

"Chechnya? What were they doing on our airplane?"

"He said they were going to New York. But first, they would go to Mexico."

Monica looked around; no one was paying them any attention. She leaned over and spoke into his ear. "He said they are working for the Organization!"

"What! Then the—"

His sentence went unfinished, for a stocky, brown-skinned man in a white shirt and khaki pants had detatched himself from the humanity on the Cali concourse and was standing in front of them. In his hand was a small card. With a start, Luis saw it had a serrated edge, like the one he was holding.

"Identificación?"

Recovering from his momentary surprise, the American traveling *incognito* lifted up his ticket-sized cardboard piece to the other man's. The jagged edges of both were a perfect match. Monica and the Colombian repeated the motions.

The fellow gestured. "Come with me!"

Luis and Monica picked up their luggage and followed the fellow out to a vehicle loading area. At an unmarked van parked alongside the curb, the Colombian stepped around and said something in rapid Spanish to the older driver.

The fellow hopped out at once and snatched the bags from the newcomers, then stuffed their parcels into the rear of the vehicle in such haste he almost lost his balance. Luis noticed he had a black, very-thin mustache that looked almost as if it had been drawn on by a pencil, like several others he had already seen on some mens' faces inside the terminal. Luis decided it must be a fashionable facial feature for males in Cali.

The man loped around and opened a side door, nodding and motioning for them to get in.

The van pulled away from the curb into late-afternoon traffic, pungent with engine exhaust.

"*'Facundo'* is expecting you," the younger man said from his passenger front seat, looking straight ahead as the vehicle shot up a ramp onto a freeway.

Luis and Monica glanced at each other, frowning—no one had yet told them where they would be going or who they would be seeing. And who was "Facundo"?

* * *

Federal Court House, San Francisco, California, at the Same Time:

Michael B. Parsley, Esq. shuffled the papers of his brief on the defense table and stood up."Your Honor, my client, Joseph Anglin, respectfully requests to the court to continue his case for six months, with just and worthy cause."

The Federal Judge leafed through his copy of the document. "I have read your request, counselor, and I have some questions. You say you have recently made contact with a party who is material to this case, and that this party is some distance from this court—that is still correct?"

"Yes, Your Honor. We are gathering sworn statements, but it will take us time to do this, and may involve some travel."

The robed jurist turned to the Federal Attorney. "Do you have any objection to this request?"

"Your Honor, I would request the court to compel the defendant to prove at regular intervals that they are making proper use of the time to prepare their case."

Even before the judge could prompt him, Parsley spoke up. "We will do that, Your Honor, and I am confident we will be ready to go to trial in six months."

"Very well, if there are no further objections, I will continue the case until March first, nineteen-ninety-three."

The judge banged his gavel.

* * *

407

The van slowed, made a left turn to an iron gate and stopped. A youth in combat fatigues brandishing an automatic weapon put up his hand. The driver leaned out. "'Facundo' is expecting us."

Nodding, the guard turned about; a bandolier of bullets across his chest caught the setting sun as he motioned at a stonework gatehouse behind him. There was shadowy movement behind tinted glass; at once the bars began swinging inward. Just as the vehicle started to move again, Luis noticed a police car creeping past on the main road. It moved on.

After passing through the gate that was now closing, the van went up a long curving drive into the most elaborate-looking layout the expatriate American had ever seen, with many Colombian *'hectares'* of lush greenery and flowering tropical plants, some on white trellises, along what looked like manicured walking trails that led into palm arbors toward the outer fences; all interspersed by enormous splashing statuary fountains, their silver sprays glistening in the low light of oncoming dusk. The whole scene was made even more striking by the red sky of sunset layered over the place; already little gas lights perched atop scrolled, wrought-iron black poles were flickering inside their glass globes. Luis glanced at Monica; her eyes were wide at the splendor of the vast hilltop estate, obviously owned by someone of great wealth and power.

As they was taking in all this, at the top of a low rise, a rambling Mediterranean-style structure loomed-up. In a few moments, the van pulled up beneath a columned entrance portico that looked Moorish. An older man in a tuxedo stepped forward and pulled open the door with a white-gloved hand, nodding as the two guests alighted onto a crimson-colored, terrazzo-tiled circular drive. The two looked around at the single-story, yellow-stucco mansion with its orange-and-brown accents that overlaid the entire top of the mountain. As they stood there while other attendants retrieved their luggage, Luis and Monica got their first magnificent view of the city of Cali, Colombia, arrayed below; its myriad shimmering lights marching off into the fading sunset. The sea of white that seemed to go on to infinity reminded Luis of the times he had looked down on the Los Angeles Basin from the Palos Verdes Hills.

"Welcome to 'Facundo's'," the man said, in the well-modulated brogue Luis recognized again from the short time he had been in Colombia. The servant noticed the two gazing down at the sights. "Cali is the third-largest city in Colombia . . . two-million people live here."

"Your things will be in your room," the man went on, as the other servants stepped through the main entrance carrying their luggage bags down a hallway. He motioned his white-gloved hands toward a pair of mahogany doors flanked by classic-styled Spanish gas lamps on the walls; potted palms, along with hanging flowering plants and ferns were arranged all about.

In the entryway foyer, Luis and Monica followed the man into a large Spanish-styled living area, into a crowd of men of various ages standing around talking among themselves and to a number of very attractive young women. Monica's eyes went wide as she noticed what Luis, in furtive glances, had already observed: all the girls were dressed in extremely provocative outfits; a few appeared to be hardly clothed at all. All the men seemed to be attired in what Luis used to call in California, "casual-natty"; understated but very expensive upon closer inspection, with lots of jewelry and gold chain accessories. He was glad he and Monica had obtained good clothes before they had left Lagos, although their outfits were nothing like the norm in this room. In one corner an instrumental combo swished away at what Luis judged to be local Colombian music; the pungent aroma of marijuana smoke pervaded the place.

"Right this way, señor . . . señorita—" the man went on over the music, as they made their way across a tiled floor that continued the crimson terrazzo scheme from the outside. Looking around, Luis observed that the place was not only big, but that all the furnishings were of very high quality—his earlier opinion that whoever owned all this was extremely rich was being reinforced every passing moment. Monica glanced at him; the awed expression her face told him her impression of these palatial surroundings matched his.

The tuxedoed man read a card in his hand, then stepped up to a rather short, brown-skinned individual in a white Cuban-style 'guyabera', holding a drink in his hand, who was speaking to another guest. "*Señor Facundo . . .*"

The man turned about, his liquid brown eyes scanning the employee in the tuxedo, then the dark-haired fellow and the small woman with him. "Sí?'

"These are the people you were expecting . . . from Nigeria."

The tanned fellow dismissed the man to whom he had been talking and looked Luis and Monica up and down with an amused expression. *"'Nigeria'*, you say?" He gave them a self-confident grin, switching his drink from one hand to another "You do not *look* like any Nigerians I ever saw! *'Fernando Ordoñez',"* he went on, nodding, his hand out, the grin continuing across his face. "In Colombia, I am known as *'Facundo'.*" There was a short pause, as if for effect. *"Everyone in Colombia knows about Facundo!"*

"Nice to meet you . . . 'Facundo'—I am 'Luis Landa' and this is my . . . ah, 'associate'—'Monica Montero'." The young woman put out her hand. The Colombian shook it, looking her over in an obvious manner.

Facundo gestured at a nearby table. *"'Coke'?"*

With a start Luis recognized the little white lines and the paraphernalia associated with cocaine. The slender rolled cigarettes arrayed on the table for the guests were marijuana. Then he remembered that the people all around them were in the big-time drug trade. "No, *'gracias'*. We are more like into 'drinks'."

Facundo shrugged with aplomb. "Ah, of course!" He motioned at a bar at one end of the open space. "Let us go and get some refreshment." He downed the remaining liquid in his glass. "I could use some more, myself."

The three worked their way between the gathered guests, ordered their drinks then moved off to a space by a glass door. "Let us go outside," Facundo said, pulling open the sliding door. The three stepped out onto a balmy terrazzo patio with a panoramic view of the lighted city below. Some other people were already there, talking among themselves, some smoking what were obviously marijuana cigarettes, taking in the splendid sight. Before them, Cali arrayed itself against the night; from far below came the faint rush of vehicle noises. Overhead, countless points of stars dotted the clear black sky.

"I have the best view in Cali," the host said, smiling, gesturing at the scene set before them.

Luis and Monica gazed down at the city for long moments. "It is a great view, all right," Luis said, sipping his drink.

Just then, a man in a policeman's uniform sauntered by, holding a drink in one hand, a "joint" in the other. Luis and Monica stared at the figure, who drifted into some shadows. Facundo noticed his guests wide eyes and spoke up. "Ah, as you see, señor . . . señorita—I have my own police force! I pay them well to be on my side!" He motioned to a nearby hilltop ridge, then at the lighted city. "Out there, are *many* police . . . *many* chiefs . . . *many* politicians—all protecting 'Papá Facundo'!"

"Protecting you from *'whom'* ?"

The man narrowed his eyes. "*Every* hombre in Colombia has enemies, señor."

For a while they stood there in the warm breeze; Facundo admiring his private view of Cali; Luis mulling over the man's comment about enemies; Monica shaking her head to herself in awe of this man who seemed to own the whole city—if not the whole country.

The Colombian broke the reverie. "You are here with the arms dealers?"

Facundo's abrupt question caught the two by surprise. "You know of us?"

The host nodded his head at three light-haired men talking to a pair of girls visible through the glass doors. "Those men are from the 'Organization', as they call it. They said two more were coming . . . a man and a woman from Nigeria and since you are the only 'man and a woman' who are here from Nigeria, you must be them!" Facundo glanced over at the coterie of cocky-acting men and the leggy, adoring-looking young women engaged in animated conversation, then back at his guests, his eyes crinkled in amusement. "You do not know them?"

Luis spoke up in a hurry. "The 'Organization' is big, so I guess we have not yet met them."

The man smiled. "Well, Facundo will take care of that!"

He nodded for the two to follow him. The man pulled open the sliding door and the three stepped up to the group. Facundo motioned for the girls to leave. At once, the young females lowered their eyes, gripped their drinks with both hands and tripped away, their spike heels clicking on the tile floor under the sound of the swishy Latin music coming from the other end of the room.

"Ah, 'Organization's men' . . . you find our Colombian women—attractive, no?"

The Russians nodded. Luis tried to appear non-commital.

"At the end of the evening, select one of our beautiful señoritas for the night—that is why they are here—to take care of Facundo's esteemed guests!" The expansive Colombian spread his hands. "The whores are *'gratis'* to you, señores." He patted his pocket. "They are already paid for—enjoy!"

The man caught Monica's frown and changed the subject. "Señores, I present to you some of your 'compadres' of your 'Organization'."

Luis put out his hand to the nearest stranger. ". . . 'Luis Landa', from Tanuta City, Nigeria, and this is my . . . ah, 'associate', *'Señorita* Monica Montero`." Once again, Luis hoped his Spanish passed muster.

"Guido Lopez", "Alex Salinas" and "Andres Martinez" introduced themselves.

"Ah! I will now leave you to get acquainted!" Facundo gave the others a nodding grin, then turned away into the crowd, where he slapped the back of a startled guest into a conversation with him.

The man who had identified himself as "Alex Salinas" looked at Luis and Monica with what to the incognito American thought to be clinical interest, then spoke. "General Retchko messaged us you were coming."

At the mention of "General Retchko", Monica gave an involuntary shudder. The man's influence was everywhere, it seemed, even extending to these strangers with whom they were now talking in this lavish mountaintop estate far removed from Nigeria. Luis, glancing at the girl, himself felt a momentary chill of uncertainty.

412

Alex Salinas nodded toward the bar. "Let us refresh our drinks and get acquainted."

* * *

Leonid Efimovich Retchko looked over Yegor Boronov's shoulder at the monitor screen. On the display, the wavy shape of a mountain was outlined from above. The engineer zoomed the perspective down to where a structure was arrayed across the very top of the peak.

"There they are," the Russian electronics expert said, pointing.

On the screen were five blinking dots in a cluster.

"They are all there, now," the bald man said, nodding, "in Cali . . . at the meeting . . . they are now talking,"

The two men watched as the dots moved about from place-to-place.

The bald man nodded; a look of satisfaction hung on his puffy, middle-aged face. "With this software and the implant chips, I will know how well they are following my orders."

"Are not the man and the woman going to become 'inactive'?"

The Ukrainian's eyes narrowed. "I will *always* know where they are and what they are doing."

17

"So *you* were the Cuban they told us about!"

"Alex Salinas", "Guido Lopez" and "Andres Martinez" gaped open-mouthed at the toned, blonde-haired young woman standing before them.

Alex told the white "Nigerians" about their Russian Special Forces connection; how two of them and one still in Nuevo Laredo had been taken prisoner by insurgents in Chechnya and had fallen into the grip of "General Retchko", who had defected from the Russian military; about Nuevo Laredo.

Guido told the others about his "wonderful schoolteacher wife" who had been shot-down by the American Navy. "I will *always* oppose the 'Amerikanskis'. . ."

The young woman mentioned that she and another Cuban woman had trained with the "Spetsnaz" units and had graduated from the special school in Moscow. "It was a very difficult régimen," Monica said, particularly the *'Balashikha Training Ground'* and the outdoor survival training in the far North.

The three Russians, all looking the part of Mexicans, glanced around at each other. Alex Salinas spoke. "I will test you . . . what was the *name* of the 'special school' in Moscow?"

Monica looked off a moment in thought. "I do not believe it had a name, we just called it, 'The Academy'—"

Alex looked around at the other two men with him and shrugged. "Who was the colonel who led the training group?"

"Um . . . *'Golubko'*—'Colonel Golubko', I believe he was."

The three expatriate Russians let out a long collective breath. "Unbelievable," Guido Lopez said, glancing at the other two, who had awed looks on their faces. "She was there, all right."

Monica turned to Luis, who looked puzzled. "We all trained under the same man in Russia."

"He was a great leader," Andres put in. The other Russians and the Cuban girl nodded in agreement.

"Did you know Colonel Golubko trained as a cosmonaut?" This was from Guido. "He told us about it one time while we were at 'Star City'."

Monica's eyes went up. "You went to 'Star City'? You rode the centrifuge?"

Guido gave a sheepish grin. "I blacked-out."

The girl grinned. "Many people did that, they told us . . . it was a real work-out, was it not?"

"*Everything* about 'Spetsnaz' was a work-out!"

Luis, not knowing what they were talking about, looked perplexed.

Alex turned to him. "Then you are not Russian?"

". . . 'American'—"

Guido looked at him with a wary frown.

"So, how did you come to be part of the Organization?"

The former Larry Landay glanced at Marisol Montoya, now "Monica Montero". "It was not exactly my idea."

Over the next two hours and several drink refills, each of the five expatriates told the others how they came to the employ of the "Organization" through Retchko and the Cartel.

Alex looked at Monica. "And you 'stowed-away' on the 'Seven-Forty-Seven'!"

The girl laughed "In a wooden box!"

"I was never so surprised in my life as when she showed up on the airplane," Luis said.

She put her arm in his. "It worked out well, for us."

'That airplane goes all over the world." .

Guido spoke up. "I found out it used to be part of Iraq's airline. It got a new name and a new job when the Organization bought it to ship paramilitary and nuclear goods around the world."

"The pilots said they used to be in the 'Soviet Strategic Bomber Forces'."

Guido nodded. "Good, well-trained, guys, I would say."

Alex looked at Luis and Monica. "You got new names, too, like we did?"

". . . and passports—very good passports and papers." Everyone nodded.

Luis looked around at the other guests. More than a few had become noticeably more tipsy or stoned-looking since the party had been going on; he had observed that keeping the lines of cocaine and the rolled joints replenished on the tables had kept the attendants busy. To him, it seemed as if the non-stop Latin music over the last little while had taken on a more incessant, pounding beat; *'orgiastic'*, even. The American was sure that Facundo had arranged everything on purpose; Luis suspected there were probably many undercurrents at work, here. As he watched discreetly, he saw that some of the scantily-clad girls had already paired-off with male guests in the direction of the bedroom wing of the huge manor house. One, he noticed in particular, had already returned and was once more working her way around the room.

He looked back at the others, who were talking about Facundo's hospitality. "So, what *are* we supposed to do, here?"

Alex, whom Luis had deduced was the spokesman for the Nuevo Laredo three, gestured for the others to draw closer. He squinted at Luis. "You speak Russian?"

The American nodded.

"Our job is to get these people to have us train their paramilitaries and to supply them with weapons. With the level of their activities, the profits to the Organization—*and to us*—will be great."

He looked over Guido's shoulder at the guests dancing to the Latin music and at others talking among themselves around the place, and went on speaking in Russian. "We have a big opportunity at Nuevo Laredo, now, with Aldrada taking over." He told Luis and Monica about the powerful new Mexican borderlord. "We can start start to train and supply his paramilitaries to where even the Mexican Army would not dare to oppose him."

Alex gave a smirk. "One of our men—'Pedro', we now call him—has taken over the training and supplying of the man's gunmen, whom we will soon turn into real soldier-type guards." He paused for effect. "Retchko and the Chief are very pleased by this."

416

The Russian acting the part of a Mexican glanced around the room to make sure no one was taking undue note of them, then spoke some more. "We must convince this man, 'Facundo', to cut a deal with us to work with Aldrada—and us—to transport drugs up from Colombia through Mexico to the border, where Aldrada will take it across to America."

The musical combo rent the air in the living room with another Colombian piece; Alex listened for a moment, then nodded his head, certain the music would continue to mask their conversation. He told a joke that made their overdone laughter appear to anyone who might be watching them think they were swapping humor.

Alex told Luis and Monica about the printing plant. "It is a perfect cover to make those people look like *'legals'* going into the 'States. . .."

He glanced at "Guido Lopez"—the former "Gennady Lychin"—and at Luis and Monica. "Those Chechens who crossed the border into Texas—"

". . . the ones who rode with us to Havana on the 'Seven-Forty-Seven'?"

"Exactly. They are now in Newark, New Jersey . . . they are preparing to bomb the 'World Trade Center' in New York— sometime about January of next year; maybe a little later, I do not know for sure."

Luis's eyes were wide. *"Bomb the World Trade Center in New York?"*

"'Ezego', Retchko's assistant—some of you may have met him—is there now with them, getting materials and helping them organize everything and build the explosives. They will use a truck-bomb in the parking garage that might bring down both buildings . . ."

Guido was frowning. "Will it not be difficult to get past their security?"

"They have found that 'security' at the 'World Trade Center' is very loose—but, if they have to, they can 'dispose' of the security people before they set off the bomb. Alex paused while a man, obviously high on something, tried without success to open the nearby sliding door to the outside. After a few seconds, the fellow gave up and wobbled on.

Satisfied there were no more possible prying eyes or ears, he went on, "Soon, I am told, 'Agent U's' men will go to *a special school in Brazil that is part of the Organization'*, where they will lose their Middle-Eastern names and accents and get new Mexican ones, then enter the United States, using the new identities we will provide them."

Luis had a quizzical expression. "Who is 'Agent U'?"

"'Agent U' is a wealthy Middle-Easterner who is working with us." Alex did not want to disclose very much to this disguised American.

Monica was curious about something. "How come it is so easy for Mexicans and all the others to get into the United States from Mexico?"

Alex gave a sneer. "The Americans need their 'low-pay' workers . . . and they are not smart enough to know the difference between a Middle-Easterner and a common *'wetback'*, as I have heard the Americans call the Mexicans."

"Ugh," Monica grimaced, "that is a terrible thing to call them."

"They have lots of other words they use to describe those 'illegals'. We will take advantage of the Americans' lack of attention to their borders to do many things to them."

Gaido Lopez looked grim. "I am looking forward to doing things to the Americans—for what they did to my wife."

Just then, a familiar figure stepping in their direction caught Alex's eye. "Ah! I see you now know each other!" Facundo was in an expansive mood. "You have more people, no?"

Alex picked up on the man's congenial frame of mind. "Si, Señor Facundo . . . we have had much to talk about!"

"Claro! Then we enjoy tonight, and tomorrow have big talk". The fellow gave a quick look around at the partygoers, then at the three single young men. "Find one of the girls for yourselves, señors, have big time with her all night and be back here tomorrow morning at nine o'clock, pronto!"

"Sounds like an order, to me!" Alex motioned for the others to go join the party, ignoring Monica's look of disdain at the man's obvious references about the other girls. For all the Cubana's admiration of Facundo's power and wealth, to her, he was sounding like a boorish cad.

Alex turned and headed toward a long-haired young woman in a very short, low-cut dress that showed lots of her tanned skin. Luis noticed that she was one of the two party girls who had been talking ealier to the Russians. The second "Mexican" made his way into the crowd of dancers, cut-in on a Colombian male and took over the attentions of the fellow's *'señorita'*.

Gaido shook his head and stepped alone in the direction of the bar.

Monica touched Luis's arm. "There is something about that hombre . . . let us go talk with him."

The two stepped to the bar just as Gaido was ordering a drink "Could we join you?" Monica said to him in Russian, taking a seat on a barstool. Luis dropped onto the unused one on the other side.

The young man looked surprised for a moment, then recognized the two. "Ah, yes, of course."

Monica glanced at the bartender, then at the young man. "What did you order?"

"Vodka. I am trying to stay as Russian as I can."

Luis hailed the bartender. "Two more Vodkas."

Monica wanted to keep the conversation going. "You said your name is—"

"'Guido . . . that is what I call myself in Mexico . . . my real name is 'Gennady Lychin'."

"My American name was 'Larry Landay'. . . I am now 'Luis Landa'."

"I am 'Monica Montero'. My name in Cuba was 'Marisol Montoya' . . . you are Russian?"

A fleeting, rueful look crossed his face that Marisol picked up. Gennady gave a quick glance over his shoulder. "*All* of us are Russians—the fellows you were talking with—we are all from Russia."

The bartender set the dripping glasses onto the countertop. The young foreigner downed a big swallow and took a deep breath, blinking.

"I have been drinking more, lately." Gennady stared at his glass, then put it down. He leaned forward, his elbows on the countertop, and put his face in his hands.

Larry and Marisol looked at each other. Marisol touched Gennady's shoulder. "You said something happened to your wife . . . ?"

Gennady, looking down, nodded, then spoke in slow, measured words. "Remember the Iranian airliner the American Navy shot down over the Persian Gulf and everybody on it was killed?"

"I read about it in the newspaper."

"My wife . . . my *new* wife—we were married only two months—was on that airplane."

Marisol suppressed a gasp. "Oh, I am so sorry."

Larry looked uncomfortable; some *Americans* had killed this fellow's bride.

Gennady went on, speaking in a low voice, hardly audible over the music from down the way. "She was a schoolteacher. She went to Iran on a 'cultural visit', or whatever they called it. Galina was on her way back to our home in Moscow when she—"

He paused to try to get himself together.

" . . . died."

He pulled a handkerchief from his pocket and wiped his eyes.

Larry stared into his Vodka; the clear, potent liquid had lost its appeal to him.

Gennady lifted a photograph from his billfold. "Here is her picture." The tiny portrait was of a young woman with short, dark hair. She was smiling. "This was 'Galina' . . . I will carry her picture with me, always."

Monica shook her head, struck by the young man's tragedy. "She was very . . . pretty."

Larry glanced at it for a moment, then looked away. She was nice-looking, all right. And his fellow countrymen had obliterated that girl.

"She was wonderful, decent—" With tenderness the Russian rubbed the picture with his fingertips. ". . . and they killed her. The Americans killed her." Gennady shook his head. "By mistake!" His words tumbled out. "They said it was all just a big mistake and they apologized! My wife is gone and they *apologize?*" Gennady narrowed his eyes at Larry and shook his head. "If it was such a big mistake, then why did all the men on your Navy ship get *medals* for shooting down her airplane?"

"I did not know about it . . . I was in Africa when it happened." Larry shrugged. "I am very sorry."

"I believe you mean it. But the other Americans did not mean it." Gennady upended the Vodka glass and emptied it. He turned to Larry again, his eyes red. "You see, I am now on a mission . . . a mission to avenge my wife . . . *a mission against America.*" He took a deep breath and shook his head to clear his thoughts. "And being a part of Retchko's Organization will allow me to try to destroy those who destroyed my wife."

"I don't know what to say."

"You do not have to say anything." The Russian shrugged. "When I was captured by Retchko's men in Chechnya, I thought it was the worst thing that could ever have happened to me. Then I found out about Galina—and nothing mattered, anymore. So I will spend the rest of my life getting even with the Americans and their damn military."

Gennady dropped off the barstool and put his hand out to Larry. "I know you are not responsible for what happened to Galina—but you have to understand my feelings." The two shook hands.

The Russian looked around at the Colombian drug kingpin's luxurious place and the revelers dancing to the frantic Latin music down at the other end of the open space. He blinked at the expatriate American. "How is it that we meet in a place like this—and now we will be working together, on the same side."

The young man moved away with unsteady steps in the direction of the mansion's living quarters.

Marisol watched him go, her face pinched. "What an unhappy person, he is."

"But he made me realize for the first time that I cannot go back to the 'States—ever again."

Marisol gave him a questioning frown.

Larry slid back onto the barstool; a glum look on his face. "Look, *everybody* back there—the courts . . . the police . . . are against me—I would never be able to clear myself." He shrugged. "I am as stuck, now, as is that Russian guy!"

"We will be in Medellín, remember? There, you will not have to worry about them. And we will be starting a new life."

Larry downed his Vodka in a hurry, hardly noticing the burn in his throat as it went down. His hand held up the empty glass; his eyes focused on the little bandage on his wrist. He shook his head. "My 'fellow Americans' may not know where I am—but Retchko does."

* * *

Madrid, Spain; the Next Morning:

The uniformed officer shook hands with Terenty. "Ah, Major Suslov, we have been expecting you." He looked at the auburn-haired young woman and the little blonde girl. "These are your wife and child?"

Terenty nodded. "My wife, Tamara, and our daughter, Larisa."

With a grin the man leaned over and enveloped the child's tiny hand. Larisa looked up at him with a grave face. "You can smile, now . . . we are friends, here! And you will have some friends to play with." He turned to Tamara. "There are other families here, with children."

The man came back to Terenty. "You will start your official duties, tomorrow. In the meantime, you can get acquainted with the embassy."

"Actually, this is my third time, here." Terenty glanced up and down the gilded hallway and through the open door to the signals office. "I practically grew up in this building; my parents were diplomats. Later, I began my military career as an 'Assistant Attaché', right there in that room."

"And now you are in charge! I am going on holiday, then to an active duty assignment." He gave a shrug. "Probably, they will send me to Chechnya—"

"I was there." Terenty caught Tamara out of the corner of his eye; she was frowning. "It is a tough place."

"Well, Suslov, you came to a comfortable posting, and I am off to who-knows-where." He touched his forehead with a fingertip, nodding. The officer turned and stepped through the open door into the room filled with electronics.

Before the door closed, Terenty pointed to the inside. "I started in there, monitoring American signals. That is still its mission—electronic intercepts, along with the usual communications with Moscow."

"It is all so . . . 'technical'."

Terenty grinned. "For us, here, it is all in a day's work." He reached for her hand. "Let us go, now, and meet the Ambassador for lunch. We are going to a place called *'Plaza Mayor'*."

* * *

Cali, Colombia, at the Same Time:

"I welcome you here to the first meeting of the *'Hemisphere Revolutionary Council'!*" Fernando "Facundo" Ordoñez stood at the head of the long mahogany table, looking around at his guests. Two dozen other men and the one blonde woman who had been calling herself "Monica Montero" were finishing their breakfasts; waiters in formal attire bustled about exchanging plates in front of them; replenishing their coffee-cups.

"I trust you are enjoying our Colombian coffee—" The man spread his arms as the others sipped their black brew, nodding. "It is the *second*-most popular product of our country!" he grinned, to a roomful of laughter. "The *most* popular, of course, is our *'white gold'* that we send out to all the world!"

It was a full minute before a semblance of seriousness returned to the gathering.

Facundo held up his hand. "The reason for our meeting, here, is to take our business operations to a new, higher level!"

He nodded at an attendant, who pulled down a rolled wall map. Larry, using the name "Luis Landa" once again, gazed at the multi-colored chart representing the area from South America

423

all the way up through Central America and Mexico to the Texas border of the United States.

"In the interest of increased efficiency, I propose we divide our responsibilities into definite areas, and share the profits." The host pointed at southern Colombia. "Here, we have the great 'coca' plantations that provide us with the raw materials. Nearby, are the extraction factories, some of which are underground or in deep forests." Facundo tapped the map. "It is here, that the government troops are least likely to bother us. You all know this, of course." The man looked around the room. "But now, I am told by my sources that this may soon change; that the government régime may try to come into this area. We must be ready for them with power that will discourage this."

There was some squirming in seats. The speaker gave a glance at Luis, Monica, and the three Russians from Nuevo Laredo, including Gennady—calling himself "Guido", again—who were sitting near each other.

"We have a solution to that problem." Fecundo surveyed the people around the table, who were mostly younger-looking men. Luis noticed all were dressed in casual, but expensive-looking, clothes, the "casual-natty" with which he had been familiar in California. The Colombian tapped the big board on the wall. The wealthy, important men around the table leaned forward. "Here is what I propose . . ."

* * *

Tanuta Refinery, at That Moment:

"You say they are now in a *meeting*? How do you know that?" General Retchko stared at the monitor in the satellite receiving station.

Boronov, the Russian electronics expert, pointed at blinking white dots on the screen. "See that pattern? They are around a table." As they watched, one of the dots moved from one side of a space to another. "Someone is standing before the others, now. According to the signal, that would be the comrade they call, 'Alex Salinas'—"

424

For some time there were no changes in position. "I believe he is giving a talk."

"He is supposed to tell the drug men about the Organization. He must be doing that, right now." The bald Ukrainian glanced at Boronov and gave a smirk."We can be here in Tanuta City and watch our employees who are thousands of miles away . . . how remarkable!"

* * *

". . . and our 'remarkable' system gives you the weapons and the training—" Alex Salinas, smiling, looked around the table at the powerful men, several of whom looked to be in a state of near-euphoria. "This will put your guard forces ahead of the regular armies of each of your countries and your other enemies." He spread his hands. "Think, comrades, what combining your forces with these weapons and technologies could mean for the protection and success of your operations!"

The drug men glanced around at each other, nodding; smiles creased their faces.

Facundo again stood at the head of the table, a pleased look on his own face. "Señors! This is the opportunity for which we have long been looking! Soon, we will be able to dictate our terms to the armies and to the governments without fear!"

"I already own the President of my country!"

"The Congress where I live is on my payroll."

One of the men was looking over a picture of an assault helicopter. "You can get us these?"

Alex nodded. "And train your pilots. Our resources are worldwide."

Another man was smiling. "No fear of attacks from the air, anymore!"

"Attacks, hell! *We* will do the attacking!"

"We can establish a military alliance of our groups across several countries."

"We can clear more land for 'coca'."

"More country people will now join us."

"The 'country' people already depend on me for their living. *They will do whatever I say.*"

One of the men was writing on a pad. "I figure we can double our profits in six months." His remark was met with nods all around the room.

Alex motioned at the Organization's people around the table. "Now, our people will meet with each of you to plan out the details and place your orders."

* * *

Plaza Mayor; Madrid, Spain, at the Same Time:

"You say you have never before been out of Russia?" The older man looked at Tamara with a lifted eyebrow.

No, 'Comrade Ambassador' . . . it is my first time out of the Moscow Region, even."

"Well, with your husband in the 'Diplomatic Section', now, I believe you will have plenty of opportunity to see the world!"

"She glanced about at their ancient surroundings. "I am enjoying Madrid, already."

A little breeze swirled across the cobblestoned square, ruffling the cloths and the umbrella-like circular canopies of the alfresco tables, most of which were still occupied by early-afternoon diners. Tamara tossed her long auburn hair out of her face and gave an admiring glance at her husband, who was wearing his dress uniform, then at Larisa, who was sitting on a booster seat, holding a juice drink in both hands, kicking her feet contentedly.

"I am trying to explain to our daughter how fortunate she is to travel at her young age."

The diplomat gave a reserved grin, nodding at the child, who was sucking on a straw with a satisfied air. He took a swallow from his mug of local beer and motioned around with the glass at the big open space where they were sitting amid medieval-like surroundings. "There is much to see in Madrid—like where we are, right now, You know anything about 'Plaza Mayor'?"

"Terenty told me he had been here, before."

426

"This is a famous place . . . tell her about it, major."

"When I was a boy in Madrid, we came down here on field trips. They told us Plaza Mayor was almost five-hundred years old."

"That old?"

As her husband went on pointing out features of the vast square that had once been the center of the old Spanish worldwide Empire, Tamara looked around at its massive, multi-story brick-and-stone buildings enclosing the space on all four sides, some clad in yellow stucco; at the heavy stonework towers that reminded her of the spires of the Kremlin back in Moscow; at the masonry arches and Renaissance-styled arcades beneath the brick facades of the big buildings all around them. At one end of the two-hundred-meter square was a pair of big stone-and-brick archways through the ground floor of one of the buildings, where they had come up into the plaza from a narrow outside street. In the center, out in the open, stood an equestrian statue.

Terenty noticed she was looking out at the enormous horse and rider sculpture. "The statue is of whoever was the king when they finished the plaza. I guess over the years there have been many big, important events here, like marriages . . . fairs— assassinations; executions—"

"Those, too?"

"It has probably been a busy place, these past five-hundred years."

The Ambassador looked at his watch. "We should be returning to the embassy, now."

He lifted his hand to get the attention of a man at a nearby table finishing lunch with some serious-looking individuals in suits whom Terenty knew were bodyguards. The fellow caught the signal and nodded at the other men. All came forward as the little gathering arose from their seats and surrounded them while the group walked back through an archway toward the awaiting ZIL limousine. When they got there, several other men, also in suits, were standing by the massive vehicle. From the way the civilian-looking guards carried themselves, Terenty recognized them as "Russian Special Forces" troops on a coveted foreign duty assignment. He would talk with them, later.

When they were seated, from his jump-seat Terenty happened to look at the backside of the front chauffeur's compartment—beneath the division glass was the same "Pavel Drubkin" manufacturer's installer plate like he had seen on the ZIL in Havana!

He casually crossed his legs and covered the engraved brass plaque with his knee. He did not want Tamara to see that her former husband had outfitted the luxurious interior of this enormous car in which they were riding.

* * *

"Perpetua Tower Hotel", Cali, Colombia; That Evening:

Alex rubbed his hands together and surveyed the papers arrayed on the bed, where the Organization's people had brought their purchase orders from the drug lords to the hotel room.

"This calls for a celebration!" The man stepped over to a small sink. "Glad this room has a wet bar." He smirked. "Facundo gave me packets of 'coke', but we are not interested in *that*, are we? I flushed it down the drain."

He reached for a bottle. "Vodka is more to our liking, is it not, comrades?" He poured the clear liquid into shot glasses and handed them out. "A little 'lubrication for the mind', I always say . . ." The expatriate Russian lifted his tumbler in salute, then downed the drink in one swallow and poured himself another, upending it, blinking, as the searing distillate went down.

"Now, to business," he went on. The others dropped into stuffed chairs around the room as he picked up the first stack of papers. "Andres Martinez—"

Andres spoke up. "The man I talked to said he wants *everything*."

"Where is he located?"

"In the east of Colombia in a jungle area—a place on the border with Venezuela." He flipped through his notes. "The man says he wants to eliminate some local competition, but his main enemies are government troops." Andres shuffled in his chair. "He wants me to train his people, personally."

"That will be your assignment."

"He says he wants the helicopters, too—and the pilot training."

Alex looked again at Andres. "You fly helicopters?"

"I went to helicopter school."

"Well, refresh yourself . . . you just became a 'helicopter instructor! You have ninety days from delivery of the goods to do it."

"Where will we get the helicopters?"

"Retchko will handle it. He has connections."

Alex looked down the pages of the next purchase order.

Luis recognized the writing on it. "That is the order from the 'Medellín' man."

"He wants multi-engine transports?"

"They will be flying drugs from central Colombia all the way to the United States."

"*Where* in the United States? That is a long haul."

"A place called *'Arkansas'*." He read the description of the place. "It is some distance inside the country. It will take special aircraft."

"Another task for the general."

Alex lifted a sheaf of papers. "Guido—"

"The Venezuela man wants everything, too . . . starting with basic-training-airplanes."

"'Training-airplanes'?"

"They are military men," Luis went on. "The man we spoke with says he is a 'front man' for the real kingpin, who is a young colonel in the Army. The fellow is in prison, right now."

"How can we help him if he is in prison?"

"He will be out in one year. Right now, his people are setting up a political party to take over the country through elections."

"No fooling! An *honest* drug man?"

"He is not into drugs, his man says. As for being honest . . . he tried a coup and got caught. Now, he will try to do it through politics—just like Hitler did."

"What *are* his politics?"

"He is some sort of socialist, I would guess. He has been to Russia. He likes Iran. Perhaps he is a communist—who cares, if his money is good!"

The man we talked to wants us to meet with the colonel in the prison."

Alex glanced at Guido. "I will send you to meet the man."

"He wants us to set up training camps for his private army, along with the airplanes."

"He is all right with the fee?"

"'No problem!' he said."

"Why are these Venezuelans wanting our help, if they are not into the drug traffic?"

"Their real objectives are the oil fields. He told us the Venezuelan oil companies send most of their crude and refined products to America—it is a huge market, up there, he said. The profits to the companies and to the government are enormous. In the same way, the 'Tanuta Refinery' finances the Organization, as I am told."

Alex grinned. "Wait until the 'Chief'' hears we are aiming at oil, here . . . we may all get bonuses!"

"The colonel wants to someday nationalize the private American and European oil companies in Venezuela . . . the man said they will wait for some years before doing it, though. He will need fighter planes, submarines and a stronger army before doing that, since the Americans may react."

Guido—the former Gennady—shook his head, frowning. "The 'Americanos' will *not* react. They are cowards . . . they shoot-down civilian airliners." His face had a stormy cast. "I want to finish this job and get back to Nuevo Laredo—I have my own private war to fight against the Americanos."

Andres Martinez got Alex's attention. "Maybe we could combine the military training in eastern Colombia with the helicopters and the Venezuela trainer-aircraft. We could do three things at once."

Alex nodded. "Good idea, since all these groups are now willing to work together. You could help them to secure an area in Colombia, close to Venezuela, and do it there."

He set down the papers. "This man, Facundo, is even richer than I had thought . . . he wants us to literally set up an army for him. He says he can recruit from the police forces, and some military people will come along with him in secret—he is well-connected to just about everybody important in Colombia, including the government in Bogotá."

The man looked through Facundo's purchase order. "This alone is worth over a hundred million American dollars!"

Alex dropped the order onto the bed and ran his hand over the little piles of papers. "And all of you got the deposits, I see." Each of the new customers had given a sight-draft as down-payment.

"The Chief will be very pleased with our work, here . . . I am sure of it."

* * *

Tanuta Refinery, at That Moment:

They are at a hotel?" Retchko, wearing a robe and slippers, stared at the screen in the refinery's satellite station.

"According to the software, they are at the 'Hotel Perpetua Tower' in Cali." Boronov moved the computer mouse and clicked onto a part of the building from overhead. "There they are . . . in one of the top-floor suites." He clicked again; the picture enlarged. "I told Alex to get a room high in the building—the satellite picks up the signals better if there are not so many floors between them and the outside."

Retchko mentally counted the flashing dots; all his operatives were there. "I would guess they are talking about the meetings they had with the drug people." The bald man glanced at the wall clock. "It is three-o'clock in the morning, here, so it must be about nine-o'clock in the evening there. We will be getting Alex's message in a few hours. I am going to bed, now."

* * *

Madrid; the Next Morning:

"I see there have been a lot of changes since I was here, last." Terenty stood at the door of the signals intercept room of the Russian Embassy looking around with the man he would

431

replace as Military Attaché. All about the walls and back-to-back in the center were consoles manned by junior officers and non-commissioned specialists.

"The main change is that now most of the data is digital." The major swept his arm around the space. "Of course, we must keep up with the Americans and with NATO, who have gone to the high-speed, broadband formats. But then, our forces have done the same thing. It is a whole new world of technology."

"I will have to brush-up on my electronics!"

"In operation, it is not all that complicated, and these men, here, are very good at what they do. All you have to do is to make sure they follow the procedures." The man paused. "I envy you, major. The job is not all that difficult, and I am sure your wife will enjoy the social life, here." He put out his hand. I will now go off to the real wars."

The uniformed officer turned away down the corridor. Terenty watched him go with a feeling of regret for the man. If he was going to Chechnya . . .

The thought was left unfinished, for at that moment, one of the decoding machines sputtered to life. Terenty watched as an officer took down a message on a tape cartridge, then put it into a printer.

When the young man turned around, he noticed Major Suslov standing in the doorway. "It is our twice-daily circuit test from the Defense Ministry, sir."

Terenty recognized the fellow as one of the Ambassador's bodyguards on the lunch trip to "Plaza Mayor" the day before. "Are you 'Special Forces'?"

The officer, wearing captain's insignia, saluted the major."Korodin', sir; 'Sergei Korodin' . . . *'Beta Spetsnaz'*—" He paused, and went on. "If I may ask, sir, how did you know I was 'Spetsnaz'?"

"Your walk, mostly—and your build." Terenty introduced himself. "You knew Colonel Golubko?"

The younger man nodded, with the suggestion of a grin. "Ah, yes, of course . . . who could forget the esteemed colonel?"

"I see you have the same impression of him as I do."

"You went to the 'States with him?"

"It is classified." Terenty did not want to discuss the mission to retrieve the *'Invisible Technology'*.

"I was in Chechnya before I came here on assignment, last year."

"I was in Chechnya, also." Terenty pursed his lips. "It was a difficult posting . . . we lost some good people . . . including my best friend. His name was 'Lychin'."

"'Lychin'?" Captain Korodin thought for a moment. "I was at 'Warsaw Treaty Headquarters' with an officer by that name."

"*Gennady* Lychin?" Terenty remembered Gennady had once told him he had been posted to Warsaw Treaty Headquarters.

"Come to think of it, I believe that was his name—you say he was *lost?*"

"Captured. The Chechens took him and two others of our squad prisoners in an ambush."

Korodin shook his head. "I was told they treat prisoners very badly. Most do not survive."

Terenty told him about Galina and the airliner shoot-down.

The younger officer sucked in his breath. "How terrible! And *her husband* disappeared, also!"

"We looked for two days, but we never found them."

Footsteps sounded in the corridor. A moment later, the Ambassador appeared in the doorway. "Ah, my new 'Military Attaché'." He nodded at Korodin, then turned to Terenty. "Come to my office and we will discuss your duties."

* * *

"Unbelievable." Leonid Efimovich Retchko fingered the pages in his hand, his eyes wide. He looked up at Boronov. "These orders, alone, are worth a quarter-billion American dollars!" He let out a breath. "The Chief' will be extremely pleased . . . what a stroke to send our people to that 'drug summit'!" He stared at the purchase orders and shook his head in amazement.

The general stepped to a cabinet. "I know it is early in the day, but we shall celebrate." He took down a bottle and two small-sized glasses. He looked at his watch. "Care to join me in a

Vodka? We can call it an 'early-lunch drink'." The bald man filled two glasses, handed one to the younger man, then downed his in one upended swallow; pouring another.

"'Comrade Yegor Ivanovich', we can have our lunch drinks 'early and often'," as they say, if our operatives over there keep sending us these kinds of purchases!" He motioned at a chair. "Take a seat."

Retchko sloshed around the clear liquid in his glass. "Tell me, how did you come to possess the plans for the 'Invisible Technology'?"

The dark-haired Russian reached for the bottle and re-loaded his glass. Grimacing from the swallow, he held up the container, squinting at it for a moment. "I was a physicist at the research center . . . we were working on the process, and were making progress, but there were some things we were unable to solve."

Retchko nodded. "At the 'Academy', we once did a demonstration of the system on a stage, using an automobile." The general narrowed his eyes, as if in thought, and went on. "I remember the machine was very big and was unable to neutralize some kinds of light waves."

Boronov nodded. "The breakthrough came when some of our 'Spetsnaz' men penetrated into the Americans' top-secret laboratory and brought out our agent with all their drawings on compressed computer files." The Russian gave a quick grin. "He said he had sabotaged the Americans' computer programs so their research would go nowhere."

Something the man had said just now interested Retchko. "You said some 'Spetsnaz' men had gone into America?"

"That is what the colonel who was in charge of the operation told us when they brought the scientist to our laboratory."

The general narrowed his eyes. "What was the 'colonel's' name?"

"Seems like it was 'Golubin,' or something like that."

"Could it have been 'Golubko'?"

"Come to think of it, I believe his name *was* 'Golubko'. He had other soldiers with him."

Retchko took a deep breath. "I knew that man when I was in Moscow." *It is a small world,* he thought.

Something else came to him. Gennady Lychin, the fellow whose wife was killed in the airplane shoot-down, and who was now working for the Organization, had been one of Golubko's men at about that time. If he had been on the mission to America to get out the scientist, he would be a qualified trainer for the drug lords' training camps. He would instruct Alex on this.

Boronov was going on. "But we were not being paid—the government had little money for salaries. Some of us had the idea to sell our knowledge on the open market."

He downed the Vodka in the glass in one swallow and again reached for the bottle. "It was then that one of the scientists made contact with 'Agent U' . . . he put us on his payroll and we supplied him with information and, later, hardware. We stole equipment and computer software from the Design Bureau and re-sold it to outside interests."

Retchko squinted at the man. "Who were some of these 'interests'?"

"'Agent U' was our main 'client'. And I believe some of it went to Pakistan . . . some to Iran, and—" Boronov looked up at the ceiling in thought—"I am sure we sent hardware to North Korea and Libya." Another pause. "We sent some prints to Brazil."

"Brazil? In South America?"

"They got a whole set of reactor blueprints, if I remember right."

Retchko grunted. This was information he would investigate further. "How did you leave Russia?"

"It was quite simple, actually. Several of us took a 'research' trip to Chechnya. There, I met up with some of *your* operatives"—he nodded at Retchko—"and made my way to Teheran. The airplane carried me out of Iran down to here."

"What about the others?"

"They went to work for 'U', at 'Tora-Bora. There, they— along with some East Germans—set up the equipment you sent him and are running the chip-implant operation with his men through the satellite. They contact me by code regularly and we exchange information."

"Does the girl, Lisa Anaya, know about any of this?"

"I have it all disguised and coded. She thinks they are 'operational tests'."

Retchko picked up the printouts of the orders from Colombia. "How did Alex send these?"

"Through his implanted 'chip'—I sent him a device that works like a 'dialysis' machine that filters blood for kidney patients, except that it is much smaller and does not actually filter the blood—it only 'modulates' the implant frequency with a digital signal containing the information. Alex scanned the purchase orders onto a small computer, then hooked it up to the dialysis machine. The blood fed the information to the chip in his wrist that transmitted it. The satellite picked up the signals from his chip and re-transmitted it to us at Tanuta City. I downloaded it and printed it out, like you see, here."

"So these orders came from Alex's *blood?*"

"You could put it that way. Is not technology wonderful?"

The bald man nodded, then went on leafing through the pages. "There are some very large items for us to supply. I must get busy . . . I will be leaving in a little while for Lagos."

Boronov understood the man's unspoken but firm instruction. He stood up and went out.

* * *

Nuevo Laredo; Late That Morning:

"*This* is where you now live?" Pedro Beltran stood open-mouthed in the central atrium, open to the sky, of the square-shaped, single-story, Spanish-style house. The young man looked around in wonder at each of the four white-stuccoed sides where heavy, dark-brown wooden doors opened into the various rooms of the girl's family's new home. Brown wooden columns held up the orange tile roofs where they projected over the inner walkways; though an open door in one of the sections came the cooking aromas of the mid-day meal.

Tatiana Castillo tightened her arm in Pedro's and led him across the sunlit, orange-tile patio to a glider-seat underneath a flowery, arched trellis. "Señor Aldrada gave us all this," she said, pulling him down next to her. "Is it not wonderful?"

Pedro cast about in amazement at the manicured flower gardens, the walkways, palm trees and at the gushing statue-fountain at the center. "Aldrada *gave* you this place?"

"He said it was a gift to me and my family for having being kidnapped and nearly being—well, 'being'—with those terrible men. He said if it had not been for me, he would not be the new leader on the border, now."

The young man remembered that Aldrada had said he would "do away" with all of Marco's men; most likely the former owner of this place had been one of those whom he had "done-away". Regardless of how they got it, the impressive house was a vast improvement over the little pink bungalow at the end of the short graveled street.

"How is your papá doing?"

The girl took a deep breath; her grip on Pedro's arm loosened. "He is feeling tired, today—I am praying to the Saints that he will better."

Just then, a powerfully-built man stepped through an arched doorway leading into the atrium. José Aldrada spotted the two sitting under the flowered latticework. "Ah, señorita, there you are . . . and Pedro." The mustachioed Mexican came toward them; in his hands was a big bouquet of carnations he held out to Tatiana with a kiss on her cheek.

The girl handled the long-stemmed flowers, beaming. "Señor Aldrada, they are lovely."

"The best to the little señorita."

"You are very kind to us, señor."

The older man gazed about at the lush surroundings. "I trust everything is well in your new 'casa'."

The girl looked around, blinking as if she still could not believe her family's good fortune, then gave the man a smile. *"Bueno, gracias."* She stood and excused herself with a blush. "I will tell *mi mamá* you are here."

When she had gone, the Mexican turned and gestured at a second individual who had eased into the garden space while they were talking. Pedro, surprised, observed that the brown, slender fellow was holding an AK-74. The armed man positioned himself in a corner of the little square.

Aldrada spoke in a low voice. "I have him and other guards hidden around the place . . . some of Marco's men are still prowling—"

Pedro was frowning. "They will be safe?"

"Just a *'precaución'* Señor Pedro." He nodded toward the door where Tatiana had gone. "You are doing *'hokay'* with the little *'muchacha'?"*

"Well, yes . . ."

The Mexican's mustache twitched. "See . . . I *told* you I would give her to you!"

Before Pedro could reply, Tatiana came back with her mother. "Señor Aldrada!" Belén Castillo smiled at the man, extending her hand, presenting her cheek for the obligatory kiss. "I am *'mucho'* pleased to have you with us."

"I wanted to make sure things are all right." The older man's craggy face creased into a grin as he lifted his white sombrero, holding an up-and-down gaze at the petite woman for a long second.

In the garden daylight, Pedro once more observed that Tatiana's mother looked to be hardly older than her teenaged daughter, a fact of which José Aldrada was also taking obvious note.

"Señor Aldrada, I cannot start to tell you—"

". . . ah, but it is the least I could do for your daughter who helped me." He frowned at Pedro, his bushy black eyebrows furrowed—a silent signal to keep quiet.

The mother went on. "Pedro told me Tatiana was there when the bad 'Señor Marco' was killed."

Aldrada, with another quick glance at Pedro, came back in a hurry. "They took her to his house, but we got there before they could do anything to her. We went away and the place caught fire."

Well spoken, Pedro thought. Aldrada had told her the truth without giving away any details, which had, in point of fact, been much more harrowing than he had let on. A look at Tatiana told him the girl would also keep the whole story to herself.

Belén Castillo touched Aldrada's sleeve. "'Por favor', you can join us for *'siesta'?"* Tatiana gave Pedro and the Mexican man expectant looks.

"Señora," the big man said, lifting his sombrero with a nod at the women, "we would be pleased."

In the stuccoed, brown-beamed dining-room, decorated in a rustic Spanish style, the mother, daughter and the two guests took seats in varnished, straight-backed chairs. As everyone was getting situated, through an open door a woman in a nurse's cap wheeled-in an emaciated-looking, middle-aged man in pajamas. She pushed him up to the end of the table and hung a bib around his neck.

"You are feeling better, today?" the man's wife queried.

The patient mumbled something unintelligible and did not seem to notice Belén Castillo's fleeting look of distress. For Pedro realized the man looked weaker now than he had when they were at the clinic in Texas; a glance around the table told him the others had made the same observation. Tatiana looked down at her hands in her lap, blinking.

An older Mexican woman in an apron bustled in just then holding in heat-mittens a big steaming tureen that she set in the middle of the table.

Belén Castillo produced a half-positive look on her face. "Enjoy!" she said, looking around at the others with a forced smile, reaching for the ladle.

* * *

Murtala Mohammed Airport Lagos, Lagos Nigeria; at That Moment:

The twin propellers of the Aero Commander wound-down to jerking stops. A rear door of the airplane opened and Retchko's foot felt for the pavement. Nodding at the pilots, he pulled his luggage bag from a side compartment and walked in the long shadows of the late-afternoon sun across the tarmac toward the airport's security office.

As he entered through the glass door into a broad corridor, a young, slender, cream-colored female came up to him and kissed him on the cheek. The general put his arm around her as she dropped her head on his shoulder for a second, smiling. Just then, Colonel Ajiboy opened his office door to the walkway and happened to see the interaction down the way between the bald Ukrainian and the light-skinned Nigerian woman he recognized.

But they had not seen him. The airport's security officer closed the door in a hurry, frowning, as the two stepped down the concourse away from him.

* * *

Nuevo Laredo, Mexico; an Hour Later, the Same Day:

"It is sad, Señor Pedro, but I do not believe your little girlfriend's 'padre' will be alive very much longer." José Aldrada leaned across the gargantuan carved mahogany desk in his office. "I spoke with his doctor specialist in Texas by telephone this morning." The man took a deep breath. "He said the man has bad lung cancer from smoking and a problem with the asbestos from the factory where he worked. I feel bad for his wife . . . she is good woman. It will be hard for her—and the girl and the boy." He tapped his fingertips on the desktop. "But I will keep my promise to take care of them because of what the girl—what was her name, again—?"

"Tatiana . . ."

"Tatiana. The little señorita's suffering from Marco's men that night gave me control of the border and I will never forget it."

Pedro pulled a pad and pen from a valise; it was time to get down to business. "We need to get started on equipping and training your men to hold on to what you now have."

The older man twitched his bushy mustache as the Organization's man started to outline the details of what the Cartel could do for him and his bordertown men. From time-to-time, as Pedro's presentation went on, the big Mexican nodded, his face creased with interest. He glanced at one of his men,

440

standing guard at the door with a rifle. "You say your group can turn our men into a military-style force?"

"Exacto."

"How long will it take?"

"The sooner we start, the quicker we can have your men ready."

"How much will it cost me?"

Pedro did some figuring, wrote a sum on the pad and turned it around to him.

"That much?" The amount was tens of millions of American dollars.

"Remember—with this, you will control every dollar and *'peso'* crossing the border, señor."

"That is true."

He was glad Alex had coached him on how to work the wealthy Mexican to the Cartel's best advantage—price sheets and order forms from the Organization's local printing office had made it easy for him. But of course the customer had not known this.

The younger man pointed at the bottom of the last printed page. "All I need is your approval right here—and a draft for the initial payment."

The older man pulled on his mustache as he read down the contract sheets, thinking things over; asking some questions. Then he took Pedro's proffered pen and put his name on the last page of the papers.

Looking straight into Pedro's eyes, Aldrada handed the document back across the desk. "My associate will prepare the payment documents." He nodded. "I want you to be my assistant and personally train my men." The Mexican held his gaze. "I will speak with Alex about this." He nodded, as if approving his own words. "I am sure he and General Retchko will go along."

The young Russian felt a flush; nowhere could he have imagined he would gain so much responsibility or power soon after arriving in Nuevo Laredo. And now he owed his *own* debt of gratitude to the girl.

* * *

Lagos, Nigeria, the Next Morning:

"Incredible."

The "Chief" leafed through the orders, blinking in amazement. "Our people did all *this?*"

"And we are waiting for one more order." Retchko popped a fistful of aspirins into his fleshy mouth and chased it with mineral water. It seemed that the headaches were becoming worse.

The leader's eyes were wide. "These orders are worth three-hundred-million dollars!"

"*Three-hundred-sixteen-*million American dollars, to be exact." Busa, who had come along with the general from Tanuta City, handed a printout of figures to the little man behind the big desk. "Our profit on these deals should be two-hundred-sixty-million, at least."

The Chief looked at Retchko. "How soon can we supply all these things?"

"I am in contact with the North Koreans for most of the conventional weapons." He fingered some notes. "Cuba is offering us trucks and helicopters, along with rifles in return for lubricants. We can get those from our fuel line of credit with Libya—the Libyans say they want more centrifuges, by the way. I will negotiate with the North Koreans for those." He again focused his eyes at the notes. "Russian helicopters and spare parts are in Libya, as well . . . the little trainer airplanes for Venezuela will be more difficult, but I believe Argentina had captured some small British aircraft from the Falklands while they were there in 'eighty-two. Perhaps we can work a deal with them. Several of our Russians have helicopter and fixed-wing experience and will train the local men to fly them." He made some more notes. "I figure we can start the deliveries in less than two weeks."

The dimunitive man behind the desk leaned back in his executive chair and tapped his fingertips together. "Very well, I want a— "

Just then, a clerk knocked on the door. "I have a message—"

"Here, boy." The stocky Security Chief put out his hand ahead of Busa's and gripped the pages. When the employee had left, he scanned down the missive, nodding. "It is the order we were expecting . . . from 'Blagron', in Mexico."

Retchko handed over the papers to the Chief'; his mouth fixed in a grin. "This means we control the man who controls the border between Mexico and America." The general kept his stare on the man across the desk from him. "The long-term profits to the Organization will be huge."

The Chief's eyebrows were up. "How did our people manage to do all this so soon?"

The bald Ukrainian sat up straight, with a condescending glance at Busa. *"I* sent them to Colombia with *my* instructions. *I* gave them the training to make the sales you see, here---they merely followed *my* directions."

". . . 'Blagron'—" the Chief interrupted, "writes here he will be the Mexican leader's 'assistant' and will 'personally' train the men—and I see he is charging them a large sum for his services."

"According to 'Alex', our leader, there, Blagron has a special 'inside' to the big fellow . . . something about our man's new Mexican girlfriend worked to our advantage."

"That so?" The Nigerian leaned back, his fingertips touching. "Maybe we should encourage *more* relationships between our people and the natives—it seems to bring us more business!"

* * *

Office of the 'Agency'; Federal Office Building, Dallas, Texas:

The orders from Watering were explicit: he, James Richard Randolph, was to go to Laredo, Texas to investigate the reputed new gang leader on the border. The agent picked up the report on what Headquarters already knew. Scanning the information, he guessed that some governments besides his own, maybe INTERNOL—perhaps even the Russians—were in on the case. But usually, the originators of such Intelligence were not revealed to field agents in order to protect those sources, which was fine with him—evidence gathered from several informants not known to each other almost always gave a broader perspective of a situation than otherwise.

According to the "Backgrounder", a man named "José Aldrada" had deposed "Marco", the long-time kingpin of Nuevo Laredo. There was evidence that there had recently been a purge of Marco followers along the Rio Grande; this Aldrada individual was supposed to be even more thorough than Marco had been.

Randolph read on with increasing interest. Watering wrote that he believed some expatriate Russians, perhaps with Soviet military backgrounds, were involved with Aldrada, who might soon have access to sophisticated Eastern Bloc weaponry. If this were true, then Border Patrol would have its hands full—nowhere on the Rio Grande were the lightly-armed Americans prepared to confront renegade Mexicans armed with such potent firepower.

The last page was even more tantalyzing. The United States Consulate General in Cali, Colombia had cabled the "Agency" about a "summit" of drug warlords that had recently taken place, there. The information—from usually reliable sources, according to the imbedded CIA agent at the consulate—included the intriguing piece that some Eastern Europeans, perhaps with military backgrounds, had also been at the meeting.

Randolph picked up the previous sheet of paper and compared it with the last one. *Eastern Europeans with military backgrounds?* Were there now *Russians* at the border working with this man, Aldrada? He took a deep breath and leaned back in his desk chair, thinking. Could these "Russians" and "Eastern Europeans", all of whom seemed to be grounded in the Soviet military, be the same persons? If this Aldrada individual should now be allied with such men of the former Soviet Union, the implications for United States national security would render trivial the usual border issues.

-18-

Nuevo Laredo; Ten Days Later:

The men with shovels stood off to the side, watching, as the hearse drove away down the narrow cemetery lane. A woman and a younger female, both dressed in black, along with an adolecent male and another man about thirty, both wearing black ill-fitting suits, hung back with a small group of others, including a priest.

As the little gathering started to disperse, an older, well-dressed man with a large mustache came forward and took the woman's gloved hand, then the girl's; turning to shake the youth's hand. He seemed to be speaking earnestly to the three; their heads were close together. The other man came up and joined them. After a short nodding conversation, the big man motioned to a black Lincoln limousine. The driver held open a rear door and they got in.

The long vehicle turned down the crunching gravel driveway past endless rows of tombstones and crypts to the main thoroughfare, then turned into the long orange rays of the late afternoon and picked up speed.

When all the mourners were gone, the men with the shovels stepped up and with hollow-sounding *"clumps"*, delivered the dirt alongside the ditch down onto the top of the concrete burial vault in the ground. In a few minutes, the grave was mounded-over. With one last look at their handiwork, the men swung the gritty shovels onto their shoulders and trudged off in the direction of a nearby parked truck.

* * *

Laredo, Texas Motel Room; That Evening:

AGENT'S FIELD REPORT SUMMARY

TO: Watering, Director of Division

FROM: James Richard Randolph, Field Agent

SUBJECT: Observations/Conclusions of the Situation at Laredo/Nuevo Laredo—

"The day I arrived in Laredo, while I was filling the gas tank of the rental car at a station near the airport, I happened to look across the roadway and noticed some men unloading goods from a delivery-type-van-truck into a mini-storage warehouse unit.

"What caught my attention were the wooden-slatted crates they were handling. Within them were what looked like strong metal cylinders. From a distance, something about the open-type boxes looked vaguely familiar to me.

"After I had filled the tank, I drove across the way and spoke to the manager of the storage place, using the excuse that I was interested in renting a space. The suspects outside were visible from where we were standing. "Looks like you're doing a good business, here," I said.

"They import farm equipment from Mexico to customers here in the Rio Grande Valley," he told me. "They stay pretty busy."

"While I pretended to be inspecting some different-sized units, we worked ourselves around close to where the suspects were unloading their truck. I managed to glance at the crates as we walked by. I am sure the metal containers in the crates were the type used to transport and store radioactive and other hazardous materials.

"While I was measuring a nearby empty unit as if to rent it, I was also overhearing the suspects talking among themselves. Their accents were Eastern

446

European, although they seemed to be passing themselves off as Mexican; perhaps Mexican-American, based on some things the manager said. I observed that all the individuals were light-skinned and had dark beards that were of several days' growth. I found out that their unit was registered to a one "Walter Macias," of Laredo. But there is no one in the city directory by that name.

"I rented a unit close by and put some of my personal items into it. I went to a furniture rental place and rented some furniture and other accessories, etc., to put in my unit to make it look like I had a legitimate need to store things. I rented a truck to do this. During this time, the suspects did not take much notice of me.

"I rented another car and parked it nearby, out of sight of the suspect's storage unit. Over the next several days, as I went in-and-out of my unit doing busy-looking work, several times the suspects were there.

"One time, I followed them in the second car (that the suspects did not appear to ever recognize) to an apartment complex across the border in Nuevo Laredo.

"The next day when they left, I again followed them in the second car. But they did not stop in Nuevo Laredo like I thought they would—they drove all the way down to Monterrey, to the airport, a considerable distance. Out of their sight, I watched them load more of the crates like the ones at the storage unit. When they had left, I sauntered into the airport cargo section and had a casual conversation with a worker. I talked to him in Spanish, of which I am fluent. Without realizing my motives, he let it drop that the shipment had originated in Havana, Cuba.

"I drove back to Laredo to the storage place, changed cars, again, out of sight of their unit. When I pulled up at my unit in my original rental car, they were already there, unloading their goods from the truck into their space that <u>appeared to have been emptied-out by someone while we were gone.</u>

"I went into the office and pretended to talk about another matter with the manager, who mentioned in passing that some other men—<u>some darker-skinned men</u>—had loaded the contents of the unit into a yellow rental truck a few hours before, which would have been while we were gone to Monterrey. Before they had driven off, he said he had told them theirs' was the busiest unit in the whole complex, but they had only stared at him without replying. The man told me that come to think of it, <u>they did not speak much English</u>. I laughed, and acted as if I passed it off. He shrugged, which suggested to me he still did not realize how interested I was in the individuals.

"Two times <u>I disguised myself as a Mexican laborer and walked across the International Bridge</u> and wandered about Nuevo Laredo. In cantinas and other places, I struck-up conversations with some of the local fellows I managed to befriend with beer and tequila. <u>I came away with some information that was quite revealing.</u>

"Everywhere I went (<u>on both sides of the border</u>), people were talking about this <u>"José Aldrada"</u> individual, <u>and a newcomer, a younger, red-haired fellow, supposedly from "another country",</u> who was his new assistant in charge of <u>"military matters."</u>

"They said "Aldrada" was getting rid of anyone and everyone who had had any connections to the former drug lord on the border; the "Hector Marco" individual.

Some of the people I talked with said they had heard that Aldrada had been behind Marco's death in a house fire, which had suited them just fine.

"In fact, <u>I was very surprised to find out how well most of the local citizens in Nuevo Laredo were taking to the new man, Aldrada.</u> Our earlier information that he was feared by the population did not seem to be correct. On the contrary, many people, including one police officer I spoke with, looked on Aldrada favorably and believed that their lives were going to be much better, now that Marco was gone.

"On the subject of police and other officials, there is no doubt that in most governmental agencies—up to and including the Federal Government in Mexico City, the local police and the local governing bodies—are at the very least looking the other way from Aldrada's activities. I heard more than once that some officials are reputedly on his payroll.

"From the outset, I kept hearing about the new <u>"military training"</u> that would start soon and that many young men seemed to be looking forward to it. I found out that <u>such "military training" had nothing to do with the Mexican Army and everything to do with Aldrada.</u> At a bar, an inebriated fellow bragged to me that he and some of his "compadres", would soon start training for <u>"Aldrada's Pistoleros"</u>, as they were already calling the <u>"paramilitary force"</u> that, from all indications, would soon come into being. <u>"Real 'Army-type training"</u>, the fellow had said, <u>"with real weapons the new military leader is bringing to us."</u>

"<u>CONCLUSIONS</u>: I could dismiss most of this as "just talk", except that I heard it consistently in and around Nuevo Laredo. "Aldrada's Pistoleros"; the "new military leader from another country"; and the "real

449

Army training and weapons" were subjects of discussions I overheard on <u>both sides of the border</u>.

"I would suggest we insert an agent into the so-called "Aldrada's Pistoleros." Something far beyond a Drug Lord's regular activities is going on down here."

James R. Randolph

* * *

Government Prison Near Caracas, Venezuela; the Next Day:

"You say you will supply our people with weapons and training?" The man in prison garb stared open-mouthed at "Guido Lopez", who was sitting at the table across from him. He glanced at a nearby guard, who did not seem to be paying any attention to them. The fellow lowered his voice to a whisper. *"All these guards are on my payroll."*

Hoping the imprisoned man sitting in the room with him was telling the truth, in low tones Guido explained how he had met the man's "compadres'" at Facundo's place and how the "Organization" would soon be helping to organize, equip and train the prisoner's followers on the outside with Eastern-Bloc weapons, including armored vehicles, assault helicopters and their auxiliary equipment. The man, still wearing his "colonel's" insignia, looked thunderstruck when Guido told him about the joint training régimen his forces and Colombian revolutionaries would soon begin in the jungles. "This is *'fantástico'*, señor! *Now* my efforts will go along with the others! We are all revolutionaries!" The animated Venezuelan seemed to be thinking as he caught his breath. "You say this 'Retchko' hombre has new-type *Soviet* weapons?"

When Guido told him the Ukrainian was former Soviet military with connections to suppliers all over the world, the young-looking man slapped his palms on the table and leaned back, grinning. He went on to tell the Russian about his ambitions to take-over Venezuela by election, then transform the country into a one-party society, using the country's oil revenues to bankroll his plans.

"We will have the *'Yanquis'* pay for their own demise!" he gloated. To do this, he told Guido, he would need a ready-made paramilitary force to back him up in the future confrontations with the regular Venezuelan military that must take place before he came to power. "This is *'perfecto'!"*

The man motioned to the guard for a paper and pen. "Mí 'compadre' in *Nicaragua* will be very interested in all this, señor." The youthful-looking colonel pushed the scrap across the table. "He is out of office, now, but will be back in power, again, I am sure." The fellow glanced at the guard, who still feigned disinterest in their discussion. "He has connections to the Russians, too, señor . . . he is true 'Revolutionary'! You must go to see him."

* * *

Between Monterrey and Nuevo Laredo, Five Days Later:

The outer fences of the Monterrey airport raced past as the van scooted beneath the "To Nuevo Laredo" sign at the entrance ramp onto the northbound freeway.

Alex glanced at his passenger."I trust you had a successful meeting?"

Guido Lopez pulled some notes from a briefcase. "I would say so, even though the Nicaragua hombre recently lost his re-election, and is out of power, now. But he says he is optimistic for the future."

"Can we help him?"

"I talked with him at his 'casa' for many hours. He told me the whole story of his struggle against the 'Yanqui Imperialists'." Guido ran down his notes and went on. "He said he has had to fight the Yanquis ever since *'Reagan'* tried to get rid of him with the *'Contras'*. He still sees the Americans as the enemy. Did you know the 'Nicaraguan National Anthem' has a line in it that says, *'Yanqui, the enemy of humanity'?"*

451

"He said the Americans had once traded with the Iranians, an avowed enemy of theirs', in order to get around laws forbidding involvement against the Nicaraguan leaders. By a complicated series of maneuvers, the Americans had sold goods, including some weapons, to Iran and used the illegal funds to support the counter-revolutionaries the Americans called the "Contras", who were fighting guerilla warfare against Nicaragua's elected, legitimate government. Then Washington got caught and it all came out. He said it had been most embarrassing for the American régime.

Guido went on. "He told me his best supporters in those days were the Soviets . . . along with Algeria, North Korea, Vietnam, Venezuela and Cuba. Especially Cuba and Algeria—they supplied him with large amounts of small-arms weapons he said were perfect for arming his citizens against the 'Yanqui' invasion he was sure would come. But the 'Americanos' had used "mercenaries"—paid foreigners—to do their dirty work."

Guido turned to the next page of his notes. "He was disappointed that the Soviets would only give him some obsolete helicopters—not the *'MIG-Twenty-One's'* he said Nicaragua needed to fend off the Americans. He said he believed the American régime bullied the Russians to not supply the jet fighters to him. But it all came to nothing when he lost the re-election."

"The Nicaragua hombre says he will visit Fidel in Cuba, soon. And he seems to have a real admiration for the colonel I spoke to in the Venezuela prison, the other day. I told him what we are doing with that group and the Colombian drug men and that we can give him a very good deal for weapons and training of his private militia. He acted interested, but I got the impression he had lost some of the fire he once had—he even talked about 'religion', of all things!"

* * *

Federal Building; Dallas, Texas:

Randolph leaned back in his chair at the Dallas Federal Building and frowned at the message just delivered to him. It was Watering's reply to the report from Laredo:

JIM,

GOOD INFORMATION ABOUT NUEVO LAREDO, BUT YOU ARE AWARE THAT CONGRESS HAS FORBIDDEN INTERFERENCE IN ANOTHER COUNTRY'S INTERNAL AFFAIRS. EMBEDDING AN AGENT INTO THE PARA-MILITARY FORCE YOU DESCRIBE WOULD VIOLATE SUCH CONGRESSIONAL DIRECTIVES. THIS IS A MEXICAN MATTER; IT IS FOR THEM TO FOLLOW-UP.

REGARDS, WATERING.

Randolph was sure the Mexicans would do nothing of the sort—if anything, they were in cahoots with Aldrada, already—but the letter left open the door for him to continue his own investigation. After he had filed the earlier report to headquarters, it had occurred to him that the "new military man from another country" could be one of the Russians Watering had earlier written about to him. He had not mentioned this to his superior. He would look into it, himself.

* * *

Tanuta Refinery; the Next Morning:

This is the 'prototype'?"

Retchko ran a stubby forefinger across the plastic-bodied disc about the size and shape of two dinner plates edged together.

"Come with me, Comrade General, and I will show you how it works." With a grin, Yegor Boronov picked up the device and motioned toward the door.

The Russian led the bald Ukrainian around to a secluded space. At a parked car, Boronov pulled a strip from one of the flat sides and laid the contrivance on the trunk lid. "You will need these," he said, handing a pair of yellow-lensed eyeglasses to the older man and putting on a pair, himself.

Then he slapped the flattened outer surface of the plastic piece with the palm of his hand.

Take off your glasses," Boronov said.

Retchko pulled away the lenses and gaped in amazement.

The car was gone!

"Wh—where *is* it?"

"Put back on your glasses."

The stocky man replaced the yellow eyeglasses on his nose.

The vehicle was there in front of them!

"Where are the controls?"

"Everything is self-contained. It cancels the complete visual spectrum—light waves—something the Russian device could not do. Our academicians refined this feature after the agent brought back plans from the laboratory in America. Now it is complete."

Boronov pulled out some keys. "Keep your glasses on . . . we are going for a drive." He gestured at the passenger-side door. "Get in, Comrade General."

In a minute the electronics expert was maneuvering the car out of a driveway onto the main road. As the vehicle picked up speed, Retchko lifted the yellow glasses and saw nothing—even his and Boronov's bodies were not there. When he dropped the plastic frames back onto his nose, everything appeared normal. The Security Chief shook his bald head, his pulse pounding. They really *were* invisible!

"How is it that I can hear the car's engine while we are talking to each other?"

"When you have the glasses on, it creates an audio path to your ears . . . whatever has become invisible outside the car, you can hear inside. Step outside, and the machine is silent, whether or not you are wearing the yellow glasses."

Just then, as they drove by some buffalo grazing alongside the road, Boronov gave the horn a long blast. The sound did not seem to disturb the animals in the slightest, even though it sounded very loud to the men inside the car.

Retchko's pulse was pounding in anticipation. "This is incredible! How soon can we get these to our agents?" He thought about the people-smuggling operation getting underway in Nuevo Laredo—this device would be perfect for it!

"A laboratory in Lagos is making them. They can have a dozen ready in five days."

The general did some fast figuring. Another air shipment was set to leave for Havana at about that time. "I want you to have them ready in *four* days."

Boronov looked to be in thought for a moment. "As you wish, Comrade General."

At the parking space, Retchko handed the yellow-lensed eyeglasses back to Boronov. "Very impressive demonstration, Comrade Yegor."

While he was making his way back toward his office, Lisa Anaya emerged from the computer building across the way and stepped across the open space in the direction of the satellite-control blockhouse. As the girl walked along, her hips swaying in a short sundress, the portly Ukrainian stared at her fluid stride, her long, creamy legs, her sinewy sandaled feet. He was sure she did not see him. And he did not care if she had a boyfriend—in particular that nobody Frank Ogawan. Betty Nkrume was still in Lagos. Very soon he would take care of some unfinished business with the young female electronics engineer.

* * *

To: General Retchko

From: Norbert Ezego

Subject: Update on Progress in New Jersey, USA

"When I first got here, I found men driven by ideology but lacking the necessary knowledge about explosives preparation and handling. Fortunately, when the Chechen men arrived from Nuevo Laredo they were able to organize the men by their skills and educational levels and start working on the project.

"Obtaining sizable quantities of ammonium-nitrate fertilizer (the explosive component) in small purchase lots so as to not arouse suspicion has been complicated. We had to find several sources in the New

York City area that were sufficiently separated from each other and buy the material in small amounts—a few twenty-three kilogram bags at a time (fifty pounds, American), which took a while, since the amount of fertilizer that will be necessary to do the World Trade Center job will be many hundreds of United States pounds. We had to buy special tanks in which to store the diesel fuel, the explosive accelerator.

"At first the Chechens were surprised at how careless the local men were about handling the materials during the mixing process. According to the chief Chechen explosives expert, a sudden movement resulting in a spark might have ignited the mixture at any time in an uncontrollable explosion that could have taken out several city blocks. This matter has since been resolved.

"To preserve secrecy and to have more room, we moved our operation to a larger rented warehouse in Newark, New Jersey. Here, we can do our business without the danger of anyone else taking notice. From here, we can even see the target "Twin-Towers", across the river in Lower Manhattan.

"One thing, however, does keep impeding our progress, in my opinion. Several times every day, all the other men stop everything and unroll towels and kneel down and start chanting. (You know my views on that sort of thing.) This causes much delay in the preparation of the explosives and of the overall project. Even so, I believe we can still meet our original planned time-frame to carry out the mission in or around January, 1993, or soon thereafter.

"Our plan is to load a rental delivery "truck" (that is what they call the "lorries", here) with the explosives and drive it to the basement garage of the buildings.

(There is a competition as to who will do the actual job.) In the morning of the selected day, they will park it next to a main support column with the timers set.

"Which column to use for maximum effect is being determined now by one of the men who has taken a job there as a cover to study the layout of the place. (By the time of the explosion, all of the involved men will have either left the United States or will be about to do so.)

"At this time, we have nearly completed mixing the materials. Packing the mixture into the containers will soon follow. The day before the mission we will load the truck (lorry) and make final preparations.

"I will be leaving for Lagos in a few days. I can meet you there. Regards to you and the Chief.

Ezego.

* * *

Tanuta Refinery; Four Days Later:

Retchko leaned back at his desk and studied the two new messages. The first, from Ezego, pleased him very much—the billing to "U" would be substantial. Ezego's report,stated that in January or February they would reap the results of their handiwork. It looked as if the "Americanskis" would be in for an "Unhappy" New Year.

The people-pipeline through Nuevo Laredo seems to be working well, based on how easy it had been to get the Chechens across the border into Texas disguised as Mexicans with the fake papers from the Cartel's printing plant in Nuevo Laredo. The smuggling system, for both goods and people, would work even better when they started using the invisible and silent technology,

457

which would be soon—the dozen devices would be aboard the next flight to Havana, bound for Mexico and then to Texas.

The hairless man lit a cigarette and picked up the second missive, which was from Busa, who was in Lagos for a while. As blue smoke swirled around him, Retchko read down the pages.

An American named *'Kip Leeds'* would be arriving in Lagos in a few days to set up an account at the "Imperial Industrial Bank". The funds would be used to make legitimate the twenty-million dollars the security men had seized not long ago at the Lagos airport from a British bank agent who had gone to the crematorium shortly thereafter. Eventually, the money, which was blackened, would go to one of the Cayman banks to be divided among the several "top men", including himself. But first, it would have to be "laundered", something with which the Ukrainian was not familiar, but he guessed it somehow made the money legal, or at the least, un-traceable. Busa was saying the American's bank account would be used as a "compensating balance" to move the money to Madrid, the first stop on its route to the Caymans. For doing this, they had told this "Leeds" fellow, who was conveniently in the petrol business in Texas, America, he would get six-million dollars. *Of course, he would not.* The Chief himself would be involved. The banker Krasheev would handle the paperwork. Others in on the deal were Busa's secretary, Mickey; along with the lawyer, "Mike" Awadube and Betty Nkrume. He had arranged the scheme so that Colonel Ajiboy would know nothing of it.

Looking ahead, he would have Ezego tail Leeds to make sure that the man did not double-cross them when he returned to America and to uncover any other worthwhile information.

* * *

Guainia Department, Eastern Colombia; Three Weeks Later:

The five dark-green helicopters pounded across the treetops and dropped, one at a time, into the clearing the new troops had hacked out of the jungle. As the aircraft arriving from Cuba *via* the seas off Baranquilla settled onto the ground, their rotor blasts throwing up leaves and small debris, the expatriate Russian, Andrey Malinovsky, now called "Andres Martinez", rubbed his hands together in satisfaction. The heavy assault helicopters NATO called "Hind" were the same type he had flown for the Soviet Union in Afghanistan. Now, the training of the Colombian and Venezuelan recruits could move ahead in earnest.

* * *

Cigarette smoke wafted around Retchko while he read the reports Alex had sent him overnight. As the bald man went along, page-by-page, from time-to-time he nodded in satisfaction—the Cartel's operations along the Mexican border with Texas and in South America were unfolding far more quickly and thoroughly than he would have ever envisioned.

The first statement reviewed the latest activities in and around Nuevo Laredo. The connection the Russian "Pedro" had made with the "Aldrada" man was bearing its first fruits: the new training camp he had supervised to be built in a canyon outside of town was now up and running. On the first day, hundreds of enthusiastic new recruits had showed up to join Aldrada's forces. Just in time, as the first supplies had arrived only the day before at the end of its tortuous journey from Cuba. The shipment had included the basic weapons and ammunition, along with hand grenades, rocket-propelled grenades, plastic explosives, land mines, security-fence materials, electronic monitors, some ex-KGB immobilizing devices seized in Chechnya—and the very important invisible technology modules, along with the yellow eyeglasses. Alex was writing that they had already tried out the light-and-sound-cancelling units with startling results. And this was just the beginning; another planeload of paramilitary supplies was bound from Lagos for Cuba this very day to be hauled overland from boats coming ashore on an isolated beach along the Mexican coast to take to the camp. The objective was to build a force that would keep the Mexican Army away from the border. Even though some of the regular Army officers were secretly on the payroll of Aldrada so as to look the other way, the

"Big Man", Aldrada, wanted to eventually have the *only* military force along the Rio Grande.

Crowds of illegals, fake papers in hand, were now pouring across into Texas, bloating the Cartel's "laundered"—(there was that word, again)—bank accounts. The general at first had been concerned about depositing Organization funds into local banks, until Alex assured him that the institutions they were using were controlled by Aldrada. In the short time the man had been in power in Nuevo Laredo, it looked as if he had taken over nearly everything.

In the jungles of Eastern Colombia, Alex wrote, Malinovsky was well along in training the combined Colombian-Venezuelan force, now that the helicopters had arrived. The former Spetsnaz officer was applying the same rigid régimen he had learned and used in the Russian Special Forces to these men, and from Alex's account, they were taking to it with enthusiasm. From his prison cell, the Venezuelan political leader had gotten out the word about how pleased he was the way things were going.

The little trainer airplanes had already arrived in eastern Colombia from Argentina. The Cartel had bought them through a dummy company; the Argentinians never did learn the actual destination of the lightly-built, yet rugged flyers that were holdovers from the *'Malvinas'* affair in the Falklands of a few years before. After the pilot training was finished, the little airplanes would fly finished cocaine out of the deep-jungle processing labs to small-town airfields around Caracas and Maracaibo on the coast. From there, the goods would go north to the huge market in the United States. Another route would soon open through Nuevo Laredo, using the fake papers and the "invisible technology".

Obtaining the helicopters and getting them down into Martinez's isolated jungle lair had been a tough matter. First, he had had to convince the Castro government to let go five of its Russian-built helicopters—with the promise of quantities of lubricants the Cartel would supply from the Libyan allotment. But the Cubans were low on spare parts; the recent difficulties with the Russians had dried-up maintenance supplies. The Cartel would have to locate more of them. India was a possibility.

460

The flight crews had had to rig extra fuel tanks on the helicopters in order to make the non-stop flight from a ship circling offshore all the way down into eastern Colombia, a distance of several hundred kilometers, considerably beyond their usual range.

They had all made it safely to their nearly-inaccessible destination, however, and from reports out of the jungle, the student pilots were coming along well in their training régimen.

Andres wrote that right away a matter of concern had come up: the lack of women. To solve the problem, he had hired some local girls to stay-over in cabins newly-built at the camp for the purpose. The complaints had ended.

In Medellin, Alex had spent some days with the local drug kingpin, who had decided that with his men's military and police experience, he would use the new weapons and supplies to bolster his ongoing operations. Alex reported he had arranged to bring down a training force in the near future to set up a camp for additional recruits. In a few days, the trio of big twin-engine transports the Cartel's operatives had located for sale at an airport in Panama would arrive and start a shuttle drug delivery service from Medellin to a small airport in western "Arkansas", in the United States. The insignificant airstrip had been chosen because it was not on any regular flight paths, yet had good highway connections, particularly to the north, toward Kansas City, and southward, in the direction of Dallas and Houston. According to the advance-man who had set up the arrangements, the locals did not seem to realize (or care) what was going on. He would soon do trial runs with the airplanes using the invisible modules. If, as expected, they proved successful in evading detection and/or pursuit by the Americans, they would be put into general use for all smuggling operations as the modules became available.

As for Facundo in Cali, the man's order, which had been very large, had already been delivered to him. After his men had finished hiding the goods in caverns, Alex, along with Andres, who would take a break from his duties in the deep woods of eastern Colombia, would go there and set up another training camp in the mountains.

Then there had been Alex's intriguing follow-up message. A young hombre who said he was from El Salvador came by Aldrada's office today, Alex wrote, and after being searched by the border lord's bodyguards, was let in to see the Head Man. The visitor—who sported many tattoos, mostly obscene, Alex noted—said he had a proposal for the "Leader of the Border", as he put it. The youthful Salvadorean said his organization numbered in the tens of thousands of mostly young people—men and women—whose intentions were to control entire cities across North America through various forms of intimidation and physical power. Whole city governments and their police departments in some parts of America were already mastered by them, he said, particularly in some towns in the southwestern United States.

What the fellow wanted, he had said, were weapons and training to become a truly effective counter to the regular *Norte* and *Centro Americano* authorities. Their group had heard about the doings of Aldrada's men along the border with Texas and wanted to investigate the possibility of joining them in a common venture inside the United States.

Retchko took a deep draw on his cigarette, thinking. If the Cartel played things right, they could parlay this ambitious fellow's desires into a vast new source of funds and influence for the Organization—an unlimited supply of enthusiastic manpower could literally be dropping into their laps. The general knew that Agent "U" was looking for recruits and troopers for his new group; such an arrangement would grant the Asian mountain man access to a whole new part of the world, including the cities and towns of North America. Coupled with the Drug Lords' rising power in South America, there was every possibility for whole new spheres of influence for the Organization.

Retchko pulled out a pad and pen and scribbled some notes. He would contact the robed, bearded man in the mountains of Tora Bora about all this.

On another matter, Busa had called from Lagos in the afternoon to tell him that the American, "Kip Leeds", had spent the past two days in the city setting up his bank account at the Imperial Industrial Bank and getting the paperwork with

Krasheev in order. Now they could move the twenty-million dollars to Spain using his cover. Busa said the fellow had no suspicion of the exact reason he had set up the accounts—the fifty-thousand-dollars he had brought were a so-called "compensating balance" on a petroleum deal that was nothing of the sort. And, of course, Leeds would never again see his money, or the promised six-million dollars commission. And if he should ever become agitated about it, he would be "taken care of" by Cartel agents *anywhere in the world* in the "usual" manner.

The bald man checked his watch—at the same airport Ezego would be boarding the KLM flight to Amsterdam at about this moment. His sources at the terminal had tipped him off a little while ago that Leeds was leaving for Texas tonight on the same plane. Ezego would tail him to his destination. From now on, it would be important for the Organization to always know the American's whereabouts.

For Retchko, there was one more thing: he had recruited Busa's diminutive servant, "Mickey—whom the Chief of Security had found to be actually quite intelligent, belying his appearance of a witless dwarf—to follow Ezego without the man knowing it. The Ukrainian had arranged for the insignificant-looking Nigerian to travel on the same flight as Ezego and the American, except that the small fellow would be in First Class, in another part of the airplane, wearing a disguise to keep Ezego and Leeds from recognizing him.

Even though Ezego's performance so far had been satisfactory, Retchko never trusted *anyone,* and having Mickey keeping tabs on him would be good insurance. Having multiple agents on the same job without any of them knowing about the others was always a good backup strategy; he had used the technique many times.

Now, the only question would be whether or not he could trust *Mickey*. He would use the others' evaluations to double-check him, as well. In the process, he would build *'dossiers'* on every one of them, in case he needed evidence for future blackmail.

One could never be too careful.

* * *

'Guido Lopez' drove the white van up to a position close behind the car in front of him. Ahead, the American guards at the International Bridge were checking every vehicle bound for Texas. Now the agent in the uniform was nodding; the gate was going up. As the front car moved forward, Guido closely followed automobile; the van nearly touching the car's bumper. In a few seconds, *both* vehicles were beyond the crossing. In his rear-view mirror he saw that the gate was going back down. A thrill of satisfaction ran through the Russian—the module on the van's top had performed perfectly! Not only was the vehicle and all its occupants invisible, it was also completely silent!

The fourteen passengers, all illegals bound for the "coyote" who was waiting for them an hour's drive ahead, sat in their seats, taking in the sights of their new country through their yellow eyeglasses. From inside the van, everything looked normal to them; in fact, they had no idea they were part of an experiment. None had been suspicious when he had handed out the glasses to them before they climbed on board, telling them to *not* take them off under any circumstances; to them the van had looked normal. But if they had taken off the spectacles, themselves and the vehicle would have vanished. As a prototype run to test the "invisible technology" in action—so far, so good.

At the "INTERSTATE 35" sign, Guido swung the van up the ramp onto the broad, four-lane highway and set the cruise control—now that he was sure the system was working, he would sit back and enjoy the scenery. One thing about American highways, he had discovered: they were generally smooth and well-marked; much better than the average road in Russia.

Fifteen minutes later, he turned off onto two-laned "Highway 83"—the instructions said the fellow would be in a blue van forty miles or so ahead in a town called, "Catarina", at the intersection of "Highway 133". The password would be "Hombre"."

In three-quarters-of-an-hour, they passed a "Welcome to Catarina" sign, and approached a marker for the other highway. Sure enough, on the side of the road, was a parked blue van. A greasy-haired man sat behind the steering wheel, smoking a cigarette. Knowing his van was still invisible, Guido decided to drive around to the other side of the block to let out the illegals.

When the thirteen men and one woman had stepped around the corner, out of the line of sight of the van, he collected the eyeglasses—at no time had they known that they and the vehicle had been incomprehensible to all others.

Hombre!" Guido called out to the man, who stepped out of his blue van.

"Hombre . . ." the fellow returned, with a quizzical look at the fistful of saffron spectacles Guido was holding. Then the man motioned to the transients, who climbed nodding, looking relieved, into the well-used vehicle.

The Russian stood watching as the blue van drove out of sight, trailing blue smoke.

In the bright sunshine, he walked back around to his own van, putting back on his yellow glasses so as to see where it was parked.

Guido decided to drive back to Laredo by a different route; he wanted to test the invisible module some more. The Russian turned the van to the right onto "Highway 133", past a sign that read, "Artesia Wells 21". 'Twenty-one "miles", he understood: the Americans measured their distances in the baffling "miles" system that only they still used. He figured it would be about thirty kilometers over to the next town; a nice little drive.

A few kilometers farther on, the silent, invisible van topped a rise. Ahead, Guido spotted a ramshackle store with gas pumps out front. A filling station! A blinking portable sign proclaimed the place to be *'Indian Joe's Store'*. He checked the guage—the tank could use a refill; this would be as good a place as any to find out some more things about the module. Guido twisted the wheel and the van bounded up to a weathered gasoline pump.

Inside the store, Tony Bitter Water glanced past the cigarette advertisements plastered on the picture window and did a double-take. Outside by the gas pumps, a man was standing as if he was "taking a leak." Frowning, the staring youth saw that a crew-cut fellow wearing bright yellow sunglasses was holding in his hand what looked like a pistol! *Was he going to rob the store?* Then Tony realized that the guy was gripping a filler nozzle, pointed slightly downward. What was he doing? The attendant reached

465

around and turned off the pump—he would have to go and see about this. An expression of surprise came onto the customer's face; he looked toward the building and saw Tony gaping at him through the glass. At once, the stranger hung up the nozzle, did a pulling motion with his left hand, lifted his foot, lunged forward and disappeared!

Tony ran out the front door. Had he imagined it? The numbers still on the pump told him that twelve-point-eight gallons had just gone . . . somewhere. The young Native American looked up and down the road, perplexed. A hundred yards away, a swirling, brownish cloud rose from the dusty pavement—moving along as if something was stirring it up.

* * *

Tanuta Refinery, the Next Morning:

Retchko hung up the telephone. The Chief had just told him he would be flying today to New York to check with the Chechens working on the "World Trade Center" project, then he would follow Ezego to Texas. This gave the general an idea: he and Betty Nkrume could also go to the 'States and look-over the new operations together. But he and the young "widow" would need passports and visas to get into America—the printing office in Lagos would have to hurry. He called Ajiboy, his uncomprehending connection in Lagos when everyone else was away, and told him to get started. Then Retchko called Betty's private telephone number in Lagos and gave her the news. She said she would be thrilled to go with him.

As he was hanging up the telephone, Boronov came in and dropped a new message onto his desk. The missive, from "U", had originated in the faraway hills of northeastern Afghanistan. The robed man's words told how pleased he would be to work with the Salvadoreans. In return for bankrolling their urban guerilla activities, he wrote, he would exact a reasonable percentage from their drug and extortion profits. Have the Organization's men in Nuevo Laredo work out the details, he said. "U" also suggested that the Central Americans should become acquainted with the temporarily-imprisoned Venezuelan colonel and his budding political operation—the two groups looked to have much in common, he believed, and, in any case, the fellow's prison term would not last much longer. If the Salvadoreans were all that ambitous, the next logical step for them would be to develop an actual paramilitary force—they could even use the new jungle training camp in eastern Colombia for the purpose. And there was one more possibility—an important one: without a doubt, Nicaragua would someday return to the revolutionary fold; a trained and armed Salvadorean paramilitary force nearby could speed up the process. There were many possibilities, "U' wrote; it was important to keep the momentum going.

The bald man glanced for an instant at the bottom paper of the sheaf from which he had been reading, then stared wide-eyed at the page, hand-written in Russian, relayed from Tora Bora through "U's"satellite connection. The message was from his Chechnya contact, the warlord to whom Retchko had secretly supplied information from Moscow, concerning Russian plans and movements. His rebel forces, the man wrote, had recently come across a *cache* of briefcase-type nuclear devices that had been developed by the Soviets and had been left behind after a Russian defeat by the insurgents. Would Retchko be interested in obtaining several? If so, he would sell them to the Organization at a reasonable price. "U" was in the process of buying about a half-dozen of the weapons, each of which was about as powerful as the ones with which the Americans had obliterated Hiroshiman and Nagasaki in their war against Japan years ago, except much smaller in physical size. They would be perfect, he wrote, for blackmailing reactionary governments or making political—or as in "U's" case, *'religious'*—statements that would be unmistakable and irresistable. He would use them himself, the rebel leader went on, except there were no worthwhile targets remaining in Chechnya.

Ecstatic, Retchko wrote out a message of acceptance and took it to the communications building for Boronov to encypher and transmit back Tora Bora, and on to Chechnya.

The Chief wanted him to pick up some of the new-type implants at the laboratory in Lagos to take with him to America. The

467

devices, just perfected by Boronov without Lisa Anaya's knowledge, were meant to be *swallowed*, which eliminated the necessity of the cumbersome wrist implants. The pill-type capsule was designed to attach itself in a person's lower intestine, from where it would transmit a constant signal through the receipient's blood to the orbiting satellite. It was possible, Boronov had told him, to knock out someone, force one of the capsules down the person's throat where they would involuntarily swallow it, thereby causing the individual to broadcast his or her whereabouts without the person knowing it. He was to take some of them to New Jersey, to the Chechens, who wanted to try them out, and a few examples to Texas, where Alex wanted to test them, as well.

* * *

Nuevo Laredo, Four Days Later:

Alex Salinas's eyes were wide. The expatriate Russian ripped off the paper from the printer connected to the blood-circulation machine that received messages from the satellite. "Comrades! This is from Retchko . . . .he is in *Texas*, he says!"

". . . Texas—?" The others looked away from the "fútbol" game on the television and gaped at their leader.

Alex pointed at Guido. "You fly helicopters?"

"Back in Russia . . . when we trained for Spetsnaz—"

"Andrey is still in Venezuela, and the general wants us to get a helicopter and attack a hospital!"

"Attack a hospital?"

Alex was reading aloud:

"'I am now in 'West Dallas', in North Texas. Our man tailed the American here. But a girl with dark, long hair saw and heard the Chief and myself. We have reason to believe she knows who we are and what we do."

"What does that have to do with—?"

Alex held up his hand continued reading Retchko's message:

"'The female, who goes by the name of 'Sloane Marie Ferry', is now in a hospital in Laredo.'"

"Why is she in a hospital in Laredo?"
Alex shook his head for silence and read on:

"The subject female has the new-type implant in her stomach that is broadcasting her location. The Chief wants you to destroy her in the hospital before she can divulge any information to the American authorities. Repeat—she is to be eliminated at once. Suggest you use helicopter assault on her room. Determine the subject's exact location and hit her with an aerial strike. Use the invisible, silent module with a helicopter. Retchko."

"But we do not know at which hospital she is, nor in which room."
Alex gave the others sharp glances. "We will just have to find out—and quickly."
"The rockets will have to use a homing device to be accurate."
"We must locate her room and put the transponder close by it."
Guido spoke up. "Let us disguise ourselves as newspaper reporters."
Alex nodded. "That is a good idea . . . while we are distracting her by asking questions, one of us can mark the target with the rocket transponder."
"There is a paramedic helicopter hangar at the Nuevo Laredo hospital . . . we can overpower it."
Alex looked at his wristwatch. "It is three-fifteen . . . we will do a satellite-scan now. Later, we will find the girl and pay her a visit."
The Russian"s brown-tinted eyes scanned around the room at the other Organization men, disguised, like himself, as Mexicans. "We will assault the helicopter hangar at eight-thirty this evening. Then, we will kill the American girl."

~~~~

PART THREE

PLAZA MAYOR

-19-

Near Los Alamos, New Mexico, at a U.S. Government Location; Two Days Later:

Sloane Marie Ferry stirred her morning coffee and gazed out the glassed-in sun-porch at the orange sunrise that was poking its face over the top of the distant purple mountain topped by a cap of white. The young woman pulled the guest-robe tighter around her slender figure against the early-autumn air of northern New Mexico.

Just then, the glass sliding door whooshed open behind her. "Ah, I see you are up, already," a male voice spoke, "mind if I join you?" James Richard Randolph, in a running outfit, set his coffee cup on the wicker table and took a seat.

Sloane smiled at the man who had brought her here on the government airliner, along with her father, Ned Ferry, and their friend, Kip Leeds, to escape the attackers who had shot-up the hospital room where she was recuperating after being rescued from abductors two days earlier. She had avoided the attack when they had moved her to a new room just minutes before the building was assaulted by a mysterious military force, apparently from the air, although no one had seen or heard any aircraft. Her little boy and the nanny, Mrs. Jackson, had arrived the previous evening from West Dallas, Texas.

"I try to have my morning coffee before Nicky wakes up . . . to keep up with him!"

The *'Federal Investigation Agency's'* Dallas Bureau Chief looked out the glassed, conservatory-like room at the distant snow-capped peaks. "Nice sunrise, is it not? I came here for the first time some years ago, during my training. They brought us here to familiarize us with this place. I've been back several times."

"What does the 'Agency' do here?"

"We sequester people in the *'Witness Protection Program'* while we provide them new identities. It's very safe and secure."

"Am I getting a 'new identity'?"

"We'll see." While Sloane looked out and sipped her coffee cup from both hands, her elbows on the table, his eyes ran up and down her slim figure outlined in the robe. For the first time since that terrible day two years ago when his wife Sabina and their son, Trini, had died in the car wreck, Randolph was finding himself attracted to another woman. Of course, he could not tell her this.

He pointed at a distant chain-link fence, backlit in the sunrise. "See that fence? It's electrified and has all kinds of warning devices."

Sloane stirred her coffee some more and glanced at the man sitting next to her. "How long have you been an agent?"

"Since I got out of college . . . sixteen years ago."

The girl did some fast mental arithmetic. He would be about in his late-'thirties she guessed. "I graduated last year—after I took off a year to have Nicky."

Sloane picked-up his unspoken question. "Let me re-fill my coffee cup and I'll tell you all about it."

Before he could offer to do it himself, she was making for the sliding door. As she stepped away barefoot, the government man could not help but observe the suggestion of her willowy figure beneath the white terrycloth robe. From what he could see, she also had nice, defined legs. With a start, he realized her long, black hair was just like Sabina's had been.

But Sloane Ferry was, in fact, quite different from his late wife: Sabina had been a high-strung Cuban-American television reporter who was always precise about things and outspoken in defense of her people and her culture; always ready to engage people on her own terms. Sloane, on the other hand, had a winsome way about herself that he found engaging; at the same time she demonstrated an admirable fortitude that had carried her through the kidnapping and the shoot-out at the hospital, two nights ago. And it was no small accomplishment that she was a licensed investigator—from his own experience with the *'Texas Investigator State Board Examination'* he knew that you had to have detailed knowledge in great amounts to get through it. Hadn't she told him she had passed the test on the first try? It had taken him two times.

After what had happened to Sabina and his son he had forgotten—that is, he had *tried* to forget—how it was with children. Since Sloane's two-year-old boy—"Nicky", she called him—had arrived from Texas yesterday, along with the older-woman nanny, he had been re-learning what it was like to be around a kid. The ache of losing his wife and son would never go away, he knew, but he must try to move on with his life.

The sliding door scooted open and Sloane came back out onto the glassed porch with a coffee pot. "Refill?"

"Of course."

She poured the black liquid into his and her cups and looked into Jim Randolph's eyes. "Nicky's father was my college boyfriend . . ."

* * *

At the Same Time:

"The read-out is coming in loud and clear!" Malinovsky called up to Alex at the wheel of the invisible white van. "The global positioning map shows we are two-hundred-thirty-six kilometers from the source of the signal."

"The radio signal from the inside the girl's stomach?"

"According to 'Ezego', the capsule-chip is designed to lodge at the appendix. Whoever has it does not know it is there—our man in Nigeria designed it—it is most clever."

Gennady spoke up. "But the instructions say it might pass-out of the person *if they had had an appendix operation.*"

"Let us hope that the girl still has her appendix! *Retchko wants her dead—*"

Blagron was looking at a map. "How long until we get there?"

Malinovsky punched some buttons on a keypad. "Four hours . . . about."

Alex glanced back. "We will stop at the 'Training Camp' after we take care of the girl."

Malinovsky did some figuring. "It is only seven kilometers from the subject's location."

"That close?"

"That is what the positioning satellite shows. It is also very near the 'Los Alamos Laboratory' where we went last winter—where we killed all those American soldiers."

"What happened to the man who was at the camp?"

"The agent we called 'Adams'? I understand he is now back in Moscow."

"Then the place should still be there, but vacant."

"It will be a perfect hiding place."

* * *

"Oh, I am sorry!" Sloane Ferry reached over and touched Jim Randolph's forearm. "Your wife and your little boy were both killed in the wreck?"

"It was the worst day of my life. I'm still trying to get over it."

"When Dominique, who was an exchange student from France, died in the fraternity fire, I thought I would go crazy—they didn't even find anything of him in the burned-down house, except the rims of his glasses. I had just found out I was pregnant. It was a hard time for me—high blood-pressure and some other things. I even had to have my appendix out while I was pregnant!" The young woman sighed. "But having Nicky was worth it. He even looks like his father—everybody says so."

The door behind them rumbled open and Kip Leeds came out. "Ah . . . we have the 'gruesome-twosome' . . . plotting nefarious schemes, I presume—"

Sloane shook her head with a grin. "Oh, Kip! You never stop, do you!"

The oil trader set his coffee cup on the table and took a seat, stretching. He nodded at Sloane, and at the agent.

"Did she give you her life's story? I can give it to you in three short words: 'smart' . . . 'clumsy' . . . 'beautiful'.'" He gave her an exaggerated look up and down.

Randolph nodded. "I can agree on the 'smart' and the 'beautiful' parts."

"You two stop it!"

Kip reached for the coffee pot. "So how long will we be here?"

"Actually, we may be leaving, today . . . I'm expecting instructions from Headquarters."

"Where would we be going?"

"To Washington State—the 'Agency' has a place on Puget Sound where we hide people."

Sloane was frowning. "Why do you need to keep 'hiding' us?"

"Until we find out exactly who these people are, we don't want to run any risks. We even have agents staking-out your places back in West Dallas. It's driving your business partner, Brad, to distraction."

Randolph stepped away and came back with his briefcase. "I want you to tell me everything about that trip to Nigeria that time, and about the people you encountered." The agent pulled out a notepad and pen and looked hard at the blond Texan. "Think carefully—even the smallest detail might be important."

"Okay . . . it all started when Brad and I got a fax from this 'Masobe Busa' guy in Nigeria. He said he and his 'associates', as he called them, had seized twenty-million dollars of 'illegal funds' at the Lagos airport and wanted to send it to an account outside of Nigeria for their 'retirement'. He wrote that I would receive six-million-dollars as a 'commission'."

Randolph smirked. "That's the classic 'Nigerian scam'."

"Maybe, but Brad and I decided to play-along to see what would happen. When I got to Lagos, they took me to the 'Imperial Industrial Bank' to deposit fifty-thousand dollars in cash that I brought strapped around my body as a 'compensating balance', as they put it. The manager was named—I'll never forget this—'I.M. Nomoah'. It sounded like, 'I Am No More'!"

Randolph and Sloane both grinned. "Go on," the agent said.

"Then, they took me at night to the 'Nation Bank of Nigeria', to a 'Doctor Krasheev', who was a 'Director' of some sort." Kip looked thoughtful. "He seemed to be really important, at least that was how the other Africans acted toward him—a real business-like, crisp, executive-type. He wore an expensive-looking suit, I remember."

"What about the money?"

"I signed some papers and then the Krasheev guy told me the money was 'blackened', and they would show me how to 'clean' it, as he put it. The next day they took me to the Busa guy's house. There, they brought a big 'strongbox—'like a 'safe'—to his living room. Outside, were Army trucks, military helicopters were flying overhead—it seemed like a whole squad of soldiers were there." Kip gave a shudder. "All those soldiers with automatic weapons! Their leader was a really tough-talking man. I wasn't sure I would even be alive, much longer!"

"You said the money was 'blackened'?"

"This is the part that really makes me believe it was a real deal. When they opened the strongbox, inside it were several dozen wrapped 'bricks'. They told me to pull out one of the 'bricks' at random and un-wrap it. When I did, I found it was made of pressed-together papers. When I took out one of the 'papers' from the middle of the 'brick', they dipped it into several trays of chemicals, and it became an American one-hundred-dollar bill! I pulled out ten bricks and took a paper from each at random and they all became real money! I know they were real, because I paid the hotel bill with two of them and spent another at the airport in Amsterdam. No questions." He stopped. "Well, at the Lagos airport one of them was dated wrong, and they wouldn't take it, but the other one went through."

Randolph frowned. "You were lucky . . . we know that some people have had serious problems at the Lagos airport with the 'departure tax' that has to be paid in cash." *I was about to say more, then thought better of it; no need to worry these people about the deadly doings I know are taking place at Lagos's International Airport.*

"That airport was the scariest place I have ever seen."

"What else happened?"

"I almost forgot . . . after they 'cleaned' the black money, Busa disappeared! A lawyer named 'Adwadube'—'Mike' Adwadube he called himself, although I doubt 'Mike' was his real name—talked to me." Kip gave a visible shudder. "He had the most horrible-looking eyes I ever saw." Kip took a deep breath. "The guy wanted one-million, six-hundred-seventy-five-thousand dollars to 'clean' all the black money—in cash! When I told him I didn't have that kind of money, he started getting impatient. It was then that I decided Nigeria was dangerous and it was time to go home."

"Anything else?"

"When the airplane to Amsterdam was loading, Nigerian Army soldiers came aboard and took off some Americans at gunpoint!"

I know that many Americans have disappeared at that airport. But I will not tell them this.

Kip went on. "On the flight from Amsterdam to Dallas, a very black man kept staring at me. When we landed, I had to lose him in a taxi. The next day, Sloane was kidnapped."

Just then, the door slid open. "Mommy!" came a child's voice.

"Nicky!" Sloane put out her arms and swept the little boy up onto her lap.

"He was asking for you." The older-woman nanny, in a uniform, stepped onto the porch, nodding to the others.

"Did you sleep well, young man?" Randolph spoke to the little newcomer.

The youngster put his thumb in his mouth and leaned back against his mother, blinking at the man.

"I think that means, 'yes'," Sloane said.

All at once, the boy slid off his mother's lap and stepped over to the government man, his arms upraised. Randolph, surprised, pulled him onto his own lap, where the child leaned back, his thumb in his mouth, exactly as before.

All the adults looked around at each other.

Kip broke the silence. "A 'bonding moment' I believe . . ."

Sloane gaped at her little boy. Then her eyes and Randolph's met.

The man flushed scarlet. "I guess he likes me."

Sloane spoke up. "He's never done that before to a strange man."

Kip grinned with a mock shrug. "Come on, Sloane, he's not *that* strange!"

It was the girl's turn to blush. "I mean, a 'stranger'—a man he's not known."

Kip kept on. "There's a first time for everything!"

Ned Ferry had stood back inside the doorway during the little scene with the boy and had seen and heard it all. Sloane's father turned into the kitchen nodding to himself. This government fellow, "Randolph", the "Agency" man, was getting along well with his daughter and his grandson, it seemed. For sure, the two had a lot in common: both had lost a loved one in an accident—*two*, in Randolph's case—and a boy child had figured in both incidents. As a result, both were trying to overcome terrible misfortune and heartbreak—and *both were detectives.* Were there possibilities, here? Would they see this mountaintop sojourn as an opening for them? Because, to him, something else was obvious: *Those three people—including the little boy—all need each other.* Perhaps he could try to help nurture things along.

In a minute, he stepped outside. "Jim—there's a call for you on the scrambler telephone."

* * *

Outside the Compound; Ten Hours Later:

The four men in paramilitary gear crawled through the tall sagegrass up a short rise to the bottom of a chain-link fence. Beyond, across a silent, pasture-like prairieland, stood a low, rambling ranch-house surrounded by barns and other outbuildings, all outlined in the setting sun. From their position at the corner of the kilometer-square layout they could see two of the four sides of the enclosed space.

"It reminds me of the armory we attacked, that time."

Another motioned to a soldier holding a device in his hands. "Are you *sure* this is where the signal is coming from?"

The second man raised himself up onto his elbows and swept a hand-held device back and forth. As he did so, a little light flashed on a display when it was aimed at a certain point. He did this several times, always with the same result. "It is coming from that direction."

By the time they had scooted the distance to the far rear corner, everything had taken on the pale cast of early evening. Directly overhead, the white semi-circle of a half-moon presided over the scene.

One of the men gazed through the fence at the rear of the moonlit buildings and frowned. "This is a strange ranch—there are no animals on it." The others cocked their ears—except for the mournful howl of a distant coyote, nothing but the silent landscape came back at them. "I do not see or hear any people, either."

"But they *must* be here!" The fellow with the detector pointed in the direction of the house. "The signal is coming from over there!"

The first man clipped a wire onto the fence. A red light on an instrument he was holding came on. "It is electrified, with sensors." He gestured for the men to crawl along the fence.

Near the rear of the complex they came to some heavy insulated electrical cables. One of the men pulled out a small torch and goggles. With some quick blue snapping flashes, the connectors parted. The light on the instrument went out."The fence is now off'," he said.

One of the men took a cutter and snipped the fence. In a minute, there was a hole big enough for a man to scoot through. The intruders crawled through the opening.

Inside the enclosure, the men loped in the direction that the device indicated.

The paramilitary with the detector held up and pointed at some grass. He walked around in a circle, frowning. "It is down there."

"*Down there?* It is supposed to be in the girl's—"

One of the men pointed at some round metal objects protruding from the ground near where they were standing. "It is what the Americans call a 'septic tank'. She passed it."

"What! The chip capsule is *underground?*" The men stared down in consternation at the spiky sagegrass.

"It became dislodged. She no longer has it inside her."

"It could not have been very long ago . . . the battery needs blood to stay charged!"

"Come on!" The men ran toward the rear door. With one smash, the barrier went down. Shining their flashlights, the paramilitaries dashed from room-to-room.

"They're gone!"

"Look!" One of the men pointed at a window. Outside, a pair of flickering headlights were coming toward the front of the house. The rumble of a big engine was becoming louder.

Alex motioned his weapon. "Let us get out of here!"

The Russians hustled past the downed rear door to the outside. As they ran across the clearing toward a barn, from the other side of the house the engine noises stopped. Brighter lights came on, illuminating the front of the dwelling.

They dropped into some deep shadows on each side behind the open front barn doors. "Shovels!" the first man whispered. With little 'clicks' the sharp-edged weapons favored by Spetsnaz troops— their former service—snapped down into position.

Through a slat, the men watched and waited, hardly breathing, as four soldiers, outlined in the lights from the front of the house, came into sight around the corner. Each was holding an assault rifle.

The Russians held back and watched as the Americans hunched closer toward the dark barn. On a signal from their leader, the adversary squad spread out and advanced toward the wide-open doors.

Just as they were about to step into the darkened interior, Alex gave a motion. At once, the four former Russian Special Forces troops sprang out, swinging their shovels. Each man took the opponent nearest him with a slashing thrust that caught the first pair in their throats with gurgling thumps. Before the other two could react to the sight of their compatriots going down, jerking, in froths of red, Blagron and Malinovsky swung the shovels at their throats. They, too, grabbed their nearly-severed necks with gagging sounds; gushing fountains of crimson.

Gennady glared at the bloody, twitching Americans on the ground. *"That is for Galina!"* His guttural voice had a vindictive edge.

"Come on!" The Russians dashed toward the open spot in the fence where they had cut through to crawl into the compound.

Just as they ran past another outbuilding, all at once the whole place came alive in more dazzling beams of light! *Security Floodlights!* At the same time, an earsplitting siren roared up across the building complex!

"Down! Down!" Alex called-out to the others. The men dropped into the ankle-high sagegrass. The leader gave quick motions toward the small building. "Over there!" The men scrambled behind the structure—a pump-house.

Alex peered around the corner and drew back. "There are more of them!" he whispered. "Fix bayonets! Weapons-safties off!"

Acting on instincts developed from the long drills back in the Soviet Union, the men drew out the long, slender blades and slid them onto the muzzles of the Kalashnikovs. Then came almost inaudible *"clicks"* as the safety levers eased off.

Around the same corner the first men had come, another enemy squad was loping toward them. From the way they were looking about, the Russians guessed the Americans did not know exactly where they were, or how many opponents they faced.

Alex gave a nod that the others picked up in the reflected light. The four men felt for the triggers of their 'AK-74's'.

The four Russians leaped up, and with triggers down, aimed their rifles at the enemy. The night was rent by the sudden flashes erupting from the muzzles and the earsplitting crashes of the un-silenced automatic weapons. And above it all were the still-sounding howls of the siren.

The Americans, who looked to be confused by the sudden onslaught, spun down, sprays of scarlet bursting from their bodies. But the last in line had dropped to the ground and was aiming his automatic rifle at the flashes before him. Flame erupted from his rifle.

Blagron jerked back and twisted to the ground, grabbing his left shoulder, gasping. His weapon clattered to the ground—a dark stain was already spreading across the upper part of his paramilitary fatigues.

The others leveled their weapons at the enemy, whose body jerked and flailed in the garish floodlight as high-velocity slugs tore him apart.

Malinovsky dropped down and ripped open Blagron's bloody shirt and stared at his compatriot's gaping, flooding shoulder. "It went right through you!" he told the moaning trooper, wiping his forehead, examining the round entrance wound and the jagged exit wound in back, that was bigger and bleeding. He snatched a pair of bandages from his medical kit and pressed them onto the wounds.

Alexei scanned about for more enemy. There were none. He motioned at the others.With Blagron in tow, they stumbled back to the hidden van. After starting the engine, Alex looked about. "Which way to the hideout?"

Malinovsky tuned the positioning receiver. "Go to the right,"

Before long, the invisible van turned off onto the hidden tree-lined roadway, now overgrown since their departure several months before. After passing though the multiple fences that the men remembered from their earlier "Spetsnaz" visit, the vehicle pulled up in front of the camouflaged entrance at the face of a hill.

Gennady pointed to a spot off to one side. "I believe the keypad is over there."

But when he pushed the button, nothing happened. "No electricity!"

Blagron, who was trying to stay alert, spoke up. "The generator is behind that hill," he groaned, gesturing with his good arm, "I put fuel in its tank, one time."

While the others waited, Gennady climbed around a rocky projection. In a few minutes, a small red light came on at the keypad.

This time when he pushed the button, a section of the hillside began swinging aside. Alex put the van in gear and drew the vehicle inside the echoing interior. Gennady located the entrance control on a nearby rocky wall. When the doors were closed, he turned on the big overhead lights. Off to the side, where Gennady remembered it from before, was the van he, Blagron and Malinovsky had ridden up from Monterrey with Colonel Golubko and the others. Gennady wondered where the colonel was now, and what he was doing.

"We will stay here," Alex announced. "Blagron will have some time to recover."

Malinovsky spoke up. "I remember there was a medical room, here."

"How about food?"

"All the rations here are freeze-dried—all we have to do is add water and heat it up," Gennady put in. "'Adams','" the fellow who was here before, showed me how he did it."

As they were unloading the van, Alex frowned. "Did we bring Blagron's weapon with us?"

No one could remember picking it up from where he had dropped it when he was shot.

"It is still there, then."

Alexei shrugged. "Never mind—it will give the Americans something to think about."

* * *

Washington, D.C., the Next Morning:

His forehead furrowed, Watering re-read the just-decoded report. *Ten of the special security guards at the supposedly-secret New Mexico compound had been found dead this morning on the grounds; six had been shot multiple times and the others were nearly decapitated. A Russian- made "Kalashnikov AK-74" automatic rifle had been discovered behind an outbuilding next to bloodstains on the ground.*

Just then, an assistant stepped through the doorway. "It's the 'White House'. The 'National Security Advisor' is on the line . . . he sounds really pissed—"

* * *

"Hood Canal" Near Seattle, Washington; Two Hours Later:

Kip Leeds leaned against the porch post, took a swallow of his morning coffee and gazed at the wondrous sight of the Olympic Mountains of Washington State in the distance, their jagged, snow-capped peaks outlined in a purple-orange hue that the cool sunrise was bringing into sharp focus. On the Hood Canal before him, a black, cigar-shaped submarine from the nearby naval base moved deliberately along the waterway, its narrow, sail-like conning tower catching the rising sun; its silver, bubbling wake following along behind it. The war-boat's lazy, vee-shaped bow wave rolled ashore along the tree-lined inlet with a liquid sigh that he could hear all the way up to where they were situated in a house on the wooded hillside.

Kip turned to Sloane, who was sitting at a table in her white robe and slippers, taking-in the panoramic view over coffee. "Nothing like this back in West Dallas, is there?"

The young woman tossed back her long black hair. "It really is lovely, here."

Jim Randolph, who had just stepped onto the porch and had heard the exchange, came over and looked out at the forest around them. "Bangor, Washington", they call it. With the naval base next door, nobody can get to us." Even as he watched, the submarine was making a slow turn. "It is headed west toward the Pacific for its next patrol," he told the others.

The government man pulled up a chair and sat down. "I was just on the scrambler phone." He turned to Sloane. "'Watering'— my boss at the 'Agency'—believes the attack last night at the place where we were in New Mexico was aimed at *you.*"

Kip spoke up. "The news said ten soldiers were killed. It must have happened right after we had left."

"But why are those people trying to attack *me?*" The girl put hands to her face. "What did *I* do?"

Randolph pulled his pad out of the briefcase. "I want to review all the details about the kidnapping and the rescue." He

486

looked straight at Sloane. "Try to remember everything . . . perhaps there is still a detail or two that would be helpful in figuring out all this."

The young woman gave a sigh. "When Kip came back from that trip to Nigeria, he sent me to his house to get a notebook . . . while I was there, somebody attacked me and knocked me out. When I woke up, I was in a motel—maybe a hotel room—with some other people."

"Try to remember who were in that room."

"Well, there were three men—one was a big black-skinned man—a mean, horrible man—he tied me up and hit me." Randolph winced. Sloane shuddered and went on. "Another very dark man was small and bald-headed—he was dressed in a nice, three-piece suit. The third man was white, and there was a young, light-skinned black woman with them."

The girl looked away, in thought. "The first man—the big guy—called the little man in the suit *'Chief'* . . . I'm sure he called him that, so he must have been their leader."

"Anything about the white man that you can recall?"

"He was completely bald—he didn't even have eyebrows! I remember he talked in a heavy foreign accent—he was also the one who told the others to 'get rid of me' . . . and it seems like one of the others called him, *'General'*—"

Randolph thought about that for a moment. "No last name?"

Sloane shook her head.

"So, we have 'General Somebody' . . . 'a big black man' . . . and the 'Chief'." What about the 'light-colored black female'?"

"She was younger than the men—I guess she was not much older than I am—and quite attractive." Sloane shrugged. "I probably owe my *life* to whoever she was. I thought they were going to kill me. But she kept talking them out of it. She convinced them to do something else."

"You said they gave you an injection and that's all you remember?"

Sloane's eyes narrowed. "Just before the shot knocked me out, I heard one of them say a word like, *'Eldorado'*."

Randolph sucked in his breath. "'Aldrada'!"

* * *

At "The Agency", Washington, D.C.:

Watering put down the scrambler telephone. The agent called to his assistant. "Get me Tarliani in Zurich on the telephone." Then he remembered something else Randolph had just told him. ". . . and find Livshits in Moscow. I want to talk to both of them—something big has come up."

* * *

In the Underground Bunker, Near Cuba, New Mexico:

"We must take all these things with us . . ." Alexei Sorbetsky swept his hand across the workbench of "GRU"-related items he had pulled from shelves and bins in the supply room of the secret cave.

Malinovsky nodded. "*Now* we will have the same advantages over the Americans we used to have back when we were working for Moscow."

"I cannot wait to use these." Gennady Lychin was poring with great interest over the Intelligence-gathering devices and anti-personnel weapons arrayed on the table-top. "My war with the Americans will now have more ammunition."

Alex spoke up. "We will take it all to the 'mini-storage' warehouse in Laredo—no need to try to get it across the border."

Just then, Malinovsky called out. "Comrades! Come and see what is on the television!" As the men trooped into the viewing room, he pointed at the big screen. "Listen to what this man is saying!"

". . . incident took place only a few miles from the 'Los Alamos National Laboratory', where fifteen or so U. S. Marines were killed in similar fashion last winter." The thin-lipped older man in the gray suit paused and cleared his throat. "All these guard-soldiers who were killed last night were highly-trained in self-defense—yet were no match for some unknown opponent

488

who took out all of them in a brutal manner with no apparent losses to themselves. I have learned it was a very rough scene up there."

A male voice came from off-camera. "What sort of place is it where these killings happened?"

"I am told it is an isolated location that is owned by the Federal Government."

"Do the authorities have any idea who was responsible for killing those soldiers?"

"I will say this: Both these attacks looked like the work of professional military assassins—perhaps from a foreign country.

"Foreign military assassins in America?"

"There are two organizations that specialize in this sort of deep-penetration killings: the Israeli Special Forces called *'Sayeret Mat'kal',* and the Russian Special Forces known as 'Spetsnaz'— both are particularly ruthless groups that strike fear in the minds of military people everywhere. I would suggest the Russians were behind this."

"Russians? What were they doing in New Mexico?"

The man shrugged. "I have no idea."

The newscast cut to a commercial; Malinovsky turned off the TV.

"We got away from that ranch just in time," Alexei said, "remember how we passed a convoy of military vehicles on the road headed toward the place? It was a good thing the van was invisible."

Blagron shifted in his seat, grimacing from the shoulder wound. "I am ready to get back to Nuevo Laredo. Aldrada wants me to continue training his men."

"Ha! Your little girlfriend wants you to continue 'training' *her!*"

"She is pure, comrades."

"Are you going to marry her? Retchko might not go along with that."

"It is too soon. But she is strong-willed, I have found out." He grinned. "It might happen."

"When are you going to tell her you are Russian?"

An uncomfortable look came over the young man's ruddy face. "I have been thinking about that."

Headquarters, "The Agency" Washington, D.C.:

". . . and Tarliani says one of his informants tells him the 'General' is 'Head of Security' of this 'Organization', as they call it—an out-and-out crime Cartel . . ." Watering spoke again into the telephone. "'Something' is about to happen in New York, but he is not sure what it will be."

The Russian's stentorian voice came back across the line in accented English."All this fits into what we also know and have passed on to you."

The American Intelligence officer went on, "Tarliani and I are going to meet next Friday in Madrid—perhaps you could join us, there."

* * *

West Dallas, the Same Day:

"Kip! I'm glad you called!" Brad Holdon's voice sounded excited. "I got a fax this morning from 'your old friend, Busa' . . . he wants you to meet him in Madrid—yes, in Spain . . . at the end of next week. He says he will have the money with him!"

* * *

Madrid, Spain, the Next Morning:

Terenty Suslov looked over his morning newspaper at Tamara, who was feeding Larisa a Spanish breakfast. "Ah, my pretty ones! You will have your first opportunity to see one of the best things about Spain—a 'festival!'" He read on, "It is at 'Plaza Mayor', next Saturday . . . oh, and I almost forgot! Colonel Golubko is coming here on an inspection trip . . . he can join us."

* * *

490

Bangor, Washington; Later That Day:

Randolph put down the scrambler telephone receiver and looked at Kip. "That was my boss, 'Agent Watering' in Washington. He says they believe this 'General' is going to be in Madrid in a few days . . . it looks as if he will be with Busa and the money! They are setting up a *'sting'* operation." The agent turned to Sloane. "They want you to be there to identify him."

"'*Madrid'*? I—I've never been out of the country. I don't even have a passport!"

"We'll take care of it."

The agent looked at the message from Busa that Brad had faxed to Kip. "This is the break we have been waiting for!"

A thought occurred to Kip. He would need a translator! Grinning, he dug into his wallet and pulled out the card of a beautiful blonde flight attendant he had met on the recent trip to Lagos.

* * *

Frankfurt, Germany, Early Evening, the Same Day:

Nixie Garten put down the telephone receiver. Her heart was pounding; she could hardly get her breath. *'Herr Leeds'*—an American she remembered from a flight to Lagos a few days before, had just called her! Could she meet him in Madrid next week for some translation work? The young woman stared at the notes she had scribbled with the information he had given her. She could hardly believe it.

* * *

Tanuta Refinery; the Next Day:

Retchko called one of the secretaries on the intercom."Get me the Russian, Lychin, on the telephone . . . yes, in Nuevo Laredo. Also Marisol Montoya and Larry Landay in Medellin—"

By tracking their chip implants through the satellite, he knew that Gennady and the others were back at the apartment across the Rio Grande from the United States. Unfortunately, as he already knew, the men had been unable to kill the American girl in New Mexico, but there would be other opportunities. Right now, he had other things on his mind.

Through orbital surveillance, he had followed the movements of his former assistant, Montoya, and the American, Landay. He would compel them to work for him on the upcoming job in Madrid.

As he waited for the calls to connect, he glanced out the window—and did a double-take. Lisa Anaya was stepping across the parking lot. The Ukrainian's eyes narrowed as he took in her swaying form, her tight, short skirt and the blouse that showed even more cleavage than usual. Remarkable, he thought, how much like her sister she looked. And he was ready to exact his payment from her for saving her life that time in the storm. Now would be a perfect time, he thought, since Betty was in Lagos. All he had to do was get rid of that damfool friend of hers, Frank Ogawan, and do the deed.

There was a "click" and a male voice speaking Russian came on the line. "Ah, Lychin . . . I have an assignment for you. You will fly tomorrow to Havana and meet the 'Seven-Forty-Seven' and come to Lagos on it . . . we will be going to Madrid next week with Busa and others *and the money* to meet the American, 'Leeds'. *'Moreno' and 'Landa' will join up with you in Havana.*" A pause, then, "Keep your Mexican disguise. I want you to work security with me *incognito.*"

* * *

Nuevo Laredo, The Same Day:

"Oh, Pedro . . . you are hurt!" When she opened the door, Tatiana Castillo's hand flew to her mouth with a gasp; her eyes went wide at the sight of the red-headed young man's bandaged arm in a sling as he stood before her on the porch. "What *happened* to you?" The girl reached out and pulled him into the parlor.

"There was a 'mis-understanding' . . ."

"But, what—?" The girl's hands were shaking.

Petr Blagron nudged the door shut; with his good arm he grasped the 'chiquita' and held her against him in a long, lingering kiss like they had never before done; through the Mexican-style blouse that dropped low on her bare shoulders, he felt the soft mounds of her chest and knew that he wanted her now and for all time. *"Mi amor—"*

The señorita pulled back, blinking, swallowing, moistening her lips; this moment of renewal had taken away her breath. She reached for his free hand. "Let us sit and talk."

The young man followed her to a sofa where they embraced once more. "I missed you very much," he breathed, caressing her shoulders and neck with his good hand, looking into her dark-blue eyes, taking in her translucent-like skin in the dim lamplight. "We went to see some people and there was 'trouble' . . . but I will be all right—"

She rubbed his cheek, her eyes still locked into his. "Oh, Pedro, If something happened to you, I would just die . . ."

A grin flickered across his face. "Señor Aldrada said the same thing about me!"

"Oh, Pedro, you are funny!" Then she saw he had become serious. "Is something wrong?"

"Tatiana, there are many things I must tell you."

The young man told the Mexican girl about his true identity; that he was from Russia (*"Moscow is 'East of here'—although I was not completely honest with you about that; at the time, I did not know how to explain it."*); that he would not be returning to Russia ever again; many things he said to Tatiana—but leaving out much that he thought might upset her. "I will be staying here, working with Señor Aldrada."

"But, Pedro—*'Petr'*, you say—*I knew all along you were not Mexican.* Your accent was not 'Hispanic'!" Her dark blue eyes flashed into his. "I talked with my mother about it—and about your red hair . . . we decided to wait for you to confess!" She squeezed his hand.

Blagron's face turned the color of his flame-hued hair. "Now *I* am embarrassed!"

The girl leaned forward and touched her lips to his; her long black hair draped over them both; a tear started down her pale face. "Oh, *por favor,* `Petr'—do not leave me, again . . . ever."

The young Russian started to say something, but Tatiana put her fingertip to his lips. "Have you heard of the *'Sacraments'?*"

* * *

Tanuta Refinery; the Next Afternoon:

Retchko glanced at his wristwatch; it was a little after three-thirty in the afternoon; she should be arriving in a few minutes. Then he took off the timepiece—he wanted nothing to interfere with what was about to happen.

The Ukrainian re-checked his plan: he had sent Frank Ogawan to "investigate" a loss of signal from a camera and sound sensor that he had deliberately disabled. He knew it would take the conscientious African some time—perhaps the rest of the afternoon—to locate and repair the problem. Then he had sent word to Lisa Anaya that he needed some papers that were on his desk —could she bring them to his quarters? She had said she would. Typical foolish female!

He reached for the aspirin bottle—today's headaches were more frequent, it seemed; in any case, right now, he needed clear thinking. The man glanced at the open bedroom door; inside, the bedcovers were pulled back.

Just then, there came a knock.

He opened the door. "Ah, yes, Lisa."

"These are the papers you wanted, general."

The fleshy European motioned for her to come inside. "I want to go over some things with you."

The young woman took a hesitant half-step forward.

"Come, come! This will not take long."

He closed the door. Without her noticing what he was doing, his fingers moved the lock-lever. "Something to drink? Tea?"

"I guess tea will be all right."

He motioned for her to take a seat on the sofa. "I already have the teapot boiling." He left her alone in the living room and stepped into the kitchen. "Sugar?" he called out.

"Yes, fine."

The bald man stepped back into the parlor and handed her a cup, taking the other for himself.

He watched as she took the first sip. Then Lisa took a longer swallow. "Tangy tea, it is . . ." She nodded in approval and upended the little ceramic cup.

Retchko narrowed his eyes. "This tea is from China."

"You said you wanted to see some papers?"

"Ah, yes." He leafed through several pages. "This antenna, here—" his fingertip ran over a diagram of a satellite dish—"will need to be re-aimed."

The young woman shook her head, blinked her eyes. She pointed an uncertain finger at the page. "You—say this dish antenna needs to—to—be . . ."

The girl's sentence stayed unfinished; her head fell back onto the sofa cushion; her hands slid limply onto her lap. Retchko kept still for a moment, to make sure she was really out.

She was. In a minute she would re-awaken and act normally—*but would be compliant and under his power of suggestion from a hypnotic drug developed by Soviet chemists for agents in the field.* One characteristic of the liquid he had dropped into her teacup was that she would remember nothing that happened while she was under its spell—*his spell.*

The girl stirred, then appeared to become awake. "Oh, pardon me—I was very tired."

The man gave a lopsided grin. *"Perhaps you should spend more time in bed, my dear."*

Off the main room she spotted the bedroom door, through the opening she could see the bed; its covers down. "There is a bed in that room . . ." Her voice sounded light; airy.

The young woman arose and started for the bedroom, tugging her blouse from her short, tight skirt. She sat on the edge of the mattress and reached down to unclasp a sandal; the fingers of her other hand fumbled with the top button of her blouse.

The older man stepped toward her, his own fingers grasping the buttons of his shirt. *Now* his time had come for which he had planned ever since he had saved her life in the storm.

At that moment, there came a loud knock at the front door!

The bald man, caught short, leaned down to her impassive face. "Stay here . . ." he hissed through nicotine-stained teeth, "you will be in my power until I *'clap-twice '*. . . only then, will you come out of it and remember nothing that happened!"

Louder, more insistent knocks sounded.

The aggravated man yanked open the door. A worker he recognized from the refinery stood before him. "Begging your pardon, general, sir, but Mister Ogawan needs some special tools."

Seething, Retchko scrambled around in a pocket and tossed the fellow a chain of keys. "One of these will open the tool-house."

The laborer looked the shoeless European up and down and glanced into the living room behind the bald man, then turned to leave. The door closed with a pronounced "click".

The portly Ukrainian padded back to where Lisa Anaya was sitting on the edge of the bed, her hands clasped in her lap, watching him with a blank stare as he came closer.

"Lie down on the bed!" he ordered.

He unbuttoned his shirt and whipped it off.

Just as he was about to undo his belt, there came a splintering *"CRASH!"* at the front door!

Retchko spun around to see *Frank Ogawan* push his way past the sagging, split-open door into the living room!

The Nigerian's eyes cast past the bedroom door and went wide. On the bed was Lisa, her eyes blinking. The girl pushed herself up onto her elbows and gaped at him, an uncomprehending look on her face. "Oh, Frank, it is you . . ."

Ogawan doubled his fists and advanced on the half-dressed Ukrainian, who was backing away. "You son of a bitch!" The younger man slammed his knuckles into the man's chubby face and flabby stomach with a pair of loud *'SMACKS!'*

Retchko sagged to his knees, groaning.

"Get up!"

On the bed, Lisa Anaya gave a shriek. Frank's two clap-like blows on Retchko had brought her out of the trance! *"What am I doing here? Frank—!"*

Then she saw the shirtless foreigner doubled-over on his knees, groaning, holding his stomach. The man was trying to stand up.

"Lisa, get off that bed!" Frank Ogawan hauled the dazed man to his feet and shoved him toward the living room. He slammed shut the bedroom door behind him.

"You sorry bastard! I have had enough of you!" He back-handed Retchko's puffy face, sending him reeling backward across the low tea-table onto the sofa; the delicate ceramic cups spun to the hardwood with a crash; his staggering feet knocked over Lisa's handbag on the floor.

Frank rubbed his knuckles. His eyes went to the little leather handbag. "The workman I sent here told me he saw Lisa's purse! That is how I knew she was here!"

The pasty European shook his head, touched his jaw.

Frank clenched his teeth and stepped forward; fists doubled. "You stupid—" The man flinched.

Just then, the bedroom door opened and Lisa came out. The girl's eyes went wide at the sight of the moaning man sprawled backward across the sofa. She stepped to Frank's side and put her arm in his.

The Ukrainian was trying to stand, with unsatisfactory results.

The office manager, breathing hard, glared at his antagonist. "We are leaving *right now!*" He tugged on Lisa's arm. "Get your things . . . we are flying out of here, tonight!"

The portly man rubbed his discoloring jaw. "I did not give you permission to—"

"Shut up!"

The "Chief of Security" hauled himself, groaning, onto unsteady legs. Lisa thought he looked ridiculous with his pallid bare feet protruding from underneath the cuffs of his baggy pants.

Retchko gave a sneer. "I could have you killed." Wincing, he put his hand to his bald temple.

A shadow on his dome confirmed to Lisa that the man shaved his head. *But why?* she wondered.

The foreigner grimaced. "Get the hell out of my sight!"

The two stepped through the splintered opening. Frank looked back. "I will send someone to fix your door!"

"Where are you going?"

"Somewhere far away."

Lisa Anaya pointed at her wrist. "We don't have the chips— so you won't be able to find us!"

-20-

José Marti International Airport, Havana Cuba; Two days Later:

Gennady Lychin stood in the shadow of the 747's wing, observing, as the forklift hoisted the last of the crates onto the cargo deck of the enormous airplane looming over him.

An old American car pulled up in front of the hangar across the way and stopped. The Russian watched as a man and a woman alighted from the vehicle with their luggage bags, laughing; the pilots had told him there would be two others on the flight to Lagos. Then Gennady recognized the grizzled-looking, middle-aged driver as the man he had met that time he was here in Havana on the "Spetsnaz" mission with Colonel Golubko and the others.

"See you again, sometime, *'Tio Trini'!*" the blonde-haired young woman was saying, leaning forward for the man to kiss her cheek. Her dark-haired companion shook the fellow's hand.

As the venerable vehicle drove off and the newcomers turned in his direction, Gennady recognized the pair as the American and the Cuban woman he had talked with that night at Facundo's hilltop house-party in Colombia.

He stepped forward as they came toward him. "*You* will be flying with us to Lagos?

The woman's eyes lit up. "Oh, Larry, he is the Russian fellow we met in Cali!"

A voice came from the open cargo door above them. The co-pilot was motioning to the group on the ground to come aboard. "We are ready to take-off!"

The forklift raised the re-united threesome up to the airplane's door, where the flight officer greeted them with a handshake. "It is good to see you—again!" He pointed toward the distant spiral staircase at the front of the cargo deck, almost hidden beyond long rows of crates. "Go take seats—we are preparing to leave, now."

The four trooped up the steps to the upper cabin. Through the open cockpit door, the captain and the flight engineer, recognizing the passengers from previous flights, waved at them.

Twenty minutes later, the gargantuan aircraft lifted from the runway and set a course toward West Africa.

As soon as the seat-belt light went off, Gennady stood up and walked to the back of the cabin to the bar next to the little-used galley. Looking about, he found a full bottle of Vodka and some clean glasses stowed in the pantry. He called up the aisle to Larry and Marisol. "Something to drink?"

The two turned about and nodded at him.

The Russian poured the strong, clear liquid into three glasses and brought them up to the others. He settled onto a seat arm in the aisle, facing the American and the Cuban woman, and took a big, wincing swallow. Gennady held up the half-empty glass, turning it around on his fingertips; his narrowed eyes staring into it. "So, you are going with General Retchko to Madrid, as I am?"

A frustrated look came over Marisol's face. "Yes, but we were supposed to be finished with him."

Larry shook his head. "His message said he had a 'one-time mission' for us in Madrid. Something about 'security' and 'a large sum of money'. We had to get tickets in a hurry to fly to Havana and catch this flight."

"I was working in Nuevo Laredo—in Mexico—when the general called me."

Marisol frowned. "I get the idea the 'Organization' is into a lot of things."

Gennady went to the rear galley and brought back the Vodka bottle with him. "Another round?" He poured some into the three glasses and took another big swallow. Larry and Marisol sipped theirs.

"We went to Nuevo Laredo to work with the new 'border-lord', there", Gennady said, ". . . a man named, 'Aldrada'. We were training his recruits and setting up a smuggling operation using the 'invisible technology'."

Marisol squinted. "I heard Retchko mention it, once—how does it work?"

Gennady described the portable, plate-sized devices and their role in spiriting people across the border. He told them about the time he pumped gasoline into the invisible van. "You should have seen the look on that fellow's face when I drove off and he could not see me!"

He reached for the bottle and sloshed more Vodka into his glass—the liquid was starting to have its effect. He swished it around and went on telling them about the two missions to northern New Mexico; the first one—the "Spetsnaz" one—to bring back the scientist with the "invisible technology" information and the other aimed at the American girl. "But she got away before we got there and I am glad, now, that we did not kill her." *I will not tell them about the midnight skirmish in the snow at the laboratory, or the shoot-out at the ranch. I no longer regret that I killed United States soldiers to avenge what the American Navy did to Galina. But I draw the line at killing females, even under orders.*

"Why were you after the girl?"

"Retchko's orders—he says she knows too much." Gennady did not want to tell them everything about why the 'Organization's' Chief of Security wanted her killed, and changed the subject. He described the mini-warehouse across the border in Laredo—in Texas. "Among other things, we stored Russian-made nuclear weapons there."

"Russian nuclear weapons in Laredo, Texas?"

"They are about the size of suitcases and briefcases—very easy to hide. They have about the same power as the atomic bombs you Americans used on the two Japanese cities. After three years, the triggers automatically de-activated, but our people found a way to re-arm them." Gennady gave a little smirk at Larry. *"There are activated atomic devices in eight of your cities, right now* . . . the last one—the most powerful one—was on its way to Houston."

Larry's eyes went wide. *"The 'Organization' has an atomic bomb in Houston?"*

"Not us . . . we are working with another group—some people out of northeastern Afghanistan. Their leader has big plans for the whole world, in particular for the Americans. They are controlling the bombs. We just brought them across the border for his men to take to the eight cities."

"*Which* cities?" Larry had not reckoned with a confederate of the Organization planning to nuke the U.S.

Gennady looked as if in thought. "I believe the men—they were Chechens, I am sure—took them to New York . . . Los Angeles . . . Chicago . . . Denver . . . Miami . . . Boston and Washington. The last one went to Houston. They are stored in little warehouses, waiting for orders. But it might take a long time for those orders to come, I was told. A decade or two, even. Perhaps longer."

It occurred to Larry that maybe it was to his advantage he would not be returning to the United States if American cities were facing the prospect of nuclear explosions.

Marisol remembered the papers she had found in Retchko's safe. "I know that Retchko was working with people in Afghanistan."

Larry spoke up. "A girl and I—she's an electronics engineer, like I am—built the satellite system that tracks the chips . . . that was why I went to Nigeria in the first place." He held up his wrist. "Both Marisol and I have one of these."

Gennady pointed at a tiny scar on his own wrist. "The same for me."

Larry looked rueful. "But I was not expecting to be made a victim of my own creation."

"That man can follow us wherever we go. He is frightening." Marisol put her glass out for Gennady to pour another round of Vodka. She held it up, eying it, then took a swallow. "I am getting a bit drunk, now, but I do not care."

* * *

Barajas International Airport, Madrid, Spain; Two Days Later:

Kip Leeds stared out the window as the Airbus pulled up and braked to a stop at the terminal—after the long haul from Seattle to Madrid, at long last, they were here. Down on the concrete in the afternoon sun, the bustle of the luggage-hauling caravans and fuel trucks was already underway.

Then he happened to see a big Boeing 747 that had been taxiing behind them turn toward the cargo terminal. Strange, he thought, the airplane had no markings on it—not even numbers.

Sloane Ferry looked around, her long black hair swishing, and grinned at Kip between the gaps in the seat-backs, and at the man who had sat next to her since they had left Seattle on the journey to the Spanish capital. Kip had watched them with interest while the airliner crossed the North Atlantic in the eastbound overnight flight, and how their sleeping heads had finally touched as the airplane flew along. *Was the girl connecting with this guy, Randolph?* Irony of ironies: Kip had always turned away Sloane because he thought he was too old for her; he had since learned that Jim Randolph was, in fact, three years *older* than he was.

Sloane watched as the parade of passengers started toward the exit at the front of the airplane and at the airport scene outside the window. Already she was missing Nicky, who had gone back to Texas with Mrs. Jackson and her father under a heavy security guard.

"We will wait until the other passengers have gone," the Federal agent said, "our Madrid operatives will take us off the plane."

Randolph turned around to Kip. "You are meeting the German girl, here?"

He pulled Nixie Garten's itinerary from his pocket. "She should be arriving from Frankfurt this evening—after the meeting."

"I will have agents watch you until you two get to the hotel."

Sloane's eyes were narrowed. "How did you find this girl . . . this *German*—?"

Did Sloane sound jealous? "Like I said, she was a 'stew' on the flight that time to Lagos. She is going to 'translate' for me."

Randolph spoke up. "Sounds like she's going to 'translate' *herself* to you!"

Except for the blackened twenty-million dollars that had been the catalyst for everything else that had followed, meeting

503

"Nixie Garten" had been the only other positive thing that happened to him on the trip to Nigeria. At the least, he hoped she would be cordial, although he found himself imagining there could be a lot more if things went right. During the long flight from Seattle to Madrid, Kip had thought a lot about the very pretty young German woman he had first seen in the airport waiting room at Frankfurt that time, whom he had labeled "Woman of Mystery", since she had been the only blonde female in the crowd waiting for the flight to Lagos. Would she still be as attractive and friendly as he remembered her having been? On the telephone, she had sounded enthusiastic. He kept thinking about the short-haired young woman who had sat next to him on part of the flight, and the alluring sway she had exhibited walking up the airliner aisle; how she had waved back at him with a smile before stepping beyond the curtain as a crewmember. Then he had found her card that he had taken as an invitation to follow-up on her. He hoped she had forgotten the preposterous cover-story he gave her that time about going to Lagos to "look for old cars"—that she hadn't believed, anyway.

But back to business. According to the fax from Busa that came in to Brad just before they had left for Spain, the twenty-million dollars for which he had signed at the "Nation Bank of Nigeria" was now in Madrid, ready for him to take and collect his six-million-dollar commission. Tomorrow, the schedule called for Kip to meet with Busa and some others from Nigeria. He knew that the "Agency", along with INTERNOL, the international police organization, and the Russian "Federal Security Bureau", were working together on an operation to arrest the suspects, whom they believed were involved with the world-wide crime cartel they were investigating.

But first, they would all meet tonight at the Russian Embassy for briefings with an INTERNOL agent, a Russian Intelligence officer, and some other operatives. Sloane would identify the people who had kidnapped her that time and left her to die in an overheated shipping crate in a truck. Thank God, she had been rescued just in time. His meeting tomorrow with the "Cartel's" men, should set the stage for the main attempt to entrap and apprehend the criminals.

Now that everyone else was gone from the airliner's cabin, some serious-looking men in sport-coats and slacks were stepping down the aisle toward them. "Randolph?" one of them said, business-like, prompting Jim Randolph to say something that seemed to be coded passwords to identify them to the men. He showed his badge to them; they did the same to the American.

The agent motioned for them to follow him to the terminal.

* * *

Two hours later, a plain white van, identified as an official vehicle only by its "Consul" license plates, followed by another, pulled-up to a gate-house where a uniformed sentry in white gloves gave his country's open-style military salute. The leading driver, in the dress unform of a United States Marine major, gave back the snappy American salute and handed some papers to the guard. After a few words between the two in English, the Russian gave a nod and another salute that was returned, the guard motioned for the Americans to drive forward.

The iron gate swung aside and the vehicles made their way up a driveway toward a white, multi-story building surmounted by the white, blue and red flag of the "Russian Federation".

As the vans drew up and stopped, two middle-aged men in business suits stepped from a low curb and approached the vehicles.

In a minute, the hosts were guiding the newcomers through the front doors into an entry foyer decorated in classical Russian style, where a dignified-looking man in a tailored pin-stripe suit with a *'boutonniere'* in his lapel met the guests, nodding and shaking their hands.

"Your Excellency—'Mister Ambassador'—we are pleased to be here." The Marine officer nodded at the man and at the others attending him. "These are the people our embassy discussed with you about the Nigerian situation."

"We are pleased to offer our assistance," the Ambassador said in accented English, with a polite nod in return. "As you know ... my country also has a great concern about this."

505

A man in a suit gestured toward a corridor leading off the main entryway "This way, if you will, please, " he said in a heavily-accented English.

As the American troupe followed their hosts down the carpeted hallway, Kip took in the gilded surroundings with its busts of famous Russians staring out from lighted alcoves; in every direction, he saw heavy-framed paintings and rich tapestries that anointed the embassy's sumptious interior.

His eyes caught Sloane's; from her expression, he knew she was impressed with the splendorous place as he was. Kip remembered from his university studies of International Law that this palatial estate in the middle of Madrid, Spain was, in effect, Russian territory.

The man directed them into a paneled room dominated by a long conference table; arranged on it were bottles of mineral water and glasses that caught the light of an overhead crystal light fixture. Already seated around the table were several men, including a decorated middle-aged military officer wearing glasses; a younger man, also in a military uniform, and some civilians, all well-dressed.

A uniformed Russian addressed the Americans in a heavy brogue. "Your credentials?"

Kip, James Richard Randolph, Sloane Ferry, the Marine, and the others on the American side handed over papers that their Madrid Embassy had supplied them. The man in the military outfit looked them over, then motioned for the guests to take seats. He nodded at a civilian at the head of the table.

A thin, balding man with a loose chin, wearing thick, plastic-framed eyeglasses arose and looked at the new arrivals. "I am 'Illya Konstantinovich Livshits', of the Russian 'Federal Security Bureau'," the man spoke in an accent. His round, fleshy mouth gave a flicker. "You Americans, of course, knew us in the past as the 'K-G-B'." The Intelligence officer made an attempt at a smile, then became serious. "I assure you that we must all now work together on a common matter of urgent importance. That is why we are here, tonight."

He nodded at another individual, a heavier-looking, dark-haired man in a tweed jacket, holding a curved smoking pipe, who stood up and looked around at the group.

"My name is 'Younce Tarliani' . . . Inspector with 'INTERNOL', the international police organization based in Geneva, Switzerland. Livshits and I—and our organizations—are here on a common quest." He looked at the Americans. "I understand you will join us?" To Kip, it sounded like a question posed as a statement.

The Americans glanced around at each other; they had been briefed earlier at the embassy and knew the basics—but not the details—of why they were here. Randolph nodded back at Tarliani.

"That is very good." The Swiss man motioned at the U.S. Marine officer. "Everyone will now introduce themselves . . ."

" . . . I am 'Major Jeremy P. Bogue', United States Marines—."

" . . . 'James Richard Randolph', United States Federal Investigation Agency—'"

Tarliani gave a start. "I have talked with your superior, 'Watering'." Livshits also nodded.

The dark-haired American girl spoke. "'Sloane Marie Ferry'. . . I am here as a witness." She glanced at Randolph.

" . . .'Rudyard Kipling Leeds . . . a witness." Kip felt odd using his full name, which the embassy had told him would be necessary at this meeting. Off to the side, a male Russian stenographer was taking down everyones' words.

The two American Military Police officers identified themselves.

Tarliani nodded at the older Russian military officer wearing glasses.

"I am Colonel 'Rodion S. Golubko' . . . 'Vityaz Spetsnaz'," he said in an accent-free American English that surprised Kip. This man—whose former-Soviet-leader-"Yuri Andropov"-looks and brusque manner seemed to embody the arch-typical, vaguely-threatening Russian he had always imagined—had thoroughly studied America, he concluded.

507

Kip had also happened to glance at the U.S. Marine officer when the Russian identified himself as 'Vityaz Spetsnaz' and was sure he had seen a wide-eyed look of surprise or extreme respect (could it have been "alarm"?) on the American major's face.

The younger Russian military man spoke. "I am Terenty Nicholovich Suslov' . . . Major, 'General Staff-Vityaz Spetsnaz'. I am 'Military Attaché' at the Madrid Embassy of the Russian Federation."

Kip saw the American Major Bogue's eyes go wide once more when the second Russian said he, too, was a 'Vityaz Spetsnaz' officer. Bogue's eyes were darting back and forth at the insignia on their uniforms, frowning, fidgeting. What was it about this 'Vityaz Spetsnaz'—about which Kip had never heard—that seemed to cause such a visible reaction in the American officer?

The thin man with the wattled neck was speaking once more in the heavy accent Kip was having a hard time following. "Inspector Tarliani and I and the Americans—" he looked down at Randolph—"have come into information about an organization that threatens us all." The man pushed his plastic-rimmed eyeglasses on his nose and went on to outline what the three crime-fighting groups—the Russian 'Federal Security Bureau', successor to the KGB; "INTERNOL" of Switzerland, the international police organization; and the "Federal Investigation Agency" of the United States, pooling their information—had learned about the Cartel. They had determined that the criminal organization was operating out of Nigeria and had world-wide connections. From time-to-time, as the Russian mentioned several names and places he recognized, Kip mentally flashed-back to the people and events he had encountered while he was there and began to understand that his trip to Lagos had been much more uncertain and dangerous than he had understood at the time.

Livshits nodded at an attendant who turned off the lights. Up on a wall, a grainy image that had been caught by an airport camera flashed onto the screen. The picture was of a man Kip did not recognize.

But when the next man's picture went up, Kip gasped aloud.

The Russian's eyes darted to the American. "You know this man?"

"That's 'Busa'!" Sure enough, the portly, very dark African's picture matched the man with whom he had gone to the banks when he had been in Lagos—the man who was supposed to bring him the documents to the airport and had failed to show-up. "He owes me fifty-thousand dollars."

"This man has stolen money from people from all over the world."

"He also owes me twenty-million dollars."

Tarliani surprised Kip by saying, "We are aware of that; we will talk about it, later."

When the next photograph went up, the American let out a long breath. "That's the guy at the bank who took my fifty-thousand dollars!"

The Russian gave the American indulgent look that Kip picked up in the indirect light of the projector. "We believe this man is the leader of the whole international operation!"

Kip gaped at the image of the bald little man in the brown, three-piece suit—the banker he had known as "Doctor Nomoah". *He* was the big boss of the crime organization the Russian Livshits was describing? Incredible.

Sloane's hand went to her mouth. "*I, too,* saw this man! He was in the hotel room the time I was tied-up!" The young woman told the others about the kidnapping.

"She almost died in the heat," Kip put in.

In the corner, the stenographer's pen scratched on his pad.

The next photograph that flashed up was of a thickset, bald-headed individual whose picture looked to have been taken in an airport lounge. Kip frowned; he did not recognize the man. The two Russian military officers sat up and stared at the picture.

Sloane gave a gasp, her eyes wide. "That's the man in the hotel room! He came in with the others!"

Livshits cleared his throat. "This is the man we are really after, 'comrades'—" As the others gave him quick looks, once more, Kip was reminded that there were foreigners in the room with decidedly different backgrounds from his own. The Russian Intelligence officer caught himself. "I mean, 'people'—"

The thin man nodded at the projectionist. "Now, we will compare this man . . ." The scene shifted to a portly, dark-haired individual walking in what looked to be a train station. " . . . with *this* man—" The second picture depicted a stocky, bald-headed individual who appeared to be stepping along in an airport concourse.

As the pictures alternated back and forth, there was a collective gasp in the room. "Exactly. *This is the same individual.*"

The older Russian officer swore under his breath. "Putridchenko!" With a stormy look on his face, he glanced at the younger military man, whose eyes were wide; then glared at Livshits. "Where *is* this man?" In the flickering light of the projector, Kip saw the older officer clench his teeth; his knuckles at the edge of the table were white; an angry-looking vein stood out on his temple.

Livshits turned to Tarliani. "You have the information on this suspect?"

The Swiss police inspector squinted at his notes in the reflected light of the projector. The picture of the suspect in his bald guise hung steady on the screen.

"Our agents in Nigeria say he is the 'Head of Security' of the 'Organization', as the Cartel is called." Tarliani frowned through his eyeglasses and went on. "He says he is a 'former Soviet general', among other things, and goes under the name of 'Leonid Retchko'. Whatever is his background, he is ruthless at whatever he does, wherever he goes . . . and from what we know, he gets around a lot."

"Where *does* he go?" The older Russian military man, still fuming, asked the question.

"We have tracked him to North Korea . . . Pakistan . . . Afghanistan . . . Chechnya—"

"Chechnya?" The younger Russian, the 'Military Attaché, blurted out. He and the older uniformed man looked at each other, frowning.

Tarliani looked over his glasses at the colonel. "You know about 'Chechnya'?"

"We were there . . . as . . . ah—part of the 'peace-keeping mission'."

The Swiss Inspector went on. "The suspect individual has also been seen in the United States . . . in Texas." He glanced at Sloane, who was following his words. "There is some evidence— not confirmed, however—that he has also been in the New York City area . . . why he was there, we do not know."

Randolph told them about the mini-warehouse in Laredo he had watched, and about the men moving goods in-and-out all the time. "I am sure our people will want to raid the place." He snapped his fingers. "My boss also told me about a warehouse in New Jersey, across from Manhattan, they are watching." All eyes went to him. "There are men around it all the time. They say they saw a man matching Retchko's description."

He fumbled in a coat pocket and pulled out a packet. "We got this telephoto picture of another individual who was there." Randolph handed it to the projectionist, who placed it on the image tray. The depiction of a very dark-skinned, muscular-looking man flashed onto the screen.

Sloane and Kip let out gasps.

"That's the guy who beat me in the hotel room . . . he's an evil man!"

"He followed me on the airplane!" Kip burst out.

Tarliani fingered through some notes. "One of our agents tells us his name is 'Ezego'—one of Retchko's top assistants—a vicious, clever man"

Randolph looked at Tarliani. "Which of your agents?"

"We have two there, now; a third agent is no longer on the case. This particular agent, *going under the name of 'Mickey'* is Busa's personal valet. *Busa treated Mickey badly and we recruited him as an agent.* The little man has told us a lot about Busa's and the banker's—the one they call the 'Chief''s'— movements . . . he even traveled to the United States, once." Tarliani looked at Kip. "One time, he warned you with a note you were in danger."

Kip gave a start. "So *that's* who left the paper under the door at the hotel! Of course!" He told them about a mysterious warning message he had gotten when he had returned from

Nigeria. Now he recognized the fellow as the stooped little African he had seen that time in Busa's living room when all those people were there with the black money!

Tarliani nodded. "He is one of our most important imbedded agents."

A photograph came on the screen of a gray-haired man in a white robe with a crown on his head, holding a jeweled rod in his hands. Kip gave a laugh, and told of how when he had left Nigeria, the fellow, who looked like some sort of "Swami", or holy man and his "harem", as he put it, had been on the flight from Lagos to Amsterdam.

Tarliani squinted at the American. "Actually, he is much more than just a "holy-man". . . he acts as a courier whom no one would suspect to transfer illegal funds back and forth from Lagos to Amsterdam, using the girls as a foil. One of our agents gave us the whole scope of his activities."

The picture of a slender young woman with medium-hued skin came up. Sloane pointed at the screen. "That's the girl in the hotel room who talked the men out of killing me! Who is she?"

"She is one of our agents."

"What! She's an *'agent'?"*

"One of our best, actually. She *was loaned to us by the British 'Secret Intelligence Service', also known as 'M-I-Six'!* She posed as the 'wife' of another agent! It was perfect cover for her to move around, a lot. Her 'husband'—*another of our 'M-I-Six' operatives*—was the manager of the refinery at Tanuta City. He got the job because he was very pursuasive when the operation was hiring a manager. She even pretended to have her 'husband' 'killed' . . . he is now in London, awaiting another assignment." Tarliani went on. "They are good—very good, indeed—even her own sister thought they were really married." She went so far as to become this man Retchko's 'girlfriend'." The Inspector gave a smirk. "She learned a lot, thanks to 'pillow-talk'. She became a 'dancing girl' for the fake 'religious man'. . . that was how she seduced Retchko in the first place. She found out that the old guy's 'temple' was a 'front' for laundering huge amounts of Cartel money through Swiss and Cayman Island banks."

There was a stir in the room. "INTERNOL is seizing those accounts, now."

Kip snapped his fingers. "Now I remember! She came into the Lagos bank when I was there and talked loudly with that big guy who later kidnapped Sloane—what was his name—?"

"Ezego."

"Then they *were* giving coded signals to Busa! But you say it was all a sham for her, since she was working for you?"

"That is correct. One more thing about that girl . . . her sister worked with Retchko, Busa, and the others at an oil refinery on the Nigerian coast, although we don't believe she was one of the criminals. We'll have more about that refinery a little later, by the way."

The next picture that came up on the wall-screen depicted a trim, very-dark man in a three-piece, pin-stripe suit. "This man is the financial brains of the operation. He goes under the name of 'Krasheev'. . . he is the head of the 'Nation Bank of Nigeria's' 'Division of 'Intercontinental Remittance'." He moves money around, using his bank as a cover through so-called "temples" the old 'holy' man has in Lagos and in Amsterdam."

Kip, who had been staring at the image, broke in. "I talked with him in his office . . . he had me sign all those papers for the black money."

Tarliani looked down at the American. "You might be interested to know that *you are entitled to all the money*—if you can clean it and put it into a bank—a *real* bank, that is."

"Are you serious?" Everyone was staring at Kip. "You mean the twenty-million is *really* mine?"

"Ordinarily, funds obtained outside the regular channels belong to the government, but this government is corrupted, so other international rules apply. The money is yours, if you can claim it."

Kip felt a pulsating in his ears; he had taken it for granted that the whole thing was a scam—now, it seemed as if the scammers themselves could be scammed—if he could get to the money. "I am supposed to meet with Busa and the others, tomorrow, about 'cleaning' the 'black money'."

"We will talk about it, later."

Tarliani nodded at the projectionist, who changed the picture. The screen flicked to a scene of featureless brown terrain as seen from above.

"These are the mountains of 'Tora Bora' in eastern Afghanistan . . . very remote."

Kip and the others frowned; what did this have to do with the Cartel?

"Somewhere in these mountains is the underground lair of a mysterious Middle-Eastern man who we believe is plotting to upset all civilization as we know it." Tarliani paused as everyone in the room stared at the picture of the nondescript hills. "But we do not yet know what the fellow looks like."

The Swiss investigator went on. "A multi-lingual agent we recruited in Libya—*a translator named 'Ahmed'*— tells us the man we know as 'Retchko' has been there."

On the screen came a telephoto shot of a very black, well-built man in a military uniform. "This is 'Colonel Ajiboy' . . . he is at the Lagos airport and seems to be one of the few 'good-men' in this whole Nigerian crowd." The projector zoomed-in on the man, who was wearing a military cap and dark glasses. "Based on our agent's reports, we believe this man is the 'weak-link', as you Americans say, in the scheme—he seems to have moral scruples, which are in short supply in Nigeria."

Randolph was curious. "Why do you say that?"

"'Mickey' told us in a coded report that the man was very unhappy about the 'disappearance' of the so-called 'Lester Nkrume' character, who was actually our agent working with 'Betty Nkrume', who played his wife for us. He also obeys Retchko's orders with great reluctance. We believe he can be turned to our side if we work things right."

Tarliani nodded and the overhead image of a factory-looking layout flicked up onto the screen."We believe this refinery— located at the town of 'Tanuta City', about four-hundred kilometers southeast of Lagos—is very much involved in the international crime operation."

Livshits spoke up. "At the request of INTERNOL, one of our *'Cosmos'* Intelligence satellites made a pass over the refinery to get these pictures and to record its electronic emissions."

The next shot showed a smaller, square-shaped building at the edge of an open parking area. "There is something going on inside this structure," Tarliani said, "from its radiant spectrum signature, we know it has electronics in it—what kind of electronics, we do not know."

The Russian Major Suslov spoke up. "My specialty is 'electronic Counter-Intelligence'." The others turned to look at him. He gave a palms-down motion to the projectionist. "Zoom down some more."

The top of the building came into more detailed relief. "See that rounded roof?" Up close, it was plain to see that the structure's topside was not flat, as it had originally appeared, but was actually dome-shaped. "There is a satellite sending and receiving system in that building, I am sure of it."

Randolph sat up straight. "That explains it!" he burst out. "One of our satellites has been experiencing strange transmissions through it . . . we knew it was coming from somewhere in West Africa. This has to be the place! But we don't know where the other receivers and transmitters are."

"I believe I can find out," Major Suslov said. "Which direction is north on this satellite picture?"

In a few seconds, an arrow pointing north came onto the top of the image.

He motioned to the stenographer. "Being an Atlas to me."

As soon as the man returned with a big book, Terenty thumbed through it to a conical-projection map of the world. Comparing the picture of the building with the arrow pointing to the north, and the map in the book, he nodded.

"Just as I suspected!" He strode up and pointed at the photo on the display tray. "Look at these. The two antennas you can see faintly underneath the plastic domes in the sun are pointed in the direction of the satellite over the equator." He glanced at Livshits, then went on, "I can tell you that our tracking stations and satellites know the American satellite is also aimed toward the west." Terenty took a deep breath. "This 'Tanuta Refinery' is sending signals back and forth through the American satellite to northeastern Afghanistan and also to somewhere in Central America—I am sure of it!"

"Then the refinery is connected with that guy up there in the mountains of Tora Bora!"

Everyone in the room let out a long breath.

"But what are the signals?"

Terenty snapped his fingers. "I believe I know." He turned to Rodion Golubko. "Colonel, do you remember how we lost contact with those three men of ours in Chechnya . . . how their 'chip implants' all at once went silent?"

While the others looked on without comprehending about what the two were talking, the older Russian sucked in his breath. "You say they have *new* implants that are being controlled from this 'Tanuta Refinery' to Central America?"

"Exactly."

Terenty and the older Russian officer stared at each other. *"Then Gennady, Malinovsky and Blagron are alive and may be with the Cartel in Central America!"*

Colonel Golubko looked at Tarliani. "But what does the refinery have to do with 'Putridchenko'—'Retchko'—as you now call him?"

"He has his office, there."

The older Russian military officer looked hard at Major Suslov, then at Tarliani. The contentious blue vein stood-out on his temple. "We would like to mount an assault against this refinery. We have a score to settle with 'Putridchenko'— 'Retchko' . . . and this 'Cartel'!"

The Swiss man's eyebrows went up. "Oh?" He glanced at the American Marine officer and back at Colonel Golubko with an enigmatic shrug. "Perhaps you soon may."

The Russian officer looked straight at the Marine major. "I would seek the Americans' assistance in such an operation, if possible. It would be in our countries' interests to work together on this common objective."

The Spetsnaz officer seemed to have caught the American off-guard. "Ah, I must check with my superiors . . ."

Tarliani spoke up. "The American, here"—the man nodded at Kip—"is to meet tomorrow morning with Busa to negotiate the black money."

The Russian Livshits motioned at Kip. "We will wire you with a special transmitter that they cannot discover. You will transmit the information to our satellite overhead and on to Moscow. Our experts there will analyze the information and send it back to us at the embassy in real-time."

Kip took in his breath; the others were looking at him. "That would be incredible—"

The Swiss police inspector looked at him. "It will be a major responsibility—but we are sure you can handle it. You will ask them questions to lead us to all the 'Cartel conspirators', and we will tell you what to say."

Sloane's hand went to her mouth; her eyes were wide. "Oh, Kip . . . be careful—"

Tarliani looked at his watch. "All right, we will break, now, and return here at zero-eight-hundred- hours in the morning."

Kip glanced at his own watch and did a double-take. "Oh, my gosh! I'm supposed to be at the airport right now, to pick-up someone!"

Major Bogue motioned at the two Marine sergeants. "Take this man to the airport and don't let him out of your sight!"

The uniformed men saluted and turned to follow Kip, who was already making for the door.

In a couple of minutes, one of the two white American Embassy vans was churning out through the gate onto the broad boulevard, 'Calle de Velasquez' as Kip read on a street sign.

"The airport is on the east side of Madrid," the driver said, as they turned left at a traffic circle and roared around a big fountain-statue. Already Kip had observed that the Spanish capital was a city of many fountains and statues.

He looked at his watch for the hundredth time. "Go as fast as you can!" If Nixie's flight from Frankfurt was on time, she would be in Customs, by now.

In a few minutes, the white van sped past a sign proclaiming the outer boundaries of the "Barajas International Airport". A little farther on, another sign, "Arriving International Flights", pointed toward a multi-storied terminal structure. The Marine driver pulled into a parking space and the three men dashed across a roadway jammed with buses and taxis toward a bank of automatic sliding glass doors labeled in Spanish, "Arriving-Passenger-Pick-Up".

Inside the cavernous open space, Kip gazed across a bustling mass of people who were looking at luggage of all description that was parading around on thumping carousels. Would she recognize him? Could he recognize *her* in this teeming throng? It had been a while since they had talked on the flight to Lagos and the lights in the airliner cabin had been dimmed. He remembered the German girl as a short-haired blonde with a smile and an eye-catching figure. Nixie had told him on the telephone that she would be wearing an orange-colored T-shirt with her first name embossed on it. He hoped it would be good enough.

On a screen he found the carousel number on which the luggage from her flight would be arriving.. Kip motioned in its direction. "Over there!" The three Americans elbowed their way through the crowd to the conveyor the monitor had indicated.

But when Kip huffed up to the undulating luggage track and looked around at the surging mass of people, there was no one in sight who looked like Nixie.

The blonde young German woman gazed down at the sprawling lights of a big city sweeping by close below the wing of the Airbus. Then came the familiar whine and the thumps of the gear lowering and she gave a shiver of anticipation—in a little while, she would be seeing him again! *But would she recognize him?* Repeatedly, she had tried to recall how the American had looked on that flight to Lagos, that time. But it had been so dark in the plane! For sure, she would have sized him up better if she had known he was really going to call her back! About all she could remember was that he had a good build and dark-blond hair. When his voice came on the line the other day, at first she had not even known who he was. *"Kip Leeds"?* The name had not registered until he had reminded her about the antique cars in Lagos. Oh, yes—the American! "Kip Leeds"—so that was who he was. And now, she was about to see him, again. She wanted a cigarette, but had promised herself she would quit. She glanced down at the orange T-shirt she had told him she would be wearing. Her name—"Nixie"—was embossed on it in bold white letters. She hoped it would be good enough.

* * *

"Passport?" The Customs officer fingered her little book and stamped something in it. But instead of handing it it back over, he motioned to someone behind her.

A hand grabbed Nixie's shoulder. "Come with me!" a gruff male voice spoke in Spanish.

"Que`?" Nixie turned and frowned. A man in a Customs uniform was confronting her.

"This way, '*por favor*'." The middle-aged man tugged her out of the line; the luggage carrier tipped up one wheel. As it straightened, the officer jerked it from her and gave her arm a shove. A woman officer came up and gripped her other arm. The two pulled the girl along at a hurried pace, elbowing others aside in the crowded place. The laces of one of her running shoes came loose, flapping along the floor of the big space as they hurried along. Wherever they were going, they were in a hurry, she realized, alarmed.

"The man pushed open a frosted-glass door. The officers hauled her into a small, brightly-lit room where another older uniformed woman was standing, cross-armed. Nixie stared at an open-type metal chair that was in the middle of the room. She recognized a gynecological seat."Take off your clothes and put them into that basket!"

"What!"

"Off with your clothes!"

The wide-eyed young woman tried to pull back from the man. "What is this all about? I am not going to disrobe in front of *him!*"

The second woman, pulling on rubber gloves nodded at a side door. With an obvious look of disappointment, the male officer turned and stepped out through the exit. There was another "click". Nixie's heart was racing. She was now locked in this cell-like room with two grim-looking women.

The matron with the gloves glared at the girl. "Are you going to disrobe—or must we rip everything off of you by force?"

In a minute the basket held her things.

"Onto the chair!"

Shaking, the girl eased onto the metal seat. Goose-bumps broke out all over her as she settled onto the cold, chromed contrivance. Through the opaque glass door she could see the vague, intermittent shapes of people in the main concourse who were moving past. Could they see her?

The full-body search was over in one minute. The woman doing the examining peeled off the gloves and nodded at the basket of jumbled garments. "Put your things back on ... you are not the one we are looking for. You are free to go."

"Just like *that?*" Nixie was indignant. "You strip me and do a search like it was *nothing?*"

Certain parts of her body felt tugged and stretched from the quick, probing examination.

"Take your things and leave, now." The hard-bitten woman's voice sounded mechanical.

Shaking, the girl pulled back on her clothes and tied her shoes. With a look of disgust, Nixie turned to leave.

Then she remembered something important. "Where is my passport?"

"Outside." A blurry shape darkened the glass door; someone was standing out there.

She pulled on the handle, almost bumping into the same Customs man who had taken her document. "Your passport, señorita . . ."

Still stung by the strip-search, she glared at him, then turned up the concourse, pulling the rolling luggage carrier in the direction of an overhead sign. 'To Baggage Claim", it read. *Was she too late?* Had this "Kip Leeds" fellow given up, by now? It was far past her scheduled arrival time. Aside from making a wasted trip, she would have missed the American—a terrible disappointment.

At the bottom of a lackadaisical escalator she encountered the bustling, bumping banks of baggage belts, surrounded by hordes of people who were staring as if mesmerized at the clunking conveyors and their thumping, wobbling cargoes.

Her throat dry, she squeezed herself and her wheeled baggage bag between people standing about and made her way toward the last conveyor, where she was supposed to meet the American. In a few seconds she would know if he was there.

Ahead, three men were elbowing around people and coming in her direction with deliberate steps—a well-built blond male in his mid-thirties, and two soldiers. The light-haired fellow was staring at her T-shirt. He was grinning.

"Nixie? Nixie Garten?"

"Kip? Kip Leeds . . . from America?"

"It *is* you!" He grabbed her shoulders, a big smile on his face, and looked her up and down, his eyes wide.

Nixie stood on tiptoes and gave him a quick kiss on his mouth. She stepped back and looked at him, blinking. "I was afraid you would not be here . . . I was late."

"I was afraid *you* would not be here. We were late, too!"

Surprised by her unexpected kiss, which he figured was probably cultural on her part, and trying not to look too obviously thrilled, Kip took a quick glance at the orange T-shirt with her name on it. *She has a nice figure, all right. With this casual outfit, she looks even better than I remembered from before, when she had worn a flight attendant's uniform.*

With obvious envy, one of the military men spoke up. "We better be going, now . . . they are waiting for us at the Russian Embassy."

Nixie gave a start. "The Russian Embassy?"

"Ah, yes, we will meet the others there." Kip nudged her in the direction of the big automatic sliding glass doors leading to the street.

Her eyes were wide as she tugged her luggage. "*'Herr Kip'* you are indeed 'well-connected', as they say."

He grinned. "One of the reasons you are here." He gave her a side glance as they hastened along. "But not the *only* reason, of course." The doors rumbled open in front of them. "I thought a lot about you. I wanted to see you, again."

"You did?" *He wanted to see me, again!*

"On the airplane I thought you were a 'Woman of Mystery.'"

Her eyebrows went up. "Oh? That is funny." *And interesting. I will have to talk to him some more about that—subtly, of course.*

He was taken by her German accent. "You intrigued me."

Before she could say something else, there was a break in the traffic and the uniformed driver called out. "Let us be moving!" he spoke loudly over the roar of a diesel bus that was pulling away.

The four bustled their way through the vehicles to the parking lot across the way.

* * *

At the curb, a black man stood with another, watching the three men and the girl climb into a van under a street-light. The vehicle's headlights came on; it started backing from its parking spot.

A Jaguar pulled up curbside and stopped. One of the men dropped into the rear seat. "Follow that van . . ." He pointed at the tail-lights of the vehicle receding into the line of traffic.

* * *

Two parking spaces behind the Jaguar, a sedan pulled away from the curb. Two men inside it focused on the white van as the vehicle with the Americans and the German girl drove out of the airport. The sedan settled back several car lengths. It would trail the van to wherever it was going.

* * *

Nigerian Embassy, Madrid; at the Same Time:

Marisol Montoya, once more as "Monica Montero" looked around and shuddered—on a wall hung an outsized oil portrait of the Nigerian military dictator in full dress uniform, his baleful eyes staring out. Her nose tingled; the musky smell of the place was getting to her.

Everyone was settled into seats in the little auditorium. She glanced at Luis; he was shaking his head slowly, as if uncertain about what was happening. Across the center aisle, Guido stretched his legs under the seat in front of him, his hands in his pockets; she got the idea he also was not happy about being here.

A very dark man in a bulging flower-print outfit like she had seen many times in Nigeria stepped to a lectern on a low stage. As the Cubana watched the fellow shuffle some papers, a comical image of a walking flower garden crossed her mind.

The man spoke in English in a heavy brogue. "From intercepts between this 'Kip Leeds' we have been tracking and the German woman, the Customs search of the female turned up nothing, but we are following her . . . we are here to prepare for when we will encounter the American."

While he was saying this, Monica glanced aside and felt cold: General Retchko, his bullet-shaped bald head reflecting the overhead lights, was stepping into the room from a side door.

523

God, she had hoped she would never again have to see him! Behind the lumpy-looking Ukrainian was the fat, grinning Busa, wearing his usual long, flowing Nigerian native outfit, and the serious-looking little bald man she knew only as the "Chief". Did he not have anything else to put on except that same brown three-piece suit he always wore? Bringing up the rear was the small, stooped African she had seen hanging around Busa a lot.

The "flower garden" was still talking. "The American has the funds with him—one-million, six-hundred-seventy-five-thousand dollars—to 'clean' the black money . . . when we have taken it from him, *we will 'take care of him' in the 'usual' manner* . . . then we will use his identity to put the twenty-million in the Swiss account using his account numbers. We will use the funds amount as a compensating balance to bring other—much larger sums—of money to the account."

So *that* was what this was about, Monica thought, glancing at Luis, whose eyes were narrowed—they were going to take a lot of money from some American and then rub him out! But why all these "security'" precautions? Across the aisle, Guido's eyebrows were furrowed. There seemed to be an air of tension in the people-packed room.

"The American will meet us at the 'Renaldo Apartments' near the 'Royal Palace'. You people"—he pointed at Guido, Luis and Monica—"will greet him and put him off-guard. When you have possession of the money, we will force him to sign some papers, then we will drive him outside the city." A smirk crossed the fellow's face. "There, our people will finish the job."

The three gave furtive, uncertain looks at each other. *They had traveled all this way just to trap an unsuspecting stranger?*

Monica saw Retchko once more glance around at her and her companions, something she noticed he had done several times, like he wanted to be sure they were all present.

Then the Latina's eyes fell on something that gave her a chill of alarm: *On Retchko's little finger was the emerald ring she had lost in the safe!*

Then it hit her: *This trap was also meant for them!* Of course! Her eyes wide, the girl sucked-in her breath. They were outsiders who knew too much! While they were here, they were also marked for death! General Retchko cast about the room. When his eyes came to Monica, they stopped once more and held their beady gaze on her for a long second.

* * *

As the embassy van made its way out of the airport, Kip's heart was pounding. The girl from the airplane flight to Lagos that time was again sitting next to him! He found himself tongue-tied. "Was your flight okay?"

She tried a smile. "I am used to flights."

In the flickering lights of traffic Kip saw her bite her lower lip. *Is she nervous?*

"Actually, I had a bad experience at the airport." She told him about the strip-search.

"My God! What did they do *that* for?"

"I do not know. It hurt."

Kip felt guilty—she was here on his invitation and already people had mistreated her. On impulse, he put his arm around her shoulder. She turned to in him. All at once, the girl felt soft, vulnerable. *Sloane had felt the same way to him that time when she had cried about her late boyfriend and he had held her. But Sloane was with someone else, now.* He glanced at Nixie, still hardly able to believe she was actually here with him. "Are you all right, now?"

"I am a little tired . . . we made two trips to London, today." *Kip's strong form next to me gives me a comforting feeling of security. I am glad to be here with him.*

Kip was impressed. "You get around a *lot* . . ."

"My schedules are better—no more Lagos trips, thank God!" She gave his shoulder a quick pat. "I even went to Dallas, three trips in a row! We laid-over there last week—did you not say on the telephone you were from somewhere around Dallas?"

"You were there? I wish I had known." Then Kip remembered he had been gone from home ever since Sloane was kidnapped and they had rushed down to Laredo to rescue her. It would have made no difference—while she was there on the lay-

525

over, he had been away. How frustrating! "Actually, I have been gone from home for some time. It's a long story."

"You live an exciting life . . ."

In the lights of the traffic, he saw she was looking at his face. "When we get to the hotel, I'll tell you about it."

The van had turned off the broad boulevard and was pulling up to a gatehouse. The Russian sentry came up; he and the Marine driver repeated their ritual as before; the gate swung aside.

The driver glanced back. "We are here to pick up some more people and go to the hotel."

Nixie's eyes were wide. "Kip, what is this all about? You talked on the telephone about 'translation', but—'The Russian Embassy'?"

"Your card said you spoke 'Russian' and 'Spanish', and I knew we were coming to Spain to meet some Russians and I don't know 'Russian' . . . so, it all fits together!"

The German girl saw a slender young woman with long, dark hair and a man who looked to be in his late-'thirties coming up. Both ducked past them into the rear seat.

As they turned down the long driveway, Kip saw the Russian Ambassador and some of his staff standing on the portico. "His Excellency" gave a wave and a nod. The second van swung in behind them. Kip saw an unmarked U.S. Embassy car at the front of the procession; another took up a position behind them.

After more formalities at the gate, the little convoy made a right turn onto the wide-laned thoroughfare.

* * *

Across the way, one of the shadowy shapes in the Jaguar parked at the curb reached for the ignition key. A heavy male voice rumbled over the sounds of the engine. "We will follow them now and see where they go,".

* * *

The second sedan that had been parked on a side street down the way drove out into the flow of traffic and fell-in several car lengths behind the Jaguar.

* * *

In a few minutes the procession pulled up to a Marine sentry at the United States Embassy. The guards noted the occupants of the four vehicles, then passed them through.

"We will pick up two more Marine guards," the driver said, then we will go to the hotel . . . we have reserved an entire floor."

The new soldiers came out and slid into the second van. The caravan moved back out onto the roadway.

Before long, the vehicles bore to the right, around the statues and fountains glistening in lights that Kip recognized from before, and headed out a very wide boulevard with an esplanade down the middle. "This is the *'Gran Via',"* the driver announced. "It's the most famous street in Madrid."

Kip stared out at decades-old, stone-faced, multi-storied edifices as they went by. On a triangle point, he picked out a two-level "McDonald's", then more fully-lit shops, banks and other businesses on the street-level of the buildings. Even though it was past eleven o'clock in the evening, all the stores were open. He saw that the buses were full of passengers, and a four-abreast line snaked up to a big motion-picture theater. Madrid looked to be an all-night city.

He saw that Nixie seemed to be taking-in all this casually. "You have been here, before?"

The blonde girl's eyes reflected the lights. "Many times."

The procession pulled up to a rear entrance of a big building. Kip recognized the familiar name of a hotel on a lighted sign. The group followed the Marines through the back door to a freight elevator.

* * *

The Jaguar passed the vans and continued on toward its pre-planned destination. A rumbling male voice spoke. "We will notify the others where the subjects are staying for the night."

* * *

The second sedan drove one block past where the vans were parked behind the hotel and turned into a parking garage.

* * *

In a minute, the elevator doors slid open. As everyone stepped out, Kip saw the number, "14" by the door. The Marine pulled a sheaf of papers from his tunic and read names loud, handing out keys; each would have a separate room on this level. Kip noticed the Marines did not have rooms; most likely they would be on guard all night.

Kip looked at his number, then at Nixie. "Which room is yours?"

"Ah, 'twelve'."

"Mine is 'ten'—we will be right next to each other!"

Nixie gave a grin. "How convenient!"

When she turned on the lights, it was Kip's turn to grin. "Connecting doors!"

An amused look came across Nixie's face. "You *will* behave, of course."

"Of course." He unlatched the suite door and stepped into his quarters. "I wasn't expecting to be practically in the same room with you!" *This could get interesting.*

She scrunched her nose at him. "I do not object—do you?"

"Of course not."

There was a knock on his door. "Mister Randolph wants everyone to meet him in his room." The Marine gave the room number.

Randolph opened the designated door. "Ah, Kip—and your 'guest'." The two stepped into the room. Kip saw that Sloane was also there. The agent motioned at a wet bar. "Drinks?"

"Lager." Nixie elbowed Kip. "We Germans are *'Bier'* drinkers."

Holding her drink, the girl with the long dark hair stepped up to Nixie and put out her hand. "I'm 'Sloane Ferry'."

"Nixie Garten."

Kip pointed at Nixie's name on the orange T-shirt. "It's written all over her!"

"Kip *said* he was meeting someone—" *She is attractive, Sloane was thinking. But who is she?*

"We met on the flight to Lagos," Kip put in. "She is a 'translator' and I knew I would need someone to 'translate' for me."

Sloane spoke up. "Kip and I have known each other for a long time." When she said that, she glanced at Randolph, who was sipping his drink; taking in the conversation. In that moment, for Sloane it was as if the book of her life had turned to a new page marked, "Future".

"Jim and I have come to know each other since all this started." She turned to Nixie. "I am here as a 'witness' on this case."

The German girl looked at the others, confused. "I do not know what this 'case' is."

Randolph cocked his eye at the blonde newcomer, then looked at Kip. "We can trust her?"

"Of course."

"Very well, this is what's going on." Randolph told her about the Nigerians Kip would be meeting in the morning; about the crime cartel supplying and training terrorists with whom law agencies believed they were involved; the black money; other things about the case.

"I was on my way to them the first time we met." Kip related to Nixie some of the events that had happened while he was in Lagos.

Sloane told about the kidnapping and the shooting-up of the hospital.

Randolph nodded at the German girl. "You should tell us about yourself."

"I was originally from Hamburg and I now live in Frankfurt with my mother. I am a flight attendant and a translator and language interpreter."

"So, you're a '*translator*'?" An idea seemed to be forming in the agent's mind. "Perhaps we could use you—would you be interested in working with us while you're here?"

The girl glanced at Kip, then back at Randolph. "What can I do?"

"Listen for side conversations we might not hear or understand—you know 'Russian'?"

"One of my languages."

"Great! One of the suspects is Ukrainian—speaks Russian. We know he is involved with the Cartel."

There was a tapping at the door; one of the Marines stood there. "Begging your pardon, sir, but the major asked me to remind you that you have an early start tomorrow morning—"

"Ah, yes, of course." Randolph turned to the others. "We will meet in the atrium in the hallway at seven . . . the hotel will deliver our breakfasts." He motioned at the military men. "The Marines, here, will be guarding our floor all night."

The guests shuffled off in the direction of their rooms.

Nixie watched Kip fumble in his pocket for his door key. "Why not go through my room into yours? It connects, you know."

"Of course . . ." *Is this an invitation?*

"We can talk."

"Sure."

He followed her into her room and settled into a chair. Nixie set her drink on the nightstand and untied her running shoes that dropped to the floor; she wriggled her toes. Kip saw that her nails were painted the same shade of orange as the T-shirt—was she always this meticulous?

She dropped back and propped herself onto her elbows. "'*Herr* Kip', why did you *really* want me here?" Her German accent had a dusky cast he had not noticed before. She raised an eyebrow and shrugged, shaking her head. "You do not *need* a translator . . . everyone is speaking English."

Once more with her, he was at a loss for words. "I—I thought I might need an interpreter."

Nixie sat up; a grin flickered across her face. She reached for her beer mug and took a swallow. Her eyes never left him. "I see."

Kip found himself floundering. "I thought it would be a good excuse to see you, again."

"I would have come, anyway—but why do you always have to have some 'excuse'? First, there were the 'antique cars in Lagos', now—*'translation' into your own language!"* Her blonde eyebrows arched upward. "Do you not have any *real* reasons in your life . . .?"

"Boy, you really know how to—"

". . . just be 'real' with me, 'Herr Kip'. I am a real person."

Nixie pulled back the bedspread and sat on the sheet with her legs crossed, facing him. The yellow lamplight cast highlights onto her blonde hair, sparkled her light blue eyes. "This is the first time we have been alone."

Kip grinned. "You're right . . . Before, we were always in a crowd." Once more he was taken by how good-looking she was; his first impression of her at the Frankfurt airport had been correct. "I'm glad you're here."

"Did you really think about me?"

"You wouldn't be here if I hadn't. How about you?"

"'Herr Kip' . . . by the way—how did you get that name?"

"My full name is 'Rudyard Kipling Leeds'. Everybody calls me 'Kip'."

"All right, 'Kip'. Of course, I never forgot about you." *He is a little older and more mature-looking than I remembered him from the airplane.*

"You didn't remember my name when I called you on the telephone."

"You never *told* me your name on the airplane. But I remembered your silly story about those 'antique cars in Lagos'. How could I forget that! I had hoped to see you when we got off the plane, but we were under guard."

"Under guard?"

She told him about airline security problems at the Lagos airport and how uncertain the flight crews had felt about their safety when they were there. "Thank God, I do not have to go to Lagos, anymore."

Kip looked at Nixie sitting cross-legged on the bed, rocking slightly as she spoke, her fingers gripping her bare toes. Being a flight attendant, he was starting to understand, was not all just fun and glamour—it could also be a downright dangerous business.

She rolled onto her stomach and folded her forearms underneath her chin. Her blue eyes looked over at him. "I am very tense and tired—would you rub my back?"

Kip eased onto the mattress next to her and sized up her prone profile. He began a slow, one-handed massage. Her torso and shoulders felt firm; tense. "You're tight."

"I need to relax . . . could you use both hands?"

Kip commenced tapping her back with his fingertips. As he kneaded her taut back, the girl's torso gave to his rhythmic ministrations; she felt exquisite under his hands. Every now and then she gave a little moan while he worked back and forth.

"That feels good," she breathed, squirming. Kip stared in admiration at the outine of her backside; the arresting female figure of the airliner cabin was now literally at his fingertips. He went on massaging, pressing and tugging her fine form. "How does this feel?"

A little moan escaped her. He looked at Nixie. Her eyes were closed

"Is this all right?" He stopped. Her breathing was soft and shallow. "Nixie?"

She was asleep.

"I guess you *were* tired, all right," he whispered.

Kip slid off the bed and slipped back into his loafers. With care, he laid the top-sheet over her and doused the lamp. The hotel room plunged into darkness except for a weak suggestion of light finding its way through the curtains from the outside.

He tiptoed to the connecting door and paused. From where he stood, he could faintly see the outline of Nixie under the bedcovers, backlit through the window curtains. Kip took a deep breath—he was responsible for her safety, he knew, since she was here in Madrid at his invitation. He looked at her sleeping form for some moments, still hardly believing she was actually here, then closed the door.

* * *

Two doors down, Jim Randolph jabbed the TV remote "mute" button and settled onto the sofa next to the long-haired brunette. The others were gone. He handed Sloane a glass of red wine and took a swallow of his own. "Here's the deal for tomorrow . . . Leeds will meet with the Nigerians in the morning. We will wire him with a Russian 'body transmitter'—a great device, by the way; those people have impressed me by how good they are, technically—the idea is to have all the bad guys in one place where we can arrest them."

Randolph gave Sloane a filtered description of the international crime organization based in Nigeria. "We believe all the ring-leaders of the Cartel will be there."

The girl shuddered. "You mean those awful people who kidnapped me were the same people I'm supposed to identify?"

"That's what we think. Your friend Leeds will be a hero if he can pull it off."

"I'm worried about him."

"We'll do our best to protect him." *But if anything goes wrong, tomorrow, the guy may be dead.* "You say you've known Leeds for a long time?"

"Since about the time my mother died. I was twelve, then. Kip was nice to me."

"And you were in love with him, of course."

Sloane felt herself flushing. "We were just 'friends'. He was 'too old' for me, he always said. Kip's about thirty-four, now. He's eleven years older than I am."

Jim gave a little laugh. "Sloane, I'm thirty-seven—I'm three years older than *he* is!"

"Oh!" She gripped the wine glass with both hands; her wide eyes stared into the drink. "That's 'interesting'—"

533

Randolph rolled his own glass back-and-forth in his hands. "Your father told me he plans to retire in a year or so. Will you take-over his business?"

Sloane took a sip of her drink. "He's mentioned it a few times."

"Could you run the show by yourself?"

"I'd need some help." She grinned. "Come and work with me . . . we could be a good team."

"I already have a job."

"We're both in the same field and we get along well, together." She looked at him in mock seriousness. "We *do* get along well, together, don't we?"

"Well, sure . . . I mean, of course, we do, Sloane—but, remember—you're my 'witness'. This is an 'official' case."

"Besides, I'm sure little Nicky would like to have you around." *I would like to have you around.*

A silence came over the room. Sloane and Jim took sips of their drinks. On the silent TV screen, a late-night Spanish comedian was laughing it up without sound.

"We could be partners, even."

Randolph glanced at her. *Partners for life? The girl is beautiful. And smart. And and she survived the kidnapping.* "I'll think about that."

"You will?" She stretched out her legs. The strappy shoes dropped to the floor. She tucked her feet underneath herself, facing him on the sofa.

"Sure, I'll think about it." He got up and poured himself another glass. "More wine?"

"Okay, a little. What kind of wine is it?"

He looked at the bottle. "*'Shiraz'*—from Australia."

"My mother was from Australia."

"That so? How was that?"

"Daddy met her on leave from the Vietnam War. It was terrible that she died so young—from skin cancer—'melanoma'. She was beautiful."

Randolph glanced down at her on the sofa. "I can see that beauty runs in the family." He sat back down and handed the glass to her. On impulse, he clicked his glass to hers. "To the future."

"The . . . 'future'—" The flush that came over Sloane was not caused entirely by the wine.

He set his wine-glass on a table. "You're serious about wanting me in your business?"

"Wouldn't have said it if I hadn't meant it. We Texans are direct, you know."

"I've noticed that. We were more subtle—indirect—back in Pennsylvania."

"I saw how Nicky took to you."

"In many ways, he reminds me of my little boy who . . . died—along with his mother."

The girl blinked and gave a tiny gasp Randolph did not pick up. For a split-second the image of a smiling Dominique—Nicky's young French exchange-student-father who had died while rescuing some fellow students from a fraternity fire—had flashed before her as it had so many times. "We both have had our tragedies." She swallowed the last of her wine and set the glass aside.

Randolph reflected a moment. "Sabina and Trini will be a part of me, always. But at some point, I just had to go on. I made my peace with the past and decided I would use their memories as inspiration to try to accomplish things in my own life." He took a deep breath. "Do you know what I mean?" He held his gaze into her eyes. "You don't know it, but you and your little boy have done a lot to help bring me out of a bad time." He looked away for a moment, then back at her. "When we talked about 'the future' just now, it was like things were changing for me—for the better." He shrugged. "Am I making any sense?"

"I thought the same thing . . . about the 'future'."

"Then maybe there was somehow a *reason* for all that happened—your kidnaping . . . even your boyfriend who was killed in the fire and me losing my wife and child in the wreck had some higher purpose—do you believe in those kinds of things?"

A wave of empathy for him came over Sloane. "I—well, maybe you're right. It is up to us to keep going." She reached for his hand. "Oh, Jim . . . you really are a lovely man." The girl leaned forward and lightly touched her lips to his.

He drew Sloane to him and enveloped her in his arms. This time, the kiss was deep; lingering. Her long, black hair flowed over them as they embraced. He kissed her neck, her face; caressed her shoulders—it had been a long time since he had held a woman like this. She felt firm, toned; he remembered Sloane had told him she was a tennis player. And she was squirming, kissing him back. He was aware of her youth; her fertility—*I could have children with her.*

In all her life, Sloane had never felt so safe and secure as in this moment with Jim Randolph. *I could fall in love with him—I have, already—maybe we could be married someday and have children to go with Nicky. But would he ever want those things with me?*

He pulled back. "I—I'm sorry . . . I don't know what came over me."

"*I do.*" Sloane leaned against him and rubbed his chest.

Jim Randolph could feel the firmness of her body; her caress.

She blinked her eyes into his; in the lamplight he saw they were misty. "Jim . . . do you realize how much we have in common?"

"I declare—you Texans really *are* 'forward', aren't you!'

"Don't blame it on Texas . . . blame it on yourself! *Any* girl would wish to have someone like you around."

He lifted her chin and kissed her nose. "You understand, of course, that this is not 'professional' behavior!"

"Who cares?" She put her arms around his neck and pulled him down for another embrace.

Randolph glanced over her shoulder at the alarm clock on the nightstand gave a start. "*We'll* care, if we don't knock it off and get some sleep. It's after midnight and we have to be up and going by six-thirty, remember?" He eased her arms off his shoulders. "I'll knock on your door, then. They're serving breakfast in the alcove." She straightened her blouse and pulled on her shoes.

In the open space, surrounded by guest rooms, he noticed the Marine guards down the way, keeping watch. "Remember, 'Miss Ferry'," Randolph said, for the benefit of the soldiers who were staring at the two, "we meet in the morning at six-thirty. We're supposed to be at the Russian Embassy at eight . . . your friend 'Leeds' is to meet the Nigerians at ten."

In a moment, she had slipped through the doorway into her room. The door clicked shut.

With a glance at the uniformed men who were gazing at him with a knowing look, Randolph stepped back down the roomy foyer to his own quarters.

-22-

A brassy clamor invaded Kip Leeds's subconscious. He groped for the telephone by the bed.

"This is your 'wake-up'!" came a woman's cheery voice, "the time is six o'clock!"

He lay back for some moments, blinking. Where was he? *Madrid.* He cast around the darkened room. Beams of light crawled around the corners of the window curtains; outside, a Spanish day had already broken. From below the fourteenth-floor window, came the muffled rumble of many vehicles down on the "Gran Via".

Through the closed connecting door, he heard Nixie's telephone ringing, then her faint, drowsy-sounding voice. She, too, was now awake.

A few seconds later, there came some little knocks on the dividing door. Kip snatched up his trousers and hopped across the carpeted floor, pulling them up, fumbling for the elusive belt; not forgetting the zipper.

He opened the door. Nixie stood blinking; her blonde hair in disarray from sleeping. "Ah, 'Herr Kip' . . ." Her voice was husky. "I—just wanted to—make sure you were—awake . . ." The young woman looked uncomfortable; she shifted from one bare foot to the other. She glanced down at the T-shirt of their little 'rubdown' session the night before and bit her lower lip.

He allowed himself an inward smile. So the girl had "'morning-after" regrets about letting him feel her up last night! "Don't worry—we behaved ourselves."

Kip remembered how one time in a college English class he had written a theme about a comely young woman in a poem who looked delectable even though dressed in disheveled clothes. Nixie, standing before him in the wrinkled T-shirt and jeans, reminded him of the poetry girl.

He glanced at the clock by the bed. "We'll have to hurry . . . breakfast is in a little while."

"I will shower, now." The girl turned toward her bathroom.

"I'll do the same." Kip closed the door and paused. Their conversation had been a stilted affair—was she having second thoughts about being here with him?

He padded to his own bathroom, hung his trousers on the door and stepped under the shower. While he soaped-up, he kept thinking about her. Was this girl into him, or not? Last night she had been a willing participant in their little massage session—he remembered it had been her suggestion in the first place for him to rub her back. Nixie must have known that he could have taken advantage of her had he so desired; without a doubt she had already been around the block a few times and knew the score. On the other hand, this girl might very well be good for the long haul, in which case there would be plenty of time for such things. Besides, he was already liking her very much; for now, he would hold off the physical stuff, which, for him, was a new attitude. As the water coursed over him, Kip found himself grinning.

His thoughts went on. Nixie's looks had attracted him from the time he had first seen her at the Frankfurt airport, and from their conversation on that airplane flight to Lagos she had shown a lively mind, as well. Maybe she had come back and sat next to him on purpose! How she had seen through his nonsensical story about the "antique cars" had intrigued him, and after last night's talk he realized she might understand him better than he had thought. Had she analyzed him while they were apart? His business partner, Brad, insisted women did that. He'd see how things went with her in Madrid before making any moves.

For now, the fact that she was taking her own shower just a few inches from him—he could hear the rumbling of the water pipes to her bathroom through the wall—was titillating.

* * *

As she soaped and scrubbed herself, Nixie heard the sounds of water running in the next bathroom—no more than a half-meter beyond the other side of the tiles of her bath, the American was also showering.

Nixie thought about last night when she had let Kip touch more of her than she would have ordinarily allowed to someone she hardly knew—she could still feel his palms and fingertips on her back. She had had to resist the impulse to roll over and draw him down to her—she was that attracted to him. But that would have certainly led to something for which she was not yet ready. For now, she would gauge his interest by how *deliberately* he came on to her—something she had not done with a man since the divorce. For she was very much interested in this American and she would be patient. *Would he be patient?*

As the water flowed over her slippery skin, the girl thought back to that first time when she had seen him in the big waiting room at Frankfurt. She had noticed him at once because he was one of only two people with light-colored hair in the whole crowd of people waiting for the Lagos flight. The other, of course, had been *her*. But that was not all that caught her attention: as she kept glancing in his direction, trying to look casual, she had wondered what he was doing on that plane to Lagos. And from what she had seen and heard from having been there several times—at his Nigerian destination, he would face great danger. Had he known that? She had decided she would talk with him during the flight. She remembered she had asked him if she could sit next to him to smoke a cigarette. The excuse had worked then, but she had since given up smoking.

And then, a few days ago, he had called her! Now, here she was—in Madrid on a mysterious mission with him and some others, of which she would soon learn her part.

Nixie turned off the water and reached for a towel. Just as she did so, the screeching of the water pipes to Kip's room came to a thudding stop; he had finished his shower, also. As she rubbed herself down, it seemed that everything they were doing was synchronized—could that be a good omen?

At some point, she would have to tell him about the divorce. How would he take it? He seemed to be a fair-minded fellow, but the last time she had brought up the subject to a man, he had gone away. She hoped Kip would understand the circumstances of the parting last year from Anton, the physical brute who hit her in places where the bruises would not show. In a matter of months, she had left him; the airline job had been the perfect vehicle to carry her far away from him and his bad attitudes. But two

540

unsatisfactory short-term relationships since then had left her disillusioned with men; the American had come along at just the right time. She did not want to do anything to endanger this new opportunity, for she saw in "Herr Kip Leeds" some encouraging prospects for the future.

A few minutes later, as she was putting away her make-up case, there came light knocks on the door. Kip stood there, grinning. "Ready for breakfast?"

The others were taking seats at tables set up in the alcove. Through big windows of the fourteenth floor the city of Madrid lay arrayed before them, painted orange in the new-day sun. The uniformed guards stood by, observing. Nixie recognized the dark-haired American girl and the man who had identified himself as an agent of their government, sitting at another table. The two seemed to be acting friendly toward each other; from their body language, Nixie suspected their relationship ran deeper than just an agent-witness arrangement. She noticed that Kip kept glancing at them. Another man was sitting at their table; overhearing his accent, she decided he must be Swiss.

The elevator opened just then and several dark-haired men in server's outfits pushed a trio of food carts toward them. In a brisk, efficient manner—almost hurried, Nixie thought—they started setting steaming plates of Spanish breakfasts before them.

Off to one side, there came a buzzing sound from one of the Marine's security telephones.

Just as Nixie was reaching for her fork, all at once the military man gave a shout. "Stop!"

Startled, everyone turned to look at him; Kip's fork with his first bite on it was already in mid-air in front of him. The soldier's portable telephone was at his ear. The man's eyes went wide and he waved frantically. "Do not eat!" He pointed at the servers, who were pushing the carts in a hurry into the elevator down the way. "Stop those men! This food is poisoned!"

The uniformed Marines ran toward the elevator that was closing. The first to get there slapped the closed double-door in frustration; the floor indicator arrow above it was already moving down. Another jabbed the button frantically. Nothing happened.

"The stairs!" Kip, the Swiss Inspector and the American agent dashed up and joined the clattering procession bounding down the zig-zagging concrete stairwell. "Those guys were fakes!" the leading soldier gasped back up at the others, as he took another quick turn, his feet drumming on the cement steps. "Hurry!"

In a couple of minutes, they huffed into the hotel's stainless-steel kitchen, where the steamy aroma of cooking food filled the air. In the middle of the space, the house detective was standing with a half-dozen indignant-looking fellows.

The contingent from upstairs ran up to them. "Where are they?"

"We are looking for them, now." The real servers were rubbing their wrists. "We found our men tied-up in the walk-in freezer." Kip saw that the employees were shivering.

Randolph spoke up. They were in the service elevator . . . did you check it?"

"No one was on it."

"Then they got off on another floor!" The American agent's eyes went wide. "Oh, my God! I know what they did—"

Kip snapped his fingers. "Of course! What did we do when their elevator started moving?"

The Marine Sergeant slapped his forehead. "We hit the stairs and ran down here—the women are up there by themselves!"

Tarliani was already making toward the elevators; the others following at his heels. The Swiss agent stabbed the button. The doors opened; the men piled in. Their weight doubled while the car shot upward.

"Let's get off at the *thirteenth* floor," a Marine said. "We don't want to open right up to them, if they are there! We can take the stairs."

Randolph nodded. "Good idea."

The doors rumbled open. Tarliani gave Randolph and the Marines quick looks. "Your weapons!" The four sergeants un-hitched their service revolvers from their side holsters; the Swiss agent drew his own *'Mauser'* from inside his coat holster; the American's snub "thirty-eight" was already out. Kip, unarmed, held back behind the others as the men advanced up the inside stairs.

On the fourteenth landing, Randolph cracked open the door for a half-second, then drew back. "Three men are holding the women at gunpoint!" he whispered. He peeped out again, then let the door close without a sound. "I see another stairwell door next to them!" The agent motioned to Kip, who understood what the other American intended. He re-traced his steps back down to the thirteenth floor, hustled across the deserted open space to the stairway diagonally across from the one where the others were waiting and climbed up once more to the next level.

He eased open the door a fraction of an inch. Out of his sight, he heard Sloane's voice. "You won't get away with this . . . the men will be returning!"

Kip's attention was on the door across the space, behind the attackers. Through the cracks, he saw Randolph give a nod.

Kip flung open the door in front of him with a loud *WHACK!* In the fraction of a second it took for the assailants to turn toward him, the other door burst aside with a hail of gunfire, catching the dark-haired men unawares! All three went down, red froth shooting from their throats. With a scream, Nixie drew back; at the same time, Sloane lunged toward the writhing leader of the trio and jammed her knee into his chest. The man went still; his nine-millimeter clunked to the floor. The other two, covered in spreading liquid crimson, were not moving.

Just then, the elevator door slid back; the house detective and two of his deputies bounded toward them. "Ah, señors!" he gasped in accented English, gazing from one inert suspect to another. The Spaniard's eyes were wide "You *killed* them?"

Tarliani spoke up. "They were holding these women at gunpoint!" He explained how they had overpowered the attackers.

"Very good work, señors!" He pulled out his portable radio unit." I will call police headquarters." The man was already punching numbers into the sender.

Kip stepped to Nixie and put his arm around her waist. Shaking, she dropped her head onto his shoulder. Jim Randolph put his hand on Sloane's shoulder and gave the young detective an admiring look.

A short while later, as ambulance crews were leaving with their unpleasant cargoes on gurneys covered with white sheets, the service elevator doors once more drew aside. Three servers Kip recognized from downstairs rolled new food carts toward the atrium, where hotel employees were clearing away the tainted dishes. "Save those plates for the laboratory!" the house detective called out. He looked around at the guests. "And your meal is *'gratis'* from the hotel."

Tarliani glanced at his watch, then at Kip and the others. "We had better hurry. We must be at the Russian Embassy in forty-five minutes!"

* * *

"You can speak normally with this on you . . ." Kip squirmed as the white-coated Russian technician rubbed glue on the small of his back and pressed the flat, inch-square, flesh-colored device against his skin. "We put the transmitter on your lower back because, if they search you, they will probably not see or feel it."

A middle-aged Russian man in a decorated uniform, whom Kip remembered from last night's meeting at the embassy as a Special Forces officer in their military, looked at the device, nodding. "We use these when we work our 'operations'."

The American thought about what kind of "operations" the crisp, military foreigner must have meant. Kip looked around the white laboratory room with thoughts of amazement. He would never have imagined he would be involved with people like these—from the "other side", as he had always thought of Russians—on a mission where the Americans and the Russians were now on the *same* side, and using *their* technology, no less.

The electronics man went on in his accented English. "Our software in Moscow will process your voice and those of the others around you and send us a display by satellite at the same time you are speaking," He held up a tiny, buff-colored, tapered device. This is the 'receiver' . . . it goes in your ear." The man rubbed something from a tube on it and pushed it, tickling, into

Kip's left ear canal. "Do not worry, after you are finished with it, we can remove it . . . no problem."

"It is far down inside your ear where they will not see it," the Russian military man said.

The technician picked up a microphone and spoke some words in Russian into it. After a fraction-of-a-second's delay, the words sounded against Kip's eardrum. "My voice went up to our orbiting satellite . . . down to Moscow . . . went through our computers . . . was re-sent up to the satellite . . . and back down to our monitor screens and your receiver, where you heard it!"

Kip glanced around at Tarliani and Randolph, whose faces mirrored his own impressed expression. No wonder these people had been such tough adversaries during the "Cold War", he thought, if this was an example of their technical expertise. The Russians looked pleased that the others were impressed.

Tarliani motioned to the American. "Come with us." He and the others followed the man down a gilded hallway to the same meeting room where they had been the night before that was now re-arranged like a small auditorium.

The thin, bespectacled individual whom Kip remembered as the no-nonsense Intelligence officer from Moscow, stood beside a white screen holding a pointer, his eyes exaggerated in size by his eyeglasses while he scrutinized each person as they come into the room.

The angular Russian nodded and the lights went out. On the screen came a picture of a row of apartments or flats. "This is where you will meet the Nigerians," he said, looking in Kip's direction, tapping the projected picture, ". . . you will walk down the sidewalk, by the park—"

* * *

Kip strode along the downward sloping sidewalk; through the black iron fence to his right was the enormous heroic equestrian statue dominating the *'Plaza de España';* from the lush little park came the laugher of picnicking children and the crunch of gravel as joggers puffed along the running track that rimmed the edge of the compact, block-square place.

He squinted into the mid-morning sun; ahead was the overpass; some distance beyond it loomed the hulking white facade of the *'Palacio Real';* the Royal Palace. A little to its left, over the treetops, soared the cross-tipped spires of the *'Almudena Cathedral'.* Somewhere in-between was the apartment row where he had been briefed to meet Masobe Busa and the others. There, he was to take possession of the twenty-million dollars and to try to delay the Organization's leading figures so they could be captured. As he stepped along, Kip realized he was tensing. "Relax!" he told himself. But he knew that the safety of millions of people could very well depend on how well he did his job in the next few hours. The tension stayed.

A resonant, Russian-accented voice speaking in English burst onto his left eardrum. "Comrade Leeds . . . do you hear me?"

"Yes, I hear you." A passing pedestrian gave him a strange look. Kip felt foolish; he must have appeared to be talking to himself. Out of the corner of his eye, he spotted the white van with the agents inside it parked halfway down a side street—at the proper time, they would swoop-in and nab the Cartel criminals.

The voice came back. "You must always be near to them for us to hear everyone speak."

One block past the overpass, he came to the intersection facing the row of apartments on the right side of the boulevard; on the corner was the florist shop he had memorized from the briefing by the bespectacled Russian Intelligence officer. Crossing the street, halfway down the block, he came to the first-floor entryway of the "Renaldo Apartments", set back from the storefronts, like he had been told to expect. "Take the inside stairs to the second level. There—according to what we know—you will meet the Nigerians," the Russians had said.

Kip spoke in low tones to those listening in the van. "I am at the apartment entrance, now." He stepped into a gloomy entryway whose cracking plaster walls contrasted with the more well-kept brick-and-glass storefronts on the outside; in the fitful light, the dingy space's peeling paint stood out. With his first breath, the dusty, musty-smelling air caused him to cough.

He gripped the scuffed banister rail and started up the steps. He was halfway up when a heavyset man appeared all at once at the top of the stairs, startling him. "Ah, Mister Leeds!"

Kip recognized the voice and the shiny face of "Masobe Busa" from when he was in Lagos that first time. Today, the man was not wearing his flowery outfit and was in a business suit.

"It is good to see you!" The African put out a ham-like hand as the American topped the second-floor landing.

Kip remembered their last parting, when the man was a no-show at the airport to give him some papers from signing for the money. "I would have liked to have seen *you* at the airport, that time."

"Ah, many apologies, Mister Leeds. I was called away on—other matters. I am sure my lawyer took good care of you, back then—in fact, here he is now."

Another very dark individual had stepped from a side room into the open space. Kip looked at him and caught his breath; in the dim light the man's bleary-looking eyes seemed to be boring through him.

The fellow put out his hand. "Mike Adwadube . . ."

"Of course." The fellow's bulging, mucosed, staring eyeballs un-nerved Kip. He wondered why the man was here in Madrid.

The three stepped into an unfurnished apartment that looked to be under renovation—cans of paint, some dropcloths and a stepladder were in one corner of the bare living room. Daylight streamed-in through unadorned bay windows that faced the street, one level below.

A dark-haired Caucasian fellow about his age and an olive-skinned young woman with short blonde hair stood by, looking him over as he came in.

Busa spoke up. "This is Mister—that is—'*Señor Landa*' and '*Señorita Montero*' . . . both are working with us."

"Kip Leeds." The American shook their hands. He thought the two looked nervous.

Kip turned and for the first time saw the big metal box in the middle of the floor—*the same strongbox he had seen in Lagos with the twenty-million dollars in "blackened" money inside it!*

Just then another very black, round-faced man in a three-piece suit strode through a doorway. Kip was sure he saw the man and Adwadube lock-eyes for a second.

Busa motioned. "This is 'Doctor Mobustu'." The Nigerian nodded at Kip but did not offer a handshake. Kip remembered him from the demonstration in Busa's living room, that time—he had been the bank official in charge of "cleaning" the sample money in front of all those people. *Why was he here?*

As silent as a shadow, a stooped little African—the same gnome-like fellow he had seen in Busa's living room, that time—loped-in behind the banker and stood by, his eyes darting back and forth. With a start, Kip remembered that the small fellow was one of the undercover INTERNOL agents about whom Tarliani had briefed them last evening at the embassy. Looking about, the American realized that several of the people he remembered from Lagos that first time were here in this room. He knew that the objective was to arrest important Cartel figures; whoever had arranged this gathering had done a thorough job.

The white man and the bronze-skinned woman, both still looking ill-at-ease for some reason, stood back, not having anything to say.

Mobustu flashed a look at Kip. "You have the funds to clean the money?"

"I want to see that it is real, before I commit it to you."

A scowl shot across the man's face. "You do not trust us?" He stood up straight. "Very well . . . " He nodded at the small fellow, who left the room.

In a few minutes, a half-dozen of the authentic one-hundred-dollar notes were laid out—crisp and clean-looking—on the floor, next to the ripped-open little pouches of chemical powder and trays. "Are you satisfied?" Mobustu sounded peeved.

Kip nodded. "I have the money you want in a bank on the 'Gran Via'."

"You did not bring it with you?"

"I didn't want to carry one-million, six-hundred-seventy five-thousand dollars with me—too dangerous. It is at the *'Sevillian Bank'."*

Mobustu frowned. "Take us there."

"I don't know if the bank is open . . . today is Saturday."

The financier's face looked fierce. "Do not stall on us!" Mobustu pointed at the white man, the woman and the little fellow. "You stay here with the money." He gestured at Busa, Adwadube, and at Kip. "Come with me."

The four went down to the street. As if on cue, a Jaguar four-door sedan pulled up to the curb. Kip saw that a Nigerian was driving. Mobustu motioned. "Get in." The car drove away into traffic. "To the 'Sevillian Bank' on the 'Gran Via'," the African said to the driver in a heavy voice.

As the automobile turned the corner, Kip got a fleeting glance of the white van carrying the Russian agents pulling away from its parking spot at the curb. He guessed it was drawing-in behind them. At the next corner, the Jaguar turned left and headed across the viaduct. Out of the corner of his eye, Kip sensed the van's shape following them several vehicle lengths to their rear.

At the "Gran Via", the car turned to the right and drove some blocks down the broad boulevard, then pulled to the curb in front of a stone-faced building. When he got out, Kip noticed that the Jaguar in which they had been riding had "Diplomat" license plates on it. *So it's a Nigerian Embassy car!* At a glance he saw the van drive on ahead and stop in a loading zone.

As they passed through a pair of elegant brass doors, Kip recognized the name of the "Sevillian Bank" on them where the Russians had told him to take the Africans. He caught his breath in alarm—for a long second, he couldn't remember the name of the man they were supposed to meet! Then it came back to him. *"Señor Alcosta,"* he told a receptionist, trying to appear calm. But his palms were sweating.

The girl lifted a telephone handset and said some words in Spanish. "I am sorry," she said, switching back to English, "but 'Señor Alcosta' is away until one o'clock."

Mobustu's watery eyes focused on a "grandfather" clock in the lobby; its pendulum swinging. "It is eleven-thirty, now . . . we will return, then."

Outside, the man was scowling. "This had better not be a double-cross." Kip detected a threatening undertone to the man's voice.

The American tried to sound casual. "Well, you know how these Spanish people are. Their *'siestas'* can take a while!" Kip's try at levity did not seem to register with the Nigerian.

Mobustu pointed at the car "Get in!" The man squinted at the driver. "Drive us around the city." Kip tensed. *What is this?*

The Jaguar eased out into the midday traffic. As they passed it by, Kip saw the driver of the white van swinging his steering wheel; the commercial vehicle was starting to move from its parking space. He took a deep breath—whatever should happen, at least they would be close behind him. Kip hoped the Africans did not notice they were being followed—he would have to trust the Russians to use good sense. His heart was pounding, his mouth felt dry; his palms were still perspiring.

A click and a hum sounded in the American's ear, almost making him jump. The accented voice came on. "We are following you . . . try to keep them talking—"

Mobustu's eyes darted about. "Go out onto the main highway. Drive fast—we will see if anyone can keep up with us."

"Kip caught his breath—*did they suspect him?*

The African's next sentence eased his concerns. "I want to see what this car can do at high speed." Kip knew that Jaguars had a reputation for fast handling.

In a few minutes, the sedan swung onto a freeway and the driver pressed the accelerator to the floor. At once, the kilometer-calibrated speedometer shot up past one-hundred-sixty. Kip did some fast figuring: they were going down the expressway at over a hundred miles an hour! A massive, orange-painted soccer stadium shot past. As they overtook and passed vehicle after vehicle, he knew that the white van loaded with equipment could never keep up with them. Mobustu, staring out, seemed to be taking in every detail.

Kip remembered he was supposed to keep them talking. "Where are we going?"

"Around."

Mobustu's vague, expressionless answer unsettled Kip. He didn't like this.

The man pointed at a big truck plaza coming up fast at the next exit. "Drive in there. I want to see about something."

Once more, Kip didn't like the tone of the man's voice—*what did he mean?*

The Jaguar pulled up into a space next to an idling semi-truck. The frowning banker turned about and pointed at Kip, who was sitting in the center back seat, then scowled at the driver and Busa. "Did you *search* this guy?"

The man's words came to the American like a thunderclap. *Were they about to discover the body transmitter and the ear implant?* A bad feeling grabbed his insides.

Busa shook his head. "No, we did not."

"Out of the car!"

Adwadube gripped Kip's forearm; it seemed to the Texan that the strong African was *pulling* him from the seat. The banker, his eyes looking fierce, came around the sedan, still pointing at Kip. "Take him inside and strip-search him! I suspect something!"

A hum came to the earpiece. "If they find the transmitter, tell them it is a nicotine patch!"

Rough hands guided Kip through the front doorway. Adwadube confronted a waitress. *"Baño?"*

The girl motioned toward the back of the crowded place where a neon "Caballeros" sign over an arched opening led to the men's room. His spirits sinking, Kip stepped along with the others. Whatever happened, now—one way or the other—it wouldn't take long, he figured. He regretted that if these men discovered what the patch was doing, the others might never know what happened to him. He thought about Nixie. He thought about Sloane.

At an oversized toilet stall, Mobustu motioned for everyone to step inside. A man washing his hands gave the five men a quizzical look, finished in a hurry and left.

Mobustu glared at Kip. "Off with it!"

The American pulled off his loafers, then his trousers and shirt.

The men looked him over. "Keep going!"

Busa pointed at Kip's lower backside. "What is this?"

" . . . 'nicotine patch'—"

"On your *back?*"

"Ah . . . the doctor said it would work better, there." Kip's heart was pounding; he could hear a swishing, coursing sound in his ears.

Mobustu rubbed his fingertips over the skin-colored disc. "You smoke?"

"I used to." Kip tried to sound casual. He had never smoked.

The African looked the American up and down. Then he jerked off the patch, causing Kip to gasp. "We will throw this away, *just in case*—" He tossed the tiny flat device into the trash can creating a rattling noise that sounded in Kip' ear. "Let us hope you do not have any 'nicotine fits'!" The man laughed at his own coarse humor. The fluorescent lights changed his yellow teeth to a hideous green cast. Kip blanched.

Mobustu looked at his watch. "Get dressed . . . it is now time for us to return to the bank!" While the Texan pulled on his clothes, the black man glared at Kip. "I am still suspicious. I will watch you to make sure you do not do anything to us. "

As he dropped back into the Jaguar, Kip spotted the white van stopped at the far outer edge of the big parking lot.

It was only as they were driving off that he realized the Nigerians had not found the earpiece. "We are still following you!" came a sudden voice in Kip's ear, causing him to give a start he hoped the others did not notice. "The ear-receiver is also a short-range back-up transmitter . . . but we will have to follow close-behind you! Nod your head if you hear us."

"We must hurry to the bank!" Kip looked at his own watch with an exaggerated nod.

"All right, we see you," the Russian came back.

"Yes, it is one o'clock, now." Mobustu sounded casual.

But the driver was giving furtive glances at the rear-view mirror, frowning. "There is a van behind us that I am sure I have seen before."

Kip stopped breathing—*after he had escaped detection the first time, was he now going to be caught?*

The Russian voice came back. "We will pull off now and return to the bank."

"I guess I was wrong," the man at the wheel said a moment later. "The van is taking an exit, now."

A minute later, just after they had driven past an entry ramp, a sudden loud burst of static and a hum came back to the tiny earpiece receiver. "Comrade Kip Leeds—we are behind you!"

A man's voice! Kip gave a start, his eyes went wide. Thank God, none of the others seemed to notice his surprise. The Russian brogue came in loud and clear. "If you hear me, rub the back of your neck . . . do not look back."

The American made a show of stretching, finishing by interlacing his fingers against the back of his neck and rubbing up and down.

"Ah, that is good. Very good." The man's heavy Slavic accent sounded re-assuring against Kip's eardrum.

"We will follow you to the bank. We are armed and will be nearby."

Kip's heart was pounding.

* * *

". . . and you have been with Busa for a long time?" "Monica Montero" was speaking in English to the little African, whom she remembered was named, "Mickey". All along, she had wondered why the bald, dimunitive Nigerian seemed to have a frightened look on his face all the time; she would probe for some answers. "How did you come to know Señor Busa?"

The older man's eyes flitted from the strongbox in the middle of the floor to the Cuban woman to her male companion. "My family lived next door to Mister Busa. There was a fire and he rescued me. I was the only one saved and he gave me a job as his . . . 'helper'. That was about ten years ago. I have worked at his house, since then."

The stooped fellow's eyes darted about, as if he was unsure about how much he should say.

Monica looked at "Luis"; a suspicion was forming. "How does he treat you?"

553

Mickey gazed out the unadorned bay window, streaked with overpaint from the re-modeling job. "Sometimes, if he is not satisfied with something I do, he will keep food from me, or lock me in my room, all day." The fellow shrugged. "I have no place else to go." He looked at them. "But I *do* reward myself at his expense . . ."

Before Monica could follow-up the man's enigmatic words, sudden thumps and bumping noises sounded from the stairs, followed by some male voices that were becoming louder.

Four men in work-clothes appeared at the top of the stairwell banister and made the turn toward the room's open door! The first fellow stepped into the unfinished space and stopped short. "Who are *you?*" he asked in Spanish. The other three shuffled up behind him.

Monica's frowned at the men. "We are, ah—looking at the apartment."

"Mira!" One of the Spaniards pointed at the half-dozen hundred-dollar bills on the floor.

Monica's eyes went wide—the banker had left the "cleaned" money out in the open!

The first workman snatched up a bill and gestured to the other men. *"Mucho dinero!"*

Fists clenched, the three others lunged forward, grinning. Mickey, his eyes wide, backed away toward the side-room door.

The Cuban girl gave the first man a quick kick, scattering the currency bills into the air. Before the fellow could react, she kneed him in his throat, sending him backward, not moving.

The twisting, leaping girl launched herself feet-first at the next intruder, catching him full in his chest! The fellow's head slammed against the wall, wobbling. He slid down, and was still.

As the other two turned to escape, Luis grabbed the nearest one's neck and squeezed-down like he had seen Monica do in a demonstration. With a strangled gasp, the fellow went limp.

Meanwhile the fourth man tried to pull himself through the door frame in a frantic attempt to get away. Monica lunged and swung her arm around his neck in hammerlock. The last of the would-be-thieves thrashed for a moment and went still. She dropped him to the floor.

Wiping his mouth on his sleeve, breathing hard, the American looked around at the inert intruders lying askew about the room. "Wow, Marisol . . . that was *some* performance!" Without realizing it, he had called her by her original name.

She grabbed Larry around his neck, shaking. "I wanted to never again have to do that!" The girl choked back sudden tears. "I want to get away from here!"

* * *

"You will deliver the money by *'courier'?*" Mobustu glared across the big mahogany desk at the well-dressed banker. "Señor Alcosta", the financier, leaned back in his high-backed leather executive chair, touching his fingertips together.

"'Si, señor . . . the 'dinero' is of considerable amount—one-million-six-hundred-seventy-five thousand American dollars—we must take special *'precauciones'*." He gave a nod at Kip. "The American bank requested us to handle it this way."

The African was frowning. "I am also a banker and this is most irregular."

"We have found that these things are best handled at places not usually associated with banks." The official-looking man tapped his fingertips some more, nodding in typical financier fashion. "We will deliver the funds to 'Plaza Mayor' during the festival, today." The Spanish man gave Kip another quick look. "Be at the food court at five o'clock."

Mobustu stood up, shaking his head. "Very well, we will be there. But this is most irregular." He motioned to the others.

Outside, the man motioned at the car. "Let us return to the flat, now."

As they drove out onto the bustling "Gran Via", Kip spotted the white van alongside the curb. It was starting to move.

* * *

Ten minutes later, Adwadube was gaping thunderstruck at the four bodies sprawled about the apartment's front room. Busa stepped gingerly over one of the men, shuddering at the dead fellow's grimacing expression. Kip held back, his eyes wide. Mobustu glared; his nostrils flared. *"What the hell happened, here?"*

Monica told how the workmen had tried to take the money and that she and Luis had overpowered them.

The African looked at the compact little woman and her slender male companion in amazement. "You did this by yourself?"

Mickey loped back into the room. "She killed three of them. This man took care of the other one. I saw the whole thing!"

Busa squinted at the Latina. "Now I remember! Retchko told me you were trained in Russia."

Kip's eyes fixed on the trim, bronze-skinned female. *Who is this little woman who just killed three men with her bare hands?*

Mobustu looked agitated. "This money is not safe, here— call the embassy and have them send a truck right away." Adwadube pulled out a cellular telephone and punched some numbers.

* * *

A half-hour later, the Africans, along with Kip, Luis and Monica stood on the sidewalk, gazing at the rear of the un-marked delivery-type truck as it lumbered off into traffic. Mobustu nodded in satisfaction. "They will carry the strongbox to the embassy."

The banker looked at Kip. "We will take you to your hotel, now." The men settled onto the sedan's leather seats; the others got into another vehicle. When the Jaguar pulled out, Kip spotted the white van parked in a loading zone. The driver looked to be talking into a hand-held device.

As they crossed the viaduct, Kip did not pay any attention to a blue van speeding past them.

"All right, here you are . . ." Kip recognized the hotel and the plaza across the broad thoroughfare from it.

Mobustu turned about in his front seat and looked at the American. "Be at 'Plaza Mayor' at four- thirty. It is near to here."

Kip got out. The car drove off. As he stepped toward the hotel's main entrance and the automatic front door slid open, it occurred to him that he had not told the Nigerians where he was staying.

One block past the "Gran Via", the boxy embassy truck carrying the strongbox turned right onto a narrow backstreet. Just as it straightened-out, a blue van swerved in front of it, brakes screeching, and came to a stop diagonally in front of the delivery vehicle!

The Nigerian truck driver jammed on his brakes. "Damn stupid—!"

His words stopped and his eyes went wide as four white men, all dressed in black, jumped from the blockading van. One of the men jerked open the driver's door and thrust a noise-suppressor-affixed automatic pistol between the eyes of the man behind the wheel. "Out! Out! Before I kill you!" the man called out in accented Spanish, "Dammit, hurry!"

A second black-clad man hauled the right-seat passenger down to the cobblestone pavement where the quaking fellow looked up the muzzle of another suppressor-equipped handgun.

At that moment, a white van swept up behind the truck, blocking it from the rear. Three more men, also dressed in black, leaped out.

The newcomers slapped duct-tape over the two shaking truckers' mouths, and shoved them to the ground. In a few seconds, the pair were strapped in a friction-type rope. One of the black-dressed men pulled open the truck's rear doors, pointed inside, then nodded—on the deck, in a pole-harness, was the gunmetal safe.

In swift seconds, the heavy steel container was loaded into the back of the blue van and the trussed-up prisoners were lying in darkness in the back of the closed truck.

Just then, a police car drew up alongside the three vehicles! Two officers with inquiring faces got out and came up, speaking in Spanish.

The black-clad men did not have time for this. One of them took abrupt, deliberate steps and swung his wrist toward the policemen's faces. There were short "hissing" sounds, and both officers slumped senseless to the pavement!

Two of the men hopped into the truck's cab. The driver clutched the transmission into gear. The procession, with the delivery van in the middle, rumbled off down the narrow street, leaving the two unconscious policemen lying beside their idling squad car; its front doors hanging open. The squawking police radio was calling for them.

* * *

"Now, we will get them all!" Retchko's broad grin seemed to ignite the small gathering around the long table in the meeting room at the Nigerian Embassy. Busa, sitting across from him, glanced at the closed door to the corridor as if to make sure the conversation was private.

Mobustu leaned across the table. "It was like the banker was reading our minds to have the money delivered to where they would all be at the same time!"

"We will have our men on the rooftops. The girl and all the others will be easy targets!"

"When the American hands over the money, we will make our moves."

Nomoah, the "Chief" was frowning. "The strongbox is back here at the embassy?"

Busa spoke up. "It should be here, now, but I have not yet talked with the drivers."

The little banker nodded; his bald head reflected the overhead lights. Then he seemed to think of something else. "We will take the passenger van to the plaza?"

Boronov spoke. "It now has the 'invisible' module on it . . . when we have accomplished our mission, we will get away to the airport with no problems." The Russian electronics expert opened a case and handed yellow eyeglasses across the table to the other men. "Keep these in your pockets. We will need these to locate the van when we are finished."

Busa squinted. "What about the others—the American, 'Landay' . . . the Cuban girl . . . and the servant, 'Mickey'?"

559

Retchko shook his head. "They know too much and are of no further use to us . . . *we will kill them there, along with all the—*"

Just then, the door opened and a very black, powerfully-built man stepped into the room.

"Ezego! When did you get here?"

The African pulled out a chair and sat down at the table. "I just arrived from New York."

"How are our 'clients', there?"

"They have about finished the explosives to blow up the 'World Trade Center' buildings."

* * *

"They fell for it!" Tarliani slapped the top of the long table and leaned back, beaming. "Now, we can arrest all of them!" The Swiss Intelligence agent looked across at Livshits, grinning. "That was a terrific idea of yours to have one of your men act as the banker and tell that African to be at the 'Plaza Mayor' this afternoon!"

"We have an account with them . . . a telephone call was all it took to get their co-operation."

Just then, the door opened and four men dressed in black, along with Kip Leeds, came into the soundproof meeting room at the Russian Embassy.

Tarliani and Livshits stood for a round of handshakes. "These are the fellows who pulled it off," the Russian said, motioning for everyone to take seats, nodding at the newcomers.

Speaking in English, the muscular, black-clad young man described how they followed the Nigerian truck to a side street, overpowered the drivers, and took the strongbox. "It was not necessary to kill them." The fellow gave a smirk. "We left them tied-up in the back of the truck. It is now parked in a loading area some blocks from the Nigerian Embassy. It will take them a while to discover what happened! The money is in our custody, now."

A black-dressed fellow tapped his wrist. "We had to knock-out two Madrid policemen."

Livshits's narrow brow furrowed. "Did they get your license numbers?"

"They did not have time."

Tarliani tapped the table. "All right . . . here is the plan: at Plaza Mayor we will situate our people at the food court." He nodded at Sloane, who had been taking in everything. The American girl, here, will give a signal when she recognizes them . . . our agents will then move-in for the arrests." The Swiss agent looked at Nixie. "You will listen to confirm the accent of the Ukrainian. He is the one we are most after."

Watering had been listening. "What if they resist?"

Livshits set his jaw. "Our snipers will shoot to kill them."

Kip spoke up. "I read in the papers this morning that there is some sort of 'festival', going on at the plaza, today."

Major Suslov squirmed in his seat."I had to tell my wife not to go there—she was planning to take our daughter to the festival. I did not tell her why."

Livshits frowned. "A complication—but our shooters are very accurate and our men will work fast. There should no difficulties."

Terenty glanced at Colonel Golubko, who was sitting next to him. "The colonel and I will be there to back-up the snipers, if necessary."

"Very good." The Russian Intelligence agent looked across the table at Kip. "It will be up to you to keep the 'target-individuals' un-suspecting until we make our moves."

The Texan, fidgeting, took a deep breath. He glanced at Nixie, who was sitting next to him. She patted his forearm.

Livshits saw the gesture. "Nervous? We teach our people to stay focused on the objective. If you do that, you will be all right." *But he should be nervous. He—and many others—may be killed in this operation.*

* * *

"Oh, look . . . a park!" Nixie took Kip's hand and tugged him across the broad "Gran Via" in the direction of the open green space.

On the other side, Kip realized it was the first time they had held hands. He looked at his watch. "We're supposed to be at 'Plaza Mayor in a little while."

"Come on—they told us we should *look* like 'tourists' . . . so let us *be* 'tourists'!"

* * *

They were not paying any attention to a pasty-complexioned man standing off to the side, watching and listening to them.

* * *

"*'Plaza de España,'*" Kip read a sign aloud, "The 'Plaza of Spain'—I guess this must be the 'center of Spain', or something like that."

The blonde young woman pointed at an enormous sculptured stone monument flanked by bronze equestrian statues. "Let us go over there . . . I want to get a picture of you by the horses!"

Kip climbed up onto a stone base next to an outsized statue of a bearded man on a horse. Nixie aimed her camera up at him. Then the two swapped places and Kip snapped a picture of her.

Kip glanced at his watch. "We must be going, now." Nixie held out her hand; the two strolled out of the park into the Saturday afternoon crowd moving along on the sidewalk.

* * *

The pale-skinned individual wove his way through the throng, never taking his eyes off the light-haired man and the young blonde woman stepping along fifty meters ahead of him.

* * *

A few blocks farther on, at an intersection, the Texan frowned—across the street, in front of them, was the row of stores and apartments where that morning he had encountered the money, the Africans, the white man and woman—and the dead men. Kip did not want to go near that place, again. He pointed at a narrow side street leading off in another direction. "Let's go that way . . ."

The two stepped up the crowded byway, lined with ancient-looking, multi-storied buildings facing across a winding pedestrian walk. The girl pointed at a tiny shop tucked into a corner. "Look . . . that place over there makes shoes!" She tugged Kip's hand.

He looked at his watch. "It's almost time for us to be at the Plaza."

"I just want to see how they do it."

The two stepped inside the tiny place where the atmosphere was heavy with the aroma of new leather.

* * *

Across the narrow way, the white man stopped and spoke to another fellow standing in a doorway, who nodded. Then he walked across to the opposite side and leaned against a door frame.

* * *

Kip spotted a clock on the wall. "We can come back, later! We must be going, now."

* * *

The three Russian Embassy security officers stood in the archway leading to 'Plaza Mayor' and looked around the great space. One of them motioned toward a nearby door opening. Inside the brick-and-stone structure—half-a millineum in age, but still strong and solid—the three men mounted an inside stairwell to the top floor. Looking up and down the bare corridor to make sure no one was observing them, the first man inserted a credit card into the door frame. The lock released and the sharpshooters stepped inside a musty, empty room. A rugged-looking young man stepped to a window and peered around the edge of some yellowed lace curtains, supressing a sneeze from the accumulated dust on the window sill.

The agent scanned the cobblestoned open arena, then located the most likely place on the other side that a sniper might use to target the outdoor restaurant below them, giving special attention to sight-lines a shooter would employ to aim straight across the open space. He turned and gauged the distance to the outdoor restaurant directly below them where his instructions told him the subjects he was supposed to protect would be situated.

Just then, loud Spanish music and the amplified voice of a female singer burst from the carnival in the middle of the vast open place. An irritation—the sounds could impede locating the source of gunfire.

He and the two others set their cases on the oiled wooden floor. With quick movements like they had done blindfolded hundreds of times, the trio assembled their 'Kalashnikov AK-74s'.

The Russian drew back the curtains of the three windows and pushed open the glass frames. To neutralize anyone who had spotted him, he smiled and made waving motions as if he was watching the festivities, then stepped back out of view of the ground. But he had a perfect sight of the facade across the way enclosing the other side of Plaza Mayor.

* * *

Outside the leather shop, Nixie reached for Kip's hand. The two shouldered their way up among the pedestrians toward a massive stone-and-brick archway across the end of the street.

* * *

The first white man nodded across the narrow cobblestoned byway. The other pale-skinned person caught the motion and started walking; both were now tailing the two targeted individuals at a discreet distance.

* * *

The young woman pointed at the archway in the ground floor of a four-story structure "There it is, up ahead—'Plaza Mayor'!"

"You've been here, before?"

"*Ja*—yes." As the two trudged up the inclined stone sidewalk crowded with people strolling along, all at once, Nixie clamped hard on Kip's hand and gave a tug. "Look straight ahead . . . do not say anything!"

Frowning, Kip started to say something, but she cut him off with a tight squeeze on his hand.

"Oh! There they are!" She pointed up the way, waving her arm back and forth. "We are over here!"

Nixie tugged her stumbling, confused male companion through the over-arching stonework tunnel into a broad open space, surrounded on all four sides by very old-looking, four-story brick-and-stone structures; some faced with stucco veneer, others with murals. Huffing, the two came to an outdoor restaurant just inside the archway and dropped into the nearest seats. Nixie was gasping. "This is 'Plaza Mayor'."

Her companion was also trying to catch his breath. "What— what was *that* all about?"

"Did you not see those men, back there?"

Kip shook his head..

"They were watching us from doorways. I saw them giving signals back and forth . . . they were going to rob us!"

"How did you know that?"

Nixie reached over and squeezed his hand. "Here, people live with those things . . . they probably had heard your American accent and followed us—but I used a trick I knew to throw them off!"

"Wow! I guess—"

". . . I see some of the others, over there."

The Texan looked about. At a nearby table, Sloane Ferry and Jim Randolph were sipping drinks from straws; a short distance over, dressed in civilian clothes, were the two Russian military men he remembered from last night at their embassy—the older-

565

looking one who looked like Andropov and the other about his own age—downing beer from outsized steins, acting casual, taking in the scene.

Looking around, Kip spotted the Russian Intelligence man and the Swiss agent at another table, watching and listening to a Spanish band playing music for a costumed *troupe* performing a native dance near the equestrian statue in the center of the plaza. The whole place was jammed with people and booths; Kip remembered there was some sort of festival taking place today in Plaza Mayor.

Nixie cocked her head while trying to overhear nearby conversations. "I am supposed to watch and listen for Russian-speaking people." The blonde girl shook her head. "Nothing yet. She stared at the dancers whirling to an energetic Spanish tune. "The music is very loud."

* * *

The assassin, dressed in all-black with a tied scarf on his head, tiptoed up the back stairway, carrying what looked like an aluminum musical-instrument case. At the fourth-floor landing, the individual inserted a pass-key into a deadbolt lock. With a creak and a groan, the un-marked door swung open to a musty hidden stairwell.

Flashlight in hand, the fellow made his way up one more level. Next to a hulking, outsized attic-fan, its swirling blades churning air at his face, the man pushed open another door. The young man stepped into a low-ceilinged room on the top floor and locked the door, using an inside latch. Hunched-down, the man loped over to a projecting dormer window that was partially obscured by half-closed storm-shutters. Opening the carrying-case, he pulled out binoculars and took a look through the narrow open space between the shutter-slats, then dropped back in a hurry. The girl with the long black hair—the main target—was sitting with a male companion at a table at the outdoor café, two-hundred meters across the plaza.

He pulled out a black, snub-barrel assault rifle and unfolded its stock into position with a muffled "click" not heard over the loud music and the merry sounds of the carnival in the plaza down below. Next, the fellow screwed a noise-suppressor onto the muzzle of the weapon, then he snapped the curved, fully-loaded magazine into the bottom of his 'Kalashnikov AK-74-U' Special Forces assault weapon. Satisfied that the rifle was ready for use, he focused the telescopic sight on the dark-haired female target. At the close distance involved down to ground-level on the opposite side of the open space, putting the shots onto the subject would be no problem. The scarfed assailant gave a smirk of satisfaction. This would be one of the easier jobs.

General Retchko had told him to watch for the American to pass the money to Mobustu, who would step away in a hurry. His accomplices, all of whom would be wearing yellow eyeglasses, would also withdraw at once. Then, the sharpshooter would assassinate everyone at the outdoor restaurant. Of course, there would be collateral deaths, but that would not matter as long as the main objective, to kill the young American woman with the long black hair, was accomplished. He scanned the scene across the way: there she was, still sitting at a table.

The sniper crouched, out of sight of those below, and aimed at the target to gauge the range. At a table, a young blonde woman was arising from her seat and motioning to a man next to her. He fixed the sights on her head and made a slight adjustment, then re-aimed at the main target.

* * *

Nixie pulled the camera from her bag. "Let us get some more pictures!" The light-haired girl gestured for her companion to stand, his back to the main plaza. She had to wait a moment while some men passed in front of her.

Kip's eyes went wide: the new arrivals were Mobustu, Busa, and the little bald man he had seen at the apartment that morning with the twenty-million dollars! None made any overt sign of recognition. Another bald African, wearing a brown three-piece suit, stepped past, along with a very white, stocky, hairless individual he had never seen before. He recognized the lawyer, Adwadube. A very dark, scowling man followed along behind the others. Kip stared at the last man and caught his breath—he was the fellow who had been on the 747 flight from Amsterdam that time, and had trailed him from the Dallas-Fort Worth airport! All took seats around an umbrella-topped table. Kip thought they were making extra efforts to look casual. A waiter came up; the American overheard them giving drink orders. The men spoke English with heavy African overtones.

Sloane glanced at the newcomers and tried to conceal a gasp. *The bald white man, the powerfully- built black man and the small fellow in the brown suit had all been in the motel room that time she was kidnapped and who had probably put her in the shipping crate to die!*

"Hey!" Nixie was motioning, trying to get Kip's attention."You are supposed to be looking at the camera!" Trying to appear casual, he forced a grin as she snapped a picture.

When Kip sat back down, he spotted, sitting off to one side, the two from the apartment that morning—the tanned, athletic-looking young woman who had killed the three men and the fellow with the American accent who called himself by an Hispanic name—"Luis", he believed it was. With them was a dark-haired young man about his own age with a mustache, who kept looking around and fidgeting like he was nervous, Kip thought. The three seemed to be taking in the dancers and musicians who were performing in the middle of the plaza.

Sitting off to another side at a sunlit table, two young priests were having animated conversation, nodding. From their small black books, Kip decided they were talking about religion.

* * * .

The white man who had been following Kip and Nixie, along with the second man from the doorway near the leather shop, sat down at a table near the archway. The pairs' eyes darted about, observing the scene. One patted his coat pocket. The nine-millimeter was there. He nodded; the other man did the same. No one paid any paricular attention to them.

* * *

568

Nearby sat four young men in turtle-neck shirts and sports coats, each drinking a beer from a mug. Kip observed that their squinting eyes kept darting about; it occurred to him that they seemed to be uncommonly interested in everything going on about them. He also noticed they were not talking among themselves. *Agents, perhaps?*

Out of the corner of his eye, the American saw the Swiss Intelligence man and the thin Russian with the thick glasses take the outdoor table next to Nixie's and his.

* * *

The assassin at the top-floor dormer window across the way nodded to himself; with a smooth "click" the safety of the AK-74-U released; he set the weapon for an initial single shot, to be followed by fully automatic fire. The man raised the assault rifle and looked through the scope. All was in readiness.

According to the plan he had mentally rehearsed, Mobustu would stand up and go to the table of the American and get the money. Then the men he was covering would put on their yellow eyeglasses and step away in a hurry. At that point, he would eliminate everyone left behind, including those of Mobustu's group the African had marked for assassination—the small, stooped black fellow; the dark-haired fellow with the mustache and his blonde female companion; the second dark-haired young man with the black mustache. He panned the gunsight; the last three were sitting at a table off to themselves. After he had killed the girl with the long straight black hair, he would rake the others, using the Kalashnikov's automatic fire. The man surveyed the scene one more time and nodded to himself. With the AK-74, it should not take more than four seconds to accomplish everything.

Even as he watched through the telescopic sight, the African banker was pushing back his seat, looking in the American's direction. It would now be only a few more seconds . . .

The sniper frowned—a reddish-brown-haired young woman and a child had stepped into the picture. The adult female looked to be talking with someone at a table in front of the target. The shooter scowled. If she did not step aside right away, his first shot would be to her head to get her out of the way, for Mobustu had stood up and was moving between tables in the direction of the American with the money.

* * *

Terenty's eyes were wide. "Tamara! What are you and Larisa doing here?"

"I knew the festival was going on, and I wanted to surprise you!" She pulled out a chair and dropped into it, still smiling. The young mother touched the older man's arm. "And I wanted to see Colonel Golubko." The little girl climbed into her step-father's lap.

Terenty glanced away; the black man was stepping toward the American's table.

Frowning, Terenty eased the clinging little one's arms from around his neck. The child looked confused. "I told you that we—" His eyes darted to the next table, where the man was now standing, speaking to the American. He clasped Larisa's hands in his and hissed at Tamara. "You must leave at once!"

"But we are already here—surely you can let Larisa stay and see the carnival!" Terenty was in a panic—his wife and the child were in grave danger.

Now it was too late to get them away! At the other table the African was already speaking with the American. A bulging envelope changed hands. The man in the suit held it, nodding.

The plan was for the four Russian Embassy security agents in white civilian turtleneck outfits to arrest all the suspects as soon as they passed the money! If necessary, they would be helped by the Americans, Watering and Randolph, who were situated at separate tables. *Two "Swiss Guards" in plain-clothes, who had watched the American with the money as he walked to the plaza in case he and his blonde female companion had needed special protection, were at another table to give additional back-up.*

Tarliani gripped the seat-arms as he saw that the envelope was in the second man's hands.

All at once the suspects slapped on yellow-looking eyeglasses and turned aside, making their way in a hurry in the direction of the archway exit! *What is this?* Frowning, Livshits nudged Tarliani, whose fingers hovered over his inside holster.

At that moment, a waiter stepped up to Major Suslov's table. *"Más cervezas . . .* something for the *'niña'?"* He leaned over and patted the little girl's head. She got off the man's lap and stood next to her mother

* * *

Behind the opposite top-floor dormer window, the sharp-shooter watched as the men, their yellow lenses glinting in the sunlight, stepped away, then break into a half-run in the direction of one of the two nearby archways leading out of the plaza.

He focused his aim on the head of the black-haired young woman. Just then, a male stepped in front of her at the table! But the fellow leaned over, once more giving the sniper a perfect shot. He squeezed the trigger and the suppressor-equipped AK-74-U responded with a muffled 'WHUMP!'

* * *

The youthful waiter raised up. All at once his head exploded in a red, lumpy froth that sprayed onto the nearby tables—the headless, convulsing torso staggered and flung itself, twisting, to the ground! With a scream, Tamara stumbled backward out of her chair and grabbed Larisa.

Terenty shoved his wife and child underneath the table and overturned a chair to shield them. Slugs from somewhere zinged and whanged about them, tearing into the brick wall behind the café; gouging cobblestones; the sounds louder than the festival music! Sloane, seated beyond the youth who had taken the rifle bullet from behind, screamed as something gray and red spun across the tabletop! Randolph, realizing they were under attack, pushed down the dark-haired girl and drew out his snub-nosed revolver. Shrieking people backed-away toward an open doorway in the building at the rear, chased by bullets zipping through the air. A busboy pitched forward and was still. Bullets ripped into the canopies over the tables; a male customer jerked backward and slumped from his seat onto the ground.

The shouts and sudden scrambling activity in the café caught the attention of the revelers in the open space. The folk tune garbled to a ragged stop; people started shouting; tripping and running as the zipping and zinging of bullets kept going. Someone pointed up at blue gunsmoke drifting from a top-floor window, gave a shout, then turned and ran.

From upper-floor windows above the outoor tables, un-silenced automatic gunfire erupted, adding to the din! On the opposite side, chunks of gouged masonry burst from the building's upperworks.

At their table, the four young men in the turtle-necked shirts pulled automatic pistols from inside their sport coats and opened fire on the dodging fugitives who were running toward the archway. With bullets snipping and whanging all around them, the other plain-clothes agents turned their weapons on the source of the gunfire that seemed to be coming from the vicinity of the roof-line across the plaza.

The bald man turned about and pointed an automatic pistol at Terenty who was dashing, hunched-down, between tables.

The disguised Gennady, crouched underneath a table off to the side with Marisol and Larry, saw the pudgy Ukrainian make the move. His eyes darted to the man's target and went wide.

"Terenty!"

The young Russian, still looking like an Hispanic male, stood up, facing Retchko, waving his hands.

"Nyet! "

Gennady dashed in the direction of Terenty, who did not recognize him. As he threw himself in front of his friend—at that instant Retchko fired his *'Walther PPK'* twice.

The bald man turned underneath the stone archway, and along with the others wearing the yellow eyeglasses, ran out of Plaza Mayor, shoving other pedestrians aside. The fugitives huffed down the stone sidewalk, past the little shops and stores, to the main thoroughfare.

There, to the astonishment of bystanders, one after the other, they lunged forward and vanished!

* * *

Inside the van, Leonid Efimovich Retchko's puffy face was contorted with fury. The hairless Ukrainian grasped a door handle as the soundless, invisible vehicle careened through an interesction, just missing a baby carriage pushed by a young woman who could neither see nor hear the vehicle. "You say the bills are *counterfeit'?*"

"I am sure of it." Mobustu the banker fingered the currency from the manila envelope Kip Leeds had given him. "And I believe they have been treated—they are already going blank!"

"Bastards!" A thunderous expression bolted across his face, turned crimson from rage, as he realized he had been duped.

From the front passenger's seat Mobustu's cellular telephone was ringing. The African listened for a few seconds, then began vigorously shaking his head.

"No! That is not possible! Find it!"

He flipped closed the tiny receiver. "They found the two truck drivers tied-up! The money is gone!"

"What!" Retchko slammed the back of the driver's seat. He turned about in his seat, then back to the front. "We are going back!"

"The driver shook his head. "No! We must go to the airport! The others are waiting for us!"

Seething, the pale European took deep breaths. "They will pay for this!"

The invisible van shot past the "Barajas Airport" perimeter and aimed at a hangar. Ahead, at the freight terminal, sat the unmarked 747, red lights already flashing on its top and bottom in preparation for departure.

Mobustu reached for the handle as the van skidded to a stop. "Bring the invisible module! We will take off right away!"

* * *

573

"Hand me the binoculars." The "ground controller" spoke to the man standing next to him.

The Spaniard aimed the spyglasses out the panoramic control tower window and focused on the 747 at the Cargo Terminal across the way. Its red rotating top and bottom lights were flashing. "The Seven-Forty-Seven'—the one without markings—is about to depart."

Another controller frowned. "What about it?" .

"They have not unloaded or loaded any cargo . . . only a few people got off one day ago and a 'Seven-Forty-Seven' is an expensive airplane to operate for only a dozen or so passengers."

Another man came up and handed a paper to the tower manager. "Here is the departure information about the 'Seven-Forty-Seven', señor . . . it has filed a flight plan to Teheran."

The airplane's rear door began closing. Then the official, still gazing through the binoculars, observed something unusual: No one was near the door. It appeared to be closing by itself.

* * *

To the chorus of shouts all around him, Terenty pushed up and stared, stupefied, at the gasping, moaning man on the ground who had stopped two bullets intended for him.

The fellow let go his grip; his eyes fluttered open. *"Terenty—"*

A bolt of recognition struck the Russian. The dark haired, mustached individual before him was—

"Gennady!"

Terenty grasped his disguised friend, who was having trouble breathing. To his horror, blood was oozing from Gennady's mouth. "He is shot!"

From somewhere Terenty heard Larisa crying. Frantic, he looked around; the dark-haired American girl was holding her, hiding her face from the sight.

"Terenty!" An agitated female came down and grabbed him. "Terenty! Are you all right?"

"Tamara! Yes!" He motioned. *"This is Gennady!"*

"Gennady! What—?" The young woman knelt to the injured man, her long auburn hair draped over his face.

Gennady coughed; bubbles of bright crimson blew out around his nostrils; a pool of red liquid was forming on the pavement beneath him. ". . . *Tamara*—"

A male voice came from behind Terenty. "This man saved your life!

"Colonel Golubko! This is 'Gennady—Gennady Lychin'!"

"Lychin!" The older man dropped to the cobblestones and gaped. He recognized Gennady's features behind the dark hair and the black mustache. "Get a doctor!"

With effort Gennady, grimacing, shook his head. "No . . . not a doctor—" His raspy voice was weak. Blinking, he looked up at Rodion Golubko, who was leaning to him. ". . .'Putridchenko' kidnapped us—we had to work for him . . ." Gennady burst into a spasm of coughing. Blood came to his lips. "Putridchenko is evil—"

The colonel took in the spreading red pool on the ground. "Be still, now, comrade."

A great wracking sob broke from Gennady. ". . . *'Galina'*—!"

Tamara caressed his face, her tears dropping onto him, oblivious to the pandemonium and carnage all about.

"They were friends," someone said to Kip.

Sounds of sirens rent the air; shouting people were running everywhere

A young olive-skinned woman knelt. "I am 'Monica'. . . 'Luis' and I are here."

Gennady closed his eyes for a moment and nodded.

A short distance away, a priest was on his knees, ministering to someone inert on the ground. Tamara arose and stepped around an overturned table toward him, just as the cleric made the sign of the cross and stood up, nodding, the palms of his hands together. She caught his eye and motioned.

The man followed her to where Gennady lay. The priest knelt and put his face to the gasping, bleeding young man and said something in his ear. Tamara dropped down and held Gennady's hand. The others stood close, their heads bowed. The dark-haired American girl, with Larisa's arms around her neck, came up, along with the two American men and a young blonde woman.

Gennady opened his eyes and focused on the man with the clerical collar who was nodding at him, his palms together. He mumbled something.

The priest looked up. "He speaks English?"

Terenty nodded.

The garbed man leaned close to Gennady. "If you wish, repeat after me—" He put his palms together and began began reciting. "I believe in God Almighty, the Creator of heaven and earth."

There was a pause and the others heard Gennady rasp out the words, with a cough.

". . . and in Jesus Christ, His only Son, our Lord—"

Those gathered by stood as the priest spoke; every few seconds Gennady would say some words; the cleric would continue.

". . . the forgiveness of sins and life everlasting . . . Amen'."

Then the priest reached into his tunic and drew out a vial of purple liquid and held it up, kissing it. "The blood of Jesus—"

He lifted the little cork stopper and put the tiny bottle to Gennady's lips. With what seemed to be extreme effort, the young man swallowed.

The priest put his palms together again over Gennady's face. "Hail Mary, Mother of God, pray for us now and at the hour of our death . . . Amen—"

The cleric looked up and motioned to the others. "Now, according to tradition, will each of you come and embrace our brother."

One after another, those gathered around knelt and hugged Gennady; each saying some words into his ear.

The priest leaned down to Gennady's face.

The young man's glazed eyes opened wide. "I see God . . ." He coughed a rasping, bloody froth. "I see Galina, waiting for me at the gate—"

There was a pause of some moments, then the priest motioned to a bystander at a nearby table.

The man gathered up something and came to him.

The priest laid the tablecloth over Gennady.

Terenty and Tamara dropped to their friend and held him. Their backs heaved.

The priest looked around at the others. *"Then, it is true: 'There is no greater love than for a man to lay down his life for his friends'—"*

-24-

Murtala Mohammed Airport Lagos; Two Days Later:

EXPLOSIONS DESTROY NIGERIAN REFINERY

(From Wire Service Reports)

(Tanuta City, Nigeria)—Reports reached Lagos overnight that the "Tanuta Refinery", at Tanuta City, on the Niger River Delta, was heavily damaged or destroyed by a series of explosions.

According to an eyewitness account by short-wave radio from the local airport, the only means of communication remaining with the isolated town, blasts occurred simultaneously all across the sprawling facility shortly after midnight. Flames were reported to be reaching a hundred meters into the sky over the kilometer-square operation, one of the largest processors of crude in Nigeria.

The witness radioed Intercontinental News that local authorities believed the explosions may have been deliberately set by unknown—perhaps foreign—saboteurs.

Colonel Ajiboy put down the newspaper and stared at the opposite wall. It was almost too good to be true: *The bad boys and the bad girl were now gone and would not be back.* It was if an enormous weight was now lifted from his shoulders.

The sudden and recent events that were the cause of his new-found freedom of action included the flight of Nomoah—"the Chief"; Busa; the little fellow Mickey; the lawyer, Adwadube; Ezego—the un-repentant thug; General Retchko and that immoral Betty Nkrume, as evil and despicable a woman as there ever was, who had had her husband killed and then took up with the hated general as his lover. All except Mickey had fled to

Teheran, he believed. With them went the enigmatic "Adept of the Terrarianists" and most of his female "temple followers". And now, the refinery was gone—and with it the Cartel and its deadly repressions.

The only conspirator left in Lagos was Krasheev, who now sat powerless and penniless since the international police had seized all his foreign accounts.

Ajiboy now had everything to himself. His pulse quickened. He knew just where to start. The Army officer swung his feet off the boardroom table where he had been reading, stood up and looked out. Through the picture window was the bulldozer parked outside for the re-grading project that was to start tomorrow. It had been a while since he had driven one of those machines, but he would figure it out.

In a few minutes the roaring scraper was clacking across the concrete—a little wobbly; slewing back and forth, here and there, as it went along, but getting along on its tracked trek toward the little cement-block building out at the edge of the parking apron—the low structure with the stovepipe chimney sticking out its tin roof.

The officer skidded the machine around, raised up the blade and put the grader in gear.

Twenty minutes later, the deed was done. What had been the "Incerator" building was now a disorderly pile of broken cinder blocks—all blackened on one side from the oven fires that had once raged within—and rusty, corrugated sheet metal now laying twisted on the ground. The squashed stovepipe was off to one side, now a metal monument to those who had been burned up in the hateful little place on Retchko's orders. The roaring, lurching machine spun around on its tracks once, twice, three times; its metal treads digging ruts in the cement surface as the operator glared at his handiwork

There would be no more cremations at this airport; no, not one—as long as he, Solomon Ajiboy had anything to do with it.

The bulldozer clattered back to its original parking place. Ajiboy cut the diesel engine.

It was then he heard the screeching of jet turbines. Out on the taxiway a small jetliner he had not noticed landing was turning onto the apron in his direction. He frowned; there was a red star on its tail. The aircraft swung about and set its brakes. Its twin engines whined to a stop.

As the Nigerian Army man stood watching, his heart pounding, the curved front door swung up and a spindly set of steps unwound toward the pavement. A man, who must have been about fifty and looking very physically fit, dropped down the stairs, followed by a younger, also well-built individual. Both wore paramilitary gear. Then a half-dozen more men, also in combat fatigues, filed out of the little jet. Ajiboy stood rooted to the spot, his eyes wide, as the serious-looking men tramped toward him.

"I am looking for a 'Colonel Ajiboy'," the older man said in American-accented English.

The African nodded, swallowing. "I am he." *What do they want with me?*

"Good." The man bored his blue eyes into the Nigerian's. "Take us to where we can talk."

"Of course . . . right this way, gentlemen." Inside the building, he directed the newcomers into the conference room dominated by a long mahogany table surrounded by leather, executive-type chairs. "Take seats." He dropped into one of the chairs. "What is this all about?"

"I will come right to the point," the trim, graying man said, "I am 'Colonel Rodion Golubko', of Russian Special Forces—'Vityaz Spetsnaz' . . . I have a proposition for you."

Ajiboy's eyes went wide at the mention of "Vityaz Spetsnaz." He had heard of them, of course.

The man gestured toward other soldiers in fatigues. "These are 'Major Suslov' . . . 'Major Grishinov' . . . and 'Major Navarin'—all of 'Vityaz Spetsnaz'. "

The officer nodded at another soldier. "This is 'Major Bogue', of the United States 'Marine Force Recon'—"

The American nodded as the Russian went on. "These other Americans are 'Sergeant Malloy" and 'Sergeant Warden', also of United States 'Marine Force Recon' . . . capable men."

Colonel Golubko saw the Nigerian man's wide eyes darting back and forth between the Americans and the Russians; a perplexed—almost frightened, he thought—look on the black man's face.

"I see you are confused, as it were, about this mixed force. I assure you we are operating on the full cooperating authority of our respective governments. Our force—our *combined* force—acting on this authority, has just completed a mission to destroy the refinery at Tanuta City."

The Russian glanced at the newspaper on the table. The story about the explosions lay face-up. "We had evidence that the refinery was at the center of an international criminal operation. Were you aware of that?"

The African's heart was pounding. He did not want to say much; as yet, he had no reason to trust these men. "I knew some of the people there were not, shall we say, 'honest'?"

"Come, colonel. Our Intelligence—" the Russian glanced around at the others, ". . . *both Russian and 'other' Intelligence*—tells us you were aware of many things. We also know that you have had—'misgivings', shall we put it—about this airport and the people behind it."

Ajiboy's mouth was dry. "What do you want from me?"

"Colonel, we are here to make you a proposition." Rodion Golubko stared straight into the eyes of his Nigerian counterpart. "I assure you this proposal is approved at the highest levels of our two governments—Russian and American . . . and there are others involved, as well, *including private concerns.*"

"Go on."

"A new anti-crime-and couter-terrorist-organization is now being put together in Geneva, Switzerland . . . it will operate outside the boundaries of international law . . . that is why our governments will—officially, at least—disavow any connections to it."

"How does this affect me?"

"You are aware, I am sure, that Nigeria has a reputation as the most corrupt country in the world. These people want to work with you to help clean it up . . . *starting at this airport.*"

Ajiboy looked out the big plate-glass window. Out beyond the parking apron was the wreckage of the crematorium he had just destroyed. "I believe the changes have already started." He told them what he had done. He was interested in their proposal—but he would also have to guard against running afoul of the current military government of Nigeria.

Colonel Golubko nodded at the Nigerian, as if satisfied with the man's response. "The new group will insert some people to work with you—to keep a liaison with Geneva. In due time, we will 'take care' of the bad men running this country." He gave a smirk and a shrug. "Sometimes people get sick and die suddenly, you know—" He let the implication hang in the air.

A grin flickered across Ajiboy's face. "Then, I would be pleased to work with this—group."

"Very good, colonel!" The Spetsnaz officer shook the African's hand. "You will be hearing from them very soon."

He motioned toward the door. The men stood and filed out.

Outside, the Russian pointed at the Ilyushin. "Have this aircraft re-fueled, if you will. We will fly now to Madrid, to leave Major Suslov and these Americans there. My other men and I are returning to Moscow."

* * *

A half-hour later, Colonel Ajiboy watched as the small jetliner arose from the runway and turned toward the north-northwest, its twin engines thundering over the landscape. In minutes, it became a dot, then vanished from sight.

The African's eyes fell on the rubble of the crematorium, directly in line with the route the aircraft had taken over the horizon. .

For the first time in a long time, there was now genuine, uplifting hope that things would become better in Nigeria. If the military men who were just here were on the level—and he trusted and believed they were—a new day would soon be coming to this lawless, forsaken country. It was if yet another weight had just dropped from his shoulders.

Ajiboy stepped through the door into rear of the big terminal building. Inside the Security Office, a squad of his men returning from the morning guard-shift were unloading their rifles.

The colonel motioned at them. "Find crowbars, and follow me."

With their commander leading, the men stepped up the main concourse. At a metal door he punched a keypad. By itself, the door creaked open into a short, dim hallway leading to a blank wall.

With a scowl, the colonel jabbed a clawed tool at an engraved metal sign. In a few seconds, the metal marker lay on the concrete floor at his shoes. The officer clapped his hands twice; part of the wall moved inward, revealing a plain room with a seat-type frame in the middle. Cabinets lined the walls.

"Tear everything out of this room and destroy it!"

The other soldiers glanced at the tarnished, now-worthless bent brass plate, covered with dust, then stepped over it:

—INTERROGATION ROOM—

~~~~

EPILOGUE

The yellow delivery truck emerged from the Lincoln Tunnel into a hazy Lower Manhattan. At the Thirtieth Street intersection, it made a turn and threaded its way along the narrow street that was jammed with midday traffic. After waiting at the intersection light, the rental truck turned onto Twelfth Avenue and rumbled down the thoroughfare that ran close along the Hudson River banks, past the gaping jaws of the entrance to the "Holland Tunnel", where vehicles of all description were nosing into the sub-surface connector; on down West Street to another turn.

A little farther, and the truck lurched into the "Delivery Entrance" of a pair of very tall and massive office buildings. On a lower parking level, two young bristly-bearded men got out. One set an electric switch that dangled outside the rolled-down rear door. The fellow nodded to his companion, and the two started walking rapidly toward a stairwell.

Outside, at street level, a car drew-up to the curb and stopped. The two dropped into its back seat. The vehicle pulled away into the traffic.

One of the men leaned forward and tapped the driver. "We must hurry—" he rasped in a guttural language, "the fuse was set for fifteen minutes."

The young man looked back and up at the enormous pair of hulking, glass-faced towers, shimmering in the haze of late morning. In a few minutes, they would come crashing to the ground, killing a quarter of a million of the infidels. Then, praise heaven, there would be no more "World Trade Center".

~~~~

DISPOSITIONS

The 'Academy'—The super-secret school in Moscow continued in operation as an adjunct of the "GRU", the Intelligence branch of the " Russian General Staff".

* * *

Colonel Solomon Ajiboy—Not long afterward, when the military dictator suddenly became ill and died under "mysterious circumstances", as the reports put it, Nigeria began taking the long-overdue steps toward becoming a real democracy. In the heady new atmosphere, Colonel Ajiboy was able to clean-out the corruption at the "Murtala Mohammed Airport Lagos" to where it now soon had a reputation as a hospitable, well-run operation where travelers were welcomed and safe.

* * *

'Ahmed', The Translator—On its way to Madrid, with the permission of the Libyan government, the 747 had stopped at Benghazi and picked up the young Libyan. He went to Tora Bora in the employ of Retchko as his interpreter. But he was unable to send any more reports to Tarliani.

* * *

Joe Anglin—His case was dismissed for lack of evidence, thanks to the unstinting legal exertions of Michael B. Parsley, Esq. Soon thereafter, he received a coded message on the little machine. The next day, he caught a flight to Medellin, Colombia. There, he joined with Larry and Marisol in a computer venture, where he is to this day. Joe married a Colombian television actress and planned to spend the rest of his life in South America.

* * *

José Aldrada and Belén Castillo—The older widower's patience was rewarded a year-and-a-half after the father of Tatiana died when they were married in a ceremony before a priest in Nuevo Laredo, Soon thereafter, the border kingpin began to turn his empire over to his step-son-in-law, Petr Blagron—"Pedro Beltran"—and went into retirement, still above the authorities, who remained oblivious of the people-smuggling operation using the "invisible technology".

* * *

"Mike" Adwadube—Mike (not his real first name) Adwadube, the lawyer with the "strange" eyes, returned to his post at the Nigerian Embassy in Madrid. He was never charged with any crimes.

* * *

The "Adept of the Terrarianists"—The bearded patriarch and the expatriate members of his earth-worshiping sect received a cold reception in Iran, a country not noted for religious tolerance. After negotiations—and a reputed substantial cash payoff—they traveled to Albania, where they re-established themselves and the group began to add members.

The Nigerian military took over the abandoned "temple" in Lagos, converting it to an Army warehouse.

* * *

Lisa Anaya and Frank Ogawan—In London, Lisa reconciled with her sister after learning about Betty's true role as an agent of the *'British Secret Intelligence Service',* known as *'MI-6'.*

Today, she and Frank are principals in a computer software company, where together they hold five British patents. After they were married, they adopted an orphan boy from Nigeria.

About a year later, they became parents of a baby boy of their own.

* * *

Yegor Boronov—The genius Russian electronics expert barely escaped the commando raid on the Tanuta Refinery, departing for Lagos a few hours before the assault by the Golubko Force that took place that same midnight. Eventually, he made his way Tora Bora, where he put his expertise to work in the service of "Agent U" and his operation, where he continued contriving deadly devices for use against the West.

* * *

Masobe Busa—The overweight African underwent gastric-bypass surgery in Teheran, paying for the operation with cleaned-up black money spirited out of Nigeria. Later, much more slender than before, using a fake passport and another name, he re-located to London and became an exporter.

* * *

Petr Blagron and Tatiana Castillo—With the breakup of the Cartel, Petr Blagron, the red-haired Russian, still using the cover name of "Pedro Beltran", was tabbed by José Aldrada to help him run his operation full-time on the border. Gradually, the older man turned the "business" over to him, even as the younger man increased the Organization's grip to include all elements of authority in Nuevo Laredo and much of the social structure across the border in South Texas.

He and Tatiana were married in the local Catholic Church. The "Best Man" was José Aldrada. Within a year, they were parents of a baby girl who had auburn hair and dark blue eyes.

* * *

The "Boeing 747"—The "Organization's" specially-equipped "Boeing 747" arrived in Teheran from Madrid with the fleeing conspirators. In Iran, it was temporarily interned, then was released to serve "Agent U". In its new employ, it was used to transport contraband goods around the world as before. In 2002, it vanished with all hands shortly after taking off on a night flight from Havana to Tripoli, Libya, that would have taken it within a few miles of United States airspace near the Florida Keys. At the Pentagon, Military Intelligence officers commended the pilots who had shot it down.

* * *

Norbert Ezego—The very black man joined Agent "U" at his "Tora Bora" hideout and became the training coordinator for the bearded man's international interests. For some years, Ezego traveled between The Philippines, Indonesia, Venezuela, Nicaragua, Equador, Bolivia, Brazil and Colombia, organizing dis-affected local men and women into anti-government paramilitary forces.

In 1998, Ezego disappeared while in the jungles of western Venezuela on a mission for the Populist colonel who was setting up a training camp near the Colombian border. Confidential reports stated he was assassinated by operatives of the crime-fighting group operating out of Geneva, Switzerland.

* * *

"Facundo" Ordoñez—After evading the govenment-led round-ups of the mid-1990's (through payoffs and paramilitary-style intimidation) that decimated several of the Cartels, the enormously-wealthy Colombian Drug Lord continued to hold sway on that country's societal, governmental, and economic structures from his hilltop villa in Cali until he was arrested in 2003 and extradited to the United States. While incarcerated in a U.S. federal prison, he was murdered by another inmate in what authorities believed was an inside hit-job orchestrated by a rival cartel.

588

* * *

Ned Ferry—The detective gradually turned his investigation business over to his daughter, Sloane, and his son-in-law, James Richard Randolph, and retired in 1999 to dote on his grandchildren. In honor of his late wife, Browning O'Bryant Ferry, he established a scholarship for Australian International students at the university.

* * *

Dominique "Nicky" Ferry—As a teenager, the boy shortened his nickname and began calling himself "Nick". After his last year of high school and before he started at the university, his parents invited Larisa Kuznetsova-Suslova, who was beginning her first term at Moscow State University, to visit them in West Dallas. The two became fast friends and eventually married; They now live in Texas.

* * *

Sloane Ferry and James Richard Randolph— After the event at Plaza Mayor, Sloane and Jim kept seeing each other. In addition, they kept up with Terenty and Tamara, whom they liked very much.

Fourteen months after Sloane and Jim had first met in a Laredo hospital room where she was recovering from the kidnapping and rescue, the two were married in the Dallas Anglican church. Ned Ferry gave his daughter away; Kip Leeds stood as Best Man.

The couple set up housekeeping in West Dallas, near Ned Ferry's investigative agency. About a year after that, Sloane presented Jim with a baby girl they name 'Margaret Browning Randolph', in honor of Sloane's late Australian-born mother, "Margaret Browning O'Bryant Ferry'.

One day, Jim Randolph received a telephone call from Watering, his former superior at the "Agency",who was now part of a private investigative venture. Would he be interested in working special assignments out of Dallas for the Geneva-based operation? He accepted the offer and joined the group.

Sometime after that, Randolph traveled incognito with the former "Spetsnaz" General Rodion Golubko to Venezuela to track-down a mysterious figure who had been reported to be organizing insurgents in the isolated wilderness along the border of Venezuela and Colombia.

Shortly thereafter, Randolph had in his hands a commendation letter from Geneva congratulating him on a job well-done—and a copy of a deposit slip for a large monetary bonus that had been deposited in a Swiss bank account for him. The man he had eliminated—the African, "Norbert Ezego"—had been an important organizer and trainer of international terrorists.

Sloane became President of the "Ferry Detective Agency". A few years later, she was appointed by the governor to the "Texas Board of Investigations", where she served two terms. Her area of expertise was the "State Board Examination" for new agents.

* * *

Rodion Golubko—Colonel Golubko became a general in 1994 and retired the next year, at which time he joined the private 'Tarliani-Livshits-Watering' anti-crime group operating out of Geneva. He is a frequent house-guest of Terenty and Tamara and is godfather of their son, Gennady.

* * *

Galina Gavrona Lychina—Following the airliner shoot-down in the Strait of Hormuz, Galina's body was never identified—all unknown passengers and crew of the doomed Airbus were buried in a common grave at Bandar Abbas, Iran. It was presumed she was one of those who was interred, there.

The U.S. Navy delivered her passport to an agency of the United Nations that worked to return personal items to the victims' next of kin. Months after the disaster, Galina's passport, still in its waterproof case, was returned to her mother in Tula.

* * *

Brad Holdon—The petroleum executive continued in the oil-trading business with Kip Leeds. In 1998, they merged their firm, "H & L Petroleum Marketing" with a larger company in Houston and took directorships. In later years, Brad was still unattached; still making pointed observations about women.

* * *

Buzzy Habbler and Jamey Suggs—The two enrolled at the "California Institute of Technology" on scholarships underwritten by the National Security Agency. The two were hired full-time after they graduated. Under heavy security clearances, they now work on the design of advanced Intelligence satellite systems for the Agency.

* * *

The 'Invisible Technology'—The United States' program was cancelled in 1993, a victim of budget cuts—a powerful Congresswoman on the "House Armed Services Committee", known to be not totally sympathetic to the military, had claimed that the concept was "unworkable" and had stopped it.

In Russia, meantime, research went on, finally achieving a measure of success. In 2013, with Russia now enjoying renewed prosperity from petroleum exports, the Kremlin was nearing production of the devices in great secrecy.

Agent "U's" organization continued to use the portable units perfected at Tanuta City by Boronov, who had gone with Retchko to Tora Bora and had set up an underground facility there to produce them. On several occasions, such as at Bali, and later in Madrid, Tel Aviv and London, unaccountable explosions causing many casualties occurred where the perpetrators were able to infiltrate crowded places unseen to set their explosives.

* * *

Colonel General Antonin Krolov—About a year after Galina's death, General Krolov and Helen Gavrona registered their marriage. Without realizing it, they spent their honeymoon in the same suite where Gennady and Galina had had theirs'. The general retired soon afterward to a country "dacha" near Tula.

In 2006, General Krolov suffered a fatal heart attack and was interred in the *'Novodevichy Cemetery'* in Moscow, surrounded by notables of Russian history. Pallbearers included Rodion Golubko and Terenty Suslov. His widow, Helen Gavrona Krolova, lives in Tula, still grieving for her late husband for her lost daughter, Galina.

* * *

Larisa Kuznetsova-Suslova—The little blonde girl grew up to become an exceptionally attractive, intelligent and personable young woman. Before starting her first year at Moscow State University, she traveled to Texas at the invitation of Jim and Sloane Randolph, who had remained long-distance friends with her parents. In West Dallas, Larisa met their son, Nick Ferry, and the two became "very interested" in each other. They eventually married and now live in the Dallas, Texas area.

* * *

N.B. Krasheev—The "Nation Bank of Nigeria's" "Director of International Remittance" was arrested by INTERNOL on a warrant issued by the United States Justice Department, charging him with Racketeering and maintaining illegal accounts in foreign countries. The charges against him were supposedly so conclusive that the government of Nigeria disavowed him and he faced the charges "on his own," as the reports put it. At this time, his fate and whereabouts are unknown.

* * *

Vasily Kuznetsov and Vera Kuznetsova— Tamara's parents made several trips to Madrid during the time the younger family was stationed there in the service of the Foreign Ministry, their first journeys outside of Russia.

In 1998, Vasily suffered a disabling stroke and passed away the next year. Tamara's mother moved-in with her daughter and son-in-law, and doted on her grandchildren, Larisa and the little boy, "Gennady, named after their late friend, Gennady Lychin".

* * *

Gennady Lychin—Gennady is buried in the *'Cemetario de Nuestra Señora de la Almudena'* in Madrid. Every year on the anniversary of his death, flowers appear on his grave.

* * *

Boris Konstantinovich Livshits—Livshits left the "Federal Security Bureau" and, along with Tarliani, Watering, and others, including Kip Leeds, set up the private crime-fighting operation in Geneva, with the avowed objective of countering terrorism outside the realm of the governments.

* * *

Kip Leeds and Nixie Garten—After the event at Plaza Mayor in Madrid, Kip stayed on in Europe for a while and traveled with Nixie to Frankfurt and Hamburg to meet her relatives. In 1993, the two married and they now have a teenaged son, Bart Leeds. Kip plays a major role with the Zurich crime-fighting group.

* * *

Bart Leeds—At the wedding of Larisa and Nick, the outgoing and handsome teenaged son of Kip and Nixie Garten Leeds

593

became acquainted with a winsome brunette Russian bridesmaid and the two planned to meet again in Moscow the next summer.

* * *

Larry Landay and Marisol Montoya—The American electronics expert and the Cuban girl kept their assumed names, "Luis Landa" and "Monica Montero" and set up housekeeping in Medellin, Colombia, where they went into the computer business and did well. They were married in a civil ceremony.

Not long after they returned to Medellin from the events in Madrid, Monica became pregnant. They named their baby boy "Guido", in honor of the young man they had known in Cali, Colombia, who had died heroically saving his friend that day at Plaza Mayor.

* * *

'Mickey'—The bald, stooped little man did not flee Madrid following the shoot-out at Plaza Mayor. Protected by American authorities, he entered the "Witness Protection Program" and now lives somewhere in the United States under another identity.

* * *

Dr. Mobustu—The director of the "Technical Section" of the "Nation Bank of Nigeria" so far has escaped the international police dragnet and is still at large.

* * *

Murtala Mohammed Airport Lagos—With the Cartel losing its grip on the airport, the new "Chief of Security", Colonel Ajiboy, began reforms that led in led to the busy, sprawling gateway becoming one of the safest and most accomodating facilities for passengers, anywhere. All traces of Retchko's "Interrogation Room", the torture chamber, and the "crematorium" were long-since gone, as were the goose-stepping soldiers, the gun-weilding ticket agents and the huge posters of the country's military dictator.

* * *

"Betty Nkrume"—whose real name was "Betty Anaya"—reconciled with her sister, Lisa Anaya, and is still an agent of the British Secret Intelligence Service, "MI-6".

* * *

"Lester Nkrume"—whose real name was "Narris Wilson"—continued his career as an agent of the British Secret Intelligence Service, "MI-6".

* * *

I.M. Nomoah, "The Chief"—The diminutive banker fled with the others on the 747 to Teheran, where he became a financial advisor to the government.

* * *

The "Organization"—The Cartel known as "The Organization" ceased to exist after most of the principals fled Nigeria to Iran and the Tanuta Refinery was destroyed by commandos. The "Imperial Industrial Bank", its monetary arm, was seized by the Nigerian government, as was the Nation Bank of Nigeria's "Division of International Remittance" and its "Technical Division". In time, most of the Cartel's activities were taken up by "Agent U's" organization at Tora Bora.

* * *

General Leonid Efimovich Retchko, aka "Semen Putridchenko"—The hairless Ukrainian made his way to the mountains of Tora Bora, where he became "Chief of Security" to the robed, bearded revolutionary in his growing, ever-more powerful organization. Over time, his brain encapsulated the radiation-caused damage, but the headaches continued to plague him.

* * *

"Alex Salinas" and "Andres Martinez"—The two Russians, who started out as "Alexei Sorbetsky" and "Andrey Malinovsky", kept their new names and eventually made their way to Venezuela, where they joined up with the populist "colonel" and his growing political party.

* * *

Terenty Suslov and Tamara Kuznetsova Suslova—Terenty continued his career with the Russian military, rising in rank to lieutenant colonel. He retired and joined the Tarliani-Livshits-Watering private anti-crime group of Geneva.

In 1994, Tamara presented a son they named "Gennady', in honor of their late, lamented friend, Gennady Lychin.

Down through the years, Tamara and Terenty maintained a cordial long-distance-relationship with Jim and Sloane Randolph, hosting them several times in Moscow, and making return visits to Texas.

* * *

Inspector Tarliani—Younce Tarliani left INTERNOL and, along with Livshits, Watering, and others, founded a private organization, based in Geneva—initially financed in large part by Kip Leeds—to fight crime, criminals and terrorism outside the auspices of governments.

* * *

Tanuta Refinery—The facility remained in ruins and the jungle eventually re-claimed it. The place that was once one of Nigeria's biggest petroleum refineries—and the centerpiece of the Cartel that organized, trained and supplied criminal organizations worldwide—is no longer visible from the air.

* * *

'Uncle' Trini Torres—On the morning of July 24th, 1993, sometime in the hours before dawn, a large raft, propeller-driven from the drive-shaft of a 1957 Chrysler "300" two-door hardtop that was lashed onto the top of it, ground ashore underneath the seaward side of the "Overseas Highway Bridge" at Marathon Key, Florida. Soon after the sun came up, a police officer was dispatched to check out a report that a group of people were milling around on the beach next to an old car that was perched atop a good-sized floatation raft. When the officer got there, an angular, bewhiskered, middle aged man stepped up. "This is America?" When the officer nodded, the fellow gave a thumbs-up, prompting a ragged cheer from the others, all of whom looked to be suffering from dehydration and sunburn. "We are here, 'señor policeman' . . . we want political asylum!" The man stuck out his hand. "My name is 'Trini Torres', señor!" He swept a blistered arm around at the others. "We left Cuba two days ago . . ."

* * *

Twenty-Million Dollars "Blackened" Money—A Nigerian Court ruled that since the money had been signed-over to Kip Leeds by an official representing the government, the money was his. Kip paid the judges one-million dollars for them to rule in his favor.

When officers seized the "Technical" section of the "Nation Bank of Nigeria", the formulas for cleaning the money fell into their hands. As per agreement, they turned over the information to Kip and he was able to convert the bills back to their original state. Then he deposited them in a Swiss numbered account arranged by Tarliani.

At the investigator's suggestion, Kip used part of the remaining nineteen-million dollars to endow the private operation in Geneva begun by Tarliani, Livshits, Watering, and others. For that, he receives a percentage of the proceeds of the booty seized by that organization as a dividend. So far, the payouts have amounted to about two-hundred-eighty million dollars, making it a very good investment, indeed.

* * *

Agent Watering—Watering left the "Investigation Agency" and joined forces with Tarliani and Livshits in the new crime-fighting venture out of Geneva, Switzerland. His most notable successes, so far, were orchestrating the assassination of Norbert Ezego somewhere in the jungles bordering Venezuela and Colombia, with a team composed of the Russians, Rodion Golubko and Terenty Suslov; the Americans, James Richard Randolph and some others; and foiling an attempt by terrorists to detonate a nuclear device in Houston.

* * *

The Underground 'Spetsnaz' Facility Near Cuba, Colorado—The secret place reposes, intact and supplied, inside its mountain lair. It is still used by Russian Special Forces as a base for carrying out clandestine operations in the United States.

* * *

"Agent 'U"—The bearded, robed revolutionary continued to operate out of Tora Bora, impervious to earlier efforts by Western Goverments to dislodge—or to even *find*—him; his name, in time, becoming synonymous with international

598

terrorism. Aided by General Retchko, along with Ezego, Boronov, and others of the former "Organization", his movement kept growing to vast power and influence, with clandestine cells and training camps on every inhabited continent—with the avowed purpose of destroying the established social, political and economic order of Western Civilization. There were reports that he was assassinated by Israeli commandos some time after the turn of the twenty-first century. But his legacy lived on.

~~~~

AFTERWORD

This story had its origins with a journey I took to Nigeria some years ago, where I encountered people and events much like those portrayed here, as well as other happenings outside the scope of this narrative that could warrant their own stories. As I told others about my adventure—that had started as a regular petroleum-related business deal that became something much more—they said it would make a good tale and that I should write about it. With that in mind, I started a short-story that soon became much bigger in scope and took me several years to research and complete in two-novel form, all the while carrying on a regular occupation.

To me, the Lagos airport was the most uncertain and un-nerving place to which I have ever been. A few years ago, a doctor who had himself been through that airport told me a security man there had let it drop that there was a secluded room where officers found it more "convenient" to beat people to death so as to not "waste bullets". Hearsay, but it would fit the reputation the place had for a long time. Now, I'm learning that things there are better these days, which is good. But people invariably bring up the ever-present and pervasive "baby-diaper"" smells—I guess those things haven't changed.

The "Academy" that figured so prominently in the story was loosely patterned after an actual one in Moscow—a super-secret, advanced "War College" for rigidly-selected officers of all branches of the military that was organized to function very much like the one in this narrative. Graduating from it was mandatory for Soviet officers who aspired to the very highest ranks; i.e., "Marshal of the Soviet Union" and "Fleet Admiral of the Soviet Union".

The "Spetsnaz" in its various units is a real organization, and continues to be—as I am informed by writings and from accounts by some former military people—the most efficient, the most effective, and the most respected of all the world's Special Forces. This is mostly due to the fact that they are able to perform missions that would be politically prohibited by most of the Western governments and they do so with a reputation for audacity and thoroughness unmatched elsewhere. The background as presented in this story about that stealthy, hard-hitting paramilitary organization is authentic insofar as I could determine, and there is a considerable body of information available. (It is worth noting that the group formerly known as "Vityaz Spetsnaz" was disbanded in 2009 and was absorbed into other units of the Force.) Anyone with an interest in Spetsnaz would do well to check out their fascinating website, along with other Internet sources. An absorbing read on the subject would be *'The Encyclopedia of the World's Special Forces'*, by Mike Ryan, Chris Mann and Alexander Stilwell, published by Barnes and Noble Books.

There was a vicious (and, in the event, unnecessary and unfortunate) fire-fight with hand-to-hand combat between U.S. Special Forces and Spetsnaz troops in the mid-1990's at a Serbian airport during the joint "Peace-Keeping" venture in the Balkans. For the purposes of the story, I moved the generally-similar incident portrayed here to an earlier year, as I also did for the Chechnya parts. The real battle went on for some hours and might well have started "World-War-Three" had it not ground to an uneasy truce when national leaders on both sides activated the "Moscow-Washington Hot-Line" (In Washington, they call it the "Washington-Moscow Hot-Line") and de-fused the issue. But for a while, its outcome had been touch-and-go. The skirmish (it was actually full-blown combat) came about because of mistakes in communication on both sides, much as is depicted here. Their counterparts in the story mirrored some of the actual participants at the event, including the acrimonious meeting in the airport over a card table between the angry Russian general and the American military officers that almost came to physical blows. One cringes to consider what might have happened had one or more of the opposing high-ranking officers been injured or killed by the other side's fists or bullets.

But, happily, things have changed greatly since those days. American troops have since marched in the "Victory Day" parade in Red Square alongside Russian soldiers commemorating the end of World War II ("The Great Patriotic War" in Russia), and U.S. Special Forces have even conducted joint training exercises in Colorado with their Spetsnaz counterparts.

In 1988 the U.S. Navy shot down an Iranian airliner by mistake over the Strait of Hormuz, killing all passengers and crew, which, with certain changes, foretold the shoot-down of the Iranian Airbus with Galina on board. On that score, one has to feel empathy for Gennady's plight: he was the tragic figure in this story and mirrored the emotional agony of the loved ones of those who lost their lives in the real disaster.

The part about hijacking the satellite channel was fictional, although "Buzzy Habbler"and "Jamey Suggs" have their egghead counterparts all over; we have all known the type.

Many thanks to the cordial staff of the *'Consulate General of the Russian Federation in Houston'* for their helpful assistance and advice on matters relating to Russian culture; in particular to Vice-Consul Tatiana Shustrova, who was a wonderful source of information concerning Russian weddings and other social customs.

As mentioned, much of the research for this story came from Internet sources (now considered to be a "legitimate" wellspring of information; particularly annotated pieces). Additionally, certain publications were useful in placing people and events in and around various locations. Among these would be the "Moscow" travelogue by *'DK Publishing'*, and the *'Lonely Planet'* book about Moscow that were vital sources of information. Three travel books about Cuba also came in handy: Frommer's *'Cuba'*; Odyssey's *'Cuba'*, by Andrew Coe; and Moon Handbooks' *'Cuba'*, an easy-to-read and informative tome by Christopher Baker.

Moving on to another part of the world, the underground complexes at Tora Bora were reputedly built by the Americans for their then-allies, the "Taliban", during their ultimately-successful war against the invading Soviets in the late-1979 to early-1990's period. After that, the complexes were abandoned, and some doubters now even question their very existence. In any case, for purposes of the story they were convenient as a place for "Agent U" and his fellow insurgents to set up their headquarters. With the "Agent U'" character, I drew upon familiar stereotypes to depict an enigmatic man driven by an intense ideology.

"José Aldrada" was fictional, but his counterparts are there. The border in and around Nuevo Laredo, Mexico and along the Rio Grande has long been a hotbed of conflict, where even Chiefs of Police on the Mexican side were not immune from abduction and assassination.

The "Facundo" character was a composite of several enormously-wealthy and influential men who are reputed to have lived in Colombia.

The Venezuelan "colonel" was fictional, although a recent President of that country would seem to exhibit certain characteristics of the storyline character.

Some sources claim that Russian-made briefcase-sized atomic devices as in the story are already in place in the United States, pre-positioned for possible future use; a thought to give one the shudders.

Madrid, the dynamic Spanish metropolis, and its landmark square, "Plaza Mayor", with a rich history going back half a millennium, provided an appropriate setting for the climax. In what other city at three o'clock in the morning are the movie theaters packed, the dashing-about buses are full, and one stands in a long line at McDonald's?

During the preparation of these books, a number of people, including Joe Barfield, Paul Caver, Tamara Gajewski, Lilia Krbashian, Mary Jo Mathews, Brian Ross, and Salem Thannoon, among others, were there with helpful suggestions and support, which I hereby and gratefully acknowledge. A heartfelt "thank-you" to Deacon Jim Hyde of the *'Epiphany of the Lord Catholic Church'*, in Katy, Texas, who gave me the proper procedure for the *'Viaticum', the 'Communion for the Dying'*. Rodrigo Aguilera's wonderful cover art demonstrates why he has become one of the most sought-after artists in the Houston area. On another front, Bobby Bernshausen and his staff at Virtualbookworm.com Publishing were helpful beyond words at formatting the manuscripts for the various editions. My wife, Cecilia, kept urging me on to finish the project. And there was Cate Kahn, who insisted that I write about the time I journeyed to Nigeria that became this story.

John S. Halbert
Katy, Texas

~~~~

www.ingramcontent.com/pod-product-compliance
Lightning Source LLC
Chambersburg PA
CBHW060239030726
47493CB00024B/1367